The Trigger

Voyager

ARTHUR C. CLARKE &
MICHAEL KUBE-McDOWELL

THE TRIGGER

HarperCollins*Publishers*

Voyager
An Imprint of HarperCollins*Publishers*
77-85 Fulham Palace Road,
Hammersmith, London W6 8JB

www. voyager-books.com

Published by *Voyager* 1999
1 3 5 7 9 8 6 4 2

A catalogue record for this book
is available from the British Library

ISBN 0 00 224711 9

Typeset in Meridien by Palimpsest Book Production Limited,
Polmont, Stirlingshire

Printed and bound in Great Britain by
Caledonian International Book Manufacturing Ltd, Glasgow

Dedication

To the memory of
The children of Dunblane, Scotland
And Jonesboro, Arkansas

Acknowledgements

Any project of this size and scope owes much to people whose names do not appear on the cover. At the top of the list is an indispensable team of publishing pros including agents Russell Galen and Danny Baror, Bantam Spectra editors Tom Dupree and Pat Lobrutto, and HarperCollins editors Jane Johnson and Joy Chamberlain. Without their contributions, we would never have been able to start this journey, much less hold on to see our journey's end.

With the principals scattered across twelve time zones, the Internet was an essential tool for keeping in touch and staying on the same page. It also proved to be a superb research tool. The Web provided round-the-clock access to an amazing wealth of information and opinion (a partial bibliography of Web sites is available at http://www.sff.net/people/K-Mac/trigger.htm). At the same time, a variety of Internet newsgroups (from rec.aviation.military to talk.politics.guns) offered both an international cast of volunteer experts and a rich tapestry of passions and philosophies in conflict.

Among the many individuals who extended themselves as a courtesy to the authors were Georgia Whidden at the Institute for Advanced Study; Dr Rick Langolf; Daniel K. Jarrell; Commander Cole Pierce, USN (retired); Dr Graham P. Collins; Major Billy Harvey, USAF (retired); Jeff Crowell; Lieutenant Colonel Les Matheson, USAF; Paul J. Adam; Robert Brown; Todd Ellner; Scott Rosenthal; and Urban Fredriksson. They are not at all responsible, of course, for any abuse of their kindness and expertise, nor for advice not taken.

Finally, the most heartfelt thanks go to those closest to hand, to the dear friends and family who provided aid and comfort throughout the long gestation of *The Trigger*. Their contributions to our endeavors have been – and continue to be – innumerable and inestimable.

Michael P. Kube-McDowell, May 1999

Dramatis Personae

At Terabyte Laboratories:
Karl Brohier, senior director
Jeffrey Alan Horton, associate director
Gordon Greene, electrical and mechanical engineer
Leigh Thayer, experimental information systems specialist
Donovan King, director of site security
Eric Fleet, security officer
Val Bowden, engineering physicist at the Annex

In Washington, D.C.:
Senator Grover Wilman, founder of Mind Over Madness
President Mark Breland
Richard Nolby, Chief of Staff
Roland Stepak, Secretary of Defense
Devon Carrero, Secretary of State
Attorney General Doran Douglas
Aimee Rochet, director of public relations
Edgar Mills, FBI Director
Jacob Hilger, director of the Defense Intelligence Agency

Elsewhere:
Aron Goldstein, owner of Aurum Industries and principal
    investor in Terabyte Laboratories
John Samuel Trent, president of the NAR
Jules Merchant, president of military contractor Allied
    General
Philby Lancaster, attorney for the NAR
Robert Wilkins, regional commander of the People's Army
    of Righteous Justice

Contents

PROLOGUE: The Chosen

With resignation, Jeffrey Horton surveyed the clutter in the hardware-filled second bedroom he and his roommate self-mockingly called The Black Hole.

Data disks and tapes were scattered under and across the several tables, and a mortally wounded CD-ROM was pinned under the caster of one of the chairs. Assorted first-generation computer components and test gear formed precarious mounds of metal and plastic in the corners. There was a jumble of cables on the seat of Horton's chair, and a sagging, badly overloaded shelf of books and manuals loomed over the large monitor like a sword of Damocles.

The normal level of chaos in The Black Hole was one that only another gearhead could love – most of Horton's friends had at least one room like it. But it was obvious from the overflowing cardboard boxes in the middle of the floor that Hal had been hitting the Silicon Valley electronics swap meets in the weeks Horton had been away.

'If it's broken, I can fix it. If it works, I can use it,' was Hal's self-proclaimed motto. It was hard for him to say no to any flea-market bargain, whether it was a $50 refractometer, a $100 argon laser, or a complete Windows-era computer for $25. Somehow, the Black Hole absorbed them all.

Resisting the temptation to paw through the boxes to appraise Hal's latest finds, Horton retreated from the room and firmly closed the door after him. The mound of dirty clothes on his bed and the accumulation of recyclables on the apartment balcony deserved higher priority than beating back entropy in what their landlord grumpily called 'an unlicensed salvage yard'.

It was then that Horton heard someone knocking on the apartment door. The knocking was sharp and impatient, as though it had been going on for a while – which it might have been, since it was competing with the white noise of the elderly dishwasher whooshing and rumbling away in the tiny kitchen.

Hastening to respond, Horton only glanced at the corridor monitor long enough to see that the caller was a silver-haired man in a long cloth coat. Releasing both locks, he opened the door to the floor stop.

'Hello – I'm looking for –' the caller began. Then he straightened his shoulders and smiled broadly. 'Well, and here you are.'

Horton was staring dumbly at a face that had no business appearing at his door. 'You're Karl Brohier,' he said, blinking and shaking his head. He had no precedent for how he should act when a Nobel Laureate appeared at his door like a campus missionary, and fell back on repeating himself. 'You're Karl *Brohier*.'

'I know,' said the older man, his head cocked at a slight angle. 'And you're Jeffrey Alan Horton.' He gestured with the bottle of wine he was carrying. 'May I come in?'

'Uh – of course, Dr Brohier,' Horton said, retreating a step and allowing the door to open fully.

'Karl,' the visitor corrected.

Horton could not allow himself such presumptuous familiarity, and so simply nodded acknowledgement. 'I have to apologize for the mess. I just got back from being away for most of three months –'

'Yes, I know,' said Brohier as he brushed past. 'How did you like it in the Midwest?'

'Uh – I wasn't ready for snow in the spring.'

Brohier grunted in amusement as he searched for a place to sit down. 'And Marsh Tolliver – how did you find him?'

Tolliver was the director of the National Superconducting Cyclotron Laboratory at Michigan State University, where Horton had gone to trade months of service as a volunteer intern for sixty minutes of cyclotron time in support of his doctoral thesis. 'He has high expectations,' Horton said.

'You are too polite,' said Brohier, settling on the one kitchen chair not piled high with mail. 'The student disease. You will get over it.'

'I –'

2

'Tolliver is a tin-god bureaucrat masquerading as a scientist – unfortunately, all too common for the top post at government sites. All of the good work that comes out of the NSCL nowadays is due to Ginger Frantala, the assistant director. I'm sure that she's the one Professor Huang spoke to to arrange your visit. Did you get what you needed out of your time there?'

There seemed to be nothing about him that Brohier did not already know. 'The results supported my thesis.'

'Excellent. I look forward to seeing them. Are you going to publish?'

'In a refereed journal? I'm not sure it merits –'

'Oh, I think it does. From what the old tiger told me – the old tiger. He loves that nickname, you know. It would do you no harm at all to arrange to let him overhear you calling him that.' Brohier chuckled to himself. 'Send your paper to *Physical Letters B*. I'm on the referee list there. I'd give it a fair reading.'

'Dr Brohier –'

'Karl,' the visitor insisted.

Horton flashed a quick grimace, then nodded. 'Karl,' he said. 'Karl, you are looking at one very confused person. I mean, it's a great honor to meet you. I've read your papers, I was delighted when you won your Nobel Prize. I consider it a privilege to be having this conversation –'

Brohier waved off the praise. 'I'm already sixty-seven years old, Jeffrey. Get to your point.'

Gesturing with both hands, Horton asked, 'Why are you here? Forgive me, but it's sort of like having Miss April show up at a frat house.'

An easy surprised laugh softened Brohier's dramatic features. 'And ask the president out on a date,' he said.

'Yeah,' Horton agreed. 'About that improbable.'

'Life is improbable – but real. I came here to ask you what you're doing for the next ten years,' said Brohier. 'If you have nothing better to do, I wonder if you might consider coming to work for me.'

'Excuse me?'

'The Nobel Prize *does* open doors – not only yours,' said Brohier. 'Not quite a year ago, a very forward-thinking man named Aron

3

Goldstein approached me about establishing a new research center. I told him there was only one way I'd be interested – if he would let me collect as many of the top young minds as I could and give them the tools and freedom to pursue whatever they thought promising.'

'Sounds like grad school without grades.'

Brohier smiled. 'I told him I didn't want to run a bottom-line-driven gadget factory, that I thought what we needed was an idea factory, working at the boundaries, pushing back the boundaries.'

'New science creates new opportunities.'

'Yes, it does,' said Brohier. 'It always has. I told him I wouldn't sign off on a business plan, couldn't tell him what we would come up with or how much it would be worth, couldn't promise him anything concrete. Then he asked me how much money I've made from my patents and licenses on solid-state memory, and I told him. He said that was good enough for him, and we shook hands.

'In about five months, Jeffrey, I will put on my administrator's hat and open the doors of a state-of-the-art research campus being built on fourteen hundred acres outside Columbus, Ohio. I'd like to have you there from day one. Are you interested?'

'Just tell me who I have to kill,' Horton said.

Brohier grinned broadly. 'This bottle contains a cork,' he said, gesturing at the wine. 'Does this apartment contain a corkscrew?'

'It did when I left.'

'Then endeavor to locate it, and you and I will kill this fine Bordeaux – and a few of our gray cells – together,' said Brohier. 'Welcome to Terabyte Labs, Jeffrey. Start thinking about what you want to work on next.' Brohier's eyes glowed with an undisguised prideful delight. 'And start adjusting to the idea that you're about to become the envy of all those who wish they could call themselves your peers.'

I: Trigger

1: Anomaly

'Vox,' Jeffrey Alan Horton said to his car. The voice-command indicator glowed on the instrument panel, and a heads-up menu appeared on the windshield. 'News, national.'

'– Attorney General John Woo is expected to release final plans for the twice-postponed murder trial against Melvin Hills and eight other members of the "God's Assassins" anti-abortion group. The defendants face five counts of murder in the deadly rocket attack on the Planned Parenthood facility in San Leandro.

'"We promise the defendants a fair trial, the court a safe trial, and the victims a just conviction."

'The unusual virtual trial is expected to be conducted entirely on the high-speed G2Net, with judge, jurors, prosecutors, and defendants at widely scattered secret locations. In January, the first jury was dismissed when several members received death threats –'

'Vox,' said Horton. 'News, local.'

'– Women's health services providers in the Greater Columbus area were reluctant to discuss any additional security measures, but Deputy Police Commander Jeanne Ryberg promised "maximum vigilance" throughout the high-profile trial.

'"We know what the Assassins are capable of, and we're not going to allow it to happen here –"'

Horton sighed. The San Leandro trial hadn't even started yet, and he was already tired of hearing about it. But the story was receiving saturation coverage, and the only relief available was to stay away from broadcast media for the next month. 'Vox. Radio off,' he said, spinning the wheel for a right turn onto Shanahan Road.

It was the time of year and the kind of clear Ohio morning when the sun rose directly over the east-west roads like an oncoming

7

fireball, greeting drivers with a blinding glare. Squinting his sleep-cheated eyes and groping beside him for a pair of sunglasses that failed to manifest themselves, Horton was grateful when he finally turned in at the tree-lined entry to the Terabyte Laboratories campus.

With a generous buffer of woods and meadow separating the research complex from the surrounding suburbs, the entrance to the complex looked more like the entrance to a park than to a world-class research center. To preserve the illusion, security at the perimeter was unobtrusive. There were no gates, no guards, no barriers – just a low-profile shadow-box sign.

But appearances were deceiving. A hundred meters in, there was a pull-off lane for remote visitor screening. Just beyond that, a pavement sensor scanned the undercarriage of Horton's Honda Passport, and a roadside transmitter interrogated his own radio-responder ID card.

Horton knew from experience what would happen if he failed either check: just beyond the first turn, he would encounter a series of barriers rising from the driveway, and be intercepted by a canary-yellow security Jeep roaring down it. Anyone who tried to go further, or to enter the campus cross-country, would be tracked by optical and thermal sensors and met by the drawn weapons of the professionally humorless security detail.

At first, Horton had regarded the security diffidently. It jarred with Brohier's insistance on calling the Terabyte site a 'campus', because fences and checkpoints had not been part of Horton's college experience at Stanford, or Purdue, or Tennessee State. But of late he had come to appreciate the quiet vigilance of the security staff – especially after the lab received one of 'Ned Ludd's' package bombs in a shipment of office supplies.

Now Horton knew all the officers by face and first name, and they in turn lent a comforting presence when, as was often the case, he found himself keeping early, late, or weekend hours. The only trouble Horton had ever had with them was during his first winter at Terabyte, when, with his own car in for brake service, Horton tried to enter the campus on a Sunday in his girlfriend's untagged electric Saturn.

His girlfriend – that was a construction Horton hadn't had need of in longer than he cared to remember. His last serious relationship had been with Kelly Braddock at Stanford. In a year and a half of dating, they had never quite gotten to the decision to live together, but between Kelly's brittle emotional defensiveness and her bold sexual openness, that relationship came to take up as much space and energy as his friends' live-in relationships seemed to. By the time Karl Brohier showed up at Horton's door, Horton was growing weary. He had begun to occasionally avoid Kelly, and to contemplate disengaging completely.

Brohier's offer had resolved that problem, though not in quite the way Horton expected it would. A few weeks later, Kelly announced she had secured a fellowship at the University of Texas. That allowed her to leave Palo Alto a month before Horton did, thereby proving to herself that she had not compromised her independence by sleeping with him. They had said good-bye without tears or concrete promises.

For a time, they had kept up with each other over the net. But netsex had proved a pale substitute for the real thing, and the real thing proved to have been the binding energy of their relationship. Lust absent, there was too little left to keep them from drifting apart, and within a few months, they were 'old friends' on their way to becoming nodding strangers.

Still, the disappearance of Kelly from Horton's life did deprive him of both an agreeable heat and a comforting unpredictability, and he made a few awkward and half-hearted efforts to replace both.

Of his several relationships that first year, the one with Moira, the owner of the Saturn, had lasted the longest. An outgoing thirty-year-old Toledo native who lived in Horton's apartment building, she had some of Kelly's fire in a softer and more accommodating package. But she lacked Kelly's enthusiasm for independence, and her principal ambition was an old-fashioned one – to marry and have children. She waited only until the first afterglow to start musing aloud about buying a house together. When she learned that Horton did not share her ambition, she wasted no more time on him.

Since then, more by inertia than design, Horton had allowed his work to swallow him whole. His recreation was limited to occasional visits to a target-shooting range or IMAX theater, plus one week-long hiking trip into a National Park each year. His social contacts outside of work were limited to netchat and two or three family holidays at his parents' new house in Columbia, South Carolina.

He told himself he did not mind his chaste bachelorhood, that the work was enough – but there was no one close enough to him to question it. He told himself he did not mind sleeping alone, eating alone, traveling alone – but the truth was that he also did not greatly enjoy it.

He told himself that there would be more time, more laughter, a fuller life later, when he had had a chance to prove himself, when work and not-work came back into balance – but he had been telling himself that for nearly six years. His thirtieth birthday was now only a month away, and it had suddenly become possible to see himself still living this way at thirty-five, and forty, and beyond.

The catalyst for all this melancholy, Horton knew, was the experiment scheduled for that morning. And the best antidote Horton could think of would be a little long-overdue success.

At the end of the snaking driveway was the main parking area and the gate into Terabyte's compound. As an associate direc-tor, Horton was entitled to one of the parking spaces inside the wrought-iron fences. He pointed the Passport toward the gate, lowering the driver's window as he did.

'Hello again, Dr Horton,' said Eric. The barrel-chested, gentle-voiced officer had been on duty when Horton left at 3.00 a.m. 'Did that catnap do you any good?'

'Not much,' Horton said, making an effort to smile. 'Have you heard anything about the status of the arrangements?'

'I just talked to the boss. We'll be ready for you at seven-fifteen,' said Eric. 'Other than me and Tim, your team has the campus to itself. The site engineer will start taking down nonessential systems at seven. It'll be as quiet as we can make it for you.'

'Thanks,' Horton said with a nod, and drove on.

'Good luck!' Eric called after him.

Horton grimaced. Luck. The team had had a bundle of it, all of it bad.

The theoretical and design work on Baby had consumed nearly a year, and construction of the experimental apparatus had taken most of six months. Now, more than two years later, the rig had yet to complete successfully a single test series. There had been a fire, computer failures, power supply problems, and a series of puzzling bugs, leading to a major redesign of the detector, two partial rebuilds of the emitter, and replacement of most of the test and measurement gear.

To be sure, the project was bleeding-edge, unmapped-territory work, and setbacks were to be expected. But even in the relaxed culture of Terabyte Labs, Horton was feeling pressure – most of it self-imposed. If he had spent the last forty months and fourteen million of Aron Goldstein's dollars chasing a chimera, it was up to him to make that assessment and close down the project. And if Suite 1 didn't produce some positive results soon, Horton might be forced to do exactly that, and admit that he had been wrong.

The Hong-Jaekel-Mussermann unified field equations had brought on the paradigm shift for which theoretical physics had been hungering through the last third of the previous century. Cosmologists rushed to embrace the so-called 'CERN system', providing as it did attractive solutions to both the missing mass problem and the age/expansion paradox.

But physics itself was turned upside down and plunged into the turmoil of scientific revolution. Reputations crumbled like fallen kings, and new heroes rose from anonymity to lead the way. The last five Nobel Prizes in Physics had been awarded for CERN system work, and no one was betting that that was the end of the string. It was an exciting time to be a physicist.

And Horton might easily have missed it. If the United States had built its Superconducting Super Collider on schedule, the essential elements of the CERN system could have been revealed nearly two decades earlier. And if it *could* be done, someone would have already done what Horton was trying to do. The window of opportunity would have closed before Horton had left primary school. The new history of physics was being written at a breathtaking pace.

But the American Congress, a body historically long on lawyers and short on vision, had canceled the SSC when it was little more than a hole in the Texas flatland. Ironically, their short-sightedness had created Horton's opportunity – if he and his team could just teach the Baby to walk.

Four years ago, at the American Physical Society's Honolulu conference on the CERN system, Horton had realized that one of the field equations in the new paradigm allowed for – but did not require – a heretofore unobserved phenomenon. That was the day that Jeffrey Horton began pursuing the stimulated emission of gravitons, the tiny bosons which were the vector of universal gravity.

His own collateral equations said that what was unthinkable in the old physics was just barely possible in the new – namely, to build the analogue of a laser for gravity. Though such a device had yet to be demonstrated, it already had a name waiting for it, inherited from the science fiction tales where it had become part of the technological furniture: the tractor beam.

And it would not stop there. Artificial gravity for long-duration spaceflight, frictionless drives, overhead cranes with no cables and no moving parts, zero-g chambers at sea level – Horton and Brohier already had a list of more than two hundred patentable applications.

When Baby came of age, everyone would want to play with him.

But Horton could not count on being the only free-thinking physicist to have looked at the CERN team's equations and seen the same opportunity. He lived in dread of logging into the Los Alamos preprint server, skimming the new high energy physics papers, and finding his hunch made real in the words and equations of someone else.

He dreaded that prospect almost as much as he did the prospect that he was wrong, and they'd all been wasting their time.

The lights were already on in the Planck Center's Davisson Lab, and both of Horton's associate project managers were busily making final preparations for the test.

Dr Gordon Greene was lying on his back on the floor, half-hidden under the refrigerator-sized transformer stage of the field generator. One corner of a faded and stained tool pouch was visible beside him, as was the Number 4 Faraday panel.

Dr Leigh Thayer was tailor-sitting in the chair at the data collection console, rubbing the back of her neck with one hand while she studied the twin displays. Her back was to Horton as he entered.

In so many ways, Gordie and Lee were a study in contrasts. He was chocolate skin on a middleweight wrestler's frame, she was tall, pale, and coltishly slim. His family's short American roots ran back to the time of Nkrumah's Ghana and had been watered mostly with hope, while her deep ones traced to the days of genteel mercantile England which had once traded in his ancestors. He was the streets of Oakland, California, and she was the upscale suburbs of Connecticut. He had needed a state scholarship to attend UC-Davis, while she had had her pick of the Ivy League before choosing Cornell.

But both had in common that they had defied the expectations of their backgrounds. Gordie had sufficiently distinguished himself at Davis to earn his way into the graduate programs in electrical and mechanical engineering at Cal Tech. And after a year, Lee had declared Cornell and her classmates a bore and, shrugging off her parents' financial blackmail, transferred to Rensselaer Polytechnic with a determination to 'get some dirt under my nails'. Even her chosen nickname was a subtle rejection of what she called 'old money affectations'.

Horton knew he was fortunate to have snared both of them. Gordie had come to Terabyte after Hughes ITT closed down its prototype shop in favor of virtual prototyping. And Lee, eight years older than Horton, had become disillusioned at Fermilab after three consecutive projects fell under a budgetary axe.

'Gordie, Lee – did either of you actually go home?' Horton asked, dropping his portfolio on one end of his workbench.

Thayer raised her hand. 'I did,' she said without looking back at him. 'Took a shower, changed my underwear, collected my fetishes and lucky charms, and came right back to finish calibrating the detectors.'

'Gordie?'

'I napped on the couch in your office for a couple of hours,' Greene called from underneath the apparatus. 'Had a nightmare about another fire in the transformer stage, decided I'd eyeball things one more time.'

'Do I detect a whiff of creeping superstition in the air?' Horton asked with a quizzical grin. 'Never mind, don't answer, I have to go light a prayer candle in the Grotto of Niels Bohr.'

Greene chortled. 'Now there's an exotic fetish! –'

'You're a pathetically lewd individual,' Thayer said, shaking her head. 'If you weren't also the best metal-basher I've ever seen . . .'

'You want me,' Gordie said to her, digging his heels into the floor and wriggling out from under the transformer stage. 'Why else would you put on fresh underwear?'

'See what I have to put up with when you're not here, Boss?' Thayer asked, spinning her chair half a turn. 'Why, if this creature and I were the same species, I'd be able to file a sexual harassment complaint as thick as his ego.'

'You both sound like you could use about ten hours' sleep,' Horton said. 'In separate beds,' he added quickly. 'I'm wondering if we shouldn't postpone this a day, come back to it fresh –'

Thayer shook her head. 'Boss, I'm planning on leaving here in three hours to go home and sleep for a week. Or go home and get drunk for a week, depending. Either way –'

Horton nodded. 'Well, I wouldn't want to have to ask you to change your plans. Gordie, how does it look? Are we going to be able to go?'

'I'm satisfied,' said Greene.

'You're supposed to say, "Dr Horton, I guarantee it – this is the day".'

'I'm willing to guarantee that if it breaks today, it'll be something that's never broken before. Is that good enough?'

Horton snorted. 'I guess it'll have to be. Lee, how much more time do you need?'

'I'm ready. All the recorders are sync'd up, and all the sensors are zeroed-in. I'm just watching to make sure Gordie doesn't undo all my hard work at the last minute.'

'Gordie?'

'Ten minutes to finish getting Baby dressed,' said Greene. 'Then we can start warming up the generator at any time.'

Horton glanced up at the clock above his workbench. 'All right.

I need to chase down some caffeine and sugar, update the experimental log before I forget what we did last night. Let's start running the checklist at seven-fifteen, and aim for starting the test series at seven-thirty.'

'Is Dr Brohier coming?' asked Thayer.

'He said he'd take a pass this time – that considering he'd been present for all the previous disasters, maybe he was jinxing us. I'm sure he was speaking metaphorically, not metaphysically –'

'*I'm* sure he just didn't want to get up this early,' said Thayer, sniffing. 'I'm half his age, and *I* don't want to be up this early.'

'Something tells me he's going to wish he'd been here,' Greene said, lying back and disappearing under the machine with the Faraday panel in hand. 'Don't ask me how I know,' he continued, his voice falling away into a horror-movie affectation. 'There's an unknown power tugging at my awareness, an inexplicable compulsion to my thoughts – I am suddenly in the grip of a mysterious, irresistible force –'

'Testosterone,' Thayer muttered.

Horton laughed, then went in search of a doughnut.

In principle, at least, the primary detector was simplicity itself.

The goal was to detect a minute, temporary local variation in the gravitational attraction between the target and the emitter. The method was to measure the deflection of the target itself – a curtain of extremely fine ribbons, each made from a different elemental metal.

In theory, when the target was subjected to the full sweep of electromagnetic radiation – from kilohertz to gigahertz, long-wave radio to short-wave X-ray – produced by the emitter antenna, the magic combination of material and frequency would cause each of the ribbons in turn to twitch toward the antenna. Horton could not predict what the magic frequencies would be. His equations required a theoretical constant that could not be derived, only determined experimentally.

In practice, the more sensitive the detector, the more fragile it was, and the more sensitive to outside influence. Even the air current created by someone walking past the detector was several orders of magnitude stronger than Brohier's most optimistic estimate of the tractor effect at experimental power levels. The first set of ribbons was torn in half by vibration when a visitor bumped into the workbench where it was being assembled.

Since then, everything possible had been done to isolate the detector. It was enclosed under a thick glass bell, with the air inside evacuated to an infinitesimal fraction of normal air pressure. Then the entire assembly was rigidly attached to a three-ton cube of black Ohio granite floating on an oil cushion.

Brohier had walked into the lab one day to find Horton, Greene and Thayer gathered in a circle around the granite cube, vigorously jumping up and down to test the shock mounting. With characteristic presence of mind, the senior director began humming the *Zarathustra* theme from *2001* as he wordlessly retreated toward the hallway.

It had been a long time since Horton had laughed that hard.

'Gordie?'

'Power supply is steady and quiet. Fingers are crossed, hat is on backwards.'

'Lee?'

'Zeros across the board on all sensors. Prayer weasels spinning counterclockwise.'

Horton glanced in the direction of the detector, now hidden from view by a semi-circle of portable radiation screens. 'Let's do it. Starting sequencer.'

'Recorders running,' Lee reported from her station.

'Output power at five percent,' Gordie reported a moment later. 'Output frequency at one hundred Hertz and climbing.'

Horton sat back in his rolling lab chair, his elbows propped on its arms, his hands restless in his lap. The experiment was now under the control of a custom program nicknamed Steady Hand, running on the Alpha 3 at Lee's console. Immune to both anxiety and anticipation, Steady Hand's primary duties were to hold the output power constant at each stage of the series, and to ensure a slow, smooth sweep through the emitter's operational spectrum.

No one spoke for several minutes. Thayer and Horton were intently watching the continuously updated displays before them.

16

Both had the power to pause the sequencer or terminate the trial with the touch of one finger.

'Coming up on the infrared notch,' Lee announced.

Horton nodded. Owing to the problem of heating the tissue-thin ribbons, much of the infrared spectrum had to be skipped. 'Here comes the first rainbow.'

From behind the radiation screens came a flare of pale red light. The light shifted quickly toward orange and kept changing until it disappeared as a pale violet cast.

'Beginning X-ray series,' said Thayer.

'I hope that was *lead* underwear you changed into,' said Gordie.

'You'll never know,' she answered breezily. 'Boss, everything still looks nice and stable to me.'

'To me, too,' he said. 'I wouldn't mind seeing a wiggle or two any time now, though.'

'Do you have a bet going with yourself about where?'

'The low end – the very long wavelengths. Dr Brohier thinks just the opposite – he thinks our emitter can't reach the necessary frequencies, up around ten to the twenty-second.' He shrugged. 'So much of the mid-spectrum's been studied to death already, the odds are that *one* of us is right –'

'First pass complete,' she interrupted. 'Negative results.'

'At least we got through a first pass,' Gordie said. 'Output power now at ten percent. Once more with feeling –'

'We've been here before,' Thayer said diffidently. 'I'm not going to get excited until we pass our previous best.'

That was twenty-eight minutes and six seconds, or nearly three complete passes, from the December 12 trial. That attempt had ended when a solid-state power conditioner failed, giving Steady Hand an advanced case of digital palsy.

'I wonder if there's some French physicist sitting in the control room at CERN right now,' Greene mused aloud, 'pumping Z particles into a simulated protostellar nebula and polishing his paper on induced gravitational clumping –'

Spinning his chair toward Greene, Horton shrugged. 'If so, more power to 'em – no pun intended. If it turns out you need heavy bosons to pump up a gravity laser, we're not going to be the ones to do it. Fermilab, CERN, KEK, even Stanford and

Brookhaven – we can't get in there, and we can't compete with them.'

'Coming up on the infrared notch,' Thayer said quietly.

Horton nodded.

A rainbow of light flared across the ceiling of the lab.

'I still think we missed a bet not making a deal with one of the smaller high-energy labs,' said Greene. 'There's always someone who's hurting for money. Macdonald, Elettra – I hear Protvino's for sale.'

Thayer sniffed. 'You just want a chance to play with a trillion electron volts.'

'Who doesn't?'

Horton stood up and stretched. 'I don't. That wouldn't help us. I'm hoping for an effect we can apply in the real world – the physics of the first three seconds of the Universe are of no practical use to anyone. If we –' He stopped in midsentence and leaned in toward the display. 'What the hell is that?'

Thayer was frowning, pulling her chair toward the control console. 'Some kind of ground tremor. Look at the seismograph.'

Before Horton could respond, a harsh alarm cut through the room, keening from the lab intercom.

'What is that – the lockdown warning?' Horton started toward the lab door. 'Reset everything to the start of the current pass,' he ordered, raising his voice over the alarm. 'Check your calibrations –'

Suddenly Horton was competing not with the alarm, but with another voice. 'All Terabyte personnel – this is Site Security. A precautionary lockdown is now in effect throughout the campus. Isolation protocols for power and communication have been invoked –'

'There goes the trial,' Greene said in disgust.

'– Please remain where you are. Do not leave the building. Stay away from windows –'

As Horton reached the lab door, the data bar on the electronic locks began to flash red, and the door itself was immovable. He grabbed the wired phone hanging beside it and punched Security. It rang an extraordinary eleven times before it was answered.

'This is Dr Horton. What's going on?'

'Dr Horton – this is Tim Bartel. Are you and your staff all right?'

'We're fine –'

'Where are you at the moment?'

'Davisson, Planck Center.'

'Good. Please stay there, Dr Horton. We'll come for you as soon as we're sure there's no danger.'

'Damn it, just tell me what's *happening*.'

There was a moment's hesitation. 'There's been an explosion on the grounds –'

'What? A bomb?'

'Bloody hell,' said Greene, eavesdropping.

'I don't know what caused it,' Bartel said tersely. 'We've got two fires burning, a couple of people hurt. But you should be safe where you are. Please stay put until we're sure the situation is under control.' Then the line went dead, the connection broken at the other end.

As Horton returned the phone to its cradle, he sighed exasperatedly, and his shoulders sagged. He looked up into the anxious expressions on his staff's faces. 'Shut it all down,' he said wearily. 'We're done for the day.'

2: Mystery

San Juan, Puerto Rico – Nine separate explosions rocked
Puerto Rico overnight Tuesday, killing one person and injuring
three others. The bombs destroyed a railroad bridge and
damaged a tour bus depot and the power substation serving
Ft. Buchanan, headquarters of the US Army South. The show
of strength by the pro-independence Macheteros came on
the anniversary of the US invasion of the island during the
Spanish-American War.
Complete story   Gov. Harrod's statement

The security lockdown ended after two hours, allowing Jeffrey
Horton to leave Planck Center. He was met at the door by an
acrid smell of something burned or burning, and by Donovan King,
the director of site security for Terabyte, in his yellow Jeep.

'Dr Brohier's waiting at the service gate,' King said. 'Get in – I
want to give you both a tour of the damage.'

Horton clambered into the back seat. 'What happened?'

'Damned if I know,' King said tersely as the Jeep jerked forward.

'Well, was it a bomb?'

'Damned if I know.'

King's answer was sobering. He was a lean, tanned veteran of ten
years with US Air Force Special Operations and sixteen in private
security consulting. In that time, he had confronted a wide range of
threats, from millennialist martyrs and Third-World gunrunners to
cuckolded husbands and corporate hackers. His quiet competence
was taken as a matter of course – which made his clear discomfiture
a matter of concern.

'What about injuries?' Horton pressed.

'Dr Horton, I understand your impatience with me, but I'd like to wait until Dr Brohier joins us and brief you together.'

Horton did not argue. He was distracted by the thin plume of grey smoke visible to the northwest. A grassy hillock intervened to keep him from seeing its source or gauging its distance, but the tang in the air told him it was nearby.

It did not take long to reach the service gate and collect Brohier. The director looked uncharacteristically rumpled, with no tie or jacket, and an unruly lock of hair over his left ear. But he greeted Horton with a relaxed smile.

'I'm glad you and your people are okay, Jeffrey. Mr King, how is Mr Fleet?'

'As soon as I could spare him, I sent Charlie over to the hospital to get a report on Eric,' King said. 'But he hasn't called in yet.'

'All right,' said Brohier, awkwardly hoisting himself into the passenger seat. 'Why don't you show me what happened here?'

Their first stop was the still-smouldering remains of the grounds-keeper's shed. The little earth-sheltered structure was a shambles, its concrete roof and overburden of earth and sod gone, its contents a blackened jumble, its sectional door lying thirty meters away, buckled and twisted. Nearby, a member of the maintenance staff stood watch beside the lab's first-response fire truck – a foam generator mounted on a Hummer chassis.

'What was Eric doing back here?' Horton asked as he peered at the remains of the tractor. 'He was on the gate when I came in.'

'He was still on the gate when this went up,' said King. 'He never got back here.'

'I don't understand.'

'Neither do I,' said King. 'Let me show you the rest.'

King took them next to the front gate. 'Eric was in the shack,' he said, gesturing. 'Nothing to see, really, except a scorch mark on the floor. Eric ended up with burns from his hip to his knee. His leg looks like it was held in a blowtorch. I have what's left of his sidearm in my office. Apparently the bits of melting nylon from the holster caused some of his worst burns.'

'Heavens,' said Brohier. 'This was caused by debris from the explosion, I take it?'

'The shack's intact, Dr Brohier. No holes in the roof, no broken glass –'

'Then what? Did he set himself on fire? Perhaps he was lighting a cigarette when the bomb went off –'

'Eric doesn't smoke,' said Horton.

'No?'

'No,' said King.

'Then what?'

'I'll show you the security video when we go inside. Maybe you can tell me.'

But first, the security director drove them past the burned-out shell of a two-door sedan parked in the outer lot, three rows south of the gate. 'We were a bit shorthanded when everything went blooey,' King said. 'Eric and the grounds shed got priority. The guys didn't get to this until the car was pretty well gone.'

'This must be how Eric got hurt, then,' said Brohier. 'There must have been two bombs, one here in front, the other in back. He must have been checking out this car –'

'No,' said King. 'Wait until you see the rest.'

'There's more?'

King drove them to the west side of Edison Center, the sprawling administrative services building, and took them inside the small security office garage, where the first-response truck was ordinarily parked when not in use. There he showed them the blackened lockbox between the front seats of a yellow Jeep which was parked in a back corner and roped off with red plastic tape. The interior of the Jeep was coated with a gritty white powder which Horton took for residue from a chemical fire extinguisher.

'We were able to keep *this* in the family,' King said. 'Jack was on mobile patrol in Number Three this morning. He was responding to the back lot explosion and reaching for his sidearm, which was in the lockbox. He ended up burning his hand on the cover of the box. I have a pretty good idea what we'll find when we get that box open – it's sealed tight, with a deadlock and probably a partial vacuum inside.'

'I'm confused – what do these things have to do with each other?' Brohier asked, frowning.

'I'm kind of counting on you to tell me,' King said.

Horton's mind was already spinning. 'Your men carry the Glock 17, right?'

King nodded.

'Anything special about the ammunition?'

'Besides the fact that there seems to have been some sort of massive misfire that I don't begin to understand? No. It's standard Remington 9mm – we don't roll our own.'

'Still, it wouldn't hurt to look at the rest of the box –'

'It wouldn't hurt, but it isn't going to happen. If you'll follow me into the office, I'll show you why.'

A minute later, they were standing in the equipment room of the security suite, staring disbelievingly at the buckled door of the gun safe. Neither the deluge from the fire sprinklers nor the fans set up to dry out the room had scrubbed the smell of burned gunpowder from the space.

'The fire started *inside* the safe?' Brohier asked.

'So it seems.'

Brohier shook his head. 'I need a cup of coffee,' he said. 'Mr King, why don't you join us in my office in half an hour. Bring the video and Mr Fleet's gun with you, and anything else you may have by then. And get someone to work on that lockbox – I think we need to see what's inside.'

'I have a forensic specialist coming in later this morning. I'd rather not touch it until then.'

Brohier nodded grudging agreement. 'In half an hour, then.'

'Director – one more thing,' King said. 'The fire inspector's waiting for me to call her back. How do you want me to handle the authorities? Invite them in, or try to keep them at arm's length?'

'That depends, Mr King. Are we looking at a crime, or an accident?'

'At this point, Director, I just don't know.'

'Then why don't we keep it closely held for a while. And I'll deal with the outside world.'

King nodded approvingly. 'I have no problem with that.'

One of Karl Brohier's qualities that Horton most admired and marveled at was his calm efficiency in crisis. While Brohier did not succeed in getting near a coffee cup before Donovan King rejoined them, he did manage to complete eight phone calls – to the township fire inspector, two members of the township council, the city editor of the *Columbus Dispatch*, the director of personnel for Terabyte, the lab's insurance officer, the chief of medicine at the Olentangy Medical Center, and the local news channel that was broadcasting live pictures of the smoking hole in the lab's back yard from an orbiting UAW.

Even more amazingly, he seemed to get what he wanted from each of the calls – namely, breathing space.

'Any further word on Mr Fleet?' Brohier asked King as the trio sat down together.

'I'm still waiting for an update from someone who's actually seen him in the ER, but the EMTs were optimistic,' said King. 'Might need some grafts, though, which is never fun. He probably doesn't feel as lucky as he was. Let me show you the recording from the gate cameras.'

Brohier and Horton watched silently as the split-screen images played. There was no vehicle at the gate, no sign of any outsider. One moment Fleet was sitting in the gatehouse, sipping a cup of coffee. Then the holster on the guard's right hip seemed to explode in a fierce roar and a searing gout of yellow flame. Screaming and thrashing frantically, Eric crashed heavily into the metal security log desk, then the side wall before falling against the door and out onto the pavement.

'Good god,' said Brohier, blanching.

Horton was shaking his head. 'That shouldn't happen. I've never seen anything like that.'

'No, it sure as hell shouldn't,' said King. 'It *looks* as though all seventeen rounds – the whole clip, with one of the rounds chambered – were involved. The gun is a wreck. The grip is nearly burned away. It looks like most of the slugs were still in the gun – half-melted, though.'

'Why is that?' Brohier asked, his gaze narrowing. 'I would think they'd have scattered in every direction.'

'The brass isn't strong enough on its own to contain the kind of gas pressures that burning gunpowder produces,' Horton explained. 'The cartridge will split and vent before the bullet acquires any real momentum.'

'So what would you call this, then – a misfire?' asked Brohier.

'No, no,' said King. 'Not a misfire, not an explosion. What we had was a gunpowder-fueled flash fire inside the body of the pistol. For a couple of seconds, it was a flamethrower instead of a firearm.'

'How do you know that's what happened?' asked Horton.

King tapped the upper left corner of the interior view. 'Eric keeps his spare clip in the log desk – he doesn't like the weight on his belt –'

'They *both* burned?' Horton asked disbelievingly.

'I'll show you the recording again. You can see the flash, and the lid of the desk jump, and then smoke from the seams.'

'Makes no sense,' Horton said, still shaking his head.

'What about the car bomb?' asked Brohier.

King nodded. 'That was probably an unfortunate choice of words on our part. Did you two see what's left of the vehicle?'

'Yes, as I arrived,' said Brohier.

'Just a glimpse,' said Horton.

'I've got a security camera recording on that, too. Take a look.'

The camera was slowly panning the nearly-empty lot when there was a bright flash inside a white sedan parked in the foreground. The vehicle seemed to jump in place, the windshield and both of its passenger-side windows blown out by a cloud of gray-black smoke that lingered over it in the still air. Then the first tongues of flame appeared, licking at the dash. In moments, the interior of the sedan was completely engulfed, and the plume of smoke turned black with burning synthetics.

King turned off the recorder. 'About three minutes later, the gas tank blew up, with the results you've already seen. Luckily, no one was there trying to put it out – we'd responded to Eric's location.'

'Which happened first?' asked Brohier. 'The misfire, or the car fire?'

'Neither,' King said. 'According to the time marks on the recordings, they happened at damn near the same instant. You can hear Eric's gun on the audio track from the parking lot. And you can see the initial flash from the car as a momentary shadow on the video track from the gatehouse.'

'Whose car was it?' asked Horton.

'Your assistant's,' King said. 'Dr Gordon Greene. I thought this might be a good time to ask him about it and see if he can shed any light.'

'By all means,' said Brohier, gesturing his assent. 'Call him in.'

King nodded. 'Maybe I should send someone to bring him here, just in case.'

'Just in case what?' Horton asked.

'In case he tries to run,' King said, his gaze and tone both level.

'Wait – this is absurd. How did he become a suspect? What do you think he did?'

'I don't really know,' said King. 'But I've got a friend in intensive care because something pretty goddamned weird happened to his sidearm. And Greene *is* your gadgeteer, yes? Don't those Cal Tech people have a reputation for pranks –'

'He's my experimental engineer,' Horton said hotly. 'But if you think he'd deliberately endanger –'

'It's all right, Jeff,' Brohier interrupted. 'We're all just looking for answers. Mr King, release the lockdown and ask Dr Greene to come here. Let's see if he knows any more than we do.'

'Boss,' said Greene, nodding in Horton's direction. 'Dr Brohier. What's going on?'

'We have some security video of the incident earlier this morning,' said King. 'We'd like you to take a look at it and tell us what you can.'

Greene shrugged his assent and slipped into a seat to the left of the monitor. 'Isn't this Lot B? I thought the shooting was at the gate.'

'This is Lot B,' said King, releasing the freeze-frame.

'Yeah, it has to be – that's my car, there. The white one.'

'Keep your eye on it,' Horton said quietly.

'What do you mean? I – oh – oh, no – oh, sweet mother of –' His eyes widened in surprise as the first flash of light and billow of smoke appeared inside the passenger compartment. Then his expression turned to one of mournful disbelief. 'Oh, hell – Boss, look at it! I still have two years of payments left –'

No one spoke, or even smiled. Fists clenched and resting on the table before him, Greene stared wordlessly through the rest of the recording. Then, when the playback ended in another freeze-frame, he dropped his forehead to his fists in an expressive display of grief.

'Do you have any idea what happened?' King asked.

Raising his head, Greene slumped back in his chair and blew a deep breath into one closed hand. 'Yeah. Tennessee.'

'What?'

'I drove through Tennessee on my way to see my brother Brandon and his new baby girl at Christmas,' Greene explained with a sigh. 'You know how they have fireworks shops at every exit along the highway, each one bigger, brighter and claiming to be cheaper than the last? I weakened on the way back north.' He shook his head. 'I had twenty dollars' worth of firecrackers in the glove compartment and fifty dollars' worth of skyrockets under the passenger seat.'

King raised an eyebrow. 'At Christmas? Why were they still in the car?'

'Because I hadn't figured out yet where I could use 'em. They're all highly illegal here in Ohio, if you didn't know. Oh, damn – illegal fireworks,' he moaned. 'My insurance company will probably use that as an excuse to deny my claim –'

'Do you have any idea why these fireworks would go off?'

Greene shook his head wordlessly.

'How were they stored? Might they have gotten damp?'

'They were still in the plastic wrap. I hadn't even broken them open.' He added apologetically, 'My neighbors live too close, and they're not particularly tolerant of loud noises. I was saving the fireworks for when Jillian and I go up to her parents' cabin on Black Lake, on Memorial Day weekend.' Greene looked to the security chief. 'Did my fireworks injure the guard?'

Lips pressed together in a line, King shook his head. 'No. It seems not.'

'Can I tell my insurance company that?' Greene asked, rising to his feet.

Brohier answered. 'Dr Greene, as a personal favor, I'd appreciate it if you'd put off reporting your loss for the time being. I don't think we need third parties asking questions when we can't answer our own.'

'Aren't the local police already involved – or about to be?' asked Horton. 'I thought hospitals had to report all firearms-related injuries.'

'Yes,' said Brohier. 'Fortunately, I have a personal relationship with Dr Giova at Olentangy, and he has accepted my assurances that the firearm was peripheral to this accident. There will be no police investigation at this time.'

King nodded approvingly. 'Excellent.'

'Well – if everyone else is fudging the facts, I guess I can do that,' Greene said. 'Wait, that is. For a little while, anyway.'

'Thank you, Dr Greene. Check in with Mr King tomorrow, please,' said Brohier. 'For now, stop by the facilities office on your way out – the manager will provide you with the keys to one of the lab's vehicles, as a temporary loan.'

Greene looked surprised. 'Thanks,' he said, as he backed toward the door. 'Boss, are we going to reset for tomorrow?'

'I don't know,' said Horton.

'I do,' said Brohier. 'No one's working here until we understand this.'

'Boss?'

Horton nodded. 'What he said.'

'Okay. I'll collect my lunch box and go home.'

When he was gone, King and Brohier exchanged glances. 'Two guns, a gardening shed, a gun safe, and a case of fireworks,' Brohier recited. 'Can you connect them, Mr King? Can you link any person or group of persons to all five incidents?'

'No. I don't like to say it, but it would be hard for anyone not on my staff to have ready access to the weapons or the safe,' King said, standing. 'Maybe I'd better talk to Eric and Charlie myself.'

'Let me know if anything comes of it.' When the security chief was gone, Brohier turned to Horton. 'Well – what do you think?'

'I haven't a glimmer of a hint of a suggestion of a clue,' said Horton.

Brohier chuckled deeply as he closed his binder. 'Send all your people home, Jeff. And then follow them out the door. I'm closing the lab until tomorrow morning to let Donovan's people do their work. You and I and Donovan will meet at seven a.m. to decide what to do next.'

'All right,' said Horton. 'Be strange to be home before dark on a weekday. Won't know what to do with myself.'

'I don't believe that,' said Brohier. 'Oh, and, Jeff?'

'What?'

'Yours was the only experiment running when all hell broke loose. Think on that a bit while you're catching up on your sleep.'

It being the middle of the day in the middle of the week, the 100-meter outdoor range at Buckeye Sportsmen's Club was uncommonly quiet. Only three of the shooting stations were occupied – two by women practicing with 9mm automatics, and one by a gray-haired gentleman risking his classic Winchester 94 lever-action rifle.

Jeff Horton picked the station furthest away from the other shooters, placed the black hard-shelled case he was carrying on the counter, and began unpacking his competition pistol. The exotic-looking Hammerli-Walther Olympia had a way of attracting more attention than Horton wanted, but it was the only gun he owned – and more gun than he probably would ever have bought for himself.

Twenty years ago, Horton's father, after gauging his children's enthusiasm for the shooting gallery at Minnesota county fairs, had decided to channel that enthusiasm into a family activity. So he purchased a second-hand Marlin carbine, an inexpensive Browning automatic, and a gun club membership – and the Horton family became recreational target shooters, or 'plinkers'.

Everyone had taken part – even Mom, who preferred the rifle and long distances, and Jeff's younger brother Tom, who became surprisingly good at speed-shooting before he was ten. But Jeff's older sister Pamela had shown a talent with a greater talent and higher aspirations. Steady, sharp-eyed, and unflappable in competition, Pamela had won a junior championship at seventeen, and earned her way onto the last two US Olympic shooting teams. The Olympia was a gun she had outgrown, and passed on to Jeff as a present four years ago.

By his own admission, Horton was not a very good shot. But the rituals of shooting had a comforting, even nostalgic familiarity, and the concentration demanded by the deceptively simple task had a calming, even clarifying effect on his restless mind. And it was, at times, Horton's escape valve for frustration. That afternoon, Horton was at the range for both reasons, and he stayed there longer than was usual for him. Only when all sixty of the cartridges his pistol case held were gone did he let the morning's events back into his thoughts.

What were you trying to say, Dr Brohier? How could it have been us?

On his way out, Horton stopped at the club's shop and cornered its ex-Marine manager. 'Bobby,' said Horton. 'Can I get a minute?'

'Hey, Dr H. Still carrying that peashooter, I see. You know, I'd love to help you spend some of your money on a *real* gun someday.'

'Someday,' Horton promised agreeably. 'I've got kind of a weird question for you. Say you wanted to booby-trap an automatic – a Glock, maybe – so the entire clip went off at once. Could it be done?'

The question brought a questioning look. 'Why would you *want* to do it?'

'I don't, actually. But I heard a story at a party about it happening to someone, and I couldn't figure out what might do that.'

'I can't imagine,' said the manager. 'Using a Glock as a lightning rod, maybe. Though you'd be better off trying it with a Colt ACP – more metal. Are you sure you heard this story straight?'

'I'm sure,' said Horton. 'Couldn't you do something to the clip, put some little hammer or pin mechanism in it –'

The manager was frowning and shaking his head. 'There's no room in there. And the weight would be off, even if you could. Wouldn't fool anybody who knew their weapon. Someone must have been telling tall tales at that party. Punch-drunk, I'd say – pardon the pun.'

'I'll try,' said Horton, frowning. 'Well, thanks anyway.' Distracted, he started to turn away.

'No problem. You need a reload today?'

'What?'

'You left a pretty good pile of brass out there,' the manager said with a jerk of his thumb. 'I was just wondering if you needed to restock.'

30

'No,' said Horton. 'Wait – yes. Do you have any .22 blanks?'

The manager looked surprised. 'Sure. Starter pistol stuff. But you don't want to put that in your Olympia. It'll just crud up the barrel.'

'I know,' Horton said. 'Let me have a box.'

Karl Brohier's three-story house in the 'executive community' draped across Claremont Hills had enough manicured lawn in front to host a croquet tournament, and enough woods in back to conceal a herd of deer. But Brohier usually seemed more embarrassed than proud when hosting visitors. More than once Horton had heard him explain how his parents' Vermont property – farm, woods and a thousand meters of lake frontage – had sold for such an outrageous sum that he'd had no choice. It was either buy a 'pauper's mansion' in Columbus or pay half its value to the government in Social Security Stabilization assessments – the new tax which reimbursed the fund out of the recipient's estate.

'My father was an old-fashioned New England conservative – he would never have stood for that,' Brohier had explained. 'He would never have forgiven me if I'd divided his legacy with our friends in Washington.'

That evening, Brohier greeted his unexpected visitor in tennis shoes, faded yellow shorts, and a oversized t-shirt bearing one of Sidney Harris's 'Dr Quark' cartoons. The director expressed no surprise at Horton's presence on his doorstep.

'Let's walk,' he said, gesturing past his protégé at the expanse of lawn. 'My doctor says I'm eight pounds overweight, and insists I break a sweat four times a week.'

'Your doctor is a tyrant,' said Horton, falling in beside Brohier. 'I know people thirty years your junior who'd kill to be as fit as you are.'

'My *doctor* is thirty years my junior,' Brohier said with a gentle laugh.

'Isn't that a little unsettling?'

'Chances are that any MD my age who hasn't retired to New Mexico to spend a fat retirement account isn't a very good doctor,' said Brohier. 'Besides – do *you* want to be cared for by someone who received their primary training in the twentieth century?'

It was Horton's turn to laugh. 'Since you put it that way –'

'Exactly,' said Brohier. 'The recipe for a long, happy life – consult with old philosophers and young doctors, consort with old friends and young women. And since I am none of these, what brings you to me tonight?'

'The accident this morning, and your little poke in the ribs afterward,' said Horton. 'I think it's possible that my experiment might have caused the accident.'

'Do you have a theoretical foundation for that thought?'

'None whatever,' Horton confessed. 'Just a compound coincidence piled atop an anomaly. Both Gordie's fireworks and Eric's gun misbehaved at the exact same second. I don't care what Mr King thinks – neither one caused the other. Two effects, which means we're looking for a third factor, the cause of both. And the only thing out of the ordinary that morning was our experiment. We'd just gone to forty percent, the first time we've been at that level –' Horton stopped suddenly. 'You're not saying anything.'

Panting slightly, Brohier stopped and turned toward Horton. 'You were doing fine without me.'

'Is there something here worth looking at?'

'We dare not overlook an anomaly,' said Brohier. 'Do you know the story of Auguste de Tocquard?'

Frowning, Horton shook his head. 'Must have missed that class.'

'A French scientist of the late nineteenth century,' said Brohier. 'He was building and experimenting with high-voltage discharge tubes. One day he noticed that unexposed photographic plates were ruined when they were stored near the tubes. So he moved them further away, for protection. Then he returned to his experiments.'

'And missed out on discovering X-rays,' said Horton, wearing an amazed grin.

'Which would have revolutionized the science of his day,' said Brohier. 'I do not know what is happening here, Jeffrey – and from what you have said, neither do you. But perhaps we, too, have stumbled on something new. The question we must answer now is, what next?'

Horton nodded eagerly. 'The theoretical work is a dead end

– too many missing pieces. I'm not sure but that the context is missing, too. I want you to unlock the lab. I want to call in my team and see if we can do it again.'

'Yes. We need to know that, before anything else,' said Brohier. 'But do you think that perhaps we can do it alone, without your team? Tonight, in private.'

'Why?'

'Because I fear that we have both been seized by wishful thinking,' said Brohier, 'and are about to embarrass ourselves as only old fools and young dreamers can. If so, I would rather it be our secret. And if not – well, we may want that to be our secret, too, at least for a time.'

It had taken Horton just five minutes to design the sensor array for the second test, and just fifteen minutes to construct it. The sensor had started life as a fence post left over from the construction of Horton's screen porch, and made its way to the lab hanging out the passenger window of his car like a dog pointing its nose at the wind.

With Brohier seeing to the doors and the security checkpoints, Horton carried the timber into the lab on his shoulder. The two men dragged a heavy table into the emitter's output radius, then secured the post to it with bar clamps. Then, as Brohier watched, Horton placed a .22 caliber blank into each of the holes he had drilled every twenty-five centimeters along the length of the post. Most of the cartridges fit loosely in the holes, dropping down till only the flanged disc of the primer end was visible. The last one had to be force-fit, and at that would only go in half-way.

'Did you bring a flak jacket for me, too?' Brohier asked, eyeing Horton's handiwork. '"Nobel Prize Winner Found Dead With Wooden Stake in Heart" . . .'

Horton frowned. 'Maybe I should take that one out.'

'Maybe you should,' said Brohier. 'And while you do, I will take the rest of that box of shrapnel out to the guards and explain that I want it, their own guns, and them at the foot of the main drive for the next half-hour. Will that be enough time?'

'Should be,' Horton said. 'We don't have to do any of the

fussy calibrations for this trial – thumbs up or thumbs down is all we need.'

By the time Brohier returned, the displays on both consoles were active, and the test apparatus' power stage was humming audibly. Horton was making final adjustments on the compact digital camcorder he had set up on a tripod in a corner.

'Ah,' said Brohier. 'That nagging business of proof. Or were you thinking to document our demise?'

'I'm thinking that if what I expect is going to happen happens, I'm going to need to sit down and watch the recording a few dozen times before I believe it,' said Horton. He straightened up and stepped back from the camcorder. 'I think we're all ready.'

'Almost,' said Brohier, and handed Horton a pair of safety glasses and a packet of foam earplugs. 'And I think I shall stand there, behind Lee's station. I'm not nearly as eager to lose that weight as I would have to be to stand any closer.'

Horton chuckled uncomfortably, then settled in his chair. He pointed a tiny remote at the camcorder, and a red light began blinking above its lens. 'May 19, 2.19 a.m., Davisson Lab, Planck Center, Terabyte Corporation campus, Columbus, Ohio. Present are Dr Karl Brohier, director, and Dr Jeffrey Horton, associate director. This is a test of a trigger hypothesis regarding the accidents on May 18 –'

'Oh, for crying out loud,' said Brohier. 'You're not on CNN, and I'm not going to live forever. Get on with it – push the damn button.'

Blushing slightly, Horton turned toward his console. 'Beginning at ten percent, low band –'

The ensuing fusillade made Horton jump in his seat. Heart racing and ears ringing, he whirled in his chair to see tendrils of white smoke climbing from four splintered holes. Two of the bright brass shells were still dancing and skittering along the hard floor – *plink plink plink*. A third could be seen buried in the soft ceiling tile.

Brohier was staring with complete disbelief. 'What the devil,' he said to himself. 'What the devil.'

Trembling, Horton reached out, grabbed the package of earplugs from the counter, and tore it open. The plugs tumbled out into his hand, and he worked them into his ear canals with the feverish eagerness of hindsight. His throat was bone dry, and for long moments he was as incapable of speech as if his tongue had been cut out.

'Ing –' He swallowed and tried again. 'Ink – increasing power, one-tenth of a percent per second.' He dialed in the changes, then turned toward the experiment before executing them.

This time he saw it – the yellow-red flash, the bright brass shell hurled against the ceiling, the tiny gray-white mushroom cloud of propellant gases, the shell tumbling back down. *Blam! Plink plink plink . . .*

A few seconds later it happened again. *Blam! Plink plink . . .*

In the grip of wonder, Brohier and Horton momentarily found each other's eyes, seeking confirmation, affirmation, celebration. *Can this really be?* Horton's demanded. Brohier's were soft with awe, as though he had long ago given up hope of the universe surprising him.

Blam! Plink plink
Blam! Plink plink plink . . .

The same pattern continued down the line until the last shell was gone. At that point, Horton's monitors told him the emitter was at less than fifteen percent power.

'Plenty of range to reach the gate and the parking lot,' Horton said, scribbling a calculation on his personal information manager. 'Even if this effect follows the inverse square rule –'

'It was as if we'd gone down the line hitting them with a hammer,' Brohier said in wonderment. He felt his way to the nearest chair and slumped into it. Mopping his brow, he said in a shaky voice, 'Dr Horton, when next you see him, you may tell Gordie that the corporation will replace his car.'

3: Secrecy

Windsor, NC – Police report few leads in yesterday's
shocking triple murder at a Be-Lo convenience store. Security
camera recordings of the crime show two masked assailants
binding their six victims with duct tape, making a pile of their
bodies, and then shooting into the pile 'as though they had all
the time in the world', according to police sources.
Complete Story

Terabyte Corporation's Columbus campus remained officially closed for nine days. But when it finally reopened, it was immediately clear to the returning staff that the campus had not been idle during that time.

'The brownies have sure been busy,' said Gordon Greene, peering out the passenger window of Leigh Thayer's boxy Skystar.

'Brownies?'

'Brownies, Girl Scouts – whoever it was that made all those shoes for the cobbler while he slept.'

Greene was reacting to the sight of a new guardhouse and gate on the main drive, adjacent to the new black asphalt parking lot that had been carved out of what had been a grassy field dotted with trees.

Near the guardhouse, blocking what had been the exit lane of the main drive, was a new cargo dock. Concrete obstacles flanked the delivery chute, which was occupied at the moment by a brown UPS van. On the campus side of the dock, a pale blue Terabyte flatbed was nestled against the wall, and two men in corporation security uniforms were transferring packages between the two trucks.

The gate and the cargo dock straddled a new fence separating Terabyte from Shanahan Road. 'Looks as though they're not going to allow any outside vehicles anywhere near the labs from now on,' said Lee.

'Seems like they're overdoing things just a bit, don't you think?'

Lee's guess was confirmed a moment later by the two gate guards who directed them into the parking lot. 'Dr Leigh Thayer, space 8,' the first officer said, affixing a responder decal to the inside of the windshield. 'Dr Greene, when you get your new car, you'll be in space 9. You can wait for an escort driver at the pavilion.'

As he spoke, the guard jerked a thumb in the direction of a covered, plexiglas-walled enclosure a few meters beyond the airport-style security pass-through. Beside the enclosure were three six-seat canopied carts that would not have looked out of place on a golf course – or, Greene thought, in an episode of *The Prisoner*.

'I think there's something we don't know yet,' said Lee, peering out the Skystar's windshield. 'Let's get up there and find out if they plan to tell us.'

Before they could pass through the gate, Lee and Gordie had to surrender their old Terabyte identification cards in favor of new and larger cards worn on a chain around the neck.

'If I'd wanted to wear a sheep collar, I could have gone to work for IBM,' Greene grumbled as they crossed to the pavilion.

Another minor indignity awaited them at the pavilion. They were not allowed to drive themselves up to the labs. That required a special key, entrusted only to the 'escort' – in this case, a thirtyish woman with an athlete's shoulders and friendly but warily alert eyes.

Neither Lee nor Gordie tried to talk over the whine of the shuttle's electric motors and the wind whipping the canopy fringe. But half-way up the drive, Gordie silently pointed between the seats at the driver's odd holster, which contained a rectangular black shape that in no way resembled a gun.

They were driven directly to and through the former main gate, which had been rebuilt with a six-sided armored guardhouse.

'Al Capone,' Gordie said as their shuttle entered the 'canal lock' entry, whose reinforced steel-bar gate arms looked solid enough to stop anything short of a military vehicle.

'What?'

'He means the new gate post,' their driver called back over her shoulder. 'It's like the gun booths little towns used to build to fend off bank robbers in the Thirties. I saw one once, in Goshen, Indiana – right on the corner of the courthouse square. Machine guns on Main Street – can you imagine?'

'Do I have to?' asked Lee.

As they were cleared through the lock, she silently pointed out to Gordie that the inner fence had been electrified in their absence.

He nodded acknowledgement. 'Reality shift,' he said. 'We're not in Columbus anymore, Dorothy.'

The escort drove them directly to the main entry of Planck Center, where they endured yet another check of their new identification cards, this time with a wand that scanned both the barcode and the memory strip across the bottom edge so the security log could compare their contents. 'Dr Greene, Dr Thayer,' the guard said with a nod a moment later. 'The Director and Dr Horton are expecting you in the conference room.'

'Don't you want to walk us there?' Lee asked archly.

'No, ma'am, Doctor,' said the guard, emphatically shaking his head. 'I'm not authorized to enter this facility.'

Jeff Horton's face brightened when his assistants entered the conference room. 'Lee – Gordie – it's good to see you.'

'It's good to see you, too, Boss,' said Greene. 'I was a little worried I was going to come in here and see Patrick McGoohan –'

As Horton and Karl Brohier burst into laughter, Greene became aware of the third person in the room – a slender man with angular features and an almost palpable air of calmness. Brohier rose from his chair and waved the stranger forward.

'Dr Greene, let me introduce you to the newest member of your team,' said the director. 'Pete McGhan, this is Dr Gordon Greene, Dr Leigh Thayer. We've given Pete the title of Co-ordinator of Special Materials.'

'Special materials?' Greene shot a questioning glance sideways at Horton.

'A euphemism for his tax return,' said Brohier. 'Mr McGhan – the former Colonel McGhan, USMC – will be in charge of obtaining, storing, handling, and preparing the samples for your new test program. Which reminds me, Dr Greene – did you receive your check? Any problems securing a replacement for your vehicle?'

'They're making me wait another week to get the color I want – which I wouldn't call a problem,' said Greene. 'I do want to thank you again –'

'No need for that,' said Brohier. 'What happened was our responsibility.'

While Greene frowned over that, Thayer stepped forward. 'Dr Brohier, Dr Horton – would one of you be so kind as to start at the beginning? Why all the increased security? And with all respect to Mr McGhan, why do we need someone new just to handle our samples?'

'Because he has fourteen years' experience working with munitions and explosives, and we don't,' said Horton. 'Gordie, we blew up your car – you, me, Lee, and Baby.'

'How?' Thayer demanded.

Horton and Brohier exchanged wry smiles. 'I don't know yet, Lee. That's why it's time to get back to work.'

First there were new and even more stern nondisclosure agreements to sign. Then Brohier and Horton showed the new arrivals the recording of the midnight tests, and took them to Davisson Lab to show them the changes.

The first and most obvious change was that the entire target assembly, including the marble pedestal, was gone. 'We've built a new test chamber outside,' said Horton, pointing toward a new all-metal door and a plexiglas viewport in the far wall.

'Twelve-inch-thick walls covered by a Kevlar and steel-plate armor sandwich, sealed and vented through a five-hundred-liter water muffler,' added McGhan. 'We tested it yesterday – big splash, very little sound or smoke.'

'We want to keep our Good Neighbor status,' Brohier explained. 'The fewer questions, the better.'

'Looks like we need to turn Baby around, then,' said Greene, studying the geometry. 'Now that we know we have to be careful where we point it.'

'Actually, we don't know that. That's your first priority – finding out what the effect envelope looks like. Pete will get you some test material that won't put you or the lab at risk,' said Horton. 'Lee, your priority is to figure out what sort of data collection we can do inside and through the port, and get it rigged up for Steady Hand.'

'What sort of samples are we going to be testing?'

'More ammunition, first – all calibers and propellants. Then the whole catalog of explosives, from Amatol to Torpex,' said McGhan. 'Everything my licenses cover and my contacts can provide.'

'And then the entire *Handbook of Chemistry*,' said Brohier. 'We need to know exactly what compounds are affected, and what compounds aren't – a very practical necessity, in the absence of any theoretical base.'

'Which is *my* first priority,' said Horton. 'We need to understand what's going on here – why what came out of this lab made something happen that natural radiation doesn't. Or doesn't where we can see it, anyway.'

'Any help from PSR Index, or the JPSI?' asked Thayer.

Horton shook his head. 'I've been searching the literature for a week now, and it looks as though this effect has never been observed before – or never been reported, at least. So I'm starting with a blank page.'

'Then we'll have to fill it with some good data, so you have something to work with,' she said, then looked expectantly at Brohier. 'Is there anyone besides the five of us who knows what we've stumbled on?'

'Not yet,' said Brohier. 'And that is the problem on *my* table. Because when we choose the sixth person, and share this with them, the world will start to change. I cannot emphasize this enough – our discretion will buy us necessary time. Indiscretion will cost us the opportunity to shape what comes next.'

His words sobered the others but his gaze measured the weight he had laid on them, and found it insufficient. 'Make no mistake,' he went on, 'no one will be able to control the future once this discovery leaves this room. We will be in the realms of politics and psychology. This discovery will rewrite the rules of power which have governed world affairs since the flintlock displaced the sword

and spear. And we will not be the ones who write the new rules –
we are merely the reason why they will be necessary.

'We did not choose this responsibility, but we cannot refuse it.
There is no turning back. What we can discover, others inevitably
will discover. You will remember today fondly as one of the last
days of the old familiar world. Your children will know a different reality.' Brohier glanced across the room at the apparatus,
then back, a kind smile softening the solemnity. 'May it be a
better one.'

4: Inquiry

Dale City, MD – Investigators are counting on an emergency dispatch center's 911 call recording to shed some light on last night's drive-by shooting in a mostly-white subdivision. The cries and screams of party-goers punctuate the 100-second recording, which begins just before bullets smashed through a kitchen window and killed home-owner Gil Dellard as he tried to report a car full of teens driving across his front lawn.

Complete Story   *911 Recording*

For the next several weeks, life in Davisson Lab was fast-paced yet deceptively tranquil.

The generator/emitter unit was relocated, realigned, and rededicated to the purpose of detonating the samples delivered four times a day by Pete McGhan. Because of the danger to McGhan if he were to approach the lab while a test was underway, his comings and goings dictated the rhythms of the test program and the daily schedule of Horton's team.

The first delivery was at 8.00 a.m., with the other deliveries following at three-hour intervals. Half-hour 'blackouts' were programmed into Steady Hand for each delivery. As insurance, McGhan called in on a dedicated line as he neared the Terabyte campus, to verify that the emitter was cold and the test chamber ready.

'Can the doctor see me?' he asked each time.

'Come on up to the office,' was the reply that told McGhan to proceed. 'Sorry, there are no appointments available,' was the reply that told him to stay outside the safety radius.

McGhan never lingered longer than was necessary to set up the samples in the test chamber and turn over the sample tags and standard yield data to Horton. Then he disappeared again to whatever undisclosed off-campus location he was using to receive, store, and prepare the samples.

'Thanks for seeing me,' he said each time as he left the safety radius.

'Please come again,' was the countersign.

The cloak-and-dagger aspects tended to elicit childish giggles and snide jokes from Horton's team – especially Lee, who'd been drafted to field the calls. 'He sounds like a hypochondriac with a drug habit,' she complained to Horton. '*I* sound like a Cincinnati madam. And if you put one word about this part in the research paper, we'll all sound like paranoid James Bond wannabes.'

'Just because you're paranoid –' Greene began.

'I know, I know.' She hunched over her console and glanced furtively to either side. 'Ve must be careful,' she said in exaggerated comic-book German. 'Ze enemy may be listening effen now. Any vun of us may haff been compromised –'

Apart from McGhan's deliveries and calls, there were few other intrusions on their work. The administrative staff protected them from routine inquiries, deflected personal contacts with a shield of plausible excuses, and took over a wide range of mundane obligations, even to picking up Dr Greene's new car and putting ready-to-eat meals in Dr Horton's home refrigerator.

Karl Brohier visited daily for the first few days, then fell out of sight after announcing he would be away from campus for a time. Exactly where he had gone and with what purpose was grist for much speculation, but not even Horton could get answers from Brohier's staff.

'He wouldn't sell us out, would he?' asked Greene. 'Make a deal behind our backs?'

'No,' Horton said firmly. 'I don't believe he'd ever do that. He's on Diogenes's mission. It's going to take some time.'

'Diogenes,' Thayer said with evident displeasure. 'You could have picked a more comforting allusion, Boss.'

'Looking for an honest man? Isn't that what we need for Number Six?'

'Boss, the one thing everyone knows about Diogenes,' she said with a sigh, 'is that he was the founder of the Cynics –'

Greene's face brightened. 'Papa! At last I find you!'

Thayer glowered at him. 'His nickname was Kayo – "dog" – because he slept in the streets. He taught his students to hold civilization in contempt. He gave up all worldly goods in a rejection of it. Boss, if we have to cast Dr Brohier as a Greek philosopher, couldn't it at least be one of the Ionians? Thales, or Anaximander?'

'I had an Anaximander when I was a kid,' Greene said. 'Kept it in a glass bowl on my dresser – till it died.'

She balled up the nearest piece of paper and threw it at his head.

As the days slipped by, the data piled up.

The first round of tests centered on ammunition similar to that in Eric Fleet's pistol – ammunition using cellulose hexanitrate propellants, or guncotton. Having little personal experience with guns, Thayer and Greene were surprised by the seemingly endless parade of varieties McGhan was bringing them. The Winchester catalog alone offered eleven powders and more than two hundred cartridges.

Blend, grain size and shape, loading, maker, caliber – any one of those factors could be the difference that made a difference, that separated a positive test from a negative one. But the first twenty samples all duplicated the anomaly with such reliability that the team began calling the last mouse-click of the test protocol 'pulling the Trigger'.

When the run of positive tests had reached thirty-two, consuming eight days, Thayer and Greene succeeded in infecting Horton with their impatience to test other materials. From that point on, they accelerated their testing by putting three ammunition samples in the chamber at once.

It made no difference in the results. Magnum and ACP, rimfire and centerfire, rifle and handgun, .218 Bee through .458 Winchester – within a fraction of a second after the emitter reached the ten percent power level, the sample cartridges would discharge, the soft brass shell splitting and curling in the clamp, the bullet crashing weakly into the catch box.

At the end of the seventeenth day of testing, with one hundred forty samples logged, ennui threatening to replace the healthy impatience of curiosity, and no sign of Karl Brohier, Horton finally reclaimed control of the project.

'That's more than enough of this,' he said to himself, closing the research log and calling McGhan. 'Pete? There's a change in the schedule. I want to do the raw powders tomorrow and Saturday, and start the Series Three materials the first of the week. Can you accommodate that? Good. Thanks. See you in the morning.'

As he logged off, he heard thin but earnest applause behind him, and turned away from his desk to find Greene and Thayer had been eavesdropping. 'Good decision, Doctor J,' said Greene. 'I was getting so bored that I was thinking about taking the new car down to Tennessee this weekend.'

'Why are men in love with explosions?' Lee asked with a sigh, not expecting an answer. 'Boss, if we're doing powders in the morning, we probably should test the exhaust and fire suppression systems tonight.'

'No,' said Horton. 'We're done for the day. And I'm taking both of you out for a decent meal.'

Greene nodded approvingly. 'Good decision number two. You're on a roll.'

'Wait till you hear number three,' said Horton. 'Both of you, take a minute to swab and fluff, and then let's get going – it's an hour's drive to Zanesville.'

'I'll drive,' Greene cheerfully volunteered.

'No, you won't,' said Horton, and Lee sighed her relief.

On the way to dinner, Horton told them of his other plans.

'With our test emitter behaving itself, I don't think I've been getting the best possible use out of you, Gordie. So tomorrow I want you to start working on a second-generation emitter,' he said.

'Sounds like fun. Parameters?'

'Take everything we've learned so far and run with it. We now know we don't need the whole spectrum, zero to infinity. Simplify. Try to give me something smaller, more efficient, sturdier, and more self-contained – in a word, something portable.'

'Portable?' Thayer asked, raising an eyebrow.

'We can't test the emitter's range at the lab – the campus isn't big enough. Someone else would get hurt, in that big subdivision on the south side of Shanahan Road, or even just driving by. We need to be able to take a test rig to a Big Empty somewhere, out West, or in the middle of Lake Erie. You can build Baby Two right into the back of a panel truck if you like.'

'Just out of curiosity, Doc – will the Trigger make gasoline explode?'

'Good question. I don't suppose you'd take a guess for an answer.'

'Sure – if it's your truck.' Greene said, grinning.

'We should test gasoline next week, then. I'll tell McGhan.'

'Probably should test kerosene and diesel fuel at the same time,' Thayer interjected. 'Unless you don't mind surprises – since there's plenty of both around.'

Horton nodded. 'Yes. And we had all three on campus the day of the anomaly, and none of them were affected at that power level. Maybe higher output levels will affect some of the materials we now think are stable in a Trigger field. If I was making any headway on the theory, I could possibly answer that. For now, all we can do is keep testing. The other advantage of having a second unit is that we could speed up the test program.'

'Every time we start Baby up, we're testing more than the sample in the chamber,' said Thayer. 'We already know it doesn't affect plexiglas, concrete, grapefruit, black lace and Spandex, carbonated drinks, the batteries in Gordie's cheap watch –'

'Black lace and Spandex?' Greene repeated, looking back over his shoulder.

'I'll explain when you're older.'

For the rest of the drive, the trio brainstormed a list of materials known to have been exposed to the Trigger field, simply by virtue of having been part of the structure, setting, or contents of Davisson Lab. But as they pulled into the driveway of the Old Market House Inn, Horton confiscated the list.

'That's it for shop talk,' he said. 'Not another word about work. If we can't think of civilized conversation, we'll eat in silence, by god – I mean to enjoy this meal. After all, it's not every day that I put on a tie.'

'Or eat something that wasn't served in colored paper and

styrofoam,' said Greene, reaching for the door latch. 'I accept your terms. Come on – I'm starving.'

With surprising ease, they talked only of pop-culture guilty pleasures, the demise of women's professional football, and dream vacations, while consuming tender meats, exotic vegetables, and most of two bottles of wine in the course of a two-hour meal. The only breach of Horton's edict was committed by Horton himself, in a toast.

'To the world's largest single-shot hand-load country-windage hide-your-children firearm, and the team what built it,' he said quietly. 'May we figure out what it's good for, and how to aim it.'

'You're a sloppy drunk, Boss,' said Thayer, clinking glasses. 'But, what you said, all the same.'

Whether it was the hour, the tranquilizing effect of the food and wine, or the sobering after-effect of the toast, there was little conversation on the way back to Columbus. Horton directed the car into the high-speed autodrive lane and let it bore westward through the moonless night while he looked out onto the darkened farms. Greene dozed, sometimes snoring lightly. Thayer watched the traffic in the self-drive lanes. A dark four-door sedan, breaking all speed limits, overtook them and melted away into the night ahead.

'Unmarked car?' Horton suggested. 'Desperate need to find the next rest area?'

'Secret government agency transporting captured alien to Wright-Patterson Air Force Base,' she said lightly.

'Ah.'

The silence seemed to be lengthening the miles, so Horton turned on the satellite radio and the last half of Count Basie's 'Kansas City Suite' saw them to the gatehouse of Greene's singles community – he had decided to taxi in the next morning rather than spend most of another hour on the road – and Stan Kenton delivered them to the Terabyte lot where Thayer's car waited.

'It was a nice place, a good meal, Boss – thank you.' Though it sounded like an exit line, she made no move to open her door.

'My pleasure. See you in the morning.'

'Can I confess something?'

Puzzled, Horton turned sideways in his seat, so he could see her face. 'Sure.'

'I didn't enjoy tonight very much –'

'I'm sorry –'

'Not your fault,' she said. 'Boss, I was nervous all the way there and back, in a way I never am when we each go our own way at the end of the night. I kept thinking, one car crash, and the status quo is safe –'

'I think Dr Brohier has enough now that he could carry on even if something happened to us.'

'I guess probably he does – but would outsiders realize that?'

'What are you getting at, Lee?'

'All evening, I've been thinking about how this work threatens the power base of a lot of people who aren't going to love us for what we're doing, and who'd surely like to stop it if they had the chance. I kept wanting both you and Gordie to lower your voices in the restaurant, even though you had the No Shop Talk sign lit. I just didn't want anyone to take notice of us. I just wanted to be invisible.'

She sighed. 'And now that I have these thoughts in my head, every sound I hear outside my condo – every time my cat gets curious about something in the middle of the night – every time I turn the key to start my car – I'm going to be nervous. Jeff, we're not going to be safe until we're no longer the only people in the world who know how to do this.'

'I don't know that –'

'You know that there're people out there who'll kill out of calculation – to further their interests, or protect them. They aren't just a Hollywood invention.'

'I suppose. I confess I haven't really thought much about it.'

'I have,' she said, her voice tight with emotion. 'My sister in Cleveland's been having trouble with gangs, because her son doesn't want to join. Their house has been shot-up three times now.' She sighed again. 'And when I was twelve, my Uncle Ted was jury foreman in a bank robbery case against the head of one of those white nationalist syndicates. The jury voted to convict.

A week later Uncle Ted was found dead, shot sixteen times, with "Traitor" painted across the windshield of his car.'

'I remember that,' Horton said in surprise. 'I remember seeing that on the news. I had no idea –'

'I promised myself –' She shook her head and started over. 'I told myself I'd never let myself get caught between someone like that and what they wanted – that I'd just hunker down in the tall grass and let the lions fight it out overhead.'

'Lee, what can I do?'

'I think I'd like to start living at the lab,' she said. 'Ernie, too, if that's okay.'

'Ernie's the cat?'

Lee nodded. 'Just until we've published, and there's not so much at stake. I could use Barton's old office – it's close to the women's lounge, and the couch is long enough for me.'

'We'll get you a bed, and a wardrobe,' he said firmly. 'And an old armchair for Ernie to claw.'

A relieved smile brightened Lee's face. 'Thank you.'

'Shall I take you around to the gate? Do you want to start tonight?'

'No – Ernie goes crazy when I don't come home.' She thought a moment. 'But I'll bring him and a suitcase with me tomorrow, if that's all right.'

'Of course. I'm pretty sure Site Services can rustle up a bed by quitting time, if I light a fire under them.'

Nodding, she opened her door. 'Thanks for not making me feel like some paranoid 'fraidy-cat.'

'There's plenty out there that's worth being afraid of,' Horton said. 'Most of us cope by pretending it's not there. You had that illusion taken away from you too damn early.' He grunted. 'And I think I just lost mine. Maybe I'll ask Site Services for two beds.'

'I'm sorry, Boss –'

'No. Don't be. Dr Brohier tried to tell us. He couldn't have been any plainer about it. And I looked right past it, with hardly a thought for anything but the puzzle, the science.' He shook his head. 'It's late. Time to go home.'

She started to climb out, then stopped and looked back at Horton with a penetrating earnestness. 'Jeff?'

'What?'

'We *are* going to publish, aren't we? Tell me we're not really working for Dow Chemical, or the Department of Defense. Tell me that Dr Brohier understands we can't just sell the Trigger to the high bidder – that there'll be a chance to use this work to declaw some of the lions. That's the only reason I didn't run away the first week.' She smiled ruefully. 'I wanted to, but Uncle Ted wouldn't let me.'

'We're going to publish,' Horton said firmly. 'And the lions are going to get the surprise of their lives.'

5: Chemistry

Lyons, France – Smoke bombs and firecrackers chased supporters of beleaguered French president Charles Fontenay from a poorly-attended election rally on Tuesday. One woman was seriously injured in a fall from an escalator. This was the ninth time in two weeks that a Social Democrat campaign event has been disrupted by the self-styled political terrorist group Mad Dogs. Police officials announced they would meet today with representatives of the three major candidates to discuss event security and 'explore troubling rumors'.

Complete Story	*Campaign Schedule*
'Mad Dog' Manifesto	*Fontenay Gaining in Polls*

When the testing moved to other materials, the first subtle clues about the nature of the trigger effect began to emerge.

A test sample of loose nitrocellulose gunpowder flared up in a single bright gout of flame. As McGhan showed them by match-burning a reference sample on the worktable, that flare represented much faster burning than would ordinarily be expected.

'It's as if there's no convection delay – as if every grain in the pile hits the flash threshold at essentially the same instant,' said Horton. 'Like the difference between heating water in a pot on a stove and heating water in a microwave.'

'That would help explain why Eric was so badly injured,' said Greene. 'And why my car went up like a bomb. Baby is very efficient at what he does.'

'I wish you'd stop calling it "Baby",' Thayer griped. 'There's nothing cute and cuddly about it anymore – if there ever was.'

'How about "Problem Child"? Is that any better?'

'Shouldn't you be down the hall, working on Son of Problem Child?'

'I only come down here when you're pulling the Trigger,' he said defensively, retreating toward the door. 'Ten minutes every three hours. I get lonely down there, all by myself. Look, I know you have a couple of hours of cleanup ahead of you – I'll leave you to it.'

The next sample was black powder – the world's first explosive, and the mainstay of armies from China to England for more than three hundred years. To everyone's surprise, the test sample merely smoked and turned gray-brown. A second test at the next power level yielded the same result, with what was left rendered inert to a match.

'It should burn,' said Horton, shaking his head. 'Black powder will catch on a spark. This is like trying to light a soggy cat.'

'We're going to have to get our samples to an analytical chemist soon,' Thayer said. 'Something queer is happening at the compound level.'

'We should get an analytical chemist set up in the next lab,' said Greene grumpily. 'Isn't there anyone on campus we can hit over the head and drag over here?'

'It's at the top of my list for when Dr Brohier returns,' said Horton. 'But I don't need a chemist to tell me that the only thing gunpowder and guncotton have in common are the nitrates. And I think we're seeing that the difference between cellulose hexanitrate and potassium nitrate is the difference between flash and fizzle.'

'I think we're going to need a physical chemist, too,' Thayer said with a frown. 'Something queer has to be happening to the electron bonds.'

'*I* think we're going to need a sample of Blasting Powder B,' said Horton. When the others looked at him questioningly, he added, 'Same basic chemistry as black powder, except it contains *sodium* nitrate. And that will give us another big piece of the puzzle.'

That afternoon, Horton and Thayer watched five grams of Blasting Powder B fill the test chamber with fragrant gray smoke. Neither the sample nor the residue ever showed a flame.

'Interesting,' said Horton.

'Indeed, Mr Spock,' said Thayer, studying her displays. 'But I want to tear that miserable excuse for a test chamber apart and rebuild it the right way. It's absurd that I can't get a spectrograph on that smoke –'

'Lee, would you look up Mr King's report on the anomaly?'

'Sure – what do you need?'

'See if it has a list of the fireworks Gordie said were in his car.'

'It's there – I remember seeing it.' Her screen flashed rapidly. 'Two dozen bottle rockets. One box M-60 firecrackers. One "Devastation Celebration" skyrocket assortment.'

'That's all?'

'That's all.' Then her eyes lit up with understanding. 'Oh! We have a little problem, don't we?'

Horton nodded reluctant acknowledgement. 'If the black powder didn't burn, and the blasting powder didn't burn, why did the fireworks in Gordie's car go off?' He pushed his chair away from his monitoring station. 'I need to stretch my legs. Be back in a few.'

The mobile emitter unit was already taking shape atop a pair of the Maintenance Section's rubber-wheeled aluminum dollies. Horton saw that the geometry of the power and control module was already well defined, and that Greene was anchoring the support section of the emitter cylinder in its upright position.

'I've never seen anyone get to bending metal faster than you do,' Horton said. 'The vertical orientation's not going to create any problems?'

'Not for me,' Greene said, sitting up and brushing the perspiration off his forehead. 'Half an hour pushing lines around with the cursor, and the CAM shop started turning out parts.'

'It's what goes on in your head before you touch the cursor that's mysterious to me,' Horton said, settling on a stool near Greene's work area. 'We have a problem, Gordie.'

Pursing his lips, Greene said nothing.

'Come on, Gordie – don't make me be the bad guy,' said Horton. 'You must have realized we'd pick it up.'

Greene wiped his hands on his overalls with great deliberation, then looked up and smiled a wry, rueful smile. 'Actually, I didn't. Until this morning I thought gunpowder was gunpowder. Who knew?'

'What was in the car?'

'An unlicensed pistol.' He snorted. 'My anti-carjacking security system. A little plastic-frame Ruger 9mm.'

'Another Tennessee souvenir?'

'Kentucky, actually,' said Greene. 'They still find a way to overlook any Federal law they don't like. And I guess they didn't like the 30th Amendment.' He leaned forward, resting his elbows on his thighs and slowly wringing his hands. 'Dr Horton – I'm sorry. I didn't know the fire was going to be kept in the family. I was afraid of that mandatory five-year term. And once I'd already committed myself to one version of reality – Doc, I was just too embarrassed to admit I'd lied.'

Horton stood. 'I guess I can weather this little surprise,' he said. 'But please don't hand me any big ones. Did you replace your security system along with your car?'

Shaking his head, Greene said, 'No. Thought about it. Decided I'd have to wait until things were clearer up here before I could assess the risks.'

'I think it's pretty clear that the lab's not going to buy you *two* replacement cars,' said Horton, letting his face relax into a lazy grin. 'So if you don't feel safe out there without a pistol in the console, you can always opt for Lee's solution – or mine.'

'What's yours?' Greene asked, cocking his head.

Horton laughed. 'Drive a car so pocket-protector dull that no one would ever think to steal it.'

A day's testing on black-powder fireworks confirmed that while Greene's cache might have helped accelerate the car fire, it could not have started it.

Then Horton's team turned their attention away from low-yield combustion explosives to high-yield detonating explosives. Pete McGhan sat them all down for a primer before delivering the first samples to them.

'Thirty-thirty rifle cartridge,' he said, placing a gleaming brass cylinder on the table between them. 'Three ccs of guncotton propellant. Powder burns in a few thousandths of a second and develops a maximum detonation pressure of a few hundred pounds per square inch.'

He placed a small putty-colored cylinder beside it. 'Three ccs of RDX, a.k.a. cyclonite. Detonation takes a few millionths of a second and develops a detonation pressure of millions of pounds per square inch. If your rifle can fire a 30-30 bullet two hundred meters, an RDX cartridge of the same size could damn near reach orbit – if there was a gun anywhere that wouldn't shatter to splinters first.

'There are more kinds of high explosive than any of you probably realize – more than a hundred readily available formulations, probably another hundred that have been used in the past and abandoned, plus a couple of dozen more that are military or industrial secrets. But most of them are built around one or more of half a dozen or so basic compounds – ammonium nitrate, picric acid, nitroglycerin, PETN, RDX, TNT. Dr Brohier's instructions were for me to provide appropriate samples from each family in the purest and simplest formulation available, then let the results guide the choice of which blends to investigate.

'Almost everything I've told you about what you've tested so far doesn't apply to what's coming up. Dynamite can burn without exploding. But the nitroglycerin in the dynamite will explode on a shock no greater than this,' he said, snapping a pencil sharply against the edge of the table. Everyone jumped. 'While Nitromex is so stable you can shoot a pistol at it or set off a detonating cord under it.

'In fact, the detonating explosives are so different from the combustion explosives, and one family from another, that I have a private bet with myself – I don't think your device is going to touch them. Any of them.

'No matter what, though, *you're* not going to touch them. I'll handle the preparation, transportation, set-up *and* cleanup – the last two wearing my Kevlar gorilla suit,' McGhan said, looking around the table. 'Dr Brohier was very specific and painfully blunt about this. I'm replaceable, and you're not. So I won't be coming into the lab anymore – I'll load the test chamber from outside, and you'll keep that access door closed and secured.

'The safety procedures we've been using, the radio calls, the blackouts, have been a drill for this,' he added as he stood and gathered up his props. 'Chances are I'd survive if you triggered a rifle cartridge in my trunk. Chances are I wouldn't if you triggered a sample of Torpex. And while I may be expendable, I'm fairly certain it would hinder the research program if you blew up your courier in the middle of Shanahan Road.'

Then he popped the putty-colored cylinder into his mouth and began to chew it. 'Peppermint, sugar-free,' he said. 'I'll be back with the real thing in half an hour.'

McGhan lost his bet by lunchtime. A one-centimeter-square cube of something called EDNA blasted the water muffler dry and cracked the test chamber's plexiglas port.

'That was way above the standard yield,' McGhan said grimly, studying the damage with the helmet of his high-collared bomb suit tucked under one arm. 'I'm going to have to trim all the samples by a quarter to a third to get back our safety margin.'

A shaken Horton agreed that that was an idea which recommended itself.

At the end of that week, Karl Brohier returned.

His reappearance was as low-key as his departure, and came with even less advance notice. The first that Horton knew of it was when the senior director poked his head into Davisson Lab, captured Lee's attention with a wave, and called out, 'Jeff? Come and see me when you have a minute.' His tone and demeanor were as casual as if he'd never left, as if only utterly mundane administrative matters were occupying his thoughts.

Horton was momentarily struck dumb, but managed to squeeze out a few words before Brohier vanished again. 'I'll be right there.'

'No hurry,' said Brohier cheerfully. 'My assistant tells me there are five hundred fourteen priority messages waiting in my mailbox.'

Despite that reassurance, Horton only waited as long as it took to call Greene in from the prototyping shop to follow Brohier across the campus to Edison Center, the administrative building.

'Ah, Jeffrey,' Brohier said brightly when Horton walked into his office. 'How is the work going? Everyone still has ten fingers, I trust?'

'Yes. Pete was a good addition,' Horton said, settling on the couch. 'He's meticulous, punctual, and only nosy about the parts that affect his job, which he does very well. Where did you find him?'

'I have a grandson, Louis, in the Marines,' said Brohier, dividing his attention between Horton and the display in front of him. 'He is not allowed to tell me his unit, but I believe it is the one trained to operate behind enemy lines for purposes of sabotage and terrorism. McGhan was an instructor for this unit until he made the mistake of sleeping with the wife of a higher-ranking officer. McGhan was charged with rape and accepted a general discharge.'

'Rape? How –'

'Apparently the higher-ranking officer provided his wife with corroborating bruises, and the incentive to lie.' Brohier smiled wryly. 'I thought the fact that that officer is still alive recommended Mr McGhan as a man of self-discipline and principle.'

'I'll say. One little booby-trap –' Horton shook his head. 'You asked how the work is going. Mostly it's going *boom*. It's beginning to seem as though if it has a nitrate compound in it, the Trigger sets it off.'

'Fascinating,' Brohier said, looking up. 'What about nitrate compounds that aren't explosives?'

'We haven't gotten to them yet.'

'And explosives that aren't nitrates?'

'No effect. But there aren't many of those. All of the most-used explosives – military *and* civil – use nitrates. All standard ammunition uses nitrates.'

'So do most farmers,' said Brohier. 'So do many people with diarrhoea – I myself had a prescription once for bismuth subnitrate, after a trip to Brazil. Did you give any thought to that?'

'Farmers?'

'Fertilizer. One farm bureau semi-trailer passing by at the wrong moment, and we'd be Breaking News on CNN.'

'Oh, god,' said Horton, his face suddenly ashen. 'Nitroglycerin. *Nitroglycerin*. I never thought about medicine –'

Brohier answered with a cheerful smile. 'I did. My doctor assures me that nitro tablets do not explode. As for the rest of the pharmacopia, well, we will look at everything in its turn before loosing this on the world.

Horton could not understand why the director was being so

casual about what to Horton seemed an inexcusable oversight. 'Dr Brohier, we've been playing Russian roulette. We have to suspend testing right away, today,' he said, still agitated. 'We can't do this work at this site anymore. We're going to need to go somewhere more isolated and work out the control issues – range, directionality. Maybe then we can come back.'

'As it happens, I've already begun negotiating for a piece of property in the West,' said Brohier. 'But, please, Jeffrey – let's not aggravate ourselves over a disaster that didn't happen.'

'It *could* have, and it would have been my responsibility.'

'We needed data,' Brohier said, gesturing. 'Even if we'd known at the outset, it was an acceptable risk. Now the picture is clearer, and we can adjust accordingly. Tell me how the theoretical side is progressing.'

Loosing a sigh, Horton settled into a chair. 'It isn't,' he said. 'The Trigger doesn't fit the CERN model of the atom. It doesn't fit the quantum model, or the Bohr model. As near as I can tell, it doesn't even fit conventional chemical thermodynamics – the yields are above book value.'

'Is that so?' said Brohier. 'Well – I will shortly be able to devote more time to this, and I confess I'm pleased you've left something for me to do.' He smiled wryly. 'I suppose I could have worded that more diplomatically.'

'No, that's all right – my ego won't kick in until it's time to haggle over the by-line. Right now the *problem* is everything. I'll be glad to have someone to bounce ideas off,' Horton said.

'The by-line will not be a problem,' Brohier said with grim humor. 'By that time, we may be more interested in dodging the blame than claiming the credit – and "Anonymous" will cover any number of us.'

Nodding thoughtfully, Horton said, 'I want to bring in a chemist, someone who can analyze the residue from our test samples and tell us what's happening on the molecular level – how the Trigger reaction is different from ordinary spark- or shock-initiated detonation. There may be someone on staff already, in one of the other research units. If not, I know someone at Ohio State who could handle it.'

'We need not bring them all the way in,' said Brohier. 'In

fact, we could spread the samples out among any number of contract labs –'

'I don't want to have to take a crash course in physical chemistry. I'd rather have one experienced person who understood the context – someone who might be able to help the two of us lay a foundation under the theory.'

'And a frail enough edifice it is, eh? Very well, let me think on it for a day. Give me the name of the fellow at Ohio State, and I'll make some inquiries.'

Horton handed over a folded piece of paper. 'Everything you'll need's right there,' he said, and jerked his head toward the door. 'I'd better get back to the lab and pull the plug.'

'Of course,' said Brohier. 'And since you have nothing to do for the rest of the day, you'll be able to come to my place for dinner.' Seeing Horton's startled look, he added, 'I have a house guest who's looking forward to meeting you.'

There was a black coupe at the end of Karl Brohier's driveway, and two men in black suits standing behind it. They eyed Horton carefully, but made no move as he drove past except to turn and watch him.

Not lab security, Horton thought, stealing a glance back in his rear-view mirror. *Private security – bodyguards. For Karl – or his guest?*

A silver Mercedes sedan was parked on the cobblestone half-circle by the house, and a slender woman in a smart chauffeur's uniform was coming down the walk from the front door. She stopped at the driver's door of the Mercedes as Horton pulled up behind it, then slid behind the wheel and pulled away as he climbed out. He peered into the sedan as it made the big turn and headed down the drive, but saw only the driver.

The presence of guards in the driveway tempered the surprise when the front door was opened by someone other than Brohier – in point of fact, by another broad-shouldered man in a tailored suit. Again there was the steady gaze, the snap appraisal, the calm alertness. 'Come in,' the man said, ushering Horton inside. 'You'll find them on the sky porch.'

Taller than it was wide or deep, the north-facing two-story space Brohier called the sky porch looked out on the upslope forest and the sky through great sloping panels of permaglass. A pair of avocado trees and a giant dieffenbachia brought the forest inside and separated a sunken tile hot tub from a casual seating area.

There Horton found Brohier and his guest, a slender man with a short-cropped full white beard and a wealth of smile lines around dark, deep-set eyes. He was casually dressed in golf shorts, polo shirt, and well-worn sandals, and had his feet propped up on the rounded edge of a low stone table.

'– I have never micromanaged your budget, Karl, and I won't start now,' the guest was saying as Horton approached. 'Ah, here he is.'

Brohier twisted in his chair to look back over his shoulder, then stood. 'Jeffrey – I want you to meet Aron Goldstein.'

Horton had already guessed the identity of the visitor. He had never met Terabyte's principal investor and majority owner, but there was a photo of Goldstein and Brohier in the director's office, and Horton had searched the hyperweb for information on Goldstein shortly after arriving in Columbus.

The most useful information had come from the *Fortune* site, which mapped Goldstein's extensive holdings – thirty-one companies in eleven industry groups, with the cash cow among them being Advanced Storage Devices, Inc., the exclusive licensee of Brohier's solid-state memory patents. The most interesting information had come from the gossipy *Microscope* pages, which had named him America's 'most ineligible bachelor', snidely commenting 'never before in our memory has anyone with so much managed to enjoy it so little'.

Goldstein stood to shake hands, then settled back in his chair. 'Do you like Chinese food, Jeffrey?' he asked.

'Um – sure. Some,' he answered, nonplussed.

'Good. Sit down, please.' Goldstein waited only for Horton to start moving before he went on. 'I want to congratulate you on your discovery. It's stunning. I've scarcely been able to think or talk about anything else since Karl told me. Which has been quite a burden on him, since I haven't had anyone else I *can* talk to.

'Of course, now I have you, too. And the first thing I want to say is, "Well done". This is revolutionary, in the same way the

60

Watt engine, the Marconi wireless telegraph, and the Hollerith tabulator were revolutionary.' He chuckled. 'I like those examples because every one of those men managed to make money while they were changing the world.'

'I confess I haven't been able to see any way of making money from this,' Horton said.

'That's all right – I have,' Goldstein said with a wave of his hand. 'Change always creates opportunities. I've acquired three companies and two hundred patents in the last ten days.' Then the twinkle of self-satisfied glee left his eyes as he sat forward in his chair. 'But that's completely irrelevant. Do you know why I created Terabyte Laboratories, Jeffrey?'

'From what Dr Brohier told me when he hired me, I assumed it was for more or less the same reason farmers plant seeds and investors buy futures,' said Horton.

'You're only partly correct,' said Goldstein. 'What I wanted was to create the Bell Labs of the twenty-first century.'

'Bell Labs –'

'Yes – the research arm of the one-time Bell Telephone monopoly. One of the overlooked benefits of that monopoly was that it paid the bills for a peerless basic research enterprise. And the twentieth century was invented there.'

'The transistor,' Brohier said. 'The laser. Cellular radio. Solar cells. Radio astronomy. CCDs and LEDs. Big Bang radiation –'

Nodding, Goldstein took over. 'Eight Nobel laureates. Thirty thousand patents – an average of one a day. And all of it the product of enlightened capitalism. In its heyday, Bell Labs was the equal and more of any university department, any government research center, and any quarterly-profit-and-loss corporate lab anywhere in the world.'

'I'm afraid we've fallen a bit short,' said Horton.

'Not at all,' Goldstein said as a distant door chime sounded. 'I could not be more pleased. Jeffrey, I long ago reached the point where I'd made more than enough money to satisfy a lifetime's ordinary desires. At which point there arises the burdensome question of what to do with the excess. Ostentatious consumption has no appeal for me. Neither does charity in the usual sense – there is no Goldstein Foundation bestowing grants on Jewish MBAs or slow-footed midfielders or the children of city bureaucrats. I do not give to save the whales or feed the birds or sponsor music in the park –'

At that point, the chauffeur reappeared, and Goldstein fell silent while she placed the blue and white picnic cooler she was carrying in the middle of the stone table. She started to remove the lid, but Goldstein raised a hand and stopped her.

'We can see to it,' he said. 'Thank you, Barbara. I expect that'll be all for tonight.'

'Yes, sir. I'm going to stay in, though, so if you change your mind –'

'We'll look in Karl's game room first,' he said, smiling tolerantly. When she had left them, Goldstein looked to the others and asked absently, 'Where was I?'

'Music in the park,' Brohier supplied.

'Music in the park,' Goldstein repeated, frowning. 'Jeffrey, money whispers to you like a whore, telling you what it can do for you if only you'll open your wallet. And if you have no shame, you can be seduced into almost anything.' Standing and moving to where the cooler sat, he began removing brown paper bags from inside it, and then white boxes from the brown paper bags. 'Karl, we're going to need three plates, and some spoons.'

'I'll collect them,' Brohier said, rising.

Cracking the lid of one container, Goldstein took a deep breath of the escaping steam. 'What do you do with a few extra billion?' he asked. 'Collect art, like Hearst? Collect women, like Hughes? Most of the examples at hand are embarrassments. When Bill Gates paid for the Ares mission to Mars, that was a stunt – nothing more than ego gratification. He was seduced into trying to buy immortality for himself and his company logo by hijacking an historic event. I promised myself I would never be that weak – and then fell under the spell of an even more fickle temptress.

'Jeffrey, I have nearly a hundred thousand people working for me, in eighteen states and seven countries. I invested in them to make money. I invested in you to make a difference. Now you've given me that chance.'

Goldstein sat on the edge of the table closest to Horton and leaned forward as though about to reveal a secret. 'Guns and bombs have been the vector of power for four hundred years. Some call a gun the great equalizer, and yet more often guns seem to me to be the great unequalizers. In the last century, guns and bombs herded Jews and gays and gypsies into Buchenwald, struck down three American presidents, killed fifty million people in war and nearly that many in peace, exterminated dozens of tribes and hundreds of species. The people with the most guns – the biggest bombs – and the greatest readiest to pull the trigger: *those* were the beneficiaries of the ingenuity of Nobel and Colt and Winchester.'

'Of course, that was business, too,' Brohier said, reappearing at that point. He carried a tray of plates and utensils to the table and reclaimed his chair.

'Yes – and as shameful a business as it was a necessary one,' Goldstein went on. 'You cannot reason with a rifle bullet fired from across the battlefield. You cannot negotiate with an artillery shell lobbed from over the horizon. You cannot compromise with a nuclear warhead screaming in from half a world away. The only answer to the gun, the only defense against the gun, has been more guns. You've given us another answer, Jeffrey. You've given us a way to tear this terrible inhuman tool out of our clenched primate fists –'

'If we take the power of the gun away from the world, what will come forward to take its place?' Horton asked, troubled.

'Perhaps chaos,' said Goldstein. 'Perhaps peace. Imagine two armies, now facing each other across the battlefield empty-handed. Will twenty-first-century men throw themselves on bayonets for god and country? Imagine the terrorist, the would-be assassin, unable to deliver his cowardly, anonymous blow from a distance.

'Now imagine Tel Aviv, Belfast, Sarajevo, Los Angeles as oases of peace, with one of your devices radiating from a tower at the heart of each city. Imagine how many plowshares we could build if we stopped buying swords. Fallen short, you say? Oh, no, Jeffrey, not at all – the Trigger is a gift of incalculable value. And I pledge to my children and yours that I'll see that its promise is fulfilled. I pledge my fortune and my life to that.'

Then Goldstein straightened up and threw his head back, eyes closed. 'So many words, tumbling over each other to get out,' he said, drawing and releasing a deep breath. 'I warned you, didn't I? Come, let's eat – that will silence me for a while, at least.'

But the food hardly slowed the torrent of words, for Goldstein was not the only one who had had no audience for thoughts burning to be spoken. And over crystal fish, Hunan lamb, and black tea, they began to hammer together the outline of a revolution.

6: Journey

Calcutta, India – A would-be good Samaritan lost more
than his car and wallet to bandits on the Berhampore road
Thursday – he also lost his idealism. British tourist Thomas
Sudaranka was on a pilgrimage to the Ganges River when he
stopped to help what he believed was an injured girl lying in
the road. Shot twice in the back and left for dead, Sudaranka
is now hospitalized with partial paralysis of his right leg.
Authorities in Murshidabad said the girl was probably a
lure for a local highway gang, and warned travelers to be
cautious.
Complete Story   _Map_

The drone of the Helio Courier's single engine increased sharply
as the plane banked and wheeled around in the sky above the
desolate valley. Ahead and to the right, Jeff Horton could see
a thin ribbon of two-lane highway meandering northward. But
there were no cars on the road, and no other signs of human
habitation.

'Where does that go?' he asked, tapping the pilot on the shoulder.

'That's Nevada 278,' the pilot shouted back. 'Runs up to I-80
at Carlin, just east of Emigrant Pass. Ninety miles of nothing.'

By then, the silver-and-red-winged Ely Air Taxi plane had swung
west and begun to descend out of the cloudless sky. By the time
they flashed over Nevada 278, they were below the level of the
enclosing mountains. 'I don't see the airport.'

The pilot pointed ahead at a dirt road paralleling a dry creekbed.
'Right there,' he said. 'Vinini Creek Road. That's as much airport as
there is in Eureka County. But I want to get a close look at it before
I put the wheels down. We had a good hard rain last month, and
you've always gotta worry about washouts.'

65

Clutching his knees tightly, Horton stared in silent disbelief at the rutted, narrow-track road as the pilot buzzed over it at no more than a hundred feet.

'That must be your ride,' the pilot called out. Horton caught a glimpse of a sand-colored Jeep Cherokee and a figure standing beside it before the pilot hauled the nose of the plane skyward. 'Doesn't look too bad. Have you down in just a couple of minutes now.'

Horton just nodded, tight-lipped.

'All this used to be government land, you know,' the pilot went on. 'Not that there's been any rush to build out here since the Feds gave it back to the state. About all we get are prospectors of one kind or another, passing through – either looking for UFOs or looking for fossils. The UFO types are the talkers, so I figure you for the other kind.'

While he was talking, the pilot had carried out a heart-stopping half-loop that brought the Courier skimming back over the road in the other direction, this time even lower. 'There's my spot,' he called out, and throttled back. The plane floated for a moment, then flared and settled, bouncing twice and kicking up a plume of yellow dust. It rolled to a stop a few dozen meters from the Cherokee.

'That anybody you know?'

Fingers digging at the catches on his restraint, Horton peered out through the thinning dust. The man standing beside the Cherokee was Donovan King, wearing dark sunglasses and a Colorado Rockies baseball hat. Horton and King exchanged brief acknowledging waves.

'Yeah,' Horton said, unlatching the door. 'Thanks for the ride.'

The little cabin of the six-place tail-dragger was warm enough by Horton's standards. But the heat that enveloped him as he clambered out of the plane was almost overwhelming. He hastened to the waiting vehicle, now idling with King at the steering wheel.

'We have air-conditioning out at the Annex?' Horton asked, turning the fan to high and directing the blast from the nearest vent toward his face.

'In the accommodation trailers. The lab building'll be another week or so.'

'Can't be too soon. Dry heat, my ass,' Horton grumbled. 'Chamber of Commerce propaganda.'

They waited as the Courier taxied eastward past them, the engine winding up for its take-off roll. 'We're going to need to get our own plane and pilot for these runs,' Horton said as King eased the Cherokee back onto the road, heading west. 'This fellow was too curious.'

King chuckled. 'That fellow *was* our pilot,' he said. 'He's garrulous, but he's harmless. We also own a one-plane outfit in Elko and a small trucking company based in Reno. We'll spread the traffic around, Doctor. And the fossil-hunter cover will help us fade into the background.'

'So that's what that was about,' said Horton, peering out the windshield at the barren landscape. 'How far from here?'

'About eight miles,' King said. 'And speaking of your ass, there's an extra pillow in the back seat – you may want it under you most of the way.'

There was no hyperbole in the warning. Before long they left Vinini Creek Road for an unnamed, unmarked track half as wide. Its undulations gave no reassurance that it had ever been graded, and the traffic which had passed that way before them could not be said to have improved it. Even at speeds that never topped fifty klicks per hour, Horton found that part of the trip all too much like an amusement park ride that went on too long.

'I'm going to recommend that we buy someone a helicopter,' Horton said, bracing himself against the dash.

'We're already planning to bring your equipment in on the Skycrane we're using for construction material. Don't want to do that more often than necessary, though. For a state with hardly any people, there are a lot of eyes watching the skies out here.'

The ride finally ended in front of a scattering of structures on the floor of a narrow, steep-walled box canyon. The largest of them was a windowless one-story cinderblock sprawl that reminded Horton of his elementary school. Half a dozen boxy mobile homes were lined up to the west, and the steel frame of a barn-sized prefabricated building was taking shape to the east. A small bulldozer, a backhoe, and three other Cherokees were nestled against the east wall of the main structure, in the narrow band of afternoon shade. A cacophony of construction noises greeted Horton as he climbed gingerly out into the heat.

'Did Dr B. really have to find a place *this* remote?' he asked, shaking his head as he surveyed the site.

'I guess the difference between few neighbors and none mattered,' said King. 'The director said he wanted a five-mile secure radius and a ten-mile safe radius. Do you want to go to your trailer or the lab first?'

'After that ride, my bladder votes for "trailer".'

King smiled, a rare sight, and pointed. 'You're in number Three.'

When Horton emerged again, King handed him a site map and a hard hat. 'Meals and recreation are in the double-wide. Trailer number Two is reserved for Dr Brohier and guests. The temporary communications shack is in Five, and the temporary security office is in Six. The construction crew is in pop-ups on the north side – we'll take over that space for staff when they've moved out.'

Horton studied his map, then squinted out into the bright haze to the north. 'What are these things?'

'Don't know. Outhouses, some here call them. There are six of them, each about the size of a walk-in closet, cinderblock construction, empty as this place was,' King said, gesturing toward the main building.

'So what was *this* place?'

'Don't know that either,' said King. 'When the last residents packed up, they took everything but the walls with them. We took photos of all the floor scars and mounting bolts we found, if you'd care to join the guessing game we've been playing.'

'What's your guess?'

'My guess is they weren't herding sheep.' King shook his head. 'There's no obvious answer, Dr Horton, which is why the game is fun. Tomorrow I'll take you out to see the concrete trenches that connect the outhouses,' he said, waving a hand northward. 'Nevada has kept a lot of secrets over the years, from Plumbbob to Area 51. With luck, it'll keep ours, too.'

As Aron Goldstein's black Dassault Falcon 55 descended into the choppy air three hundred meters above the Potomac River, Karl

Brohier turned his recliner toward the nearest oval window and searched the sprawling cityscape for its familiar landmarks.

Having no great fondness for politics or for bustling, traffic-choked cities, Brohier had only been to Washington, D.C. three previous times. The last, eight years ago, had been for a friend's funeral. The time before that had been to be paraded in public by politicians and then have to beg for funding of basic science research in front of half a dozen review committees – for Brohier, an experience hardly more pleasant than a funeral. But the first and most enjoyable of his visits had changed the course of his life.

At a time when wealthier school districts were sending plane-loads to Europe, chartering Caribbean windjammers, and white-water rafting in Canada, it was all that Champlain Valley Union High School's graduating class could do to manage a fifteen-hour bus ride down from buttoned-down Chittended County for three days of sightseeing in the nation's capital. The chaperones made up for that indignity with a light schedule and liberal curfew.

'We're not going to decide for you what you want to see,' Mr Freebright, the class advisor, had said. 'Every one of you has a guidebook, a Metropass, a trip buddy, and a mind. If you don't lose any of them, you'll go home having had a trip to remember.'

Brohier and his best friend Tom Lange had passed up the out-of-boundaries expeditions to various Maryland sin spots, where drinking, gambling, and topless dancers could be pursued. Instead, they had divided their free-exploration time among the Smithsonian, the Museum of Natural History, and the US Naval Observatory.

The attraction of the last was the chance to look through the thirty-two-inch reflector at Jupiter's moons or a solar prominence, but gray clouds and a summer drizzle had stolen the opportunity.

Disappointed and looking to salvage the time spent waiting in line for the tour, the young Brohier had become fascinated by the Master Clock of the United States and the scientific magic behind it. Cesium oscillators, hydrogen masers, satellites, and synchronizers opened an unlikely door to wonder – one which led him to relativity, radioactivity, and nuclear science. After a summer of testing the waters through heavy reading, Brohier had reported to the University of Vermont and promptly changed his major from the safe career path of computer science to the uncertain one of physics.

He had managed to keep the news from his parents for a year and a half, and then to resist their intense pressure to correct his 'error'. After distinguishing himself in an undistinguished program, he won a graduate fellowship at MIT, where both the competition and the intellectual stimulation were of a higher order. But it was the right time – his mind never quicker, his hunger never sharper than in those days – and by the end of his two-and-a-half years there he stood out in that company as well.

It had gotten harder after that: the disaster at the University of Texas, where a clash of personalities with the department chairman and the distracting complexities of first love and first loss combined to make him a doctoral dropout. The five years as a lab drone in TRW's materials science lab, a gift from Tom Lange but a prison for Brohier's curiosity. Then the second try at a Ph.D., at Stanford, where every other candidate was younger and seemed quicker, and Brohier felt like he was running uphill trying to catch up. The first shot in the CERN revolution was still five years away, and Amy Susan a few more beyond that, and zero-phase solid-state information storage nearly two decades down the road.

But he had started on that road here, and now – against his better instincts – he had followed it here again.

The cabin of the Falcon 55 shuddered as the landing gear extended and locked in place. There was nothing but water beneath them, and the water seemed very close. Then suddenly there were rocks, a patch of brown grass, and the runway threshold. Tires kissed the concrete gently, then again more firmly. When the nose wheel settled, the cabin began to vibrate with the roar of the Falcon's three engines as the thrust reversers were applied.

Brohier looked across the cabin at Goldstein, who was still napping peacefully, his slight frame almost swallowed up in the ultracushioned chair. *I hope you're right about this, my friend*, he thought. Neither Brohier nor Horton had anticipated involving anyone from the Federal government this early, and both had profound reservations about involving the military at all. Just the knowledge that the Pentagon was less than three kilometers away gave him chills.

It was what Horton called the 'Hangar 57 scenario' that haunted him – the fear that with one wrong word to the wrong person, a convoy of black vans filled with Special Operations troops would swoop down on the Terabyte campus and cart away everything. It had taken Goldstein hours to convince them that 'friends in high places' did not belong to the same class of imaginary creatures as unicorns and mermaids.

'There are people at every level of this society who can and will help us,' Goldstein had insisted. 'And we'll need as many of them as possible with us when those who *will* oppose us realize the danger.'

'We'd better be damned sure which kind we're talking to,' Horton had said.

'The man I want to bring in will not betray us. As elected officials go, he's an oak among reeds –'

'Faint praise, in my book.'

Goldstein had grown irritated at the carping. 'You scientists are such naifs about politics. You only know these people from CNN, and barely even that,' he had snapped. 'I've known this man as a man for twenty years, and I've never known him to act rashly or compromise his principles. What's more, *his* power base is not threatened by this – very much the reverse, in fact. And if he *does* come aboard, I expect his contacts to be of inestimable value to us.'

'Then why not tell us his name?'

'To protect him in the event that he chooses not to involve himself – because he *is* my friend.'

In the end, Brohier's presence on the plane, and at the meeting to come, was the price of consensus. Horton would not agree to let Goldstein make a private approach to an unnamed unknown without the reassurance of knowing Horton's interests would be represented there – and Horton did not know Goldstein well enough yet to take that reassurance from him.

It was, on some level, an unreasonable, even an irrational demand, since Goldstein could easily have had hundreds of secret meetings with anyone he chose in the weeks since Brohier had brought him the news. But so much was at stake that even Brohier's trust wavered at times, and he was glad to have a reason to insinuate himself into the process.

As the Falcon 55 came to a stop at the VIP gate, Goldstein opened his eyes and stood. 'Made good time,' he said, glancing at his watch. 'Did you get any rest?'

'I can't sleep in planes,' Brohier confessed.

'My job would kill you, then,' Goldstein said with a cheerful smile.

In a remarkably few minutes, they were in the back seat of a silver Mercedes that was humming north along Washington Memorial Parkway. Almost before Brohier realized it, the Pentagon loomed up on the left. Goldstein caught him looking out at its bland, imposing, implacable face as they drove past.

'Are you still worried?' Goldstein asked.

'Not about you, Aron. I never was worried about you. I'm worried about losing control of this,' Brohier said. 'I don't want the responsibility – I don't want to have to make these decisions. But I'd rather it be me – us – than a lot of people I can think of. And a lot of *them* live and work in this city.'

Goldstein nodded. 'I'll tell you something I learned a long time ago about the Washington gang. The good news is, away from the cameras, they're just like the people back home who sent them here. The bad news is, away from the cameras, they're just like the people back home who sent them here. No better, no worse – just a great deal more visible, and their mistakes have a longer reach.'

Smiling wryly, Brohier said, 'That's kind of funny. This friend of yours – to keep my thoughts in the green zone, I've been trying to imagine that someone I know and respected went and got themselves elected – someone like my father, say.'

'*Mr Smith Goes to Washington*,' said Goldstein. 'Karl, let me say something I didn't want to say in front of Jeffrey, given his state of mind at the time. This meeting tomorrow – this man – we need him badly. At this moment, this is a frail conspiracy.'

'I've thought about that,' Brohier said. 'Our secrecy works against us. We could be swept up in an afternoon, and it would all be over.'

72

'Ah, but unlike you, and even me, my friend has too much stature to be easily silenced,' Goldstein said. 'Unlike Jeffrey and his people, he's too visible to just be made to disappear. He can't be intimidated, and he won't let himself be compromised.' He turned away toward the window and gazed out across the Potomac toward the Lincoln Memorial. 'And he'll ask the right questions, loudly and in the right places, if *we* disappear.'

'That's very comforting,' said Brohier. 'Aron – your friend – it's Senator Wilman, isn't it?'

Goldstein nodded silently, and the gesture was reflected in the tinted glass. 'How do you feel about that?'

'I think I feel all right about it.'

'Good. Still,' he added absently, 'I think we will not tell him about the Annex. That will be our insurance policy.' Goldstein turned to face Brohier's questioning look. 'In case I *am* wrong about him, or about how far our adversaries would go.'

7: Strategy

Hong Kong, China – In a last-ditch attempt to end sixteen days of anti-Beijing demonstrations, the new military governor of the Hong Kong Special District today declared a twenty-hour daytime curfew that permits travel only between home and work. Governor Han Lo announced that Chinese army commanders are now authorized to shoot to kill if 'treasonous disrupters' defy the order. At least a dozen demonstrators and five police officers have died in earlier confrontations in the city's Botanical Gardens and along the Victoria waterfront in the University area.

Complete Story   *Hong Kong Since Unification*
Han Lo Bio   *Stay On the Story with Sky-Scan*

Grover Andrew Wilman's suite in the Humphrey Senate Office Building was typically the first on that floor to come alive each morning, and the last to close down each evening. The official work days of his top administrative aide and top legislative aide began at seven a.m., which was early enough by Congressional standards. But they often found that their boss had beaten them there by an hour or more, and with terrifying efficiency had already done a morning's work before their arrival.

On most mornings, Wilman's self-assigned first task was answering what he called the 'mad dog' mail. The educational and lobbying efforts of his disarmament advocacy coalition, Mind Over Madness, generated a steady stream of critical, often hostile mail – video, audio, and text. Even after the anonymous, unanswerable screeds were filtered out, there were hundreds of messages a day from people who felt compelled to tell Wilman exactly how deluded, misguided, ignorant, disloyal, and just plain wrong he was.

'Gets my blood moving better than any amount of coffee,' he explained when questioned why he took the trouble to answer messages that others would ignore. 'And it surprises them so much when they get something back from me personally that sometimes they actually stop to reconsider. Besides, I have an irrational belief in the power of reason.'

Early morning was also a good time to teleconference with his allies in Europe. Mind Over Madness had chapters in forty-one countries, and legislative partners – like Wilman, signees of MOM's Common Sense Declarations – in almost half of them. Of course, that alliance made Wilman a favorite target of the Christian ultra-nationalists and the internationalist-conspiracy fringe.

Somehow, Wilman took it all in stride. On one level, it was only noise. On another, it was confirmation that the message was getting out. That, plus the parallel stream of supportive letters and the occasional conversion of an opponent, was enough to confirm him on his course. His crusade was no poll-driven, short-horizon, media-savvy re-election ploy. It was a principled long-term commitment to changing how people thought about conflict. He knew better than to judge the progress of that effort by the 'mad dog' mail.

Wilman's office was as unconventional as his politics and as doggedly confrontational as his Senate floor persona. The standard desk accessory for senators was a large American flag, positioned where visitors could not ignore it and cameras could not miss it. In Wilman's office, that prime space was occupied by a framed blowup of his favorite Mind Over Madness print ad – the controversial 'corpse collage' of morgue and crime-scene photos with the bold caption GUNS DON'T KILL PEOPLE above, and a sardonic (THINK ANYONE'S STILL BUYING THIS?) below.

Elsewhere in the room, the usual honorary degrees and personal photo gallery were likewise absent, their spaces taken over by the words and images of heroes and pioneers of the peace and disarmament movements. It was Wilman's private hall of fame, a shrine to a philosophical ideal which, for more than a century and a half, had been running a poor second to the reigning *zeitgeist* – Man as killer ape, and evolution red in tooth and claw.

The only images of Wilman himself were the caricatures in

two framed political cartoons and a glass-covered photograph of Wilman with his tank crew on the sands outside An-Najaf, Iraq. Framed beside the photograph were his captain's bars, service medals, and honorable discharge certificate.

I have the moral right, the photograph insisted. *You cannot invoke cowardice, or disloyalty, or fear, and then dismiss me – you must engage the moral issue in our challenge.* And a year earlier, that photograph had spoken loudly enough from campaign ads to give Wilman a razor-thin victory and another six years as Oregon's senior senator.

'No other state in this Union would have sent you to Washington,' his Democratic opponent had said in his private concession call. 'And no other state would have sent you *back* there once they realized what they'd done. Still and all, for the trouble you cause the Republican leadership, and for the good you try to do by rubbing our noses in the shit, I almost don't mind losing to you. And if you tell *my* party chairman I said so, I'll see to it that your incestuous little nest of morally bankrupt technocrat pansies never gets another hundred bucks in dues from my wife.'

It was the essential Wilman paradox, encapsulating not only the campaign, but his entire career in politics. His friends and allies resented him and his enemies admired him for exactly the same traits: his stubborn singlemindedness, the characteristic bluntness in the service of a penetratingly insightful mind, and his uncompromising commitment to principle over practicality. In the words of the leading news magazine *In Touch*, he was the prototype anti-politician.

'He breaks rules considered sacrosanct, but knowingly, out of necessity rather than defiance,' the magazine's political editor had written in introducing Wilman's profile. 'He makes mistakes considered fatal, yet survives, because passion is something rare and therefore treasured in this usually bloodless city.

'Grover Wilman makes us at once proud and uncomfortable, as though we know the truth of his words but despair of living up to his ideals. At no time in my thirty-year memory of these halls has there been such a grand iconoclast or an intellectual of comparable consequence in Congress. Patently unelectable as

President, he is now at the peak of his power – and when the masses tire of his somewhat preachy message, as they inevitably must, L'Enfant's city, this writer's beat, and our national dialogue will be the poorer for his absence.'

Indifferent to the praise, Wilman sent the editor a copy of the piece with 'as they inevitably must' circled in red and a hand-written note scrawled across the bottom:

If civility is a fad, civilization is a fantasy. Is that really the best you can offer your children?

'For me, this is the one that rocks,' said Toni Barnes. The graphics designer touched the controller and brought a different ad dummy to the conference room video wall: a monochrome photograph of eight adults standing in a circle, each holding a revolver to the head of the person to his left. 'We can use something like "Feel Safe Now?" as the hook line, and "The Killing Stops When We Stop It" as the sell line.'

'I still like the first one,' said Evan Stolta, Mind Over Madness's senior strategic consultant. He reached out and returned a photo of a three-year-old in tiny fatigues, holding an assault rifle, to the screen. 'Hook and sell in four words – "Now he's a man". Simple, strong.'

'Stop thinking like a Yalie lib,' said Barnes. 'There are a lot of people out there who won't catch the tone – they'll think that's *cute*.'

'There's nothing we can do to help the irony-impaired,' Stolta said, annoyed by the dig. 'What do you want – smoke coming from the barrel and a second kid lying in a puddle of blood?'

'Let me see it,' said Senator Wilman, who had been sitting back in his chair listening to the brainstorming.

Frowning, Barnes turned to her digitizing easel. In a few moments the black-and-white image acquired color. Not long after, it acquired a corpse.

Wilman was already shaking his head when Barnes turned to him for his opinion. 'No, no, no. We've never faked a victim in any of our material, and that's not nearly strong enough to make an exception. But I like the color. Why are we falling into this Wiesenthal-Bergman high-art rut lately? These people we're trying to reach don't live in a monochrome world, and we have to connect with them where they live.'

'We –' Stolta began, but couldn't find an opening.

'Toni, your circle-of-insecurity would work just as well in color,' Wilman went on. 'Better, because the people will look like family and neighbors, instead of characters from a film noir murder mystery. You can move the light source around if you want to play with the emotional subtext. Show me something by the end of the day.'

Barnes nodded, and began closing up her easel. With barely a beat, Wilman turned his attention to Stolta. 'Evan, what happened to what we talked about last week – going after the content providers? We can't possibly buy or beg enough bandwidth for these spots to compete with the program libraries at Turner and Sony and Bertelsmann. They're going to have to do something to help us.'

'They don't want to talk to us,' Stolta said, shrugging his shoulders.

'Of course they don't,' said Wilman, standing. 'They're sitting on hundreds of thousands of hours of program material that's based on the premise that men maiming, torturing, and killing other men is entertainment. But it's your job to figure out how to get them to talk to us.'

Stolta was shaking his head. 'They have an enormous investment in inventory –'

'An inventory of poison. We need them to start looking at those libraries as liabilities, not assets,' Wilman said sharply. 'We need to help them see that there's an ethical dimension in what they're doing that goes beyond supply and demand. And if that means beating on closed doors and closed minds until they open, that's what we're going to have to do. Now, if you're too burned out for that kind of fight –'

'Put me on your schedule for Friday,' said Stolta. 'I'll try to have some ideas for you by then.'

'Good.' Wilman checked his watch. 'Late for my meeting. System?'

'Ready,' said the conference room controller's synthesized voice.

'End meeting log.'

'Verified,' said the room. 'Do you wish me to abstract and distribute minutes?'

'No. Archive only.' Then Wilman looked up and flashed a sympathetic smile at the others. 'This road is uphill all the way,' he said. 'And that's hard. Sometimes when I get discouraged, I think about renaming the coalition the Sisyphus Society. So far I've managed to get over it before having papers drawn up, thank goodness – it's a name only a Yalie lib could appreciate.' He winked in Stolta's direction, and his smile brightened enough to put a twinkle of puckish humor in his eyes.

'A lost opportunity,' said Stolta. 'Just think of the jazzy animated logo we could have had for our Web sites.'

Wilman laughed as he picked up his portfolio. 'I'll be back in the office in an hour. If something urgent comes up before then, Marina knows how to get in touch with me.'

A light breeze was blowing across Arlington National Cemetery, taking the edge off what was warming up to be a quintessential oppressively-humid Washington summer day. Even so, Wilman was perspiring freely by the time he walked from the Sheridan Gate to the gentle hill where the remains of Dayton Charles Arthur Deich rested in the shade of a hundred-year-old maple tree. The tree interrupted a line of white marble headstones, and its spreading roots had pushed Dayton's headstone a few degrees askew.

Over the last year, the sole visitor to Dayton's grave had been a private of the 3rd US Infantry, who paused there briefly to place a small American flag in front of the headstone in preparation for Memorial Day. Through this annual tradition, The Old Guard remembered and honored his service and sacrifice. But the chances were that no one else did.

Dayton had died half a world away and more than half a century ago, a draftee corporal who fell during a bitter Korean winter and an even more bitter defeat – the bloody retreat to Hngnam-ni. Dying at twenty-one, he had left no descendants. The closest of his living cousins was three generations and five states removed.

But Dayton was not alone in fading from sight. As Korea's youngest veterans passed from the stage, Dayton's war had crossed the line from memory to history. Now distilled down to a Cold War skirmish which boasted no patriotic songs or triumphant images, it had lost all its pain and passion.

Even the most basic facts had left the collective consciousness. Rare was the civilian who knew more about Korea than could be gleaned from the classic television comedy set there. Ridgway and MacArthur, Pusan, Inchon and the Yalu – their emotional resonance was gone.

But it was the same for all of Dayton's neighbors in the old graves on the hill in Section 20. Even those who fought in a Good War could not count on visitors to break the settled solitude.

We give you this little piece of the earth, Wilman thought as he neared the two men waiting for him at the maple tree, *allow you this little claim in a realm you no longer inhabit – to what end? An exercise in propaganda, sanitizing the truth. The honored dead in their final rest, with no hint of what they did, what they endured, to earn that dubious honor. No blood, no torn and broken bodies, not a weapon anywhere in sight – just row after row of sterile white stones, lying by their silence. I hate this place more than any other I know –*

Karl Brohier frowned. 'Is that him?'

'That's him,' said Aron Goldstein, nodding.

'He doesn't look happy.'

'I don't expect he is.'

'Maybe we should have just picked him up in your car and gone for a ride around the Beltway,' said Brohier. 'That would have been private enough, wouldn't it? More private than this. One cheap audio telescope, and –'

'I know how he feels about Arlington,' said Goldstein. 'This is a better way.' He moved toward Wilman with a smile and a hand offered in greeting. 'Grover! Thank you for meeting us.'

'You said it was urgent that we talk,' Wilman said, looking past Goldstein. 'I know you. Where do I know you from?'

'That's not important,' said Goldstein. 'Come, let's sit. Karl, the blanket.'

They settled in the shade on a red-and-black stadium warmer, looking for all the world like three brothers lingering a time at a family gravesite. 'What do you have for me, Aron?'

'Would it brighten your day any if I could offer you the prospect that there would never be another grave dug in this cemetery except to bury an old man like me?'

'I don't quite know what you mean,' said Wilman, frowning. 'But the casualty rate in the US armed forces is the lowest it's ever been – even when we put forces in the field, the machines do most of the fighting, and combat deaths are so rare that they all make the news. That half of the battle's nearly won, Aron. Casualties are no longer acceptable.' He nodded in the direction of the Pentagon, hidden from them by distant trees. 'Now if only we could get them to care that much about the Hutus, or the Brazilians.'

'That's expecting too much,' said Brohier.

'Why?' Wilman demanded.

'Men have willingly killed other men's children for ten thousand years. Makes more room on the planet for their own.'

'Oh, Christ, don't invoke Darwin to me,' Wilman said in disgust. 'I've heard a lot of sociological drivel about The Other, and I'm telling you that the only thing it means is that sometimes we can't hear the wives and mothers crying.'

'Explain what you mean.'

'Happily. Tell me what you remember about Desert Storm.'

'Desert Storm? Gracious, that was – you know, there are great gaps in my awareness of current events over the last sixty years. I was having my crisis at Bell Labs, I think.'

'I was in an Abrams M1-A1,' said Wilman. 'Go on – whatever you remember.'

'You'd think I'd remember more, since every TV everywhere I went seemed to be tuned to CNN for what seemed like a month straight,' Brohier said with a frown. 'We had the stealth fighters, the smart bombs, and Schwarzkopf. They had Saddam Hussein, Scud missiles, and an air force that ran away to Iran. It wasn't much of a contest, as I recall.'

'No, it wasn't.'

'And the Iraqis set the oil fields on fire, didn't they? When they left Saudi Arabia.'

'Kuwait.'

'Right. Kuwait. So, how did I do?'

'You remember what most people remember,' said Wilman off-handedly. 'It was a Good War. Our cause was just, we won handily, and almost everyone came home.' He gestured at the seemingly endless field of headstones surrounding them on every side. 'Not many here who died that winter. And that's too bad –'

'What?'

'– Because the Good War is a lie. Desert Storm was a horrible little war. And the most horrible thing about it was how little of the horror made it back to Frogleg, Mississippi. We went to war for Big Oil and the divine right of someone else's king – not for self-defense, not for democratic principles. The press treated it like a video game, and the people treated it like a television miniseries.'

Wilman shook his head. 'In the span of six weeks, we killed at least twice as many Iraqi soldiers and civilians as the US lost in fifteen years in Vietnam. But we didn't see the mothers crying, so it didn't mean anything to us. The Good War.' He snorted derisively. 'The Good War means that only strangers with funny names were blown to bits.'

'Grover – what if it all could have been avoided?' asked Goldstein. 'What if the Kuwaitis had had a border that no Iraqi tank or Iraqi soldier could have crossed without being disarmed?'

'And what if the Iraqis had known that in advance?' Brohier added.

Wilman studied their expressions for a long moment before answering, as if trying to gauge their seriousness. 'The Iraqis had excellent long-range artillery, and a lot of it. A fortified border wouldn't have stopped their army, just altered the tactics. Are you asking me how high the price would have had to be to dissuade Saddam?'

'No,' said Goldstein. 'I'm asking if the war could have proceeded at all if tank rounds and artillery shells exploded before they reached their targets, if bombs and missiles blew up in mid-air, if rifle and pistol magazines caught fire when the infantrymen got within a thousand meters of the border.'

Frowning quizzically, Wilman said slowly, 'Well, there are still such things as arrows, catapults, and the phalanx. I don't know that the second century was a great deal more peaceful than the twentieth. Still and all, your scenario would certainly have upset a lot of apple carts, Saddam's included. But is it anything more than a fantasy?'

'That's an interesting question,' said Goldstein. 'Let's call it a thought experiment rather than a fantasy and play with it a while longer. Let us suppose there were a technological means by which these results might be achieved. How might you go about introducing it to the world stage, if your goal were to put an end to war? In whose hands would you want to place it?'

'I don't want to play the game,' said Wilman. 'Do you have this thing, or don't you?'

'We have it, Senator,' Brohier said quietly. 'We call it the trigger effect. We call the device itself the Trigger.'

'Theoretical or –'

'No,' said Goldstein quickly. 'The prototype is operational.'

Wilman's whole body shuddered involuntarily. He looked away from the other two men, his gaze unfocused. 'My god,' he said finally. 'An anti-weapon weapon. The essential tool the UN's blue-helmet army has needed for fifty years.'

'And the tool every tyrant will want to disarm his opposition,' said Goldstein. 'How do we keep it away from the tyrants?'

'We probably can't. So we'd have to make sure everyone has it,' said Wilman. 'How difficult is the device to make? How small can it be and still have useful range? How expensive are the components?'

'It's too early to really answer those questions,' Brohier admitted.

'That isn't very useful –'

'But it's the truth. Listen, the first lasers were big, power-hungry, finicky, and expensive. But after just a few decades of development, twenty dollars bought you one that ran on penlight batteries and fit in a shirt pocket. We don't know how far we can scale up or down from the prototype. We probably won't know that for quite a while.'

'This discovery – was it wholly within Terabyte? You own this discovery free and clear?'

'Terabyte has never taken a dollar of government money,' said Goldstein with stiff pride.

'Good,' said Wilman. 'Not that it would matter in the long run. If they want you, you belong to them – and they'll want you. How's your security been?'

'As tight as we could make it,' said Brohier. 'This conversation is the biggest risk we've taken.'

'I doubt that. And how did you manage to test your prototype on artillery shells and tanks?'

Brohier and Goldstein exchanged glances. 'Well, we haven't, actually,' Brohier said. 'A little problem of access.'

'You're going to need to solve that problem,' Wilman said. 'If you don't know the limits and capabilities of your system, you're going to get people killed – the wrong people.'

'That's why we came to you, Grover,' said Goldstein. 'Because we know you share our outlook on how this should be used – and because you know both Washington and the Pentagon from the inside. That's why we'd like you to come aboard. That's why we want your counsel.'

Wilman frowned. 'The first I'll give you. If some day these Triggers of yours were as cheap as televisions and as common as wristwatches – well, I could let myself dream of living long enough to see *that* world. But whether I know either Washington or the Pentagon well enough to help make that happen – that's highly questionable. Which makes any counsel I might offer of dubious value.'

'Why not let us judge that?' asked Brohier. 'We haven't promised to *take* your advice, after all.'

That brought a surprised laugh from Wilman. 'No, you haven't, have you? Very well. I think it's your duty to inform the President, just as Einstein informed Roosevelt about the possibility of the atomic bomb –'

It was Goldstein's turn to be surprised. 'But, Grover – five minutes after we do, the Pentagon will slap a Top Secret sticker on it.'

'Yes, they will.'

'And you still think we have an obligation to hand it over to them?' Brohier demanded. 'How does that help move us toward disarmament? It's more likely to move us toward a *Pax America* – if we're the only country that has the Trigger, we'll end up being the only country that has armies.'

'Karl is right, Grover,' said Goldstein, his face flushed. 'I am as patriotic as any man – I love this country – but I sure as hell am not going to give some young Caesar a magic formula for empire-building. And you cannot tell me that the Chairman of the Joint Chiefs is going to share your enthusiasm for making Triggers as common as televisions.'

'No,' said Wilman. 'I can't. But hear me out. We need to be clear about the objective. It isn't to keep this discovery away from our government and its armed forces – because you can't. If our intelligence assets don't dig it out, they'll grab it when you start to hand it out. Do you think that'll give you more influence, more moral authority, more bargaining power than you'll get going to them first?'

'Probably not,' said Brohier. 'But –'

'Of course not,' said Wilman. 'You're not trying to keep this from them. You're trying to make sure they don't take it from you. If we make them discover us, we'll validate their every worst suspicion. But if we come to them with this, and remind them of all those peacekeeping missions that weren't so peaceful, some of them will realize "We can use this to save some of our kids". And then we'll get the Trigger tested in ways you never could on your own, against the full range of military munitions.'

'At the cost of losing control of it,' said Goldstein. 'This doesn't belong in the hands of the people who're pointing the guns. It belongs in the hands of the people the guns are pointed at.'

'You never had control of it,' said Wilman. 'It's scientific knowledge – it belongs to everyone. How many labs around the world could start building a Trigger today, if they had access to your information?'

Goldstein looked to Brohier. 'I don't know,' the scientist said slowly. 'Thirty – forty? Maybe more.'

'And how many of those labs are capable of making the fundamental discovery on their own, next month, or next year?'

'Probably a third – maybe half of them.'

'So how much will that "Top Secret" sticker really mean?' Wilman asked. 'It's meaningless reassurance for our leaders.'

'It represents a year's head start, or more,' said Brohier. 'A year in which we could march into Mexico and unseat Cardeña, or annex Western Canada, or take back the Panama Canal –'

'But, Karl – we could do any or all of those things today,' said Wilman. 'Our military has the best of the best, and enough of them to dominate any battlefield on any continent. But we don't do a tenth of what we *could* do with that power. Why? Because we know we'd make lousy conquerors – we'd pull our punches when it comes time to shoot dissenters and hunt down the resistance. And because modern industrial democracies don't start wars – they're bad for business. Do you really think there's anyone at 1600 Pennsylvania Avenue harboring a secret desire to ride triumphantly into Vancouver?'

'I don't want to take the chance. There've been adventurers in the White House in the past. There may be again, sooner than we imagine.'

'There are no risk-free alternatives, Karl. And I'll say this – if I had to pick any existing government of any major power to trust with this for a year or two or five, I'd pick this one. They may not do the *right* thing, by our lights – but I'd take the chance that they won't do the *wrong* thing.'

'I wish I shared your confidence.'

'I know these people, Karl. So does Aron – ask him his opinion of the President,' said Wilman. 'And there's something else to consider – if this discovery of yours reaches Baghdad and Havana and Phnom Penh and Kiev before it reaches our people, someone's sure to use it against us while we're trying to catch up. You have to picture the Trigger in the hands of the people who're trying to hurt you, not just the people you're trying to help.'

'I believe Grover is correct, Karl,' Goldstein said gently. 'We need to talk to the President.'

Brohier shook his head. 'This is not what I pictured at all.'

'Well – I would not have you thinking me a trusting innocent, Karl,' said Wilman. 'Aron – if you decide to talk to the President, I would be happy to make the arrangements. But before that day, there are two steps I would urge on you. One is to use the secure application procedure to apply for a patent on the Trigger technology. That'll complicate any attempt to edge you out.'

'The Pentagon vs. the Patent Office? What's the line on that fight?' Brohier asked sardonically.

'What's the other?'

Wilman ignored Brohier, addressing himself to Goldstein. 'The other is to give me – give MOM – a copy of the plans, all the technical information. And a list of those labs, too.'

'Why?' Brohier demanded.

'Because you can't unring a rung bell,' Wilman said grimly. 'Because they can swear you to secrecy on threat of imprisonment for treason, but they can't get back the words that have already left your lips. Because I might be wrong about all of this, and have to do something to try to undo the damage. You might want to make plans of your own along those lines, just in case.'

'Wouldn't that be treason, too?'

'Perhaps,' said Wilman, turning his head and looking out across the headstones. 'What happened to our breeze? The air is suddenly heavy. I'm dreading the walk back.' He rose to his feet, and the others followed suit. 'Dr Brohier, a pleasure meeting you – you see, I remembered after all,' he said, turning back and managing a polite smile. 'My congratulations on your new discovery. Who knows, perhaps your next Nobel will be the Peace Prize. Aron, come see me in a few days, tell me what the two of you have decided. Dr Brohier's not ready to decide today.'

'Is that unreasonable? The price of being wrong is very high,' said Brohier.

'Yes, it is,' said Wilman. 'And I can't promise you that I'm right. I know that we're prepared to be the policeman of the world. But are we prepared to walk that beat with an empty holster? That, I don't know. When you change the rules, you change the game. Gentlemen.' He nodded at them, and started back down the hill.

Watching him go, Brohier ran his fingers back through his hair and sighed. 'Aron – did he just take over?'

Goldstein paused in the business of folding the blanket. 'No. But he would, if we asked – or we lost our way, or our will.'

'So he's going to be standing behind us with a spear, exhorting us to glory?'

'Something like that.'

'And this was part of your plan?'

'He is a tiger,' said Goldstein, glancing in the direction Wilman had gone. 'We need his strength.' He brushed perspiration from his forehead with the back of his hand. 'And I need a drink. Let's go.'

They picked their way in silence through several rows of headstones before turning and following the aisle between two rows. In ten sweltering minutes they were at the car, parked inconspicuously in the congestion near Arlington House.

On the way to the West Gate, a signpost for Roosevelt Drive caught Goldstein's eye. 'Does anyone know, would Einstein have done what he did if Hitler hadn't already invaded Poland?' he asked.

'Yes,' said Brohier, holding a handful of ice to his neck. 'He actually wrote his letter to Roosevelt about the bomb the month before. It took Sachs three months to deliver it.'

'Oh,' said Goldstein. 'Never mind, then.'

'No, no – that was exactly the right question,' Brohier said. 'I was reading *Out of My Later Years* on the way here, wondering what Einstein had thought about that letter later, after the Manhattan Project, after Hiroshima. And I learned something I hadn't known, and wouldn't have guessed. Einstein and the Hungarian conspiracy – Szilard, Teller, and Wigner – they wanted to stop Hitler, yes. But they were also idealists, pacifists. They thought that the discovery they were bringing to Roosevelt was going to put an end to *all* war, not just to *that* war.'

'No –'

'Yes. They believed that the atomic bomb would bring about world government, and through it world peace.' Brohier glanced sideways at his companion and smiled ruefully. 'Something to think about, eh?'

Goldstein's only answer was a gloomy countenance and the sound of gin cascading over crackling ice.

8: Amity

Chicago, IL – Calling Schwab Rehabilitation Hospital 'a monument to gang violence', executive director Amafa Jones pleaded Friday with city officials to act decisively to end the South Side's war in the streets. 'Something's terribly wrong when a gunshot scar is considered a badge of honor,' she said in testimony before the City Council. 'Our wards are full of kids who'll never walk again.'

Complete Story	*Chicago Gangs on the Net*
City Crime Statistics	*Police Chief Responds*

'Chief Assistant Junior Auxiliary Mushroom reporting for duty,' Gordon Greene announced as he entered Engineering 04, where the portable Trigger unit was nearing completion.

Looking up from her work, Leigh Thayer regarded him with a wary expression. 'Mushroom?'

'Sure – you know, kept in the dark, fed lots of –'

'I've been getting my breakfasts from the cafeteria,' Thayer said dryly. 'You might want to check the routing on your meal requests.'

Greene laughed easily. But his expression turned serious as he dropped his sleeping bag and red-and-white sports bag near the door and approached her. 'No, seriously – aren't you feeling like we're completely out of the loop here?' he asked. 'Brohier and Horton are off who knows where talking to god knows who, cutting deals and making arrangements that we're going to have to live with –'

'I'm feeling like we still have a lot of work left,' she said. 'And if we don't hear from the boss for a few more days, that's fine with me, because then I won't have to tell him we're not done.' She pointed past Greene at the bag. 'What's that?'

'A pillow, six shirts, a dozen pair of underwear, a toothbrush, and twenty-three Anthony dollars tied in a handkerchief.' When she looked at him blankly, he added, 'I'm running away from home.'

'Oh,' she said. 'So you're finally doing the sensible thing – moving in. I don't know why you didn't do it two weeks ago.'

'Why, that's very gracious of you to offer your hospitality, Miss Lee,' Greene said. 'I'd be most grateful if I could stay with you for a spell. I won't be a lick of trouble.' He peered into the portable control console and quickly assessed its partially assembled state. 'How about I knock out a lateral brace and mounting bracket for that processor board?'

'As long as you don't block access to the backplane,' she said. 'I don't want to have to take it completely apart to field-service it.'

'Can do,' Greene said, already crossing the room to the design engineering station linked to the polymet prototyping lithograph down the hall. 'Yeah, you were right,' he called back as he settled there. 'It just didn't make sense to go home. Not after twelve-hour days. I was kidding myself that I could still have a life.'

'Couldn't get any dates at midnight?'

'Couldn't stay awake through them. It was ruining my reputation.'

Thayer snorted. 'I wouldn't count on getting my life back soon, if I were you,' she said. 'The hole spacing on that bracket is sixty millimeters.'

'Got it.'

As the bracket took shape on the screen, Greene ran through a mental checklist of the tasks which Horton had left to them.

The project data had been collected, encrypted, and archived to two secure off-campus sites. The prototype Trigger had been broken down into sections and boxed for transport. The test samples were tagged, indexed, and resting securely in three compartmented aluminum cases.

All that was left was to pack up the main control console, a job that was waiting on the arrival of a custom wooden crate and a couple of strong backs borrowed from lab security. The portable emitter unit had passed its low-power checks and was ready for the first round of system checks as soon as its controller was ready.

That left as Greene's sole remaining project one he had added to the list himself – making 'Baby Two' not merely portable but operationally mobile. 'There just may be places we'd want to put this where you can't run an extension cord,' he had explained.

So he found himself distracted by what amounted to primitive technology – a pair of high-output Caterpillar diesel generators. Delivered as a single integrated unit complete with rubber-tired trailer and a sound-insulating shell, the DuoCat 1500 had been designed as an emergency services generator, with automatic switching from primary to backup.

The rebuild that Greene was carrying out sacrificed that redundancy in the name of doubling the output. At the same time, he had decided to replace the power conditioning stage, hoping to filter and stabilize the output to something closer to laboratory standards. His best guess was that he had four days' work ahead of him – and, at that, he expected to be finished a day before Lee.

'I'm going to go collect that bracket for you from the tank,' he said, pushing his chair back. 'And drop my stuff off in Conference B. Say – do you happen to know where they put that comfy sofa from Barton's office?'

'Oh, it's still there. They took out the desk instead, to make room for my bed.'

'In that case, can you spare it? I don't want to ask Site Services to bring in another bed –'

'Ernie – my cat – sleeps on it –' Thayer began.

'Oh,' Greene said with an offhanded shrug. 'Never mind, then. Plan B. Dr Brohier must have something in his office worth borrowing.'

'That's all right,' she said, to Greene's surprise. 'Ernie will adjust. Just drop your bag in my room for now. I'll help you move the couch later.'

Almost from the moment Greene had arrived at Terabyte, he and Lee had fallen into a foolish and annoying rivalry that had they been twenty years younger would have been taken for flirting.

91

It played out as one-upmanship – a futile contest between two gifted minds to force a compliment from the lips of the other, coupled with a stubborn determination not to give the other that satisfaction.

After so many months, the rivalry had little blood left in it. It lingered as a tic, a running joke which neither of them took seriously but neither of them would give up. Horton called it Let's-Poke-Each-Other-In-The-Eye-With-A-Stick, and sometimes chided them when he caught them at it.

That night, however, it was Thayer who caught them. 'We're doing it again,' she said, sitting back on her stool and switching off her test gear.

'What?'

'The only reason we're still working at ten to ten is that you don't want to be the first one to admit that you're tired,' she said. 'Well – I'm tired. I've been inside this little box all day, and my eyes won't focus anymore.'

Greene laid down his tools. 'I suppose you think this proves that you're the mature, responsible one.'

'Not at all,' she said breezily, standing and stretching. 'I proved that last week by staying here working when you took off early for your snipe hunts.'

'As if it's my fault that I'm popular with the ladies,' he said, joining her as she moved toward the hallway.

'Of course you're popular with the ladies. You pay in advance, and you leave early.'

Greene winced. 'Ouch. Victimized by a grievous low blow, the white king staggers, gasps his surrender, and topples off the board,' he said, play-acting his own narration as he went. 'Mercifully, he lands on a comfy couch.'

'Ever gracious in victory, the red queen invites the vanquished king to share a Molando's barbecue pizza at her table.'

'Did you already order?'

'Half an hour ago. It should be at the gate in ten minutes.'

'Ha! So we're really knocking off because you got hungry? Yes!' he chortled, going into a mock victory dance. 'I take back my surrender. Oh, the flesh is so weak sometimes –'

*   *   *

The pizza vanished in short order, as did a large bottle of Vernors which Thayer produced from her tiny refrigerator.

'Thank you,' Greene said. 'That was good – too good. I'm going to need to run the fence a few times first thing in the morning.'

'You could do it now, and give the snipers a chance to practice with their nightscopes.'

'You are so thoughtful,' he said, and patted the couch he was sitting on. 'I guess we'd better get this moved, so I can thoughtfully leave you alone.'

'Maybe we can just leave it where it is.'

Greene cocked his head questioningly and waited for her to explain.

'It hasn't been that easy for me to sleep here,' she said, seemingly embarrassed by the admission. 'I thought about this today – and I'd rather have you in here where I know what you're up to than out there making strange noises in the middle of the night. If you don't mind, that is.'

He shrugged. 'I suppose that'd be all right. Unless you sleep with the lights on, or have some sort of unnatural relationship with your cat, or something like that.'

'No,' she said, amused. 'Of course, I may change my mind when I find out what sort of strange noises you make in *here* in the middle of the night.'

'I'm housebroken, I never snore, and I've taught my spiders not to bark.'

'A prince among men,' she said. 'Let's give it a try, then.'

There were a few awkward moments as they prepared to turn in. Lee was momentarily startled when Gordon, apparently oblivious to her presence, stripped down to a pair of white boxers before slipping into his unzipped sleeping bag. A few minutes later, when Lee returned from changing in the women's lounge, Gordon caught himself being unaccountably curious about how her knee-length nightshirt draped her body.

Darkness relieved both of them of their embarrassment, but did not erase their awareness of the other. The silence seemed meaningful somehow, as though it were waiting eagerly to be broken, as though it had an awareness of the moment which transcended theirs. Greene fought against the temptation to read

93

more into her tentative invitation, and in doing so had to confront a cache of unexamined thoughts.

I always told myself it was because we have to work together, that we didn't need that complication. But it's more that you deserve better than a six-week wonder that ends after we've been to bed a few times, and I don't know if I have more than that in me.

The office was an inside room with no windows, and Gordon could barely even make out Lee's outline on the bed against the opposite wall. But he listened to her turning on her side, adjusting her pillow, releasing a settling breath. *What are you thinking over there? Did you expect any different? Are you disappointed, or relieved, or is it just an arrogant fantasy that you're even aware of me?*

Greene sighed, and then wished he could snatch the air back, because the sound seemed all too loud and meaningful in the darkness, too like an invitation. And because he had created that opening, and feared that she would avail herself of it, and knew that there were questions he could neither answer nor gracefully deflect, it became necessary for him to be the one to break the silence.

'Lee?'

'Mmmm.'

'There's something I've been meaning to ask you –'

'What's that?'

'Do you *really* think babies are cute?'

'Why do you want to know?'

'Just exploring one of those men-women boundaries. I don't have any sisters, you know. Two older brothers. Sean doesn't want any kids. And Brandon has this new baby that cries all the time, and as near as I can tell he doesn't even think *she's* cute yet.'

'So what good would my answer do you?'

'I just wondered how universal this baby thing is, how much starch there is in the stereotype. Whether all women are drawn to it on some level, even women who're happily single with successful careers.'

'Ah – I get it now. This is one of those summer-camp slumber-party first-week-in-the-dorm conversations.'

'Right.'

She was slow to respond. 'It sounds like you already believe the stereotype, or you wouldn't ask the question.'

'I can see as readily as anyone that men and women are built to different specifications, if that's what you mean.'

'For example?'

'I've never seen guys cluster around a stroller the way women do. Brandon calls Molly his babe magnet. That's why he doesn't mind taking her for a walk, or shopping.'

'Your brother sounds like a charmer.'

'Well, he's only twenty-six. He won't be sentient for another couple of years.'

Lee chuckled savagely. 'What does that say for you?'

'"Danger, danger, Will Robinson –"'

She laughed. 'What was – is? – your mother like? Since you have no sisters to set a better example –'

'I'd say that being a mother was my mother's first and best destiny, and she knew it. She stayed home with us until the youngest of us – me – entered high school. I remember I was turned around enough at one point to feel guilty about that. She told me that we didn't keep her from doing anything she wanted to do more, because there wasn't anything she wanted more. I don't think those were just words.'

'Was she a Family First covenantor, then?'

'Oh, no,' he said, chuckling. 'There was nothing political about it. She was just being mom.'

'That helps me understand the context of the question,' she said. 'So what kind of answer do you really want? General or specific? Sociobiology or psychology?'

'Ladies' choice.'

'How quaintly old-fashioned of you,' she said, yawning involuntarily. 'I guess I'd say it's a confidence-point-nine-zero generalization. Most women are drawn to babies, and most of them can't even tell you why. But there's that other ten percent. I *have* had a couple of friends over the years who avoided babies like they were booby-trapped.'

She stopped a moment, then added, 'But now that I think about it, both of them came from screwed-up homes – one abusive step-father, one alcoholic mother. And both of them had cats. Maybe it's a confidence-nine-five generalization, after all.'

'Then there *are* exceptions – no cats, no horses, no dogs, and no regrets –'

'You're mixing up at least four different kinds of women,' she said. 'The relationship between women and dogs – big dogs, anyway; little dogs count as cats – is nothing like the relationship between women and their cats, or women and their horses. Mind you, I'm not saying there isn't some compensation and displacement involved in all three of them. These are relationships, not possessions.'

'So if cats are substitute babies –'

'*Some*times,' she cautioned. 'And dogs are sometimes solicitous lovers. – Not literally,' she added hastily.

'Not usually, anyway. And horses –'

'Horses – horses are complicated.' She thought a moment. 'I think horses manage to evoke all the kinds of human relationships there are, from the purely mercenary and utilitarian to the profoundly personal, even sexual. The horse can be mother, father, friend, child, lover, devoted servant – not to mention the powerful wild thing held captive between the horsewoman's legs, kept in check by harness and whip and the rider's will –'

'I'm guessing you watched *Xena* when you were a kid.'

'How did you know?' He could hear her smile.

'Lucky guess,' he said. 'But, still, you say there are exceptions – women who simply aren't drawn to motherhood and babies, who haven't filled that space with substitutes and aren't running away from their own terrors.'

'Yes. Which is why you can't make one rule for all women, why women have to be able to choose.'

'And are you one of them? The exceptions?'

'Ah – so you do want the personal answer, after all,' she said, sighing. 'No. I like babies fine. I *do* think they're cute. I wish I'd been able to be around more while my sister's kids were little. And I haven't given up hope of having one or two of my own. – Don't read anything into that.'

'Wouldn't think of it.'

'Just for the record, you could have been a little less eager to agree,' she said, and sighed. 'I'm not what men want. I know that. And I'm not interested in trying to be what men want. – No, that's not really true. I understand it well enough, and I'm not one of those women who find the whole thing disgusting. It just doesn't come naturally to me. I'm a tone-deaf siren, a wallflower at the mating dance. And I do wonder why men can't want me for me. I'm smart, I don't defer, and I didn't put making babies number one on my list of priorities. Does that disqualify me somehow?'

'It shouldn't,' he said. *It doesn't. Now give me a clue or three about what you want, and where you think you might find it –*

There were two messages waiting for them in the morning. The one from Brohier advised them that he would be remaining in Washington for a few more days. The one from Horton asked for their best estimate of when Baby would be ready to travel.

'Something's happened,' Gordon said. 'They've made some kind of deal.'

'That would be good news, wouldn't it? Or did you want to live like this forever?'

'It's *not* good news. Brohier's going to hand the Trigger over to the Pentagon, and Horton's going to stand by and let him.'

'You don't know that. The boss promised me –'

'It's inevitable. If they were thinking globally they'd be in New York, visiting with the Secretary General of the UN. Look, Brohier's not in Washington to cruise Embassy Row. He's in Washington because he's a nationalist at heart. He doesn't want to do anything that might weaken his country.'

'And that's a problem for you?'

'It's seventeenth-century thinking, not twenty-first-century thinking. Strong armies, strong city-states, strong walls. But there are no walls anymore. We have a global culture and global commerce built on science and technology. Every attempt to politicize scientific knowledge has been an unmitigated disaster. Information wants to be free.'

'What do you expect from them? Dr Brohier is as proud of his National Medal of Science as he is his Nobel Prize.'

'Brohier is a throwback,' Greene said with disgust. 'Look, I expect Brohier and Horton to think about the politics of the Trigger. I expect them to act like *Homo sapiens sapiens*, not Americans. We're supposed to be outgrowing our tribal mentality, not reinforcing it.'

'Are the two mutually exclusive? It's perfectly reasonable to make sure your own home is safe before charging off to save someone else's.'

'But giving the Trigger to the military amounts to hoarding the fire hoses and then wondering why our neighbors' houses are burning down. Come on, Lee – I know you can't want this to end up in the same warehouse with the Ark of the Covenant, the cold-fusion turbine, and the Roswell UFO.'

Lee was shaking her head. 'You're so paranoid that you're starting to make me feel normal by comparison. No, I don't want to see the Trigger used to make the powerful invulnerable – it's good for people like Nkrumah and Moraña and Son Lee to have to worry about finding themselves on the wrong end of a gun. But I can't believe that we'd give the Trigger to people like that.'

'You don't think our government still plays the game of propping up our friends and weakening our enemies? I didn't think you were that much of an innocent.'

'Gordie, I'm not naïve about politics, I'm bored to tears by it – there's a difference. Church politics, city politics, national politics, international politics, it's all the same, just an endless pissing contest punctuated by the occasional bloody brawl.'

'You can't pretend the outcome doesn't matter –'

'It's as inconsequential to me as the outcome of the next Ohio State football game –'

His face showing mock horror, Greene made a cross of his forefingers and held it up before him as though warding off a demon. 'Heathen child!'

'It's my heretic heart,' she said agreeably. 'As far as I'm concerned, you could call the whole season off, and apart from the quiet and the improvement in the traffic near campus, I'd hardly notice the difference. Which is pretty much how I feel about elections, family feuds, hostile takeovers, superhero comics, professional hockey, and action movies. I'd keep the Olympics, but get rid of the national uniforms – everyone represents themselves. No medal counts.'

98

'You're a totally alien creature.'

'I thought we agreed on that last night,' she said. 'Gordie, seriously – maybe I *am* naïve to trust the promise the boss made me, that we'd see the Trigger used to liberate rather than oppress. But it seems to me that making a disarmed world work is going to require a lot of trust, and I'm willing to take that chance. We *have* to be willing, or we're dead at the start.'

'Except Horton isn't in Washington – Brohier is,' Greene pointed out. 'What kind of promise did *he* make you?'

She had no ready answer for that, save a frown. 'It doesn't matter anyway,' she said, turning to her work. 'What could we do, even if we had proof you were right? Arrange an "accident" that'll destroy the lab and kill us? Run away with Jeff's babies and see how long we can keep one step ahead of the FBI? Publish the notes and specifications on the Internet and let chaos come?'

'I'd be willing to think about at least two of those.'

'Well, I'm not,' she said, turning back toward him. 'Like it or not, we're committed to this course. And if the first mass-produced Triggers are built by TRW and installed in the White House basement, the Pentagon courtyard, Air Force One, and the Social Security Data Center, so what? It's a Trojan Horse, Gordie. Because you can't use the Trigger in self-defense without disarming yourself at the same time.'

'They'll find a way around that.'

'By the time they do, we'll have the size down to a suitcase and the price down to a good deskstation, and Triggers will be everywhere, creating little oases of sanity,' she said. 'Or maybe we'll have boosted the range so much we'll just build three great big ones and park them in Clarke orbits a hundred and twenty degrees apart. That's something Washington can make happen, and Tehran can't.'

'It's worse than I thought,' he said gloomily. 'You're an optimist, too.'

'Bite your tongue,' she said sharply. 'The optimist only sees the up side, just like the pessimist only sees the down side. I'm a meliorist. I see the possibilities. You have to have hope, Gordie. The kind of stars-in-your-eyes, feet-on-the-ground hope that lets you see a better world hiding in the shadow of this one – and warns you that only hard work will bring it into the light.'

By the time she finished, Greene was eyeing her with a curious expression that seemed one part skeptical amusement and three parts surprised admiration, or perhaps the other way around. 'You really are something else, Dr Leigh Thayer,' was all he said, in a voice so carefully neutral that it didn't reveal which way the balance finally tipped.

'Funny, that's what it says in my FBI surveillance file, too.' Her gaze narrowed, but her eyes betrayed her with a twinkle. 'But how would you know that, unless – you're one of *them*.'

'Hah. I'm not just one of them – I'm the *original* one.'

'Just as I suspected all along,' she said, her face relaxing into a smile. 'Look, what do you want to tell the boss about the timetable? I should have my part wrapped up by the end of Friday – Saturday noon at the latest.'

'Tell him ten days.'

She squinted questioningly at him. 'I thought you were closer to being finished than that.'

'A week, then.'

'Gordie, what's this about? You're just tinkering with the power trailer now.'

'I think we need to burn in the portable – at minimum power – for seventy-two hours before we move it. Bounce it around a bit, too.'

'Why?'

'So we'll know we can count on it during the move.'

'Still thinking about FBI agents in pursuit?'

He shrugged. 'About what else is in those shadows. We might as well have the benefit of our own creation, both here and when we leave here. I'd rather have it and not need it than need it and not have it.'

'You're sure you're not just digging in your heels and trying to slow down the Terabyte express?'

'I'm sure,' said Greene firmly, then added, '– though I'm not saying I wouldn't if I thought I could.'

She nodded understandingly. 'I'll tell the boss that the prototype is ready whenever, and the portable will be seven to ten days. He won't question it. He knows it's only the two of us here, and that we're doing the best we can.'

'I don't want to ask you to lie for me –'

'I won't,' Lee said. 'I'll just say we're not quite ready.' She glanced around the lab, now stripped of not only every personal touch, but all traces of the work that had been done there, and sighed lightly. 'This was the job of a lifetime. And it's over. I know that. But I'm not quite ready to leave.'

9: Colloquy

Algiers, Algeria – Opening ceremonies of the World Islamic Progress Conference were disrupted by a deadly rocket attack that killed thirty-two and wounded scores more, including visiting Egyptian President Mohamed Khaled. In retaliation, Algerian Prime Minister Zaoui ordered ground and air assaults on Hassan Hattab strongholds in Z'Barbar and Tipaza. Later, in an interview on CNN, Zaoui denounced 'the blood merchants of France and America' for selling advanced weapons to the anti-government insurgents.
Complete Story   Anti-Terrorism on WIPC Agenda
Khaled Addresses Conference From Hospital Bed

None of the three men waiting restlessly in the Oval Office anteroom was a stranger to the White House, but none of them were accustomed to being treated like beggars at the back door.

Before his anti-gun activities made him a political leper, Grover Wilman had been one of the Republican Party's rising stars. Coming late to politics, he offered a mature visage unburdened by a long legislative pedigree, and found himself cast as the worldly-wise war hero. Between Congressional briefings, legislative strategy sessions, and media events, he had logged more than sixty visits to 1600 Pennsylvania Avenue, most during the first term of President Evans.

Because power has always and everywhere courted wealth, and wealth invariably returns the favor, Aron Goldstein also knew the White House well. He had been favored with invitations to social events and State dinners by four successive Presidents, including Evans. In a deft and delicate balancing act, Goldstein had managed to preserve his virtue while retaining both their interest and his access. By neither begging for favors nor buying them, he achieved a reputation for integrity which made him more welcome in those circles than any mere money-man could be.

By contrast, Karl Brohier had only been inside the White House on two occasions, but both had been red-carpet events. The first had been President Engler's campaign-season 'cattle call' of Nobel Prize winners. In that now-infamous embarrassment, Engler had tried to claim credit by proxy for America's scientific successes. Minutes later, Bartlesmann, the recipient of the prize for medicine, pointed out from the same South Lawn podium that Engler had cut the Federal science budget in half, and killed the program under which Bartlesmann himself had received his doctoral training.

The second occasion, when Brohier accepted the National Medal of Science from President Evans, had been a quieter but considerably more dignified affair.

But all of that had been before Mark Breland moved into the Oval Office.

The first man since Kennedy to move directly from the Senate to the Presidency, and the first 'people's President' since Teddy Roosevelt, Breland had – for better or worse – broken or rewritten most of the rules about how Washington worked. Neither Evans nor Engler would have allowed the likes of Wilman, Goldstein, and Brohier to be kept waiting for nearly two hours for a pre-arranged audience. But this was Mark Breland's White House, where nothing was as before.

Breland's personal charisma was often likened to JFK's, but the resemblance ended there. He was from the Senate, but not of it, and his wealth was 'new money' and self-made – Breland had been a star pitcher for the Philadelphia Phillies for more than a decade. With an engaging smile, an old-fashioned work ethic, and a one-two punch consisting of a disheartening fastball and a wickedly deceptive slider, Breland pitched the Phils to three World Series, collecting two Cy Young Awards as the best in the game.

But Breland was unimpressed by celebrity, including his own. Throughout his career, he had quietly turned down all endorsement deals, even when they would have doubled or trebled his substantial annual salary. Then a frustrated athletic-shoe company tried to borrow Breland's fame without using his name or image in a clever ad featuring blurred action shots, shadowy figures, darkened locker rooms, the sound of running footsteps, and a grandfatherly narrator who began each spot by drawling, 'Yessir, he was the best I ever saw –' Instead of suing the company, Breland shamed them with a memorable press conference that produced an even more memorable quote:

'Why should anyone care what kind of shoes I like to wear? I'm the only one walking on my feet. And doesn't everyone here know that it's the walking, not the shoes, that gets you where you want to go?'

It was a national audience's first glimpse of the plain-spoken, common-sense populism that would come to define Breland's public reputation. And it was not the last time he would break the rules. In an era when major league rosters might change completely in a span of only two or three years, he played his entire career for one team, and chided his fellow players for valuing money more than loyalty, saying, 'No mercenary was ever a hero. You can't expect to be cheered when you change uniforms in the middle of a battle.'

And after posting his one losing record in what had become a nightmare season for the whole team, he apologized publicly to the fans and gave back his salary in the form of refunds – $2.71 per ticket for every game he appeared in, mailed or credited to every ticket purchaser on record.

'I'm lucky enough to be a grown man playing a boy's game,' said the note accompanying the refund checks. 'I'll take your money again when I've earned it on the field.' Eight teammates followed his lead. And the following season, the team regained its competitive form and reclaimed first place.

In part because of moments like those, when an off-season wrist injury prematurely ended his career, 'Breeze' was *the* marquee player in professional sports. In the news coverage of his retirement, the most frequently applied adjectives were 'genuine' and 'honorable'. And his fame had spilled over into the mass cultural consciousness, placing him in that elite group of athletes instantly recognizable by millions who had never seen him play.

When Breland called the chairman of the beleaguered Pennsylvania State Democratic Party and told her that he wanted to run for the Senate, party officials had been jubilant, thinking that they finally had a horse they could ride back to respectability. But somewhere along the way, the roles of horse and rider got turned around. Behind Breland's golden reputation were dual degrees in literature and political science, an incisive and decisive mind, and an unwavering conviction that the country's problems were solvable through a generous application of industry and compassion.

'These are my family values,' he said on election night, the phrase somehow sounding fresh on his lips, 'the values that were my parents' greatest gift to me, the ones they taught me by example. You work hard. You protect and provide for your family. You put your responsibilities before your desires. You lend a hand when someone's struggling, listen and hold a hand when someone's hurting, speak up when someone needs guidance, stand up when the truth needs a friend.

'None of this needs explanation, or justification. Everyone here understands. Everyone knows it's the right thing to do. These are the values of communities that work, of tribes, villages, neighborhoods, towns. Our challenge is to extend those values to communities the size of states and countries, and in time to the whole globe.'

It was a message that wanted a wider audience. It found that audience six years later, when Breland asked to be entrusted with the job of President of the United States.

He asked the people, not the Democratic Party. One term had been more than enough to make clear that the qualities which endeared Breland to his admirers vexed and infuriated the party leadership. He was too direct and not nearly beholden enough for their liking. Breland would not play The Game, would not bow to the icons and mouth the mealy platitudes, would not keep his place or mind his tongue. The party could neither control him nor silence him. He did not need the party, and both of them knew it.

The party needed him, and both of them knew that, too.

Though jaded Beltway insiders dismissed Breland as a lightweight and discounted his chances of making it as far as the nominating convention, he was good copy – as quotable as he was quixotic. And his words struck a chord, not only with early adopters across the political spectrum, but with some of the jaded press covering his unconventional campaign of ideas. February's joke became, in turn, May's longshot, August's surprise nominee, and November's poll-defying President-elect.

Breland's first act the next morning was to announce that he wouldn't accept the Presidential salary of $250,000. 'I'm a rookie in this league,' he said. 'Let's wait and see what kind of year I have.'

And so far, it had been a strange and wonderful year, as Breland continued to break the rules and upset expectations.

He had canceled most of the pomp of Inauguration Day, including the parade – putting the focus on the democratic miracle of the peaceful transfer of power, and on the theme of his address, 'We can do better.' Within two months, the press that had loved Breland the candidate was beating Breland the chief executive about the head and shoulders with that phrase, mocking his ad hoc administration for a series of missteps great and small.

But instead of resorting to the usual White House tactics of denial and distraction, Breland crossed up the press corps by publicly agreeing with them.

'Yes, we've made mistakes. Did anyone here expect me to pitch a perfect game on opening day?' he asked a roomful of journalists and a national holovee audience. 'Because *I* didn't expect it. It just doesn't happen – which I'm sure you know, since most of you folks have been following this sport longer than I've been playing it. But I'll tell you this: more than once in my career, I've been wild early, found myself down a couple of runs to a good team, and gone on to win. Leave me in the game, coach. I'll be all right.'

Allergic as they were to folksy metaphors not of their own creation, the Washington press remained cool – but the public was charmed. Breland's approval rating went up eight points, and had remained high despite the best efforts of his enemies.

But you're still missing the plate with your fastball, Wilman thought crossly, rising to go question the appointments secretary once more. But before he and his accumulated annoyance got there, he was intercepted by Breland's chief of staff, Richard Nolby – the man who had arranged their visit.

'Senator,' Nolby said breathlessly. 'I'm terribly sorry. This situation in Algeria has had us hopping all morning. But the President is free now – if you and your companions will follow me?'

*   *   *

One thing that had not changed during the Breland tenure in the White House was the power geometry of the Oval Office.

Visitors who were there to be flattered, impressed, intimidated, or humored found Breland behind sixty inches of flame oak desktop, ensconced in front of the famous curved windows in what he and his aides had dubbed 'the hot seat'. Visitors who were there to negotiate, brainstorm, debate, or conspire had their meeting with Breland in what he called 'the pit' – a pair of claw-footed davenports facing each other across a glass-top accent table. A matching armchair, which Nolby had never seen Breland use, made the pit into a U that seemed more intimate than the room that surrounded it.

For more than an hour, Breland had been perched on the front edge of one of the davenports, listening raptly as his visitors laid out the details of an astonishing discovery. The science was beyond his ability to comprehend, but the implications were not. Every goal he had, every problem he faced, every hope he harbored had suddenly been rendered irrelevant. These three men – unprepossessing in appearance, naïve in outlook, unpolished in presentation – were sweeping away Breland's game plan, rewriting the future before his eyes.

Everything you know is wrong –

'I can see that I'm not going to be getting a full night's sleep for a while,' Breland said, shaking his head. 'I hope you'll understand when I say that I'd like to witness this Trigger effect myself, at the first opportunity –'

'As would I,' said Wilman.

'Everything we've told you is the truth,' said Goldstein with a hint of indignation.

'Did I suggest otherwise? It's not doubt you were hearing,' Breland said. 'You and Dr Brohier arrived at my door with enough credibility to tell me the incredible and keep me listening. But I confess to the childish desire to touch the miracle.'

'We'd be happy to arrange that at your convenience,' said Goldstein, looking mollified.

'Well – it's hardly the most important thing to be settled,' said Breland, and looked to Nolby. 'I suppose we should have General Stepak in to hear this, and Carrero,' he said, naming the Secretaries of Defense and State.

'At the very least,' Nolby said. 'Though we'll have to be careful to keep this information tightly compartmentalized. Dr Brohier, who else knows about this?'

'Does it matter?' Brohier asked with a raised eyebrow. 'In the long run, there are no secrets in science. The universe will not cooperate in a cover-up.'

'Richard wasn't thinking about a cover-up, I'm sure,' said Breland. 'But I have no doubt you've already –'

'Wasn't he?' asked Wilman sharply. 'Mr President, there's only one reason we're here. And that's because you, more than any other person, have it within your power to see that this discovery is used for the benefit of the human species, for the advancement of civilization. These men are patriots, as am I – but none of us came here to offer you anything as transitory as a technological edge over our enemies. The Trigger isn't something to be "compartmentalized" – it's something to be shared, to be spread around the globe until it's in the hands of everyone who can benefit from it. And if you're not of like mind on this, we'll make our apologies for misjudging you, and take our leave.'

'Just because we aren't at war doesn't mean we have no enemies,' said Nolby, unmoved. 'Just because there are no troops massing on our borders and no warships off our coasts doesn't mean our enemies can't threaten us. And with old Soviet nukes in at least twenty countries, the threat is extremely potent. Remember Srvestibad,' he said, invoking the name of the first city since Nagasaki to vanish under a mushroom cloud. 'We don't want one of those in Florida or Texas or California.'

'I remember Oklahoma City,' said Wilman. 'The guns that most threaten us are our own. The fanatics who most threaten us are home-grown.'

'No.' Breland shook his head. 'Oh, that threat is there –'

'Not merely a threat,' Wilman said. 'We've just become numb to the bloodshed when it happens in ones and twos. Shoot ten in a restaurant or a post office and we'll pay attention for an afternoon. Kill fifty by blowing up a railroad bridge and the *City of Chicago* and we'll pay attention for a week. But eleven thousand gun murders every year pass beneath our notice – until it's a sibling, a friend, a child –'

'If we were losing eleven thousand young men a year to firefights in rice paddies or jungles or sand dunes, you wouldn't be shrugging it off,' said Goldstein. 'But because it's in vacant lots, and bedrooms, and bars –'

'I don't shrug it off,' said Breland. 'Though perhaps there's something to the charge that we're numb to the bloodshed, or at least inattentive. But I wish I could tell you – hell, I wish I could tell CNN – how much our intelligence agencies have done for this country over the last ten years, how much pain they've spared us by keeping those weapons away from our borders. There've been so many sacrifices, so many heroes, that no one's ever heard about.'

'The Trigger can make the CIA's job easier,' said Wilman. 'But if all we do with it is protect our own, then shame on us. There are innocents dying every day in Panama, in Korea, in Angola, in Bosnia, because of the detritus of wars that ended half a century ago – a hundred million mines waiting in the dark for a child's footstep. There are places in the world which haven't known a day's peace in a hundred years, because guns and bombs drown out all other forms of dialogue.'

Breland smiled wryly. 'You are a passionate and persuasive man, Senator. One might think you've done this sort of thing before.'

'Home field advantage,' Wilman said lightly. 'No apologies.'

'Of course not.' Breland glanced sideways at Nolby, then fixed his gaze on Brohier. 'You want me to start a disarmament race.'

'Yes,' said Brohier. 'Yes, exactly.'

'Forgive me, Mr President, but that's the worst kind of foolishness,' Nolby said. 'You can't change human nature. You can't eliminate conflict. It isn't the weapons – it's us. It's greed, and lust, and rage, and someone standing in the way of what we want. War was invented long before gunpowder, and murder long before war. Take away the guns and they'll use knives and clubs. Take away the bombs and they'll use poison and fire. This doesn't touch the impulse that leads to murder, that leads to the order for the infantry to advance.'

'I pity you,' Goldstein said, though his expression spoke more clearly of contempt. 'You live by choice in a bleak and hopeless world, and use your pessimism as an excuse for inaction.' He looked to the President with a steady, challenging gaze. 'But even if Mr Nolby were right, and our species is condemned to create murderers and warlords, the least the rest of us can do is make it as hard for them as we possibly can.'

It was Wilman who answered the challenge, and his words made Goldstein and Brohier both stare in disbelieving wonder.

'Mr Nolby *is* right. It's dishonest to pretend otherwise,' Wilman said. 'Without war, we'd hardly have any history. Without murder, we'd hardly have any fiction. We are flawed, and the flaw is a failure of empathy. We are unable to give the suffering of others the same weight as our own mild discomfort. We block the pain of others from reaching our nerve endings, lest we find ourselves impelled to do something to relieve the pain.

'But Mr Nolby is also wrong. He discounts the significance of learning, the possibility of enlightenment. I could not now bring myself to do for you, President Breland, what I willingly and unthinkingly did for another President, half a lifetime and half a world away. I learned from my experiences, and so must we all. Do you have children, Mr Nolby?'

'Three sons.'

'Ah, well, then at least you have some foundation for your pessimism,' said Wilman. 'If you come home tonight and find your sons beating each other with sticks in the back yard, you will want to talk to them about respect, about other ways of solving disputes, about the rules of your household. But while they're trying to absorb the wisdom of your advice and the earnestness of your warnings, won't you also take away the sticks? In fact, won't you do that *first*?'

He did not wait for an answer, turning next to Breland. 'I welcome the revolution. I want to see how it changes things if our presidents can no longer napalm a jungle or machine-gun a crowd, if all that the general's tanks can threaten is what they can run over, if the worst the premier's planes can do is drop rocks. I want to see if a commander will send an army into battle knowing that the very weapons his soldiers carry will likely kill them. I want to see if that army will march into battle unarmed.'

'Haven't you made the strongest man in the tribe king, then?' asked Breland.

'In some respects, likely so,' said Wilman. 'Sir, I won't promise you an egalitarian world. Dominance hierarchies will not disappear – they'll be strengthened. And so it should be.'

'This is a good thing?'

'It's the express lane of the road to peace. One of the most insidious things about guns is how they inspire the ambitions of weak men – how they lead them to fight when they properly ought to submit, and to keep fighting when they should accept stalemate. Nature's been turned upside down by these weapons. Imagine what rutting season would be like if the bucks were armed with shotguns.'

Breland showed a rueful smile, and Goldstein laughed uncomfortably. By then, Nolby was openly scowling. 'Then you mean to betray your country, to surrender the planet to the Chinese?' he demanded. 'Because our military technology is the counterweight for their numbers. Take away our technology, and the balance of power shifts to them. And the Romans built an empire with nothing but the phalanx and the oared galley.'

Brohier rescued the moment for Wilman. 'President Breland, I can tell you that the Chinese physicists are just as capable of making this discovery as we were,' he said. 'In fact, I can't offer you any reassurance that they didn't make it five years ago. We are as likely to be a little behind as a little ahead.'

'So they could be building these devices now.'

'It's entirely possible.'

Turning to Nolby, Breland said, 'It's not clear to me what other options there are, Richard. But I'll listen to your suggestions.'

'I have none,' Nolby confessed. 'But I find this whole business unsettling – deeply unsettling.'

'"Unsettling" is a good word,' said Breland. 'It looks to me as if this will "unsettle" a great deal. Dr Brohier, can you stay in Washington for a few days?'

'Under what terms?' asked Wilman.

Nolby and Breland exchanged glances.

'Well – I suppose Richard will insist that I get your signatures on a security oath –' the President began.

'He can insist all he likes,' said Brohier, interrupting. 'I'm no more trustworthy with my name on a piece of paper, and no less trustworthy without.'

'Of course,' Breland said. 'But you can understand that –'

Brohier had no patience for verbal balm. 'Mr President, you don't own me – and no one owns a scientific discovery. You have no business asking me for a commitment when you're not ready to make one yourself. When you decide what you're going to do about what we've told you today, then I'll be ready to decide what I'm going to do. In the meantime, I'll take a room, and give you your few days. But only a few – I hate jostling with tourists, and I hate socializing with lawyers, which sharply limits how long I can stand this town.'

'Would you be interested in going up to Camp David, Dr Brohier?' asked Breland, unfazed by the remonstration. 'No tourists, and I can have the lawyers driven off before you get there. You're a Vermont man, if I remember correctly – I think you might enjoy the mountain and the woods.'

'A prison with a view?'

'Dr Brohier will stay with me at Hollow Oak,' said Goldstein. 'If that's agreeable to everyone.'

'Given what's at stake, I'd like to see the Secret Service on the grounds,' Nolby said.

'To watch us, or watch over us?' Brohier said sharply. 'Never mind. Aron, this time, will you let me run the trains?'

The President looked puzzled, but Goldstein wrinkled his nose in contemplation and allowed, 'Maybe one slow freight.'

Brohier nodded and looked to Breland. 'We'll be at Hollow Oak.'

'We'll accept an escort, if you insist on providing one,' Goldstein said with polite cheer. 'But no agents on the grounds,' he added sharply. 'That's my home, Mr President. And I choose not to live in a fortress. I recommend that notion to you.'

As a rule, Mark Breland did not have trouble being decisive. Indecision was a fatal flaw in competitive sports, and the purposeful self-assurance he had displayed on the mound was woven into his nature.

To be sure, his decisions were not always right. But Breland would rather be wrong in a hurry than agonize his way to a state of ambivalence. Soon after his arrival in Washington, his staff and

112

the media alike had taken note of his uncanny ability to quickly size up the options, run out the likely consequences, and make a choice he was willing to live with. Breland's fans, looking at his best decisions, called it 'incisiveness' – his detractors, looking at his worst, called it 'impulsiveness'.

But the decision facing Breland now was causing the gears of his analysis engine to seize.

The options were clear enough. The government could take over and build the Trigger for its own purposes, step aside and allow Brohier and Goldstein to take it to market, or draw down the black curtain and bury the secret in the vaults of Yucca Flats.

But the likely consequences of those choices were frighteningly complex – like trying to look fifty moves ahead in a chess game where each side had five hundred pieces. By the time Goldstein and Brohier left, Breland was feeling humbled by the situation, ill-prepared for the responsibility.

It was not the first time he had felt that way, but it was the first time in a long time. As a sixteen-year-old high school sophomore, he had found himself the starter in a state tournament game, thanks to a car wreck that injured two of the team's senior pitchers. He hadn't expected to play, hadn't studied the opposing hitters, hadn't been mentally or physically ready, and their top-ranked lineup had stung every pitch that wasn't wild during a half-inning that had gone on forever.

In the loneliness of a deserted locker room, a teary-eyed Breland had vowed never to be caught out again, never to bring less than his best. Until that day, he had coasted on raw physical talent, never working harder than his notion of 'fun' allowed. From that day forward, he set out to make certain he was always ready for the next level, the next opportunity, the next challenge.

Breland outworked everyone that fall and winter, made the All-State First Team as a junior, was a first-round draft pick out of high school but took Florida State's scholarship instead of a million-dollar contract. He played four years and graduated with eight SEC records, a degree plus six credits toward a master's, a multimillion-dollar contract, and a nickname – 'Breeze', because he made it all look so easy.

He never liked the nickname, thinking that it meant they

couldn't see the work. It was a nickname better suited to the boy he had been than the young man he had made himself into. But, still, when Breland was called up to the big club after smothering Triple-A for half a season, he was ready. Nothing had changed when the game became politics and the arena Washington – the day he started running, he was ready to win, and the day he won, he was ready to get to work. Even his harshest critics gave him credit for working hard.

But at that moment, he was his own harshest critic, and the only answer he had for the uncomfortable feeling of looking up at a problem that seemed to dwarf his resources was to work even harder.

Breland spent most of the afternoon querying the Library of Congress, using the broad-band terminal in his private office. The lead topics were criminology and military history, though industrial chemistry and the Manhattan Project also commanded his attention. By early evening he'd worked up a number of questions he wanted to put to human experts. He picked up his phone, and the parade to the White House gate began.

Wherever he could, he picked the brains of his visitors without revealing the existence of the Trigger to them. It saved considerable time on a night when most of the men and women Breland summoned spent an hour or more impatiently waiting for him in an anteroom, wondering about the urgency under which they'd been called away from their personal lives.

When his questions couldn't be posed any other way, Breland spoke speculatively about disarmament without specifying the means, or in airy what-if generalities about the future of weapons technology. Only to his last two visitors of the night did Breland offer a full explanation as preamble.

His conversation with FBI Director Edgar Mills began just before midnight, and it was after one before Breland finally posed the first of his two questions to the somber-faced former field agent. 'Director, if this technology reaches the hands of ordinary folks, what kind of impact would it have on crime?'

'Reaches them how? At the price of a new Mercedes, or the price of a cheap suit?'

'I wouldn't be surprised to see both ends of that scale over the span of a few years.'

Mills nodded, rubbing his nearly bald pate. 'We had ninety-three bombings last year, not quite two hundred dead. A quiet year, comparatively. At Mercedes prices, maybe we alter the script of fifty of those incidents – and end up with five hundred dead –'

'What?'

'Because not every bomber means to kill. But you're still going to have ninety-three explosions, except now some of them are going to take place in the streets at rush hour instead of in a deserted clinic in the middle of the night. And there isn't going to be time to make that phone call and empty that office building. In fact, maybe we end up with three or four bombings a week instead of two, because we won't have as many opportunities to catch some of these people before their timers hit zero, and because this gadget will make competent bomb-builders out of the klutzes – whereas today, sometimes we catch a break because amateurs make mistakes.'

'But once word starts to get around that their own bombs are going to kill them, won't that alter the equation?'

'I'd expect it to alter the tactics,' Mills said with a frown. 'There are a lot of ways to deliver a bomb-sized parcel besides walking it up to the front door yourself. Messenger services, UPS, dupes and mules – just find someone who goes where you want the bomb to go and strap it under his car. Now, at middle-class prices, maybe we alter the script of seventy incidents, and end up with two hundred explosions and three thousand dead –'

'Why?'

'Because middle class people live and work closer together than the Mercedes people do. From what you say, this device is a detonator that's live all the time, with invisible wires that reach out hundreds of yards – you and your bomb drive past one installed in a mansion's front gate, and you and maybe a security guard or a gardener die. Drive past one installed in an apartment house entryway, and you and maybe a hundred residents die. The simple fact is that the more of these things that are out there, the more carnage we'll have. This thing would make bombs more dangerous for all of us, not just for the would-be bombers.'

'You don't think people will change their behavior when faced with changed circumstances.'

Mills sighed. 'Mr President, we've been changing the circumstances for two thousand years, and we still haven't run out of people willing to be criminals.'

Breland nodded slowly. 'But this device would also make guns less dangerous. How would you balance that against what you've already said?'

'Oh, that's where the *real* trouble begins,' Mills said, shaking his head. 'Partly because this is how that device will end up in that apartment house entry in the first place, because people will be thinking about guns instead of bombs. But mostly because there are five hundred million guns in this country, and the people who own them are rather attached to the idea that they're going to work when they need them. The Second Amendment is a high-voltage live wire, Mr President – they don't come any hotter. Don't touch it. If you do, your Presidency will be dead.'

'You believe that gun owners are equally attached to those fifty thousand shooting deaths a year?'

'Sir, this may sound cold, but so long as it's someone else's family doing the bleeding, yes. They'll tell you that a third of those shootings are suicides, and whose fault is that? They'll tell you that a third of those shootings are gangboys killing each other, and good riddance to them. And they'll try to tell you that the victims left over are a tragedy, but nothing compared to the number of people who would have been victims if they hadn't been armed, if the bad guys had no reason to be afraid.'

'Are they right?'

Mills drank the last of his coffee before answering. 'You know, when I'm visiting East L.A. or the Tenderloin, I think like a cynical old cop, and wonder how I could ever be foolish enough to think we're anything more than savages. And when I'm visiting Sydney or Toronto, I feel like I've discovered a lost world called Civilization, and I wonder why the hell we Americans don't expect more from ourselves. But it really doesn't matter, Mr President, because the gun owners believe *they're* right. You'll never move them, and they'll never forgive you for trying to take their guns away. Besides – if you can disarm them, they can disarm you, and we can't tolerate that. Not here, not now.'

Giving a tired little sigh, Breland eased back in his chair. 'Director

Mills, I was going to ask you for your recommendation on how I should handle this, but I think you've already made that clear – still, if you'd care to summarize –'

Mills stood, preparing to leave. 'Speaking for the FBI, I'd rather deal with the problems we have now than the ones this technology would bring. Lose it. Destroy it. Don't go there.'

The President's conversation with his final visitor, National Security Advisor General Anson Tripp, was much shorter. Now practiced, Breland was able to condense his briefing to little more than ten minutes. Tripp was able to condense his answers even further.

'General, if this technology reaches the battlefield –'

'We'd better be the side that brings it there.'

'So your recommendation would be? –'

'Build it, figure out how to beat it, and then throw a blanket over it.'

'A secret weapon.'

'Yes.'

'Wouldn't there be some deterrent value to making it known that we had such a device?'

'Mr President, there's very little that's more fleeting than a tactical advantage due to a technological advance. There's also very little that's more valuable. If we don't keep it a secret, it won't be available as a weapon.'

When Tripp left, the anteroom was finally empty. Breland took his unsettled thoughts for a slow walk on the dark South Lawn. Pausing near the fountain, he looked out across the Ellipse at the stout spire of the Washington Monument, which was bathed in a soft yellow glow reminiscent of moonlight. He tried to peer not merely out into the quiet night, but into the shadowed future.

Breland was in shouting distance of fifty – too old to have delusions about the depth of the footprints he was leaving on Washington. Like most of his predecessors, he had received an intensive education regarding the limits of presidential power. Looking for insights, he often ended the day sitting in his robe in his private office, reading from his collection of presidential memoirs, especially those of the men for whom the tourist maps listed no monuments. He had come to the conclusion that while presidents sometimes missed an opportunity for greatness, no president could create such opportunities – the moment came to them, driven by events outside the White House walls.

With a certainty he could not explain, Breland knew that his moment was here. In another fifty years, the only remaining trace of his having passed this way would be the consequences of his decision about the Trigger – doubly so if it was the wrong one.

He told himself he cared less about being remembered well than about doing well, and it was probably true. He had told the voters, 'We can do better,' and now his deeply-held and boldly-stated meliorism would be tested – a test devised by a crotchety genius and delivered by an idealistic tycoon, both of whom clearly viewed him with the skepticism due an unproven youth. To the extent that pride was part of what moved him, it was tied up in not wanting to disappoint those who looked to him to lead – whether they looked like fans, or sounded like fathers.

But it was far more important to rise to the moment and seize the opportunities it offered. Getting it right mattered. Each life touched dozens more, and the line between living and dying, between healthy and crippled, between joy and fear, could be crossed in an eyeblink. Monuments did not matter. Suffering mattered, because it was real, and so often unnecessary.

And considered in that light on the deserted White House lawn at three in the morning, Breland realized with weary relief that it was all right if this particular decision took a little longer. He could give himself permission to rest, to close his eyes with the question still unresolved, and take it up again tomorrow. Tomorrow would be soon enough.

The White House was full of moles, and some of them wore the livery of Secretary of State Devon Carrero.

Twenty-two years in the diplomatic corps, including high-profile posts in Bonn, Beijing, and Tokyo, had schooled Carrero on the value of information, and instructed him well in where it could be found. Any change in the President's schedule, any unusual visitors, any meetings which did not appear on the daily bulletin provided to the media, were reported swiftly and discreetly to Carrero. Knowing that most of what really mattered in official

Washington took place out of sight, Carrero studied the city as though he were leading a legation in the capital of a foreign power, ever alert to the kinds of cues which inevitably foreshadowed change.

The media had dubbed Carrero one of the 'ringers' on Mark Breland's team. Breland had not been in politics long enough to accumulate either friends or obligations in significant numbers, and he had filled out his Cabinet with veteran Capitol insiders who owed their positions not to friendship with the President or even long party loyalty, but to their experience, expertise, and connections. That this was considered remarkable said something about the practices and priorities of Breland's predecessors.

But as a newcomer, Breland was only fitfully observant of inner-circle rituals and etiquette. Carrero had suffered the first few slights in silence. But when he had found himself out of the loop on the Rwandan intervention – with the ambassador to the UN not only holding the spotlight that should have been his, but mishandling the responsibility – Carrero elevated his normal level of inquisitiveness to outright spying.

'I want to do everything I can to prevent any further embarrassments,' he told his sources and himself. 'Those of us who've been here longer have to help the President succeed. But I can't do that if the President doesn't call on me, and I can't step forward and volunteer if I don't know what's going on.'

But that grey and windy spring morning, the picture was coming together slowly. The growing roster of visitors was mysterious indeed – among them, two sociologists, a psychologist, the top historian at the Library of Congress, the vice president of the American Chemical Society, the president of the demolition contractor CDI, half a dozen Pentagon types (including a major general in command of the Army War School), and Carrero's own coodinator for counterterrorism, Donald Lange.

More worried than angry, Carrero called Lange into his office. 'Don, I'd like a report on your meeting with the President,' he said, drawing on his experience to offer a convincing smile and affect a disarmingly casual tone.

'There wasn't a lot to it, Mr Secretary,' Lange said. 'The President asked me for some facts and figures on trends in international terrorism –'

'What kind of facts and figures?'

'Number of active terrorist groups, number of incidents per year, deaths per year – nothing that I don't put into the annual report, except that the annual report's six months out of date. He was very interested in trends and patterns in methodologies, asked me a number of questions about that.'

'Who else was there?'

'Most of the time, no one. Chief of Staff Nolby was in and out a couple of times. I saw the secretary of defense on my way in, but he was gone by the time we finished.'

'What about a stenographer?'

'No, there were no minutes kept. The President made a few notes, that's all. Come to think of it, that is a little odd, isn't it?'

Carrero ignored the question. 'How was this meeting arranged?'

'I got a call this morning asking me to come down. I thought it was a joke – even in Washington, calls that begin "This is the President" aren't all that common. Didn't you know about this? I would have notified you if I'd had any reason to think you weren't in the loop –'

'No, I knew,' Carrero said quickly. 'I just wanted to make sure everything came together properly, given the short notice.'

'Oh,' said Lange. 'So can you tell me what it's about?'

'I'm sorry, Don,' Carrero said with an apologetic smile. 'I'm not at liberty to go into that right now. You understand.'

'Of course. Well, if there's any other way I can be of help –'

'Thank you.'

Pacing in his office, Carrero totted up the score: secretary of defense, chief of staff, counterterrorism, military brass, psychology and sociology, industrial leaders. It added up to a terrorist threat – a credible and imminent threat, probably to a chemical manufacturing site. He drew his phone from an inside jacket pocket and paged his secretary.

'Clara, would you get me Richard Nolby?' While he waited, he walked to the window and looked out across the city toward the White House. *Amateurs*, he thought gruffly. *Too many amateurs.*

'Mr Secretary, I have Mr Nolby.'

'Thank you, Clara.' He pressed a button, and heard the ambience change as the digital scramblers came up. 'Richard, Devon. What the hell is going on over there? I want to see the President, and soon. If what I've been hearing travels any further, we could be looking at a very serious situation –'

Nolby objected, but Carrero would not be deterred. The chief of staff was a flyweight, a doorman. It was not his place to decide policy or control the Cabinet's access to Breland. And if he thought it was, then he deserved to be put in his place by those who knew better.

'I'm coming up,' Carrero said. 'Tell the President to expect me. And don't even think about having me held up at the gate – unless you really want our disagreement to have a much wider audience, because I will *not* go away quietly.'

A glow of hope slowly replaced the surprise in the Old Lion's eyes as he listened to Breland, and as it brightened the decades seemed to fall away from his face.

'This is wonderful – far beyond anything I could have hoped for – Mr President, we *must* have these devices for our embassies. How long will it be until they're available?'

Breland shook his head. 'I haven't decided yet if we're going to build them – or if we do, how we'll use them.'

'You haven't decided, or you haven't announced? No, that's not your way, is it,' Carrero said. 'Then may I say a few words, Mr President, against the possibility that my perspective hasn't yet been heard in your deliberations?'

'Go ahead.'

'Thank you.' The diplomat's gaze narrowed, and the weight of his years returned to his countenance. 'Mr President, I do not like funerals. I especially do not like being an old man at the funeral of a young man or woman. And the hardest days of all are when I must attend the funeral of a young man or woman who died doing a job I sent them to do.

'Mr President, our missions are under siege. We have no great adversaries, but ten thousand sworn enemies. There are incidents every day, injuries every week, and the constant awareness that we are the prime target for the disaffected. An embassy is an outpost in hostile territory. When we forget that, we place at risk the people we send there to serve.

'The diplomatic corps overseas pays the price for the decisions made here. And a steel gate and a Marine guard detachment aren't enough protection. I don't think I need to remind you, but I will, because these are our people dying. Eleven killed by a rocket in Athens – three of them had been guests in my home. Ambassador Warton murdered by a sniper. A car bomb in Ankara, with state security looking the other way. Sofia. Tashkent. Jakarta. My memories go back as far as Nairobi and Dar es Salaam.'

'So do mine,' Breland acknowledged.

'Then perhaps you've noticed that we're no longer shocked when these attacks occur, no longer capable of outrage. My department has shipped bodies home from twelve countries in the last ten years.' Carrero hesitated, his mouth working wordlessly. 'One of those bodies was the man my daughter was pledged to marry – an analyst named John Dugan, killed when a mob stormed the embassy in Amman. A bright, gentle, funny man. I would have like to have seen his and Jeanne's children.'

Drawing that close to his family's own loss, Carrero seemed to shrink into sadness for a moment. But lurking just behind that sadness was anger, and in the moment he took to reach for his glass of water, it steadied him.

'Mr President,' he said in a soft voice that was all steel, 'you cannot ask these people to risk their lives in service to their country and not do everything in your power to minimize that risk. Anything less than that is shameful, unworthy. If this device can disarm a mob, detonate a bomb while it's still blocks from the front gate, destroy a rocket in midflight, then we must build it, and we must use it. Conscience demands that of us.'

Then Carrero struggled to his feet, waving off a proffered hand. 'You've listened politely, Mr President, and I won't make it necessary for you to be rude. I know how to make an exit as well as an entrance. I only ask that before you decide, you be certain of how you will feel when the next bomb goes off or the next rocket flies – and that you agree to accompany me to the funerals. Good day, Mr President.'

The door had scarcely closed behind Carrero when it opened again to admit Nolby. 'Is everything all right, sir?'

'We had a good conversation,' said Breland. 'And we need to

thank Secretary Carrero for showing us where we've been careless. We need to get out of this fishbowl.'

'We'll need a cover story.'

'Work one up,' the President said. He picked up his phone, and in a few moments he was in touch with Hollow Oak. 'Mr Goldstein, this is Mark Breland. I've made my decision. Will you and Dr Brohier join me at Camp David to discuss what comes next? Good. No, I'll notify the Senator. Yes, we'll arrange transportation.'

He logged out and looked up to find Nolby regarding him with an unhappy frown. 'What?'

'You're going to build it.'

'Yes. You still have misgivings?'

'More than that. This thing scares me to death. I don't think we're smart enough to understand all the ramifications.'

'There's a tremendous amount of work to be done,' Breland said, nodding. 'But I'm convinced we have to pursue this. We'll take it a step at a time, and keep a short leash on Wilman and Goldstein. We won't just throw it out there. I find this every bit as overwhelming as you do, Richard, but it's the right thing to do. And I'm going to need your help if we're going to do it the right way.'

'I'll be here. I'm still on the team,' Nolby said, acquiescing without enthusiasm.

'Good. Then let's get the rest of the team together and get on the bus. We'll want Stepak, Carrero, Mills, and, I think, Davins from NSA.'

'We probably should include the vice president.'

'No. There's nothing Toni can contribute to the project right now.'

'All right. Harvey Tettlebaum, then,' Nolby said, naming the science advisor.

Breland shook his head. 'Let's get everyone who already knows about this sitting at the same table before we start talking about who else should be there. No one gets brought into this now unless we *need* them to be part of it.'

'Have you gotten Senator Wilman to agree to that yet?' Nolby said challengingly. 'I think the man is a real threat to security. Dr Brohier might be one, too.'

'They came to us, so they want something from us,' said Breland, rising to his feet. 'We'll work it out. Let's get the wheels turning.'

The setting for the first meeting of what Nolby had waggishly dubbed the 'Trigger Guard' was as unprepossessing as any Karl Brohier could have imagined. As the well-weathered wood and multiple layers of paint betrayed, Cabin C dated from Camp David's origins as a mountain-top youth retreat. The surface of the long table bore so many scars that it was useless as a writing surface, and a carelessly placed glass was in danger of tipping over.

The men seated at the table matched the informality of the setting. The baseball jersey tucked into the waistband of Breland's jeans was faded and stained. Goldstein wore a Georgetown University sweatshirt with the sleeves pushed up past his bony elbows. Nolby had hidden his receding hairline under a black ball cap bearing the Oldsmobile logo, and his comset peeked out of the front pocket of a heavy cotton lumberjack shirt. A World War II era B-25 menaced the room from General Stepak's t-shirt. Even the ever-proper Carrero had forgone his suit and tie for a designer-label polo shirt, though his black dress shoes had fared poorly in the soft ground left by an overnight rain.

Nor was there any Robert's Rules of Order ritual in Breland's manner. When a slightly breathless Edgar Mills finally appeared, the President simply made his way to his chair, and waited for the others to notice and follow suit.

'Mr Nolby has agreed to take notes,' he said. 'You're welcome to do so as well, but understand that your notes will be classified documents, and you'll have to handle them accordingly.

'Some of you recommended to me that the Trigger not only be classified, but completely erased. But the fact is that we don't have a long enough reach to suppress this discovery. We can really only deny it to ourselves, not to the Chinese, or the Indians, or the Russians.

'So my decision is that we're going to move as fast as we can to develop it, and at the same time work as hard as we can to control it for as long as that's possible. But let's not delude ourselves. In my very first intel briefing as President, I was told I could assume that material marked Confidential would be compromised in six months, Secret in eighteen, and Top Secret in three years. So that's our window of opportunity. In three years, this technology will be everywhere.

'I'm authorizing an expanded research effort, an extensive testing program, and immediate production,' Breland said, eliciting an approving nod from Brohier. 'I intend for us to build them as tactical weapons for the armed forces. We'll build them as counterterrorism shields for government facilities here and abroad. And if the research effort produces results, there's the prospect of making use of the Trigger in the public realm.

'I'm asking Terabyte Laboratories to provide two prototypes at the earliest possible date, so we can start to find out how useful it is in its current state of development.' Breland looked toward Brohier.

'I would think we could manage that in a matter of a few weeks, Mr President.'

'I imagine we'll need at least that long to figure out who will have custody of them, and where they'll carry out the testing. Dr Brohier, I wanted to ask you – do you think it might it be possible to place a Trigger unit in orbit?'

'For missile defense?'

'No – aimed at the ground. To target a hot spot, much the same as the Forest Service fights fires with aerial tankers. Think how differently Kosovo would have played out if we could have simply disarmed the Serbs.'

An unfamiliar rush of optimism brightened Brohier's eyes. 'Obviously there's a range issue to deal with, and the current version doesn't give us the option of aiming. We'll have to look into that, Mr President. I can't say it's not impossible, but it's a worthy question.'

'Then let's put it on the list,' said Breland. 'Dr Brohier, I want your people to stay with this. I propose we reimburse Terabyte for its costs to date for this research, and contract with you and your research team for your continued services. I'm not sure who you'll report to, but I can't see any reason why you can't personally continue to head the unit. It will need to grow, though, and quickly. And I don't think Columbus is the place for that. Are you still interested?'

'I had girded myself to fight if you tried to push me out, Mr President.'

Breland laughed and turned to Goldstein. 'Mr Goldstein, we're going to need to build these systems somewhere. Perhaps you could be persuaded to convert or set up an appropriate production facility.'

'We'd be happy to bid for the job, Mr President.'

'That won't be necessary. Now, Senator Wilman –' He shook his head. 'I'm grateful for what you did in bringing these men to me. But I honestly don't know what role I can offer you in what lies ahead.'

'Take my calls,' said Wilman. 'I'm going to be your conscience, President Breland. You need someone who doesn't owe you anything to make sure you play between the lines – to make sure you remember that this isn't about the White House, or the *Washington Post*, or the next election, or posterity, or making the Pentagon brass happy. I think you already know all that, but good intentions have a way of getting twisted around in this neighborhood.'

'So they do,' said Breland. 'Very well. I accept your offer. You'll all be staying, then?' He counted nods, then stood. 'Richard has some paperwork for you, then, and once that's taken care of we can roll up our sleeves and get after the details. There's a lot to do.'

As the President stepped outside, Nolby slid a sheaf of papers in front of Brohier and laid a pen atop them. 'Three documents, three signatures,' the chief of staff said. As Brohier pulled the first one toward him and fanned to the last page, Nolby added in a low voice, 'You never answered my question. How many of your people know? I'll need a list by the end of the day.'

Looking up, Brohier held the chief of staff in a level gaze. 'Mr Nolby, I make promises for no one but myself. The people you're talking about work at Terabyte, not *for* it – we don't own them. I'll take your offer to them. And they'll make their own decisions.'

'But Terabyte owns this discovery, doesn't it? You do have that much control over them.'

Brohier laughed derisively, scrawled his name, and pushed the

126

security oath across the table. 'It's not that simple, Mr Nolby, not with people who are accustomed to thinking for themselves. You can get their signatures on all the papers you want, but it's still a lot like making bullfrogs promise to stay in a bucket.'

10: Exigency

Philadelphia, PA – A family argument over the dinner menu flared into domestic violence and ended in a deadly shootout in a southside neighborhood late Friday night. Dozens looked on as Malia Jackson, 24, fled her Fourth Street row home in tears and then opened fire on her boyfriend, Raymar Rollins, when he followed. 'That girl had no choice,' one neighbor protested when police took Jackson into custody. 'Her man beat her every weekend. He was a bad character.'
Complete Story   Domestic Violence Hotlines
Murder or Self-Defense? A Newsline PeoplePoll

The phone woke both Leigh Thayer and Gordon Greene from a dead sleep, as it was meant to under such circumstances. The call was announced by the special high-frequency alarm for the Emergency Code, which overrode all filtering and forwarding instructions Lee had in place for her personal number.

Only three people had Lee's Emergency Code – her sister Joy, her half-sister Barbara, and her father. The only one who'd ever used it was her father, to tell her that her mother had had a heart attack. The shrill, nerve-jangling sound echoing through the darkness of the ersatz dormitory portended equally dire news, and Lee's hands were already shaking as she fumbled for the folding phone. The tiny yellow data screen told her that the caller was Barbara.

'Yes – hello? Barbara?'

The words that came back to her were lost in a wail of pain punctuated by broken, racking sobs.

'Barbara, what's the matter? What's happening? Talk to me, hon –'

Across the room, Gordon had turned on a reading light and sat up on his couch. He said nothing, but his furrowed brow and intent eyes showed his concern.

Once again, Barbara's sobbing stole most of her words. Lee managed to catch 'Elise' and 'window', but the rest conveyed nothing save the depth of her sister's fear, or shock, or terror.

'I can't understand you, hon. Try to calm down – take a deep breath, let it out slow. That's it – you can do it. Get control. Easy. Breathe. Remember to breathe. Now tell me what happened to Elise. Is she hurt?'

'She's – she's –' There was a catch in Barbara's voice as she fought back another outbreak of sobs. 'No. No. She's not hurt. She's not hurt.'

'That's good. Is Tony all right?'

'Tony – Tony's okay.'

'And you're not hurt?'

'No. Nobody's hurt. But it was so close –'

'Are you at home?'

'Yes. Yes. The kids are finally asleep. I hope they're asleep. I made them move to the basement. Oh, Lee – I thought it was over. I thought we were done with this. But it's happening again. They almost shot her, Lee – they almost shot my Elise.' Saying the words tested Barbara's control of her emotions, but she struggled on through deep, shivery sobs. 'She was on the couch watching TV. The bullet missed her head by six inches. Six inches –'

'Who shot at her?'

'Those damned White Kings,' Barbara said, fury in her tone.

'The gangs are after Tony again?'

The fury dissolved into despair. 'What am I going to do? What am I going to do?'

'Tell me everything that's happened.'

Over the next few minutes, Lee painstakingly pieced together the story. She already knew that not quite two years ago, Tony – then fourteen – had been approached by an Iranian-led gang called the Scimitars, then taking over the drug traffic at Tony's high school. When he refused to join, the windows of Barbara's ten-year-old car were shot out as it sat in her driveway. Further confrontations had mercifully been headed off by a Cleveland Metro drug enforcement unit 'street sweep' that put most of the Scimitars in jail.

But a new gang calling itself the White Kings had lately taken shape in the neighborhood. The White Kings were positioning themselves as the protector of the Caucasian majority against the Middle Easterners and African-Americans who predominated in several surrounding neighborhoods – all served by the same high school where Tony was now a sixteen-year-old junior. There had been beatings and brawls as the White Kings asserted themselves in a bid for respect.

Once again Tony had been approached; once again he had refused. And once again he'd been warned that refusal was considered betrayal, and would not be tolerated. As before, the warning came in the form of gunfire – in this case, a single bullet fired through the living-room window an hour after dinner, a bullet that buried itself in the wall over the couch and showered a terrified nine-year-old Elise with plaster dust as squealing tires boldly marked the retreat of the shooter.

'Did you call the police?'

A bitter laugh. 'I called the police. A half-hour later I called them again. They finally got here an hour later, and treated it like a joke.'

'What do you mean, a joke?'

'Apparently if you're not selling drugs or spilling blood, our police aren't interested. One of them actually said, "Well, no harm done, eh?" He suggested I might want to put heavier curtains on the front windows, and keep them drawn.'

'They aren't going to go after the gang?'

'They're not going to do anything. Oh, they didn't admit it to my face, but they might as well have patted me on the head and said, "There, now." Not that Tony helped any.'

'Let me guess – he wouldn't name names.'

'He told the police he didn't know who'd approached him, said he wouldn't recognize them, said he didn't see the car. Oh, god, Lee, that's almost the scariest part – he's known these boys for years. Some of them were in his church basketball league. What am I going to do? Am I supposed to tell Tony to

130

go ahead and join, wear their white cap and beat up blacks and yellows? Am I supposed to wait for them to come back and kill one of us?'

'No. Neither,' said Lee. 'Here's what you're going to do – first thing in the morning, you're going to put Tony and Elise in the car and come down here. You can stay at my apartment – I'm not using it. You'll have plenty of room.'

'I can't do that,' Barbara wailed. 'The kids have to go to school –'

'What's more important? Their health or their attendance record?'

'I'll lose my job – I don't have any more personal days for another two months. Besides, what's the point? Oh, Lee – it's generous of you to offer, but it doesn't solve the problem. The White Kings will still be there when we go back, and the police still won't be able to protect us.'

'Who said anything about going back? We'll put the house up for sale, and go up there in a few days to clean it out. No, even better, I'll pay to have it done – you don't have to spend a minute more there.'

'This house is all I have,' Barbara said in a voice that was close to becoming a whine. 'Even though I probably owe more on it than it's worth. I can't afford to sell it. I can't afford to buy a house in Columbus.'

'You can afford one in Plain City, or West Jefferson, or Johnstown, or Carroll. There're a lot of little towns around here, very reasonable. And I'll help. I never understood why you stayed in that house when Jonas left you –'

Barbara had begun to sob again. 'You never will understand. Both my children were conceived here, born here, took their first steps here. You don't just throw that away.'

Her patience exhausted, Lee snapped, 'Oh, grow up, Beebee – do you want to be able to add "both of my children were murdered here" to that list? Then you could make it into a goddamned shrine –'

'I don't deserve that,' Barbara said plaintively. 'You shouldn't talk to me like that – I called you for *help*, Lee –'

'Then why won't you take it when it's offered? Pack your bags, gather up your kids, and come make a fresh start down here.

131

Come on, Barbara – face reality. There isn't anything up there worth holding on to, and that includes your job.'

'I'm sorry if my life doesn't come up to your standards,' Barbara said, her tone suddenly cold. 'You don't have any respect at all for me, do you? Nothing about me and my kids counts with you, is that it? My job, my house, my feelings, our friends –'

Lee was barely aware that she'd stood up and was pacing the dimly-lit room. 'Are any of those things worth Tony's life? Elise's life? Your life? Do you want Tony getting a gun of his own and trying to solve your problems for you? Six inches, Beebee. Six inches is all that separates a second chance from a funeral.'

Now her sister was crying again. 'It's too much. There's just too much. I can't do it, Lee.'

'You don't have to do it alone –'

The sobbing deepened, and started to steal her words again. 'How can I tell them? I'd just be admitting my whole life's a failure. How can I just run away after fifteen years? What kind of example is that? How can I tell Tony that that's the right thing to do?'

'Because sometimes it *is* the right thing to do. Beebee – I'm begging you – all these other things you're going on about are just pride getting in the way. For once in your life, be practical. You can't protect those kids there, and the police won't – don't make Tony think he has to do it for you. Please, Lee – come to Columbus. Come tomorrow. Come tonight. Please.'

'I don't know,' Barbara said, her voice a frightened whisper. 'I don't know. I have to think. I'll call you.'

'Beebee –'

The connection closed. Exasperated, Lee threw the phone down on her bed and looked across at Greene. 'She makes me so *angry*,' she explained, aware that her entire body was tense and jangling.

Gordon nodded silently. 'Tell me the half I didn't hear. I want to make sure I have the whole picture.'

Half an hour passed before Lee was ready to talk to him.

For the first few minutes, she stewed restlessly – pacing the room, rummaging in the small refrigerator without finding anything that suited her mood, scrubbing her face to redness in the adjacent women's lounge, sitting on her bed brushing her hair so vigorously Gordon could not believe it could be anything but painful. Finally she put down the brush and picked up the phone. 'Personal agent,' she said. 'Search: Cleveland Heights, Ohio. Police. Emergency dispatcher. Connect.'

There followed a short, brutal education in the nature of the police mission and the limitations of police power. Gordon watched surprise, indignation, dismay, and finally despair paint Lee's face.

Yes, the police were aware of gang activity in Cleveland Heights. Yes, the street patrols were aware of the shooting incident at Barbara's house. No, they could not offer any promise of protection – the police investigate crimes, they don't provide bodyguards. No, detectives were not actively investigating the incident – on an average night, there were at least a dozen reports of gunfire. Yes, in an ideal world – but, no, this wasn't one, and there was hardly time to investigate the shootings that sent victims to the hospital or victims to the morgue.

When that conversation was over, Lee was still giving every sign of being at once unapproachable and inconsolable. She stood hugging herself near the door, head lowered, eyes burning a hole through the floor with an intent but unseeing gaze. Gordon had the distinct impression that if he tried to throw a comforting arm around her shoulders, Lee would snap it off and gnaw on it.

Then she was on the phone again, this time to her younger sister Joy in Bakersfield, California. Barbara had apparently not called Joy, allowing Gordon to get most of the information he still needed as Lee brought her up to date. The two sisters then commiserated about Barbara's lifelong tendency to become paralyzed in a crisis, and that seemed to take some of the tension out of Lee's face.

'Exactly – that's it exactly,' Lee said in response to some observation by Joy. 'As if she has no survival instincts whatever. She's the squirrel who sits in the middle of the road staring into the headlights of the oncoming truck, instead of running for the shoulder. Hmm? No, I don't think it's even that she expects to be rescued. She's just completely overwhelmed.'

But Joy had no suggestions Lee could seize on, no solutions to her dilemma. The sisters agreed that it was the wrong time to involve their father, who had his hands full caring for Mom, and was a thousand miles away in Florida in any case. With that as precedent, it quickly became clear that the only help Joy was prepared to offer was commiseration and a call to Barbara in the morning to try to persuade her to accept Lee's offer.

When she put down the phone after that conversation, Lee's armor of anger had vanished, replaced by the momentarily lost look of someone who was even then realizing the cavalry was not coming. She tried one last call, to Barbara, but it rang a dozen times without answer. She left a message with the network voice-mail forwarder, but there was little life in her voice as she recorded it: 'Barbara, this is Lee. Please call me.'

Then she settled back onto the edge of her bed, folding the phone and setting it aside.

'Maybe that means she's in the car, on the way here.'

'No,' said Lee. 'Barbara's not capable of just going out the door and dealing with the details when she arrives. She'd never leave home without talking to me – confirming I was going to meet her, setting a time, getting directions, asking if she should bring pillows, and the like.'

'So you think –'

'I can't think that. What she probably did was turn off her phone, so the kids wouldn't be disturbed – they need a good night's sleep, after all, if they're going to get up tomorrow and go to school.' Lee shook her head. 'I love her dearly, but sometimes I just want to slap some sense into her.'

Gordon nodded. 'But first, there's the little matter of getting the squirrel out of the street.'

'I have to go up there,' Lee said with a sigh of resignation. 'I have to wake her up somehow – I can't let her endanger those kids again.'

'Okay,' said Gordon. 'Then we'd better stop talking and get to work.'

'What? What are you thinking?'

'I don't know why you aren't thinking it, too,' said Gordon. 'These thugs are going to want to know if the message got through. If tomorrow morning Tony tells them to go stuff themselves, they'll be back tomorrow night. And we'll be waiting for them.'

134

'That's crazy, Gordie –'

'No, it isn't. We can have Baby Two ready to roll by noon. I just need to put together the collimator I've had rattling around in my head for a week or so, while you wire in a couple of quick-and-dirty controls for the truck cab. We can be up there by the time the kids get off the bus.'

'The Boss will never agree to this.'

'A good reason not to ask him.'

'What, you think we can just drive out with it?'

'Yes.'

'They'll shoot us. And then Brohier will fire us. And then his friends in the sheriff's office will throw our corpses in jail, for good measure.'

'You know, you're starting to sound a lot like your sister,' Gordon said quietly. 'Why are you looking for reasons not to try?'

Her eyes widened in surprise as the thrust found its target. 'You think I don't want to help her? They'll stop us at the gate, Gordie.'

'No, they won't,' he said. 'I've already had the truck out of here three times, twice with Baby Two inside – and the last time with the generator trailer riding out back.'

'Why?'

'I've been worried about the roadability of the system. I had to know that taking it across a grade crossing wouldn't put it out of action.'

Lee stared at him with dark suspicion. 'Aren't you a little ahead of schedule on that? Gordie – have you been planning to steal it?'

He shrugged. 'I've been trying to do my job, that's all – to make sure we're ready for any surprises. I've been trying to protect us,' he said. 'That's why I've been running it every night, too. A little extra security.'

'What? How?'

'Timer module, right on the actuator. Don't kick yourself, you'd have to be a lot more paranoid than you want to be to have spotted it.' He chuckled. 'You almost caught me on Tuesday, though, when you got up early.'

'Son of a – I thought it seemed awfully warm in the bay that morning. I even checked to see if the climate controls were working.'

'I had it plugged into the generator trailer that night. The climate controls can't really keep up.' He smiled conspiratorially. 'So – are we going to do the right thing, or the safe thing?'

'Explain something to me first – why are *you* willing to take this risk? She's my sister – that's my niece and nephew – but you've never even met them. What's your stake in this?'

Greene pursed his lips. 'She matters to you. That's enough for me. I don't add things up the way everyone else does, Lee.'

'Is that what you're going to tell the Boss when we get back?'

'I'm going to tell him that we took the system out for a real-world field test. And if protecting your sister and her kids doesn't seem like a good enough reason to him, or Dr Brohier, then I'll know they're not the kind of people I want to be working with anyway.'

'Then why not ask them?'

'Because we'd run squarely into a wall of worries, and we don't have enough time to knock it down. Once we're back safely, though, they can't say, "Yeah, but what if –"' He smiled. 'Which is the secret of why it's easier to get forgiveness than permission.'

Lee was shaking her head. 'Maybe once I'm there, I can talk her into moving down here –'

'Have you ever?'

'Have I ever what?'

'Talked her into doing the sensible thing when she seemed set on doing the familiar thing, or the expected thing. How many times has she been hit by the car, and how many times have you managed to get her to run for the curb?'

'I've never been able to do that,' she said gloomily. 'She always gets hit by the car.'

'Then why are we still sitting here yapping?' he said, rising to his feet. 'We have a lot to do.'

True to Gordon's prediction, it was only a few minutes after noon when he and Lee climbed into the cab of the unmarked white truck. Behind them in the locked cargo area was the Trigger unit, resting on a foam sheet and secured to the tie-downs with

136

wide straps. Behind the truck, attached to the tow hitch, was the bright orange generator trailer.

With his hands resting lightly on the steering wheel, Gordon looked sideways at Lee. 'Ready?'

Her nod was less than wholly convincing, but Gordon reached for the ignition switch anyway. The truck's big engine whined, coughed, and came to life. 'Try not to look so guilty,' he said, and eased the truck into gear.

There was no trouble at the inner gate. Tim Bartel was in the gatehouse, and he waved them through as soon as he'd recorded the number stenciled in black on the side of the truck. The guards at the street gate were unfamiliar, but they showed no special curiosity as they logged the two researchers out and allowed their vehicle through the double barricades.

'Told you so,' Gordon said as he guided the truck out onto Shanahan Road. But there was no sign of relief in Lee's expression.

'What?' he asked.

'I'm thinking about Eric. He's still in the hospital, isn't he?'

'Last I heard. Burns like that take a long time to heal.'

Lee looked away out the window. 'I don't know if I can do that to someone – knowingly.'

He reached over and squeezed her hand. 'You don't have to,' Gordon said. 'I know how you feel about that kind of confrontation. All you have to do is take your sister and her kids to a motel – convince her she needs to let things cool down for a couple of days. Just keep them away from the house. The way we've rigged things up, I can do the rest.'

'And you're okay with that?' she asked, turning back toward him.

'I am,' he said, reclaiming his hand so he could turn south, toward the freeway. 'Lee, these thugs set the ground rules when they picked up a gun and pointed it at your family. I'm not going to lose sleep if that boomerangs on them. Are we going to hurt them? Perhaps even kill one of them? I damn well hope so. Are you okay with *that*?'

'I can't seem to let myself admit to feelings like those,' she said quietly. 'Which isn't the same thing as saying I don't have them.'

'I'd worry more if I *didn't* feel this way,' said Gordon. 'Anybody who terrifies a nine-year-old kid, waves a gun in the face of a teenager, brings this kind of fear into a family that's minding its own business – they've earned whatever comes. Haven't they? Haven't they? Barbara's whole world is under attack.'

'Yes.'

'Then let's not be coy about this – this thing in the truck behind us is a weapon, and we're going up there to strike back.' Then his tone softened. 'But I'll do it alone if you want. You don't have to be there. I can still leave you here.'

'No,' Lee said. 'Keep driving. But stop talking. I want to keep pretending for a couple more hours. I want to hold on to my illusions just a little while longer.'

Gordon and Lee started talking again north of Brunswick. By the time they reached the exit for US 20 and Cleveland Heights, they had a plan. At the core of it was a decision to conceal from Barbara the real reason they were there, and in doing so to give her an alibi that would shelter her from any consequences of their actions.

They parked within sight of the East Cleveland diet clinic where Barbara worked as a records and claims clerk, and Lee called her from there.

'Barbara Thayer-Cummins, please,' she said, glancing sideways at Gordon with a look that said here we go, across the Rubicon. 'Thank you. – Barb, this is Lee. Listen, I caught a ride north with a friend – I'm just a few minutes away. No, I just want to do what I can to help. How late do you work today – until six? Okay, where are the kids going after school? – Margie is right across the street, isn't she? That's awfully close, if they come back.

'– No, it's really not fair, even though Margie was brave enough to offer. That's more than a good neighbor. – Listen, I have a motel room in Mayfield Heights, at the Budgetel just off Two-Ninety-One. Can you get away long enough to collect the kids and bring them over to the motel? I'll watch out for them until you get off work, and then we can have dinner together and figure out what to do. – No, I don't know my room number yet. I'll be there before you, though. All right – I love you, too.'

A minute later, they saw a woman emerge from the clinic,

look around nervously, then scurry across the parking lot to a well-traveled sky blue sedan – an '02 or '03 Saturn, Gordon thought.

'That her?'

'That's her,' said Lee, her left hand moving to the industrial-grade control box resting on the seat between her and Gordon. There were only three switches on the box: a pushbutton to start the generator, a click-detent rheostat to activate Baby Two, and a shuttle knob for pointing the new collimator head toward a target.

Barbara's sedan headed south, and they followed, the height of the truck cab allowing Gordon to lag a few car lengths behind. This was the part that worried him the most – the family still on the street, and him with no idea where the White Kings were, or if they were bold enough to attack in daylight. Every vehicle that drew near to the Saturn was a potential threat, and the margin for recognizing and responding to a real threat seemed wholly inadequate. All through the short drive, Gordon was sorely tempted to activate the Trigger preemptively. Only the near-certainty that doing so would leave a trail of chaos and injured innocents stopped him.

Instead, he brought the truck up in the outside lane and rode in the Saturn's blind spot, denying that place to any other vehicle, and giving himself and Lee a clear view of any cars that might pull up behind or beside her sister. When Barbara turned off the boulevard onto a one-lane, one-way street, Gordon followed, again falling back a few car lengths.

'This is her street, coming up on the right,' Lee said.

'Turn on the generator,' he said, tightlipped. 'Just in case there's someone waiting for that car to show up.' He opened his window in time to catch the muted cough of the DuoCat turning over, then hauled firmly on the wheel to make the turn onto Seaton Road.

'Which house is hers?'

'Fourth one on the left – the white salt-box, before the yellow duplex.'

'See anything out of place?'

'No.'

'Keep looking,' he said, studying the big rear-view mirror. 'I hope she called ahead to tell the kids to expect her.'

'Looks like she did – here they come.' A slender girl and a taller, wider teenaged boy had appeared on the stoop and were already running across the postage-stamp lawn toward Barbara's car, its brake lights glowing bright red.

'No one behind us,' said Gordon. 'See anyone in any of those parked cars ahead?'

Her fingers were nervously caressing the rheostat. 'Nothing.'

In a few seconds, the children had clambered into the back seat, and the Saturn began to accelerate. 'Don't relax,' he said. 'That next intersection would be a good place to box them in.'

But they rejoined the busy boulevard and turned east toward Mayfield Heights without incident. Gordon allowed himself a glance at his companion, and found her visibly perspiring. 'A little tense?'

'I kept thinking someone was going to sit up in one of those cars, and I'd freeze up and have to watch them being shot to death in front of me.'

He smiled. 'You should have played more *Doom* when you were a kid – honed those combat reflexes.'

'I hated that game.'

'Ask me if I'm surprised.' He looked in the rear-view mirror again. 'No one followed us out of the subdivision. Unless we're just unlucky enough to bump into the bad guys –'

'Let's pretend we're superstitious, and not sit here generating failure scenarios for the cosmos to borrow.'

'Fair enough,' said Gordon. 'Okay, I see the motel sign. I'm going to go ahead and pass her now, so I can drop you off. I'll wait until she leaves to go back to work, and then come in and talk to Tony. Make sure she parks away from the street, tail-first. And tell her to take a taxi here after work, or get a ride. I don't see these thugs as having a lot of ambition, and I know a Saturn's about as invisible a car as there is, but let's not assume they're idiots as well as thugs.'

Three hours later, Gordon and Lee were parked at the curb near the west end of Seaton Road. Their nervousness had been replaced by a quiet, almost fatalistic determination. They had enlisted Tony in their conspiracy, and – as Gordon had suspected he could – the youth had told them much more than he had admitted to the police. With his help, they knew what cars they were looking for: a white Camaro convertible, and a forest-green Eddie Bauer Explorer.

'They make a big entrance every morning at the school parking lot, honking, burning rubber,' Tony had told them. 'The Camaro belongs to Frosty – Steven Frost. The four-by-four is John Nolan's. They have permanent parking spots together in the first row – everybody knows, and nobody else dares to park there. They sit there revving their engines for five minutes, and there's twenty girls – all lookers – down there surrounding them by the time they're done. I don't get it.'

Also thanks to Tony's help, they were confident that they were not looking in vain.

They had told him as little as possible about what they were planning, but, even so, the hard part had been persuading him to stay behind. With the reckless arrogance of young men everywhere, he was eager to be part of the hunt, picturing himself in the moment of victory, tasting his tormentors' humiliation, craving his redemption. Only Lee and Gordon's combined resistance blunted his eagerness.

'You need to stay with your family, and comfort and protect them,' they had told him. 'We can't do that job as well as you can, and you can't do our job as well as we can.'

But he had remained dissatisfied, until he found a way to play a part.

'You want to be sure that they show up at the house tonight, right? You're staking out the place in case they come back.'

Gordon had confirmed that much to him.

'Then call me when you're set up there,' Tony had said. 'I'll make sure. I know what will bring them out.'

That call had been made half an hour ago. Now twilight was settling over Seaton Road. Children were disappearing from the yards, and adults from front stoops and porches. Security lights came on at side doors and in back yards, and dogs came inside for the night. Blinds and drapes were drawn as a defense against the dark, hiding the bluish glow from televisions and computer monitors. Two of the three streetlamps began to glow dully. By the time they warmed to full brightness, the street was deserted, abandoned to the creatures that owned the dark.

Holding hands in silence, Gordon and Lee waited for them to emerge.

Time crawled. They heard a distant siren, and then another.

'Car wreck,' Gordon said under his breath. 'Or a fire.'

He watched in his rear-view mirror as a car turned onto Seaton Road, heading toward them. Its headlights momentarily blinded him, and he held up a hand to shield his eyes and hide his face. 'Wait,' he said, feeling Lee's urgency beside him. As the car trundled past, he saw that it was a red four-door sedan. It turned into a narrow driveway further down the street and disappeared into a carport.

A scruffy dog padded across the circle of light cast by the nearest streetlamp.

'Would this be a good time for you to explain what a sister of yours is doing living in a neighborhood like this?'

'Half-sister.'

'Go on.'

Thayer sighed. 'My father visited Cleveland thirty-odd years ago on business and carelessly left some sperm cells behind.'

'Ow.'

'Barbara's mother didn't use up all her bad judgement sleeping with my father – she let my father's lawyers inveigle her into signing a support agreement that might have sounded generous, but wasn't even fair. Even at that, the annuity was a magnet for deadbeats – two husbands, two live-ins, two more babies. Then Barbara got twenty-five thousand dollars when she turned eighteen – supposedly for college, but not nearly enough. She bought a car instead. She still drives it.'

'So she wasn't exactly brought into the family fold.'

'No. Mom never has acknowledged her. My father does so grudgingly. I'm easily the closest to her – maybe because I'm pretty much an outcast myself. Joy is the Good Daughter, doesn't want to make Mom angry or Father uncomfortable. She has too much to lose.'

142

The sound of a helicopter beat down on Seaton Road from somewhere up above.

'Are we going to wait for them to start shooting?' she whispered.

'Only if that's what it takes to be sure it's them,' he whispered back. 'They already started shooting, remember?'

A car turned onto Seaton at the far end, starting the wrong way down the one-way street. Gordon pushed Lee down, then ducked down behind the dash himself before the approaching headlights could give them away. Gordon tracked its progress by the moving shadow of the windshield pillar, and sat up just in time to see a minivan slide past.

'False alarm,' he said. 'Just someone looking lost.'

Another siren keened in the night.

A car with squeaky brakes appeared and parked on the street, six car lengths ahead of the truck.

In the moments between, time seemed to have stopped.

'The generator's going to give us away,' she whispered.

'Sssh,' he said, and squeezed her hand. 'They'll never hear it. This kind likes their cars loud and their music louder.'

'I don't think they're coming.'

'They're coming. It's a head game. They think they've got Tony sweating, while they're off somewhere juicing themselves up for sport.'

'How do you know so much about this?'

'I had exceptionally poor judgement when it came to friends, once upon a time.'

She looked away to her rear-view mirror. 'I hate this.'

'Just wait,' he said.

The creeping, interminable minutes had finally carried them close to midnight when Gordon heard a short-pipe dual exhaust clear its rumbling throat.

'Convertible at the corner,' he said, touching the shoulder of his dozing companion.

'What?'

Then the Explorer glided into view, following close behind the Camaro. 'Here they come,' Gordon said. 'Get down.' Heeding his

143

own admonition, he ducked out of the glare of the Camaro's headlights. His right hand fended off Lee's left and claimed the Trigger controls. 'Let me,' he whispered.

It seemed to take forever for the two vehicles to pass where Gordon and Lee were parked. The bass grumble of the Camaro seemed to stop right outside Gordon's window, which he had left open a few centimeters for both air and sound cues. For an agonizing minute, he feared that they'd become the target – that the gang had become either wary of the truck, or curious about its contents.

Fragments of an animated conversation, thick with slang and profanity and punctuated with wild laughter, reached him through the cracked window. Gordon strained to decode what he was hearing, and suddenly realized that behind their bluster, they were spooked by Barbara's house being completely dark. While sneering at Tony's supposed cowardice, they were hanging back, wondering about an ambush.

It was for just such a possibility that he had taken the home security remote from Barbara's car while she was inside Lee's motel room. The system was unsophisticated, but he did not require much from it – merely a way of drawing them in, the equivalent of a pebble tossed in the dark. Digging in his jacket pocket with his free hand, he found the remote and pressed the top button. Almost instantly, the porch and living-room lights came on.

That was all it took to goad the gang into action. There was a whoop and a shout from inside the Camaro, and it surged forward, tires squealing and smoking. 'Stay down,' he whispered sternly to Lee, then sat up as the Explorer passed.

With cool deliberation, Gordon assessed the situation in the street ahead. There were four White Kings in the convertible. One was standing up in the back seat, shouting unintelligible taunts toward the house and waving a pair of pistols in the air. Another gang member was hanging out of the right-side window of the Explorer, clinging to the roof and cradling some sort of larger weapon. In moments, both vehicles would be directly opposite the house.

Gordon waited no longer. A single long thumbpress started the generator. The collimator atop the Trigger was already pointing down the street toward his targets. With a slight twist of his wrist, he brought the Trigger to life, dialing up the power one click at a time.

There was one short burst of gunfire, the hollow popping of a small-caliber automatic – Gordon thought it came from the Explorer. The glass panes in the storm door of Barbara's house disintegrated as though smashed with a hammer. A second gun, its bark deeper, harsher, spoke once, twice. He heard gleeful laughter.

In the next moment, everything turned. The Explorer was suddenly lit brilliantly from within by yellow-white fire, almost as though several flares had gone off in the middle of the back seat. There was barely any sound from the eruptions, no more than the dull *whump* of a pillow whipped against a mattress. But the laughter and taunting cries turned to screams as the vehicle swerved sharply, then screeched to a halt. Gordon could clearly see the contortions of the passengers as they tried to escape the fire and flee the vehicle.

At the same time, the Camaro began to speed up. But it had not traveled more than a few car lengths when its trunk erupted in a fireball so intense that Gordon felt the heat of it on his face. Moments later, the Camaro careened into a parked pickup truck with the sickening sound of rending metal and shattering plastic.

'As ye sow –' he said grimly. 'Now maybe the police will take notice.'

Lee, now sitting upright beside him, wide-eyed and white-knuckled, said nothing.

As the flames climbed higher and the screaming continued unabated, Gordon started the truck's engine. The burning vehicles had Seaton Road blocked, so he used the first driveway to turn the truck and trailer around. He left the truck's lights off until he reached the corner and turned right. From that point on, they could pretend innocence.

'That was horrible,' she said, hoarse and dry-voiced.

'More horrible than burying your sister, or one of her kids?' he said.

'I feel dirty.'

'Don't. They came there to Tony and his family. They got hurt instead. Simple justice, directly meted out. Would you rather it had been Barbara?'

She slumped against the door and stared out at the night, glancing nervously at the rear-view mirror when she heard sirens in the distance. 'I just wish Tony hadn't told us their names.'

11: Military

Cleveland Heights, OH – A minor car crash on a quiet
residential street turned into a killer conflagration Monday
night when a trunkful of illegal guns and ammunition
erupted in flames. Three members of the White Kings race
gang, including alleged gang leader Steven 'Frosty' Frost,
were killed. Four other gang members were hospitalized
with extensive burns and other injuries. State police are
investigating the incident, which destroyed three cars and
caused minor damage to several nearby houses.

Complete Story　　　　*Casualty List*　　　　　*Gun Safety Tips*
Race Gangs Selling Nostalgia, Not Drugs

Committees being one of the least efficient decision-making mechanisms ever devised, it had taken six days of twice-a-day meetings to
hammer out the details of what was now called Project Brass Hat.
But at last the operational plan had been finalized, the memoranda
of agreement drawn up, the executive orders signed, the black-
budget draws authorized, and the committee finally dispersed.

Karl Brohier was on his way back to Columbus to begin ramping
up the research effort. Aron Goldstein was on his way to North
Sioux City, South Dakota, where the closing of a computer
assembly plant had left a technically skilled workforce and a
hundred twenty thousand square feet of work floor idle. Grover
Wilman was on his way back to the Senate, where the bipartisan
Defense Advisory Committee was about to admit a new member
to its ultrasecret meetings.

That left the White House quartet – Breland, Nolby, Carrero, and
Stepak – with what looked to be the hardest job: selling Project
Brass Hat to the Pentagon. And the key to that was General Roland
Stepak, USAF (Ret.), the first secretary of defense since George C.

Marshall to bring general officer rank and command experience to the office.

In a twenty-six year career, Stepak had logged nearly ten thousand hours in a variety of aircraft, including the top air superiority and strike fighters in the world. He had been an air combat instructor, an F-22 squadron leader in Namibia, and a wing commander during the Taiwan Interdiction – though, typical for a pilot of his era, he had flown only sixty-two actual combat sorties, and recorded no air-to-air kills. Stepak owed his reputation more to his brand of confidence without ego and leadership without arrogance than to heroism in the air.

Since leaving the cockpit, he had returned to Keesler to lead the 2nd Air Force in its training mission, returned to Japan as commander of the fighter-dominated 5th, added a third star to his collar and moved up to commander of the Pacific Air Forces, and finally came home to take over the Air Combat Command at Langley – considered the prestige assignment among the major commands.

Interspersed with those assignments had been three turns in high-visibility staff positions at the Pentagon, where his diligence and quiet competence won him respect from the headquarters staff. By the end of his second year at Langley, he was considered a dark horse candidate to eventually return to the Pentagon as Air Force Chief of Staff.

But then his wife of twenty-two years, Peggy Ashford Stepak, learned that the persistent headaches which had plagued her for several months had a tangible cause: brain cancer. The morning after they received the news, the general put in for immediate leave – he had nearly half a year accumulated – and for retirement as of the expiration of his leave. In all but name, he quit on the spot, violating the standing protocols regarding the orderly transfer of command. By noon, he was off the base, out of uniform, and at Peggy's side for the follow-up MRI. It was the single most selfish act of his career.

The three years which followed were the best of times and the worst of times, as the general and his wife played catch-up on a lifetime of postponed promises and deferred dreams. Peggy's final six months were an agony for both of them, until at last saying good-bye was a small mercy.

Five years later, President Breland had plucked Stepak from the private anonymity he had fallen into, rescuing him from a lingering grief and an unfocused restlessness. The appointment, and the work that went with it, had renewed Stepak.

Some days Stepak's countenance still seemed clouded by the darkness of an unspoken regret or a melancholy memory, but it never touched his work. He had been as diligent and thorough in preparing Breland for that morning's meeting with the Joint Chiefs as he would have been preflighting his F-22 for a sortie over the Formosa Strait.

'Don't expect to get a clean read from the Joint Chiefs at this first briefing,' Stepak cautioned the President. 'The service chiefs, especially. There's an inherent conflict in their posts – they're your advisors, but they're also the senior commanding officers for their respective services.'

'Which way do you think they're going to fall on this?' Breland asked, patting his copy of the agenda book, with the words TOP SECRET embossed on the locking leatherette cover.

'In all honesty, sir, I think you're going to have some trouble,' Stepak said. 'Above and beyond the implications for foreign policy and national security, you're changing the conditions of the exercise in ways which threaten their identity. They're human beings. They have thirty years' time in. Behind the gold stars and the ribbons, they're pilots and grunts and swabbies. They know what the people who have to do the actual fighting have at stake, and they identify with those people.'

'How bad could it get?'

'My guess is that it'll be "Yes, Mr President" while they're still recovering from the shock and trying to get on top of this news. But once they've had some time to think about it, you'll start to feel their resistance. Whether that'll be today or sometime down the road, I don't know.'

'First assess the battlefield intelligence, *then* deploy your forces.'

'First look over the defense, *then* call the snap count,' Stepak said with a quick smile. 'Something else – realistically, they're probably going to resent being kept in the dark until after some of the decisions were already made. They may wonder why this didn't come through the National Security Council.'

'Isn't it obvious? Just the bare mention of the NSC would probably have spooked Goldstein's people. Besides, the only statutory member who wasn't part of the Brass Hat committee was the Vice President.'

Stepak nodded. 'Are you planning to involve her at any time soon?'

'No,' said Breland, and shrugged. 'Truman wasn't told about the atomic bomb until after Roosevelt was dead.' He caught the surprise in the secretary of defense's expression, and added, 'It's not that difficult for me to come up with scenarios which end with my being impeached for treason. No?'

'I wish I could say I thought you were overstating the risks, Mr President.'

'I'd be a tough sell. I can think of too many folks up on the Hill who'd view my allowing this discovery to disarm our military as nothing short of treason. I'm sure I know what Ben Twilly's counsel would have been – destroy the research and make the Terabyte people disappear,' he said with a rueful smile. 'And he could probably manage to round up a posse of like-minded citizens.'

'Possibly so.'

'But if I can keep Toni at arm's length, maybe she could survive my impeachment. Which I think would be to the good of the country – if everyone wakes up some morning to discover that they have a President that no one voted for –' He shook his head. 'Let's see if we can avoid running that particular experiment in representative democracy.'

'I'll concur on that, Mr President.'

'Which brings me back to what you were saying earlier,' said Breland, standing and emerging from behind his desk. 'Just what form might that "resistance" take? Do you think there's a chance that the Joint Chiefs would resort to direct action?'

'Against you?'

'Against me. Against us. And please, an honest answer – I need more than a glib reassurance that it's never happened here.'

'It's not a glib reassurance,' Stepak said. 'These men take their oaths every bit as seriously as you do yours. This isn't like schoolkids mumbling their way through the Pledge of Allegiance at the start of classes.'

150

'I accept that – but it doesn't rule out the possibility of a fundamental difference of opinion. The oath they take is to the Constitution and the Presidency, not to any particular president. There has to be a limit to how long they'll stand by and do nothing. I'm asking you how close you think we are to that line.'

'It doesn't matter where that line is, or what side of it you're on,' said Stepak. 'It's not the place of the Joint Chiefs to remove you. You may not understand that, but they do. You're speaking truthfully about human nature – but the whole point of a soldier's training and loyalty is to defy human nature. That's the only way you get men to run *toward* where the bullets are coming from – when any rational person can see that the sensible thing to do is run *away*.'

Breland was frowning. 'You know all of the current Chiefs personally, don't you?'

'Yes. I count two of them as friends. But I'd say the same thing if they were all strangers,' Stepak said firmly. 'Mr President, if you were facing impeachment, and there was an angry mob coming up Pennsylvania Avenue with the intention of accelerating the process of removing you from office, every one of those men would willingly and unhesitatingly place themselves between you and that mob, would give their lives if necessary, to see that you lived long enough to be impeached. There was no coup when Johnson and McNamara were bungling the Vietnam War, no night of the generals when Nixon was sullying the presidency or Clinton was selling it. You have nothing to fear from that quarter.'

Breland was taken aback by the earnest passion of Stepak's reproof. He retreated a step and sat down on a corner of his desk. 'My apologies, General Stepak,' he said softly. 'I got confused for a moment about which team is wearing what color.'

'No apology is necessary, Mr President,' said Stepak. 'It's my job to make sure that you don't forget anything important. – Now, to answer your question. You don't need their consent. You only need their obedience, which you'll have, whatever your orders. You're the commander in chief – it's *your* responsibility to get it right, theirs to get it done. Moreover, the chain of command doesn't pass through the service chiefs – it goes directly from you to the major commands, through me. So even if the chiefs were of a mind to thwart and defy you – which, I'll say again, isn't going to happen – they would have to overstep their authority to do so.

'No, what you can expect is a war of words,' said Stepak. 'If they think you're wrong, they'll argue with you – and a full-out assault by the combined chiefs is nothing to sneer at. They'll argue as hard and as long as you let them – and it's a good idea to let them, because the one thing they can do to seriously hurt you is resign.'

'Go on.'

'If you bring them a policy they think is dangerously wrong, and if you leave them feeling that you weren't willing to hear them, or to defend your decision in front of them –'

'I'll put them in a position where the only option their conscience will allow them is to resign.'

'Yes. And the simple truth is that if you suddenly lose two or three people from the JCS, Congress will notice, and so will the entire force structure. You don't need that. This is going to be difficult enough *with* their full commitment. Technically, you don't need their consent – but practically, you do need their experience, their insight, and their leadership, all fully engaged.'

'It's not enough if they just run out and take their positions,' said Breland. 'I need them to have their heads in the game – I need them to play hard.'

'Exactly, sir. And if I may add a personal opinion –'

'By all means.'

'You owe it to the country to give them every chance to convince you that you're wrong.'

'Are you saying that you think I am?'

Stepak raised his hands in a gesture of profound ambivalence. 'Mr President, I don't know. The only way I get any sleep these days is by telling myself over and over that it could be worse – it could be *my* decision. Maybe the right place for the Trigger is at the bottom of a thousand-foot shaft, with five hundred feet of concrete on top of it. I just don't know.'

Showing a wry, lopsided smile, Breland admitted, 'I've had a little trouble sleeping myself.'

'You'd have to be inhuman not to,' said Stepak. 'Even after a week of talking about it, I can't really say I've grasped the full reach of the changes to come if you follow through on Brass Hat. I know this much – no one's life is going to be untouched. And if you do follow through, no presidency in this country will have left the country, the *world*, as profoundly changed as yours will. I just wish I had the wisdom to know if we'll be changing it for the better, or for the worse.'

'Except that isn't the choice we face,' said Breland. 'We can act, or we can wait to be acted on. One of those at least gives us a *chance* to try to control the outcome. And that's not a hard choice for me, even if the attempt ends badly. We can't wish this away – what if some Chinese physicist met with the Premier the same morning Brohier came to me? It'd be an abdication of responsibility *not* to move forward.' A relaxed, reassuring smile came to his lips. 'To use one of those sports metaphors you're so fond of, Roland – it's crunch time, and I want the ball in my hands.'

The concealed door to the outer offices opened just enough for Nolby to poke his head in. 'Mr President? It's time.'

Breland glanced back over his shoulder at the clock behind his desk. 'So it is. General?'

'I'm with you, Mr President,' said Stepak, standing. 'And I want you to know I mean that.'

'I know you do.'

The formalities of roll call complete, General Donald Madison, Chairman of the Joint Chiefs, dismissed the recording secretary from the conference room.

Clearing his throat, Madison pushed his personal organizer back from the edge of the conference table and laid down his stylus beside a thick, secure-sealed white envelope. An identical envelope rested in front of each of the men seated at the table. The envelopes were personalized, dated and numbered; the one by Breland's right hand was marked *Copy 1 of 8*. The contents had been prepared by Stepak, under Breland's close supervision and subject to his personal editing.

'This special meeting has been called at the request of the President,' Madison said in his phlegmy rumble of a voice. 'The information he's brought us is compartmentalized Top Secret – there are to be no notes taken, and no minutes kept. The briefing materials will be collected at the end of the meeting.' He looked across the expanse of wood at Breland. 'Mr President, the floor is yours.'

'Thank you, General Madison,' Breland said with a nod. 'Gentlemen, I'm here not only to brief you, but to consult with you. I've recently learned that there now exists a technological means to neutralize most conventional weapons.' It was a natural pause line, but Breland was aiming for a matter-of-fact presentation, not a dramatic one, and went right on. 'This discovery was made by American scientists earlier this summer. They constructed a working prototype and carried out a series of preliminary tests. Those tests confirm that the device, which we are calling the Trigger, detonates or destroys nitrate-based explosives and propellants at a distance.

'In consultation with the secretary of defense, I've already ordered an expanded research effort aimed at refining the Trigger device and establishing a theoretical foundation for its extraordinary effect. I've also ordered the immediate production of one thousand examples of an interim Mark I Trigger design based on the prototype, which has an effective range reported to me as "no less than five hundred meters".

'One hundred of the Mark I units are reserved for an expanded testing program, to be carried out by the Defense Advanced Research Projects Agency and the Redstone Arsenal in cooperation with all three services. I've directed General Stepak to see that every weapon and munition currently in inventory, conventional and nuclear, is tested for susceptibility to the Trigger effect. However, I have to tell you that our expectation is that all conventional munitions *will* be susceptible.

'No one currently cleared to know about the Trigger has access to detailed technical information about the design of current nuclear munitions, so their susceptibility is less certain – but on general design principles, considered likely. With your assistance, we may be able to settle that question before the end of this briefing.

'Together, these three operations – research, production, and testing – constitute Project Brass Hat. But they only address the most immediate need to discover the limits and capabilities of this new technology. There are many more issues and challenges

154

which need to be addressed, many of them crucial questions related to national security and international relations.

'We're fortunate to have a chance to address them before being confronted by this technology on a battlefield. We have a window of opportunity in which to rethink our battlefield concept, and shift our tactics, our weapons mix, and even our force structure, to remain effective in the new combat environment.

'But that's only the beginning. The morning after I learned about the Trigger, I woke up with the realization that everything I knew was wrong. This discovery calls on us to develop a new concept of "security", one which doesn't depend on our having more and bigger weapons than the enemy. We have a window of opportunity in which we can rewrite the definition of "deterrence", and reconsider the need for traditional means of force projection.

'Just think, Admiral Jacobs – an unarmed freighter with a Trigger unit aboard would be more secure in a war zone than the heaviest cruiser or the fastest carrier. In fact, the freighter might be a greater threat to the cruiser than the cruiser would be to the freighter.

'Just think, General Moorman – we have before us the means to create an entirely new concept of a national border. With the Trigger standing guard, we can create open borders in places where open borders have never existed – the Middle East, the Far East. Open borders without fear of attack. Because the Trigger can give us borders that a friend can cross at any time, but an enemy can never cross.

'Beyond all that, I also see one great opportunity that transcends our own legitimate needs to protect our people and our allies – an opportunity to save twenty thousand lives a year, to save hundreds of thousands more from a lifetime of suffering.

'Because despite the treaties of '97 and 2000, there are still more than a hundred million live mines lurking in the ground in Cambodia, Kosovo, Afghanistan, Bosnia, Chad, the Ukraine – you know the list as well as I do. Despite the ban, there are still more mines put *into* the ground every year than there are taken out. And all across Europe, central Africa, southeast Asia, the unexploded munitions left buried by a century of warfare are still percolating to the surface.

'We can put an end to that threat. We can stop the slaughter of the innocents. Just think, General Hawley – a squadron of Trigger-equipped helicopters should be able to cleanse an acre in minutes, an entire country in a few weeks. We now have the capacity to turn battlefields back into the farms and pastures and playgrounds they were before the armies showed up. Humanity may not have learned yet how to stop brawling amongst ourselves, but we finally have the means to clean up after ourselves. And we'll do more good for more people – and for our country! – by being the janitors of the world than we ever have as the policemen of the world.'

But despite all Breland's passion, eloquence, and earnest enthusiasm, it remained a tough room, a distant audience. The demands of etiquette and the expectations of discipline assured him the Joint Chiefs' full attention, but they absorbed his words with scarcely an outward reaction. Breland was not interrupted once by the poker-faced chiefs, whose body language – which approached sitting-at-attention – gave him little more to go on.

'I've said enough to set the context,' he said, settling back in the padded-armed chair. 'Please open your briefing packets now. You'll find an overview of Brass Hat, a summary of the test results to date, an outline of issues and opportunities, and a preliminary list of questions regarding the impact on national defense. If the Chairman has no objection, I'd like to invite you to take as much time as you need to review what's there, and then we'll come back together and begin the hard work.'

'I have no objection,' said General Madison, to the sound of secure-seal tabs snapping and Tyvek rustling.

Breland nodded and rose, his eye on the crystal tumblers and pitchers of ice water at the far end of the table. His exposition had left him dry-mouthed, with the first hint of the widely-noted rasp that frequently came on him when he found himself talking at length. But as he turned away from the table, someone cleared his throat and said, 'Mr President, I don't need any more time to know what I think of this.'

Breland turned back to find General Hawley standing at his seat, a single finger touching the briefing packet. 'Very well. Go ahead, General.'

'I think it's madness,' said Hawley. 'You've obviously decided not only to develop this weapon, but to deploy it – not only to deploy it, but to do so in as public a manner as possible.'

'That decision *hasn't* been made,' said Breland. 'But I won't mislead you, General – it's clearly the option that offers the most opportunities to alter a potential enemy's behavior.'

'I can tell you the first behavior that'll be altered,' said Hawley. 'Ten minutes after news of this reaches Beijing, Premier Denh will order an all-out effort to buy or steal the Trigger secrets. Every scientist working on Brass Hat is going to need to be locked up where no one can find them. Every one of those Mark I units is going to need a twenty-four hour guard made up of the most bribe-proof people we can find. Every Trigger you take out of the country is going to need a platoon of Marines to protect it. And even if you do everything right, within ten years, the Chinese, the Iranians, the Iraqis, the Pakistanis, and anyone else who really wants the Trigger will have it.'

Breland nodded calmly. 'That would be the expected outcome – wouldn't you agree, General Stepak?'

Stepak nodded gravely. 'Everyone here knows there's nothing more transitory than a military secret,' he said. 'In my opinion, any deployment scenario eventually leads to universal proliferation. The only variable is the timetable.'

At the far end of the table, General Moorman was flipping through the pages of the briefing packet. 'Does building a Trigger require any exotic materials or exceptional technology?' he interjected. 'Perhaps we can slow the rate of proliferation by controlling the means of production – as we did with nuclear weapons.'

'I'm afraid not,' said Breland. 'Once they know the fundamentals of the design, any country that can build high-powered microwave transmitters can build Triggers. Which means, essentially, every industrialized nation. And since we're not talking millions of dollars per copy, those who can't build them will likely be able to buy them.'

'Then I'm more mystified than ever,' said Hawley, pushing the packet away from him as though it were something distasteful. 'Mr President, I'm completely at a loss to understand why you're proposing to dismantle the preeminent military force of the twenty-first century.'

'Dismantle?' asked Admiral Jacobs. 'A submarine equipped with this device would be virtually invulnerable.' The appeal of that idea was evident in the voice of the former fast-attack submarine commander.

'And completely useless, Mark. Your *Sawfish* couldn't even carry a deck gun.'

'Wait – but this is a directional effect, yes?'

'No, sir,' said Stepak. 'The Trigger field is omni-directional.'

'Surely there's some way to shield our own magazines –'

'Not that we now know of,' admitted Stepak. 'We have to do more testing, but the available evidence is that the field penetrates all ordinary materials. The primary limitation on the Trigger appears to be range – which is principally a question of available power.'

'You see, Admiral? You see?' Hawley prodded.

'Well, what are we supposed to do, then?' Jacobs exploded, looking to Breland for an answer.

'I'll tell you what you're supposed to do – disarm the entire Fleet, or mothball it,' said Hawley. 'Better yet, mount battering rams. General Moorman, you'll have to rearm all your tanks with bayonets. General Brennan, you'd better call your Warfighting Laboratory and tell them to lay in a supply of crossbows. And I'll be able to send everything but the recon squadrons to the graveyard at Davis-Mothan.'

He turned on Breland with angry eyes. 'Start building these things, Mr President, and you're throwing away everything that makes this country strong and keeps our people safe,' Hawley said. 'We have a technological advantage in every dimension of the combat cube – air, sea, land, undersea, and space. We enjoy an absolute numerical advantage against every possible adversary except China. And even against them, we can establish absolute battlefield dominance – right up to their front door, if need be. Push this technology into the mix, and we lose all of that.'

'The Chinese can raise an army of ten million, a hundred million, and hardly notice if they lose them all,' said Moorman. 'What are we going to do when they cross into South Korea, into Vietnam – when they take Vladivostok, and Taiwan, and start looking across the water at Japan?'

Breland was unfazed. 'Gentlemen, it seems to me that those are exactly the kind of questions *you're* going to need to help answer.'

The Vice Chairman, General Heincer, spoke for the first time since the meeting began. 'There have to be other options. An intermediate strategy – fast development, but no deployment – all-out effort on alternative weapons, but a maximum effort to contain and suppress this discovery –'

Shaking his head, Breland said, 'Unless someone's been keeping secrets from the President again, we don't have enough people in China to prevent them from discovering this on their own – or even to know if they've discovered it already.'

'The President is correct on that point,' said the Chairman. 'We are tracking nearly eight thousand Chinese agents in the US. We have barely two hundred agents in China.'

'Maybe it's time we evened things up,' said Admiral Jacobs. 'March 'em out to the end of Santa Monica Pier, point toward Beijing, and wish 'em a nice swim.'

'And when Beijing responds by expelling every American businessman –'

'That'd be all right by me,' General Moorman grumbled. 'It's gotten so you can hardly buy anything for under a hundred bucks that isn't made in China. They're making our toys, our clothes, our tools – last month, my wife even found an American flag, one of those little desk flags, that was made in China. And that was at the Base Exchange. I couldn't believe it.'

'Believe it. Be glad for it. That's part of the answer to General Hawley's challenge, General,' said Breland. 'We're China's biggest trading partner. And Japan is number two. We're more valuable as customers than as conquests.'

'That won't help Vladivostok much,' said Jacobs. 'Or Taiwan. Hell, they take Taiwan, and we'll just have to buy that much more from them.'

'You're missing the point,' said Breland. 'In the long run, it doesn't matter if the Chinese factories are full of kids being paid slave wages. In the long run, it doesn't matter if the ruling circle is full of rabid expansionists. The real meaning of all of those billions of dollars we're sending to China is that there are now powerful voices inside China with a strong interest in staying on good terms with us.'

Jacobs answered with a derisive snort. 'All we've been doing is paying for their military build-up.'

'Which is about as smart as paying for your wife's divorce lawyer,' said General Brennan. That brought a laugh that took some of the edge off the tension in the room.

While he listened, Breland had reclaimed his chair and settled into a determinedly relaxed posture. 'Gentlemen, I respect the dedication and experience you bring to the great responsibility of ensuring the security of our country,' he said. 'It's your duty to take the darkest possible view of our adversaries, the most cynical interpretation of their acts, the most skeptical view of their words.

'It's my duty, however, to balance the worst possible scenario against the best possible scenario, in search of the most likely. We don't fortify our northern border against the possibility that some Canadian Prime Minister might decide he wants a port on Lake Michigan. We don't search every trunk, cooler, and hat box coming across the Friendship Bridge, looking for Canadian terrorists with suitcase nukes.

'Now, China is no Canada. They keep building Long March ICBMs. They keep cloning Soviet missile cruisers and arming them with Silkworms. They keep upgrading their air force with Su-27 and MIG-31 knockoffs. They keep spying on us and our friends. They keep six million men in uniform. In short, they keep acting like they expect to find themselves in a scrap against someone a lot like us.

'The question is whether they expect to start that scrap.'

'What are you talking about?' asked Moorman.

'Every one of you has a counterpart in China. What do they tell the premier about us?' Breland asked. 'When they look at the United States, with our technological superiority, our absolute battlefield dominance, our allies on their doorstep, our super-silent boomers which we *promise* aren't lurking in the Kuril Trench and the Bering Abyssal, our hypersonic SSTOs which we keep assuring them aren't bombers, maybe they get to feeling just a little bit uncomfortable, a little unsure of *our* intentions. It's just possible they'd welcome a chance to stop spending four hundred billion yuan every year on guns and bombs.'

The Chairman leaned forward and rested his folded hands on the table. 'No offense intended, Mr President, but I hope you're not telling us you belong to that school of woolly-headed internationalists who believe that people everywhere are the same, and every conflict is the result of a misunderstanding.'

'No offense taken, General,' said Breland. 'I hope you're not telling me that you belong to that club of testosterone addicts so in love with big fast toys and noisemakers that they can't imagine giving them up.'

'Now, just a minute –' Jacobs began.

'I'm not finished, Admiral,' Breland said sharply. 'The fact is, we've been extremely successful playing under twentieth-century rules. But if we keep on fighting the last war, we're going to find ourselves wearing red and marching in straight lines across the meadow while our enemy mows us down from behind the trees. Does anyone here want to fight the twenty-first century version of the Battle of New Orleans – as the British?

'Gentlemen, the rules of the game are changing. They've already changed, in fact. You don't have to like it, but we all have to deal with it. I know it's going to be a painful transition – but I have to believe that if we apply all the experience and dedication and talent we can call on, we can be successful under the new rules, too.

'But we have to be smart, and we have to be flexible. We have to be able to break our own tendencies, and we have to be willing to redefine success. It may not mean technological superiority and absolute battlefield dominance. It might mean giving up the capacity to start a war in exchange for the capacity to prevent one. It might mean a hundred little victories no one notices instead of one big one that gets written about for a hundred years. It might mean a new kind of conflict, and a new kind of peace. And if we're *very* smart, and a little lucky, it just might mean a safer, saner planet for all of us.

'That's what I expect from you, gentlemen,' Breland said, meeting the eyes of each chief in turn. 'I expect you to find the path that gets us from here to there. I expect you to figure out how to keep us as safe as possible along the way. I expect you to rise to the challenge of the hardest job any President has ever handed this body – and the most tantalizing opportunity fate has ever handed our country.

'No, we won't forget that we have real enemies, that greed and cruelty and hate keep evil alive in human hearts. But we also won't forget that there never has been a war that left the world a better place – that even the "good" wars exact a terrible price in both blood and treasure, in lost years and squandered lives. If there can be another way, a *better* way, let us be the ones to uncover it. Now, you may call that woolly-headed idealism if you like – but I call it hard-headed human compassion. And if you can't locate a fund of that to draw on, then you've forgotten why we wanted the guns in the first place.

'Now – are there any other questions? General Hawley? General Moorman?' He looked from one face to the next, searching for the men behind the insignia, the humanity behind the duty.

'Not a question, but a comment,' General Brennan said at last. 'Over the years, the Warfighting Laboratory has looked into a lot of alternative weapons for Special Forces – compressed-air guns, hurling sticks, shock prods, various martial arts devices, and so on. Those files, eh, would probably be worth a second look now.'

Nodding, Breland said, 'Consider it on the list of things to do.'

'I have a question,' said General Madison.

Breland swiveled his chair toward the head of the table. 'Go ahead.'

The chairman drummed his fingers on the table for a long moment before responding. 'Those other nine hundred Triggers – what plans do you have for them?'

'Well,' Breland said, 'I confess I find the thought of putting one in every high school in Los Angeles for a month or so very appealing.' Then he shrugged. 'But, actually, those decisions are waiting on input from all of you.'

'Then I have a few thoughts in that area, Mr President,' Madison said. 'Some allocations that I'd like to propose receive priority.'

Sitting back in his chair, Breland caught a sideways glance from Stepak that said *I think the worst is over.* 'Go ahead, General. It's as good a place as any to start.'

12: Apostasy

London, UK – Constable Clarence Whitehead closed out
an era today when he added a leather holster and a black
Webley & Scott pistol to his uniform before setting out
on his daily foot patrol in the Docklands. Though London's
famed bobbies have had the option of carrying firearms on
regular patrols for years, the recent murder of two officers in
Shropshire led Scotland Yard officials to make it mandatory.
'I've got regrets,' said Whitehead, a 25-year veteran, 'but I
don't see as the Inspector had much choice.'
Complete Story   *Walther Revives Webley Name*
Sociologist Says American Cinema Brought 'Gun Cult' to UK

The day for good-byes had finally come, and Donovan King had
chosen it well.

The day was a cloudy autumn Saturday, and the stiff breeze
had a winter's bite. With the top-ranked Penn State Nittany Lions
in town for a showdown with the Buckeyes, the entire city of
Columbus awakened to thoughts of football. All across the region,
Ohio State fans began the rituals and ablutions which would lead
them to their seats in the stadium and in front of television screens.
The patterns were as predictable as a sunrise: as the sports bars
filled, the roads emptied. As kickoff neared, the stores became
deserted, the beer flowed and the heady energy of anticipation
grew. The police were occupied, the populace distracted.

At Terabyte, Saturday began with the arrival of a yellow Ryder
tractor and semi-trailer at the gates. The truck was driven by
a two-man team from Terabyte's expanded security force, and
accompanied by a forest green Chevy Tahoe sport-utility and a
silver Honda sedan. All three vehicles bore plates from different

163

states, and all three drivers wore casual clothes – both signs of Donovan King's attention to the smallest details in planning a safe but unobtrusive move from Columbus to the West Annex.

Even on a lightly traveled highway, it would take more than a casual observation to realize that the three unremarkable vehicles made up a caravan, or to guess that anything more valuable than household furniture was being transported. To complete the illusion, the last three meters of the trailer would be packed high with ordinary moving boxes filled with what had been the contents of Leigh Thayer's apartment.

While the crates containing the prototype and its instrumentation were loaded into the trailer, three teams from the lab's engineering staff went to work on the vehicles. Working quickly enough to beat the twenty-minute update cycle, they removed the unsophisticated Ryder and Hertz global positioning system trackers, transplanting them into Terabyte vehicles. Those vehicles, with their identification numbers spoofed to match those of the caravan, would never leave greater Columbus.

In place of the trackers they removed, the engineering teams installed Terabyte's own military-grade GPS-III secure-duplex trackers. Identical systems had been installed overnight in the two largest crates, against the possibility that they might become separated from the truck or each other en route. It was all part of King's promise to Brohier:

'I'm going to make sure it's easy for you to monitor the entire move, and damned hard for anyone else to.'

The caravan rolled out the gates again a few minutes before kickoff, with King himself at the wheel of the lead vehicle. Brohier saw them off, then crossed to where Lee and Gordon were waiting and watching, near the main entrance to Planck Center. As he approached them, he noted their starkly contrasting body language – Gordon perched casually on a low wall, bare-headed, coat wide open, while Lee stood stiffly half a dozen paces away, hands buried in her ski jacket's square pockets, collar rolled up and a crocheted hat on her head.

'That's one, Doctor,' Gordon said.

'That's one,' he agreed.

'I was kind of surprised to see King leave now,' said Gordon, hopping off the wall. 'I would have thought he'd stay around until the second caravan was away.'

'No, this was always what he planned,' Brohier said. 'Listen, you two – we're looking at a lull of an hour or so now, and I spoiled the chief cook's day by making her come in. How about one last lunch in the grille, for old time's sake?'

'Sure,' said Greene. 'But I'll eat Lee's hat if you can name three of Josie's specials – when did *you* ever patronize the campus cafeteria?'

'Whenever there was six or more inches of snow between me and something better,' Brohier said cheerfully. 'Lee?'

'I could use something hot,' said Lee, and shivered. 'Even something from the Terror-Bite Girl.'

The deserted cafeteria seemed cavernous, tomblike – every clink of glass and flatware, every word above a whisper carrying to the four corners. Conditions were perfect for eavesdropping, except that the only conversation underway was the one at the table where Lee was seated.

Mercifully, even that conversation was largely Karl Brohier's monologue. The director seemed to be aware of how uncomfortable she and Gordon were with each other, of the way their easy banter had given way to a chilly, awkward silence, and smoothly took over the burden of filling the silence. Lee had never seen him quite so garrulous.

Brohier told them a series of physicist jokes so groaningly bad that the cumulative effect had them both laughing out loud. He reminisced about his one chance meeting with Stephen Hawking, about embarrassing himself in front of John Wheeler, about his tumultuous internship under John Bardeen at Bell Laboratories.

'I took that internship hoping it would lead to a job at the lab, and once I was there I wasn't shy about telling them so.' He laughed and shrugged. '– My father used to tell me, "Always ask for what you really want – you might get it." I had to discover on my own that the style points counted.

'Dr Bardeen was brilliant, one of the few legitimate geniuses I've known – and he had just accepted his *second* Nobel Prize in Physics. And here I was, younger than either of you, the ink barely dry on

165

my doctorate, totally clueless about the etiquette and politics at that level, and totally in love with my own ideas, in love with *new* ideas.

'I wanted to impress Dr Bardeen. And I tried to do it the same way I'd done it all through school – by showing my teachers I was just as smart as they were. Or smarter. I kept treating the internship like it was Wilkenson's graduate seminar – with a paycheck. Well, surely you can see this coming – Dr Bardeen and I could never seem to agree on anything, including how smart I was. We had at least one full-blown, high-theater argument a week, and I never won a single one. I got used to going home feeling like I'd been exposed as an idiot.

'But I was a stubborn idiot. And the less success I had, the more frantic I was to find some way to correct Dr Bardeen's mistaken opinion of me. By the end, I must have been completely obnoxious.

'I came to Dr Bardeen's office that last day, itching to reopen an argument we'd had a few weeks earlier – as I recall, something about Fahy's approach to modeling the properties of complex materials from first principles. Old news, now.

'In any event, I never even got started. He told me that the lab wouldn't be offering me a position. Then he told me he'd enjoyed our arguments, that he thought I'd helped make it a "lively" year – which I could only hear as his way of saying I'd provided valuable comic relief. Finally, he handed me his letter of recommendation.

'I was afraid to open the letter in front of him. I didn't even want to open it when I was alone. I sat there in my kitchen, staring at the envelope, realizing all my mistakes. I did a year's growing up in the hour or so it took for me to reach a point where I thought I could read the letter without crumbling.'

He took a sip of his ice water before continuing. 'Dr Bardeen's letter was two sentences long. It said, "Karl Brohier will do important work someday. I recommend his employment without reservation."'

A startled laugh escaped Lee's lips. 'No!'

'Oh, yes. But there's more – he'd written me a note, and stuck it to the bottom of the letter. "An old bull and a young bull don't belong in the same pasture. Don't take it personally – and don't

166

stop pushing. Good luck – J.B."' He smiled a quiet smile. 'I still have that little yellow square of paper.'

'I guess he knew talent,' said Gordon.

'Or perhaps it was just a self-fulfilling prophecy,' said Brohier. 'No one was more surprised than I when Dr Bardeen's prediction came true – well, perhaps my parents. My parents must have been astonished to learn that I ended up doing anything of consequence. But that's another story.

'I lived under the weight of those expectations for fifteen years before I managed to turn one of those wild notions Dr Bardeen had dismissed into the first working example of solid-state memory,' Brohier said, and smiled ironically. 'It took me that long to finally win an argument with him.'

'Did you call him up and say, "I told you so"?' asked Gordon.

'Unfortunately, there was no opportunity to. He had died a few months earlier. Of course, honor would have compelled me to admit that he'd been right about all the other wild ideas – so perhaps it's just as well.'

Brohier picked up a napkin and began wiping his fingers, even though he had hardly touched the food in front of him. 'It seems to me that you two are living my life backwards. You have already done your most important work, at a very young age. The weight of its consequences is just now settling on you, and it isn't easy to see what can ever lift that weight.'

He knows, Lee suddenly realized. The thought tightened the muscles of her ribcage, squeezing out the air, and paralyzed her face in a rictus of apprehension.

Brohier went on, 'I made my biggest mistakes – the ones that proceed from naïvete, and ignorant idealism, and egocentrism, the ones of which we can say, "I was young – I didn't know any better" – I made them when the only person affected by them was me. You no longer have that luxury.

'I want you both to know that I feel great sympathy for you – sympathy limited only by the extent that your mistakes cross over the boundaries of my responsibilities. I warned you once before that what lay ahead of us was harder than the part that lay behind us. Well, what's the saying? Today is the tomorrow you worried about yesterday.'

Brohier glanced at his message watch, though whether to check the time or the display Lee could not say. 'The second caravan should be here now,' he said, standing. 'Time to wrap this up.'

The relocation plan had seemed innocent enough when Donovan King had presented it to Gordon and Lee in the director's office. The prototypes would travel separately and under escort, with the original Davisson Lab unit masquerading as household furniture, and the portable unit's truck-and-trailer repainted as an electrician's van. The details of their routing King chose to keep to himself, but Gordon guessed that neither would follow a direct route, or complete the journey in the same vehicle in which it started out.

Lee and Gordon would likewise travel separately, each in the company of a bodyguard. Gordon's first stop was Atlanta, Lee's Minneapolis, but the full itinerary and ultimate destination were still unknown to them – their tickets were in the custody of their traveling companions until boarding time. Gordon imagined that King had some scheme worked out to cover their tracks – a ticket swap at a plane change, perhaps – that would make it seem as though they had gone somewhere else.

'By Monday afternoon, you'll all be reunited at the Annex,' King had promised.

But then King drove off with the first caravan, which started Gordon wondering. And then Brohier started talking as though he were saying good-bye to more than Columbus, which turned Gordon's wonder into worry. Edging past Brohier in the hallway, Gordon ran ahead to the entrance and out into the courtyard. A single glimpse was enough to tell him how wrong everything had gone.

Baby Two's truck and trailer had, indeed, been repainted. It now blended in perfectly with the other olive drab vehicles flanking it, and the green-uniformed soldiers standing guard with M-16s at all four corners. The vehicles carried the markings of the 612th Engineer Battalion of the Army National Guard. Gordon's tools, which were supposed to have been loaded aboard the truck, were still sitting on the sidewalk fifty meters away.

His face suddenly flushed with anger, Gordon spun on his heels to confront the director. 'You son of a bitch – you lied to me –' he growled.

'Yes,' Brohier said. 'As you did to me. And we'll talk about it in my office, in just a few minutes.' He brushed past Gordon and raised a hand, calling out, 'Captain Brandt!'

'Damn it, come back here!' Gordon took a step toward the older man, but then Lee caught up to him and grabbed his arm.

'Don't,' she said, tight-voiced.

He shook off her touch and retreated a step. 'Don't you understand what this means?' he demanded, sweeping an arm in the direction of the convoy. 'He's turning our work over to the goddamn Pentagon.'

'I understand what it means,' she said harshly. 'It means we screwed up, and he knows it. It means he trusts them more than he trusts us now. *We* are on the way out, and I can't say we don't deserve it. Go on, keep after him, maybe you can get him to turn us over to them, too. What would it be, Gordie, espionage or treason? Or maybe just three counts of first-degree murder.'

Taken momentarily aback by the intensity of her assault, Gordon could not find a comeback worth voicing. Chafing at his impotence, he watched in silence as Brohier stood talking with what was obviously the officer in charge of the convoy. As the two shook hands, Gordon belatedly realized that the captain's camouflage uniform bore no unit insignia.

'Why would they have the National Guard make this pickup?' he said under his breath. 'Answer – they wouldn't, so they're not. Probably Army Intelligence. But no one'll wonder at seeing a few weekend warriors out on the highway – and they can go right to Camp Perry, or Camp Grayling, offload Baby Two onto a V-22 tilt-rotor, and take it anywhere.'

'It doesn't matter,' said Lee. 'It's out of our hands.'

Gordon slowly shook his head. 'I don't accept that.'

While they were talking, the captain had climbed into one of the three waiting HMMVs. There were no orders shouted, but engines began roaring to life, and the four sentries left their posts, scattering one to each vehicle.

'Accept it,' Lee said curtly as Karl Brohier backed out of the driveway and rejoined them. The lead HMMV lurched forward, and the other vehicles followed with crisp precision. Gordon felt the anger returning as Baby Two's truck passed in front of where the trio was standing. But neither he nor anyone else said anything until the convoy had passed through the inner gate and disappeared down the drive.

'Let's go talk about you,' said Brohier, and turned away toward his office without waiting for their reply.

Brohier was waiting for them behind his desk. 'Sit,' he said, gesturing. 'I have one more story to tell.'

Gordon and Lee exchanged glances, then sorted themselves into the two closest chairs.

'Last night, I had a call from a member of the Joint Chiefs,' said Brohier. 'He was trying to evaluate a report he received from the NSA, which now has its ears up for any hint of anything that might be related to your discovery. Of course, they weren't expecting to find it in the *Cleveland Plain Dealer*.' He turned his desk display toward them. 'The security logs show that you and the truck were off campus when this happened, Dr Greene. The truck's mileage – well, this is not a court. You and I both know that this was your doing.'

Greene glanced briefly at the news item displayed on the screen. 'Yes,' he acknowledged. 'I *am* sorry about the fires. The collimator didn't work as I thought it would.' He shrugged. 'Truth is, I don't really understand this Trigger field very well yet – not once it leaves the emitter, anyway.'

'You understood the effect it would have on that car full of kids.'

'That car full of kids with guns,' Greene corrected. 'Yes, I did. But don't fool yourself – those "kids" didn't deserve to be labeled with a word that evokes five-year-olds saying "Mommy, I want a hug".'

'So you say,' said Brohier. 'But as I said, this is not a court, and I am not interested in your justifications.'

'Why are you only talking to Gordie?' Lee said. 'I was there, too.'

Brohier raised an eyebrow in her direction. 'I have no information about that.'

170

'What are you talking about?' she demanded, sitting forward on her chair. 'The guard must have logged us both out. It's my sister we went up there to help. It's more my responsibility than Gordie's. He did it for me.'

'You don't need to do this, Lee,' Gordie said quietly. 'Dr Brohier, I drove the truck. I pushed the button. I did it on my own initiative, and for my own reasons. Nothing else matters. The weight falls on me.'

'Gordie –'

But Lee was ignored by both men.

'Do you think you know how much weight that is?' Brohier asked. 'We have a one-time opportunity to make certain uses of the Trigger, preemptive strikes if you will – an opportunity that will vanish as soon as knowledge of its existence becomes commonplace. I choose not to offer specific examples, but suffice it to say that there are some actors on the stage who can't be given a chance to rearm. And there's one obvious countermeasure against the Trigger that some governments are not above using – placing prisoners, hostages, in their armories as human shields. The lives of *good* people are at risk, Dr Greene – good soldiers, and innocent civilians. The kind of people we want the Trigger to help, not harm.

'Now, you may be thinking that what you did in Cleveland Heights was done in exactly that spirit – a preemptive attack in the defense of good people. But by acting unilaterally, by taking untested equipment into the field, by putting the second prototype on the road, unprotected, by attracting public attention and handing the police a curious puzzle, you may have done incalculable damage.' Brohier tapped the top of the display with his forefinger. 'There's no telling how many people are out there tonight thinking, "Hmm, I wonder what happened here". And the moment the first one figures it out, our window of opportunity starts to close.'

'I think you give people too much credit,' said Greene. 'No one cares. It's already old news.'

'I'm sure the Cleveland Heights police department cares,' said Brohier. 'And we can't afford to have their investigation reach Terabyte's front door.'

'It won't,' said Greene. 'No one saw me. Not even the targets. Everyone thinks it was an accident – a car wreck.'

'You can't promise me that. You don't know if there was a video camera in an upstairs window, a man out walking his dog.'

'It was clean, I tell you,' Greene insisted. 'There's no way this comes home to you.'

'No? Then explain why the NSA called me,' said Brohier. 'You put us on record. All the essential elements are there. And just knowing something is possible is motivation enough sometimes.'

'That's why I decided to turn the portable system over to the Defense Department now. It was always going to go to them for testing, but I thought it best that it disappear now – and do so in the hands of people who can slam the door on a mere city detective's curiosity.'

'I suppose you expect us to disappear now, too,' said Lee.

'If that's all I needed of you, I'm sure one call would be enough to make it happen,' Brohier said. 'No, I have something harder to ask of each of you, now that you've had your moment of selfishness – I need you both to set aside your personal baggage and do the right and necessary thing.'

'As you define it?' Greene said challengingly.

'As I define it,' said Brohier. 'Dr Thayer, would you mind stepping out into the anteroom for a minute or two?'

'She can stay,' said Greene. 'I don't mind.'

'I do,' said Brohier. 'Please, Dr Thayer.'

'You don't have to let him push you around, Lee,' said Greene, coming to his feet as Lee did.

'It's all right, Gordie.' Her fingertips lightly grazed the back of his hand as she passed him.

When the door closed and the two men were alone, Greene turned back to the director. 'Well?'

'You are an excellent engineer, Dr Greene,' said Brohier. 'But you're only an average hacker, and the NSA has whole buildings full of people who are better at it than you are – better at it than almost any freelancer. It's a point of pride with them that when they sift cyberspace, they don't miss very much. In addition to this news clip, they also found the extra copy of the research database you banked in pieces all over the net. And one of our people found the Trojan horse you tried to attach to Terabyte's employment records – the one that would have published the database to half a dozen servers when your termination was posted.'

'I had to try,' said Greene.

'No, you didn't. You had to trust – and you weren't up to it.'

'Are you going to turn me in? Or do you expect me to turn myself in?'

'Neither. I'm going to give you another chance,' he said. 'Another chance to rise above your cozy cynicism, and to show that you're worth trusting. Does it still matter to you to protect Dr Thayer?'

He thought hard before answering. 'Yes.'

'Even if she doesn't know that you're doing it?'

'Even if.'

'Then what I need you to do is resign, today –'

'What does that accomplish?'

'To begin with, it means I won't have to put your name on the list for FBI background checks, because you'll never officially be part of what the Trigger project has become,' said Brohier. 'I don't have to explain why I fired you – you simply decided you weren't interested in relocating with the project.'

'Is that all you want? To avoid embarrassment?'

'No.' Brohier slid the right drawer of his desk open a few inches and plucked something from it. When he slid it across his desk toward Greene, the engineer saw what it was: a ten-gigabyte solid-state data block. 'I want you to hold onto that.'

'What is it?'

'It's a copy of the Trigger research archive, identical to the one you tried to hide – same encryption scheme, same password lock,' said Brohier, leaving Greene blinking in surprise. 'If you leave us the way I'm asking, voluntarily, without a cloud hanging over you, I believe I can ensure that no one we work with will wonder if you might be hiding something – or from something.'

'I don't understand. What do you expect me to do with this?'

'Hold on to it. Hide it. Wait a year. If, after a year, nothing has happened, or the wrong things are happening, take that to Senator Grover Wilman and his group, and help them put it to good use. But give us that year to start things moving. Give us that year of opportunity.'

Greene leaned forward in his chair and picked up the memory block, holding it gingerly between thumb and forefinger. 'How do you know I won't publish this tomorrow, and then just disappear?'

'I'd like to be able to say that I simply choose to trust you,' said Brohier, closing the drawer. 'But I also know that you must realize if you do, it'll all come out – and Lee will be the one hurt, because they'll be able to reach her. She'll pay the price for your egotism.'

'So Lee's the hostage in *your* armory, eh?'

'I'm giving you a chance to choose, Dr Greene – which is frankly more consideration than you've earned.'

Frowning, Greene let the memory block drop into the palm of his hand. 'What are you going to tell the NSA?'

'As little as necessary. That you were asked to archive the research offsite. We can let the fact that you tried to add another copy for yourself pass without comment.'

'And the Cleveland Heights police?'

'Didn't you assure me no one saw you?'

'I did,' Greene said. He stared for a moment at the memory block, then slipped it into a pocket. 'Where are you sending Lee? Is she still going to the Annex?' When Brohier hesitated, Greene patted the bulge in his pocket. 'If you're going to trust me with this –'

Brohier acquiesced. 'If she agrees, she's going to follow Baby Two to the DARPA test site, and spend a few weeks training some people to operate and maintain the system. Then she'll join us at the Annex.'

Nodding, Greene stood. 'That will be hard for her,' he said. 'An out-of-cocoon experience.'

'I know,' said Brohier, following suit. 'But if you can carry your weight, I'm sure she can carry hers.'

'I have the feeling you'll make her believe she ought to try.' Greene released a sigh that dropped his shoulders and carried away his coiled defensiveness. 'Dr Brohier – if this year goes the way you hope it will –'

'Then you'll be able to color me amazed,' Brohier said with a half-grin.

'I was just wondering –'

'I know,' said Brohier. 'The answer is yes. If we don't need you for something more important a year from now, you can come back in.' He offered his hand.

A year's probation. A year's penance. Little enough for what I did – what I was ready to do. Greene took the director's hand.

'Good luck,' he said, with unexpected feeling. 'I'll see you next October.'

13: Enginery

Paris, France – Hunting for a special gift for the folks at home? At the biennial European Defense Exposition, which opened its doors to invitation-only customers on Monday, you can try out and buy Iranian tanks, French armor-piercing rockets, and Chilean antitank mines. 'It's just like any other trade show,' said Henri Dessault, organizer of the week-long event. 'Glitzy booths, salesmen in suits, beautiful models, and silly giveaways. Except for the product demonstrations, it's actually rather boring.'

Complete Story   *Top 10 Arms Exporters*
Secretive EDEX Attendees Speak Softly, Carry Big Checkbooks

The first of the Mark I systems rolled out of the Brass Hat plant in North Sioux City five days before Christmas. It had a formal and unpronounceable Pentagon designation (XM9M1, for Experimental Munition 9, Mark I) and a serial number (0001-1), but was otherwise a close twin of the hand-built prototype portable. The only changes of note were the replacement of the three-kilowatt Caterpillar DuoCat with the US Army's battlefield-tested Advanced Tactical Quiet Generator with the Toyota cold decoupling fuel cell, and the addition of military-standard safing mechanisms to what was now being called the firing controller.

Numbers 1 through 10 were delivered without ceremony into the custody of the 41st Tactical Battalion, 3rd Combat Engineering Division. The 41st had been newly reorganized for the job of transporting and deploying the Mark I Triggers; the job of protecting them would go to a new cross-service security division still being assembled. The first stop for all ten units was a reopened Cold War era airfield in North Dakota, where they underwent a live systems checkout and two days of hot testing.

By New Year's Day, Number 1 was installed in the basement of the White House. Several times in the following week, it was quietly activated for a few seconds at a time, so its output could be carefully calibrated. When that process was complete, its protective halo enclosed the entire White House, the east face of the Executive Office Building, the west face of the Treasury Building, the Pennsylvania Avenue pedestrian mall, East Executive Drive and the tourist entrance, and half of the South Lawn.

The hard decision was how to use it – as a primary defense, or a backup to the existing security systems and procedures. After long discussions with the Secretary of Treasury and the head of the Secret Service, Breland overruled both of them and approved a plan for round-the-clock operation.

'I've always thought Americans should be able to look at these grounds and see a house, not a fortress,' he said. 'What kind of example does it set if I ask others to put down their guns, ask them to trust this technology, but refuse to trust it myself?'

That meant Breland was now to be guarded 'in the bubble' by a special unit of Secret Service agents who'd been thrown into intense training with shock wands and compressed-air guns. At the same time, the sharpshooters yielded their snipers' nests to agents armed with 500-pound pull crossbows – an elite group that soon would take to unofficially calling itself the Company of St George, after the medieval crossbow society that once protected the English sovereign.

Conventional weapons were not completely abandoned in the new security scheme, but they were pushed outside the Trigger's threshold perimeter. The White House air defense unit, armed with the new Raven shoulder-launched antiaircraft missile, was moved to the rooftops of the Department of Commerce and the General Services Administration. And to back up the 'Secret Service Elite', fast-response teams with traditional firearms were posted in the Executive Office Building and just inside the South Lawn fence.

After weeks of drill and rehearsal, the new security system quietly supplanted the old during Breland's State of the Union address.

Trigger Number 2's destiny was to occupy the back of a sleek black van with tinted windows, government plates, and its own built-in CDFC generator. Nicknamed 'The Caboose', the van was slated to follow close behind the presidential limousine in every motorcade, effectively becoming part of the limousine's armor.

Even though there had been no aerial intercept tests yet, Numbers 3 and 4 were placed in the cargo holds of Air Force One and Air Force Two – President Breland's aerial yachts, and, in the event of war, his flying command posts. Since the twin 747-200s were unarmed aircraft, only modest changes in operating procedures were required – affecting only the Secret Service contingent and the selection of survival equipment normally stowed aboard.

Number 5 was delivered to Camp David, Maryland, and installed beside the communications trailer adjacent to the main house. The boundary of the gun-free zone was marked by a ring of small blue pennants. The retreat's security forces retained their weapons, maintained their fences, and respected the Trigger boundary – one demonstration, with six 9mm rounds pressed into a grapefruit that was then rolled across the boundary, was enough to enforce the warnings.

Number 6 went into the bowels of the US Capitol, though not without some joking about whether or not Congress actually represented a valuable national asset.

Number 7 was installed inside the Supreme Court building, and heartily welcomed by the head of security there. The fight over the National Firearms Registration and Responsibility Act – known to supporters as 'little Brenda's law' and to opponents as the 'gun-grabbers' license' – was not over. It equaled or surpassed the fight over abortion in ferocity, and gave every sign of persisting as long. Eight years had passed since the Souter-led Court had ruled the NFRRA constitutional in *Jefferson vs. United States of America*, and the death threats and demonstrations had hardly abated. In fact, the annual 'Show Your Gun' march and rally on the anniversary of the decision had grown larger and more alarmingly boisterous every year.

Trigger Number 8 had been allocated for the Pentagon, and the Joint Chiefs had developed four different plans for using the system at the famous structure. Ultimately, however, they decided not to implement any of them. The official reason was that it could not be done without destroying so many traditions and stepping on so many toes that the Trigger would quickly become the worst-kept secret in military history.

But Breland suspected that, behind that undeniable truth, the chiefs were expressing a deep-seated fondness for the familiar. Though there were actually far fewer firearms inside the Pentagon's walls than most people would have expected, the chiefs and generals simply weren't ready, Breland thought, to see their subordinates standing guard with broomsticks – much less to surrender their own service sidearms.

Given that precedent, there was less surprise when the FBI Director declined the offer of a Mark I to protect the Bureau's headquarters at 10th and Pennsylvania. But she requested four units for tactical evaluation, a request which was placed near the top of the Brass Hat committee's lengthy Candidate Allocations list.

It was no surprise at all when the CIA Director also declined the offer of a Trigger for the Company's well-protected headquarters complex upriver in Langley, Maryland. But he, too, apparently saw the potential of the system, and requested ten units for the Directorate of Science and Technology. That request Breland viewed with a somewhat jaundiced eye, wondering what assurances he could secure that those units could be kept out of the hands of the Operations Directorate.

The principal weapons of the National Security Agency were technology and cryptology, which the Trigger did not threaten. Nevertheless, with most NSA facilities – including the headquarters – located securely within the perimeter of the Army's Fort Meade, the director's answer was 'Thanks, but no thanks.'

So Numbers 8, 9, and 10 were reassigned to the next three highest priorities drawn from the FBI's official Domestic Terrorism Threat Assessment and the Cold-War era National Disaster Recovery Plan – the Federal Reserve Board, the Social Security Administration, and the Internal Revenue Service's central records center.

'Making the world safe for tax collectors was not exactly what I had in mind when we started this,' Breland said dryly as he signed the transfer authorizations. 'I got the latest numbers from FedStat this morning – thirty-five thousand deaths by gun last year – a hundred thousand more gunshot injuries. I want to do something to protect *those* people, not the Beltway elite – we were already safer than they are. Someone reassure me that we haven't lost our way so soon.'

'The next fifty Mark Is – a month's production – are going directly to Utah to expand the test program,' said Richard Nolby. 'We won't have a chance to really address the civil sector until March.'

Breland sighed. 'I know I was there when it was decided, but do they really need so many at once?'

'Yes, Mr President,' said General Stepak. 'Truth is, they could use a hundred or more – up until now, they haven't been able to do any tests which might damage the only working example they have, tests that actually simulate combat conditions. And, in any case, the special security units are a few weeks from being ready. We're going to need them when we start going outside the kind of tightly controlled environments these first ten Triggers went into.'

Propping his chin on his hand, Breland spun his chair a half-turn and stared out the window at the snow flurries dancing above the South Portico. 'I guess I'm just impatient, General,' he said. 'I can hardly stand to look at the news now – every shooting, every terrorist bombing, seems that much more sense-less and tragic, knowing that there *is* something that could be done.'

A hundred miles west of Provo, Utah, the vast expanses of the Great Salt Lake Desert belonged to the engines of war. Over the decades, hundreds of new and exotic weapons had come to the Utah Test and Training Range to prove themselves. Hidden by sheer isolation from curious eyes, the white salt flats had been bombed, burned, strafed, shelled, gassed, sprayed with noxious chemicals, and littered with the debris from shattered drones, smashed tanks, and doomed aircraft.

In the remote southwest corner of the UTTR was a cluster of hangars, shops, garages, and barracks which those who lived and worked there called the Fortress of Solitude, and the Pentagon called the Desert Test Center. Here the newest and most secret weapons underwent their auditions. Weapons which passed muster typically became part of the inventory. Those which did not typically vanished back into the anonymity of 'file and forget' – the fate of classified projects that not even the enemy was interested in.

Lieutenant Colonel Roger Adams, commander of the DTC, was hoping that the XM9M1 Trigger would be one of the latter. And if it could be done without violating the test protocols, he was determined to see the system fail – because its success would be a nightmare for every battlefield commander.

Far better for everyone if his report could be summarized in four words: *Not reliable. Not effective.*

So far, the clocks for the Continuous Operation Duration Test had reached the 200-hour threshold with all eight systems still up and running. But even that test was being made as challenging as possible, with two units mounted on shakers, two being fed dirty power, and two being dialed between 1% and 100% every thirty seconds. With luck, they'd all expire well before reaching their initial design target of a thousand hours.

The most crucial test, though, was to begin that morning. At 07.00, three tracked vehicles had trundled out of Building 9 and headed north to the test area. The first was an HMMWV equipped as a camera platform. The last was a Bradley Fighting Vehicle which mounted a small forest of antennas instead of the standard 25mm cannon.

Sandwiched between the Hummer and the Bradley was Ground Test Article 1 – a boxy sloped-fronted M113 armored personnel carrier, remotely controlled by an operator in the Bradley. And inside GTA-1 was Trigger 00013. (Adams was not above enlisting the power of superstition in his cause.)

The test area was sixty kilometers from the Fortress of Solitude, but the jolting cross-country run was actually the first hurdle. Waiting for GTA-1 on the other side was a murderous gauntlet it was not expected to survive – first a high-density minefield, then a series of five fire zones, each boasting higher-powered weaponry than the last.

At 08.30, Lieutenant Colonel Adams and test coordinator Captain Dionne Weeks boarded a UH-60M Black Hawk helicopter, from which they would observe the test. Before long they caught up with the test caravan, now waiting motionless on the desert outside a flag-marked boundary. Both officers donned headsets monitoring the command frequency, and moved to the Black Hawk's large side windows with binoculars in hand.

'Test Control, this is Test Command,' said Weeks. 'You may proceed. Over.'

'Roger, Test Command. All stations, prepare to activate GTA-1, on my mark.'

From their hovering helicopter, Adams and Weeks watched as the Hummer and the Bradley retreated a few hundred yards from the M113. When the activation order came, they had an unmatched view as a great semi-circle of the minefield ahead of the M113 suddenly erupted, with at least fifty plumes of white crystals and dust thrown up from the former lake bed. The cleared area was easily three hundred meters from one side to the other. When the M113 started forward, the circle became a great arc moving ahead of the vehicle like a bow wave.

'That's incredible,' Weeks shouted to Adams, shaking her head. 'It looks to me as though the only way a mine could touch that APC is if the driver took it into the minefield before he turned on the Trigger. An armor column with one of these at the point wouldn't even have to slow down. I'd say the M58 is now obsolete,' she added, referring to the combat engineers' current mine-clearing system.

'No surprises,' Adams shouted back crossly. 'This is just what we would have expected from the static tests.'

'Yes, sir – but it's still something to see.'

There was a brief pause when the M113 cleared the minefield, allowing camera and other recorders to be reset and the Black Hawk to crab closer to the first fire zone. Then the order to proceed crackled over the headsets, and the elderly APC rumbled forward. As soon as it passed the first marker flag, a gunner 500 meters away opened up with a 40mm automatic grenade launcher – single shots at first, then short bursts, then a sustained ten-second fusillade of more than a hundred rounds.

To the Army sergeant whose finger was on the trigger, it seemed as though every round was on target – except that after the flash faded and the breeze blew away the smoke, the APC was still rolling. But the camera crew following in the Hummer and the observers aloft saw something quite different. From their perspective, the grenades exploded more than two hundred meters away from the vehicle, as though they were striking an invisible wall. GTA-1 suffered no greater punishment than a light hail of shrapnel.

'Well, *I'm* impressed,' Weeks shouted. 'A Mark 19's supposed to be able to take out an armored personnel carrier.'

Frowning darkly, Adams made no reply.

In the next fire zone were more infantrymen, armed with two Silver Dragon wire-guided antitank missiles. Their marksmanship was impeccable, the explosions louder and more spectacular, but the net effect was the same. Secure inside its mysterious shield, GTA-1 ambled on.

Waiting in the third fire zone was a Bradley Fighting Vehicle mounting the most powerful antitank weapon available to the infantry, the TOW 2 wire-guided missile. Its warhead was powerful enough to penetrate the frontal armor of a main battle tank, and should have gutted a lightly-armed vehicle like the M113. But it, too, expended itself uselessly against the Trigger field, the force of the blast so muted by distance that all it did was momentarily rock the APC sideways.

'If I wasn't seeing this for myself –' Adams muttered under his breath. 'Test Control, this is Test Command – what frequency is the Abrams using?'

'Combat 1 for C&C, Combat 2 for monitor, sir.'

As the APC moved into the fourth fire zone, Adams leaned forward and changed the frequency of the radio to Combat 2. New voices crackled in his ears as the M1A2 Abrams tank prepared to fire its deadly-accurate 120mm cannon from a point-blank 800 meters away.

'Gunner, APC, HEAT,' ordered the tank commander.

'APC, HEAT, aye.'

'Target is green,' said Test Control.

'Gunner, fire!'

'Fire, aye.'

A billowing gray-white cloud pierced by a gout of crimson

fire erupted from the barrel of the tank as the enormous shell sped toward its target. The detonation of the high-explosive shell was wild and terrifying, the shock wave making the Black Hawk shudder. But although the blast bent an antenna and shoved the APC half a meter sideways on the crumbly salt pan, it did not cause any critical wounds.

'Gunner, APC, sabot.'

On hearing that, Weeks jerked her head around to stare at Adams. 'Who added that to the test routine?' she demanded.

'I did,' said Adams.

'APC, sabot, aye.'

'But there's no explosive charge in a sabot round. It's strictly a KE weapon – you *know* what's going to happen.'

'Gunner, fire!'

'Yes, Captain,' Adams said.

'Fire, aye!'

Moments later, all that was left of the test article was an oily scorch mark a dozen meters across, a tall plume of black smoke and a quiet rain of metal fragments onto the desert.

Against a background of cheering from the tank crew came the message, 'Test Command to all units, looks like we're done for the day. Secure all weapons, lock all data recorders, and return to base.'

'Colonel Adams, I don't understand,' Weeks shouted, tearing off her headset. 'We had an Apache loaded with Hellfire missiles waiting in zone five.'

'Let's not do this here, Captain,' Adams said, his eyes steely. Removing his own headset, Adams leaned forward, tapped the pilot on the shoulder, and signaled to him to head back.

'Where, then?'

'Wait for the operations debriefing.'

When the helicopter landed, Adams silently bade her to follow him with a jerk of his head in the general direction of his office. Behind closed doors, he turned to her with arms folded over his chest. 'First, let's make sure we both understand that I'm not under any obligation to explain myself to you.'

'Understood, sir.'

'Fine. Then this is the operations debriefing. What's your gripe?'

'Since I'm the one who signs the first line on the test report that goes back to HQ, I was hoping that maybe you could give me the benefit of your reasoning.'

Adams looked out the window. 'What do you think the result would have been with the Hellfires?'

'Well –' She pursed her lips. 'If the 120mm HEAT didn't do the job, chances are that the Hellfires wouldn't, either.'

'In which case right now there'd be a hundred and twenty-some soldiers who'd witnessed a miracle, a tin can transformed into an indestructible tank with an invisible shield – a hundred and twenty minds starting to chew on the idea that there's something out there that can take their best shot and keep coming. I'm not accusing anyone of disloyalty, Captain Weeks, but I don't think they'd all be able to keep from talking about it. And I don't want that idea getting out there in the ranks. I can't imagine anything more destructive to morale.'

'So you gave them the big finish, to reassure them.'

'I did,' said Adams. 'Captain, maybe I can't make them forget about everything they saw back there – but half a miracle doesn't make half as good a story, and the difference might just be enough to help them keep their mouths shut. As for your report, tell it straight, but keep it simple – I overruled you on the test protocol, because I wanted the entire munitions inventory included.'

Weeks took a moment to digest that. 'You know, sir,' she said slowly, 'if the Trigger had more range, it's the Abrams that would have been burning.'

'Make sure that makes it into your report, too, Captain,' the colonel said with a nod. 'But you'd better not repeat it anywhere else.'

On a clear, cold January morning, two aircraft roared down a runway at Nellis Air Force Base and climbed into a velvet Nevada sky. Test 11 was made up of a mismatched pair – an elderly Navy F-14 and a sleek Air Force F-22 – but they formed up together and turned to the southeast with the easy grace of the well-trained performing a familiar task.

The test sortie was carefully scripted, the aircrews well briefed.

Still, not every question had been answered, and some could not be asked.

One was about the target aircraft itself. While most target drones were retired fighters, Test 11's sortie was against a QT-1 Jayhawk, a one-off based on a common twin-engine jet used to train transport and tanker pilots. Even the test director had acknowledged that oddity with a little joke.

'Yes, it's going to seem like going after a Southwest Airlines commuter out of Salt Lake City,' the general had said. 'So be sure we don't.'

The mystery was heightened by the weapons loadouts, which were unusually heavy for a test involving a single drone of any type. Captain 'Mojo' Thorne's Tomcat was hung with both Phoenix and Sparrow missiles, while Captain 'Rhino' Oatley's Raptor had both Sidewinders and AMRAAMs tucked away in its internal bays. All of the missiles had live warheads. Each fighter also carried a full load of ammunition for its 20mm Vulcan cannon, in a high explosive/lead/tracer mix.

'Loaded for bear, Mojo,' one of the armorers had said, asking without asking.

'We'll bring back what we don't need.' Thorne had replied. Privately, he had said to his back-seater, 'Seems like they want a month's data from one sortie.'

The prospects for getting it, though, seemed dim. They had been told the target would carry an experimental electronic counter-measures package, referred to only as 'the package'. Its principles and capabilities had not been alluded to, much less disclosed. But, experiment notwithstanding, nothing in the air should be able to withstand the onslaught programmed in the sortie script – least of all such a thin-skinned, glass-jawed target.

It was not their place to ask for or expect explanations. They would fly the mission like professionals, light up the drone, and leave the rest to the managers.

Accelerating to the high subsonic, the tandem covered the distance to the first waypoint over northwest Utah in a matter of minutes. Wheeling around to the south, they turned on their long-range attack radar and climbed to the specified altitude. Almost at once, they picked up the target drone, which was circling over the range. The Raptor pulled out and fell behind the Tomcat, which was assigned to take the first shot.

'Flagman, Mojo,' said Thorne, calling the test controller.

'Mojo, Flagman. Go ahead.'

'Test 11 is home on the range. Calling Judy.' With that word, control of the intercept passed to Thorne.

'Roger, Mojo. Proceed. Range is hot.'

'Contact, twenty left, forty-five miles.'

'That's your bogey.'

When his Radio Intercept Officer called thirty-five miles, Thorne selected a Phoenix missile. At thirty, he said, 'Fox one,' and thumbed the firing pickle.

As the stout projectile jumped off the rails and accelerated to its supersonic cruising speed, the two fighters broke off into a tight check turn to the left, maintaining their distance from the target as the script required. The Phoenix closed that distance so swiftly that only the Tomcat's RIO, twisting her head sideways, saw the explosion with the naked eye.

'Direct hit!' she said excitedly as the bright yellow flash collapsed into an oily black cloud. 'Splash the drone!' But in the next instant she saw that the drone remained on her radar display. 'Mojo –'

'I see it. Flagman, Test 11. Do you have a tally on the drone?'

'Test 11, Flagman, negative splash, drone is still alive. Range is cold.' A long two minutes later, the controller came back. 'Test 11, range is hot. Proceed.'

The second Phoenix roared away toward the horizon. Again there was a yellow flash, a snarl of black smoke – and again the drone flew on, apparently unscathed.

Closing to a distance of twenty miles, the Tomcat loosed the first of its medium-range Sparrow missiles. Still the drone flew on.

'Rhino, check victor,' said Thorne, and switched his own radio to the VHF intraflight frequency.

'Toop,' his wingman acknowledged.

'Rhino, whatever they've got hung on that bird, I want one.'

Before Rhino could answer, there was a sharp, chastening response from a new voice, that belonging to General Thom Vannigan from the Office of Defense Technology. 'Test 11, this is Goldenrod. Knock off the chatter.'

'Copy, Goldenrod,' said Thorne, swallowing hard.

The last of the Tomcat's missiles was as ineffective as the first, and the flight vectored away to set up for the Raptor's turn at bat. By that point Thorne had decided the 'the package' was not only affecting guidance, but causing the missile warheads to detonate prematurely. He expected the F-22's AMRAAM, with its large directed fragmentation warhead, would end the exercise.

But it did not happen that way. Four times the Raptor's weapons bays opened, and four times the test controller reported, 'Negative splash.'

'What the hell is that thing?' Thorne muttered to his RIO. 'Eight clean intercepts, eight warheads, and it's still out there?'

'Maybe it isn't,' she said. 'Maybe it's a damn ghost.'

'We'll find out in a minute, if they keep to the script.'

It took five orbits in the loiter circle for the range safety officer and the test controller to both give their approval.

'Test 11, Flagman.'

'Flagman, Mojo.'

'Mojo, close for guns.'

Almost eagerly, the fighters hurried along the trail their impotent missiles had blazed. Before long, the dot in the tracking circle became a bright red silhouette, and the silhouette a recognizable plane.

'It really is a T-1,' Thorne said, bleeding off speed. 'A goddamned Beechcraft.'

'Hardly seems sporting, Mojo,' said the RIO.

'No honor in the kill,' the Tomcat pilot agreed.

The headphones crackled. 'Test 11, target is hot. Cleared to engage. Watch your separation.'

'Copy, I am engaging the target. Rhino, give me some room.'

As the Raptor peeled away, Thorne zeroed in on the drone. Calling, 'Guns, guns, guns,' he began firing the prescribed one-second bursts at the maximum effective range of his cannon. It seemed to him that the first few bursts exploded in midair like Chinese firecrackers, as though against an invisible wall.

But something was getting through, because pieces of the Jayhawk began to fly in every direction. Just before Thorne broke off, the drone disintegrated just forward of the engine pods, and

188

the shattered pieces spun out and tumbled toward the salt-frosted desert eight thousand feet below. Wheeling back toward Nevada in a knife-edge turn, the silent aircrew searched the ground for explanations.

Rhino finally made the call. 'Flagman, splash target. Test 11 returning to center, over,' he radioed, then looked sideways out his bubble cockpit as he eased into formation with the Tomcat.

'Rhino looks just as pixilated as I am. What the hell did we just see here?' asked the RIO.

Thorne shook his head in answer to both her words and Rhino's questioning look. 'I know this much – this is gonna be a hard one not to be able to talk about.'

As far as Jeffrey Horton was concerned, the smells of the Nevada desert were hot asphalt and concrete dust – the sounds, rivet guns, ratchets and rumbling diesel engines. The Terabyte Laboratories Annex had been continuously under construction for six months, and there was no end in sight. The finished space was already over-crowded, and there were seventy more technicians and engineers already hired but not yet on site, simply because there was no place for them to work.

Everything had changed, and was still changing. The jouncing cross-country ride Horton had endured was a thing of the past. An extra-wide two-lane asphalt road had been laid down across the scrubland, and more than a dozen tractor-trailers used it every day to bring in more tons of construction material and equipment. There were five new dedicated lab buildings arrayed to the south and east of the original structure, and an entire village of Cardinal manufactured apartments had grown up inside the main gate to accommodate the more than sixty people now living at the Annex.

Everything was different than Horton had thought it would be, and few of the differences were to his liking. The weeks when he'd been the only member of the Columbus staff at the Annex had been hard – long hours of uninteresting work, unpleasantly hot weather, makeshift quarters with few familiar comforts, a suffocating burden of responsibility, and an isolation that ground at him more with each passing day. He'd survived it in surprisingly good humor by telling himself it was temporary, that soon the old team would be reassembled, and work would be fun again.

It hadn't worked out that way.

Lee Thayer now ruled her own ten-thousand-square-foot kingdom and an eighteen-person Instrumentation & Measurement team. She had most of them working on the crucial but – so far – intractable problem of detecting and gauging a Trigger field without pyrotechnics. Outside the lab, she kept to herself. Horton hardly saw her except for the twice weekly team meetings, at which she rarely smiled and never laughed. Horton had no inkling of what had taken all the presence and playfulness out of her, and so far she hadn't given him any opportunities to ask.

While Lee was only partly there, Gordon Greene had never shown up in Nevada at all. According to Brohier, he'd opted out at the last minute, saying he preferred to change jobs rather than change locales. Unprompted, the director had wondered aloud if a woman was part of that decision. All Horton knew was that he'd left Greene three messages, but never heard back from him.

The new engineering physicist, Val Bowden, had twice as much space as Lee, and had turned it into a fully equipped Experimental Assembly shop – complete with CAM machinists, hardware engineers, PROMgrammers, composite spinners, and burn tanks. So far, Bowden's team had scratch-built four Mark I variants, one for Lee, one for Horton, and two for the test range. Bowden was personable and talented, and he'd gathered an equally talented group around him – his fourth Mark I was forty percent lighter than his first, and a third more efficient. But at this point, he was strictly a colleague, and Horton missed his wise-cracking, cynical friend.

Even Brohier was a changed man. In Columbus, he had seemed content behind his desk, resting on his considerable laurels and letting the science staff do the heavy lifting. His visits to the various labs were polite and perfunctory, and he typically evinced more interest in the results than in the work. But since coming to the Annex, Brohier had been revitalized. He had claimed for himself the problem of shaping, aiming, and shielding a Trigger field, and taken an aggressively experimental approach that was keeping Bowden's shop hopping.

Horton presided over the least space and the smallest staff. His Theoretical Modeling group occupied six small offices encircling a modest conference room. He had brought in two technical researchers, a mathematician, an administrative assistant to keep the files straight and the research record current, and a young physicist with some interesting thoughts about information theory as applied to the CERN system.

They met informally every morning for an hour or two to share ideas and generate new ones. The brainstorming sessions helped keep them mentally fresh, but the pressure was enormous, since any substantive progress would have immediate dividends in the work of the entire Annex. Though inspired persistence in the experimental sections had yielded some advances, a sound theoretical understanding of the phenomenon was still the keystone of the edifice they were trying to build.

Alas, progress was slow. Horton's stock characterization of his group was 'good chemistry, so-so physics', and took most of the blame for the latter on himself. Many afternoons found him hiding in his office, feeling overwhelmed by the task before him, fighting the conviction that his ability to think clearly was fading, and that the leap of inspiration necessary to solve the puzzle was beyond his capacity.

The self-doubt waxed and waned, but never vanished. More and more, it looked to Horton as though the Trigger discovery had been a lucky accident, and someone else would have to be the one to explain it. That was why he had started to press the director on the subject of publishing their findings, or at least circulating them privately among colleagues who might take an interest. But Brohier would not consider it.

'*Mathematical Physics* isn't interested in phenomenological anecdotes – and I don't see how it will advance our work to publish in *Ripley's Believe It Or Not*,' Brohier said. 'In any event, our contract with the Defense Department prevents us from publishing without their blessing – which won't be forthcoming, not at *this* juncture.'

'I can't understand why you agreed to that –'

'Do you not understand the concept of "national secret"? We'll publish when doing so doesn't carry such a high risk of compromising the President's efforts, of compromising international stability –'

'Which might be fifty years from now – or never.'

'– In the meantime, the government agreed not to squash or contest our patent applications on the Trigger device.'

'They agreed we could keep what was ours, so long as we didn't tell anyone about it,' Horton said. 'Somehow I can't see the parity there.'

'If you think that was no small concession, you haven't had enough contact with the upper echelons of government – any government,' Brohier said. 'Taking what they want and telling themselves that it's in everyone's best interest is a well-ingrained reflex. Only the most honorable manage to resist it. We're fortunate that one of them happens to be President at the moment.'

'And three years from now, if Breland isn't re-elected?'

'Three years from now this will be a different world – and I would not care to sign my name to any prediction more specific than that. No, if you need more skull power, Jeffrey, you can recruit it – you're barely at half your authorized head count, and I speak with some confidence when I say that no one would question a request from you to double it.'

'You can't get the best people to sign on under these terms – not when I can't even tell them what it is I want them for, not when I can't even tell them *where* the work is, except that it isn't in Cambridge or Palo Alto.'

'Maybe you can't, and perhaps even *I* can't,' Brohier agreed. 'But I wager the President can. If there's someone you know you want –'

'I wish it were that easy,' Horton said. 'I wish I could hand you a list of ten people I *know* could help. But how do I know what kind of expertise we need when I can't even properly define the problem? We might as well be looking for experts in *meta*physics.'

Brohier chuckled. 'Perhaps so. Nevertheless, I want to point out one other option. Washington already has a very large number of scientists under contract, working for every branch of the civilian bureaucracy, the Pentagon, and all the agencies and contractors. And while bona fide theoretical physicists might be a bit thin on the ground, I'm sure that there must be *someone* out there in that mix with the skill set you're looking for – and that Breland would be more than happy to send him – or her – to us. Seniority wouldn't be an issue, either – we could go right to the top of anyone's staff chart. Think about it.'

An interruption rescued Horton from having to admit that the idea activated his professional territoriality. The interruption came in the form of a courier from the secure signal shack – in local parlance, the telegraph office.

The four officers assigned to the signal shack were, as far as Horton knew, the only military personnel at the Annex. Horton called this one The Tailor – his business suit and blue tie were so unconvincingly out of place that he might as well have been in uniform.

'Do you want me to leave?' Horton asked.

'Nothing in this that I won't tell you tomorrow at the round-up,' Brohier said, signing for the magnetically-sealed portfolio. Before the door had even closed behind the courier, Brohier had entered his security code and was removing the documents within. He skimmed the cover page, grunted once, and glanced at the next sheet. 'Well,' he said, and retreated to the chair behind his desk.

'What? What is it?'

'The Pentagon's wish list,' said Brohier. 'From the timing, I'd guess that it reflects the results of their testing with the early production units.'

'And?' Horton asked, settling into a nearby chair.

'Oh – nothing too surprising. They want it smaller, lighter, and less power-hungry. They want increased range – fifteen hundred meters as soon as possible, three thousand as soon as possible after that.'

'No hint there that they know that their first two wishes are inherently contradictory.'

'No hint,' Brohier agreed. 'They also want a way of shielding or blocking the Trigger effect, or a way of making it directional – or, ideally, both.'

'So they won't have to give up their own weapons to use it.'

'Presumably.' Brohier's gaze skimmed down the page. 'This one's signed by the President, not Stepak.'

'Karl – we can't give them what they want.'

'It's a wish list, as I said. They don't expect it all on their doorstep in the morning.'

'That isn't what I meant,' Horton said, leaning forward. 'The minute we give them directionality, the Trigger stops being a defensive weapon – stops being a force for disarmament. If our military has a directional Trigger, they get to keep all their weapons, and take away everyone else's. If the law enforcement agencies have a directional Trigger, we're looking at the same game – they get to keep all of *their* weapons, and take away all of ours. Karl, that wasn't the plan – was it? Or *was* it?'

'No.'

'Then what are we going to do?'

'Work on the wish list,' said Brohier, gently placing the President's memo on his desk. 'But when Christmas Day comes, just to be fair, we give presents to everyone.'

'Are you really prepared to do that?'

Brohier smiled ruefully. 'I suppose I can forgive you a touch of skepticism. But I have a conscience, too, Jeffrey – even if it comes with a complex set of loyalties attached. I want to give my President and his people every chance to live up to my high opinion of them. But I'm not such a naif that I couldn't anticipate the possibility that they'll disappoint me. Yes – I'm prepared for that eventuality. I've been preparing right along.'

Drawing a deep breath and releasing it slowly, Horton sat back in his chair. 'I think you should tell me more about that.'

Disappointment crossed Brohier's eyes. 'I hadn't realized you looked on me with such deep suspicion, Jeffrey.'

'Oh – no, that's not why I want to know,' said Horton. 'You see, I've wondered, now and again, if I wasn't stopping myself – not letting myself see the answers, because I can't control what others will do with them. And I've envied you your apparent self-assurance – without realizing that there was more to it than reckless optimism. If I know what you know –'

'Then you can come to the problem with a clear conscience.'

'A clearer one, at least,' Horton said, then grinned. 'Besides, if something should happen to you, there should be someone else who knows where you put the Santa Claus suit.'

'Catastrophic single-point failure mode,' Brohier said thoughtfully. 'Very well, Dr Horton – welcome to my little conspiracy.'

14: Opportunity

Port Arthur, Tasmania – Gunshots fired from a passing truck
scattered a crowd of more than a thousand gun control
advocates rallying at the Port Arthur Victims' Memorial.
Eleven people were injured, one seriously, and the memorial's
ceramic frieze was struck by two bullets. Police are looking
for three men in a tan 'road-worn' Range Rover. 'I guess they
must have figured we wouldn't be shooting back,' said event
organizer Chad MacKee, of Hobart. The 'Enforce The Laws'
rally was one of many being held on the anniversary of the
1996 massacre of thirty-five people by gunman Martin Bryant,
which led to Australia's universal gun registration law and the
ban on self-loading firearms.
Complete Story   Mass Murder and Madness
'I Remember' Flashback: Port Arthur Massacre
US Still Leader in Guns, Homicide, Suicide

The 641st Tactical Brigade, an independent unit of the United
States Army Intelligence and Security Command (INSCOM), made
its first appearance as the second phase of Trigger deployment
began. In a small miracle of military efficiency, 641 Tac BG had
been created from scratch in just four months, and for only one
purpose – to protect the myriad of Mark I Triggers wherever they
might be placed.

The Mark Is which had previously been deployed in the
Washington, D.C. area had gone to locations which were already
among the most secure on the continent. What's more, only
two of those ten sites were 'hot' sites, ones where the Trigger
was active around the clock. Out of sight and protected by the
existing security, each of those ten units had only been assigned
an operations team from the 115 Sig BT.

But the wider deployment which was planned brought with it a much higher risk of attracting the curiosity of people outside Brass Hat. Stepak had told the President that the secrecy of the project could not be guaranteed once Phase Two began – it was only a matter of time before someone 'not on our Christmas card list' would learn of the Trigger's nature and existence. And once that happened, it was inevitable that someone would try to steal a working example to study, copy, and turn against the American government, the military, or the public.

'It would be the perfect terrorist weapon against an armed enemy,' Stepak had pointed out. 'And frankly, sir, we are the most heavily armed target in sight.'

'Then we'll just have to make damned sure that every one of these things is guarded well enough that no enemy can get to one,' had been Breland's answer.

But Breland had been surprised to be told that what he asked was impossible. 'We can't put enough men around one of these to prevent a sufficiently determined enemy from getting his hands on it,' Stepak had said. 'Not unless you'd agree to have them all stored at one of our ICBM sites. What we *can* try to do is make certain that by the time they reach a Trigger, it's of no use whatsoever to them.'

That conversation had been the genesis of 641 Tac BG. Its first members were one hundred and fifty Army Special Forces troops drawn from three veteran companies at Fort Campbell, Kentucky. To them fell the task of devising a training program for the seven-man squads that would soon be called the T-teams. In two weeks, a plan was in place. Two weeks later, the cadre – now tasked with implementing its own plan – started receiving its first class of trainees at Fort Sill, Kansas.

The intent behind the T-teams was to put a two-man guard on a Trigger unit around the clock – four-hour watches, one on, two off. By and large, it promised to be dull and unglamorous, the kind of 'stationary post' assignment that many Special Operations troops not only dreaded, but silently considered beneath them. It took no special training to be a guard-post gargoyle, and the roving 'head-knockers' of the Military Police got little more respect.

But if the boredom ever broke, the T-team would likely find itself having to use nontraditional weapons at close range to resist a numerically superior force – a job for the toughest, calmest, and most intensely focused troops available. Reflecting that, a majority of the first class of recruits came piecemeal from the elite Special Operations units of all four services – Green Berets, Seals, Army Rangers, Recon Marines.

If it looked no further, 641 Tac BG would have cannibalized all those units by the time it reached its full strength of seven thousand troops. So the first class of two hundred and fifty, like the ones that would follow, reached beyond Special Operations and drew on regular infantry and Airborne units as well.

The three-month training program took some of the traditional strengths of Special Operations troops and built on them. Physical training and hand-to-hand combat were part of the daily regimen, but no more so than fighting off monotony and maintaining mental alertness.

A folding, quick-loading crossbow and a compressed-air short-barrel carbine that could fire fletchettes or gas ampoules were added to the weapons qualifications list. In the meantime, the cadre kept testing other exotics, including a pistol-like cyanosilicate 'glue gun', which was startlingly effective but too prone to clogging to rely on.

Some of the 'packages' – as the Triggers were referred to on all documents and throughout training – would be mobile, and all of them had to be protected in transit from the factory. So the training command took over a twenty-mile stretch of the brand-new automated interstate being built west of Nashville, and put every recruit behind the wheel of both the transport and escort vehicles for anti-hijacking drills and high-speed driving practice. The 'road work' caused more washouts than any other element of the training.

More than two dozen buildings and other facilities at Fort Sill, ranging from an ammunition bunker to a four-story office building, were converted into mock deployment sites, and each training unit was assigned regular watches at one of them. They were not told about the concealed cameras monitoring them, or the group of cadre members assigned to carry out sneak attacks against them – a role which quickly but somewhat mysteriously earned that group the nickname 'the Spanish Inquisition'.

It was not until the third month, after most of those who would

197

wash out were gone, that the 641 Tac BG recruits were shown a mock-up of a Mark I Trigger unit. Only then were they made aware of the second dimension of a T-team's responsibility – to destroy their Trigger if they could not protect it. They were introduced to the special thermite castings – one each for the controls and the emitter – which had been devised for the purpose, and schooled in the streamlined arming procedure.

Finally, soberingly, the T-teams trained with the interlocked jaw-clench and hand-grip dead-man switches which would both allow the team to keep fighting as long as possible, and assure that death would not prevent them from fulfilling their ultimate responsibility. By the time they received their new battalion patches and individual team assignments on graduation day, every member of 641 Tac BG understood the stakes in a very personal way – and why, for what was being asked of them, no mere gargoyle would do.

Unannounced and unexpected, Karl Brohier poked his head around the corner of the door to Jeffrey Horton's office. The associate director was sitting with his back to the door, hunched over a digitizing easel two-thirds of the size of his desk.

Brohier had never gotten comfortable with the easel, which was, ironically, a product of the Aleph Instruments Division of Aron Goldstein's little empire. He much preferred the tiny notepad he carried everywhere and the enormous whiteboard he'd insisted be installed in every Terabyte conference room. But the easel had two advantages that attracted many younger scientists – it could both record and erase itself.

But Horton did not look comfortable, either – and there was not much on the board to either record or erase. Brohier cleared his throat. 'You have a little time?'

Horton stole a glance back over his shoulder, then straightened and turned. 'Sure.'

'Good. Go pack a bag.'

'Pardon me?'

'We need to go to Washington.'

The prospect of escaping the Annex lit up Horton's face. 'I finally get to meet Santa Claus?'

'No, you get to meet the Grinch. The corporate patent attorney just forwarded the PTO examiner's first action on our application covering the Trigger – rejected.'

'On what basis?'

Brohier chuckled. 'The same one they use to reject applications for perpetual motion machines and reactionless drives – fails the standard for usefulness on the grounds of operativeness. Fails the test of patentable subject matter on the grounds of unsubstantiated scientific foundation.'

'They don't think it will work.'

'Right. They want us to submit a working model.'

'We can't do that – can we?'

'No. We're going to file an amended application for reconsideration, but first you and I are going to go talk to the examiner.'

'Can't we do it on the wire?'

'The Patent and Trademark Office doesn't have military-grade secure conferencing. Have a winter coat?'

'In a box somewhere. Why?'

'Find it. Ten inches of new snow on the Mall.'

'Lovely. I'm looking forward to it.'

Retreating toward the door, Brohier sniffed skeptically. 'Meet me at the helipad at three – with coat.'

'And files?'

'No. We sent them a small mountain already. Our problem is making them understand what they read.' The door started to close behind him.

'Say – Karl,' Horton called after him. 'Are we allowed to travel together now?'

A wry smile crossed Brohier's face. 'Oh, sure. We'll have an escort – but they're only worried about us being grabbed, not killed. As far as Brass Hat is concerned, we're expendable now. We even get to fly straight there – no cloak and dagger, no double switches, no side trips to Kalamazoo. And you can have my peanuts – I can't digest them anymore.'

By then, Horton was standing. 'Don't let anyone ever tell you that you don't know how to plan a vacation, Doc. I'll see you at three.'

*   *   *

Patent Examiner Michael Wayne was a year younger than Jeffrey Horton, but was already at the top of the Patent Office's internal hierarchy.

A short man with a shock of wild red hair, Wayne had outspoken opinions about 'tabloid science' and 'crooks with degrees'. From the first, he had taken special pleasure in dissecting and rejecting applications from the 'under-educated egotists who either think that we're idiots or don't know that they are.' Though nominally the senior examiner in engineering physics, Wayne was, by his own choice, the primary review examiner for the applicants the office informally dubbed 'exotics', and Wayne called the 'fanatics'.

'They don't have any idea how much they don't know,' he would expound on the slimmest provocation. 'They can quote Clarke's First Law, but they don't understand the First Law of Thermodynamics. They've heard somewhere that Edison flunked the third grade and Einstein needed help with his math homework, and they think that means the world's waiting impatiently – checkbook in hand, of course! – for their invention.'

Wayne reserved special contempt for any applicant who dared use the word *revolutionary* on the forms or in an interview: 'They make mistakes any second-year science student would catch, and when you point them out, they cry conspiracy – General Motors, or Exxon, or IBM has the fix in, protecting their stockholders. True Believers think they're *this* close to being billionaire tycoons, but they have a union man's contempt for big corporations, and the hard work it takes to build one.'

Though his formal authority was limited to training supervisor for his own section, Wayne's attitudes had influenced the entire Engineering division, and the collection of 'perpetual motion' machines on his credenza was a Third Floor landmark. The irony of that – apparent to others with longer tenure, but not to Wayne himself – was that he had risen so quickly through the grades in part because the Marchmont scandal had swept a small army of senior examiners out of their offices and onto the streets.

In retrospect, it was easy to see how the Marchmont situation had developed. None of the names on the application titled Enhanced Energy Devices had any face credibility – neither the individuals nor the University of Wisconsin-Whitewater, where they were all students or instructors. The subject of their application had even less credibility – the Office had rejected more than three hundred cold fusion devices and processes over a span of nearly two decades. The whole application had the smell of a college prank, a hoax brewed up from beer and chutzpah.

The only problem was that the EED worked. By all rights, Peter Marchmont and his graduate practicum in chemical engineering should have received the world patent for the decoupling hydrothermoelectric generator.

But Toyota received it instead, based on an application filed in Tokyo seven months after the Marchmont application was received in Washington. And as the first Toyota Waterfall electric commuter sedans – with their thousand-kilometer range and inexpensive quick-replace plug-in fuel cells – began rolling off assembly lines in Kyoto and Tennessee, heads rolled in Washington.

The Director, all five Associate Directors, and all sixteen Technical Section Managers were fired in President Engler's 'Black Friday' purge. But that was only the overture. When the Supreme Court gave the green light to *Marchmont vs. US Patent and Trademark Office*, the Office quickly settled out of court – and then vigorously cleaned house. More than two hundred senior review examiners were fired over the rejection of a patent application only five of them had ever seen.

'We are going to war against a deeply-entrenched culture of that's-not-how-I-learned-it skepticism,' said the new director of the Office, a business-school graduate and former Merck executive. 'The cutting edge of science and technology comes to our front door – we have to be ready to welcome it, and speak to it in its own language.'

Wayne missed the irony of his position because his reading of those events was different than that of most of the survivors. 'It's not that the examiners were too skeptical,' he explained to his trainees. 'It's not that they were hidebound and behind the times. It's that they got it wrong.

'Walking into this building in the morning is like walking into a room where the floor is covered with precious black pearls and poisonous black beetles. You're supposed to stomp on the beetles and pick up the pearls. And if some day you can't tell the difference, you'd better not do anything until you can. The Marchmont examiners stomped on a pearl – a big one, a beauty. I have no sympathy for them. When you say "No", don't be wrong. It's as simple as that.'

'So, gentlemen – you intend to file an amended application on your Remote Pyrotechnic Detonation Field Device?'

Something in the examiner's tone of voice prompted Horton and Brohier to exchange glances. 'That's why we're here, Mr Wayne –'

'*Dr* Wayne.'

'My apologies,' Brohier said, following the examiner's lead and sitting down. 'As I was saying, Doctor, that's why we're here – to make sure you're aware of the special circumstances surrounding this application, and see if we can come to a meeting of the minds that will assure –'

As Brohier was speaking, Wayne picked his card up from the desktop and squinted at it. 'Special circumstances, yes – excuse me, but in exactly what capacity are you here today?'

Brohier blinked in surprise. 'I'm the Director of Terabyte Laboratories –'

'But you are not a named inventor on this application, is that right? Or do you anticipate amending that part, too?'

'I hardly see a reason –'

'Good. So long as you understand that adding your name adds nothing to the application – the defects in it would be unaffected. As for your taking part in this review –' Wayne shrugged. 'It's a bit irregular, but I can overlook it. Dr Horton, where is your patent attorney?'

Offended on behalf of his mentor and taken aback by Wayne's police-interrogation style of questioning, Horton stammered through his answer. 'I, uh – the corporation's patent attorney is based in Cincinnati. I understood that the issues, um – the issues were technical and scientific, not legal. We have the attorney's release –'

'As you wish,' said Wayne. 'I'll just note that you declined to have your attorney present. Now, about that amended application – as I'm sure you saw in the notice, I'm requiring you to submit a working specimen with any amended app. I've also judged your technical disclosure to be inadequate. This time, you'll need to provide citations to published papers in refereed journals establishing the validity of your operating principles.'

The smug superiority in Wayne's voice kept Horton's slow burn alive. 'I'm afraid it won't be possible to show you a working specimen –'

'In that case, why not save my time and yourself some money, and file a declaration of abandonment instead – what?'

'– without authorization from the Joint Chiefs of Staff,' Horton continued. 'Turning one over to you is out of the question.'

'This is a government project? I saw nothing about that in the application. If you're an employee of the Federal government, you may not even be eligible for a patent –'

'It's a private project by a private research firm,' said Brohier. 'Now classified, on the President's orders. That's why Dr Horton applied for a secret patent.'

'I don't see how *any* patent can be granted. This is completely irregular.'

'We're strangers here ourselves,' said Horton, thinking he saw Wayne's arrogance wavering. 'How can we help each other?'

The overture was sharply rebuffed. 'This isn't a mutual assistance society, Dr Horton. For a valid patent, I have to certify that the invention you've described is both novel and usable. Since you say you can offer me neither a demonstration nor an explanation of its function –'

'Would you accept certification by General Thom Vannigan, head of the Pentagon's Office of Defense Technology?' Horton asked.

'Are you representing to me that working specimens of this invention have already been delivered to the government –'

'Yes.'

'*Working* specimens?'

'Yes.'

An annoyed frown appeared on Wayne's face. 'Then tell me how it works. If your explanation's satisfactory, perhaps I can drop the requirement that you submit an example.'

Horton allowed himself a little laugh. 'We don't know how it works yet. We only know that it does.'

'That's not acceptable,' Wayne said, shaking his head. 'Not acceptable. A patent must be specific as to process –'

Brohier leaned back in his chair and grunted. 'I told you to just tell 'em that was classified, too.'

'Dr Brohier, if that's your contribution to this meeting –'

'Dr Wayne, what would you have done with an application for a patent on the atomic bomb in 1945? Or radar in 1939?'

'I would have approved them,' the examiner said unhesitatingly. 'They were significant technical advances with a sound theoretical foundation. You, on the other hand, are pulling a rabbit out of a hat – and you won't show me the rabbit or the hat. My hands are tied. Your patent would never stand up to a challenge. I earnestly doubt any other PCT signatory nations would issue reciprocal paper on it.'

'I'm not planning to seek patent protection overseas,' said Horton.

'Not even if your American patent is eventually published?'

'No.'

Now looking completely perplexed, Wayne folded his arms over his chest. 'Then what exactly is the point of your application? If the technology's classified, you can't benefit from a patent anyway – your only customer is the Pentagon. Is this just an ego issue? Or a money hunt – are you chasing some sort of bonus from Terabyte?'

Horton glanced sideways at the director before answering. 'Dr Wayne, I don't think my reasons are germane to the application and review process.'

'No – you're right. They aren't. But I thought you might want to offer me some motivation to read the procedure manual as creatively as you wrote your technical disclosure.' He covered his mouth with his right hand and blew a sigh through it. 'Do you have that certification from General Vannigan with you?'

Horton produced a security-sealed Tyvek envelope and passed it across the desk. 'It's a read-once,' he cautioned.

Nodding, Wayne tore open the seal and studied the letter within. It was already beginning to disintegrate when he sighed again and placed the letter on his desk. In less than a minute, it crumbled to a fine white powder, unreadable, unreconstructable.

'Sorry about the mess,' Horton said, gently breaking the silence.

Wayne waved the apology away. 'These are – special circumstances, as you said, Dr Brohier,' he said slowly. 'Classified technology – an immature theoretical domain – a patent which won't be published unless and until the Pentagon approves the release. All that's really required is to preserve your date of precedence in the event this does become an open patent.' He drummed his fingertips on the desktop, making the dust dance. 'Based on the, um, supplementary documentation presented here, I can approve a provisional – ah, provisional and conditional patent.'

'The condition being –'

'You'll have to provide an amended technical disclosure, setting out the theoretical basis for the device. If you don't do so before the restrictions are lifted and the patent submitted for publication, the patent will be invalid – withdrawn.' Wayne sat back in his chair, hands folded in his lap. 'That's the very best you're going to get from me, gentlemen. I suggest you take it.'

As Horton listened to the pronouncement, he felt the weight of expectations pressing down on him more heavily than ever. But Brohier stood up and offered his hand and a cheerful smile. 'Very good. Thank you, Dr Wayne. That will suffice – yes, that will do nicely.'

Brohier had built some slack into the schedule for their return – enough, he told Horton proudly, to allow for an early but leisurely dinner at Mamarand's in Alexandria.

After seven months, every meal away from the Annex – even their hasty lunch in a Denver airport tavern – was a palate-cleansing pleasure. But Mamarand's was a surpassing delight in any context, a four-star Capital landmark that had held the allegiance of Washington notables for nearly two decades.

Horton threw caution to the wind and opted for one of the notorious 'cardiac cut' specialties, the bacon-wrapped Twin Filet. 'If I thought this would taste half as good tomorrow, I'd order another one to take with us,' he told Brohier.

'If I thought my body would forgive me for it by tomorrow, I'd order one to have now,' Brohier said, eyeing his own light fish entree with regret.

Mamarand's walls were papered with autographed caricatures of famous customers. The few tourists lucky enough to get a table – always before seven – invariably gave themselves away by gawking or giggling. The regulars only took notice of new hangings.

'Are you here somewhere?' Horton asked. He had been entertaining himself with a third glass of cabernet and a little game of seeing how many faces in a row he could recognize without recourse to the autographs.

'Me?' Brohier chuckled. 'Jeffrey, out in the real world, the typical Nobel Prize winner is a news story with a half-life of twelve hours. I'm not famous. At best, I'm answer B on question one hundred ninety of someone's cultural literacy test.'

But as though in direct refutation, they were interrupted half a dozen times before the end of their meal by late-arriving diners stopping by the table and greeting Brohier by name.

Horton knew none of them. After the ritual introductions, he found he also knew of none of them. But having Brohier explain to him who they were after they'd moved on toward their own tables only reinforced Horton's feeling of living a disconnected life. Each cheery greeting nudged him further into a dour dissatisfaction. He fell silent, and Brohier misread the silence as fatigue.

'You know, I was thinking that it's really not necessary that we return tonight,' he suggested gently. 'We can take a couple of rooms at the Northwind, and recharter in the morning. It'll do us good to let someone pamper us a bit – the jacuzzi, a massage, plush towels, a king-size bed.' He chuckled to himself. 'I think when we get back I'll hire someone to put little chocolates on everyone's pillows.'

Horton doubted a single night of luxury would leave him any more enthusiastic about returning to the Annex. 'Let's do that – the Northwind, I mean, not the chocolates.'

Dabbing at his mouth with his napkin, Brohier fished his comset out of an inside pocket. 'Let me see what I can arrange.'

But nothing touched Horton's melancholy – not the spectacular view of the capital's brightly-lit panorama of monuments from his hotel window, nor the blistering heat of a long four-head shower, nor the indulgence of a room-service Shrimp Cocktail For Two at midnight, nor the plush comfort of the long white hotel robe, nor even 500 channels of music, theater, and film delivered through a shadow-box holowall.

When a hard swim in the hotel pool did nothing to urge him toward bed and sleep, Horton realized he was prolonging the day as a way of postponing the morning. In that same moment of clarity, he also realized what had to change. That was how Horton found himself standing in the corridor in his robe at five minutes to one, tapping at the door to the other suite.

'This will only take a minute,' he promised when Brohier finally opened the door and squinted sleepily out at him.

Brohier grunted crossly and retreated from the doorway, allowing Horton to enter. 'I would have thought you'd have been asleep two hours ago. *I* was. This couldn't have waited until morning?'

'I really need to resolve this now, Karl – if I don't, I don't know if I'll even be here in the morning. The way things are right now, I don't think I could make myself get on that plane with you.'

The door closed behind Horton as he was speaking, leaving only the pale glow from a lamp dimmed to night-light intensity. 'All right,' the older man said, the annoyance leaving his voice. 'What do you need from me?'

'A change. I'm not having any fun beating my head against the wall. I don't know what the reason is, and I've lost interest in trying to figure it out. The fact is I'm stumped. I've gone mentally stale. No, it's worse than that – I've developed a bad attitude about the whole business.'

'Do you want out?'

Horton felt himself tempted, but pushed the thought away. 'I wondered if I could interest you in swapping problems?'

A sardonic chuckle rumbled deep in Brohier's throat. 'Why do you think I'd be any more successful? You can't know how much harder it is for me to concentrate than it was when I was your age. Maturity has nothing to offer the physicist, Jeffrey – nothing that makes up for the wear on the instrument.'

'Why do you think I'll believe that you're not interested, that you haven't been thinking about it all along?' Horton shot back. 'You can stop respecting the territorial boundaries. I just erased them. You gave me every chance to put it together on my own.

Well, I can't do it. I'm asking for help – exactly as you said I should. I should have done it months ago.'

'Do you think I would have kept silent if a worthy thought had strayed into my consciousness? Really, Jeffrey, you have too generous an estimation of me, and too harsh an assessment of yourself.'

'I don't think so. Even if you can't solve this yourself, you can bring together the people who can. You know everyone in the field, and they know you. There's no one who won't take your call, respect your confidences, trust your word –'

'Oh, there are a few,' Brohier said, smiling wryly. 'More than a few.'

'Not as many as would do what I did, and jump at a chance to work with you. I know you expected more from me –'

Brohier sighed. 'That you could say such a thing makes your case for you – you need a change of scenery. Trying too hard is a mistake that can sabotage you in almost any field. So, very well, then – I accept your proposal.'

'Thank you –' The rush of relief was more intense than Horton had expected.

'Not because I expect the problem to yield to my superior brain,' Brohier added quickly, clapping Horton on the shoulder, 'but because it *does* interest me, and because we are friends. And you're right about something else, too. We are separated by two generations, and I can reach out to my peers and down to the younger physicists more easily than you can reach up to them. So I'll do that, and we'll see what we see.' He shrugged. 'It may well be that it just isn't time yet.'

After that, sleep came easily.

15: Trickery

Kupang, Timor – A peaceful 'March of the Forgotten' turned into a bloody massacre Wednesday as Timorese security forces loyal to embattled President Gusmao fired on a crowd of more than two thousand demonstrators as they approached the government offices in central Kupang. The death toll was estimated at 'more than forty', with as many as 200 others injured. A spokesman for Gusmao called the marchers 'brigands' and 'Indonesian terrorists' who were exploiting the island's economic difficulties.
Complete story   Timeline: Tangled History
1996 Nobel Prize 'brought no one peace'

The brainstorming sessions during which the bulk of the Basing & Deployment Site Manifest had been generated had been some of the liveliest and curiously enjoyable meetings of the Brass Hat team. But when it came to assigning priorities to the more than 14,000 candidates, consensus proved impossible past the first hundred places. In the end, the prioritization was primarily the work of General Stepak, after consultations with the President and the service secretaries.

Escorted by their T-teams and ops units, Triggers went to the Air Force for installation in Global Hawk battlefield intelligence drones, E-8D Joint STARS flying radar stations, and KC-10B Extender tankers – all unarmed aircraft crucial to the twenty-first-century concept of war. The Navy had plans to turn four Sturgeon-class attack submarines into torpedo-interceptors for its precious aircraft carrier task forces, and was toying with reviving the Pegasus hydrofoil patrol boat as both an attack platform and a defense against sea-skimming cruise missiles.

On the ground, the Army wanted every cavalry squadron to

have two Trigger-equipped M113A3 armored personnel carriers to serve as mine-clearing combat vehicles. The Marine Corps was evaluating the system's usefulness in amphibious assault, as a means to clear a path through fortified and booby-trapped beaches. It planned to create test beds using Osprey tilt-rotors, Super Cobra helicopters, and its Navy-operated LCAC air-cushion landing craft.

Over the years, a variety of offices in the law enforcement and intelligence communities had invested many thousands of man-hours in creating exhaustive lists of the possible high-value targets for attack by terrorists and hostile forces. These threat assessments and targeting analyses amounted to a classified catalog of vital national assets, from communication and transportation infrastructure to key research centers and records archives. The FBI and the Pentagon had both provided the Brass Hat committee with their lists, and from them Stepak selected one-of-a-kind civilian and military sites in almost every state.

America's space industry received a priority allocation, from the Venture Star launch centers in Florida, California, and southern Texas to satellite dish farms in nine states. And Stepak wanted to go further than that – all the way to orbit. He was pressing the NASA Administrator to equip the agency's six SSTO orbiters with Triggers and order the commercial fleet to follow suit. In the last two years alone, there'd been one confirmed and three suspected cases of airliners shot down on takeoff or landing by Stinger-type shoulder-launched missiles.

But the NASA Administrator was resisting. None of those incidents had taken place in the United States, he argued, and every kilogram of payload was precious now that eighteen people were living aboard the expanded International Space Station. Stepak had scheduled a meeting between President Breland and the NASA chief to resolve the dispute.

The secretary of state had no such reservations. Every American embassy from Dhaka to Gaborone was slated to receive two Triggers, along with a special addition to its Marine guard contingent. Most of those Triggers would be deployed cold, as insurance against the unpredictable vicissitudes of Third-World politics. But half a dozen would go hot from the start, as insurance against the unpredictable violence of political terrorists.

Neither Breland nor Stepak was ready to turn control of a Trigger unit over to any law-enforcement agency, even the FBI. But staging depots – dubbed 'rental agencies' by Richard Nolby – were being prepared at six sites scattered around the continent. Each would be the home base for as many as a dozen mobile Trigger teams, available for loan to local and state police and the FBI for specific raids and investigations.

The President's pet idea for the Trigger was to use it as 'a filter in the flow', to intercept weapons in transit. 'There are places people already know you can't take a gun, places they already expect to be screened and searched,' he told Stepak. 'They don't need any further warnings for us to make sure that they follow the rules. No more road-rage shootings. No more letter bombs. No more courthouse rampages or schoolyard feuds.'

Nolby tried to convince Breland that the actual number of such incidents was too small and the number of necessary deployments too high to justify an allotment from the first thousand. But Breland was unmovable.

'The numbers may be small, but their impact isn't,' he said. 'Every killing like that makes the news, lingers in people's memories. Kids shooting each other outside math class – letter bombs killing middle-aged professors – airliners full of French students blowing up in midair – these are the sort of moments that tell people life is insane, that their world is turning wrong. That's what makes them afraid.'

On hearing that, Nolby remembered that Breland's childhood home of Williamsport was just a few miles from Montoursville, the hamlet that was hit so hard by the Flight 800 tragedy. Rather than rehash the still-controversial verdict or argue with the emotional memories of the young Breland, Nolby acquiesced. Restricted-power Triggers and Kevlar blast boxes went into the baggage-handling systems of forty-four airports and the sorting systems of the Postal Service's central mail facilities.

But Stepak did manage to persuade Breland that the schools would have to wait until those placements could be made openly. The presence of soldiers could not easily be explained away, and, as Stepak observed, 'Absurd as it is, injured kids are almost always seen as innocent victims And if they're the good guys, we're the sneaky bad guys – which is not how we want to introduce the Trigger to the public.'

Senator Grover Wilman followed all these developments through his monthly meeting with the President and biweekly updates from the Brass Hat team, which then became the basis of his own classified reports to the Joint Congressional Committee on Security.

He did so with a growing dissatisfaction, one that the President's reassurances did less and less to assuage. Wilman had his own list and his own priorities, and as month after month passed without him seeing them reflected in the deployments, he began to wonder if he ever would. By the time the July meeting approached, Wilman had thoroughly lost all faith in the promises Breland had made at that momentous first meeting.

Before the end of that month, the 500th Mark I would roll out of the South Dakota plant and into the hands of 641 Tac BG. Contemplating that fact, Wilman decided that he had been patient and reasonable long enough.

'Mr President, have you been shining me on?' Wilman said as they sat down together in the Oval Office.

'Excuse me, Senator?'

'I think you heard me clearly enough. Have you been "handling" me? Are these little meetings your way of neutralizing me, given that you wouldn't go along with the recommendation to just have me killed?'

'No one ever made such a suggestion, Senator,' Breland said, his gaze narrowing darkly. 'Not where I could hear them, anyway.'

'No discussions of whether I could be trusted to stay quiet and play by your rules? No intimations that I have stronger loyalties to the MOM than to the Congress, that I'm an internationalist peacenik dressed up as an American hero? If not, there should have been – it's all true. I've been on my very best behavior, Mr President. Better than *I* would have thought me capable of. To sit on something this big for eight months – well, sir, I can only say that I'm feeling very pregnant.'

'Is this the beginning of a confession? Are you going to make it to nine?'

'I would think that depends on your answer to *my* question, sir.'

'Senator Wilman, I'm grateful for your patience –'

'I'm sure,' said Wilman. 'But will it be rewarded, or is this whole Brass Hat exercise nothing but an extended joke at the expense of the people I care about?'

'I'm afraid I don't understand –'

'I'll put it plainly. Are you ever going to do anything *constructive* with the Trigger?'

Breland frowned. 'I know you're getting all of the deployment reports, so all I can think is that you and I mean different things by that word –'

'Then I'll be glad to explain what I mean. Active rather than passive. Pro-active rather than reactive. Positive, affirmative, transformative, risk-taking, do-something interventions that affect people's lives, that *save* people's lives. I thought you had a visionary understanding of the power and potential of the Trigger. I'm still waiting to find out if I was right. You have the hammer and the anvil in front of you – do you ever mean to use them?'

A flash of annoyance intruded on Breland's features. 'We have more than four hundred Mark Is in the field. They're not warehoused in an armory somewhere.'

'They might as well be, for as much good as they're doing,' Wilman said. 'You've turned a miraculous breakthrough into a goddamned homeowners' insurance policy. We're protecting billions of dollars of concrete and metal, safeguarding all our precious collections of toys and souvenirs – and forgetting all about people. Good lord, most of the Triggers you've deployed aren't even turned on. If there's a hundred of them hot right at this moment, I'll do naked cartwheels on the Mall.'

'Every site has its own set of considerations, Senator. I don't really understand what you expect from me.'

'Try thinking about eighteen thousand four hundred and nine corpses.'

'Where does that number come from?'

'The Center for Health Statistics at the CDC, yesterday afternoon,' said Wilman. 'That's how many people have tried to stop bullets with their bodies since the day Dr Brohier and I came to see you. That's how many murders, suicides, and fatal accidents you've tolerated. That's the price of timidity, and secrecy, and passivity.

'Of course, that's just us Americans – and we're not even officially at war with anyone. I can't begin to tell you how many Europeans, and Africans, and Asians have stepped on mines or gotten in the way of a border squabble or a little uncivil unrest. I expect our twenty thousand are just the down payment.'

Breland's angry frown declared his displeasure at being lectured to. 'Now you're sounding like a True Believer, Senator, and I'd thought better of you than that. You can't expect us to stop all the killing –'

'We can make it much harder than it is now. But we have to want to do it. We have to try.'

'We *are* trying –'

'The hell we are, Mr President. The hell we are. All we're doing is digging in our heels against change. Hold on to our edge. We're scared to death that Mao was right, that all political power does grow out of the barrel of a gun – and that we're about to lose ours.'

Rubbing the back of his hand across his mouth, Breland said nothing. In the silence, Wilman changed seats to move closer to him.

'It's the most natural thing in the world, Mr President, to want to protect your own,' he said, sitting forward on the edge of the couch. 'It's just not good enough for this century, or this office. We have to care as much about a dead black teenager in Atlanta as we do about a dead white baby in Beverly Hills. We have to care about mortars fired across the Congo at Kinshasa as though they were being fired across the Mississippi at Kansas City.

'How big is your tribe, Mr President? Who gets the benefits of membership? Just soldiers and politicians?'

'No – no, of course not –'

'Then why are we protecting our wealth and power when we could be protecting our people?'

Breland stared, blinking. 'You did warn me you'd scorch my feathers, didn't you,' he said, and shook his head. 'Grover, we're not really at odds here. Your ethics and mine could get along in close quarters. People are more important than things. Lives are

214

more important than ideology. And I do believe that humanity *is* one family – even if it's a dysfunctional one.'

'You say that, but you've sent nine-tenths of the Trigger production to addresses that begin with "Fort" or end with "Base".'

'Because they're ready to make use of the system *now*. The civilian population isn't. We have a huge public education job ahead of us –'

'Is that your excuse for going so slow?'

'So slow? What are you talking about? We're deploying them as fast as Goldstein's people can make them.'

'Then why haven't we ordered a second thousand, and a third? Why aren't we pushing Goldstein to increase capacity as fast as he can? Why are we being so goddamned *timid*?'

'Timid?'

'Timid,' Wilman said emphatically. 'It's all baby steps and half-measures. Look, your notion about filtering the social flow – that's *exactly* the sort of thing we should be doing. But you didn't go nearly far enough.'

Breland turned his palms upward. 'Tell me what I missed.'

'For starters, all the loaded handguns in glove compartments and under car seats. Congress passed the Merck-Martinson law ten years ago, and people are still being shot down after a fender-bender, murdered for making a face at the driver in the next lane. Why didn't Merck-Martinson put an end to that?'

'I think it's because of something called "probable cause",' Breland said, attempting a wry smile.

'It's because Merck-Martinson doesn't help the police find those guns before something happens. But the Trigger can. It can put bite in what's been a toothless law. It can be to gun control what radar and the automated highway were to traffic control.'

'What exactly are you advocating here?'

'Nothing more than what you did with the post offices and airports. Everybody who drives eventually crosses a bridge, passes under an overpass, takes the tunnel, goes through a toll booth. If you put enough Triggers at the choke points, you could get all the guns off the road.'

'It'll only destroy guns that're loaded. And cause some dandy traffic accidents in the process.'

Wilman shrugged. 'It's not as if they haven't heard of Merck-Martinson – you can't carry a loaded weapon in a moving vehicle.'

'So you think we can go ahead and destroy everybody's ammunition, even if they're obeying the law, even if the ammunition's safely tucked away in a lockbox the driver can't reach – even if it causes a fire that destroys the family car –'

'Mark the screening zones. Light 'em up like truck scales. Big red signs every hundred meters for a kilometer. Big red stripes across the road. Let them know what's coming. Give them a place to dump their ammo before they reach the edge of the zone – we don't want anyone hurt. That's –'

'We can't do that, Grover. You know we can't do that.'

'Why? And don't tell me it's because of the Second Amendment. Ask your Attorney General about *Miller vs. US*.'

'It's because we're not ready for CNN,' said Breland. 'The Pentagon is dead-set against any disclosure until they have an effective defense and a substitute for gunpowder in hand.'

'And when did this become their decision?'

'It's not. It's mine.'

His face relaxing into a thoughtful expression, Wilman sat back on the couch, draping one arm across the backrest. 'Was that the decision you wanted to make, Mr President?'

Surprise bloomed in Breland's eyes. Without answering, he stood and crossed the office to his desk, where he scooped a root beer-flavored hard candy out of a bowl. 'I don't know why that isn't an easy question to answer, Grover,' he said finally.

Wilman nodded. 'Mr President, I think I owe you an apology. When I suggested that you'd been trying to "handle" me – I was off target. I respectfully suggest that you're the one who's been handled. No shame in it, sir – they're experts.'

There was an audible crunch as Breland's teeth ground down on the candy. 'I knew they were going to try,' he said. 'I knew that that wasn't my St Crispin's Day speech – knew that if I got too far out ahead of them, I'd find they weren't following. But I thought I was on top of it, Grover.' He sighed, and the last of the candy disintegrated between grinding molars. 'Maybe they worked me better than I realized.'

'It was a fine speech. You got their attention. The deployment program is proof of that – it's got their stamp all over it. They couldn't make the Trigger go away, so they took over. And they tell you perfectly reasonable things about how doing it any other way will make all hell break loose.' Wilman managed a thin smile. 'An argument strengthened by the fact that they're right – it will. I look forward to it. They dread it. You –' He let the word hang as a question.

Breland sank down against the edge of his desk. 'Give me an idea. Something we can do now, so you'll know my heart is in the right place.'

'I get a dozen ideas every day, reading the news,' said Wilman. 'Denis Sassou-Nguesso is at the top of my list at the moment. I'd love to see you give him a call, tell him that he has twelve hours to get everyone out of his Cobra compounds, and then send an F-117 into the Congo with a Trigger in its belly – has the Air Force managed to fit a Mark I into the internal bay yet?'

'Still working on it.'

Wilman looked disappointed. 'It's just as well. He'd probably pack the camps with opposition hostages – if he could find any that the Cobras haven't already killed. Of course, we could always do it *without* the twelve-hour warning –'

'Next idea,' Breland said firmly.

'Well – if you're not ready to go public, how would you feel about spreading a little disinformation?'

'Go on.'

'There are too many people involved in Brass Hat to keep it black ops for long. I don't get your intel reports, but I'd wager every government that cares has now heard of Brass Hat, and some have gotten deep enough inside to get the cover story – that this is a follow-on to Shortstop, intended for mine-clearing operations.' He paused, looking to Breland for confirmation. 'You always did have a good game face.'

'Just for the sake of your argument, let's assume that you're right.'

'Well, then the next obvious thing is to back up the cover story with a demonstration,' said Wilman. 'Get the boys at INSCOM to cook up a photo-op prop of some sort that we can sling under a Black Hawk – lots of shiny metal, plenty of antennas and blinking lights, even give it a magnetic field and some radio emissions to make it convincing to the Chinese.'

'And the real Trigger is tucked away inside the helicopter?'

'Exactly. The L model of the Black Hawk should be able to lift both with no trouble. You call a press conference, announce your initiative against land mines, tell them you've established a special unit of the Army dedicated to humanitarian demining, and cue the helicopters. It'll be great television, Mr President – top of the news. And it'll give the Pentagon another few months' cover. A little bit of truth can make a wonderful lie.'

Breland pursed his lips. 'General Madison and the Joint Chiefs won't like giving away even that much.'

'Fuck 'em,' said Wilman, startling Breland with his coarseness. 'Ask them when was the last time they visited a prosthetic clinic in Bosnia, or attended a village funeral in Afghanistan. Ask Madison if he thinks these secrets are worth his right leg, or his granddaughter Macey's life. A hundred and fifty *million* mines waiting in the ground – approaching a thousand casualties a week. And both numbers have been going the wrong way for twenty years. You can *do* something about it, Mr President. Please – do something about it.'

Rising up from the desk, Breland pointed an accusing finger at Wilman. 'This is what you wanted when you walked in here.'

'Yes, sir,' Wilman admitted cheerily.

'So *you're* the one working me now.'

'No, sir. I'm the one shaming you.'

Breland sighed. 'You're doing a good job of it.'

Showing a rueful smile, Breland circled around behind his desk. 'You know what the biggest surprise about this job has been, Grover? How hard it gets to be to do the right thing, even with the best of intentions. How hard it can be to do *anything*. It's almost as if every time one of those doors opens, a little more Potomac river-bottom muck leaks in. Before you know it, you're hip-deep in it, and you can hardly move.' Leaning forward, he touched the intercom key. 'Mrs Tallman, would you find General Stepak and tell him I need to see him?'

'Do you want me to stay for that?' Wilman asked after the acknowledgement came.

218

Breland shook his head. 'Not unless you brought a shovel with you. – You do know the story of the city fella, the farmer and the mule?'

'"First, you gotta get their attention,"' Wilman said, chuckling as he stood up. 'Good luck, Mr President.'

That afternoon, pursuing an impulse, Wilman sent a present up to the White House – a long-handled shovel with brightly chromed yoke and toe. It had originally been made for ceremonial ground-breakings. Wilman had a large decal of the Presidential Seal added to the flat of the toe.

But he didn't know if he'd misjudged the man or the moment until his next visit to the White House, when he found the shovel mounted on the wall to the left of Breland's desk. A black-and-yellow sign more appropriate for a factory had been hung beside it. It read FOR EMERGENCY USE – DO NOT REMOVE.

A surprised and delighted grin was still taking shape on Wilman's face when Breland handed him the new mid-month Brass Hat summary report.

'Item Two,' he said, then paused a moment to let Wilman's eyes scan to it. 'Have a favorite country?'

The heading for Item Two was *Brass Hat Demining Initiative.* Wilman looked up, his gaze grateful. 'No favorites, Mr President,' he said pointedly. 'But I have always wanted to see more of Cambodia.'

Breland nodded. 'Cambodia it is, then. And I take it it's all right to include you in the travel arrangements?'

'I wouldn't miss it.'

'You shouldn't,' said Breland. 'I'm planning to publicly credit you, and I want to find out if you blush.'

The perspiration had barely begun to cool on Gordon Greene's bare skin when the alarm on his comset began to sound.

The alarm was a surprisingly unobtrusive noise – in part because he had left it set in Carry mode, and in part because the jeans he had been carrying it in were lying in a jumbled heap on the floor ten feet away, near the bedroom door. Half vibrating rumble, half low-pitched buzz, the alarm was no louder than the breathing of the naked woman curled up against Greene's right side. Moving slowly, Greene disengaged himself from her embrace, replacing his shoulder with a pillow under her cheek, his body warmth with a blanket drawn up to her shoulders.

It was not tenderness or affection that guided him, but rather a combination of politeness and his desire for privacy. As in most encounters during which strangers become lovers, the last hour had been about mutual selfishness, not intimacy. Her need not to be alone and his need to slake his hunger for touch had made the arrangements, negotiating with measured promises by the cold light of a hot dance bar eight blocks from campus.

For all that, they had meshed well, their bodies fitting easily together for hard kisses and all that followed, her intensity matching his, her body glowing to his touch, his body answering the call of hers. The final coupling had been feral, vocal, febrile, wanton, and they had collapsed together on the damp sheets afterward with no thought of regrets – in fact, with very little in the way of thoughts to disturb the pleasant haze of sense-memories and a swift descent into sleep.

Then came the alarm. Greene had remembered at once why he had set it, and found it was still reason enough to give up the agreeable pressure of Kiera's softness against him. He escaped the bed with a single squeak from its springs. By then the alarm had ceased, but he snatched his jeans up with one hand as he slipped out of the room, and paused in the hallway to climb back into them.

There was enough illumination filtering through the blinds from a security light outside for Greene to find his way to the swivel chair in his study. When he touched the trackball, the hundred-centimeter display awoke from Sleep mode, throwing enough light onto the desk for him to see his split keyboard – an antique accessory that required an arcane skill, but still Greene's first choice for talking to his system. Most of the interesting things that could be done with a computer required giving up the cozy conveniences of a multimedia interface – and at the machine level, syntax mattered.

All of his newsagents were active and showing new retrievals. Since there was still a little time before the scheduled broadcast from Phnom Penh, Gordon started to skim the waiting messages.

There were so many entries in the Explosion queue that it almost seemed as though the earth should be reverberating beneath him. A truck bomb in Colombo, mines in a busy road in the Jordan Valley, a rocket attack in Algiers, mortar duels outside Bogotá – these were routine. Greene had skimmed hundreds of reports like them in the last month alone. Fifty-year-old American cluster bombs killing farmers north of Ho Chi Minh City, a suicide bombing aboard a German train, live 105mm artillery shells found in a Kentucky landfill – these at least offered some novelty, though no spoor of Greene's quarry. And now and then there were stories Greene could only call macabre and bizarre – a booby-trapped casket at a burial service in southern Italy, or the 'homing donkeys' smuggling grenade launchers over the mountains into Greece.

Occasionally, inevitably, his newsagents' context parsers would hiccough, and offer Greene a lighter moment – an article on a 'explosion' in fire ant populations in Missouri, or a Devonian cometary impact in Nevada. Those were balanced by the stories Greene could not shrug off, the senselessly cruel, the shamelessly brutal. The mental pictures stayed with him for days – of fragmentation grenades hurled into the middle of a crowded church in Manila, of a bungled letter-bomb murder in Grozny that killed a one-month-old girl in her mother's arms.

But nowhere yet had the newsagents found evidence of the Trigger being used as he had been promised it would be – of would-be bombers killed by their own bombs, of despots deposed and armies deprived of their armories, of thugs and punks and wiseguys stripped of their finely machined blued-steel masculinity. The bleeding and dying, the suffering and crying continued unabated, on every continent, in every country, with only the most poignant and dramatic deaths even registering on the conscience and consciousness of strangers half a world away. All was as it had always been.

Greene did not despair, because he was enough the cynic that he had expected no better. Even so, he felt the lost opportunity more keenly with each passing day – felt it for himself and for those he had called friends, and for her who was never far from his thoughts. A noble gesture wasted, a year lost, and lives disrupted without purpose. It was not from the surrender of hope that his

221

disappointment came, but from the sacrifice of good intentions. They had fallen on hard ground, and it looked more and more as if he would have to step forward and tend them.

That prospect seemed so certain, in fact, that Greene's preparations were already well underway. He now had three encrypted copies of the Trigger file secreted on remote servers, all physically located outside the United States. Two of those copies were wrapped in a digital envelope addressed to more than a hundred public distribution sites, from newsgroups like alt.peace and sci.physics to preprint servers in sixteen countries. The third was targeted at nearly two hundred private mailboxes belonging to disarmament activists and the Terabyte team's peers around the world – physicists of every flavor, experimental engineers, and the research directors of unencumbered high-tech companies.

All in all, Greene calculated that his efforts – incorporating the newest and sneakiest tricks of direct-mail spammers – would spawn no fewer than ten thousand copies of the massive file by the end of the first hour. Depending on the speed and effectiveness of any Pentagon interventions – roadblocks, packet assassins and cancelbots being just a few possibilities – there could be half a million copies or more in circulation by the time they found and shut down the source servers. And at that point, it would be too late. Too many recipients would have taken note of the digital elephants Greene had dropped off at their front doors. It would be impossible to make them all go away.

The threat that most concerned Greene now was the knock at the door that came without warning. *He* was the weakest link – a classic single-point failure mode. So he had set up all three of his caches with 'dead-man' mailers, their schedulers set three days ahead. If something happened to him, so that an innocuous net "ping" failed to reach his mailers at least once every three days, everything would be set in motion without further involvement on his part. That same mechanism would give Greene a head start – a few hours, a few days if he wanted to risk it – in which to fade into the shadows, if and when the call came.

But the reason he was sitting in front of a terminal in the wee hours of the night – instead of cuddling the woman in his bed, as any sane man would – was to find out if just possibly all that work had been in vain.

A few minutes before two, as he was closing his newsagents, he heard the living-room floor creak. 'Hey,' she said softly as she approached.

'Hey,' he said, bringing CNN up and muting the sound. 'You're a light sleeper.'

'Not as light as you, apparently. What are you doing – posting a review to alt-dot-gotlucky-dot-com?' she murmured, wrapping her arms around his bare chest from behind.

'Keeping up with current events,' he said. 'President's on a tour of the Far East.'

'I've known guys who had to smoke afterwards, and guys who had to eat afterwards, and guys who had to jump up and brush their *teeth* afterwards –'

'That's endearing.'

'Intensely,' she said, as a CNN LIVE EVENT bumper appeared on the screen. 'But if you don't come back to bed, I'm going to have to go home thinking I got passed over for a politician – and a dopey-looking one, at that.'

With a touch of his left hand, Greene started a video capture. With another, he brought up the volume. With his right, he squeezed Kiera's hand, stopping her from pulling away. 'Fifteen minutes and I'll be all over you again.'

She giggled. 'This gets you hot?'

'Well, you know about the genetic link between testosterone and explosions, right?'

The introductions over, President Breland was beginning to speak.

Kiera peered over his shoulder at the screen. 'You're expecting explosions?'

'That's the rumor. Not at the podium,' he added quickly. 'They're going to clear a minefield.'

'Isn't that dangerous? And doesn't it take a long time?'

'Usually. That's why this is news.'

She looked at the screen and saw only talking heads. 'Fifteen minutes? You promise?'

'Twenty, tops.'

She kissed the top of his head. 'Maybe I'll go take a shower, then.'

'What Napoleon said to Josephine.'

'Hmm?'

'Don't.'

She made a surprised noise – but not a displeased one. 'Don't keep me waiting.'

'I won't.'

When she was gone, Greene allowed himself to smile. He'd gotten his first glimpse of the air-cushion vehicle at rest in the background, behind the President. The smile broadened to a delighted grin when the first closeup came. When a mock blueprint followed it to the screen, Greene sat back in his chair and started chuckling quietly in the dark.

'"Harmonic Demining Vehicle",' he whispered to himself. 'I like that. Like the phoney antennas, too – and those big Leslie speakers fore and aft. Very cheesy. Harmonic demining – yeah, that'll do.'

Greene had misjudged his own degree of glee and fascination. More than an hour passed before he finally tiptoed back into his bedroom. When he did, he found Kiera sound asleep and snoring lightly. He intended to make amends in the morning, but she left the bed early and did not return, hiding in a long shower and then keeping him at a distance until she could escape.

To his surprise, Greene found he did not particularly mind the lost opportunity, or regret the broken promise. He did not try to detain her, or explain himself. His first thought that morning was to wonder how the event was being reported on the leading headline services. His second thought was about Leigh Thayer, and about the suddenly improved prospect of seeing her again.

'Before Pol Pot and Lon Nol, before America's secret war and Cambodia's brutal civil war, this was a farm,' President Breland said to the cameras that carried his image around the globe. To his right was the Chairman of the Supreme National Council; to his left, the director of the Cambodian Mine Action Center. 'These fields produced rice, and the woods beyond them yielded firewood and fruit.

224

'This was not a factory farm, or a state cooperative, or even a cash cropland. This was the family farm of Ngos Tran.' Breland looked down the platform to where the thin, hunched-shouldered man stood barefoot, in jacket and *sampot*. 'He, and his eight siblings, and his parents, Poth and Ravi, worked these flooded fields for their own survival. If in a good year there was enough extra to fill a cartful to sell at market, they counted themselves blessed.

'But then the soldiers came, and Mr Tran lost a brother to a bullet. In time, those soldiers were driven off by other soldiers, and Mr Tran lost a second brother – recruited by bayonet, and never heard from again. Again and again, four different armies have skirmished over this land, which lies too close to the Mekong River and the Kâmpóng Cham road to escape their attention.

'The armies are gone now, but their calling cards of death remain – dozens of plastic-cased antipersonnel mines, hiding under the water, hiding under the mud. One killed Mr Tran's oldest sister. Another took his father's right leg. No one lives off this land now. No one grows rice here. It's too dangerous, even for desperate and hungry people.

'But the mines in Cambodia are not just one family's tragedy – they are a national tragedy. There are more amputees here than anywhere else in the world – one out of every two hundred people. Four hundred civilians are killed every month, in what the Khmer call peacetime.

'Why doesn't someone do something? Someone has been trying. For more than a generation, the Cambodian Mine Action Center has run one of the best organized, most dedicated, and most successful demining programs in the world. Working one step at a time, one mine at a time, the CMAC teams – more than three thousand men and women, most of them trained by CMAC – have removed more than seventy thousand mines, and cleared more than six thousand square kilometers of land. And every square kilometer the CMAC clears allows fifty refugees to return home.

'But despite their unceasing efforts, there are still eight million mines concealed under Cambodian fields, waiting along Cambodian roads and trails, hidden in Cambodian forests. These fields have been red-flagged, on a list of sites to be demined, for nine years.

225

The CMAC – the people of Cambodia – have done all anyone could ask to rid their country of this scourge. They need and deserve our help – and help is what we have brought.

'Behind me is a remarkable machine – the first of what I promise will eventually be hundreds of Harmonic Demining Vehicles, which I intend to see put to work everywhere that our help is welcomed. Using principles of sound energy which will be familiar to anyone who's ever attended a concert, the HDV can do in an hour what would take a platoon of trained deminers a week – and without the terrible casualties all too often suffered by these brave volunteers.

'This land has seen too much blood spilled, and lain fallow for too long. It's time for Mr Tran and his family to return home to their village and to their fields. That is why I have asked the US Army's newly-formed 318th Engineering Brigade to bring their first HDV here, and to demonstrate to the world that the era of the mine is ending. Mr Tran, I hope these will be the last soldiers that are ever seen in your fields.'

Breland turned away from the podium and made a signal – a circle drawn in the air with his forefinger – to the Army lieutenant standing at attention with his crew in front of the HDV. The lieutenant answered with a salute. As he and his men climbed aboard the vehicle, Breland allowed himself to be steered to one of the five chairs sheltered by three large sloping panels of clear acrylic shrapnel shield – a concession to the Secret Service, who had wanted Breland to make his speech from a studio in Phnom Pehn.

There was a rustle and murmur of anticipation as the HDV's turbines wound up, and the air-cushion vehicle rose up off its collapsed rubber skirt. With its ducted steering fans all spinning, it turned and approached the boundary markers. As it neared the first flag, another sound was added – the basso thrum of the high-output speakers, which reached Breland's ears almost as a pulse, even though he knew it was a continuous sound.

Almost at once, half a dozen small fountains of earth and water erupted from the abandoned rice paddy in an arc just ahead of the HDV. The individual explosions, muffled by the overburden, were barely louder than their scattered echoes, but they nevertheless caused the hundred or so spectators to start, and then – inexplicably – crowd closer. As the HDV glided forward over the edge of the field, the explosions continued, to the delighted applause of his hosts.

When the vehicle paused at the treeline and then turned to begin a second, parallel pass, Breland could see that the air-cushion skirt was splattered with Mekong mud, but there was no sign of any damage.

'How many of these can you lend us?' asked the Supreme National Council chairman, leaning close to Breland.

'We're organizing them in squadrons of four,' said Breland. 'I was hoping you'd allow me to station two squadrons here. My experts tell me that they should be able to have all the lowland areas cleared by the end of the year.'

'By the end of the year –' the Chairman echoed, marveling.

Just then, without warning, a single huge explosion erupted just a few meters inside the edge of the flagged area. Something hard rattled against the shield, and the entire platform shook. Breland flinched reflexively, then started to stand, his ears ringing. The explosion had curtained the HDV from his eyes behind a solid wall of mud, smoke, and water.

He was grabbed by two Secret Service agents, who clearly meant to take him to the floor shielding his body with their own. But he shook them off angrily as Colonel Grassley of the 318th came running up to the platform.

'What's happening, Colonel?' he called, helping the CMAC director to his feet.

'UXO, Mr President – unexploded ordnance. Probably an artillery shell or mortar round that buried itself in there. Sounded like a big one – the Chinese copied the Russian 82mm towed mortar, could have been something like that. Could even have been an iron bomb we left behind.'

'Is the HDV damaged?' But by then he could see that it wasn't – though now well-painted with mud, it was still moving forward, passing close by a small crater that was quickly filling with water.

'No, sir. Do you want us to continue?'

The commander of the Secret Service unit stepped forward and tried to take that question, but Breland was quicker. 'Absolutely, Colonel. Clear that entire field.'

The Secret Service was now at Breland's elbow, angry and insistent. 'Mr President, we have to move you back –'

'I'll sit back down, John,' he said in a low voice the microphones did not catch. 'That's as far as I'm going to let you move me.'

In another ten minutes it was over. There were no more big explosions, and only a single medium-sized one, which Grassley identified as an antitank mine. In all, some three dozen 'poppers', as the director of CMAC referred to the small antipersonnel mines, detonated in the first sweep of the field. The HDV made a second sweep at right angles to the first, but not a single additional explosion ensued. It appeared that the first sweep had been one hundred percent effective, locating and destroying every threat lurking under the surface.

As the HDV settled onto its skirt in the parking zone, Breland jumped down from the platform and crossed the road to congratulate its crew. His Secret Service detail hurried nervously after him, hoping his next stop would be the Presidential helicopter, and a quick trip back to the safety of Singapore. But as Breland was finishing with the crew, he saw that Ngos Tran had also left the platform, and was walking haltingly toward the red flags, all alone in his wonder and uncertainty.

It was then that, on impulse, Breland made the gesture which almost every news editor around the world would choose as the defining image of the day. Crossing the ground with long but unhurried strides, he joined Ngos Tran where he stood.

The two men could hardly have been less alike, or from more different worlds – West and East, city and farm, broad-shouldered and thin, tall and stooped, empowered and impoverished, a President and a peasant farmer. Neither could understand a word that the other spoke. But in a few gestures, they made their meaning clear.

Is it really safe? Tran wanted to know.

Come – see for yourself, was Breland's answer.

Side by side, the two men walked past the flags and into the soggy field that half an hour earlier neither of them would have dared enter.

228

Before long they were joined by the Cambodian officials, then others from the platform, all rushing to demonstrate that they, too, were not afraid. But the others were irrelevant. The cameras barely paid them any mind.

It was Ngos Tran's tearful gratitude – looking up at Breland and clasping both his hands, the two men standing ankle-deep in the mud – that would earn photographer Milos Thurban a Pulitzer Prize.

And it would earn President Mark Breland inestimably more.

16: Perplexity

Nagasaki, Japan – Seismic tracings 'prove without a doubt' that China conducted an underground nuclear test in violation of the Comprehensive Test Ban, according to the director of World Nuclear Monitor. 'The bomb transients are unmistakable. This was a new design, with a higher yield than we've seen before,' said Dr Ray Milius. 'I expect it's the warhead for the DF-10.' The Chinese Space Agency test-fired its new long-range rocket last month. But officials in Beijing insist that the seismic event, centered near the Lop Nor nuclear test area, was an earthquake rather than an explosion, and that the Dong Feng 10 was designed as a booster for the Lotus manned spacecraft.
Complete Story   State Dept. 'reviewing Data' Video: DF-10 Launch
Japan's Premier Protests   Was Test Meant as 'Warning' to Russia, US

Dr Leigh Thayer's control and measurement team was in command of the test range for the afternoon. It had prepared more than 400 samples of materials being evaluated as Trigger shields – from metals to crystals to liquids to inorganic compounds rich in nitrogen. Each material would be tested in three thicknesses – one, three and five centimeters – and at two distances – ten and twenty-five meters.

Lee called these test sessions the Scramble, because the predominant image of them was of the entire team scattered across the test range, carrying sample trays and hurrying from one test pad to the next. The tests themselves only took a few seconds each, so it seemed as though they were in an endless cycle of set-up and collection.

There were now a total of twenty test pads laid out in two arcs to the north of the main lab. Lee had asked for more, so more materials could be tested at once. But after watching the first Scramble shortly before he left for Princeton, Brohier had ruled against her request.

'As things are, you have one person per material – very orderly, little chance of error,' he had told her. 'Go beyond that, and all you'll do is increase the chance of a mistake.'

Mistakes were not the threat they had been in the beginning, because they were no longer using explosives in their testing. Instead, they used the closest thing to a workable Trigger detector that had yet been devised – Leigh Thayer's 'puff caps'.

Analogous to a reagent strip or radiation badge, the caps consisted of a plastic panel bearing a fabric disc impregnated with a solution derived from black powder. When exposed to a Trigger field, the caps erupted with a readily visible puff of fragrant smoke.

The information they provided was strictly binary – yes or no, Trigger detected or not – and the caps were consumed in the process. Nevertheless, unlike the pyrotechnic poppers, which had cost one of Lee's assistants the tip of two fingers, the caps could be handled with no special training, and the test cycle shortened by half. They were also nearly noiseless, which meant that testing days no longer sounded like the Fourth of July. The Pentagon saw potential in them as perimeter alarms, so Goldstein was rushing them into production, and Lee had applied for a patent.

But Lee was still looking for the breakthrough that would allow her to build a proper detector and strength-meter for Trigger fields. The two problems – shielding against the fields and taking their measure – seemed inextricably linked. Up to the limit of a Mark I's range, the Trigger field appeared to pass through any amount of matter as if it wasn't there.

She had tested with poppers suspended a hundred meters down a well-shaft and placed on the far side of a granite ridge. They had tested with the well flooded and the emitter swathed in lead. They had sealed a popper inside a box made of depleted uranium. The results – all positive – destroyed all notions of propagation based on the behavior of any form of electromagnetic energy. Whatever it was that came from the emitter of a Mark I Trigger found rock as transparent as air.

231

Because the Trigger's interaction with matter was so weak and selective, it was inevitable that Horton and Brohier started looking at neutrinos. The CERN model had relegated those mysterious ghost particles to the status of the interplanetary ether, dismissed as a mere bookkeeping convention of an immature theoretical model. Even so, neutrinos remained attractive. For most of two weeks, Horton had talked of almost nothing else.

In their last days on the theoretical stage, neutrinos had been the strangest of the many strange creatures in the subatomic zoo. With their variable mass, fractional spin numbers, candy-store variety, and the bizarre ability to pass through the entire mass of the Earth as though it wasn't there, neutrinos were the last Holy Grail of the Standard Model physicist – and the last hope of Jeffrey Horton.

The hope was that somewhere in the experimental record there lurked, unremembered and unrecognized, another Trigger anomaly. It had troubled Horton that he had been unable to connect their discovery with any naturally-occurring phenomenon.

'I'd give my right arm for a good look at this thing from another angle,' he had told Lee at dinner one evening shortly after she arrived at the Annex.

'You'd have to find someone who actually wants your right arm first.'

Horton was already humorless by that point. 'You know what I mean. What we do in here with technology ought to mirror something that happens out there without it. I'm uncomfortable with the lack of natural analogues. If this is a real phenomenon, where are the observations it should be helping us explain?'

'Horton's Paradox,' she had said. 'What did the literature search turn up?'

'Nothing,' he had said with a shake of the head and a disgusted expression.

'Maybe you searched the wrong literature,' she had suggested. 'Maybe you want *The Weekly World News* instead of *Physics Today*.'

'Do you think I'm above resorting to phenomenology at this point? Maybe I didn't go all the way to the tabloids, but I purposely left the search parameters as open as possible. I made sure they caught all of the fringe science and parascience.'

'And?'

'You don't want to go there.'

'Come on – tell me.'

'The search agent kept trying to tell me that spontaneous human combustion was a good match on my criteria.'

She had chortled with delight. 'Oh, it is!'

'It is not,' he had said tersely. 'There's not a single documentable case with witnesses – no preachers immolated in the pulpit, no matter what you've heard. As near as I can tell, all of the "best" cases involve a reclusive elderly woman who was overweight, lived alone, liked to tipple, and smoked.'

'Hmm. Doesn't sound like you'd need Sherlock Holmes to draw you a picture.'

'And the forensic science is either anecdotal or nonexistent. You've never seen such credulous reporting –'

'Sure I have,' she had said. 'I was raised an Episcopalian.'

'Withdrawn,' he had said with a wry smile. 'But still, if we need Mary Reeser or Mrs Oczki to make our case –'

'Well – what about "fires of suspicious origin"? Someone must keep records.'

'Someone does – the National Fire Data Center. We covered this ground while you were still in Utah, training the Army operators.'

'And?'

'The best we could do is a definite "Maybe". NFDC tracks two million fires and explosions a year, and one out of five is "cause unknown". We hired a private arson investigation company to go through NFIRS database for possibles. They came back with a very long report, and none of it was anything I could use. Not enough information, not reproducible, no patterns that held up to close examination.'

'No proof.'

'In a word.'

'It has to be out there somewhere.'

'If we're asking the right questions,' Horton had said. 'One of the truths I'm still reasonably sure about is that matter and energy interact. But I'm starting to wonder if whatever's coming off that emitter is neither matter nor energy.'

'You have any other suspects?' she had said, surprised.

Horton had frowned and shook his head.

That question was now Karl Brohier's to worry over. Within three weeks of returning from Washington with Horton, the director had packed his bag again, this time for the Institute for Advanced Study in Princeton.

In his absence, Horton had become a presence again at the Annex, showing welcome signs he was returning to his old form. No longer a hermit, he had evinced renewed enthusiasm for his work, some of which spilled over as an almost intrusive interest in Lee's work as well. He had spent most of a week going over her unit's records and talking to her staff about the detection and measurement problem.

And at the end of that week, he had delivered what amounted to an old-fashioned pep talk to her staff.

'If you can detect it, we can deflect it. If you can measure it, we can modulate it,' he told them. 'Stay focused – stay committed. If you can, stay optimistic. We all have trouble with that one sometimes. But your work may well hold the key to everything we're doing here. If you find something that interacts strongly with a Trigger field, we can have shielding the next day, and directionality the day after.'

Horton's involvement was coming late in the day from Lee's perspective, but she was surprised to find that his enthusiasm even buoyed her own mildly discouraged spirits. And she was pleased when Horton showed up at testing control half an hour before the second Scramble was scheduled to begin. It reminded her of the old days, before Baby – a time which, like many new parents, she looked back on with some selective nostalgia.

'Anything I can do?' Horton asked.

'I'm accepting donations of synapses in good condition,' she said. 'Did you know that the last brain growth spurt takes place right after puberty? After that we're coasting – and coasting is downhill.'

'I did know that.' He smiled broadly. 'I even developed a pet theory about how our life paths are decided by how we use those last few billion connections – academics or sex.'

'You must have looked around in grad school and realized just

234

how many really bright people haven't a clue about relationships,' she said, regretting the touch of bitterness that crept in
unbidden.

'I could see it as early as high school honors math,' Horton said.
'Only two of us went to the prom, and they went with each other.
Diana and Kim. Got an extra headset?'

She pointed. 'Bottom drawer.'

They were too busy for conversation soon after that. Lee ran the
final checklist herself with a brisk efficiency that kept everyone
hopping. Horton distinguished himself by managing to stay out
of her way, which she appreciated more than any help he could
have offered.

The actual test was an anticlimax. With the test range cleared,
Lee brought the Mark I up to ten percent for fifteen seconds. All
of the test strips were sealed inside small resin boxes lined with
the test material; there were no vent plugs, so there was no puff
of smoke, no sound. When the green light went out again, one
of Lee's crew brought the electric truck back from outside the test
radius, and the numbered boxes were gathered up and taken away
for examination later.

As that cart drove off, a second arrived, carrying another batch
of samples. There was another short lull at testing control as they
were being placed.

'Did Dr Brohier say anything to you about how long he expected
to be in New Jersey?' asked Lee.

'He said it wasn't as terrible a place as people liked to say, and
not to be surprised if he was gone a few weeks.'

'Think we'll hear from him while he's gone, this time around?'

'Not unless he has something,' Horton said. 'He's just not the
chatty type.'

'Did he give you any clues about why he went there – I mean,
who in particular he was planning to talk to?'

'Well – he has plenty of friends on the faculty. Buhl and
Esterovich, particularly. But all he actually said to me was that
he'd been wondering if we'd been pushing on the wrong end
of the stick, if what we needed wasn't a new physics, but a new
mathematics. I took that to mean he was going there to talk to
Reichart and Wu.'

Both names were familiar to her. Reichart was faculty in the School of Mathematics, and a recent Wolf Prize winner. Wu was a visiting member in the School of Natural Sciences, and a notorious free-thinker whose critiques of the CERN model were as much a part of his reputation as his own work in stellar physics.

'The by-line's going to be as long as the paper by the time we have this all figured out,' she said lightly.

'I'm more worried about it ending up published by *Kreskin's Journal of the Bizarre*,' Horton said.

'Could be worse – you might get invited to appear on *Wonders of Nature*,' she teased. The ratings leader of Phenomenal!, an infotainment channel devoted to fad religions and paranormal pseudoscience, the lowbrow daily *Wonders* featured a voluptuous former model turned neoEgyptian priestess as hostess. Her undraped assets (bared by her neotraditional garb) might not have given rise to the show's title, but certainly accounted for much of its audience.

'It's a hope worth grabbing onto,' Horton said straightfacedly.

She laughed, and swung the headset mic toward her mouth. 'This is Lee in the booth. Ready for round two. Call off by stations.'

A few days later, it was much harder to find any humor in their situation. Lee and Horton were finishing their inventory of exposed samples from the third Scramble, and facing up to the reality that the results had been no different from those of the first two. None of the shielding materials had worked; all of the puff caps had been destroyed.

Horton sat back in his chair and surveyed the line of tables filled by opened test boxes. 'Guess we're going to need to reorder, eh?'

'Jeffrey, I want to talk to you about that.'

He noticed that she no longer called him Boss. 'I'm listening.'

'I've already worked my way down the periodic chart and back again. Given unlimited time and money, I could work my way through the *Handbook of Chemical Compounds*, too. But that doesn't seem to me to be a good use of either. Not without *some* encouragement from the tests we've already done, some direction that shows a little promise. But the only materials that interact with the Trigger field blow up or disassociate. And even there, I don't understand the process – I can't even prove anything's being absorbed. It's a dead end, Jeffrey. This damned thing –' She shook her head, frustration denying her the words.

'Have we gotten a good survey?'

'Absolutely.' She thumbed the stack of test reports. 'Metals, non-metals, transitionals, noble gases, actinides, sulfides, carbonates, cobalt complexes, phosphates, resins, alloys – Geri's a good chemist. She understood what I wanted.'

'So what do you want to do now?'

Lee sighed and looked away. 'I suppose we could stand to work the metal-organics a bit harder. And I've been shying away from liquids, because of the handling problems – so many of them are reactive. We could go there, I suppose.'

'Okay,' Horton said encouragingly.

'What I really want to do is get out of here for a while,' she said plaintively. 'Is that possible? You had your holiday. Or am I still on probation – house arrest?'

'Hmm? What are you talking about? What do you have in mind?'

'How far is it to Las Vegas?'

'By chopper, close enough for a night on the town. If you drive, you'll want a three-day pass.'

'It's no fun going to Las Vegas alone,' she said, looking at him hopefully. 'That's for gambling addicts and showgirl wannabes. I'm neither.'

'You know more about it than I do – I've never been.'

'Neither have I.'

'Reason enough,' Horton said, rising. 'You grab your toothbrush. I'll roust the pilots from their card game.'

17: Festivity

Sacramento, California – Six workers died Saturday night when fire broke out in a confined basement area of the State Capitol. Capitol Park Director Beth Markham said there was 'no structural damage' to the historic building, and the upcoming session of the State Assembly would not be affected. Markham said the contractors were installing cutting-edge air-quality equipment intended to help preserve the Capitol's museum-grade artifacts when they apparently sparked the blaze. The casualties included two US Army engineers supervising the installation.
Complete story

Horton and Thayer immersed themselves in the glitter and spectacle of Las Vegas with the reckless glee of runaway children with a borrowed credit card. They hired a white Cadillac limousine at McCarran International Airport, and told the driver – a breezy, tuxedoed Louisianian named Ruby – their intentions. By the time the limo reached The Strip, Ruby and her cellular RedCarpet city guide had secured them a suite at Bellagio and tickets to the two hottest casino shows.

The early show, at the Luxor, included a sumptuous dinner served by bronzed 'temple slaves' wearing mock-gold jewelry and short colorful skirts that owed more to Hollywood than to Egyptology. The spectacle that followed depicted the rise and fall of the First Kingdom, and was built on the twin foundations of prurience and ufology, highlighted by an on-stage Nile flood, a sybaritic orgy, and the destruction of the Great Temple at Karnak by a departing spaceship.

There was just time enough between shows, Ruby told them, to catch one of The Strip's most enduring crowd-pleasers. She dropped them at the curb in front of the Treasure Island Hotel's Buccaneer Bay just as the first twelve-pounder from the *HMS Britannia* roared, belching crimson flame and silver smoke. The crowd of 500 lining the bridge cooed in delight, then cheered as the privateer *Hispañiola* returned fire.

'Do you ever wonder why we find guns and explosions so attractive as entertainment?' Lee asked as they watched the playlet unfold. 'Or is that something that testosterone just understands instinctively?'

A deafening cannonade from the *Britannia* sent pirates and planking flying in the air, and Horton held his answer until the pirates had triumphed and he and Lee were back in the limousine.

'I do wonder about it,' he said. 'There's something visceral, to be sure. The bright lights, the intense colors, the loud sounds, the pressure wave against your chest —'

'That explains fireworks. Not war movies.'

'That's tied up with something primal, I think. Something deep in the animal mind. All those myths about Big Men — fathers and kings and warriors —'

'The friend with the gun is our champion. The enemy with the gun is the killer beast,' she mused.

'And slaying the beast without being harmed confers heroic status — the protector and provider.' He shook his head and dropped his voice, mindful of the driver. 'It's an old script — going to be strange to see what it looks like when we're done rewriting it.'

'What are we going to do for entertainment?' she said with a little laugh. 'Half the writers in New York are going to be out of work.'

'Aren't they already?'

'Okay, then the *other* half will be out of work, too.'

Horton shrugged. 'There's always historical fiction.'

A hopeful smile appeared on her face. 'Just think, Jeffrey. Maybe in a thousand years, a "Western" will be a story set between the invention of the flintlock and the invention of the Trigger — a moment in time when the rules were different. A colorful era, a fascinating one, a rich source of legends and folklore — but fundamentally tragic and brutal, with no reason for anyone to regret its passing.'

Horton reached across the wide leather seat and squeezed her hand. 'A nice thought. Hold tight to it. If we can ever manage to look back with that much clarity – well, we'll have learned something, then, won't we?'

'It could happen,' she said with conviction. 'When's the last time you heard anyone defend the genocide against the American Indians, or wish they were living in Tombstone, circa 1880?'

'Oh – I'm sure we could find someone. People get nostalgic for the oddest times – there are weekend medievalists, Civil War reenactors –'

'But most people think the present is a better place to be,' she said, looking out the window at the bright bustle of Las Vegas. 'And I think most people still will, fifty years from now.'

Fifty, I'll grant you, Horton thought. *It's the next five I have doubts about.* But he said nothing, leaving her optimism hovering over them like a pleasant scent on the night air.

It was not in Jeffrey Horton's nature to let himself enjoy a demonstration of stagecraft for its own sake. He took his rewards from matching wits with the professional tricksters, and in piercing their illusions to discover the reality beneath them. Long before he had entertained any thought of a career in science, his two great curiosities were special effects and stage magic – two domains where deception is the highest art, and reality becomes elusive.

When Horton's parents had taken him to see David Copperfield in Cincinnati as a present for his ninth birthday, they had taken his rapt attention for youthful wonder. In fact, he had spent the entire performance trying to penetrate Copperfield's bold, stage-filling illusions. On the drive home, Horton had done his best to spoil them for the rest of the family by telling them everything he had discerned or deduced. When many of the same illusions appeared on one of Copperfield's network specials, Horton had recorded it on CD-R and studied it until he could narrate a thorough dissection.

At thirteen, his favorite film was *The Stunt Man*, which audaciously manipulated reality not only for the audience but for the protagonist – a desperate Steve Railsback dancing at the end of a godlike Peter O'Toole's string. Horton's favorite book was *ILM: The Art of Special Effects*, an expensive Christmas gift from his mother's brother, in which the secrets of virtually every popular film of Horton's youth were revealed. He watched every behind-the-scenes documentary he could, to the point that his brother Tom claimed Horton's favorite show was *The Making Of*.

But it proved to be an obsession with diminishing returns. The more Horton knew, the harder it was to fool him, or even surprise him – the workaday tools of magicians and effects technicians alike changed slowly, and true innovations were rare.

Pixar mattes were better than bluescreen mattes, which were better than rear-projection mattes, which were better than knowing that a scene in *The Wizard of Oz* had to end when it did because Dorothy was about to dance face-first into a giant matte painting. But they were all tricks designed to place real actors in unreal surroundings – and they were all equally unbelievable once detected.

So it was with every tool in the standard repertoire of magician and technician alike. And since Horton was uninterested in using what he knew to fool others, there had come a point where he needed a new set of puzzles to test himself against.

He had found them in Mr Tompkins's sophomore honors physics, where he was first introduced to the notion that science was an ongoing inquiry with unanswered questions, and not merely a catalog of things already discovered. The latter had hardly engaged his interest; the former came to consume him.

Reality itself proved the grandest and most fascinating illusion of all – solid matter was largely empty space, stationary objects were in constant motion, straight lines were actually curved, most of the Universe was invisible, matter created itself spontaneously from vacuum, time was a variable, and every answer led to more questions.

With those and even more paradoxical mysteries to occupy him, he had never been bored since – not one day in twenty years. A holiday church service, a long line at a state office, a charity telethon, a garrulous grandaunt, a cross-country car trip, the proceedings of any legislature, a round of golf – Mr Tompkins had effectively immunized him against all such tedium. His thoughts were unfettered even when duty or etiquette held his body in thrall, and there was always someplace more interesting for his mind to go.

So Horton had let Lee choose their entertainments for the night, because it mattered more to her than to him what the choices were. But because Las Vegas was at its heart a mirage in the desert, illusions were its stock in trade, and all of Lee's choices had been working to reawaken the thirteen-year-old inside him.

The shows at the Luxor and Treasure Island had shown him that he now was able to appreciate artistry in execution, and not just creativity in design. Putting a hundred-thousand-gallon flood and a set-destroying conflagration on the same stage half an hour apart was no small accomplishment – doing it twice a night and a dozen times a week was stagecraft of a very high order. Placing an audience smack in the middle of a sea battle – Lee had sworn she had heard the cannonballs flying overhead, and Horton had seen that she was not the only spectator to duck reflexively – was as bold as the demolition of the *Britannia* was complete.

But it was during their final stop that everything came together for Horton, that the past and the present, work and play, intersected and merged. *EFX* had been the MGM Grand's showpiece for two generations, its several incarnations the fulfillment of a solemn promise that inside the doors of the Grand Theater awaited something that could not be seen anywhere else – not on any other stage, in any studio theme park, on any screen. *You must come here*, it whispered, and come they did, expecting not merely the best show on The Strip, but on the planet.

Perhaps it was because Horton did not bring those expectations with him to his seat, or because the wizards of illusion had had fifteen years to further polish their craft. All he knew was that for the first hour, he watched with the edge-of-the-seat joy he had never quite mustered as a child. Like the grand finale of a fireworks show, the stunts and tricks came so closely spaced that there was scarcely time to appreciate them, much less to analyze them.

It was an ostentatious display of technical virtuosity, a continuous parade of sights and sounds seamlessly bound together by grand music and the theme – it did not deserve to be called a

242

plot – of a time-traveler skipping through the highlights of five billion years of Earth history.

But midway through the show – shortly after the Yucatán asteroid had fallen from the sky and struck beyond the horizon with a blinding flash – Horton was suddenly yanked out of his suspension of disbelief. It was not the shaking of the ground underfoot or the blast of hot wind in his face, or the jungle being flattened before him, or the massive smoldering tree trunk that toppled out over the first dozen rows that did it.

It was, rather, the lone pteranodon circling mournfully overhead, looking down on a devastated landscape, on the twilight of its era. Horton saw at once that the pteranodon wasn't an animatronic prop hanging from a wire, or a radio-controlled model, or a film projection, or any other trick of stagecraft that he recognized. The creature was flying above the ceiling, and was as real to Horton's eyes as any bird on the wing had ever been.

Hologram, he thought as the pteranodon flew off, vanishing into the gathering darkness of the great cloud that foreshadowed the end of the age of dinosaurs. But Horton had never seen synthetic holoanimation with such detail or on such a scale. What's more, there had been no sign of a laser or other illumination in the darkened auditorium.

Transmission holograms, mounted in the ceiling and lit from above –

Horton spent the rest of the show watching for the effect to be repeated. He was rewarded for his diligence at the start of the finale, which depicted a techno-utopian future in the spirit of *Popular Science* of the 1950s – complete with flying cars overhead and a horizon-to-horizon architectural showcase of a megalopolis.

Both effects were, if anything, more convincing than the pteranodon, if only because the shapes were simpler and the scale more familiar. Horton hardly noticed as the finale built to its climax. He was pondering the difficulties of creating those images – the incredible calculating power required, first to model the images in sufficient detail, then to derive the interference patterns for the digital holographic writer. Making a photorealistic hologram of an imaginary object taxed the most powerful graphical workstation. Making a photorealistic animation was several orders of magnitude

243

more demanding. The complexity of the diffraction grating –

'Interference,' Horton said aloud, then clapped a hand over his mouth as Lee stared at him. He offered no explanation, ignoring her questioning look. But as the audience rose for a standing ovation and the cast began taking their bows, he edged toward the aisle. 'I have to make a call,' he said, and headed for the exit. 'I'll come back and find you.'

The secure comset in his back pocket could have handled the task from Horton's seat. What he was seeking was privacy. He had to go all the way back to the limousine to find it, chasing Ruby out to the sidewalk.

'General Stepak – yes, here, too. Moon and dark and all,' he said. 'General, I want the last two Mark Is that came out of the plant diverted to the Annex. At the gate at oh-eight-hundred, if possible. Yes, I know there are some located closer to me. But I need two that are as nearly identical as possible.'

When Horton rejoined Lee in the casino, she demanded an explanation. He demurred, saying, 'I'll tell you when we're back in the suite.'

'Are you trying to avoid spoiling my night out?'

'I'm trying to avoid ending it prematurely. It's bad enough that one of us is still thinking about work.'

'Why – who did you call?'

'Management,' he said. 'Trust me – this will keep until you've had your fill of Las Vegas.'

She acquiesced, but contented herself with only one more stop – at New York, New York, where the recreation of the Coney Island amusement park was scheduled to be demolished in the spring. Coaxing Ruby to accompany them, they rode the roller coaster three times in succession, spun madly on the Tilt-A-Whirl, laughed their way through a mirror maze, and rode the Ferris wheel for the panoramic view from on high. Still thinking them a couple, Ruby insisted they go on the Ferris wheel alone.

'The ultimate carnival midway,' Horton said, leaning out over the side of the swaying car and looking out along The Strip.

'Are you going to tell me now why we're going back early?'

He told her. She did not argue. Their last view of the city that night was from the company helicopter as it wheeled about over McCarran International and headed home to the Annex.

The Triggers arrived a few minutes after nine, delivered by a five-vehicle caravan and a platoon of uniformed men who looked decidedly unhappy about releasing the units to Horton's custody.

By midafternoon, Val Bowden had the units carefully aligned and securely mounted side by side on the test pedestal at the south end of the test range. Thayer finished installing her hastily improvised controller synchronizer under floodlights.

'Two controls, amplitude and mix,' she explained to Horton. 'I've calibrated the two units as closely as I can without being able to directly measure the field strengths.'

'We can refine it as we go, by trial and error if need be. Do you have enough puff caps?'

'What sort of grid do you want?'

'Fine. One per square meter.'

'Well – I've had three people working on caps all day. Triple our usual batch. I don't know if they're dry yet, though.'

'Find out, would you?'

'You want to run a test now? I thought we'd have to wait till morning.'

'I can't wait,' Horton confessed.

'Are you that confident?'

'No – I'm that insecure.'

It was nearly midnight before the grid was ready. By then, word had spread, and a crowd had gathered. It seemed to Horton that everyone who was not working on the test was waiting and watching – the entire Annex staff gathered by the test range, their anticipation as palpable as the chill of the desert night.

At 12.20 a.m., Thayer reported to Horton that the test grid was ready – fifteen hundred puff caps laid out in a thirty-by-fifty array fifty meters from the test pedestal. Horton turned to the manager of the test site.

'Do we have enough light for the recorders? We're not going to get any other data off most of those placements.'

'There's enough light,' he promised. 'The low-angle floods should give us ideal coverage – better than daytime.'

245

'Okay,' he said. 'Clear the test range.' As the five-minute-warning horn began to sound across the compound, he turned back to Thayer. 'Any reason not to do this?'

'None that I know of.'

At one minute, a second, more urgent siren sounded – the signal that all Triggerable material should by then be beyond the safety radius of 500 meters. At thirty seconds, the test range's audio, video, and infrared recorders began receiving data.

'Take it up slowly, now,' Horton said to Thayer, who was standing at the synchronizer, her hands on the controls.

'I know the test profile, Boss,' she said. 'Honest, I do.'

Horton retreated, joining Val Bowden at the plexiglas-shielded observation rail a few meters away.

'Are you a betting man, Dr Horton?' the engineer asked.

'Not even in Las Vegas,' was Horton's answer. 'But this isn't gambling – it's guessing. And your guess is as good as mine.'

A sharp electronic chime counted down the last ten seconds. Then Thayer counted off the power setting, one percent at a time.

The many tests done at that site had conditioned everyone's expectations – the front edge of the fifty-meter grid reached reaction threshold at fifteen percent, the back edge at forty percent, with fifty percent observed as the redline for test purposes.

So there was an audible gasp of surprise from the previously hushed onlookers when the center of the first rank of the grid erupted in smoke just after Thayer called out, 'Six percent.'

She hastily added, 'Holding,' and lifted her hand from the amplitude control. 'Boss?'

'I counted five cells,' Horton said into his headset mic. 'What did you get?'

'The same,' Bowden said.

'I didn't see it,' Thayer said with a sigh. 'I wasn't expecting anything yet.'

'Take it to seven percent, step-wise,' he said, signaling Thayer with a lifted hand.

'Resuming, step-wise,' Thayer acknowledged.

It was eerily quiet on the test range, considering the number of people gathered there – so quiet that many of them heard the faint *pfffft* as the caps in the next three ranks of the grid erupted. It took a moment even for the most observant to realize that *only* the center of the next three ranks had gone – the rest of the first rank still had not reacted. It took a moment longer for the quickest-thinking observers to realize what it meant – but only a moment. Scattered whoops and cheers erupted in the wake of that realization.

Horton was not among those cheering. Still withholding judgement, he ordered, 'Eight percent.'

This time no one could mistake what was happening – the twin Mark Is were slicing a path through the middle of the grid, leaving the cells on either side undisturbed. The Trigger field had become a Trigger beam – and the celebration became more certain of itself, the cheers full-throated, the scattered applause solidifying.

'Should have made that bet, Dr Horton,' said Bowden, clapping him on the back enthusiastically.

'Don't jump to conclusions,' Horton said, stubbornly clinging to his fatalism. 'Nine percent, Lee.'

But a scant few minutes later, even Horton had to accept the evidence of his eyes. At fifteen percent power, the beam cleared the center of the grid all the way to the last rank. The remainder of the cells were still unaffected.

'Change the mix, now – minus one,' he called. That would reduce the output of the A unit by one percent, while increasing the output of the B a corresponding amount.

The 'beam' swung to the left, taking out most of two files in the back half of the grid.

'Minus two.'

More cells on the left side erupted in smoke, clearing the grid to the edge. The audience had begun to thin by then, the cold driving people inside.

'Plus two.'

The right rear quarter of the grid erupted as the Trigger beam swept across it.

'Boss, I think with a little practice, I could write my name with this thing,' said Lee. 'But I'm going to start building a better controller first thing tomorrow.'

Horton stared out at the floodlit test range. The initial euphoria of accomplishment had already faded, replaced by a vague but growing apprehension and the accumulated fatigue of a long day and a longer chase.

'That's enough for now. Shut it down, Lee. Send everyone to bed, with my thanks,' he said. 'Val, put out the word – department heads will meet in Conference C at eleven to review the test data.'

'Are you going to call the Director now?' Thayer asked.

Horton nodded. 'He'd expect me to.' He drew a deep breath of cold air and released it as a sigh. 'See you at eleven.'

'Boss –'

Her voice stopped him in the middle of turning away. 'Hmm?'

'This was a good catch. Congratulations.'

Horton waved a hand dismissively. 'It was just luck. If you hadn't dragged me away to Vegas –'

'Newton and the apple. Archimedes and the bath. Luck favors the prepared mind.' She smiled. 'But maybe it favors the relaxed one, too. So I'll take a little of the credit when you talk to the Director.'

'At least there won't be any trouble about the bill,' Horton said, then laughed. 'I charged everything to the firm, right down to Ruby's tip.'

18: Equity

Pontiac, Michigan — Eleven-year-old convicted murderer Austin Williams heard himself described as both a 'sociopath' and a 'regular kid' as the sentencing phase of his trial began Monday. The four-foot-six-inch fourth-grader faces a potential life sentence without parole for the shooting deaths of his mother, Bernice Fortune, and two teenaged neighbors last October. Williams' aunt, Helen Battrick, pleaded for leniency, saying that the youth 'just thought he was playing a game' when he used his mother's semiautomatic pistol to fire at students disembarking from a school bus in front of his house.
Complete story   Court transcripts
Young Perps Trial For Police, Jurors, Parents

Karl Brohier did not mind being awakened early. He welcomed the news of the breakthrough, and was eager to see the data for himself. He returned to the Annex in time for breakfast the next morning.

By then, there was more news. It came out of a long afternoon devoted to a low-tech but effective method of mapping the reach of the double-barreled Trigger. 'Dowelsing,' Thayer called it, and Horton thought the appellation an apt one. The mapping exercise involved scattering as many warm bodies as could be dragooned into helping around the periphery of the test range. Each volunteer had a short dowel with a piece of puff-cap material wedged into a slit in one end.

The dipole Trigger was activated at a given mix and amplitude, and the 'dowelsers' started walking toward the test pedestal, holding the dowel out in front of them. As each staffer's test strip started smoking, they stopped walking. Eventually, they formed a human map of the boundary of the field in that configuration. A photo was taken, the Trigger shut down, the dowels reloaded, the Trigger reset, and the process repeated. Over the course of the afternoon, a complete picture of the capabilities of 'The Twins' emerged.

The hot zone ranged in size from five to eight meters, depending on the angle of deflection. That angle was limited to about nine degrees in either direction – past that point, and the interference between the units seemed to collapse, and The Twins acted like a standard monopole Mark I.

They also discovered a second hot zone, one hundred eighty degrees removed from the one over the test range. 'Someone compared the dipole to a bazooka that fires in both directions at once,' Horton explained to Brohier over Belgian waffles and strawberries. 'You have to be real careful where you point it – which I think will limit its usefulness.'

'Not appreciably. Point it up,' Brohier said at once. 'Put it in an underground turret, twenty meters down, and you can forget about the hot zone behind you. Or put it in a plane and point it down. They'll find ways, Jeffrey. Be sure of that. Have you determined the range yet?'

'No,' Horton said. 'But it's going to be a big jump over a Mark I.'

'Let's see if we can't get at least an approximation by the end of the day.'

'If we do, we probably won't get anything *else* done today.'

'I'm not sure there's anything more important. I want those numbers, and the Joint Chiefs want every bit of improved performance that we can give them.'

'How long do you think we can hold back before we give them anything?'

Brohier looked at Horton with surprise. 'I had assumed that you'd *already* reported. Why do you want to hold this back?'

'To give the rest of the world some time to start catching up,' Horton said, confounded by Brohier's surprise. 'Even with the plans, it's going to take months for anyone else to start producing Triggers.'

'I see. You're talking about our friend – the insurance policy.'

'Of course I am. Karl, I thought we'd already settled this. With this Mark II, the Pentagon gets the best of both worlds. They can keep the weapons they have, and take everyone else's away. Which is why *I* assumed that you'd already given our friend the go-ahead.'

'What? No – oh, no. I really don't think that's necessary,' Brohier said. 'Look at the progress they're making on demining – tremendous progress, in just weeks, with only a handful of units out there, and more coming all the time. I don't think we're going to need that disaster insurance, Jeffrey. I think we're right where we hoped we'd be.'

'Then you and I must have been hoping for different things,' Horton said. 'I wasn't planning on giving the government a way of taking everyone else's guns and keeping their own.'

'Jeffrey, what do we gain if we disarm the police, the armed forces – handcuff the President – chaos, son, nothing but chaos. This needs to be handled carefully – deliberately. It needs to be coordinated – orderly –'

'All under one roof.'

'Exactly. I trust Mark Breland,' Brohier said. 'I trust Roland Stepak. They're good men, Jeffrey. They want what we want.'

'What about Grover Wilman?'

Brohier shrugged with his hands. 'He's an extremist – an ideologue. What he wants is unrealistic. Global disarmament would just mean chaos – kindergarten without a teacher.'

'Someone needs to be able to enforce order.'

'Yes. Because human beings want that. We need limits. We respond to authority. Humane discipline –'

'And if one kid is hurting another kid with a toy –'

'You take the toy away. You do understand, then.'

'Not in the least,' said Horton. 'I didn't hear any of this before you went to Washington with Aron. I didn't hear anything like this when you came out here and told me about your contingency plans.'

'That was a mistake on my part. But it'll be corrected.'

'"Corrected"? Who's been talking to you, Karl? Whose words are these?'

'Now, Jeffrey –'

'You say you trust Breland and Stepak – fine. What if, in two years from now, it's another Nixon and Haldeman instead? Or one of the rabid dogs from the Hill? Do you really think it can't happen here? We weren't supposed to rig the game for our side, Karl – we were supposed to referee it. Same rules for everyone, remember? What happened?'

'I've been made aware of – certain issues we overlooked in our enthusiasm.'

'What do you mean?'

'The kinds of enemies we face. The real evil that threatens us. People you've never heard of. Stories that don't make the newswires.' Grimacing, he shook his head. 'Things I wish I didn't know.'

'Made aware by whom?'

'I had visitors in Princeton. General Stepak came up to talk to me, along with a colonel from Army Research.'

'Why did he do that?'

'I – they were interested in my progress. And Stepak wanted to introduce me to Colonel Weiss, because he'd just assigned him as a liaison to the project.'

'They didn't say anything about security?'

'Well – the General did ask for some reassurance about how much I was sharing with my peers at the Institute.'

'Because they've been worried about Wilman. They probably figured that they could get you to think you were doing the right thing by telling them what you knew about his intentions.'

'Now, I'm certain they have better sources of information on the Senator and his activities than me,' Brohier demurred.

'But you *did* talk about him.'

Brohier was beginning to lose his equanimity, and his tone became defensive. 'It ended up being rather a long conversation. We went through two pots of coffee.'

'Come on, Karl – think it through. They wondered about the research archive. They wanted to know how many there really were, who had them. Am I right?'

'No – no. The colonel gave me a number I could use if I discovered a breach of security,' Brohier said slowly. 'It was an afterthought – they were ready to leave –'

'Until you told them Wilman has one. You did, didn't you? That was your "correction".'

'If you had heard what I heard –'

'Did they ask about Gordie?'

'No,' Brohier said. 'God help me, Jeffrey, I told them about him on my own.'

Horton slammed the table sharply with his open hand, startling diners at several other tables. For a painfully long moment, his anger would not allow him to even look at Brohier.

'Jeffrey – you have to understand –'

'Don't ask me for that now,' Horton said curtly. 'When was this "conversation"?'

'Perhaps a week ago – let me see, it was a Tuesday –'

'Son of a bitch.' Horton rubbed his eyes vigorously, then threw back his chair and stood up.

'Where are you going?'

'Maybe they haven't grabbed him yet. Maybe they're holding off until they're sure they can grab every copy of the archive at the same time.'

'You're going to contact him?'

'I'm going to try. If you have a problem with that, I guess you'd better call Colonel Weiss and turn me in, too.'

'No – no. Go. Do it now. Jeffrey, I'm sorry –'

The older man's distress was so naked and palpable that Horton's hard feelings toward him unexpectedly softened. 'They've studied us pretty well, it seems,' Horton said gruffly. 'I guess I'm about to find out just how well.'

Neither Jeffrey Horton's personal data carrier nor the Annex's corporate carrier would complete a call to Gordon Greene's number. The former reported that Greene was off net, and volunteered to forward a voicemail message when he reactivated his service. The latter reported that Greene's number was not a valid account.

Horton did not believe either story, and tried two *à la carte* gypsy carriers – and heard two other variations. One baldly pretended to *be* Greene's answering machine, though the voice wasn't even close.

The other – the Libertarian-owned ComFree – straightforwardly advised Horton that 'a state or Federal law-enforcement agency has issued an Article 209 block-and-trace order for this subscriber's account.' Horton vaguely remembered that Article 209 had been added to FCC rules as a tool for rooting out digital pornography. 'We at ComFree believe that Article 209 is unconstitutional. We object to this oppressive intrusion on free and private communication, and urge you to add your voice to the Free Speech campaign. To download an intelligent mailing list, press the *Yes* key –'

'I guess you won't need to give 'em my name after all, Karl,' Horton muttered to himself as he broke the connection.

There was one other option, though it did not offer Horton the certainty of knowing that he had been successful. Anticipating the possibility of being cut off, Greene had provided Brohier with a short list of aliases, a code phrase, a verification key, and a short primer on sending anonymous mail.

'If I have to vanish myself, these are the accounts I'll be checking – all international, so they should be untouchable.'

It did not take long to get the messages ready to go – Horton had set up a secure file in his personal communicator the same night Brohier had given him the information. But when the moment came, Horton hesitated. If Gordie was already in custody, if Army Intelligence had already gone through his files and records, all Horton would be doing by sending the activation was implicating himself. Trying to call Greene was a completely innocent act. Issuing him marching orders, however –

'The hell with it,' Horton said aloud, pressing a key. 'Come on and arrest me. It's my patent, goddammit – and I'll give it away if I want to.'

The isolation of Dr Gordon Greene from his net resources was nearly complete at the moment Horton sent his alert. Three of Greene's five alias accounts had been discovered through a search of payment records, and a fourth had been found through a National Security Agency penetration of a poorly-protected server in Santiago. Every outgoing message was being monitored; every incoming message was being filtered or spoofed in real time by an NSA traffic simulator.

Greene was aware of none of this, any more than he was aware that he was also being watched from the apartment above and followed when he left the complex.

For the moment, he still had his freedom, and his weekly routine took him all over the city. Regular stops included the Ohio State University library with its digital stacks and netlinked carrels and a by-the-hour virtual teleconferencing service whose private booths attracted the business of clients who appreciated the discreet billing. He was also a familiar sight at more than a dozen other well-connected but less reputable enterprises. They ranged from an Undernet nightclub with wide-open links to uncensored offshore shock sites to a CD-publishing kiosk in Worthington that was agreeably casual about the copyright status of the data it was burning.

All of those could be explained either by Greene's lifestyle or the contract consultancy work he had been doing since leaving Terabyte. But each of them also gave him an opportunity to poll his aliases via a third-party account, an opportunity he made sure to avail himself of once a day.

Gordon picked up the message from Jeffrey Horton at a coffee-and-crullers franchise cafe called Hot Bytes, where every tabletop had a large supertwist LCD built into it – an old technology, but one that made it difficult for anyone to read over your shoulder as you sipped and surfed. He did not know who had actually sent the message, or that it was the sole survivor of five that had started the journey together.

But the names it bore – names he himself had chosen – foreshadowed its contents. The sender's name was Pandora. And it was addressed to one Michael Armstrong – the name of a character in an ancient spy movie, that of an American physicist who was both a defector and a double agent.

The body of the message consisted of two words, both the title of that film and an assessment of where things stood.

It read, *Torn Curtain*.

It meant, *Publish the archive without delay*.

His face offering no hint of the turmoil in his gut, Greene did so without hesitation or wasted motion. Linking his personal communicator to the cafe's open ports, he used the Armstrong account to activate his failsafes and rogue publishing agents. When some of the expected acknowledgements did not appear, he weighed his options, then re-sent the activation commands through another alias account. Insurance, Greene thought, though he knew the price for it might be high.

Then he headed toward home, which was barely ten minutes away, to collect an already-packed bag and then vanish from Columbus.

It was a mistake, though he realized that too late. He should have left without the bag, or taken it on his errands with him, and to hell with appearances. But he did not, and they were waiting for him. He was intercepted on the sidewalk outside his apartment by four men in civilian clothes but with Army Intelligence identification cards. Moments later an olive-drab van pulled up at the curb beside them.

Greene did not try to flee or resist – there was no point. All of his personal ambitions, already barely sustained against his pessimism, had vanished the moment he received Pandora's message. He asked but one question as they took him into custody – 'How did I do?'

'Not so good,' one of the intelligence officers said with cheerful arrogance.

After that, Greene had nothing to say. There was no point in arguing with the drones. If and when he found himself face to face with their masters, then he would speak his mind.

In the back of a black limousine headed uptown to the United Nations, President Mark Breland asked much the same question of General Stepak. But Breland received a more thorough – and honest – answer.

'Eleven minutes and change from the time Greene issues his marching orders to the time our counterattack begins. In that eleven minutes, he managed to spawn more than six thousand copies of the archive – pretty good work, given the size of it. He apparently thought ahead and found big pipes and fast pumps. The distribution was scattershot – e-mail, preprint servers, news servers, FTP. A little of everything.'

'How many of the six thousand have been purged?'

Stepak glanced down at the screen of his communicator. 'Not quite all of them,' he said. 'Cancels took out all the public ones, and the NSA is sitting hard on the afterchatter – there won't be any

"Please repost" and "What happened to –" messages. But they're still working on a few dozen hard-to-reach traceables – I think all of the copies still outstanding went to dial-up mail accounts, most of them offshore.' He saw Breland's frown, and added, 'The rest of the world doesn't live online quite as much as this country does. An inconvenience.'

'So the NSA has to wait for the next time those people connect to make a try at burning that file.'

'Yes. And we really should make a personal visit to each of them to make sure those copies don't have copies. That'll take a National Security Directive from your desk.'

'Draw it up,' Breland said. 'Is that the extent of the damage?'

'No. There were about thirty hits on the preprint server at *Physics Today* before we closed it down –'

'Thirty? In eleven minutes? Is it always that hot a site?'

'No. It looks like Greene passed the word in advance to some friends that they should keep an eye on that server. He may have done the same with all of the public copies.' He shook his head. 'Mr President, the section chief is telling me that even when they get finished going through the transaction logs of every machine along the line, they can't guarantee that there aren't thousands of private copies, off net, out of reach.'

'How is that possible?'

Stepak shrugged. 'The information-wants-to-be-free generation hasn't quite died off yet. Some anonymous servers really are – they throw away the transaction data. Greene used several of them. But the section chief promises me that they can keep this thing from moving over the net from now on – proactive is more efficient than reactive.'

Breland reached for his glass. 'Of course, the longer we do that, the more obvious it'll be that we're doing it – people are going to notice that their messages don't show up, that their mail doesn't get through.'

'Yes,' Stepak admitted. 'And anything we try to do about *that* just makes it all snowball even faster. Besides which, it can still move hand-to-hand, and we won't see that at all.'

'Perils of a free society,' Breland said. 'All we can do is what we can do. Let's make sure everyone remembers where the line is, and which side of it we work on. Send the section chief a copy of the Bill of Rights.'

'Mr President, this is an extremely serious situation –'

'General, I hope you don't expect me to start locking people up over this.'

'Not even Dr Greene?'

'What does it accomplish?'

'If we make an example of him, we might not need to detain very many others. A knock at the door – two FBI agents explain that certain classified material has been stolen and placed on the net in a virus by a man now under arrest, facing serious charges – and would they cooperate by allowing our technician to search their computers for this virus –'

'You're talking about knocking on tens of thousands of doors. Do we have the manpower? Is it even worth the effort?'

'I think I can give you a reason why it is. The archive Greene put out isn't the same as the original we got from Brohier.'

'What do you mean? How was it different?'

The distinctive architecture of the United Nations was now visible ahead of the limousine. Somewhere inside it, the Secretary General was preparing to present Breland with a humanitarian award for his spectacularly successful demining campaign.

'Greene's been adding to it. More than three hundred pages of ideas about how to modify the Mark I design – what to do to make it more powerful, more efficient, more compact,' Stepak said, his voice conveying his alarm. 'He's provided complete CADCAM drawings for a medium-power unit that would fit in the trunk of this car. He talks about avenues of research that he thinks might lead to a suitcase-sized mass-production version. All of this could be extremely destabilizing.'

'It probably will be, General. And sooner rather than later. The veil is getting a bit tattered. We're going to have to go public soon. I think it's time to start deciding how we want to handle that.'

'And in the meantime –'

'Let the NSA pull as many weeds as it can.' He sighed. 'Is there solid law to support Greene's detention?'

'The Espionage Act of 1917 is still in force, and clearly pertains.'

'How long can you hold him without charging him?'

'Ah – I'll have to confirm this with the Attorney General, but I believe it's thirty days. Why does it matter, sir? There's more than enough evidence to not only indict, but convict.'

'I'm not going to let someone face the death penalty for trying to reveal a secret that I'm going to turn around and reveal myself a few weeks later. That's an awfully high price for simply beating me to the punch,' Breland said as the limousine turned into the UN's west entrance.

'But, Mr President –'

'Besides,' Breland went on, 'from the sound of it, what we really want is to have this man back on the team, working for us. So here it is, General – the FBI has thirty days to use Greene as a stick to beat the bushes – what will that be, March 19? I'll schedule an address to Congress for that morning – and that afternoon, Greene goes free. Tell him that, and see that he's treated civilly in the interim. No, don't argue with me about this – just see it done.'

'Yes, sir. What do you want to do about the Terabyte people?'

'I'll take care of it when we're done here.'

'They have to be involved,' Stepak said. 'Brohier was vague to the point of deception about how Greene got his copy of the project archive, and Horton sent Greene a coded warning that apparently precipitated the release. It's clearly a conspiracy to commit treason.'

'You'd like to see all three of them charged.'

Stepak nodded. 'Absolutely. Sir, it doesn't matter if what a traitor gives the enemy is something the enemy could have eventually gotten on his own. They should be removed from the project at once and put away where they can't do any further damage.'

The limousine eased to a stop at the curb, and Breland raised a hand to prevent the Secret Service agent on the sidewalk from opening the door. 'That isn't going to happen, General. Let me be absolutely clear about this – the Trigger is no longer a secret. We will deal with that reality. I never intended for it to be a secret forever.'

'But allowing these people to give it away willy-nilly –'

'Try to understand: I don't need, we don't want, and you can't sustain a technological hegemony. It's completely proper for us

259

to share what we know. It's *necessary*, if the Trigger is to fulfill its potential. And there's precedent. You may not be aware – I wasn't, before some recent reading – that our government went public with a detailed report on atomic weapons just days after the Japanese surrender.'

'The situations are hardly analogous, Mr President.'

'No, they aren't,' Breland agreed. 'The Trigger is a defensive weapon that only threatens armed attackers. General, the interests of our people and the world's peoples are best served by allowing the Trigger's proliferation – not by seeking its suppression. It's inhumane and immoral to continue to withhold it.'

'As an ideal, in an ideal world, yes, but we have to be practical –'

'Now, General – we've had nearly a year to try to make certain that we're not surprised by this nor placed at a disadvantage. How many people who might have been saved were sacrificed as the price of our caution? It's not only that we can't help Chechnya protect itself against Russia, or India against Kashmir – keeping this a secret means we can't do half of what's possible to protect our own people.

'So who are we serving by holding back? Obviously, ourselves. Our jobs, our reputations, our attachment to our ability to project force anywhere at any time.' Breland shook his head. 'General, the fact is, I feel like a fraud, coming here today to accept their praise, knowing that what we've done is only the hundredth part of what we could have done. Have you read Gil Elliot – *The Twentieth Century Book of the Dead*? A hundred and ten million killed by the machinery and the privations of war. We can do better. We *will* do better, if I have any say in it.'

'I understand, Mr President.'

'I sincerely hope so, General.' He signaled, and the limousine's door was opened from outside. Before he climbed out, he leaned closer to Stepak and added, 'Because if men like you aren't ready for the twenty-first century, it may not get here until the twenty-second.'

There were no happy faces among the quartet squeezed into the paint trailer. Brohier looked positively dyspeptic; Horton still wore hard lines of anger around his mouth. Thayer's features conveyed a far-away sadness, while Val Bowden's face had not yet lost the wide-eyed pole-axed surprise that had settled there as he learned the unsuspected secrets of his employment.

It had not been a long argument, but it had been a draining one all the same. Horton had spoken first, and set out his unwavering position: 'We can't give the government the Mark II – not today, not ever. We have to tear down the test unit and destroy every record of yesterday's tests – and quickly. If we don't move fast enough, we'll lose the opportunity. And anyone and everyone who knows enough about the operating principle of the Two to recreate it – most especially the four of us – has to swear to whatever god they fear most that they'll never hand it over to these people.'

To his surprise, it was Lee who had opposed him most strongly. 'There are too many people on site who know pieces of the puzzle – there were five hundred witnesses the other night,' she had said. 'What we should be doing instead is backing up Gordie. The Annex must have a thousand different links to the outside. We should use them while we have them, and keep using them until we're completely frozen out. We need more weight, not more secrets – we need Senator Wilman on the late news, and Dr Brohier on the early news.'

But no one else thought they could mount such a campaign quickly enough to make a difference. Horton eventually won over Thayer with the indisputable fact that his plan required none of the outside cooperation that hers did.

'We can see this through on our own,' he said. 'It's all right here on our turf, within our reach.' When he added a promise that her proposal would be his second priority, she acquiesced.

But when they emerged from the trailer, they were hailed almost immediately. 'Dr Brohier! Dr Horton! Stay right there, please.' It was The Tailor, one of the signal shack's out-of-uniform Army officers, running across the Annex's west lot toward them. 'Call off the hounds, Lieutenant – I've found them all,' he said into a collar mic as he closed with them.

'What's all the excitement, son?' Brohier asked, stepping forward to meet him.

'We've been paging you and looking everywhere for you for the better part of an hour, sir,' said The Tailor, panting and perspiring freely. 'You have a call, at the signal shack.'

'Who does?'

He pointed at three of them in turn. 'Dr Brohier, Dr Horton, and Dr Thayer. Sorry, Dr Bowman – the President didn't mention you.'

'The President?' asked Horton.

'Yes, sir. He's been holding while we look for you. If I could ask you to come quickly –'

The glances that the quartet exchanged among themselves ranged from skeptical to apprehensive. 'Pass the word that we'll be right along,' Brohier said, manufacturing a polite smile. 'All four of us.'

Four was more of a crowd in the booth than it had been in the paint trailer, and the back row was still jockeying for a comfortable position when the signal unscrambled and Mark Breland appeared in front of them, seated at his Oval Office desk.

'Good afternoon, Doctors –'

Before Breland could complete the greeting, Brohier interrupted him. 'Where is Dr Greene? Is he in Federal custody?'

Breland blinked in surprise, then laughed lightly and shook his head. 'Very well,' he said. 'First things first.' He looked up, past the camera, and said, 'Doctor?' before vacating his chair.

A few moments later, Gordon Greene sat down in his place.

He was wearing his familiar bemused grin, and looking off to the right. 'Say – what's the going rate for a chance to plant cheek behind the big desk? Five-thousand-dollar donation to the party?' Then he looked into the camera lens. 'Would somebody please screen-capture this? My parents will want to hang it on the dining-room wall.' He looked off to the right again. 'Can I get the Prez in this shot?'

In the distance, Breland laughed.

Lee fought through her surprise first. 'Gordie, are you all right?'

'I'm fine now,' he said. 'Missed you.'

'What are you doing there?'

Greene sent an inquiring glance off to the right, and they heard Breland's voice answer it. 'Go ahead – tell them.'

'Okay,' he said. 'Consulting. Going to want to get you in on it, too. The Trigger goes public in a month, and the folks here seem pretty serious about wanting to show it off properly.' He leaned back in the big chair, hands folded over his abdomen. 'I think everything's going to be all right, gang. Even if I can't quite believe I said that.'

19: Guaranty

Bonn, Germany – Investigators are still searching for
explanations in the wake of Tuesday's suicide bombing
aboard a Berlin-Bonn high-speed monorail train. Chilling
security camera images showed a young man in a business
suit shouting hate slogans to the half-filled carriage moments
before the blast, which killed twenty-two commuters and
destroyed a thirty-meter section of the southbound track. 'This
is not supposed to happen here,' said a DeutschRail official.
Complete Story   *Casualty List*   *Blast Video*
Getting There: Trains Rolling, But Schedule Cut

Given that the well-connected could choose among more than
a thousand licensed feeds of round-the-clock news, commerce
and entertainment, plus a cornucopia of nearly 60,000 unregu-
lated Undernet channels, it was a challenge for anyone, even the
President of the United States, to get the simultaneous attention
of more than a few percent of the populace.

To be sure, not everyone who could call themselves American
qualified as 'well-connected'.

A few percent simply did not care to be. Some of that number
actively campaigned against what they called 'netmind', which
Pull The Plug founder Michael Adamson defined as 'that state
of electrode-in-the-monkey-brain masturbatory overstimulation
which elevates amusement over all else – in particular, ambition
and achievement.' But most of the dissenters simply withdrew to
one of the small wireless villages of the Welcomer movement.
There, only analogue communications technology was allowed –
and that principally to maintain contact between the scattered villages, and to see that Earth continued broadcasting to the stars.

For one family in seven, the elementary net services included

264

with a basic household telecommunications account were either all they could afford or all they cared to master. News 1, News 2, Talk 1, Talk 2, Arts 1, FedFacts, NetSearch, NetTeach, NetAgent, and MultiMail put the basic elements of interactivity in the living rooms of the two flavors of underclass that had resisted eradication – one economic, the other intellectual. Ironically, it was the very paucity of their options which made these people the easiest to reach. They were the principal receivers of cablecasting, passive sponges for the advertiser-supported feeds.

But premium connectivity was an investment middle class families budgeted for, upper class families took for granted, and every model of enlightened education depended on. Net literacy made them participants rather than spectators, and opened the doors of digital and virtual libraries around the globe. It also fragmented the audience into a billion pieces, leaving very few of them passively taking an unfiltered feed in real time.

No media event of the new millennium had yet commanded as much as a fifty percent share of the connected audience. The last event to attract even a ten percent share of the online audience was the World Cup final between Scotland and the United States, three years ago – a thirty share, the Santa Rosa earthquake that dropped the north span of the Golden Gate eight years earlier.

Even knowing the difficulties, Mark Breland wanted better than that for his address to the nation, and he pressed his staff hard to make it happen.

'This is something people should hear first-hand, unedited – families listening together, the whole sports bar watching, every screen in the electronics emporium carrying the same feed. Like Roosevelt's fireside chats and the landing on the moon,' Breland said. 'I want a chance to talk to everyone directly, so they first hear about this from my lips, and not from some predigested and regurgitated second-hand abstract.'

'You can't change people's habits,' Chief of Staff Richard Nolby said dismissively. 'People won't put their lives on hold to sit and watch a talking head. Even a three-dimensional talking head in a virtual one-on-one. As soon as they try to ask a question, they'll know it's a lecture, not a conversation. No, I think we'll be doing well to get a fourteen share – getting the four top entertainment licensees to agree to carry the speech was a breakthrough. And I think we can still get Financial Newswire and WorldMarket to window your speech on the ticker feed, which would push us up over sixteen.'

'It's not enough,' Breland said.

'Our saturation advertising doesn't start for another hour, and will build right up to the opening gavel,' said Aimee Rochet, the director of public relations. 'I still think we have a chance at twenty. And the post-event propagation will be very extensive – I'm modeling it with the Accelerated algorithms, which means seventy percent event awareness within three days.'

'I want seventy percent by the closing gavel,' said Breland. 'By tomorrow, I'm going to be either a hero or a villain to millions of people who haven't given me a second thought since the election. I want a chance to win over as many of them as possible – I want them to remember where they were when they heard about this. It has to be the number one topic of conversation in bedrooms and chat rooms overnight and on the trains in the morning.'

'You're asking for mass media numbers, and there are no mass media anymore,' protested Rochet. 'It's all narrow casting and interactivity.'

'Don't the licensees have any contractual obligations in the area of civic service? Isn't there any way to *make* them carry the speech?'

'There's the Emergency Broadcast System,' said General Stepak. 'It's never been used to stream real-time multimedia on that scale, though – test announcements are text and audio only. If we flag this for EBS, we might end up choking everything off.'

'*That* would be a disaster,' Rochet said quickly. 'Zero share watching, one hundred share annoyed.'

'Can you do a small-scale test this afternoon?' Breland asked, looking at Tettlebaum, the science advisor.

Tettlebaum was momentarily startled to find a question directed at him. 'We could, Mr President. But a small-scale test won't tell us anything. The scale *is* the potential for trouble.'

Breland grunted his dissatisfaction and turned back to the others. 'Other than this unmeasurable possibility, where's the downside of invoking the EBS? Why haven't we talked about this before?'

'Even a successful EBS broadcast will annoy millions,' said Rochet. 'The Undernet community hates having its servers frozen for any reason at any time. They barely tolerate thirty-second tests – a twenty-minute speech will have them organizing for impeachment, if not revolution.'

'Forty-five minutes,' Breland corrected. 'Maybe a little more.'

Rochet winced. 'Are you serious, sir?'

'Why shouldn't I be?'

'Why – Mr President, I can promise you fourteen, maybe sixteen, at the opening. But if you run on for forty-five minutes, you'll be lucky to hold a five share through to the end. And you will *not* get the kind of next-day numbers you want. Moreover, if you start in the negative, you will *never* turn it back to the positive. That's just expecting too much from people.'

'On the contrary – I don't think you expect enough from them,' Breland answered. 'I also don't think you understand the stakes – and I accept responsibility for that. You're planning to watch tonight?'

'Of course, Mr President.'

'Good. Someone tell me this: do we pay licensees for their loss of revenue when they carry the State of the Union address?'

'No. Which is why you can't get anyone with an entertainment license to carry it,' said Rochet.

'Are we paying Dreamworks and Sony-Fox and Alliance to carry me tonight?'

'Yes, sir.'

'Then let's pay them all,' Breland said. 'Notify the licensees that we'll be invoking the EBS for one hour beginning at nine-thirty tonight. Advise them that if they keep their systems up and the feed uninterrupted, we'll reimburse them their usual revenues – plus a twenty percent bonus – for technical services. The channels that already agreed get a fifty percent bonus.'

'Are we dropping the ad campaign, then?' Rochet asked.

'Absolutely not. All the EBS can do is put me on their screens. You still need to put them in the seats,' said Breland. 'As for the Undernet, start getting the word out now that we're going to need their bandwidth for a while this evening. A properly worded advance warning should mute at least some of the indignation.

And we need to be sure to invite them to come over to the other side – we can drop some heavy-handed hints about the Trigger and the Greene letter without naming either.'

The director of public relations was looking nonplussed. Breland had always been a difficult client, but even he rarely rejected her advice this completely. 'Sir – meaning no disrespect, but are you sure that this address can carry the weight of the expectations you're trying to create?' she asked. 'Wouldn't it be better to go at this a little more slowly, target the most sympathetic audiences first, and then use them to pull the bandwagon down Main Street?'

Breland had written his address himself, and Rochet was not among the very few who had seen even part of it. But if she was trying to win herself a preview, she failed miserably.

'You don't need to concern yourself with that,' said the President. 'Making the pitch is my job. You deliver their eyes and ears. It's up to me to deliver their hearts and minds.' He smiled and shrugged with a studied nonchalance. 'And if I can't, maybe I don't belong here. Now, get to it – you have just about twelve hours left before we start finding out.'

Mark Breland had debated with himself for days, trying to decide on the best setting for his announcement. Should it be an address to Congress from the podium of the Senate chamber, with the pomp and formal setting of a joint session? That added the unpredictability of a live audience – 539 men and women who owed him little, and from whom he would be asking much.

Should it be from the Oval Office, which evoked just as much authority but closed the distance to the width of the big desk? Some of his predecessors had used that illusion of intimacy to their advantage, but others had lost stature in trying, making themselves seem ordinary – or, worse, petty and pathetic.

There were other options, of course. Breland considered several seriously, including originating the 'cast from a hospital emergency room, the front steps of a police station, the streets of the District of Columbia, a firing range at Fort Knox, a studio with a small 'town hall' audience, and a schoolroom full of children. On Nolby's prompting, Technical Services offered to give the address the full film-school FX treatment, dropping Breland into as many digital landscapes as he needed to make his points.

In the end, he settled on the Senate chamber – in part because it was the most High Church of all his options, but primarily because he knew that the likelihood was that his toughest audience would be right there in the room with him. But standing behind that high podium and looking out at their faces as the obligatory applause faded and they settled into their seats, he wondered if he had made the right choice.

Speak through the camera, don't make a speech at it –

'"We hold these truths to be self-evident – that all men are endowed by their Creator with certain inalienable rights, among them life, liberty, and the pursuit of happiness."

'You all recognize the words. These are the ideals of the American experiment, the ideals of the Founders of this nation, the promises that America has always held out to its citizens and to the world – life, liberty, and the pursuit of happiness.

'But none of those ideals can be met, none of those promises can be kept, if we do not have the essential prerequisite of security.

'This is why one of the great common themes of human life everywhere is the hunger for security. This hunger is expressed in many aspects of our lives – we pursue the security of our nation, the security of our homes, the security of our children, security in our jobs, security in our relationships.

'Each of us may define this blessing differently. Some of us may need more of it, and others less. But rare is the human being who has deliberately arranged his life so as to refuse it completely.

'Because if we do not have that security, we live in fear. We fear for ourselves, and for those we love. We fear loss, and suffering, and death.

'But what we call security is not just the absence of fear – it's the antidote to fear. It's the confidence that allows us to set aside our darkest thoughts and embrace our brightest hopes. It's the prospect of a tomorrow worth looking forward to. It's the key that opens the door to the endless possibilities of our lives. It guarantees nothing – but it allows for everything that matters.

'There can be no "good life" unless we satisfy this first and most primal need – to know that, at least in that moment, we are safe. All of the best things we humans are capable of – music, art, literature, athletic achievement, philosophy, invention, charity – take place in the sheltered spaces we create.

'We are in such sheltered spaces at this very moment. None of us would be here in the Senate if we felt threatened by being here. None of you would be watching if a stranger was rattling your front door, or there was the smell of natural gas in the room.

'But our sense of security is a subjective state of mind. It is less a matter of *being* safe than of *feeling* safe. We feel secure here, but there *could* be a terrorist bomb secreted under someone's seat, its timer ticking away. You feel secure where you are, but there *could* be someone skulking outside, figuring out how best to get at you.

'The interesting thing is the way that even just saying such things alters our perceptions for a moment. Did you think about reaching under your seat, or listen for the ticking? Did you think about going to make sure the front door's locked, or draw a deep breath to sniff the air?

'I'm sure that many of you did. We react to the mere mention of a possible threat as if it were a threat. We reevaluate our security constantly, just as we do when driving in heavy traffic on the freeway. We try to stay within a personal comfort zone – not too fast, not too slow, not too close. In like fashion, we try to live in a personal comfort zone.

'But consider this – if you stood up right now and went outside to the street, picked a direction at random and started walking – alone, and dressed just as you are now – how many blocks would you have to go before you began to lose that sense of security, before you began to feel anxious, uncomfortable, afraid? Do we know what's out there? Do we know if we're in danger? Uncertainty is the enemy of security.

'Two tragic miscalculations are possible. One is to believe your-self in danger when you are safe. The other is to believe yourself safe when you are in danger.

'As a nation, we are haunted by both.

'More than any other people at any other time, we Americans have tried to find security through the gun. Our guns make us feel powerful. They make us feel safe. Or do they?'

There was a small stir at the right side of the chamber as a door opened and a man entered. The stir grew quickly to commotion as more and more of the audience noticed the hunter orange vest he was wearing, and the carbine he was carrying in front of him. Angry shouts of protest and calls for the sergeant-at-arms could be heard as the man climbed the steps to the lower level of the dais and approached Breland.

One stride short of the podium, the gunman stopped and raised the carbine to his shoulder, pointing it directly at Breland's head. There was a collective gasp, and then an anxious hush settled over the chamber as the cameras locked on the bizarre tableau.

'It only takes one gun in this room to change the perceptions of all five hundred and forty of us,' Breland said. 'It only takes one gun to shatter our illusion of security. What you see before you is the equation of fear – the unarmed, helpless before the armed. And for all of our history, there has only been one way to balance that equation.'

Reaching behind his back, Breland found the military 9mm automatic tucked in a belt holster and drew it.

'What the hell!' someone exclaimed from the upper dais – it sounded like the Speaker of the House, Breland thought.

He raised his right arm and pointed the pistol at the gunman's face. The chamber erupted again in surprise and consternation.

'You can see the answer for yourself – the equation neatly balanced,' Breland said, raising his voice over the tumult. 'The only answer to a gun is another gun. We can build walls and lock doors, but a wall is only a way to hide, a lock only a way to delay. The only answer we have found to a gun is another gun. Mutually assured destruction, the same principle which we depended on through the Cold War – only on the smallest possible scale. Two men, two guns. Equilibrium. Security.'

They were all listening now, shaken out of their complacency and their comfortable habits of thought by his unconventional theatrics. 'But is this truly security?' he demanded, gesturing toward the weapons with his free hand. 'Do you feel as safe now as you did when you thought there were *no* guns in the room? I must tell you that I personally find this a more precarious peace –'

271

There was a scattering of uncomfortable laughter at that, which Breland accepted with a smile. 'It strikes me that there are many more things that can go wrong now, and with much graver consequences. It seems to me that my gun does not give me back what his gun takes from me.

'I will say that again – my gun does not give me back what his gun takes from me. At this moment, I am not as free as I was when neither of us was armed. I am not as safe as I was when neither of us was capable of killing with a twitch of the finger.

'Would I feel any better if I knew that ten, or fifty, or a hundred of you were also armed? Would that make this chamber a civil society again? Or would it only increase the number of threats I have to worry about, the chances of an accident, the prospect of a misunderstanding?' He scanned the front row for a familiar face. 'Senator Baines, when you were arguing the assisted suicide bill with Senator Kastin last month, do you think it would it have helped advance the dialogue if you'd both had automatic rifles handy?'

That brought hoots and wicked laughter, for the debate over the Loomis-Figer bill had been the most heated and acrimonious in many a year. Standing at his seat, Baines called out, 'I suspect it might have shortened it, Mr President.'

Not every broadcast microphone caught the comment, but they all caught the ensuing wave of laughter that broke the tension in the chamber. As it subsided, both the President and the orange-clad gunman lowered their weapons.

'The truth is, it's only when we have real security that we can enjoy true freedom of speech. If we fear being silenced by a gun, our freedom is compromised.

'It's only when we have real security that we can enjoy true freedom of assembly. If we fear being made a target by terrorists, our freedom is compromised.

'It's only when we have real security that we can devote our energies to bettering ourselves and building a future.

'Several months ago, news of a startling new invention was brought to me – an invention which gives us, for the first time, another answer to the gun raised against us. I have been obliged to consider whether we can be more secure – as a people, as a nation – if we put that invention to use.

'After long consultation with my Cabinet and my conscience, I have concluded that the answer is yes.'

He walked around the podium to the edge of the dais and laid his pistol down there. The gunman came forward, close on his heels, and laid the carbine down beside the pistol.

'Sergeant-at-arms, please take these away,' Breland said. As the sergeant-at-arms started forward uncertainly from the back of the chamber, Breland turned to the orange-jacketed man. 'Thank you for your assistance, Major Imhoff.'

Imhoff saluted smartly and left the dais. By then, the audience was buzzing with anticipation. Many of them had made the connection between his words and a month's rumors and denials. Breland could almost hear the whispers: *The Trigger – he's talking about the Trigger. The Greene letter* wasn't *a hoax –*

'That's better,' Breland said, reclaiming the podium and the floor as the sergeant-at-arms collected the weapons. 'I feel better without that gun in my hand – and without the other one pointed at me. Because I don't want to live that way. I can't imagine many of you do, either.

'I've come to realize that the security our guns give us isn't the genuine article. It's a deception – a shadow of the real thing. An armed society is not a polite society – it's a murderous, terrified society. Bosnia in the last century – Kashmir and Egypt in this. And America in both.

'The gun is the first choice of our fearful for self-protection. It's also the first choice of our criminal population for forcing their will on us.

'What choice does that leave the rest of us? We can become gunslingers ourselves – or refugees, fleeing from the streets, hiding in our homes, moving out of the war zones.

'But either way, we can still end up a casualty. And so many have – too many have.'

The enormous screen on the wall behind Breland had been displaying the Presidential seal. Now it changed to a digital map of the fifty-two states, white on a blue background, with the states outlined in black. Small red dots began to appear – seemingly at random, but for the fast-changing counter, its large numerals also red, which appeared below the peninsula of Florida at the same time.

'There is no solemn black marble Wall for the casualties of our uncivil war – their small memorials are scattered in city cemeteries and church graveyards from Atlantic to Pacific,' Breland said. 'But I wish there were such a memorial, because then I could forget all the statistics and simply point you to it, and ask you to walk it from one end to the other. By the time you were finished, you would understand why something must change.

'But the memorial itself would never be finished. It would quickly dwarf the Vietnam Memorial. In fact, we would need to add a section as big as the Vietnam Memorial every single year.

'And it has been going on that way for nearly a century – our own Hundred Years War.

'Even in the worst years of that terrible Vietnam conflict, the death toll in the jungles and rice paddies of Southeast Asia was less than half the death toll in the streets and homes of America. It took fifteen years of combat to put the names of some fifty-eight thousand veterans on The Wall. In those same fifteen years, America buried nearly half a million civilian casualties of our home-grown war – nine times as many.

'Even if we took the first day of the new millennium as the starting point for our Citizens Memorial, we would need a wall long enough to completely surround the Reflecting Pool – and the wall would have to be five meters high.'

Behind Breland, the counter was still running, the dots still appearing. There were ugly crimson blotches now over the locations of the largest cities, but even the least populous state had a scattering of red.

'Every year, our guns kill as many as AIDS did at its peak, more than our cars do, twice as many as alcohol does, four times as many as illegal drugs do.

'Last year, the death count was the third highest in our history: forty-six thousand, three hundred forty-one.'

Pausing, Breland turned to look up at the display as the last five thousand-odd victims were marked on the map. The chamber was

274

absolutely hushed. He would learn later that even the newsfeed commentators had observed a respectful silence.

'It would take three days just to read their names from this podium. It would take many months to tell you all their stories. But I can't allow them all to remain numbers, nameless, faceless.' He raised his hand, pointing a laser controller at a dot in southern Idaho. A digital zoom turned the dot into a photograph of an owlish-looking Caucasian man, with unruly blond hair and a broad grin.

'John Carpani, age thirty-two – an award-winning teacher of English and the drama club sponsor at Manning Central High,' Breland said, and clicked his controller. A second photograph opened, to scattered gasps and exclamations – this one showed Carpani lying face-down in a parking lot, his shirt stained with the blood that was puddled beneath him. 'John was shot twice by a sixteen-year-old student named Michael Pace, who had brought his father's shotgun to school to kill his former girlfriend.'

Another click, and a dot near Houston expanded into a photograph of a black-haired, round-cheeked Hispanic girl with a frozen gap-toothed smile. 'Juanita Ramirez, age five.' Another click, and they saw a small, still form huddled in the dirt in front of a wood-frame three-apartment bungalow. 'Juanita was struck by a stray police bullet when a high-speed chase – a carjacking – ended half a block away. She had been playing with her dolls in the yard, with her older brother watching from the porch.'

The next click was near Los Angeles, and introduced them to a bespectacled Asian teen named David Chen. 'David was an honors-track straight-A student at Point Reyes Preparatory Academy. One week after he gave the salutatorian address at his graduation, he tidied his room, took a .357 automatic from a locked cabinet in his mother's office, and committed suicide in the woods behind the family home.' The grisly police photo showed that half of Chen's head was gone. 'David left his father a note apologizing for disappointing him, and his mother a note apologizing for the mess.'

The final click revealed a middle-aged black woman named Julia Myers. 'Julia was on her way to a ReadiMart for milk and bread when someone stopped her, robbed her, and then shot her through the neck. It took her half an hour to bleed to death on the sidewalk, unable to call for help. Her three children still cannot understand why anyone would kill her for a twenty-dollar bill. That happened only ten blocks from the Capitol, just two weeks ago.'

Clicking Julia's photographs away, Breland turned back to face the chamber. 'I ask you to reflect again – how much security do we really have? An honest answer would be: not enough. Not enough by half.

'Could the old answer have saved these people? Would more guns have made their worlds safer? I don't believe so, though others may feel differently.

'But this I do believe, with all my heart – there are certain places that shouldn't have to be made into armed fortresses to be safe, certain places where guns are simply not welcome,' Breland said. 'Our schools, our churches, our streets, our public transportation, our courts and government offices, our homes, and, yes, even our legislatures – these should be sanctuaries.'

That brought the first genuine applause of the evening – and perhaps because they had been holding back, it grew into a standing ovation which lasted more than a minute.

'I will now confess to a small deception,' he said when they had satisfied themselves. 'I wasn't afraid when Major Imhoff had me in his sights – because I knew that his gun wasn't loaded. I knew that not because of his assurances, but because this building is protected by the invention of which I spoke – the LifeShield.

'If Major Imhoff had tried – by accident or design – to enter the Capitol grounds with a loaded weapon, he would have received a rude surprise. The ammunition in his weapon would have been violently destroyed the moment it made contact with the Life-Shield's protective field. His weapon would have been destroyed or rendered unusable in the process, and he would have been lucky if he had not been injured himself.

'The LifeShield gives us a means to disarm a threat without taking up arms ourselves. The LifeShield protecting the Capitol is but one of nearly five hundred which are already in use at government and military facilities around the world. The LifeShield is also the secret technology behind America's humanitarian campaign to rid the world of land mines and the unexploded munitions of the twentieth century's wars.

276

'That is only the beginning of what we can and will do with this miracle of science. But I want to say something first about what we *will* not do.

'We will not touch the Second Amendment. We will not take a single gun from any rightful owner. There will be no LifeShields in the woods – game hunters may continue to hunt as they always have. There will be no LifeShields in the gun clubs and on the ranges – sport shooters will continue to plink and pull to their heart's content. We will not come into your house and carry away the firearm in your nightstand – much as we might wish otherwise, the burden of personal defense remains with you.

'But we *will* do everything we can to make your children safer. We *will* work to make the streets outside your homes safer. We *will* make a start at erasing this shameful stain from the fabric of American society. Forty thousand dead! We can do better. We *must* do better.'

It would have been an applause line, but Breland did not wait for it. The red blots across the map of the nation had begun to fade when Breland first spoke the Trigger's new name. Now they vanished completely, and were replaced by a large and unfamiliar symbol superimposed over the center of the map – a stylized white dove with outstretched, sheltering wings on a United Nations blue circle.

'Tomorrow morning, sites which are already protected by the LifeShield will bear this sign prominently at every entrance. This is not the dove of peace – like the real bird, this dove is aggressive in the defense of its territory. This dove is both a warning to aggressors, and a protector of innocents. And she will become a familiar, and – I hope and believe – a welcome sight.

'This morning, I instructed the directors of the LifeShield project to expand the existing production facilities so that they can deliver a total of fifteen thousand units by the end of this year. I intend that we use them to keep guns and bombs out of places where they plainly do not belong.

'We'll put them in urban schools, so your children and their teachers will have a shield against gang violence and adolescent rage. There will be no more massacres like the one at Henry Ford High.

'We'll put them in post offices and courthouses and government buildings, so you can open your mail and conduct your business without fear of terrorism. There will be no more tragedies like Oklahoma City or Austin.

'We'll put them in airports – in time aboard the planes themselves – so you can travel freely and in confidence. There will be no more Flight Two-Oh-Nines.

'We're going to allocate one tenth of the production – a tithe, if you will – for churches and temples and synagogues, so that they may enjoy the protection of both god and science. There will be no repeats of the Beth El bombing.

'– And by the way, the cost of these units has already been paid by a generous gift from an anonymous donor – not a single tax dollar will be diverted for this use.

'I also have decided to give samples and the specifications for the LifeShield to our friends around the world – to begin with, Great Britain, Canada, Israel, Germany, and Japan.

'We'll keep looking for ways to use the LifeShield here at home. There is no intrinsic right for *anyone* to carry a bomb or a fire-arm onto Federal public property, whether it's the highways and bridges of the Interstate system or our national parks, monuments, and museums.

'To support these efforts, we'll continue to expand production, until we reach the point where we've run out of ideas and built a surplus of spares. At the same time, we will mount an aggressive research project aimed at reducing the size and cost of the LifeShield, so that placements which aren't possible now become possible in the future.

'Those are some of the things we're going to do.

'Now – here's what you can do.

'First, you can help us think of more ways to save more lives. A national toll-free number and a free Web site have been set up to take your suggestions for public placements.' As he spoke, the routings appeared on the display behind him. 'We want your knowledge of your own neighborhoods, your passion for your families and your community, and your compassion for your fellow citizens to help guide us.

'Second, you can ask your governors, your mayors, your legislators

278

to participate in LifeAssist. This is our plan to sublicense production of the LifeShield to state and local governments, so they can take steps to provide you locally with the same quality of security that we intend to provide in the Federal sphere.

'Finally, beginning six months from now, some of you will be able to buy a LifeShield yourself from a licensed manufacturer, and use it to create your own sanctuary.

'At first, sales will be limited to the owners of large multifamily housing, such as apartment buildings; financial institutions, such as banks; public accommodations, such as hotels; retail establishments, such as malls; and commercial properties, such as office towers. I want those owners to be able to offer a firearm-free environment to their tenants, their clients, their customers, and their employees – to use it in their advertising and their recruiting. Nothing will help spread the blessings of the LifeShield faster or farther than old-fashioned competitive American capitalism.

'But we will lift that restriction as quickly as we can, and reduce the price as often as we can. I look forward to the day when the LifeShield symbol is as commonplace as an auto-club sticker or a credit-card logo, when a gun-free environment is no longer a saleable curiosity, but a basic expectation, like air conditioning or handicapped accessibility.

'I want to be very clear about something – tomorrow is not the first day of the Utopian States of America. The LifeShield will not make us a more moral people, or resolve the conflicts which all too often explode into violence. It's not a magic wand that will erase homicide or suicide or stupidity or cupidity overnight. It's not a guarantee – it's only a tool that we can use to build a better society. We'll have to work hard and grow fast. We'll have to accept some compromises and make some adjustments in order to make that society real.

'But they are, I believe, lesser compromises than the ones we are already making – think of all the places that you've become accustomed to metal detectors, bag searches, armed guards, and of all the times you've found yourself afraid. They're trivial adjustments beside the adjustments of the forty thousand families each year that are losing a father, a mother, a child, a sibling, a spouse.

'Benjamin Franklin warned us, "They that can give up essential liberties to obtain a little temporary safety deserve neither liberty nor safety." The ghost of Franklin can rest easy, because the LifeShield defies that old equation of trading liberty for safety. We can and we will have more of both. That is the promise of the LifeShield, and that is my promise to you.

'Thank you – and bless you all.'

The standing ovation which followed was unprecedented in the history of Congress – or, at the very least, unsurpassed within the memories of the longest-tenured observers who witnessed it. It had no detectable partisan tilt, and went on for more than ten minutes, continuing even after Breland left the dais – whereupon he was immediately surrounded and nearly overwhelmed by the glad-handing Senate and House leadership and other front-benchers. All the formal etiquette of the chamber had vanished in the burst of enthusiasm that filled it.

Then Senator Grover Wilman appeared from nowhere, and bent his shoulder to the task of clearing a path for the President. With Wilman's help, Breland slowly made his way up the center aisle to the double doors and the more practiced assistance of his Secret Service detail. In Breland's wake, with throngs jamming the aisles and the floor, the Vice President abandoned parliamentary procedure and unilaterally gaveled the session closed.

Aimee Rochet and Aron Goldstein were waiting for Breland in his limousine. The latter was beyond words, but clasped the President's hand fervently with both hands and thanked him with eyes bright with tears.

'That was – well, that was incredible, sir,' said Rochet, removing her eyescreens. 'The share we were guaranteed, we bought that, but the ratings – the numbers kept going up from start to finish, as if people were calling their friends and saying, "Are you watching this?" I was wrong, Mr President. I was wrong, and you were right.'

Breland settled back into the cushions with an exhausted smile. 'I'm afraid it's much too early to be sure of that, Mrs Rochet. But thank you, all the same.'

'I mean it sincerely,' she said, leaning forward toward the vehicle's communications center. 'Is there any particular feed you'd like to monitor, sir? For the reaction and analysis?'

'Leave it off, please,' he said. 'If all they're talking about is my little Mexican standoff with the major, I don't want to know about it until tomorrow.'

'It'll be less frothy in the morning,' she agreed. 'I'll have a real solid sense of how it played and where it's going by, say, ten o'clock. Can we meet then?'

'Put it together. I'll be there,' the President said, and closed his eyes.

There was no sleep that night for most of Aimee Rochet's staff. If they weren't monitoring and analyzing the public dialogue, they were doing their best to shape it.

Immediately after the speech, the Stand-Ups were the busiest, making themselves available for push interviews on the newsfeeds and snap debates in the virtual town halls.

As the night wore on and the formal postmortems ended, the burden shifted to the Sit-Downs, who'd begun working the Undernet message boards and public chat rooms hours before the speech. With their flags of allegiance discreetly furled and their anonymity protected by sprites, aliases, and the NSA's best smoke and mirrors, the Sit-Downs seeded and highlighted the themes Rochet wanted to see emerge.

To that end, Rochet kept tabs on an evolving list of headers, taglines, and catchphrases that were playing and propagating well. 'Our kids don't belong on battlefields' and variants headed the list, with the technically inaccurate 'This isn't gun control – it's bullet control' and the ungrammatically blunt 'dead people don't need rights and got no freedoms' strong early contenders.

The observer-analysts carried the freight through the wee hours of the night, tabulating and classifying, watching for the crystallization points where discussion hardened into argument and opinions began to break toward both extremes. That was when the uncertainty collapsed – almost as though it were part of a quantum wave function – and the minority and majority positions became defined.

True to her promise, by ten o'clock the next morning, Rochet had an extensive report prepared for Breland and the other principals at the meeting – Nolby, Stepak, Attorney General Doran

Douglas, FBI Director Edgar Mills, and National Security Advisor Anson Tripp.

'We have an extremely dynamic situation this morning,' she said. 'High profile, high investment, record high deviations. Seventy million touches on the suggestion site – and one out of ten left a message.'

'It's going to be a long, long time before we have seven million Triggers,' said Nolby.

'Most of the messages aren't suggestions – they're expressions of support. I'm mailing each of you a summary and excerpts so you can see what the up side looks like. The numbers are excellent for women generally, married-with-children, and men over forty.'

'And the down side?' asked Breland.

'Something that emerged very early was a high uncertainty value where geopolitics were concerned. You didn't say much about military affairs, foreign relations – you gave them a full diet of domestic. But the audience included our men and women in uniform, our veterans, and all of their associates – people who know enough about military matters to ask hard questions.'

'The same sort of questions we've been asking for the last year, I imagine,' said Tripp.

'Not having been privy to those conversations, I'll leave that analysis to others,' said Rochet. 'But we're going to need a fast follow-up to speak directly to those issues –'

'How fast?' asked Breland.

'By the end of the day, if at all possible. And I'd recommend you consider someone with solid ties to the uniformed side of the Potomac – we want that face credibility working for us. General Stepak would be my suggestion, though anyone from the Joint Chiefs would meet the requirements.'

'With your permission, sir, I'll get together with General Madison and work it out,' said Stepak, looking to Breland.

'Fine.'

Rochet nodded approvingly. 'I have some data you should look at, General – perhaps when we're done here,' she said. 'Now, we come to the major action points – three hard areas, and one soft one.

'The first hard area is a self-inflicted wound. You've raised public expectations dramatically, Mr President. You've also made them look at something that they don't want to see, and told them that their world is a nastier and more dangerous place than they previously cared to notice. From this point forward, we're going to be fighting to live up to those expectations.

'Everything that happens will be measured against the ideals you've identified yourself with instead of against yesterday's realities, and there's a very real danger of a Gorbachev scenario – where instead of getting the credit for progress you get the blame when it doesn't happen fast enough to suit them. There's a number of things we can do to work on that, but it'll take a total team effort to keep every run-of-the-mill shooting from coming back on you as an accusation of failure.'

'Consider me chided,' said Breland. 'Continue.'

'Yes, sir,' Rochet said. 'The second hard area was completely predictable – the Second Amendment crowd isn't buying your reassurances. They think you're after their guns. The most immoderate voices think you've sold your soul to the internationalist left, and that this is the opening round of the fight they've been expecting for fifty years – the Federal government trying to disarm the American people before surrendering sovereignty to the Secretary General of the United Nations. There's a lot of talk about mounting armed resistance, though there's been substantially more shouting than shooting so far.'

'*Has* there been shooting?'

'I'd classify the incidents we're monitoring as individual shows of defiance,' said the FBI Director. 'No deaths or injuries.'

'How many incidents?'

'Sixty-three – two-thirds of them west of the Mississippi.'

'I wouldn't be surprised if either the moderate elements or the ammunition manufacturers are in court before the day's out, looking for an injunction against the Trigger – I mean, the Life-Shield,' said Attorney General Douglas. 'But we're already preparing responses to the anticipated grounds. I doubt that anyone'll be able to hold up the program for more than a week or so, if that.'

'My biggest concern is that we keep these conspiracy theories contained on the fringes, where they're preaching to the converted,' said Rochet. 'We have to be very conscious to avoid missteps which might seem to give these charges any validity.'

'Good luck,' said Mills. 'These people will believe what they want to believe, with or without what passes for evidence with them. Besides – they might be right. We *might* be after their guns, if the heavy weapons that've been disappearing from military arsenals for the last ten years are ending up in their hands. There's no good reason anyone living in Iowa or Idaho needs an antitank rocket or a SAW.'

Breland had heard enough on that subject. 'The third area?' he asked Rochet.

'Criminal opportunism,' she said. 'Crime rates, murder rates, might actually get worse rather than better in the short term, once the LifeShield becomes a credible threat to their ambitions.'

'People are openly talking about this?' Breland asked. 'About running out and killing someone while they still can?'

'Enough to light the storm lamps,' she said. '"Don't delay – off the bitch today." Saw that one myself, in a misogyny chat room.'

'Free speech is wasted on some people,' Stepak said with open disgust.

The FBI Director leaned forward and rested his crossed arms on the edge of the table. 'Staying on point – if I'd armed myself with some sort of aggression in mind – knocking off a bank, settling a score, whatever – I might be rushed into acting now if I thought I could lose my opportunity later. It's completely plausible.'

'Use 'em or lose 'em,' said Tripp, nodding agreement. 'We could be looking at this in the international arena as well.'

'How do we handle it?' asked Nolby. 'This is not just a matter of perceptions – this is a real threat.'

'Maximum vigilance, immediate response, assured consequences,' said Mills. 'We beat the bad actors to the draw as early, as often, and as publicly as possible, until the word gets around that this just isn't a good time to test the system.'

'Which might be exactly what the conspiracy fringe needs to sell their hokum to Mr and Mrs America,' Rochet pointed out. 'I won't presume to tell anyone here their business, but I can tell you that those newsclips of police in black combat gear breaking down doors doesn't help us with the public.'

'We'll come back to this,' said Breland. 'You said there was a soft spot?'

'Yes, Mr President – a big one, right in the middle. There's a lot of residual skepticism. You kept talking about the dragon, but in the end, you didn't show them a dragon, or even one good snort of fire from behind the rocks. They don't have to understand *how* the Shield works, but they're going to need to know that it does.'

'Which brings us to the question of the day,' said Breland. 'Weighing all the factors, do we want to go ahead with the Chicago demonstration?'

'It's not a demonstration to the Chicago police department,' said the attorney general. 'There've been six people killed by the Cabrini Green snipers, including a paramedic and a police sergeant. The snipers have been using the media to taunt the authorities. It's going to end in blood, on a live national feed, unless we give them an alternative.'

'I'll take that as your nonbinding recommendation in favor of proceeding,' said Breland. 'Let me hear from the rest of you.'

The tally was five in favor, one – Rochet – against.

'I'm glad to hear so much support for the option I've chosen,' said Breland. 'Director Mills, will you make one of the FBI's street tactical units available?'

'We can have a team there in an hour,' he said, turning a faintly mocking gaze on Rochet. 'I'm afraid our spring fatigues aren't in yet, though, so we'll have to go with basic holiday black.'

Am I the only one in this room not trying to get Breland impeached? Rochet wondered. 'Mr President, if we're going to do this in public, may I suggest that we at least do what we can to try to build a positive mystique around the LifeShield and its crews. Even if it means a delay of a day or two –'

'It's covered, Ms Rochet,' said Breland, and smiled. 'I think you'll be proud of us when you see.'

20: Publicity

Winona, Mississippi – A small band of armed gun rights advocates blockaded the northbound lanes of Interstate 55 near Exit 185 for two hours on Wednesday, creating a 40-mile-long traffic jam. Shouting 'Wake up, America!', the demonstrators fired rifles, shotguns, and pistols in the air. 'The LifeShield is the nose of the camel,' said Winona mayor Tom Mullins, who led the demonstration. 'The Feds won't stop until they've confiscated every firearm and disarmed every household.' State police responded to motorists' complaints, but made no arrests.

Complete story   *Commentary: Guns & The South*
Post Commander Defends 'low-key' Handling

Tower 11 was the last ghost of Cabrini Green – a fourteen-story concrete monolith rising from a desolate treeless tract of urban desert. A monument to misplaced public charity, Tower 11 and its now-demolished neighbors had been built as Federal subsidized housing. They soon turned into shameful vertical ghettos, a case study in the tragedy of the commons, and a symbol of everything that was wrong with the cities of America.

For all the misery they inflicted on their occupants, and all the embarrassment they represented for their creators and caretakers, the towers of Cabrini Green had lingered a surprisingly long time on the South Chicago skyline. Even after Cabrini Green was finally closed, boarded up, and fenced off, the stark, windowless towers stood for nearly another ten years as one redevelopment scheme after another fell through.

Only when the city finally agreed to subdivide the parcel and the Federal government agreed to share in the demolition cost did the towers begin to come down. Tower 11 had been only a week away from a visit by Controlled Demolition when it was occupied by something calling itself the African Heritage Army, who claimed 'moral ownership' and announced plans to turn Tower 11 into a museum of gang history and 'the twentieth-century nigger reservations.'

Whatever official sympathy for those goals the squatters might have found was squandered in an afternoon. Impatient with the lack of serious attention from both the press and the polls, 23 Jordan Nkrumah went to the top floor of the tower and began sniping at cars on the nearby northbound Dan Ryan Expressway.

An enraged amateur with a cheap Chinese-made assault rifle, Nkrumah had little control over what he hit at that distance. He simply kept firing, through half a dozen clips, until the freeway was deserted and the tower ringed with police cars, a helicopter was circling overhead, and he was the story of the day on CNN Breaking News and the Chicago newsfeeds. It was then that he learned that his bullets and the high-speed accidents they spawned had killed five and injured nine more.

That was when Nkrumah became Captain Michael Kaminski's problem – and vice versa.

Kaminski was a seventeen-year veteran of the Gary, Indiana, and Chicago police departments, serving the last five years in the 'headline bureau' – the heavily-armed, combat-trained Selective Response Team. For the last two years, he had served as CSRT commander, handling such high-profile cases as the meat-packer bombings (traced to the Animal Life League) and the Field Museum hostage situation (resolved with only a single fatality among the creationist extremists).

It had fallen to Kaminski to inform Nkrumah, in their first contact, that most of his victims had been black, including an eight-year-old and a woman pregnant with her third child.

Nkrumah had been unapologetic. 'They are martyrs to the cause of truth, and their deaths are on the heads of our oppressors,' he said. 'We will write their names boldly on these walls.' When Kaminski asked what Nkrumah hoped to accomplish by murdering black children, the squatter replied, 'A slave is invisible to the king until the slave bloodies the king's nose' – a line he repeated in his next (and last) conference-call media interview.

Then Nkrumah had rebuffed Kaminski's appeals to surrender and avoid further bloodshed. He vowed that he and his army – which he claimed was a hundred strong – would not be moved until the Federal government promised to 'guarantee justice for the black prisoners of war who died in Concentration Camp Cabrini.'

Nkrumah's African Heritage Army and Kaminski's Selective Response Team had been locked in a standoff ever since. Nkrumah's band – which Kaminski suspected numbered no more than twenty – held the high ground and had a thousand open windows to fire from. They were also armed with sticks of industrial dynamite – from which they had improvised grenades to thwart the SRT's only attempt to enter the tower in an armored personnel carrier.

But the police controlled the perimeter, meaning no food, water, ammunition, or reinforcements were reaching the AHA. They also controlled the airwaves, as least insofar as anything originating from within the tower – Nkrumah had been completely silenced. Even so, the story had not gone away. And the continuing press attention meant continuing pressure on Kaminski to resolve the situation.

Knowing that there was no way to assault the tower without risking a Waco, Kaminski had resisted the pressure. He hoped that hunger and a late-winter chill would eventually soften Nkrumah's resolve. But when sporadic sniping from the tower claimed two more casualties, a second assault was planned.

Then the director of the Chicago office of the FBI had called with an unlikely proposition, and a few hours later the President had made an extraordinary announcement – giving Kaminski a chance to revise the assault plan one more time, and bringing him to the perimeter gate to await the arrival of the cavalry.

There were more than two dozen news witnesses waiting there as well – part of the price of the FBI's help was giving advance warning to the press and site access to three pool camera teams They reacted to his arrival like steel filings to a magnet, and he gave them the quote they were looking for.

'I hope Mr 23 Jordan Nkrumah was watching someone's news-feed last night, so we can keep the explanations short and get every-one here home in time to say "Sleep tight" to your kids,' Kaminski said. 'In a little while, we're going to take away Nkrumah's guns, and a little while after that he's going to be behind bars, answering for the lives he took with those guns.'

'What about the moral rights of the squatters?' someone shouted to him from the back. 'Do you expect them to be able to get justice from prison?'

'The politics don't interest me. Child murderers have no special claim to moral rights that I can see,' Kaminski called back. 'And yes, I expect them to get justice – considerably more justice than they gave Donnie Stavens, or Vernon Thagard, or Jonita Walkey –'

Just then, sirens announced the approach of the LifeShield Assist team. Rather than the ominous keening of the typical American emergency vehicle, it was the more neutral two-pitch trill Kaminski associated with old British crime movies. The sound turned all heads (and the headset-mounted cameras along with them) away from Kaminski and toward the street.

Moments later, a pair of white vehicles – an all-terrain scout car and a four-wheel-drive panel truck – pulled up at the gate. The scout car had four weatherproof speakers mounted on its roof; the truck, four black antennas half a meter high. The vehicles had large blue LifeShield emblems on the hood, roof, and doors.

The five-man crew that piled out of the vehicles was dressed in the same color scheme – white jumpsuits with LifeShield emblems over the left breast and on the right shoulder. One of the five also had a gold circle ringing his emblems; and it was he who pressed forward through the news witnesses and introduced himself to Kaminski.

'John Grodin, team coordinator,' he said. 'Any changes from what you sent us this afternoon?'

'No changes.'

'Do you have your safety perimeter established?'

'At two hundred meters. We're ready to pull back on your signal.'

'Then let's do it,' Grodin said. 'Are you riding with us?'

'I'd like to.'

'There's a seat open in the lead car,' said Grodin.

Kaminski thumbed his lapel mic. 'SiteOpCom to all units – clear the blue zone. Repeat, clear the blue zone and assume your Baker Hot positions.'

As the others fell back, the tiny caravan moved forward to the edge of what had been the tower's playground. 'You want the honors?' Grodin said, handing Kaminski a comset.

'I already have all the publicity I can stand,' said Kaminski. 'It's your play.'

Grodin accepted the phone back with a nod. 'They're not answering,' he said after a time. 'Not to worry, we'll get his attention.' Using his thumb, he entered a code on the comset's keypad. 'Attention, occupants of Cabrini Green Tower Eleven,' he said, and his words boomed through the night from speakers atop the car. 'Attention, Twenty-Three Nkrumah and the African Heritage Army. This is John Grodin with LifeShield Assist Team Thirty-one. Please listen carefully – this will be your only warning.

'As of now, your weapons are more dangerous to you than they are to us. I can detonate your explosives and destroy your ammunition in a second, with the press of a single button. That's fact one. If you fire on my vehicles, I'll push that button. That's fact two. If you're standing too close to your weapons when I do that, you're going to get hurt. That's fact three.

'I don't expect you to take my word about this, so I'm prepared to offer a demonstration. You have two minutes to place something from your arsenal – loaded gun, explosive, it doesn't matter – at the far end of the hallway on any floor of the south wing. You pick the floor, you pick the weapon, and then you get everyone clear. When two minutes are up, I'll activate the LifeShield and destroy that weapon from here.

'After that, I'm going to wait three minutes, and then start dialing up the power. You can use those three minutes to lay down your weapons and walk out of there, or you can stay. Either way, five minutes from now, every explosive in that building is going up.

'One minute to the demonstration.

'There isn't anything you can do about this. You only have one choice to make – put down your weapons and live, or keep holding and die. Fire on my team and you forfeit the choice. Don't think the walls will protect you. Don't think you can hide yourself or your weapons. Don't think you can run. The LifeShield will be everywhere, inside and outside.

'Thirty seconds.

'Come out unarmed, and you will not be harmed. Cling to your weapons, and you're going to the hospital, or the morgue. Your choice.

'Ten seconds.' He carried the countdown to zero, then switched channels. 'Tech One, this is Team Director. Do you have a range to the south corner, first floor?'

'Range is one-seven-two.'

'Make your range one-nine-zero and prepare to initiate.'

'One-nine-zero, aye.'

'Initiate.'

There was a bright flash from a fourth-story window, followed an instant later by a concussive thunder that made the car vibrate. A hail of concrete fragments rained down on the barren ground. When the breeze blew the cloud of fine dust away, the spotlights showed a gaping hole high on the wall of the tower.

'Attention, occupants of Cabrini Tower Eleven,' said Grodin. 'You now know that I'm telling you the truth. Your weapons are no longer of any use to you. Your weapons are now a grave danger to you. You have three minutes to abandon them and surrender yourselves to the authorities. Exit the building through the west entrance and walk directly toward the LifeShield vehicles. Do not try to carry a weapon out of the building with you –'

'There,' said Kaminski, pointing. There was movement at the west entrance – a figure that appeared in the ruined doorway, then disappeared again. Moments later, two women emerged, picking their way across the splintered plywood panels which had once covered the entrance. Shielding their eyes against the bright lights directed toward them, they started uncertainly in Grodin's direction.

'That's right – keep coming,' he said. 'Two minutes.'

Others followed. By the time the countdown reached zero, twenty-four people had emerged from the tower and been escorted away by flak-jacketed members of Kaminski's Selective Response Team. But it quickly became apparent that Nkrumah was not among them. He had ordered his followers out, but defiantly stayed behind himself.

Kaminski made one last attempt to call Nkrumah's comset, but the squatter did not respond.

'Do we have enough to declare victory?' asked Grodin. 'No casualties so far, which would please the people *I* work for. Or do we carry out our threat and give Nkrumah what he wants? He might have enough ordnance up there to bring down big pieces of that building.'

'I don't think he's the kind to give up *his* life for the cause,' Kaminski said. 'Not to mention that he's too smart to leave himself with no other options.'

'You think he thinks we're bluffing?'

'I don't think he's standing over his armory waiting to find out. My bet is that he's down at ground level somewhere, and unarmed.' He thumbed his lapel mic. 'TacData, this is Kaminski. We're looking for one more. Anything on infrared or audio?'

'I had some audio transients in one-fourteen about two minutes ago.'

'Might it have been a comset ringer?'

'It might have been,' the tech agreed.

Kaminski thumbed his command radio off. 'We have him,' he said to Grodin, then gave the order to go in.

Team Red Five found Nkrumah cowering near the window in the ruins of apartment 112, waiting for the explosion, ready to vault the sill and run. Team Red Two found his cache of weapons against an outside wall on the sixth floor, where it would have provided a mighty diversion to cover Nkrumah's attempted escape.

'Like I said – smart,' said Kaminski as he and Grodin's team watched Nkrumah being taken away in handcuffs. 'Smart enough to come out of this alive.'

'I'm glad we had a smart one the first time out,' said Grodin. 'Can you live with the fact that he didn't give you a chance to kill him?'

The question surprised Kaminski. 'Yeah,' he said after a moment's thought. 'Yeah, I can. I could even get used to it. I don't suppose you can let me keep that thing.' He jerked a thumb in the direction of the LifeShield van.

'Sorry,' said Grodin. 'But they'll get you one of your own eventually. This is only the beginning.'

*   *   *

The core of the Annex team – Karl Brohier, Leigh Thayer, Jeffrey Horton, and Gordon Greene – had come to Washington for the Trigger's unveiling. All but Brohier had been in the gallery itself for Breland's speech, as guests of the President. In fact, had Brohier not objected on their behalf, Breland would have taken that opportunity to credit them with the discovery and introduce them to Congress and the world.

'You don't want to be celebrities yet,' Brohier had said at a White House luncheon the day before.

'You're not enjoying the food, Karl?' Gordie had called from the other end of the table. 'I'm pretty sure I'm the first person from the neighborhood to get seated at this restaurant.'

'Believe me, Dr Greene, I understand. I know how seductive it can be to find yourself here, somewhere that previously only existed for you on TV. This is *fun*. It is, isn't it? Being invited to the President's tea party. Just being in his company makes you feel like Somebody. Of course, you're not *really* somebody until you can be blasé about coming here.'

Even the President had laughed at that.

'We still have work to do, and the spotlight won't make it easier. The theoretical foundations aren't there yet. We haven't *earned* the spotlight. We don't have good answers to important questions. Every one of you can think of peers who forgot to make sure they had it right before they went to the press. I promise you, the country – the world – will find out soon enough who we are. No one else will get the credit – or the blame – for your discovery.

'Now, I wouldn't ask any of you to turn down the chance to be here. But this week, please take my counsel, and stand a little to one side. The President's kind enough to give us that choice – I think because he understands that it can be a most unwelcome spotlight.' Breland had silently gestured with his glass at that. 'In a little while, we'll know if we're heroes or bums.'

Heeding Brohier, they had stood a little to one side, and not felt the sacrifice too keenly. They had been feted privately by the White House and by Aron Goldstein at his estate, welcomed by Grover Wilman at Mind Over Madness, and briefed by a four-star general at the Pentagon. They enjoyed government drivers on call and five-star accommodations, and no ticket or reservation was too hard for the President's social secretary to secure.

Brohier had only stayed in Washington long enough to host a private Terabyte Annex party in his hotel suite the night of Breland's address. Half-drunk on champagne, he praised the members of his team effusively, toasted them repeatedly, and revealed an unexpected command of the ribald limerick. The next morning, he returned to Princeton.

The others lingered, tempted by Breland's offer of A-list access to whatever landmarks they chose. For Gordie, that meant a peek at the Cold War era Situation Room and an unhurried after-hours visit to a deserted Air and Space Smithsonian; for Horton, a floor tour of the Mint and a chance to watch a sunset through the stained-glass West Rose Window of the National Cathedral. Lee spent an entire day poking through drawers and cabinets at the Smithsonian with the paleontology curators at her elbow.

'The road not taken,' she explained, and the others seemed to understand.

No matter how many different directions they went during the day, they watched the news together each night, most often in Horton's hotel room, to see what they had wrought. In the week following Cabrini Green, there were half a dozen more LifeShield raids and sweeps. All were carefully chosen to offer the most unambiguous and unsympathetic villains, the most egregious flaunting of civil authority, the greatest threat to innocents, the greatest likelihood of success, and the best opportunities for favorable media play.

In Roswell, north of Atlanta, police cleaned out a designer drug factory, collecting more than a dozen automatic weapons. Near South Bend, Indiana, a white anarchist enclave surrendered after the LifeShield unit disarmed its perimeter guards and blew up a ring of mines and booby-traps. In Brooklyn, a Chicano gang house went up in flames, driving its unarmed occupants to the street and the waiting police.

Nine hostages were released unharmed after a bungled bank robbery in Amarillo, Texas, when the would-be robbers' guns caught fire in their hands. And a joint FBI-RCMP operation thwarted a Quebecois separatist group building bombs meant for

294

trains passing through the Sarnia Gateway and Coleman Young Tunnels spanning the Detroit River.

Unexpectedly, each day's reports left the three of them less and less satisfied with their handiwork – especially the last, in which eleven separatists died. After Horton turned off the screen, he looked across the room at Lee and Gordie and gave voice to what both had been thinking.

'It's still pretty crude, isn't it,' he said soberly. 'Messy. It'd be so much better if we could find some way to tune it so high explosives just fizzle the way propellants do. I really don't want our Baby to keep killing people.'

'Vacation over, Boss?' Gordie asked.

He nodded. 'Vacation over.'

They were back at the Annex by noon the next day.

21: Piracy

Taipei, Taiwan – Acting on a tip from a would-be robber, the fraud unit of the National Police arrested four men and two women for selling phony LifeShield devices. Also seized in the raid were more than five thousand of the one-kilogram 'LifeGuard' necklaces, which feature a calculator-like 'system controller', an array of blinking lights, and a low-pitched hum. The robber, bleeding from a gunshot wound to the right leg, complained to arresting officers that the device had failed to disarm the clerk of the Every Happiness Pharmacy.
Consumer Fraud: Newest Growth Industry
Legit LifeShield production 'going great guns'

It was inevitable, everyone involved in Brass Hat understood, that somewhere, sometime, a Trigger would kill an innocent civilian.

It was inevitable, everyone conceded, that when it happened for the first time, the media would give it saturation coverage, and offer every credentialed critic all the air time they wanted to tear into Breland and his LifeShield policy.

But no one quite realized just how thorough a disaster it was going to be, because no one managed to anticipate a tragedy as preventable and painfully personal as the sinking of the *Mutual Fun*.

For nearly three years, the US Coast Guard had been trying – with little success – to deal with a piracy problem along the middle Atlantic Coast and its inland bays and waterways. There had been more than forty incidents from Absecon to Hilton Head, most involving pleasure motorcraft. There appeared to be at least three criminal groups operating in overlapping territories, boarding moored cabin cruisers or luring them in with false distress flags, then destroying their radios, disabling their engines, and stripping them of valuables. With anything from a few hours to a few days head start before the crimes were even discovered, none had yet been captured.

But the stepped-up vigilance of the authorities had had an unexpected consequence. In a recent and vicious turn, several boats had simply disappeared – seized or sunk, with their occupants, the only witnesses, left to drown. And with the line between property crime and murder now crossed, nothing was unthinkable. The sole survivor of one such attack, picked up after eighteen hours in the water near the mouth of the Chesapeake Bay, reported that his wife and her girlfriend were taken by the pirates, who leeringly intimated that hours of sexual torment awaited their captives.

That lurid story lit up the newsfeeds more brightly than all the previous incidents combined, overwhelming the ongoing efforts by the boating industry and the waterside resorts to blunt the danger to their livelihoods. Thus it was that Commander Robb of the Cape Charles Coast Guard Station proposed placing a LifeShield aboard a twelve-meter trawler and using it both as bait and as a floating checkpoint.

'When you get right down to it, the reason we haven't been able to find any of the pirates is because they're hiding in plain sight, ordinary-looking people with ordinary boats – and there're too many boats on too much water with too much shoreline for us effectively patrol it all,' he had explained to the commandant of the Coast Guard. 'It's much easier for the pirates to keep track of us than the other way around. But we know these raiders are well-armed, and every boat-owner knows that firearms are prohibited on the water. If we play the pirates' own game, and set up out there in the high-traffic areas, eventually we'll catch them coming or going.'

'First try decoying them into coming after you,' the commandant had ordered in giving his blessing.

Robb had complied, but only with the letter of his instructions, not the spirit. With eleven unsolved piracies within the Bay alone, he had no patience with the prospect of weeks or months of stakeouts with a single Trigger-equipped decoy boat. Far better to take the more aggressive course, and secretly search hundreds of boats a day.

So after going unmolested during a single night anchored near Tangier Island in Pocomoke Sound (the site of one piracy), and another night spent in Mobjack Bay (where the cruiser *Daddy's Toy* had disappeared), the trawler *Sea Me* moved out to the Intracoastal Waterway. It dropped anchor near the southbound channel, within sight of Fair Port. All of the traffic heading oceanward from the Potomac or down from the upper bay passed through those waters, making it an ideal checkpoint.

The third boat to approach the *Sea Me* in the first minutes after the Mark I went hot was a ten-meter Cross & Davidson sport cruiser belonging to stockbrokers John and Jinx Morgenstern of Fredericksburg, Virginia. Next to the floating palaces that the pirates had been targeting, the Morgensterns' modest craft was an unlikely target. They also had no plans to sleep on the water – this long-planned trip with old friends was to end in Virginia Beach before nightfall. The chances of them crossing paths with the Chesapeake pirates were accordingly modest.

But because John Morgenstern was a prudent man, he had taken the precaution of adding a flare gun to the hand-held flares aboard the *Mutual Fun*. And because John Morgenstern was a frugal man, he had retrieved the perfectly good twenty-year-old Heckler & Koch 37mm flare kit from his late father's boathouse rather than buy a new 'safety launcher' at a premium price.

In the Coast Guard's closed-door inquiry into the deaths of the Morgensterns and their friend Thomas Welch, Commander Robb would admit that he had not read the LifeShield technical briefing before authorizing the pirate hunt. He would allow that although he had ordered a test with a 'clean' boat carrying standard-issue Coast Guard flares and rockets, he had not devoted enough thought to the possibility that there would be other boats on the bay carrying prohibited or outdated pyrotechnics.

But at the moment *Mutual Fun* reached the boundary of the Trigger field centered on *Sea Me*, no one on either boat realized the danger represented by the black case Morgenstern had tucked away in the life-jacket locker behind him.

The only danger on Morgenstern's mind was a mild violation of etiquette should he bounce the tan-hulled trawler with his 25-knot wake. He was reaching with his right hand to back the twin throttles off when the lid of the locker blew open with a bang, exposing a fierce magnesium-sweetened fire.

Loretta Welch was sitting closest to the locker at that moment. Surprise and an instinctive urge to flee from the intense heat carried her out of her chair and into a jolting collision with Jinx, who was lunging for the boat's fire extinguisher. The collision knocked Jinx back and carried Loretta over the side of the boat. Her shriek was cut short by the water that closed over her.

Investigators were never able to determine the exact sequence of events after that. Curiously, when the trawler reached Cape Charles, the sound-actuated video recorders were found to have malfunctioned, leaving no official record of the accident.

But witnesses aboard nearby boats reported an explosion that was, in the words of one, 'pure Hollywood' – a two-stage crimson and yellow billow with oily jet-black highlights. It rose thirty meters into a cloudless blue sky as tiny bits of wood and fiberglass debris rained down onto the surface of the bay. Even from barely a hundred fifty meters away, there was nothing anyone aboard *Sea Me* could do, except move in and pluck a dazed Loretta Welch from the water, then wait for the Coast Guard search and rescue helicopter to arrive.

When news of the incident – still publicly unconnected to the Trigger program – reached the Oval Office, Nolby pleaded with Breland to let it remain a regrettable accident.

'It's completely deniable,' Nolby insisted. 'There's no reason to tell anyone that we provided the spark that set off that explosion – and every reason not to. Liability torts, conspiracy nuts – instead of feeling safe and secure, you're going to have people being afraid when they see the LifeShield symbol. I beg you, Mr President, if this initiative means anything to you, leave things as they are – this accident will be archive dust in a day or two.'

'There's one reason you seem to have overlooked, Mr Nolby – we were in the wrong. Commander Robb secured his Trigger through the Joint Chiefs instead of through the FBI assistance-request clearinghouse – it didn't get the kind of risk review it should have. The trawler was unmarked, the checkpoint was unannounced – those people didn't have any warning that they were sailing into a Trigger-controlled zone. When you come right down to it, this was an unprovoked assault by elements of the American uniformed services on innocent citizens. Do you seriously expect me to overlook that?'

'You can discipline those responsible without putting your own neck in the noose. It can all be done quietly.'

Breland held his Chief of Staff in a frosty gaze. 'Was it your impression, Richard, that I thought protecting the people – my bosses – from the truth was part of my job?'

'In the service of a greater good, sometimes, yes.'

'And what good does it do to compound a mistake with a lie?'

'I'm not asking you to lie, sir – I'm urging you to bite your tongue –'

'Is that a meaningful distinction for you, Mr Nolby? Is that the way your moral calculator works? Why should I assume the secret will stay a secret?'

'It's well-contained at the moment, Mr President.'

'Only if you assume that everyone who knows or will know is a friend of this administration and of LifeShield. Can you assure me that that's so?'

Nolby sighed. 'No, sir.'

'Then all the lie does is double the damage from a later revelation – and double the temptation to make that revelation. "What did you know, Mr President, and when did you know it?" Throw me into that tar pit, and I'll never be seen again,' Breland said. 'Have Aimee schedule a press conference for five o'clock. If your conscience can't stand that much honesty, you can put your resignation on my desk by that time.'

'I wasn't making myself understood, Mr President – my apologies,' Nolby said stiffly. 'I'll put Aimee on alert.'

The next morning, with Loretta Welch's name on millions of lips and her face on dozens of newsfeeds, lawyers representing the National Association of Riflemen descended on the Federal Court for the District of Columbia to ask the judges to declare the technology known as LifeShield unconstitutional.

'"– In the hands of the government, this technology represents a *prima facie* violation of the Second Amendment guarantees; in the hands of the public, it represents a grave threat to life, liberty and public order,"' Attorney General Doran Douglas read from the display of her comset. '"The plaintiffs ask that this Court order an immediate injunction against any further use of this technology; further, for the destruction and dismantling of all existing examples of this technology; and finally, for a permanent ban on the manufacture, ownership, and sale or other transfer of the plans, specifications, component parts, or operational examples of this technology."'

She set the device down and looked across the tea table to the President. 'I'm a little surprised that they didn't ask for you and your staff to be mindwiped.'

'Who says that they're finished?' asked Breland flippantly. 'Are you aware of the NAR making any sort of back-door approach to us in advance of this filing, any attempt to open a dialogue or a negotiation?'

'No,' said Douglas. 'But, then, we didn't make any sort of back-door approach to them in advance of your presentation to Congress.'

'I suppose I did set the ground rules, after all,' said Breland, smiling wryly. 'What do you think they really want?'

'I think they really want everything,' said Douglas, reaching for her coffee. 'They're providing Loretta Welch with legal assistance for a wrongful-death suit. And I hear that they've contacted the Patent Office – I think we can expect some sort of action against the Trigger patent, which is hanging by a thread anyway.'

'They want a time machine,' said Breland. 'They want to make it all go away.'

'Ideally, yes, sir. Though I don't imagine they actually expect to get everything they've asked for. The court would have to gut the First Amendment to give it to them.'

'They might be willing to make that trade,' Breland said. 'Where does this go from here?'

'A hearing next Tuesday on the request for the preliminary injunction. That'll be before Judge Virginia Howarth – an Engler appointee, but more level-headed than that suggests.'

'Predictions?'

'I expect that she'll reject the request for injunctive relief, but the case itself will be a nasty scrap.'

'How long will all this take to settle?'

'Could be three months if it's fast-tracked, could be three years otherwise. With SCOTUS's current backlog, there's not much likelihood of anything in between. Of course, if Howarth rules for our side, we have no reason to go fast track.'

'You can control that?'

'Well – we can apply to the Supreme Court for a writ of *certiorari*. That amounts to asking them to step in and hear the appeal themselves. Of course, the other side is free to do that, too. I expect they will, if they lose with Howarth. And given the issues in this case, if either side asks for it, it'll probably be granted.'

'Good. I want this settled quickly. Can we bypass the District Court trial, too?'

She cocked her head and looked at Breland questioningly. 'Mr President, I wouldn't even consider starting down that road unless I was absolutely sure where it ends.'

'And you're not.'

'Only reasonably sure.'

Breland nodded. 'All right. I want to talk to the plaintiffs. The NAR leadership – president, board of directors, whoever's making the decisions.'

'I see.' Douglas frowned. 'Sir, what do you imagine such a meeting might accomplish? I can't think what you could say to them now that could make them decide to drop their lawsuit – just the reverse, since they'll probably interpret our request as a sign that we're worried about the case, or the political heat, or both. It'll be like showing wolves a lame leg.'

'I don't intend to try to talk them into dropping the case,' Breland said. 'Can you set it up?'

Douglas sipped at her coffee before answering. 'John Samuel Trent,' she said finally. 'He's the power there. I'll have someone arrange it. If his lawyers will go for it.'

For most first-time visitors to the Oval Office, being ushered into that storied sanctum evoked the humility of a penitent entering the Vatican, the awe of a fan entering Graceland, or the gleeful pride of a young man allowed to sit with the council of adults for the first time. But for John Samuel Trent, the predominant feeling was of confident anticipation.

The organization's First Vice President, a legendary action star of the television era, had tried several times to dissuade Trent from accepting the President's invitation. 'There's nothing he can give us,' she had said that morning. 'There's no prestige in being summoned to the White House like a dutiful servant. If he wants to talk to us, let him come down to Fairfax and ring the bell at headquarters.'

'No, no – you don't understand. You may relish the thought of Breland begging on our doorstep, hat in hand, but it's infinitely sweeter to see him humbled in his own house,' Trent had answered, collecting his coat. 'I've been waiting for this for eighteen years – eighteen years of watching presidents who were our friends take us for granted and presidents who despised what we stand for chip away at our rights. Now a wounded president reaches out to us, asking for mercy, asking for our help. I wouldn't miss for anything the chance to walk into hell and give the devil our answer.'

But the audience for Trent's moment of delicious *schadenfreude* was going to be much smaller than he had allowed himself to hope for during his short drive into Washington. He had envisioned Breland holding court with a retinue of Cabinet members and senior staffers gathered behind him to bolster his prestige. But there was only one other person with Breland in the Oval Office, a youngish man of such low status – one of the Secret Service's new ninjas, perhaps – that the President did not even trouble to introduce him.

'I thought this room was bigger than this,' Trent said, settling into a chair after a perfunctory handshake. 'It must be something about the camera angles, I suppose – I'm a big fan of political movies, you know. Especially those charming post-Watergate films where the President turns out to be the villain. Have you ever seen *High Crimes*?'

'I suppose we all enjoy fiction that confirms our prejudices about the world,' Breland said. 'My tastes in classic movies run more to stories where good men have to make hard choices than where they have to make a good shot – *To Kill A Mockingbird,* or *Casablanca.*'

'Or *Mr Smith Goes to Washington*?'

'Touché,' said Breland. 'A palpable touch.'

Trent smiled broadly. 'Let's get to it, then. Why did you ask me here? To try to make our troublesome lawsuit go away, I assume.'

'No, not at all –'

Trent heard the denial, but discounted it, confident that a more oblique and face-saving appeal was coming.

'– I welcome your challenge – in fact, I've asked the Attorney General to do what she can to expedite the progress of the case through the lower courts. I want all the uncertainties resolved as soon as possible.'

'She's not telling you you can expect to win, is she? If she is, fire her – she's obviously incompetent.' Trent tossed his hand dismissively.

Unexpectedly, disconcertingly, Breland smiled. 'I'll tell her you said so. But the fact is that I'm well acquainted with the arguments she's going to present in Baltimore on Tuesday, and I don't see how your side can prevail.'

Trent crossed his arms over his chest. 'You're baiting me.'

'Not at all. You obviously expected this meeting to be adversarial. But when it comes to the Second Amendment, we're on the same side.'

With a hot flush climbing his neck and quick anger balling his fists, Trent sprang up from the couch. 'You're a bald-faced liar, Mr President – and you must think I'm a fool.'

'On the contrary. I think you're a dedicated advocate of personal liberty, and a vigilant defender of the Second Amendment –'

'Don't compound your insults with empty flattery,' Trent said with cold fury.

'– But your world view is, I'm afraid, out of date,' Breland persisted. 'There's nothing in the Second Amendment to guarantee that arms technology would or should stand still. There were no selective-fire automatics, no laser sights, no centerfire cartridges in the eighteenth century. The NAR isn't defending the right to bear flintlocks and black powder – you want Americans to have all the benefits of two hundred fifty years of refinement and invention. Am I right?'

'Yes – while you want to deny us those benefits. You want us disarmed and compliant –'

304

'You're missing my point, Mr Trent. Disarming someone is a violent act –'

'Exactly. And this is violence against sixty million gun owners, and two and a half centuries of democracy.'

Breland gestured toward the couch behind the NAR president. 'Please, Mr Trent – if you would hear me out.'

Liking the sound of what he took for anxious pleading, Trent settled back into the cushions. 'Only because I'm curious about how you've deluded yourself into expecting victory.'

'Because the LifeShield – or the Trigger, as it's also known – is a weapon,' Breland said softly. 'And the Second Amendment protects private ownership of it just as strongly as it protects ownership of rifles and handguns. We'll win because you can't use the Second Amendment to privilege one class of arms over another. You have a right to your firearms. Your neighbor has a right to a LifeShield. And it's no business of the courts if your neighbor's weapon turns out to trump yours.'

The audacity, the arrogance of Breland's tactics left Trent blinking and momentarily speechless. 'You're shifting the ground. There are no LifeShields in private hands,' he sputtered. 'They're all in the hands of the Federal Bureau of Intimidation, and the Central Interference Agency, and the fascist gun-grabbing police forces you're making out of our armed services. This isn't about individual rights – it's about the government trampling individual rights. It's about you murdering Loretta Welch's husband.'

'That's beneath you, Mr Trent,' Breland said, but without evident rancor. 'That was a screw-up, a tragic concatenation of mistakes. You know as well as I do that the courts have never used the Constitution to limit how the Federal government can equip its armies – or how government at any level can equip its police. Armies and police exist to apply force. Sometimes that power is misused. I understood this to be the reason you call gun ownership the "First Freedom".'

'It's exactly that,' said Trent challengingly. 'A man who can't defend himself, who can't protect his home and his family, has nothing – no rights, no freedom, no property.'

'Then help bring *this* power to those people,' Breland said. 'We're standing on the cusp between yesterday and tomorrow.

We can't change that – neither you nor I. That's why I asked you here – to make sure that you understand that it's out of our hands. No man – not even a president – stands against history.'

'I don't see it that way at all,' said Trent lightly. 'You've lost twenty points in three days – and I've gained half a million members. You're defending the slaughter of innocents, and I'm defending the Constitution. You think people are afraid of guns – I know they're more afraid of their government. And we've analyzed the firearm death statistics – your plan can't possibly prevent more than ten percent of those deaths. You've overpromised, and we're going to make sure the nation knows it.'

He chuckled, a sign his confidence had returned full force. 'How many factories are building these things – one, two? What's so irresistible about history that those factories can't be closed? Are there so many of them that we haven't enough torches to cut them up, or enough smelters to melt them down? No, Mr President – it'll be easier to stop this than you think.'

'You're already too late.'

Trent jerked his head in the direction of the new voice. 'What did you say?'

'I said, "You're already too late."' The young man advanced several steps from where he had been standing. 'Right now, there are at least eleven production lines in operation around the world. I know of five more that'll be up before the end of the month – three of them in Canada, and owned by my employer. And there're at least thirty labs working on improvements – the Japanese are already testing a design that's a third smaller and has a fifth fewer parts. America isn't the world, Mr Trent. Maybe the Supreme Court will be afflicted by sunspots, and we'll be the last to benefit from the Trigger, instead of the first – but it will happen.'

'Who is this?' Trent demanded of Breland.

The President stood and invited the newcomer into the circle with a sweep of one hand. 'John Trent, may I introduce Dr Jeffrey Horton, associate director of Terabyte Labs and principal inventor of the Trigger.'

'And former life member of the National Association of Riflemen,' Horton said, dropping his membership card onto the table in front of Trent. 'While you're counting heads, make that a net gain of a half-million minus one – I have no interest in belonging to an anachronism. And that's all you'll be, as irrelevant as a muzzleloader encampment or a reenactment of the Battle of Shiloh, if you keep closing your eyes to what's happening – what's already happened.'

'I see,' said Trent, coming to his feet. His hands were trembling with barely-suppressed fury. 'I hope you enjoyed your little deception, Mr President. And I hope you enjoy your blood money, Dr Horton. I trust that you'll be profiting handsomely from betraying your country.'

Horton shook his head. 'You never have understood, have you?'

'Understood what?'

'That the reasons you love your guns are exactly the same reasons others hate and fear them,' said Horton.

'What are you talking about?'

'It's the *power* – that terrible, concentrated power in your hands, at your command. The power to kill in an instant of rage, or impatience, or greed, across a room, across a street. There's a *djinn* inside the gun that obeys you – and because it does, others must, too.'

'A philosopher,' said Trent curtly. 'I despise philosophers. They delight in making the simple obscure.'

'No,' said Horton. 'A physicist. But I'll accept the definition anyway.'

'It doesn't matter,' said Trent. 'You can't even see the erosion of individual rights that you and your kind have engineered. Those issues obviously don't matter to you. So we're done here.'

'Not quite,' Horton said sharply, taking a step to block Trent's path to the door. 'I want to correct your mistaken assumption about something – I'm not earning a penny from the Trigger patent. I donated it to the public domain almost two months ago – a free license. That's part of why things are moving as quickly as they are. It's true that I got paid well while I was working on it, and someone'll make money selling it, but if you think this is about money or politics – well, you're very wrong.'

Incredulous, Trent stared at Horton as though he had revealed himself the devil incarnate. 'You won't be satisfied until you've taken every last gun away from us, will you?'

Horton tucked his hands into his back pockets and showed a weary smile. 'You still don't get it – it's not about the guns. But you're right, I'm not satisfied,' he said. 'I won't be satisfied until Triggers are the size of a briefcase and every shop-owner can afford one. I won't be satisfied until they're the size of a comset and every home-owner can afford one.

'Hell, I won't be satisfied until they're cheaper than a good handgun and just as easy to conceal. So you say you won't feel safe carrying your Glock on the street in such a world? Then turnabout really is fair play. We haven't felt safe with you carrying it in this world.'

Drawing a deep breath, Trent summoned all of the contempt he could muster and slathered it over every word of his rebuttal.

'You have to be two of the most foolish men this office has ever seen,' he said, circling toward the exit. 'Your little toy won't protect you from a mugger with a knife, or your daughters from a gang of rapists. It won't turn away a gang or slow down a Chinese division. You're living in an imaginary world where people want to get along – I'm living in the real one where they covet everything you own.'

By then he was at the door, with his right hand closing on the doorknob. 'And you're either insane or hopelessly naïve if you really think a hundred million Americans are going to stand by and let you take away their guns and their god-given rights.'

It was a perfect moment – the best presence-of-mind-parting-words-slam-the-door exit he had ever managed, or could ever hope to.

Too bad, Trent thought as he drove away, that to share it with anyone he would have to also revisit the nightmare of the darkest morning of his life.

22: Alchemy

The wonderful thing about Triggers/
Is Triggers are wonderful things/
Their insides are made out of widgets/
Their outsides are made out of zings/
When bombs go boom! and ammo foom!/
You'll know I'm having fun/
But the most wonderful thing about Triggers is − /
I have the only ONE

NSA INTERCEPT LOG
Search Key 00062883Hit: A3H07HB   *Rating: 99%*
Classification: Folk Doggerel, Derivative
Sender: Anonymous   *Propagation: Netwide*

The lawsuit aimed at stifling the Trigger had offended Jeffrey Horton on both a personal and a philosophical level. Claiming that Trigger technology was unconstitutional seemed to him to be of a piece with the Pope silencing Galileo or Tennessee forbidding the teaching of evolution. It was a small-minded, short-sighted, self-serving absurdity, and he had found himself bursting with eagerness to denounce it as same.

'All of their justifications are just sugar-coating for anti-intellectualism,' he had grumbled to Dr Greene after reading the NAR's court filing online. 'If they had their way, it'd still be muskets and flintlocks. This is the twenty-first century, not the damned eighteenth.'

'Don't tell me, tell them,' Gordie had replied. 'I'm not the one who said you had an ugly Baby.'

Taking the suggestion to heart, Horton had contacted the White House to offer his assistance in responding to the lawsuit. That had led to a long conversation with the President and the longer flight back east for the confrontation with John Trent.

It had not gone quite as he had expected. Horton had wanted to see for himself how Trent's mind worked. The President had wanted Horton there as a resource he could call upon. Neither of them had anticipated Horton would play quite so large a role in what transpired.

But by the time he jumped into the conversation, Horton had built up a full head of righteous indignation. In venting it, he had satisfied himself for the moment, but he had also irreversibly crossed the line about which Brohier had warned him. He had walked out of the shadows into the spotlight, and placed himself right beside the President.

The day after his confrontation with John Trent, a gun rights Web site outed Dr Jeffrey Horton as the inventor of the Trigger. Most of the article was polemic and character assassination, easily shrugged aside. But the biographical material sent a chill down Horton's back. To judge by the errors and omissions, most of it seemed to be drawn directly from the AAAS Directory and Terabyte's own publications. But there were also three photographs of him – including a vidcap of him sitting in the gallery for the joint session of Congress – with sighting circles and crosshairs superimposed.

Immediately below his photos appeared his former address in Columbus, along with a map of the driving route from there to Terabyte's Columbus campus.

'We can make that page go away,' said FBI Director Mills at a hastily arranged meeting that included the President and the director of the Secret Service. 'But they've already accomplished their goal – we can't stop the information from spreading. The mainband news organizations will probably have it by this evening, if they don't already.'

'So what do I do?' Horton asked, looking to Breland.

'It's up to you,' the President said. 'You can decide to make yourself available, or you can decide to make yourself scarce. My suspicion is that it won't much affect how much they talk about you, but it might affect what they say.'

'He still has a safe harbor in Nevada,' said the Secret Service. 'No one knows about the Annex yet. Maybe just going back there is the best idea.'

310

The director of public relations was vigorously shaking her head and edging forward on her chair. 'I've already fielded three direct inquiries about the identities of certain people who've been under our wing this week, and there others are nosing around,' Rochet said. 'I say we step right up and answer the questions, let them have a peek at Dr Horton, maybe even allow a press conference – *then* let him high-tail it back to Nevada.'

'They'll eat him up,' said Mills bluntly. 'Nothing personal, Dr Horton, but you have no experience with what passes for journalism here.

Speaking forcefully, Rochet said, 'I've always believed that it didn't matter whether the natives were preparing to feast you or roast you, you're better off helping make the arrangements than leaving everything to them. I think we can spin this very nicely, if Dr Horton agrees. He's a pleasant-looking young man, smart, well-spoken, no political baggage, no extreme agenda – why let them demonize him when we have the truth on our side? This static over the Morgensterns isn't changing any minds, just giving the opposition something to rally around. We can give our people something to rally around, too – an unassuming hero. What do you think, Doctor?'

Horton searched their faces for an answer. 'I wouldn't want the rest of the team to think I was trying to take all the credit,' he said slowly.

'You'll talk to them beforehand, explain the situation.'

Nodding, Horton added, 'But I also don't want to let what the *Ammo Locker* said go unchallenged.'

'Absolutely right,' said Rochet. 'You shouldn't give them the last word. It's all about perceptions.'

'I was thinking it was about the truth,' said Horton.

'Not often,' said Rochet. 'But we always try to start there.'

'Was that a decision, then?' Breland asked Horton.

'I think so,' he said.

'Good,' said Rochet, standing. 'Why don't you come with me to my office, then, and we'll get to work.'

Like a Picasso drawing figures in mid-air, Aimee Rochet was an artist working in the transitory and insubstantial – impressions, perceptions, and, when necessary, illusions.

Overnight, she put together an event which was not merely a political debutante's coming-out party, but a hero's coronation. When the Commerce Department balked at rushing through a National Medal of Technology for the Trigger developers, she rummaged through the White House archives and found paper authorizing an earlier incarnation, the Presidential Medal of Progress. She lined up an enthusiastic audience big enough to fill a wide shot by tapping the middle-level staffers of the State Department. The two living American recipients of the Nobel Peace Prize were rushed into town to sit in the front row and be seen shaking Horton's hand.

The frothy speeches for the President and his honoree were whipped together by the usual suspects on staff, but she personally rehearsed Jeffrey Horton on his, and then rewrote his remarks to make them simpler and more in keeping with his natural rhythms. She hand-picked the media representatives who would be allowed to take part, and gave a three-hour scoop to a particularly friendly correspondent from Bertelsmann Worldwide. At a morning breakfast, she coached Horton through what she thought was a successful mock press conference. And when the time came, she personally moderated the real thing.

The only thing Rochet couldn't do, she thought regretfully as she looked out at the thicket of raised hands, was answer all the questions for Horton. He shared Breland's faults – he was too real to memorize a polished answer, too honest to avoid the political potholes. Unlike Breland, he was an amateur. She could only hope that he wouldn't wound himself too badly.

She pointed, thinking, *We open with the big bear*. 'Yes, Richard, you have the first question.'

'Dr Horton, Senator Wilman says that the LifeShield is the answer to a pacifist's prayers. Have you discussed this with either Senator Wilman or god, and do you think global disarmament is a realistic goal?'

Come on – just like over eggs and pancakes – you don't have to answer them all –

'I don't know Senator Wilman,' Horton said. 'But I'm pretty sure that god is on the side of peace. Whether global disarmament

312

is realistic or not, I can't say. I can tell you that the LifeShield team will be happy if our discovery moves the world in that direction.'

Not bad, she thought. *Now the vicar –*

'Dr Horton, Alfred Nobel made his fortune selling TNT to both sides in a series of nineteenth-century wars. Would you accept a Nobel Prize for discovering the antidote to dynamite, or would you consider that blood money?'

'Nobel told his friend, the Countess Bertha von Suttner, that he wished he could produce a machine or material that would make war impossible. He seems to have been thinking about deterrence – mutual assured destruction – but I don't think anyone who's honored by his Foundation has any reason for misgivings.'

Very nice. Here comes the fondler.

'Dr Horton, would you rather win a Nobel Peace Prize or the Nobel Prize for Physics?'

'I don't think about it,' Horton said. 'My business is science, not awards.'

Ohh, the fondler won't have anything nice to say about you tonight, you took away his moment. Let's have one from the college press –

'Who are your idols, Dr Horton?'

'I don't think people in my line of work can allow themselves to have idols. But I owe a debt to every teacher who taught me, and every pioneer who worked out a piece of the puzzle and passed on that knowledge to us.'

Oh, I could kiss you. Let's see, let's see, the giggler should be safe –

'Would you describe yourself as a genius?'

'No. I just work hard.'

Just a few more and we're out of here. All right, Monsieur –

'Dr Horton, what do you know about a net document concerning something called "Trigger Mark I"? It purports to be a complete set of instructions for building what sounds very much like the LifeShield. Can you tell us whether that's authentic or a hoax? Did you have anything to do with it?'

While Horton gaped, Rochet smoothly stepped in. 'I'll remind you that Dr Horton simply can't comment on the specifics of his research until restrictions related to national security are lifted. That includes confirming or denying rumors from the net.' *Quick, who – oh, Lady Flowerhat –* 'Eleanor.'

'Dr Horton, what would you like to say to Loretta Welch and the Morgenstern children?'

Shit – see if you ever get called on again, bitch – 'Dr Horton joins the President in expressing his condolences –' she began.

'No, it's all right, Aimee – I'd like to answer,' Horton said. 'I'm sorry it happened. I wish it hadn't. It was a bad day in the lab when we heard. I hope the people who are handling the LifeShield in the field learn from it. But when I lost a friend in a plane crash a long time ago, I didn't blame the Wright brothers. When those Challenger astronauts died, I don't think anyone thought it was Robert Goddard's fault. Every new technology brings both risks and benefits. I don't think we can ask for guarantees.'

Stop talking, stop talking already. I need a graceful exit – 'Last question to Tania, up here.'

'Dr Horton, have you talked to your sister? I understand she's an Olympic shooting medalist.'

'She is,' he said. 'I'm very proud of her. No, I haven't had a chance to talk to Pamela.'

'Do you think she'll approve or disapprove of what you're involved in?'

Horton looked surprised. 'We've always supported each other. That's the kind of family we are. I don't see why that should change.'

Good enough – With that, Rochet hustled him away into the White House, told him he'd done splendidly, turned him over to a supernumerary, and then hurried away to the press wing to try to knock off the rough edges. By the time she came back, she knew enough to steer him to some of the best of a mixed but mostly favorable set of notices. They channel-surfed together in a White House media center for a short time, until Horton stood up, shuddering, and pronounced, 'I can't take any more. I hate my voice.'

She smiled and said, 'By tomorrow you won't have one – you'll just be a video clip under someone's voiceover –'

He laughed at that.

'You know, you really did all right,' Rochet said, and hugged him. She had seen a lot of post-press conference meltdowns, and not only among beginners. 'In fact, if you made yourself available for a few more days, you could do a lot of good for our side. Let me know, Doctor.'

He agreed on the spot, and bore up well during a whirlwind week of carefully staged high-profile appearances. So Rochet was as surprised as anyone when, nine days after returning to Nevada, Dr Jeffrey Horton wrote himself approval for an indefinite, unpaid leave of absence, drove out of the Annex in a Terabyte vehicle, and vanished.

Alerted by the gate guards that Senator Grover Wilman was on the plant grounds, Jules Merchant met his old friend in the reception lobby of the Allied General administrative center.

War had thrown them together three decades ago, and shared memories of roaring through a desert night in a sixty-ton Abrams tank had bound them together. But they had taken different paths after the war, and politics had kept them separated for more than a decade. The chairman of what was both the world's largest arms manufacturer and the country's top military contractor could not be allowed a personal relationship with a man who was both the Senate's most outspoken maverick and the planet's best-known disarmament advocate.

But a friendship formed in fire lasts forever, and Merchant's greeting and smile were both warm and genuine. 'Grover,' he said, opening his arms to a back-patting clench. 'Do me a favor and don't tell me how long it's been.'

'It's good to see you, Jules,' said Wilman. 'I believe you're the first person I've seen in the last twenty minutes who isn't gaping or glaring at me.'

Merchant laughed easily. 'Ah, you've been getting the what-the-hell-is-he-doing-here look,' he said. 'I've been getting the flip side of it ever since I told my staff you were coming up. But everything changes if you wait long enough, eh? Come on – I've got wheels out front. I want to take you out to the test track and show you something.'

The chairman's wheels were attached to a low, wide five-seat vehicle that despite its neutral brown color had 'battlefield' written all over it – spare fuel cans in a sheltered central well, global positioning system display in the dash, obvious firing positions protected by angled armor on both rear corners, and a roll-bar that incorporated a two-axis mounting ring for a light machine gun.

'This is the replacement for the Hummer?' Wilman said, swinging a leg over the high splash-board that passed for a door and pulling himself into the second seat.

'Yeah – this version answers to "Fiver", or Forward Infantry Vehicle, Recon/Patrol. Also for the five-man fire team – driver, stand-up gunner, spotter-loader, and two riflemen watching your back. We started delivering them last May – current contract is for thirteen hundred units in all versions. It'll hit a hundred klicks on the flat, climb a fifty percent grade, ford anything shallower than the turbine's air intake. But you know all that, I suppose – you led the fight to cut back the buy from fifteen hundred to thirteen.'

'It was nothing personal, Jules,' Wilman said. 'And I never said Allied General didn't deliver value for money.'

'I know,' said Merchant, gunning the turbine engine and pointing the vehicle at a driveway that disappeared into the woods to the west of the parking lot.

'First time I've seen one in person, that's all.'

'Well, the Fiver isn't what I want to show you,' he said. 'Have you gotten far enough into the black files to read up on something called Basilisk?'

'No. I've been busy with other things.'

Merchant nodded. 'Well, you being an old tanker, I thought you might appreciate a peek at the prototype. I couldn't have shown this to you before you were moved up onto the black-budget committee, you know.' He slowed for a checkpoint as they passed through a double gate into the high-security test area. 'Have you ever seen one of those crazy events where people compete to see how far they can drive a snowmobile across open water?'

'Sure,' said Wilman. 'Though you have to wonder who the first guy was who decided to try it, and why he thought it was a good idea.'

'I just figure it was a sixteen-year-old somewhere – drunk or extremely bored. Or both. Anyway, that's Basilisk – named after

316

the lizard that runs across water. Essentially it's a Bradley CFV on diet pills and steroids – synthetics everywhere, plastic armor, a sealed chassis that's close kin to bathtubs and lifting bodies both, and the new GE high-output turbine that's a big brother to the one under the Fiver's hood.'

'You're talking about a light tank that can swim?'

'"Swim" isn't the verb I'd use. But here we are – Shed 7. You can see for yourself.'

With Merchant yielding the wheel to an AG test driver, they followed the Basilisk at high speed to a remote section of the test range that offered hills, brush, a natural river, and an artificial lake. There the Basilisk's test crew put on a demonstration that brought a wide-eyed elemental joy to Wilman's face – the look of a boy reveling in the noise and power of big machines.

The Basilisk climbed rock walls, bulled down a small tree, flew along a rough road, and then vaulted the river without slowing down, throwing out a jet-plume roostertail of water behind it. To close out the demonstration, the Basilisk crossed the small lake at its widest point, then turned around and started back. Half-way across, it slowed to a stop, dropping deeper into the water but remaining securely afloat. With tracks wheeling in opposite directions, it spun through a full turn clockwise, then counterclockwise. The turret swung round and the 25mm cannon fired at a target off to the west. The recoil barely left the Basilisk rocking as it surged forward, climbing up out of the water as it picked up speed and headed shoreward.

'Try that in any other vehicle,' Merchant said proudly.

'Can it handle sloping banks?'

'Of course. So long as it reaches the water right-side-up, it's not going under.'

'Well – I'm impressed. An amazing machine,' Wilman said. 'We wouldn't have needed them in Iraq, but most anywhere else – you've got the mobility of a hovercraft without the hockey-puck effect.'

'Thank you,' Merchant said. 'I thought you should see it before it goes the way of the B-49 – chopped up for scrap or consigned to the Museum of Historical Curiosities.'

'What?'

Merchant inclined his head to the right, and the two men fell into a slow walk along the concrete beach of the artificial lake. 'The Basilisk was intended to replace both versions of the Bradley. But I got word Monday that the order for the next six prototypes is on hold, and the entire production run is in question – the Pentagon is reevaluating all development and procurement of all weapons platforms. Every contract that has brakes in it is squealing to a halt.'

'No great surprise, is that, considering?' Wilman asked.

'No. But it looks like a lot of them will never start up again, including this one. And if we don't get a domestic production run of some size, we'll never get an export license, even for sale to friendlies – which means the end of a new platform that might have put $20 billion on our side of the trade ledger and kept six thousand skilled workers on the job. We don't have anything for them if this falls through.'

'Are you telling me this to make me feel guilty, or are you asking for something? And if you are, are you sure it's something I have to give?'

'I'm asking for a compass reading from a friend – nothing more,' Merchant said. 'Grover, I spent most of last week in Vail, talking privately with some acquaintances who have similar concerns. At the end of it, we couldn't agree on how to respond. We went away – let's say deeply divided, and in a high state of anxiety.'

'If these acquaintances were named Burton, Lightner, and Sullivan, that's understandable,' said Wilman, naming the CEOs of the other three American defense conglomerates. 'You have a lot of responsibility – a lot of influence over people's lives.'

Merchant stepped in front of Wilman and stopped short, facing him. 'Grover, you know I don't care about the politics – I'd just as soon be building Caribbean cruise subs and RVs for Mars if that's what governments wanted to buy. Allied General builds cutting-edge vehicles for any environment – land, sea, air, space. It's our customers who insist on weighing those vehicles down with weaponry.'

'"If wishes were starships . . ." I know you believe that, Jules. And on the strength of old friendship, I'm willing not to argue it, at least not now.'

'Thank you,' Merchant said. 'The hell of it is I've got a hundred and seventy-five thousand people who depend on the theory of armed deterrence to pay their bills and cover their kids' subscriptions to college. So I have to ask – is it too late to derail this train we're on?'

They had the privacy of isolation by then, two hundred meters around the curve of the lake from the vehicles and their crews. Wilman threw a glance in that direction, then said, 'Much too late, Jules.'

It was the answer Merchant had expected, the one that validated the position he had taken during the Vail sessions. 'Then do you have any ideas about what we do now? We're talking about seventy billion a year in government contracts drying up – twenty-five billion a year in arms exports disappearing.'

'If you're looking for sympathy, Jules, you should have known I'd be a tough audience,' Wilman said. 'You're the Four Horsemen of the Apocalypse – Allied General, Boeing, Lockmar, United Textron. You've done very well for yourselves on the suffering of others. If you're going to be the ones suffering now – well, frankly, it's hard for me to work up much outrage.'

'We won't really be the ones hurting, Grover. We can slash payroll, close plants, write down canceled projects, until we've shrunk to whatever size the rest of our business can support. I'd have a harder time of it than the other three – more than half of AG's business is military. But even we can probably survive in some form.'

'So what is it then, Jules – the value of your stock options? What's the reason for the "high state of anxiety"?'

Merchant shook his head. 'I'm surprised you have to ask that. The "Four Horsemen" have major facilities in sixty-three locations in thirty-two states. It'll be the economic equivalent of a Los Angeles earthquake, a Lower Mississippi flood, and a Florida Coast hurricane all in the same week. You're going to be looking at a hundred thousand layoffs in the first wave alone – most of them high-skill, high-pay jobs that support professional-class families.'

'We've gone through cycles of this sort of thing in the past – contractions in an industry, trade dislocations, technology shifts,'

Wilman said. 'It's temporary. After a year or two, the economy reabsorbs the talent.'

'And loses the special capabilities, the synergy, the technological and intellectual muscle that you get when you concentrate talent in one place. Grover, I'd like to try to keep as many of those people at work as possible. I'd like to keep the teams together and keep them on task.'

Wilman wrinkled his face in distaste. 'You're talking about make-work, corporate welfare. "Let's buy a few more bombers a year to keep the Palmdale plant open, let's build an aircraft carrier we don't need to hold Newport News together." But you do that when you think you'll need that muscle later. And, this time, I don't know that there's ever going to be a "later" like that.'

'That's exactly what I want to talk about,' Merchant said. 'About what else we could use that muscle for. About whether we're sure that we're never again going to need to know how to build a fast-attack submarine or a stealth bomber, and about what we might want to do with ourselves while we're waiting to find out.

'But not about welfare, Grover – not about making things we have no use for, or taking twice as long to make things we do need. I'd just like to sit down with the President and talk about the possibilities.' Merchant hesitated, then decided to turn over his hole card. 'I'd like a chance to talk to him about a manned mission to Europa – about putting a spacecraft in orbit, a crawler on the ice and a sub in the ocean. Do you think he'd be willing to listen?'

Wilman's wondering eyes proclaimed that he had finally heard something unexpected – and inviting. Whether it was the idea itself or the prospect of converting one of the Four Horsemen from acts of chaos to acts of creation, Merchant did not know. But Wilman's words opened the door wide enough to give him hope.

'I don't know if the President would be willing to listen,' the senator said slowly. 'But I would. Do they let you have enough space for two chairs and a hatrack somewhere around here?'

Merchant laughed. 'Yeah, Grover – they do. All the coffee I can drink and a key to the men's room, too.'

'If you take them up on the first, you're going to need the second – especially at our age.' He clapped a hand on Merchant's shoulder and turned him back the way they had come. 'Well, gunner – let's go talk about what we're going to do after the war.'

It's out of our hands now.

When Mark Breland had offered those words to John Trent that morning four months ago, it had been with a purely intellectual understanding of their verity. Now he had all the evidence he needed of his own prescience. There were no longer any 'normal' days – something totally unexpected, and yet at the same time completely understandable, seemed to be happening all the time.

'On good days,' he explained to Stepak, 'being President used to be kind of like trying to steer a rickety minibus down an unfamiliar mountain road at high speed while three aunts and a mother-in-law simultaneously try to give you advice about your driving.'

'And now?'

'It's more like learning to surf,' said Breland. 'And surfing isn't something we do a lot of in Pennsylvania.'

But the metaphor was more than the punchline of a joke to Breland. His control was that tenuous – the forces that powerful and turbulent – and he seemed to spend all of his time falling off, climbing back on, or precariously clinging to his balance.

Sometimes events merely sprang to the top of the news queue, complete and remote, suitable only for expressions of wonder or disgust, celebration or regret. Others demanded a place at the top of the President's daily agenda, and occasionally lingered there demanding continuing attention. Breland placed the two assassination attempts – one domestic, one imported – in the former category. The impeachment attempt – by general agreement, a much closer call – belonged to the latter.

Breland had survived all three attacks, but he had other wounds, and they were not healing. Rising expectations had battered his approval rating. An unlikely coalition of civil libertarians and uncivil Libertarians, patrician industrialists and industrious Patriots, was sniping at him from both ends of the political spectrum, with a sophisticated mailing campaign and a coordinated protest campaign the principle weapons.

Even with the election more than two years away, a second term seemed a lost cause, and by Nolby's order was simply not spoken of in the President's presence. The staff's focus, as defined by Vice President Toni Franklin, was 'curing the foundation'.

We cannot control what happens when we are gone from here, or when that day will come, she explained in the memo that became known as the Eulogy. *We cannot be assured of completing what we've begun. We cannot be assured that our successors will honor either our intent or our efforts. All we can do, in the time remaining to us, is to make the most of our presence. If all we leave behind are plans, they are easily ignored. If all we leave behind is a hole in the ground, it is easily filled. If all we do is hoard workers and supplies, they are easily diverted to other causes.*

But if we commit ourselves to this goal and no other, enlisting help wherever we can find it, I believe we have enough time to place in the ground a solid foundation for peaceful disarmament, with pilings that go all the way to the social bedrock. And if we diligently tend and watch over our foundation until the concrete has cured, and is ready to bear all the weight we intended for it, then those who follow us will have as much trouble dismantling it as they will ignoring it. It will be a permanent fixture on the political landscape, a reminder of the new possibilities. What our successors decide to build there will be influenced by what we've done to prepare the ground, and their choices will be visible for all to see, and judge.

It may be that it's not yet time for this vision to become a reality. But we can change the nature of the argument forever, and provide those who share our vision with a symbol and an example around which they can rally. It may be that it is not within our reach to hasten the future – this is still a young country, stubbornly short-sighted at times. But we can still be the voice of the self-fulfilling prophecy, the midwife if not the mother of a new age. Our commitment and our example will ensure that the future, when it comes, will bear more than a passing resemblance to our ideals of a safer, more civil society.

This is what the moment asks of us. This is what the President needs from us. Make every day count.

Printed on fine bond letterhead instead of electronically mailed, individually hand-signed by the former Alabama senator and hand-delivered by her to nearly three hundred desks in the Executive Office Building, the Eulogy memo had far more impact on the staff than Breland could ever have guessed. There were a handful of defections and resignations, but those who remained closed ranks around the President and tried to shelter him from the storm raging without.

Ironically, one of the sheltering havens they found for him was Western Europe. Breland was more popular in Cologne than in Chicago, more respected in Bonn than Boston. All of the European Union nations had long ago resolved their issues regarding private ownership of firearms – and resolved them in favor of public safety. It was hard for the typical citizen of England or Germany or France to grasp how an American President could find himself in trouble for offering a long overdue solution to what they viewed as an ugly stain on America's character.

But there was more to Breland's popularity than sympathy for someone seen as wrongly maligned. Most of those same EU nations had struggled for decades with urban terrorism, and Breland's gift of the Trigger had given the police a powerful new weapon against the car bomb and the package bomb. And unlike in America, there was no resistance to using the Trigger creatively and aggressively.

Offspring of the Mark I were buried under dozens of intersections in Paris and three other French cities, creating confinement grids that made it difficult to transport a bomb any distance through the city. Checkpoints with massive blast deflectors were placed along the approaches to train and highway tunnels in the Swiss Alps. Large areas of London, Belfast, Geneva, Amsterdam, Rome, Warsaw and Berlin – some as extensive as forty square blocks – were evacuated and screened for unexploded ordnance, then placed under permanent protection by a Mark I array.

Creating these 'safe zones' was a calculated risk, and there were some casualties, despite metal-detector and magnetic anomaly sweeps beforehand – a thirteenth-century church, San Francesco, in Bologna and a ten-year-old government services center in Bonn both partially collapsed into the craters left by deep-buried aerial bombs, and in London a fire caused by a V-1 warhead exploding under the basement badly damaged a block of flats near Parliament Square. But the safe zones, marked by Breland's blue-and-white dove symbol, were so popular with tourists and residents both that those losses did not derail the program.

At the same time, all across the European continent, fields and forests by the square kilometer were being swept clean of bombs and shells left behind by almost two centuries of warfare. A startling amount of aging ordnance proved to still be in the ground, and the work became something of a spectator event, producing spectacular visuals for the newsnets on a regular basis.

Outside the EU, similar 'anti-terrorist protocols' and 'interdiction zones' began to appear along the Nile, where the new democratic government of Egypt was eager to lure Westerners back to the pyramids and temples; in Sarajevo, which was determined to recreate itself as the beautiful, cosmopolitan city it had been before the first civil war; and in Singapore, which surrounded itself with what amounted to a Trigger-field moat and declared itself 'the island city of peace'.

Elsewhere in the Far East, the governments of more than a dozen island nations from the Solomon Islands to the Philippines were calling on the United States and Japan to return and clean up not only the battlefields but the territorial waters on which they'd fought, and the US Navy had begun testing a towed Trigger array off Guadalcanal. The premier of a reunified Vietnam made the same appeal to the governments of France and the United States.

Viewed from Eureka County, Nevada, or Princeton, or the Goldstein estate in Maryland, all this activity seemed like a thoroughgoing vindication, a guarantee that there would be no turning back.

But the view was different from the offices of Senator Wilman and Mind Over Madness, of General Madison and the other Joint Chiefs, of Anson Tripp and the National Security Council, of Devon Carrero and the geopolitical analysts at the Department of State. They were concerned not with cleaning up after the last war, but with preventing – or, it became necessary, winning – the next war. And it was not yet clear to anyone whether the Trigger could help with either.

No one in those circles believed that peacable demonstrations of the technology alone would make the Trigger a credible deterrent to aggression. It was widely held that someone, somewhere, would have to put armed forces on the move and on the line. 'It will take a

Hiroshima,' was the chilling phrase that had achieved currency.

And so they waited, preparing for what they considered the Trigger's real test, knowing that if their response was too slow or too feeble, it would have to be done again. They waited for the rumblings of aggression in a place they could reach in time and in strength, rumblings loud enough that no one could miss when and how they were silenced.

They waited, frozen in an uncertain standoff with an undeclared opponent. They waited, and while they waited the training went on, preparing unarmed pilots and sailors and soldiers to face an invading army, an advancing fleet. If the Trigger did not work, many lives in the special Tactical Intervention units would be forfeit.

The waiting finally ended on June 6, when President-for-Life Hosan Hussein demanded that Syria, Saudi Arabia, and Kuwait cease construction on a series of slender fifty-meter-tall towers located just inside their borders with Iraq.

'We know the true purpose of these structures,' Hussein declared in a chest-pounding national address. 'We know that the claim of a defensive shield is a lie. These towers are being built so our enemies can spy on us, so the infidels can peer into our villages and cities and streets and homes and mosques. These towers are being built so our enemies can beam destructive energies into our bodies as we sleep, energies which will cause cancers to grow and steal the life from our unborn children.

'We will not allow these assaults to take place. We will not accept these insidious invasions of our sovereign lands and our sacred places. The towers must come down. If those who plot against us do not abandon their course and destroy these evil weapons, then I will send our brave pilots and soldiers to smash them down and scatter our enemies on the sands.'

To back up his ultimatum, Hosan Hussein sent two armored divisions supported by artillery and antiaircraft batteries south to within a four-hour drive of the Al-Rafah crossroads on the Saudi border, where more than eight kilometers of the tower array stood completed. But before the columns of tanks had even reached those encampments, a mixed squadron of F-22 Raptors and F-117B Nighthawks had flown half-way around the world and landed at Al-Hayyaniyah, just forty minutes from the border.

The aging Nighthawks carried the military version of the Mark I in their internal bays, while the Raptors carried the long-range Mark II in an oversized underbelly pod. But even the crews of those aircraft wondered silently how much eight aircraft carrying no missiles under their wings, and cameras instead of guns in their noses, could do against more than one hundred tanks. They listened to Breland's public warning to Hussein with no hope that it would be heeded.

The next morning, the Iraqi forces moved to within an hour of the border, and Hosan Hussein issued another ultimatum, this time including the United States in his roster of villains. 'We will not wait to be your victims, or needlessly endanger our fighting men. We will not be diverted into lengthy negotiations or slowed by empty promises. The towers must come down now.'

By nightfall, the last of the construction crews working along the Saudi border had packed up and withdrawn.

At 2.00 p.m. Washington time, Stepak and Tripp interrupted President Breland in a meeting with news of what looked like the Iraqi push. 'We have new satellite data,' said Stepak as they hurried through the corridors toward the situation room. 'The Iraqi units near Al-Rafah are moving east at high speed, and six more divisions are coming down the Al-Basrah road toward the Safwan entrance into Kuwait.'

'So Kuwait was the target after all,' said Breland, studying the map. 'Al-Rafah was a feint.'

'So it appears,' said Tripp.

'How long?'

'We're projecting that the western forces will probably cross into Kuwait along the Wadi al-Batin, where the array is still under construction. If they keep up their present pace, they can cross just before dawn local time. The eastern forces can reach Safwan an hour sooner. The grid *is* active there.'

'Rockets and artillery?'

They reached the situation room as Breland was asking his question, and the secretary of defense went directly to the theater map. 'In position to reach Al-Kuwayt – here, here, and here.

326

And as this scenario is developing, Mr President, we expect to see them used.'

Stepak hesitated, then turned to face Breland. 'I know you intended to wait until the tanks crossed the border, so there'd be no question that Iraq was the aggressor. But if the GA-30s have chemical warheads, we could be looking at ten thousand dead in Kuwait City. If they have biologicals, the bidding starts at thirty thousand. Do we wait until the Iraqis put the artillery in play, or do we go after them preemptively?'

'How fast can we respond once they start? Can we get close enough to wait on the first muzzle flash?'

General Hawley stepped forward to take the question. 'The Nighthawks don't have much capacity to loiter on station. The Raptors have more, but, frankly, we don't have enough planes there to cover all the bases – or to cover the likely losses if we do expose our aircraft that way.'

'Do we have any other aircraft we can bring in?'

'There are six Trigger-equipped strike fighters on the *USS Truman*, in the Mediterranean,' said Admiral Jacobs. 'They're too far out. There are six more on the *USS Reagan*, in the western Indian Ocean – with midair refueling, we could just get them over the Iraq-Kuwait border by dawn, but the timing is tricky – we need a Go within the next half-hour, and they won't be able to linger.'

Breland settled into his chair at the circular conference table. 'I need to hear recommendations,' he said. 'Don't expect me to call the pitch.'

'Very well, Mr President,' said Stepak. 'Our recommendation is that we violate the border and act preemptively. General Madison proposes to send one flight of F-22s and one flight of F-117s after the artillery in Iraq, with the attack timed to take place thirty minutes before the armor units reach Kuwait. The other four aircraft at Al-Hayyaniyah would pursue the armor column from Ash-Shabakah and intercept them at the border. Four aircraft from the *Reagan* would be sent to intercept the eastern column at Safwan.'

'Projected losses?'

'Twenty percent. Three aircraft.'

'Can they get the job done?'

'I'd rather have twice as many aircraft, and some top cover for them,' said Madison. 'But we'll do our damnedest to get the job done with what we have.'

'Can we be sure this isn't another feint?'

'Not if we shoot first.'

'I'll want to issue another warning.'

'Then projected losses double, and I can't guarantee the results. I would counsel strongly against it. You already told them we're there, and you told them why. Letting them know we've seen through the feint gives away an edge we probably need.'

Tripp appeared at Breland's right elbow. 'And, sir, consider –' he said in a low voice. 'What if you warned them again, and they actually stopped? Does that give us what we want?'

His implication was as distasteful to Breland as the prospect of initiating hostilities on Iraqi territory. Pushing his chair back, he walked up to the theater map and studied it, his arms crossed over his chest. But the map was only colored pixels, an eccentric chessboard with exotic pieces. He had to force himself to see the human beings – the American pilots, the Iraqi tankers, the Kuwaiti soldiers and citizens, the artillerymen expecting to be fifty kilometers from the fighting.

We do *need a Hiroshima, after all. Damn them for not believing,* Breland thought bitterly. *Damn them all for being willing to raise the club – and obliging me to knock it out of their hands. And that means no half-measures – it has to be done with enough authority that they never pick it up again. Damn them all –*

'I authorize the plan outlined by the Secretary of Defense,' he said without turning from the map. 'Send the planes into Iraq.'

The planes came racing through the near-total darkness of a moonless predawn morning, skimming four abreast two hundred meters above the desert. Neither radar nor sentry saw them, angular black shapes knifing through the sky, outrunning the sound of their own engines – not until it was too late, and hellish pillars of fire marked the location of ammunition trucks which had been poised to feed the great steel cylinders of the long-range artillery.

From inside the cockpits, each thunderous explosion below seemed to lunge upward at them, grasping for the delicate flight surfaces, hurling shrapnel at the spinning turbine blades, the soft bodies of the pilots. The worst of the concussions shoved their planes around in the sky like a thunderstorm cell. But the speed of their passage carried them safely away from harm, as though they were riding on the leading edge of chaos.

Breaking into pairs, they made four more runs over the gun emplacements and the adjacent encampment, both now starkly lit by fierce fires. The last of these was made in silence, as there was nothing left on the ground below them that could threaten the planes – or anyone else.

Along the Az-Zubayr road, four more ghosts chased and caught a different quarry – a long and badly strung-out support convoy following a two-mile column of Russian- and Indian-made armor. With one Nighthawk flying just above and to the right of the road and another just above and to the left, a single pass was enough to leave the convoy in ruins. The Ravens, trailing behind as spotters, found nothing to aim their Mark IIs at, and no reason for a second pass.

When they caught up with the armor column, they found it dispersing, scattering off the road and into the sand. It made no difference. In less than two minutes, every tank was a flaming coffin. The token machine-gun fire directed at the planes in the first seconds did no damage, and even with radioed warning from the convoy behind, neither of the mobile antiaircraft guns managed to fire a single shell at the low-flying attackers.

The third element of the interdiction force, the Navy contingent from the *Reagan*, arrived late at Safwan, their unforgiving time-table ruined by half a dozen minor snafus and a midair refueling problem. Dawn had already broken when the flight finally made contact with its targets.

But to the amazement of the pilots, the Iraqi column – number-ing more than two hundred twenty tanks and other vehicles – was neither driving into Kuwait nor fleeing back the way it had come. Instead, it was stopped dead on the road a kilometer from Safwan, a ragged double line of vehicles in clear sight of the Kuwaiti border post. And on either side of the road, scattered across the barren land but keeping well clear of the tanks, were hundreds, perhaps thousands of Iraqi soldiers on foot.

It took several radio calls over the next several minutes to sort out the mystery. Eventually, though, the circling pilots received confirmation from the Kuwaiti forces at the border that the improbable prospect before them was in fact the strange reality – the soldiers on foot were the tank crews, who had abandoned their vehicles rather than be blown up inside them.

'Flight, they obviously got the word on what they could expect. Let's not disappoint them,' said the sortie leader, and led his wingmates down.

It was, at last, the end of the beginning. In less than an hour, a dozen unarmed aircraft had dismantled a modern armored invasion force, methodically destroying its equipment and, more importantly, breaking its will. But it was the story of the battle that wasn't – the events at Safwan, the incredible images captured by combat videographers on the ground – which confirmed for believers and skeptics both that a new era had dawned, and there would be no going back.

II: Jammer

23:

'If you have a nation of men who have risen to that
height of moral cultivation that they will not declare
war or carry arms, for they have not so much madness
left in their brains, you have a nation of lovers, of
benefactors, of true, great, and able men.'
— *Ralph Waldo Emerson*

From the first day it was filed, the National Association of Riflemen's lawsuit against the Trigger had received special handling.

Judge Virginia Howarth of the D.C. District Court had needed barely two weeks of testimony and four days of deliberation to reach a ruling upholding the NAR's position: citizens had a right to guns, but no right to Triggers. Her blanket injunction forbade the use of any Federal funds to develop, manufacture, or deploy the Trigger. But she had infuriated John Trent by, in virtually the next breath, setting aside the injunction pending the appeal.

'Why?' he had demanded of his lead lawyer, Philby Lancaster. 'She gives with the one hand and jerks it away with the other. Isn't she one of ours? Who else does she owe?'

'She's only been sitting for three years,' Lancaster had answered. 'This is too big for her, and she's obviously passing the buck to the appellate courts. Don't worry about this. The weight of the decision leans toward us. And the real action starts now.'

Within days, no fewer than nine petitions for a writ of *certiorari* were filed with the Supreme Court, including the expected one by Doran Douglas on behalf of the Justice Department. The Court responded by reaching down and claiming the case before the District of Columbia Court of Appeals had even scheduled motions.

Once in the highest court's hands, *NAR vs. US* was pushed to the top of the calendar, leapfrogging more than two dozen other cases already on the docket. Oral arguments were heard barely ten weeks after the case was first filed. In a rare departure from form the Court had approved Rule 28 motions from both parties, and extended the time allotted from the usual half-hour per side to forty-five minutes.

In an even stronger break with tradition, the Supreme Court had even allowed representatives of four of the record number of groups filing *amicus curiae* briefs to also argue before the justices. Gun Owners of America and the Second Amendment Alliance had appeared in support of the NAR, while Mind Over Madness and HCI had stood up for the gun-grabbers. Trent had been pleased by the contrast that presented.

'Judge them by the company they keep,' he had said when interviewed by the media on the eve of oral arguments. 'Patriots and lovers of the Constitution support our position. Socialist internationalists and statist propagandists support theirs. Disarming America has been on the far left's agenda for fifty years. I'm confident the Supreme Court will not join them in committing treason.'

No case since *Roe vs. Wade* had attracted so much public interest. A public affairs foundation turned the transcripts of the pleadings into a three-hour docudrama literally overnight; when it was published, so many people tried to access it that the Oyez Project servers crumbled, and the producers had to resort to a sponsored broadcast at fixed times. Even so, it topped the ratings for the week.

All the urgency fostered expectations for a swift ruling, but it did not come. Month after month slipped by, until Court watchers were united in the belief that the justices were badly divided, possibly hopelessly deadlocked.

As the scheduled end of the Court's annual session neared, Lancaster relayed to Trent a rumor that the justices had not even decided who was to write the opinion – which, if true, raised the prospect that the Court might adjourn on June 1 without issuing a ruling, and take the case up again in the fall.

'How can this be so hard for them?' he demanded of Lancaster. 'What possible issue could they be stuck on? The plain language of the Second Amendment gives them everything they need. The

Founder's own words – George Washington, "Firearms stand next in importance to the Constitution itself." James Madison –'

'Please, John – not the whole conservative book of quotes. I wrote the brief, after all.'

'I know that,' Trent said with a sigh. 'But, god almighty, Philby, Judge Howarth got it right in a tenth of the time they've already had. – Except for the stay, of course.'

For the first time, Lancaster was unable to exude confidence. 'The government's argument may be causing problems for the strict constructionists on the Court,' he said. 'We're in a realm the Founders never imagined. There's talk that the justices are divided not two ways, but three. Compromise comes hard to that body. We could end up with strange bedfellows and a tortured decision that pleases no one. I think we should be prepared.'

'And in the meantime, the Feds are laughing up their sleeves – the factories humming and the trucks rolling and new Trigger installations going online every goddamned day,' Trent complained bitterly. 'Isn't there anything we can do to get the stay lifted? Isn't there any way to reach the Court? Should we be out there on the front steps every morning, six or ten or twenty thousand of us?'

'Oh – certainly. And be sure to bring plenty of guns to wave, like they do at that stupid demonstration every year. Scaring the justices is always a good idea,' Lancaster said acerbically. 'John, we talked about this months ago – there's a fucking Trigger in the basement of the Supreme Court itself. If our people do *anything* that makes the justices feel like they need it there to protect them from the likes of us, it's over. Over.'

'Maybe they should disqualify themselves from the case. Conflict of interest.' Trent's tone was sulky.

'You'd better tell me you understand, John. One mistake, and we throw away the edge the eight years of fuss over NFRRA gives us. The justices aren't hermits. They know how passionate you folks are, and the Court *has* to be leery of kicking off another long-running controversy. You are reaching them by being patient, reasonable, and civil. Stick with it. And do everything you can to clamp down on the free spirits until we get the ruling.'

'And what if the opinion goes against us?'

'Then we analyze the justices' thinking, and go at it again from another direction.'

'So Plan B is more of the same.'

Lancaster snorted. 'Burn me for heresy, John, but when you have good lawyers, you don't need guns.'

June 1 came and went, and the Supreme Court neither issued an opinion in *NAR vs. United States* nor recessed for the summer. No announcement was made, no explanations offered, as for the first time in more than two decades, the Court extended its session. The phrase 'hung court' made its first appearance in a CNNLaw report, and soon was heard everywhere.

John Trent weathered the crush of media attention in the weeks preceding and following June 1 with outward calm. Everyone wanted to know what he thought, and he was sternly prevented by Philby Lancaster from actually telling them.

'This delay should alarm no one. It should tell us that the Court recognizes the very grave issues at the heart of our complaint, and is according it the seriousness it deserves,' Trent said, standing before a newly-dedicated monument to Revolutionary War Militiamen in Brandywine, Pennsylvania.

'I'm absolutely confident the Court will come to the right decision – right for the Constitution, right for the country, and right for our citizens, whose rights are paramount in a free and democratic nation,' he said a week later, standing beside a poster-sized facsimile of the Bill of Rights hanging in the lobby of NAR headquarters.

'The way I see it, Jay, there can't be anyone in Washington more eager to wrap this up than the justices themselves – it's summer in Washington, and those robes have to be hot,' he said a week later in a VR appearance on *Altered Egos*. It was a good line, even if it was only a set-up, and the laughter was bolstered by the fact that the producers had given him the scantily clad Biblical David as his avatar on the virtual set.

'Speaking of robes,' Jay cracked back, 'if there are any Monicas over there in the law clerk corps, please call, because we'd like to know if this really is a hung court –'

Away from the cameras, Trent was increasingly restive. He

complained bitterly to other NAR executives about the shortage of courage and conscience on the Supreme Court, and the lack of honor in the legal profession generally. He derided Philby Lancaster and the rest of the NAR legal team as professional leeches who would cheerfully lose a case to keep a hungry client's wallet open. He could scarcely bear to mention Mark Breland, Grover Wilman, or Jeffrey Horton by name, but when he did, he liberally peppered his comments with angry words like 'traitors', 'lying bastards', 'murderers', and 'cowardly whores'.

Ironically, Trent found himself spending much of his day listening to even more venomous rants and forcing himself to counsel moderation. By virtue of being first to the courtroom, the NAR had become the gravitational center of the fight against the Trigger. It seemed as though the top officers of every gun-rights organization with more than three members expected to have a chance to bend Trent's ear – whether to offer him unsolicited advice, praise and encourage him, commiserate with him, or bluntly excoriate him for timidity.

He suppressed his growing doubts and told them all what Philby Lancaster had told him, that as long as the outcome hung in the balance, their interests were best served by what amounted to a ceasefire – no threats, no violence, nothing but polite demonstrations and gentle persuasion. He took some ridicule for that, but he steeled himself against the criticism and persisted.

'We don't want those justices checking the news and coming away thinking that America needs the Trigger,' he told the commander of the West Montana Militia.

'We don't want those justices thinking that the three-piece suits are fronting for a collection of thugs, mutts, hotheads, mean drunks, and bullies,' he told the president of .45 Caliber Freedom.

'We want the Court to know that America is a civilized country filled with responsible gun owners. We want 'em to know that our firearms are saving lives and protecting our liberties and providing family recreation,' he told the chairman of the Arizona Committee of Correspondence.

With patience and persistence and sometimes a pretense of brotherhood, Trent persuaded most to sign on to the 'civilized ceasefire' concept. He did it even though he knew that some of them nevertheless considered him weak, soft, timid. A willingness to kill for the cause was, in their eyes, the only real measure of manhood. And those who had lost all faith in what they believed were corrupt courts and sham trials made it clear that they were ready to resort to violence.

Trent could identify with that frustration, but found it difficult to even talk about taking the next step. The toughest tests, though, were his meetings with the extremist militias. It was a small mercy that not many of them came calling. Some had established separatist communes and severed all contact with the rest of 'Amerika'. Many others viewed the NAR with the high contempt due all collaborators.

But several times since the case reached the high court, Trent had found himself sitting across a table from a man of morals so repellent and mindset so alien that it made him squirm to think of him as an ally. They brought him offers he did not want to hear: to assassinate the managers of Aron Goldstein's factories, to take the Chief Justice's six-year-old great-granddaughter hostage, to poison the White House water supply, to hijack an airliner and crash it into Trent's target of choice.

He did not know if they had the wherewithal to deliver, or if it was just bluster, and he did not care to. The line Trent would not cross, the line his visitors helped define for him, was the line between acts of patriotism and acts of revolution. He would not condone destroying the nation to preserve it – that paradox, which Trent associated with the Inquisition, seemed to him a kind of madness.

Ironically, it was out of these sessions that Trent emerged with his blackest moods, his most uncompromising fury toward Washington. 'You need to start treating craziness like a contact poison, John,' his senior administrative aide kidded him. 'Don't go in there without gloves and a mask.'

'That's not it,' Trent said, unable to laugh about it. 'Do you know why I end up this way? Because I can't forgive the President for giving people like that fuel for their paranoia. Tyranny isn't the only threat to what I love. Anarchy is every bit as dangerous.'

*   *   *

338

The voice came from behind him in the lobby – pleasant, assured, and unfamiliar.

'I wonder if we might have a frank conversation together, John Trent.'

Trent spun around to find a nattily-dressed older man standing one stride behind him. His glance went first to the usual places of concealment for a man wearing a well-tailored summer suit, then to assessing the man himself. Several centimeters shorter than Trent, the stranger had a full head of silver hair, a Princeton ring, and a slight paunch that the tailoring could not quite mask. Trent gauged his age to be sixty.

'I'm sorry, do I know you?'

'Possibly,' the man said, edging closer. 'In any case, I have some information that will be of interest to you.'

Trent frowned. Being recognized in public and approached was nothing new, especially lately, but he had run out of patience with it. 'Look, I'm here with friends, to hear the orchestra. If this is Association business, I'd appreciate it if you'd call the office tomorrow.'

The stranger's response was to take Trent firmly by the elbow and turn him toward the corridor leading to the offices of the concert hall. 'Please,' he said, 'I'm afraid I can't sit through the Mahler. My tastes run to the Italian romantics – I came for the Rossini, and to see you.'

'Might I have your name, then?' Trent asked, allowing himself to be led.

'How rude of me,' the man said. 'I am Angelo DiBartolo. Come – in here.' DiBartolo had unlocked the office of the sales manager, and stepped aside to allow Trent to enter first. When Trent shied, looking back down the hall for Jerry, his driver and bodyguard, DiBartolo added quickly, 'No, no, we're friends, Mr Trent, please let go of your pulp-fiction prejudices. Your driver and my driver are having a cigarette outside, so we can have a little privacy.'

'You're *that* Angelo DiBartolo,' Trent said. 'From Baltimore.'

The other man shrugged resignedly. 'I have people who try to keep my face and name out of the news. Unfortunately, they aren't always successful. Come, please, and perhaps we can still get you back to your seat for the first movement.'

Trent turned on the light as he entered, and DiBartolo turned it off again as he pulled the door shut and locked it again. There was enough light streaming in from a streetlamp to make the room a grey and white world.

'You said you had information for me –'

'Yes, you see, I've been taking a very personal interest in your lawsuit,' DiBartolo began.

'Why? Speaking frankly.'

DiBartolo smiled. 'You could say that applied violence is to my business what advertising is to General Motors. So any possible change in business conditions is of great interest to me. And in pursuing my curiosity, I've now heard something which I'm sure is of interest to you. The Supreme Court will hand down its opinion on Tuesday morning –'

That was three days away. 'How can you know that?' Trent demanded.

'I have a friend, someone who is extremely close to the Court.'

'Look, how can I –'

'Are you not interested in knowing the outcome?'

With a sick feeling, Trent swallowed hard and fell silent.

'The Court will split five-four,' DiBartolo went on, 'to overturn Howarth and allow the use of the Trigger to continue. They will issue four opinions in all, including three from the majority. Liggett will write the principal opinion.'

'You're telling me we've lost.'

'Regretfully, yes. I hope that the advance notice will help you be properly prepared to respond.'

There was no reason to believe DiBartolo, save perhaps one: Supreme Court Justice Joseph Anthony Perri, formerly of the District Court for the State of Maryland and the 4th Circuit Court of Appeals, and currently the junior member of the October fraternity. 'This news is – reliable?'

'Absolutely reliable,' DiBartolo assured him.

Trent turned away and grabbed the back of a chair with a fierce grip that left his fingers bloodless. 'What's the price of this information, Mr DiBartolo? You offered it before I told you if it was of any value to me.'

'Don't concern yourself with that, Mr Trent. There are no

340

obligations attached. In fact, I want to ask if we can do anything more for you –'

'More? What, a hit on the President?' Trent's tone was sarcastic.

'You misunderstand me, Mr Trent,' said DiBartolo, though there was no indignation in his tone. 'I would never sanction such a reckless act. There are *rules*. One doesn't take retribution on a man simply because he opposes you. There must be a sound business purpose, some clear profit to be gained. That, or it must be a matter of honor.'

'What, then?' Trent demanded, spinning toward DiBartolo. 'What are you offering? You come here and tell me they beat us. What do you think you're going to be able to do for us now? I'm afraid I'm not very good at reading between the lines.'

DiBartolo shrugged. 'An unarmed man on the road always knows that he's in danger. An armed man behind a castle wall isn't always so wary. In time, you see, all the castles fell – to artillery, to siege, to corruption and betrayal. There is a way, Mr Trent, and someone will find it.' He invoked the air with his right hand. 'But in the meantime, there are expenses. I would like to make a contribution toward them. This is something we can do –'

The offer pricked Trent's ego, and the wound bled a sharp-tongued resistance. 'We can pay for our own lawyers. Or any other professional services we might require.'

'As you wish.' DiBartolo raised his hands as though in surrender. 'But if you should need help securing other resources – someone who knows the secrets of artillery or the ways of siege engines, as it were – I hope you'll feel free to call on me. My people take some justifiable pride in their expertise in that area.'

The glow of the corridor light through the pebbled glass of the office door dimmed momentarily, once, twice, three times. 'Ah, there's the call – you see, the intermission is just ending, you've missed nothing yet. By all means, please, rejoin your friends. I myself am eager to go home and see my family. Thank you for your courtesy, Mr Trent. I wish you well.'

John Trent said nothing to anyone about that meeting for two days. By the time Mahler's 2nd Symphony was over, he had calmed himself enough to hold his tongue, and convinced himself that he would wait and see what Tuesday brought rather than go out on a limb on the basis of DiBartolo's word.

But early on Monday morning, the treasurer of the NAR came into Trent's office with a worried expression and a handful of printouts.

'Look at these,' he said. 'In the last hour, nearly a million dollars has been posted to the general administrative account – all wire transfers, all between forty and a hundred thousand dollars, all from donors we've never heard from before. International Liberty Fund, Sophia Aiello Foundation, Friends of Freedom, something called the Maritime Enterprises Holding Company, half a dozen individual EuroUnion citizens plus two Caribbean accounts that might be hiding just about anyone – did you have a good weekend and forget to tell me? None of these donors contacted us for our account information. How do I handle this?'

'I had an awful weekend, thank you, and I'm expecting an even worse week,' Trent said curtly as he came to his feet. 'Allocate the money to Education and Outreach. We're going to spend a lot of it in the next twenty-four hours. Kenneth!' The last was a shout directed at the outer office.

His administrative aide came running. 'Yes?'

'Call in the council. We have work to do.'

The netmail action alert tree worked perfectly. By dawn on Tuesday, the vanguard of the Justice Day demonstrators was streaming into Washington aboard a small fleet of tour buses and charter aircraft.

Converging on the west end of the Mall, the buses disgorged their human cargo near the Lincoln Memorial, then headed off to gather more. March captains gathered the new arrivals into groups of two or three hundred, and led them east along Constitution Avenue toward the Capitol. That route took them past the windows of the White House, and many marchers shouted jeers across the Ellipse. But they were otherwise well behaved, and while the park police on horseback watched attentively and seemed to be doing a great deal of talking on their radios, they kept a comfortable distance and did not try to interfere.

342

By 8.00 a.m., there were more than ten thousand outside the Capitol, milling on the grassy eastern tip of the Mall in sight of the Supreme Court half a block away. By then the parade along Constitution Avenue had grown to a thin but unbroken stream, and the shouted jeers had been replaced by a wordless but equally challenging display of clenched fists and one-fingered salutes. The signs and placards reading JUSTICE NOW! and FREEDOM NOW! finally arrived, and soon were in evidence along the full length of the Mall.

Every side street seemed to have at least one police unit parked and watching, but still there were no confrontations. The march had taken the authorities by surprise, and while they were no doubt uncomfortable watching the crowd swell, they had no ready strategy for preventing it.

There were cameras evident from the beginning, some feeding NAR-friendly sites and others belonging to press outlets friendly to their cause, but the march officially became an event when two of the 'Big Five' netcasters put the story at the top of their portals. It cascaded quickly from there to the smaller providers, and the buzz spread even faster throughout Washington: 'Something's happening on the Mall.'

Just after nine, normal morning traffic and the influx of curious locals slowed traffic flow near the Lincoln Memorial to near-gridlock, and the city police responded by trying to close Arlington Memorial Bridge. Almost immediately, the half-dozen officers whose vehicles formed the barricade found themselves caught between more than a thousand demonstrators disembarking from buses stopped on the Virginia side of the Potomac and more than three times that number marching in relief from the Mall. But the imminent clash never came. After a hasty consultation with headquarters, the barricading vehicles were hurriedly removed, and in a complete reversal the police began directing traffic to help the buses get through.

Supreme Court announcements were ordinarily made at 10.00 a.m., and John Trent had hoped to have the two blocks of park and street which separated the Capitol steps and the courthouse steps completely filled by his people before then. That proved too optimistic – there were bottlenecks everywhere, and the small delays had a way of compounding each other – but it did not matter. No announcement would be made in the face of what must have looked like a prospective riot. Only a few of the organizers knew that anything unexpected had happened, but when CNN1 reported that the justices had been hustled out of the city by the Secret Service, a loud cheer went up throughout the crowd.

'Vacations, hell – they didn't want to face us!' a man wearing an Airborne beret hooted. 'We spooked 'em!'

All morning the buses kept coming, with the entire Mall west of 14th Street turned into a drop-off zone and marshalling area. The parade east to the Capitol became an uncountable throng that kept spilling over into both Constitution and Independence Avenues, the thoroughfares flanking the Mall. Fearful of an incident, city police closed both routes west of 2nd Street. In minutes, the marchers gleefully claimed them for their own.

When a rumor spread that Breland was watching from the South Portico, a chant of 'Traitor – traitor – traitor –' went up in its wake. One reporter described the chanting as 'loud enough to rattle the White House'.

At the Capitol, the hard-working march captains tended to a mostly-patient crowd that now numbered more than a hundred thousand. Looking after its own interests, the National Park Service lent unexpected assistance in the form of a water truck and two flatbeds filled with portable toilets. A podium finally went up on the Capitol steps just before noon, with wireless repeaters scattered through the crowd all the way to the Supreme Court.

'What do you want?'

Coached by the march captains, the part of the crowd standing before the Capitol shouted back, 'Freedom now!' and thrust their signs and placards high into the air. A moment later the part of the throng nearest the Supreme Court answered with, 'Justice now!'

'What are you here for?'

'Freedom now!' The sound of their massed voices echoed off the high marble walls.

'Justice now!' The sound of their massed voices shook the crowded street.

As the chanting went on, John Trent climbed out of the back

344

seat of the dark blue Cadillac parked just outside the barriers on the circle drive and started walking toward the podium. With some help from a dozen or so plants who'd been expecting his appearance, he was noticed and recognized, and the crowd started applauding as it parted to let him pass. By the time Trent reached the stairs all of the cameras and most eyes were on him, and as he mounted the stairs to the podium the chanting turned to cheering. He held up his hands for silence, then leaned forward to the mic.

'This is the greatest nation on the face of the earth,' he said, and a roar of approval erupted from his audience.

'This is the greatest nation in the history of human civilization,' he said when it subsided, and the second roar was louder than the first.

'I love this country,' he said with a catch in his throat, and the throng went wild, answering his love with their voices for an unbroken minute.

'This city is not what makes America great. These grand buildings do not make America great. You – the American people – make us great.'

They applauded themselves enthusiastically, as late arrivals continued to pack in at the edge of the crowd.

'And the contract we have with each other makes us great. The contract that allows us to assemble here today, unmolested. The contract that allows us to freely speak our minds, uncensored. The contract that promises freedom, unfettered. The contract that provides for justice, uncompromised.

'This contract, this Constitution, that guarantees our right to defend ourselves and our families and our nation from those who would prey on us.'

He paused and swept the crowd with his gaze. 'What is it you want?'

Loving it, the crowd shouted as one, 'Freedom now!'

'Make sure they can hear you inside!'

'Justice now!'

'What are you here for?'

'Freedom now!'

'They need to listen to you!'

'Justice now!'

Trent pointed in the direction of the Supreme Court. 'There are nine justices in that building over there who seem to be having trouble understanding our contract with each other.' There was booing, but Trent did not stop to indulge it. 'They seem to be having trouble understanding that it was armed citizens who created this nation, and armed citizens who've strengthened and preserved it for nearly two hundred fifty years. They seem to be confused by the plain language of the Second Amendment – which I'll wager you all know by heart.'

It was ragged, but impressive all the same. The cameras panned the crowd and found rapturous faces while they recited the words of the Second Amendment.

'The good news is that there are plenty of people in this building who do understand,' Trent told them. 'And right now I'd like to introduce you to some of our friends.' He turned and looked up the stairs at the group of nine Congressmen descending toward the podium, and began to applaud.

The crowd's response was little more than polite, but it didn't matter – that moment was wholly for the media. Four senators and five representatives. Seven men and two women. Three Democrats, four Republicans, and two Progressives. Six whites, two blacks, and an Asian. America in a microcosm. The best 400,000 dollars I ever spent, Trent thought.

He shook hands with each of them, then brought Senator Gil Massey to the podium.

'John Trent is right – this is a great country. And John Trent is a great American!' Massey said, beaming in expectation of the applause that followed.

'I came here today to tell you that as the ranking minority member on the Senate Judiciary Committee, I will shortly introduce a bill to outlaw the Trigger now and forever –'

His words were lost in a kaleidoscope of joyful noise that dwarfed every outburst which had preceded it.

Protecting his sound bite, Massey repeated himself at first opportunity. 'I say, to outlaw the Trigger now and forever! No matter how the High Court rules. This device is as un-American as a sneak attack! It says, neighbor, I don't trust you. It says, mugger,

346

rapist, murderer, pick me, I want to be your next victim. Well, I say that's crazy. I say these things belong at the bottom of Boston Harbor with the King's tea! We don't need them!'

Trent smiled and applauded through eight more occasionally tortured invocations of patriotic imagery, then reclaimed the podium with the Congressmen forming a half-circle behind him.

'Will you help?' he asked the crowd. 'When you go home tonight, will you keep this memory alive? Will you cast one eye on Washington while you go about your daily business? Because Senator Massey will need you. Representative Baines-Brown will need you. I'll need you. This will be an all-out fight. With Breland in the White House, this bill will need a veto-proof margin. Will you help us get it?'

There was a roar of affirmation, and as it faded, someone in the crowd began singing loudly, 'God bless America, land that I love –'

The singer was a plant, but, even so, by the final chorus, a chill ran down Trent's back, and there was a lump in his throat.

Afterwards, while the gathering was being slowly reabsorbed by the buses and the surrounding city, there were interviews to do – a seemingly endless string of them, starting with the gray eminence of newsmedia, Bill Moyers of ABCDisney. Then, finally, there was a chance to escape from public view, drop the mask, and quietly celebrate. He chose a private dining suite at Alexandria's low-key Mondrian Inn for the setting, and NAR lobbyist Maria Nestor for the company.

'That was beautiful,' she said, greeting him with a kiss on the cheek. 'You throw a great party.'

Her perfume lingered in his nostrils as she circled the table and sat down. 'You did the heavy lifting,' he said, pouring her a glass of cabernet. 'I couldn't be more pleased. Senator Massey! That was a coup. And what a fine lineup of mannequins to go with him.'

'I enjoyed being back in my comfort zone. The High Court is hard to scare and harder to buy. But Congress is a whore.' She laughed. 'I should know.'

By the time they were finished with a leisurely five-course dinner and a thorough mussing of the king-sized bed and each other, the Mall was empty. A city the size of Madison, Wisconsin

– perhaps even Riverside, California – had appeared overnight in the middle of Washington, spent the day in the park, and then quietly departed, without a single arrest and with little more than some well-trampled grass left to testify to their presence.

I hope the right people got the message, he thought, climbing back in the Cadillac and waving his driver on. *This time, we were content just to be heard. This time. This time, we left our guns at home. This time. Pay attention – add the pieces up – I can put two hundred thousand people on your doorstep any time you make it necessary. You don't want to make it necessary.*

Expecting the NAR decision to be released in the morning, Trent had made plans to spend the night in Washington, so he could make himself available to the cameras again. But it seemed that someone else was thinking about the empty Mall as well. As the car neared the Hotel Americana, Lancaster called with the alert.

'This is it. They're releasing it at 8.00 p.m.,' he said. 'I'm on my way over there – they only gave us twenty minutes' notice.'

'Did they say anything about the timing?'

'They say it was delayed from this morning by a printing problem.' He snorted derisively.

Trent and his driver sat in their car in the driveway of the Americana, waving off the doorman and car valet and listening to the news together on Iridium Radio. There were four different opinions, two with only a single signer. They added up to a 5-4 vote to reverse the DC District Court.

Justice Joseph Anthony Perri, Trent noted with interest, voted with the minority.

'Bastards,' said Jerry, smacking the steering wheel with the heel of his hand. 'Rubbing it in our faces. Couldn't even give us a few hours to enjoy what happened today.'

'No rest for the wicked,' said Trent, who had not extended the benefit of his foreknowledge to his driver. 'Well, there's no reason to stay in town now. Let's go home, Jerry. Fredericksburg, not Fairfax. I'm think I'm going to let myself go fishing in the Rappahannock tomorrow.'

The red Ranchero pickup followed them all the way from the Americana to the Interstate 395 on-ramp, including a side trip through Arlington National Cemetery which Jerry tossed in just to see how interested the driver of the pickup was in them. He seemed very interested in them and not at all in the cemetery, which troubled Jerry enough for him to mention it aloud.

'Could be media, I suppose,' Trent said, glancing back. Dusk was disappearing into night, and there was little to be seen except a pattern of lights – headlights above, fog lamps below – that left a vague impression of a high-ground-clearance vehicle. 'I've made myself unavailable since before the decision was announced.'

'It's not really a media sort of vehicle, Mr Trent. More of a trouble sort of vehicle. Maybe I should call security for an escort, head for Fairfax instead so they can get to us early.'

'You like to drive fast, don't you, Jerry?' Trent said, settling back into his seat. 'Let's just keep going.'

The driver obediently pushed the Cadillac to 120 kilometers per hour. 'He's fallen back a little, but he's still there.'

'Maybe he just wants to shake my hand,' Trent said, then chuckled to himself. 'Or maybe he was part of the march and didn't get his travel money.'

'I would really be more comfortable calling for an escort, sir.'

'If he's still back there when it's time to leave I-95, then I'll worry.'

But just past Quantico, the red Ranchero moved up behind them and started to press. Jerry responded by pushing the big Cadillac harder, opening up the gap again – and, a few minutes later, running them right into a well-disguised two-car block on the quiet stretch between Stafford and Falmouth. The Ranchero came roaring up quickly to seal them in – minivan ahead, black coupe on the left, guardrail and ditch on the right, pickup behind.

'Son of a bitch,' Jerry muttered. 'I should have seen that –' Trent heard the Velcro rip as Jerry yanked up the passenger cushion and retrieved the Beretta .45 ACP concealed there. 'Hang on, Mr Trent, I think we're going to have to play bumper-cars.'

'Wait,' said Trent. 'They may just be punks, with no idea who we are.'

'So much the better. Mr Trent, I think you should get down.'

'There's no air bag on the floor, Jerry.'

'I'm not going to let us crash, Mr Trent.'

'It's not your driving that concerns me, Jerry, it's theirs.'

Just then, Trent's comset began chiming in local mode. As it did, the front passenger window of the vehicle beside them was rolling down, revealing a laughing young man who raised his own comset to his ear and gestured. The youth's shaved head and enormous mutton-chops were instantly recognizable, as was the cackle Trent heard when he answered the page.

'Hey, got any fucking mustard?'

'Bowman –' Trent's slow-burning ire at the Patriot Fist commander made the name come out a growl.

'No? Maybe check your shorts, you'll find some there! How'd you like that, Mr President?'

'I'm glad to be able to help entertain you. Is there anything else you want?'

'Yeah, we gotta talk about some stuff. Have your boy take the next exit, we'll find a quiet spot.' The connection terminated as the coupe's window rolled up and the vehicle surged ahead.

'Do we have a problem here or not, chief?' asked Jerry.

'Apart from the fact that Bob Bowman is high half the time and paranoid all the time?' Trent asked. 'Probably not.'

'What do you want me to do?'

'Follow them off at the next exit. But don't be too trusting, all right?'

After several minutes of wandering the winding roads on the outskirts of Fredericksburg, the lead car in the caravan pulled in at a deserted roadside park and boat launch along the Rapidan, just past Fox Run.

'I thought for a minute we were going to end up at the reservoir,' Jerry said as he shut off the engine. 'Do you want the pistol?'

Trent shook his head. 'No. Just stay in the car, act nonchalant. I have a big enough credibility problem with this guy as it is.'

When he climbed out of the car, Trent was momentarily taken aback by additional familiar faces. The driver of the Ranchero was Mel Yost, the fiftyish publisher of *Washington War Crimes*, 'a newsletter of the American Resistance'. The minivan had borne Zachary Taylor Grant to the meeting. Everywhere he went, the tall, bearded founder of the Hedgehogs militia wore camouflage pants, a flak vest, and a large silver cross on a neck chain.

'Did we get your heart going pretty good back there, Johnny?' Grant said with a hearty laugh. 'We'd have had you – bang bang. Just a rehearsal, though – lucky you.'

'You shouldn't tease my driver like that,' Trent said. 'He loves a chance to bend some sheet metal. What's this all about?'

'Well, you were nice enough to invite us all to your place to tell us what you thought we should do,' Grant said. 'It's only polite for us to return the favor.'

'Nice place you've got,' said Trent.

'Come on, let's not drag it out,' said Bowman, flinching nervously. 'The next SRA satellite will be passing overhead in eleven minutes. And let's go into the fucking trees – sound carries across water.'

Without waiting for their agreement, Bowman led the way. Yost followed with a penlight flash, while Grant fell in beside Trent. 'Johnny, one of the things I wanted to know is how serious you are about that show you put on today.'

'Serious enough.'

'Really? It's not just fresh-scrubbed-face cover? You're going to count on the same scoundrels who passed Brady I, Brady II, the ugly guns ban, national registration, and the Stoke-Williams liability act to rescue you? Now, see, you made a liar out of me.'

They caught up to Bowman at that point, and in doing so also to the sound of urine splattering against a tree trunk.

'Geez, Bob, what are you thinking? Now they'll know you were here,' said Grant.

'What? Hey, there's no DNA in piss, is there? Shit –'

Grant laughed heartily as the younger man frantically tried to staunch his flow and zip up. 'You spoiled everything, Bob. We can't kill Johnny now.'

'You're a cruel fuck, Zack,' said Yost. 'Bob, don't listen to him – there's no DNA in urine unless you've jerked off in the last twenty-one days.'

'Christ,' said Bowman, and Grant laughed even harder.

'I guess that means I owe you a favor, Bob,' said Trent lightly. 'Zack, I've got people waiting on me. Can we take care of business

351

before that satellite gets here and photographs our cars together? What's this about?'

It was Yost who stepped forward to answer. 'We wanted to give you a chance to come in with us, now that your lawsuit went in the dumper. We're going to work together on another strategy, a little more direct.'

'A lot more direct,' said Bowman, making a pretend gun out of his hand and 'firing' a shot into the darkness. 'I'm tired of waiting. Right in the face, all the fucking traitors.'

'Why me?' Trent asked.

'Two reasons, Johnny,' said Grant. 'Because you'd be useful – you're national, we're local, you're respectable, we don't want to be, you're well-connected, we wouldn't join any club that would have us. And second, because you just got kicked in the face by the conspiracy, so it's real clear to you now that they're not going to let it happen.'

'You can't beat them playing by their rules, because they have the game rigged. Like Las Vegas, only worse,' said Yost. 'So we're going to play by our rules.'

Trent pursed his lips. 'If I ask you what kind of targets you have in mind, will that affect my status here?'

' "I have a little list – they never will be missed –" ' Bowman said, sing-song.

'No, Johnny, you're square with us,' said Grant. 'But before I tell you, make sure the answer makes a difference. Are there some targets you'd be ready to sign on for, and some you wouldn't? If so, you'd be getting in at the right time. We have a target-rich environment and a lot of decisions to make.'

For the first time since the Ranchero had appeared in the rear-view mirror, Trent was gripped by an acute feeling of peril. He was not completely confident that the wrong answer would not put him face-down in the Rapido, and so he tried not to answer at all. 'I'm going to need to think about it, guys.'

Grant frowned and shook his head. 'I don't think we can do that. It's like Bob said. We're tired of waiting.'

'I don't get why you're not more fucking *angry*,' Bowman said, kicking a rock. 'Man, you ought to be jumping at the chance we're giving you. Why haven't you been thinking about it all along? *I* have. We're going to do something, not just suck up bandwidth like you did today. Maybe you don't really want to win. Or maybe you're just a fucking coward.'

'Say, Bob, how much longer till that satellite is above the horizon?' Grant asked.

'What?' Bowman peered at his watch. 'Goddammit –' Pushing past Yost, he bolted for the parking area.

Grant and Yost shared a chuckle at Bowman's expense. 'Don't say it, Johnny, I know – he's deeply twisted. But he has very good access to toys,' Grant said by way of explanation. 'What's your answer going to be, Johnny? In or out? We're going to make some noise, I promise you that.'

'Then you're going to need me to keep on doing what I do,' Trent said on impulse. 'High-profile, high-road, voice of reason, good citizen working through the system. It's the best cover you can have. Let me be blunt – if something goes wrong and the Feds take down Bob Bowman, he's replaceable, and the public thinks, well, that's one crackpot. If something goes wrong and they take down John Trent – well, I can't risk that for anything but the highest stakes. And I don't think we're there yet. Which doesn't mean I'm not going to wish you luck.'

Then he held his breath.

Grant and Yost exchanged glances. 'All right, John,' Yost said, and offered his hand. 'You hit them high, we'll hit them low – and luck to you, too. You won't hear from us again.'

The skin on Trent's back crawled all the way back to the parking lot. When he was safely back in the car, he broke out in a cold sweat. 'Let's get out of here, Jerry.'

'What happened?'

'You know better than that, Jerry.' He settled back in his seat, wondering if his hands were trembling because he'd been afraid, or because, under the fear and revulsion and contempt, some part of him had been tempted.

24:

'I am proud of the fact that I never invented weapons to kill.'

– Thomas Alva Edison

In the ten months since Dr Jeffrey Horton's face first appeared in the newsfeeds, both his life and his appearance had dramatically changed.

In the days following his unveiling as the inventor of the LifeShield, his face had been everywhere. He had agreed to interviews, taken part in debates, testified before Congress, and appeared at the United Nations with President Breland, where they received a standing ovation from the General Assembly.

But immediately after that, he had disappeared – not only from public view, but from what had been his life. Taking an indefinite leave from Terabyte, he traded in his hermitage at the Annex for the life of a wanderer. Since then, he had had no home base to speak of, renting a hotel room in Vancouver for a week, a camper in the Great Smoky Mountains for a fortnight, a lakefront cabin in northern Minnesota for a month, and so on – leapfrogging here and there across the North American continent with no clear purpose beyond going where he had not been and seeing what he had not seen.

He carried with him only that which he could fit into a hiker's backpack – little more than a few days' change of clothes, a few essential toiletries, an extra pair of comfortable shoes, his comset and reader. The toiletries included neither razor nor scissors; he had grown his first beard, and let his wavy hair grow long.

'I look like the very cliché of a tree-hugging eco-terrorist,' he had written to Lee, one of his very few contacts at Terabyte. 'It's wonderful, because respectable people who might recognize me keep a wary distance, and the eccentric and disreputable types who actually approach me don't care who I am, as long as I'm willing to listen to their advice, or their complaints, or their philosophy, or their dreams. I listen, because these fringe folk are interesting, with refreshingly unlikely and discordant perspectives on the world. I'd forgotten just how *differently* people can think, and how few of them are burdened by thinking the way the lab-coat-and-doctorate set does.'

In a note to Brohier, he had added, 'I feel like I'm reconnecting with the real world – or maybe connecting with it for the first time. I didn't realize it when we were having those conversations about what our work would mean to Society, but my theoretical model for people was as flawed as our model for physics turned out to be. But I guess that's what comes from collecting all your samples in your own back yard. I overestimated the influence of reason, and underestimated the influence of passion. And I completely missed the fact that intelligence can serve either one equally well.'

Horton had been in the Mayan Peninsula, perspiring profusely after a long climb up the steep stairs of a 1,600-year-old stone pyramid, when he received Brohier's excited invitation to come to Princeton and share in a theoretical breakthrough. But Horton was not yet ready to talk about physics – he had only activated his comset in order to find out more about the structure which he was sitting atop, and about the people who built it. So he had let the invitation go unanswered.

But despite his best efforts to prevent it, Princeton kept intruding on his consciousness, threatening to give direction to his directionless journey. It insinuated itself into his thoughts like an elephant in the living room – impossible to ignore. Either going to see Brohier foreordained the end of his journey and the resumption of his professional life, or it represented something he was avoiding. And neither admission was acceptable to Horton. The only escape from that psychological double-bind was to make Princeton just another stop along the way, a side trip off a road heading somewhere else.

So in his second week in Cape May, Horton took a break from watching the late-winter storms lash the piers and stone jetties. Locking up his third-story apartment with all the ritual of someone who intended to return, he hired a jet taxi out of Wildwood to Philadelphia. There he caught a nearly empty Amtrak commuter train to Princeton Junction, from which he rode the rattly, superannuated 'dinky' shuttle onto campus. There was a ground taxi at the station, but Horton elected to walk the last leg of his pilgrimage, declaring indifference to the damp chill in the gusty March breeze.

But as Horton was following College Road between the deserted golf course and the theological seminary, he realized that he had contrived to create a sort of Zeno's Paradox for himself – the closer he got to his destination, the more slowly he approached it.

Does it still bother me that much? he wondered. *Is this choice or coincidence?* Unable to answer, he picked up the pace.

As he drew nearer to the Institute, Horton was taken aback by the names of the streets: Hegel Avenue, Newton Road, Einstein Drive. Only the last of the three men so honored had ever walked these streets, but the names alone made Horton feel as though he were entering another world – an island enclave where the names of great thinkers had more resonance than the names of soldiers and politicians.

But, then, that was what the Institute's benefactors had intended to create – a haven for pure intellectual pursuits, unpressured by academics, uncompromised by commercialization. The Institute had no laboratories, no curriculum, no tuition, no degrees – but it had excellent libraries, long wooded trails, and a remarkable record of success.

Horton found it humbling enough to consider the aggregate brainpower of the current faculty. But even that stellar assemblage paled beside the roster of past faculty and alumni, which read like a history of the last century in science – not only Einstein, who had closed out his career and his life here, but C. N. Yang, John Von Neumann, Kurt Gödel, Freeman Dyson –

I am unworthy to enter your house, sahib – Horton thought self-mockingly, standing before the sign at the foot of the main drive.

He had to give his own name at the reception desk in Fuld Hall to gain admittance to the Institute's buildings and directions to Brohier's office. That was something he had taken pains to avoid in the course of his travels. But there was no flicker of recognition, no raised eyebrow – just the reserved Old World courtesy and New World efficiency of a well-trained staff.

'This is your visitor identification, Dr Horton. There's no need to wear it – just carry it with you. It also serves as your cafeteria pass, should you decide to take a meal while you're here.'

'Transmitter?' Horton asked, turning the thin silver disc over in his hand.

'Linked to our security systems, yes. But it's only to tell us that you're an authorized visitor – we won't be keeping track of where you go. It expires at eleven, though, when the Institute closes to visitors.'

Horton nodded and slipped the disc into his breast pocket. 'An early night for Cinderella. One-Seventeen, you said?'

'Yes, Dr Horton. I've already informed Dr Brohier that you're here.'

'Guess I'm in for it, then, eh? Retreat cut off.' He found a wry smile. 'Thank you for your help.'

The hallway was carpeted with a soft pile that absorbed the sound of footsteps. The doors and moldings along its length were a dark-grained hardwood with a faint sheen – real wood, not synthetic, that remembered a thousand dustings, cleanings, and re-oilings.

A year ago, Horton would probably have missed the life in the wood. Now it spoke to him not only of attention to detail, but dedication to principle – of an unwavering investment in bringing the best out of the best, and of a place where there was always enough time to do things right.

Suddenly, Horton was ambushed by a wistful envy for those privileged to call this mecca home, and an unexpected eagerness to hear what Brohier had uncovered here. A moment later Horton saw him, emerging from the corner office at the end of the hall, raising a hand in greeting and starting toward Horton with an uneven gait that favored the right leg.

'Karl,' Horton called, hastening his steps.

'You came.' Brohier was beaming joyfully. 'I'm so glad – I've so much to show you. Wherever have you been?'

'I took the long way,' said Horton. He pointed at Brohier's leg,

357

then surrendered that same hand to a hearty handshake. 'What did you do to yourself?'

'Fell, on the woods trail. My own fool fault. I went walking after the first snowfall, with the wrong shoes. It's nothing now – just a bad habit I haven't broken.' But when Brohier took Horton by the elbow as though to steer him toward the office, Horton realized that he was being drafted to serve as the older man's walking stick. 'How long can you stay? Did they find you a room? I could make space for you in my cottage – it's nothing like Columbus, mind you, but big enough for the two of us.'

'We'll talk about that later,' said Horton. Out of the corner of his eye, he noticed the number on the door they were passing. Half-turning, he gestured with a thumb. 'Wasn't that –'

Brohier's glance followed the gesture. 'Einstein's office? Yes – his last one. One-Fifteen Fuld. Here, I'm right next door.'

'How is that?' Horton reached for the knob.

'Pardon?'

'Well – it seems like it could be intimidating. Like working down the hall from god.'

'I find it inspiring,' said Brohier, releasing Horton's arm and making his way to his desk. 'The stories they still tell here about him – he's become a real person to me, instead of an icon.' Then he laughed as he settled heavily into a chair. 'Besides, it's Harry Beuge who's carrying the weight of comparison. I only have to *pass* Einstein's office every morning – he has to *work* there. Which may explain why he's over here six times a day.'

Horton joined Brohier in his chuckle. 'There *is* something about this place, though, isn't there,' he said, dragging a chair up.

'This building is touched by greatness, by genius – it's in the bricks, the plaster, the air. I draw a deep breath every morning, hoping to borrow some.' He leaned forward conspiratorially. 'When I'm feeling impish, I tell someone there's a morphological field over the campus – there's been so much deep thinking done here that it's now easier to do it here than anywhere else. Last week I said it in front of the Director.'

'You invoke Sheldrake to the Director of the Institute? You're a brave man.'

'I've committed worse sins here than that.'

'Such as?'

'I've been holding out on them, waiting for you.'

'You shouldn't have. You didn't owe me that.'

'Oh, there's been plenty to do. I've had to go back to school, to learn some chemistry.'

Horton blinked in surprise. 'Chemistry? You? The man who earnestly explained to me over a bottle of Bordeaux that chemistry was a trade for people without enough imagination to be physicists?'

'The very man,' said Brohier. 'As many times as I've said words to that effect in front of witnesses, I'll probably have to make a public recantation at an annual meeting of the American Chemical Society. But look behind you – right there on the top shelf is the place I started, Pauling's *Nature of the Chemical Bond*. A first edition, in paper, no less – hand-corrected by Pauling himself.'

Horton stole a glance back over his shoulder. 'Isn't there a multimedia edition yet?' he asked, unimpressed by the artifact.

Brohier wrinkled his nose in disgust. 'Oh, of course – and it's awful. All cluttered with three-dimensional animations and other extraneous nonsense. I sent it back after a week. This, this I've had checked out of the Natural Sciences library since August.'

'Slow learner?'

Brohier bleated a laugh. 'Oh, thank heavens. There was only one thing that worried me more than the thought that you were never coming back –'

'The thought that I was, but my sense of humor wasn't?'

'Just so. You were frightfully earnest for the longest time, you know.'

'Well – it was my first time,' Horton said with a rueful smile. 'I'd never changed history before.'

'We're not finished yet, Jeffrey,' Brohier said, sitting back. His eyes had the eager brightness of a parent anticipating his child's first glimpse of the Christmas tree. 'Don't you want to know why I've been reading Pauling?'

Pursing his lips, Horton hazarded a guess. 'You figured out something about the Trigger and bond energies –'

'Because you and I have to rewrite Pauling. Because the whole fundamental model, the core metaphor, has to change. I know

359

why the Trigger works, Jeffrey. I know what you did right – and why you kept hitting theoretical dead-ends.'

'Well – give, then!'

Brohier looked past Horton to make certain that the office door was closed. 'We were hidebound old farts, Jeffrey – trying to shoehorn our new wonder into the pinched shoe of yesterday's fashions. We weren't thinking nearly radically enough by half. Understandable, really – no reflection on us. I think we've all been fooled into thinking that the revolution has already come and gone, that the CERN system was the paradigm shift we'd been waiting for. But it wasn't the shift – just the tremble beforehand.'

Shaking his head, Horton said exasperatedly, 'I'll be damned if you don't take your own sweet time getting to the point.'

Brohier's eyes widened in indignation – whether mock or real, Horton couldn't discern. 'You keep *me* waiting for months, and now you begrudge me a few minutes? Arrogant youth. You'll sit there and be quiet for as long as it takes. I have a right to enjoy this.'

'Sorry,' Horton said with a sheepish, lopsided smile.

'I may forgive you,' Brohier said. 'Or I may drag it out another twenty minutes just to spite you. Now, where was I?'

'Paradigm shifts. The fundamentals of the model. Rewriting Pauling.'

'Paradigm shifts,' Brohier echoed. 'Jeffrey, in the CERN model, why is there such a thing as matter?'

'Pardon me?'

Brohier repeated his question.

'I don't think the CERN system says anything about *why* matter exists,' said Horton, shaking his head. 'All it addresses is *how* – the matter identity of energy as a collapsed wave function, the stability of the collapsed field state, the asymmetry of the initiating factors for transitions. But that isn't the answer you wanted, is it.'

'No. Look at the picture we physicists have painted. Energy is energy. Matter is energy. What else is there? Forces – which are transmitted by vector bosons, which are particles, and particles are matter, and matter is energy. So why is the universe so complex? Why does it not consist of nothing more than the white light of god, pure and undifferentiated? Why should there be air or stone or tree, desk or wall or me or thee?'

'The Kastenmach equations –'

'Describe how – they do not explain why.'

Horton sat forward in his chair. 'Karl, maybe I'm missing your thrust, but aren't we outside of the realm of science here? I thought teleology was something we fobbed off on the Humanities Department.'

'We're outside the realm of matter-energy physics,' said Brohier, 'but not outside the realm of science.'

'What else *is* there?'

Brohier's eyes sparkled. 'Now we're asking the right questions. What else, indeed! What is the factor which collapses the primal energy field into so many discrete field states – four forces, a dozen elementary particles, a hundred elements, a hundred thousand compounds? What is the essence of differentiation that allows a drawerful of pencils, a sky full of snowflakes, a beach full of sand grains to exist – with each element of the set retaining its individual character and separate existence, without sacrificing the underlying identity of form?'

'Why, we're talking about the effects of quantum indeterminacy, aren't we? Stochastic variation. It all depends on how complete a description of the subjects you specify. The sand displays unity at certain resolutions, and variation at others.'

'Too subjective. Either there are a billion grains of sand, or there aren't. They exist independent of perception, or because of it. Choose.'

'I'm voting Materialist in this election,' Horton said. His face bore a quizzical expression, and he followed his answer with a question. 'Are you trying to say that what gives them their identity, their existence, *is* the specification of their properties?'

A satisfied smile crept across Brohier's face. 'Yes, exactly, Jeffrey. The "what else" is information. Information organizes and differentiates energy. It regularizes and stabilizes matter. Information propagates through matter-energy and mediates the interactions of matter-energy. It is the mind of creation, the antidyne to chaos.'

Horton was staring through the floor as he grappled with

361

Brohier's pronouncement. 'If the universe consists of energy and information,' Horton said slowly, 'then the Trigger somehow alters the information envelope of certain substances –'

'Alters it, scrambles it, overwhelms it, destabilizes it,' Brohier said. 'And crudely, too. The units we're building now are unimaginably wasteful – like hitting a computer with ten thousand volts of lightning to change a few bytes of its programming. It was a fluke, pure serendipity, that somewhere in the smear of informational noise describing your prototype were a few coherent words in the language of resonance mechanics – the new science of matter. You stumbled on the characteristic chemical signature of certain nitrate compounds, which picked your signal out of the air like a ham radio operator finding a voice in the static.'

'But if we can learn to read and write in that language –'

'You see now why I said we need to go back to Pauling and start over.'

The idea was too big, and had snuck up on him too fast. Horton felt his resistance mounting. 'Are we just playing word games here, or do you actually have a representational system worked out?' The inflection of the words conveyed more skepticism than Horton had intended.

'Why, Jeffrey – you wound me. You know it isn't science until you can say it in numbers.'

This time, Horton saw the twinkle, and knew that the affront was pretense. Pushing the sleeves of his sweater up to his elbows, he rose from his chair.

'Good,' he said. 'Let's go to the whiteboard. Show me the math.'

They spent nearly two hours at the giant whiteboard hanging low on the common wall with 115 Fuld. For most of the first hour, Brohier sat in a secretary's chair and rolled back and forth with a fat black marker in hand. For most of the second, Brohier sat in the middle of the office, from where he could see the entire board as a whole, and debated with Horton as the latter edited and annotated the board with a bright red marker.

Finally Horton, too, retreated from the board. He surrendered the red marker to Brohier as he joined him.

362

'Well?' Brohier prodded. 'What have you decided?'

'I've decided you should buy me dinner,' said Horton. 'An expensive dinner. You can charge it against the prize for your second Nobel.'

'Oh, foo – that kind of talk is extremely premature,' Brohier said with a dismissive wave of his hand. Horton could tell that Brohier was pleased, nonetheless. 'Just tell me that it sings for you.'

'It does,' Horton said, resting a hand on Brohier's shoulder. 'I can't find a wrong note. Not that I'm the most critical listener you'll run into. But if it ends as well as it begins – Karl, it's a hell of a piece of work.'

Brohier beamed and patted Horton's hand. 'Thank you, Jeffrey. Now wipe the board, will you? And we'll go find you some dinner.'

The Institute's meal hall was not quite what Horton had had in mind for a celebratory dinner, but he conceded to Brohier that theirs would not be the first such taken there.

'Indeed. Besides,' Brohier assured him, 'there's nothing second-tier about the food here. The Institute takes very good care of our stomachs, as well. Go on, look – tell me the last time you saw a menu like that on campus.'

Horton saw quickly that Brohier was not exaggerating. The entrees – which apparently changed daily, since the menu bore that day's date – spanned five continents and more than a dozen cuisines.

In a replay of Horton and Brohier's last dinner together, while they were waiting for their food, Horton had to endure two introductions and an intrusion. The introductions were to Barbara Glennie-Golden, the round-cheeked grandmotherly Distinguished Visiting Professor in Historical Studies, and Roger Petranoff, the vulture-necked chairman of the mathematics department.

Neither scholar was anything but polite, but Horton still squirmed as he smiled his way through the encounters. He was too conscious of his own notoriety to relax, and Glennie-Golden's parting words only heightened that sensitivity.

'You know, young man, you've certainly made my field more interesting,' she said, pausing by his chair. 'The lions of the economics school of historical analysis were sleeping peacefully, thinking that they were at the top of the food chain – and now you've stirred up the hornets of the technology school, and they've been making the lions mighty uncomfortable.'

'And what are you, Barbara – lion or hornet?' asked Brohier.

She laughed. 'I'm the sterile crossbreed.'

The intrusion came in the person of Samuel Bennington-Hastings, an exuberant physics post-doc from Cambridge who looked young enough to make Horton feel old. 'So, you're the legendary Trigger man,' he said, slipping into one of the empty seats at the table. 'Does this mean our secretive Dr Brohier is finally going to let the rest of us play with the new toys?'

Brohier snorted good-naturedly. 'Dr Sam thinks I've been holding out on him.'

'Not at all, sir – on the whole department,' Bennington-Hastings said. 'Dr Brohier asks a thousand questions for every one he answers. When I ask him what's the trick inside the magic box, he just smiles like the Buddha.' He reached across the table and patted Brohier's stomach. 'He's starting to look like the Buddha, too.'

Brohier rapped the young scientist sharply across the knuckles with a spoon, then sent a sheepish look in Horton's direction. 'Since I hurt my hip – it's winter, after all. And the food *is* good –'

'I just hope you're keeping excellent notes, so Dr Horton doesn't spend the rest of his career deciphering Brohier's Last Theorem. It'd be better still if you'd come with me to the fitness center at sunrise, for Hatha yoga and twenty-five laps. Then you'll live forever – maybe even be famous someday.'

'If I have to get up at sunrise to run laps, Dr Sam, what's the point of living forever? – I think this is our food coming.'

With a wink, Horton leaned toward Bennington-Hastings. 'What you don't understand, Sam, is that Karl here doesn't know what's in the magic box. See, the truth is, I've been carrying him for twenty years. He's only here to spy for me.'

'Oh, splendid, I'm beset by liars on both sides. A fine thing this is for the upward march of science.' He stood up as the waiter reached the table. 'Eat, yes, eat, may your arteries harden to stone and your manhood dangle like an empty snakeskin.'

364

Brohier laughed heartily. Horton stared after Bennington-Hastings with an uncertain grin and a wondering look. 'What *was* that? *Who* was that?'

'Well, Dr Sam would tell you that he's descended from a long, distinguished line of English eccentrics, and that John Cleese is his spirit guide.' Smiling broadly, Brohier shook his head. 'Don't ever tell him, Jeffrey, but I find him a delight. He's a gifted mimic, and completely irreverent. He has half a dozen different characters living in his head, and he'll shift into any one of them without warning – you got a little taste of the one I call Dr Bombay there at the end. But don't underestimate him. Dr Sam tutored me in combinametrics when I first arrived. He's a very bright young man. And I wager he'll be sitting in the center of the front row when we present our paper on resonance mechanics.'

Horton said nothing to that, and it proved the last time either of them spoke of work while there was still food on the table. Instead, Brohier quizzed Horton about his travels, and Horton surprised himself by finding he had entertaining anecdotes to tell about himself.

'Have you kept in touch with Lee and Gordie?' Brohier asked over dessert.

'About as well as I have with you,' Horton confessed. 'How are they doing?'

'As far as I can see, the Annex appears to be on an even keel. It seems as though they cancel out each others' deficiencies as managers.'

'That's not what I was asking about.'

'Oh,' said Brohier. '*That.* At last report, they were inching toward each other at a pace which makes glaciers seem nimble.'

'Really? That much progress? Whose report was that?'

'Lee's.'

'Ah – the pessimist's version. If we had Gordie's version, we could find the average, and then we'd know what's really going on.'

Brohier snorted. 'I suppose you haven't kept touch with any of the Washington people, either, then.'

'No. I walked away, and they didn't chase me very hard. I didn't even get a Presidential Christmas Card.'

'I don't think Breland sends any,' Brohier said over a quiet smile.

'Just my luck. I should have taken a souvenir when I was up at the White House.'

'They'd have you back,' said Brohier. 'They're not running from this. You have friends there.'

'There and where else?'

Brohier grunted. 'You gave up watching the news too soon.'

'Did I? Breland is going to lose big this fall.'

'Probably,' the older man said. He dropped his crumpled napkin on his empty plate. 'But that's politics, Jeffrey. You're not being judged by the same standards. And you shouldn't take on guilt that isn't yours.'

'People are still doing horrible things to each other out there, Karl.'

'I know.'

'Some of them made possible by what we gave them,' said Horton. 'That man in Denver, the one who used the courthouse Trigger as the detonator on his suicide bomb –'

'His choice, Jeffrey.'

'And the two other women he killed?' Horton shook his head. 'I used to watch the news and think, "A Trigger could have saved those people." Now sometimes when I let myself watch, I find I have to think, "A gun could have saved those people."'

'Ah. St Paul?' The name evoked a month-old headline of horror – a neighborhood gang rampaging with chains and metal clubs in a Trigger-protected strip mall, killing a seventeen-year-old and severely injuring a dozen other shoppers. The irony was that the LifeShield had been installed in response to an escalating turf war over that mall, a war which had seen half a dozen shootings on or near the property.

'And Birmingham Heights, and Louisville, and South Boston.' Each name carried an echo of a tragic brutal crime.

'This is a period of transition, Jeffrey. Mistakes are going to be made. Anywhere that the gun was an easy answer, people are having to make adjustments, having to address underlying issues. Guns were Band-Aids, and some wounds require more attention than that. You can as easily say that a ninja could have saved those people, and it would be just as true.'

'I don't know,' Horton said. 'It just seems as though the water gets muddier all the time. People are having second thoughts about whether they wanted this.'

Brohier shook his head vigorously. 'No, no – *you're* having second thoughts. Look, production has been expanded ten-fold in less than a year, and there's still a six-month waiting list. Do you know the biggest problem the committee's dealing with at the moment? Counterfeit LifeShield signs. They've been popping up all over – people are that eager for the benefits of the Trigger.'

'But if they use it as recklessly as they were using guns –'

'Some will. You have to accept that. My solid-state memory microcards have been used to smuggle documentary films into China and send a million-volume library to Mars. They've also been used to pass child pornography hand to hand, smuggle corporate secrets out of IBM, and hide criminal bookkeeping from the FBI – and those are just a few that I know about.'

'So it's the user, not the tool.'

'Exactly.'

'Remind me why we didn't find this point of view convincing when the tools in question were guns and explosives.'

'Because some tools are too dangerous to give to chimps or children,' said Brohier. 'Because a tool designed to kill when used properly is a threat to everyone, and making more of them doesn't change that – every household having a gun is almost as frightful a prospect as every country having a CBN missile battery. Or ought to be, to anyone with any sense.' He frowned. 'This melancholy of yours is a byproduct of idleness, Jeffrey. And I know the cure for it – getting you back to work. Let's talk about where you're going to sleep tonight.'

'Cape May.'

'You're going back to get your things?'

'I'm just going back, Karl. This is your work, not mine.'

'There's more than enough to do for two of us. For ten of us,' said Brohier. 'And it doesn't have to be done here – you could work in Columbus, or at the Annex – I may need to go there myself soon to supervise the start of testing.'

Horton shook his head as he pushed back from the table. 'Offer it to someone else. I gave up my claim on the way back from Washington, remember?'

'And I've dutifully kept it in a jar on my desk, waiting for you to get over your funk and ask for it back. What the devil is going on with you, Jeffrey?' Brohier fumed, struggling to his feet and fumbling with his coat.

'I don't want to have this conversation, Karl,' Horton said. 'And it's time for me to go.'

Turning away, Horton started for the exit with long strides. It took a supreme effort for a hobbled Brohier to catch him.

'Jeffrey – *Jeffrey* – stop,' Brohier said, grabbing for the younger man as they reached the double doors leading to the path back to Fuld Hall. 'You've already missed the last train, so you might as well hold still for this. And, frankly, I think you owe me a little more consideration than you're giving me.'

Looking past Brohier, Horton saw Bennington-Hastings watching curiously from the other end of the short hallway. 'All right. But out there,' he said, jerking his head toward the doors.

They settled on the steps just outside, using the doors and the cold to secure their privacy.

'I'm just trying to understand, Jeffrey,' said Brohier. 'Most people in our field go their entire careers without an opportunity like the one we have. And a lot of them are a damn sight smarter than either of us, just not as lucky. We're looking at a scientific revolution, not just a social one. I don't understand how you can walk away.'

Horton shook his head. 'I'm just not ready to come back yet.'

'I see,' said Brohier. 'Nothing more to it?'

'No.'

'I see. Well, I'm reassured. I was afraid that you had some silly notion that you weren't worthy to be part of this. I was worried that you might be feeling that you didn't deserve either the acclaim or the blame that you've already received, that you felt the most you could claim for yourself was being the first on the scene of a research accident.

'Because if any of those fears turned out to have any foundation, I would have had to tell you you were being an idiot – that every one of us who ends up in the spotlight feels a touch of impostor syndrome from time to time. The only ones who don't are egotistical incompetents like Tettlebaum, whose self-image depends on the title and the office and the newscams and seeing themselves quoted online.'

Horton scuffed at a patch of ice on the second step. 'I might have needed to hear that, if I'd been thinking along those lines.'

'I probably wouldn't have stopped there,' said Brohier. 'I'd have wanted to remind you that people like us didn't choose this path to become famous – it was because we wanted to know things that no one could tell us. So the cure for impostor syndrome isn't to give up the work – it's to focus on it until you forget there's an audience, and you don't know or care what they're saying about you.'

Horton's chin-high sigh blew a plume of icy condensation up into the air. 'Sometimes it's hard not to care.'

'What are they to you, Jeffrey?' Brohier said with a shrug. 'What do they know about you?'

'Some of them know a lot,' Horton said with a shiver. 'Come on, I'm cold – let's walk.'

They started down the path in silence, both of them knowing Horton was not finished.

'The morning after the President and I had that press conference in the Rose Garden, my father called me,' Horton said at last. 'Now, you have to understand that my father never calls any of the kids, and if he should happen to answer the phone when I call, chances are the first thing he'll say is, "Hi, Jeffrey – I'll get your Mom." It's not in his nature to chat, or nag, or intrude – it's not that he doesn't care, it's just that –'

'He doesn't ask for anything he doesn't want to give,' Brohier suggested.

'I suppose that's it,' Horton said. 'I would have said he believes that there are boundaries.' They'd reached the side entrance to Fuld Hall, and Horton stopped there. 'So he calls me that morning, and being my father, he comes right to the point. "There's something I have to know, son – in all those Saturdays the family spent at the range, with hundreds of people walking around with guns, did you ever meet anyone you found scary or dangerous? Did it make you nervous being there?" And I had to tell him no. Those are good memories – some of the best I have.'

Brohier cocked his head quizzically. 'He assumed you'd been working on the Trigger by choice? That it was a personal crusade, and that he might have had some part in your taking it up?'

Tightlipped, Horton nodded. 'Then he said, "I wish you could have remembered that yesterday, and said something about it to the President. But, thank you, son. Your mother sends her love."

'And that was the end of the conversation. But I kept hearing the things he didn't say, all the rest of the day – and a lot of days since.'

'That he disapproved?'

'No, much worse than that,' said Horton. 'That he was hurt and puzzled and disappointed, as if by doing what I did I'd attacked the family, sat in judgement on our friends. He couldn't say any of that, of course, because he loves me.'

'And because there are boundaries.'

Horton nodded slowly. 'I'm sure that I'm going to work again, Karl. I just think it's going to have to be on something else.' He tried a smile, but it came off as wistful at best. 'I guess it doesn't matter how old you are – a kid still wants to know his parents are proud of him.'

'I understand,' Brohier said. 'And a parent can be the most difficult audience to please. I had a father myself, as it happens.' He hesitated, then added, 'I won't ask again – but if you change your mind, don't be too proud to tell me.'

'I think I can promise that, Dr B.'

'Good.' Brohier took a step toward the warm, inviting brightness of the main lobby, then stopped abruptly and turned back. 'Jeffrey – if I can presume, and speak as a mentor rather than a friend –'

'Of course.'

'Just make sure you're someone *you* can be proud of. Don't give that up just to win approval from someone else. I learned the wisdom of this from watching *my* father.' Then Brohier shook his head and grunted, a single joyless laugh. 'The pity of it was, he never quite learned it himself. – Did you want to stay with me tonight, then?'

'I thought I'd check on a late airport shuttle. Or rent a car and drive to Cape May. I might enjoy that, actually.'

Brohier nodded. 'It was good to see you, Jeffrey. Safe trip home – wherever that might be.'

In the end, Jeffrey ended up spending the night at a motel near campus, and taking the first train out in the morning. But even so, when he finally reached his apartment, he was struck by the realization that, whatever it was to him, it was very little like home.

He said good-bye to it the next day, journeying on.

25:

'War contains so much folly, as well as wickedness,
that much is to be hoped from the progress of reason;
and if any thing is to be hoped, every thing ought to
be tried.'

– *James Madison*

The change had been swift, sudden, and final. The day after
Toni Franklin had been brought in from the cold on the Trigger
project, the National Security Council had formally taken over its
management from the ad hoc Brass Hat committee.

There was no paperwork involved, since Brass Hat had had no
official status. And since three out of the four seats in each body
were occupied by the same people – President Breland, Secretary
of State Carrero, and Secretary of Defense Stepak – the significance
of the change wasn't immediately obvious. On the surface, in fact,
the ramifications seemed inconsequential.

The meetings moved to a different conference room in a different wing. Since there was no longer a need to account for the
President's time, the meetings could be held more often, and were
– twice weekly instead of once. They could also run longer, and
did – frequently consuming an entire morning or afternoon.

But the issues were the same, and the headaches were the same.
The NSC still had to juggle the dual threats of passive resistance
from the Pentagon and active resistance from Congress. It still had
to wrestle with a fast-developing, constantly changing security
situation both inside and outside of the country's borders. And,
just as before, it found that no amount of diligence guaranteed an
end to surprises.

Still, there were benefits to the change, if you knew where
to look.

The easiest to see was the replacement of Richard Nolby with Toni Franklin. That forced the chief of staff to the sidelines where the Trigger was concerned, neatly resolving a nagging problem for Breland. He had been increasingly uncomfortable with Nolby's ambivalence about the Trigger. The former senior aide to the Speaker of the House was the only true Washington insider on Breland's staff, and Breland found his obsession with calculating the political advantage of every scenario offputting – contrary to what Breland saw as the spirit of the undertaking.

Now Nolby had been marginalized, and in a way which left him no room to complain to Breland about the demotion – the Vice President was a statutory member of the NSC, and the issues surrounding the Trigger clearly placed it under the NSC's purview. Franklin's contributions as a fence-mender on the Hill and a logjam-breaker in meetings only sweetened the deal.

The change that displaced Nolby also pushed Grover Wilman farther away from the decision-making. The formal security protocols surrounding the NSC made it impossible for Breland to casually include Wilman, or even to brief him in detail afterwards. That development had pleased General Madison and the Joint Chiefs, who had viewed Wilman as an iconoclast at best, and a traitor in the ranks at worst.

But far and away the most significant consequence of the shift was that it made the substantial resources of the NSC and its professional staff available to Breland. He was no longer dependent on the good will of the Joint Chiefs for opinions and expertise in the military realm, no longer even dependent on his own ability to ask the right questions. The NSC's analysts were good at thinking up the questions on their own, including questions which trampled on the toes of spit-shined shoes. Moreover, when necessary, the NSC had the knowledge, the connections, and the authority to reach inside the Pentagon for answers.

One example of a question Breland would never have thought to ask: whose career aspirations were threatened by the Trigger, and how did that map against the resistance among the generals and admirals? Analyst John Miller's monograph pointed out that the 'combat commands' which were most affected by the new technology were traditionally the fast track to moving up the chain of command. His unblinking case studies embarrassed two generals for putting turf and status ahead of readiness and security.

Better information, however, did not necessarily mean welcome news. And the white paper authored by senior analyst Wendell Schrock and titled THE NEXT WAR was anything but welcome. At the instigation of Harris Drake, the President's assistant for national security, Schrock and three assistants had investigated the response of all four services to the prospect of facing an enemy equipped with the Trigger. The day before Schrock presented the paper to a meeting of the NSC, he gave Breland an informal Oval Office preview that made the President feel like he was hearing the complete story, plainly said, for the first time.

'We looked at three different scales of engagement: global superpower conflicts, theater conflicts, and skirmish conflicts. We considered each in light of two different scenarios – one in which the United States retains its current monopoly on the long-range, point-target Mark II Trigger, and one in which we fail to do so. That gave us a total of six different conflict models.

'Within each of those models, we looked at our readiness to cope with Trigger-equipped adversaries in all four sectors of the combat cube – land, air, sea, and space.

'Our overall conclusion, Mr President, is that in every conflict model but one, we are no more than six months away from reestablishing a level of battlefield domination comparable to that we enjoyed before the Trigger appeared. Within six months, we'll have the ability to overwhelm Trigger-based defenses and use our conventional weaponry to apply any degree of destructive lethality appropriate to our objectives.'

'The exception being –'

'The exception being a global superpower conflict with a China which has Mark II technology. In that model, we're twelve to sixteen months away from restoring a decisive advantage.'

'Let me be certain I understand – are you saying that we're at most six months away from neutralizing the Trigger as a deterrent factor?'

'Yes, sir.'

Breland heard that as *My successor will be able to start a war with impunity.* 'How is it that we've managed this so quickly?'

'If you'll look at Section Two –' He waited while Breland scrolled his reader. 'There are really only two tactical issues presented by the Trigger. One is predetonation of explosive projectiles – principally torpedoes, cruise missiles, AAMs, and artillery shells. To deal with that, we're building missiles with higher-yield warheads and different fragmentation patterns. The goal is to make sure that we can get a kill at the Mark I's effective radius. This is proving very do-able.'

'A bigger bang – that's all?' Breland said, frowning.

'It's the kind of challenge the hot weapons designers love, sir – packing more into less. And we have some excellent people at NAWC and the Marine Warfighting Laboratory. In some applications, we're replacing conventional explosives with some of the exotics which contain no nitrates – we can expect more of that as time goes on. In other cases, we're completely removing the warheads from our missiles, and replacing them with inert mass. After all, throwing a rock up the tailpipe of a SU-27 works just about as well as throwing a bomb.'

'I suppose if a bird in the engine can bring down an aircraft –'

'Just so. Now, the other issue is the accuracy and lethality of kinetic-energy weapons. It isn't a matter of range, because every combat firearm except for our service sidearms already has enough range to fire from outside the effective radius of the Mark I. The problem is strictly one of hitting the target – the *effective* range of some of our weapons is less than the Trigger radius, and our experience in combat is that most kills take place at even shorter distances.'

'And how are we dealing with that?'

'A number of ways. Changing the mix of weapons in an infantry unit, so there are more heavy weapons like the SAW, and more sniper rifles – and, of course, you change your tactics at the same time. Taking the explosive rounds out of the belt-loads for automatic weapons and aerial cannon. To a limited extent, supplementing conventional firearms with flechette weapons and electric railguns. Changing the loadings of our ammunition to get non-explosive expansion, fragmentation and edge-cutting from the slugs.'

'That's all it takes? These changes sound – almost trivial.'

'They're adjustments,' said Schrock. 'The real change is at the theater tactical level. Apart from the limited range, the real vulnerability of the Triggers is their susceptibility to EMP.' When Breland's face showed no recognition, Schrock added, 'Electromagnetic pulse. A side effect of a nuclear explosion.'

Breland blinked. 'What?'

'All three services are preparing to bring new generation tactical nuclear warheads back to the field. The Air Force has two versions under development – one for air combat, and one for ground support, using a cruise missile platform. The Navy's looking at both versions, one for antisub and one for antiship. They may want something for air combat, as well. The Army is working on nuclear-tipped shells for both the 120mm and 150mm platforms – both rocket-assisted, so they can get the altitude and standoff distance you want to have, even with a baby nuke.'

Then, belatedly, Schrock read the disapproval on Breland's face. 'Of course, all these projects will need your approval for both testing and deployment – you'll have to rescind Directive 99-15.'

'Don't we have some sort of treaty obligations to observe?' the President asked crossly.

'Actually, no, sir. Congress never ratified SALT IV – we've been observing its provisions voluntarily. We can bring tactical nuclear warheads back to the field any time we choose to.' He hastily amended, 'Any time the President chooses to.'

'And what happens if we find our forces are too close to the opposing forces to light off a nuclear artillery shell overhead?'

'Sir, preventing that situation from developing is one of the necessary changes in combat doctrine. The new doctrine would call for holding conventional units back from the front until the area has been depacified.'

Making the world safe for war, Breland thought, reacting to the ugly neologism with an involuntary shudder. 'What if the enemy doesn't cooperate with our new doctrine, and refuses to keep a respectful distance?'

'The new doctrine calls for decisive engagement –'

'Decisive? That would mean preemptive, wouldn't it? And with nuclear weapons. *The Next War*, indeed – and a fine little war it'll be.' He flipped the reader in the direction of the table, where it spun to the edge before stopping.

'Sir, if I could remind you that this is a report on what we found, not what we recommended –'

Breland raised a hand. 'Yes. Yes – and I'm glad to have it. You've done good work here. I just hate what it means – what it says.' He looked toward the map wall and, sighing, combed the fingers of both hands back through his hair. 'Mr Schrock, next time your desk is clear, figure out for me why we're working harder to make this go away than we are to use it. Tell me why we can't let go of the power to kill.'

'Sir –'

'Um?'

'Was that strictly rhetorical?'

Breland sat back in his chair. 'No – go ahead.'

'I've spent a lot of time over on the other bank – including ten years in uniform before I went civilian. It's absolutely true that some of those guys – and a few of the gals, too – are in love with the power. Big machines, fast machines, the thunder, the power to destroy. It's *fun*. You can make a fetish out of the machinery of war, and never see the blood. You don't have to be in uniform to do it, either. Air shows, fireworks, action movies –'

'But? –'

With the light touch of a single finger, Schrock pushed the President's reader back to the center of the table. 'But I think those types are the exception – and that they're pretty well held in check by the others.'

'The others being? –'

'The others being the ones who realize that nobody wants to fight, but somebody needs to know how. That's what's going on here, Mr President – professional soldiers figuring out how. They do it because it's their job. And they do it well because they have to do the fighting and the dying when men like you decide when and why. At least, that's how it works here. – No offense intended.'

'None taken. Were you heading somewhere?'

'I thought so.' Schrock paused. 'Maybe our modern technological wars are a little too clean and tidy – you never get splashed with the blood of the man you just killed. Maybe our last ugly, personal war is too distant a memory to properly chasten us. But I still think they'd gladly let go of that power the day you can persuade them we no longer need it – the day that giving it up doesn't put everything they love at risk.'

'I guess that's the question, isn't it? What they love most.'

'Forgive me if this sounds like recruiting babble, but I think most of them love the same things we do. I think they love their lives, their families, their freedom much more than they love the guns and the bombs and the killing. If you can give them an alternative, Mr President, if you can give them a way to protect the one without the other, they'll take it. I know they will.'

'And the Trigger isn't it?'

Schrock shook his head. 'No. For what it's worth, I happen to have considerable sympathy with your vision. I'm sorry to say that I don't think the Trigger is enough to get us there.'

Breland stood, signalling that the briefing was over. 'If you're right, Mr Schrock, that just means we have to work harder. Thank you for your efforts on this report – and for your frankness. You've opened my eyes to some issues I've been neglecting. I want you to keep on trying to do that.'

'I'll do my best, Mr President,' Schrock said with a nod. As he stood, he reached up and touched his lapel, drawing Breland's attention to the silver pin he wore. The face of the pin was in the shape of a Q, with an arrowhead pointing to the right. 'Are you familiar with the figure?'

'I'm afraid not. Your unit insignia?'

'More like my fraternity pin. It's a creation of Theodore Sturgeon – a neglected writer of the last century,' said Schrock. 'It means, "Ask the next question." I wear it to remind me what I'm supposed to be doing.'

'If you don't mind my asking, what "fraternity" would that be?'

'I don't mind. I belong to the Alliance for a Humanist Future – the Futurians.' When he saw no recognition on Breland's face, Schrock added quickly, 'It's not a proscribed organization. We have a social and technological agenda, not a political one.'

'Which would be what, exactly?'

Schrock smiled. 'Actually, you borrowed our mission statement for your speech last year: "We can do better." Made me reach for the zoom, to see if *you* were wearing one of these.'

'Well – as you can see –'

Waving off the demurral, Schrock said, 'It's not important. Member or not, we consider you part of the alliance. And when you see one of these – and you might be surprised where you do – you'll know you have a friend there.'

It was a curious ending to a disturbing conversation. Breland did not know what to make of Schrock or his intimations, so he set them aside until he could learn more about the so-called Futurians.

But he knew that the information Schrock had brought him meant trouble. It was difficult enough to hear that the path he had chosen would not take them to the summit – not least because he had begun to suspect it himself. It was far more distressing to discover that, far from moving the world toward disarmament, the Trigger might be pushing it back toward not only the proliferation but the use of nuclear weapons.

That kind of backsliding was intolerable, completely unacceptable. The question Breland had no answer for was what, if anything, he could do about it.

The President was not the only person in the District of Columbia harboring a growing apprehension about the direction events were taking. At the Mind Over Madness offices in Georgetown, Senator Grover Wilman was fretting over reports from a completely different realm.

Months ago, Wilman had effectively abandoned the duties of his Senate office, placing his staff on autopilot after the manner perfected by the Stennises and Thurmonds. On the insistence of his chief of staff, twice a week Wilman reported to the Capitol instead of to the brownstone three-story two blocks from the University. But it was strictly for appearances – behind his closed door, he was teleconferencing with MOM's staff in Kuala Lumpur, or Prague, or Nairobi.

His voting attendance had dropped below thirty percent, and would have dropped lower if it were not for the new remote voting rules. Wilman could not be moved to take the time to actually cross

Constitution Avenue and appear in the Senate chamber. Coming to the outer office, where the vote-verifier sat alone on a small desk, was the biggest concession he was willing to make for the sake of appearances. The Trigger campaign was all that mattered to him, and the moment would not wait.

So he left it to his Congressional staff to answer the mail, and handle the constituent problems, and fend off the callers and visitors who thought themselves important enough to have a claim on the senator's time. It was the work of the foundation's staff which had his attention, and which was the source of his concern.

At Wilman's instigation, Mind Over Madness had taken on the task of easing the transition to the new paradigm. In a span of just four months, it had tripled its budget, dipping deeply into its endowments to fund a presence at every point where the intelligent application of money could make a difference. Their efforts went far beyond attitudinal advertising and working the wires. They were trying to provide as many answers as possible to a problem the Trigger created – how the law-abiding and nonviolent could protect themselves from the bullies in their lives.

MOM's money was paying for studio space and instructors for free martial arts training in the sixteen metropolitan areas which accounted for sixty percent of all gun homicides and armed assaults. The curriculum had been developed under MOM's sponsorship, and consisted of six techniques for disabling single attackers and two for dealing with multiple attackers. Graduates as young as nine and as old as seventy-three had already successfully defended themselves, and the press had coined the phrase 'citizen ninjas' to describe the phenomenon.

The nonprofit retailing arm of the foundation had vastly expanded its operation from an Internet publisher and storefront (The Peace Library). MOM was now buying the entire production run of stun batons, shock-boxes and chem-sprays from five different personal defense companies – all but one owned by Aron Goldstein.

They were reselling those nonlethal weapons at cost – not only on the Net, but through StreetSmart kiosks in hundreds of malls. The low prices and the near-monopoly kept the lines long, even though nearly one in four applicants who passed the criminal registry check were rejected after an interview with a counselor.

In the entertainment realm, Mind Over Madness had endowed the annual Pax Prizes – $100,000 cash awards in eight different media to writers whose work best exemplified the notions that entertainment did not require exploding bodies and dramatic tension did not require drawn firearms. Taking an even more active role, MOM had bought a small multimedia production company, renamed it PaxWorks, and hoped to turn it into a major content producer in both interactive and performance media.

But, distressingly, beneath this ambitious edifice cracks were starting to appear in the foundation – one after another after another.

The first came to Wilman's attention in a report focusing on crime patterns. He called in the analyst – a fourteen-year FBI veteran volunteering in the Georgetown office – to question him more closely.

'As I read what you sent me, after an initial dip, we're not seeing decreases in the targeted crime categories. We're seeing steady or increasing numbers and a shift in the victim population.'

'That's correct.'

'What's happening at street-level? Take me beyond the numbers.'

The analyst shrugged. 'Contrary to popular notions, most criminals aren't stupid. If there're fifty bank branches in town, and the twenty biggest are protected by Triggers, the rest of them are going to get extra attention. And because the average take is down –'

'You get perpetrators who work three days a week instead of two.' Wilman frowned. 'This is what's driving the traffic in counterfeit LifeShield signs. People who aren't protected yet want to have that sign out there saying "Go rob someone else."'

The FBI analyst nodded. 'Along the same lines, if the merchants' association turns West Avenue Mall into a LifeShielded property, the bangers are going to start hanging at Northland Mall instead. And when the Star-Bellied Sneetch Tribe finds that The Cat In The Hat Gang has already staked a claim to Northland, you get a turf war that you probably wouldn't have had before.'

'So to whatever extent people would rather relocate than give up their weapons, the Trigger aggravates the situation by artificially restricting the supply of territory and increasing the demand.'

The analyst nodded again. 'The effect is of concentrating the remaining weapons in an ever-smaller area, and things get worse rather than better for those who inhabit that area.'

'Ghettos for violence.'

'In a manner of speaking.'

'So is this strictly a transitional phenomenon? What do you expect to see, say, three years from now, when Northland and most of those little banks are LifeShielded, too?'

'The wolves always look for the cripples and stragglers. There isn't any projection I've seen that brings us close to having entire cities being protected. I'd expect the status quo, only more so – two societies, two cultures, the haves and the have-nots.'

Another crack showed up in a longitudinal study of the economic impact of the Trigger, which included a comprehensive catalog of Trigger-related products. Reviewing the update one day, Wilman found an item with a new-item flag which was troubling enough that he had to verify it himself.

At a digital shop based on a server in the Cayman Islands, Wilman found a database called Safe Passage offered for sale by an organization called The Resistance. The database was a catalog of LifeShield installations in North America, offered as an unlicensed add-on for GPS navigators and other trip-routers. If the database was accurate, anyone who had a copy could smuggle explosives or ammunition safely between almost any two points on the map.

Wilman arranged to have a surrogate acquire a copy of Safe Passage, and then turned it over to the NSA for analysis. It proved to be a clone of the supposedly secret database used by LifeShield Transport to make deliveries, twenty-four days out of date but one hundred percent accurate and complete. The leak was plugged ten days later with the arrest of an LST driver and depot manager in Idaho, but Wilman was not reassured. Neither the digital shop nor The Resistance could be touched, and there was enough money chasing that kind of information to assure that someone else could be bought.

'So let's undercut them, and take away the profit motive,' said Wilman's senior strategic coordinator. 'If we openly market a list that's ninety-five percent complete for ten dollars, how many people will cross the line to pay a thousand dollars for that last five percent?'

'It's not the information that matters,' said Wilman. 'There aren't even a hundred unmarked Trigger installations. The liability issue makes it impossible to have stealth installations in public places, at least here – we would if we could, but we can't. No, it's the sales pitch, the reason for putting the data together this way that matters. People are starting to find work-arounds. And there's damned little we can do about that.'

The next crack appeared in an urgent teleconference called by the Atlantic States field coordinator in the wake of deadly bombings in Baltimore and Manhattan.

'People have caught on to the fact that they can use the Trigger as a fuse,' the coordinator told Wilman. 'And it enormously simplifies making and planting a bomb.'

'None of that fuss with timers or fuses or remote controls.'

'No technology at all. Making a bomb becomes a matter of gaining access to an explosive, and then concealing it in the trunk of someone else's car or the cargo compartment of a bus or train or a parcel – anything that someone *else* will take care of moving. And this approach has the added psychological impact of making people paranoid about entering LifeShielded space – for just that moment, they wonder if they're riding with a package of death, one of these so-called "hitchhiker bombs".'

But most alarming to Wilman, because it spoke to the attitudes of the mainstream rather than the criminal fringe, was a crack that he discovered through his own resources.

For nearly two decades, the Algonquin Saloon had clung to a tenuous existence on a side street three blocks from the Georgetown University campus. A cross between an Internet newsgroup, a old-fashioned talk show, and an even older-fashioned British pub, the Algonquin catered to two endangered vices – caffeine and live, face-to-face conversation.

It was the creation of one man, Martin Groesbeck, an energetic and voluble former journalist who'd retired 'rather than go over to the enemy' when the *Washington Post* was purchased by

DisneyNet. Groesbeck had an ear for issues, a trustworthy face, and a knack for drawing out the occasional shy or intimidated visitor to the Algonquin's seven circular tables. Through the marriage of an idiosyncratic vision and sheer stubbornness, Groesbeck had managed to create and sustain a unique community he proudly called 'a seven-ring intellectual circus'.

He threw strangers randomly together at the nine-seat tables, and sat in to fill an empty space or 'stir the soup' at a sluggish roundtable. He wrote and published a daily house broadsheet called *The Real Slow News* which highlighted social and political issues, copies of which were known to turn up far from Georgetown. He wandered from table to table in the early evening, scattering fire-red *Devil's Advocate* cards – each bearing a controversial proposition in Groesbeck's distinctive handwriting – on tables as conversation-starters.

Groesbeck delighted regulars and offended newcomers with his 'bouquets and brickbats' policy, under which he tore up the checks of customers whose participation kept things interesting and doubled the bills of customers who were conspicuous spectators or tedious bores.

Saturday evenings were reserved for guest presenters, an event Groesbeck promoted as 'Nights of the Roundtable'. Applying his own idiosyncratic standards, he offered 'interesting people' from all walks of life (no politicians need apply) a chance to test their ideas in front of a roomful of articulate critical thinkers who gave no points for credentials. Considering that he only offered a token honorarium, a surprising number of the invitees accepted, leading to some of the Algonquin's most memorable moments.

But as a business, the Algonquin was a grand failure, despite the full houses most weekday nights and every Saturday. The turnover was too slow and the average per check too low to do more than break even.

Wilman found the Algonquin too valuable to risk seeing it replaced by a pottery shop or a piercing emporium. Of all the places he frequented in and around Washington, it was the only one where he could be sure that what he was hearing was unaltered by his celebrity or his position or the speaker's ambitions. Not even within the foundation offices could he be confident of that. The Algonquin was his touchstone, his bellwether for public opinion – the sort of well-grounded, passionately-held opinions which had staying power as memes.

That was why Wilman had found ways, indirect and anonymous, to funnel money into Groesbeck's pocket and keep the Algonquin's doors open – grants, private gifts, a book contract, a short-term consultancy. If necessary, Wilman was prepared to do more: to set up a trust which would buy the property and hire Groesbeck to manage it.

But for now, he could walk through those doors as a regular but not a rescuer, and sample both an opinion and a vintage Pepsi. Or, if time was at a premium, he could come early in the day, sit at the serving counter in the back, and squeeze the sponge that was Martin Groesbeck.

'What do you hear that's new, Marty?'

The big man turned away from the chrome taps he was polishing. 'Order something, and we'll talk. Let's see, you take your caffeine cold. I've got some Royal Crown Draft in. Cuban sugar, American spring water, concentrate from Canada.'

'Glass-bottled?'

'Metal cap and all.'

'Dig one out of the ice.'

'I like a customer who doesn't ask "How much?",' Groesbeck said with a smile, plunging a hand into the cooler. 'So what's the keyword today, Grover? Breland?'

'We can start there. How's the "internationalist conspiracy" selling?'

'Not very well – but, then, this isn't South Dakota. People here have actually *been* to other countries – and I don't mean Niagara Falls or Tijuana.'

Wilman chuckled. 'And these worldly and enlightened folk are saying –'

'It's been an interesting evolution. Breland's actually been doing a little better. Two months ago, I never heard anyone defending him – he had supporters, mind you, but no defenders. They were still looking for a defensible position.'

'Have they found some, then? I thought the Bringer of Chaos and Enemy of Liberty camps had command of the field.'

'They forgot to set up pickets around the high ground,' said Groesbeck. 'The defensible position is forgivable idealism. Every time Breland comes back to his we-can-do-better theme, a few more people in the Bringer of Chaos camp seem to realize that he's serious about it, and that he was serious all along.'

Wilman cocked an eyebrow. 'Bringing him what, exactly? Grudging respect?'

'Integrity points. The secret agenda all the cynics were ready to impute to him, or his handlers, or the Trilateral Commission, hasn't materialized – his agenda is right out there in the open, and was from the beginning. More civility – less killing.'

'Which, on second consideration, is starting to sound like not such a bad idea to them?'

'To an extent.' Groesbeck bent forward, resting his forearms on the serving counter. 'What I'm hearing sounds like the reluctant admiration we reserve for someone who sets a standard we're not quite sure we can aspire to.'

Wilman nodded slowly. 'We have to temper our approval somehow, as a hedge against being called on to follow the avatar.'

Groesbeck patted the countertop with the flat of one hand. 'Just so. In Breland's case, he stands accused of thinking too well of us. You see, he's handicapped by having been surrounded all his life by nice people. Early exposure to villainy broadens one's horizons, or so it's said.'

'Sounds like the conclusion of someone who lives in Newsworld, or Movieworld,' said Wilman. 'The real world isn't nearly as violent as either of those places. Most people can get from one end of a day to the other without seeing or laying hands on a gun. – Which includes most gun owners, if they're being honest.'

'I won't argue the point,' said Groesbeck. 'I know my father owned a shotgun, and my mother had a revolver. But in twenty years of living at home, I never saw either one of them – and I was a nosy kid. Still, I could find you an argument, if you wanted one.'

'Without going to South Dakota?'

'Sure.' Groesbeck pursed his lips. 'Two nights ago, there was a fellow at table five going on at length about why the LifeShield program was a "disaster". He wasn't the most eloquent customer in the house, but he was very upset about those condo rapes in Milwaukee –'

'The week after the condo turned on its LifeShield,' Wilman recalled. 'Three men who lived there were arrested.'

'That's the one. I remember that this fellow said, "Not everyone with a gun is a bad guy. Not everyone without one is a good guy. A bad guy without a gun can still do a hell of a lot of damage. A good guy without a gun can't always stop it from happening."'

'Did he carry the table with that?'

'Seemed so to me.' He paused. 'Grover, for a couple of months after Breland's speech, I kept hearing variations on "It's a shame they didn't have a Trigger" – talking about some killing in the news, some tragedy that didn't have to be. There was a woman at table five that night who said something I hadn't heard before –'

'"It's a shame they didn't have a gun."'

Groesbeck looked at him with surprise. 'Were you here, and I just missed you? Yes, that's what she said – with exactly the same mixture of anger and regret that I used to hear from the others.'

'I wasn't here,' Wilman said, and drained the last of the soft drink. 'All I had to do was think of the last thing I wanted to hear – nostalgia for the good old days, when real Americans kept pistols in their nightstands.'

'You can't get away from the fact that if one of those victims *had* a gun –'

'– Somebody would probably be dead,' Wilman finished. 'Maybe one of the rapists. Maybe one of their victims.'

'And maybe those three men would have just stayed in their condo, drinking away their self-pity,' said Groesbeck. 'You can't escape the fact that some guns did some people a world of good, and the Trigger's taking those guns away, too. I know, you like the tradeoffs – but, then, none of those women was your daughter.'

'No,' Wilman said. 'Just like none of those men was my son. I don't want my daughters raped, Marty – but I don't want my sons shot to death, either. Why should I have to choose between those alternatives?' He stood up from his stool and gestured at the empty bottle. 'How much?'

Groesbeck grunted. 'Just hand over your debit card. – But, much as I need the money, in the future you might think about asking the price before you commit yourself.'

'When the price makes a difference to me, I do,' Wilman said, surrendering his card. 'But not every decision can be made with a calculator. – In fact, I doubt that any of the important ones can be.'

In theory, there were eight different ways for Karl Brohier to reach Jeffrey Horton.

The standard comset Terabyte Laboratories issued to its employees was a Celestial 3000 Personal Office – which, by no coincidence, incorporated Terabyte solid-state memory and was built in a factory owned by Aron Goldstein. The Cee-Three would accept voice, flat video, page, and priority page signals in real time, and store voicemail, 3-D video, fax, and hypermedia for playback on a base station. And with three-band global pointcasting, Celestial claimed that its customers enjoyed 'universal connectivity, from pole to pole and mountain to sea'.

But there was nothing Celestial could do about a customer who muted the ringer, disabled the pager, and allowed his mailbox to fill up with sex ads and get-rich schemes. There was no technological recourse when a man simply didn't want to be reached.

For more than a week, Brohier had peppered Horton with urgent entreaties to come back to Princeton. The longer they went unanswered, the more anxious and impatient the director became. Toward the end of the week, he was driven to violate his own security rule for unpublished work. Trusting Celestial's kilobyte encryption, Brohier sent Horton the key equations he wanted to discuss, hoping to tempt his protege into at least a long-distance collaboration.

'I have taken this as far as I can on my own, Jeffrey,' Brohier said in the attached message. 'I need the Ruyens transformations verified, and some help with the beta combinametrics. Then it will be time to bend metal, as the engineers say.

'We thought we had already seen the whole opera. When you look at these files you'll realize how naïve we were. Everything that's happened so far amounts to no more than the overture. I hope you will help me write the finale – but if you choose not

388

to, understand that I will have to turn elsewhere. I can't bear the thought of leaving this work unfinished. As it is, I can hardly keep from dancing a giddy jig around every physicist I see.'

But to Brohier's disappointment, even that appeal did not bring any response – not even regrets and good wishes. He allowed forty-eight hours to pass, then reconsidered and extended his personal deadline another day, but to no avail.

Even then, it was difficult for the director to bring himself to turn his back on Horton, and he took a long slow walk through the Institute woods to think it through.

It was impossible for him to be angry. More so than with any of the other bright young talents Brohier had recruited at the founding of Terabyte, his feelings toward Horton had taken on something of the flavor of the relationship between accomplished father and promising son. Whether Horton realized it or not, he was the heir apparent, the son Brohier expected to eventually take over the 'family business'.

And just as it would be for a father, it was hard for Brohier to know that Horton was struggling, and harder to realize that there was nothing Brohier could do to help him through it. In a way, Brohier felt that he had failed Horton – failed to prepare him for the weight that had fallen on his conscience.

And yet, who could have anticipated where it would lead? How often had a theoretical physicist even needed a conscience?

After all, it wasn't science which had transformed the world, but the marriage of technology and capitalism. The ignorant might blame science for the ills and evils of the modern era, but that was a case of mistaken identity – no research scientist ever polluted a water table with PCB, or performed a third-trimester abortion, or denied someone insurance based on a genetic screening, or turned the Internet into a covert way of peering into private lives.

Real scientists were invisible outside their own circle of peers. Even Nobel Prize recipients barely registered on the public consciousness, as Brohier well knew. A Heisman Trophy or an Oscar counted for far more – there was no market for Heroes of Science trading cards. Status was still measured in arcane units: by-lines, citations, appointments, grants.

No, apart from the occasional entrepreneur like Sagan or Pauling, it took the heavy hand of politics to raise a scientist to the status of household name, and to confer a moral polarity on the research they pursued. Einstein gave Roosevelt the roadmap to an atomic bomb. Eisenhower injected Salk's vaccine into the arms of twenty million schoolchildren. Von Braun and his Germans built Kennedy a moon rocket.

And Jeffrey Horton handed Mark Breland the Trigger.

Though he himself had played a role in that, Brohier's own conscience was clear. He harbored a lifelong contempt for those who resorted to violence to resolve their problems, and especially for those who used violence to trump decisions made by rational or democratic means. Like many of his calling, he both lived in and believed in a meritocracy, in the triumph of superior ideas and the leadership of superior men.

The enemies of civilization were the terrorist, the bandit, the assassin, the bully, the anarchist – precisely because of the way petty men of no accomplishment could bring the good and great low with the squeeze of a trigger or the push of a button. It was a perversion of the natural social order, a kind of rabid egalitarianism that would not tolerate another's success.

In Brohier's eyes, violence was not merely the last refuge of the incompetent. It was the gloating revenge of the sore loser.

The quintessence of civilization was the concept of good sportsmanship, and its principles were easily understood – graciousness in victory, acquiescence in defeat. They could be seen in the way outgoing Presidents surrendered their offices, the way Oscar losers applauded winners, the way victors showed mercy to the vanquished. They could even be seen in a gentlemen's duel that ended in death, because that contest had rules which were binding on both sides.

But terrorist violence – the shot from the dark, the bomb in the mail, the blackmailing threat – was the antithesis of civilization. And, by Brohier's lights, class violence was indistinguishable from terrorism. That was why the director had been lenient with Lee and Gordie after the Cleveland incident. Brohier had no brief for gun-wielding thugs out to terrorize good people who were playing by the rules.

Still, he was under no illusions. Civilization was hard, and terrorism was easy. The tension between order and chaos was ubiquitous and eternal. Brohier knew in his heart that logic and reason were easily drowned out in the human dialogue by the insistent voices of passion and self-interest.

Even so, he firmly believed in the bootstrap theory of progress – that even a minority committed to reason, to excellence, to the high principles of civilization, could make a difference. Society was not led from the middle, but from the top – by the ideas of the thinkers, the discoveries of the explorers, the creations of the inventors, the words of the philosophers, the marvels of the builders, the sacrifices of the pioneers.

As he was fond of saying: rudders are, as a rule, much smaller than the ships they steer. Leverage mattered.

Leverage, and which hands were on the wheel.

That was what the Trigger represented to Brohier – leverage. Leverage that could be used to turn society in the right direction, toward a saner and more civil existence. And if it was not enough leverage, or if more hands were needed to hold the wheel steady in rough seas, then it was incumbent on him to do what he could to help.

In the end, that was what swung the decision – an obligation deeper and stronger than that which his feelings for Horton could command. Sitting in the sun on a bench at the edge of the woods, he realized that he had waited for Horton as long as conscience would allow. It was necessary to go forward without him.

On his return to his office, he wrote a brief note to Samuel Bennington-Hastings:

When you have a few minutes, I'd like to talk to you about something I've been working on.

It seemed as though Brohier had barely lifted his hands from the keyboard when the young mathematician opened his door and poked his head in.

'Testing Ashby's interdimensional transport, Dr Sam?' Brohier asked with a raised eyebrow.

Bennington-Hastings beamed a bright smile. 'I was afraid that you'd be planning on eating your usual dinner, and –' he touched his chest and made a guttural sound like an explosion '– I'd find you face-down in the smashed potatoes.'

Brohier laughed. 'Come in, Dr Sam. Come in and take a look at this.'

There was no trace of the playful sprite when Samuel Bennington-Hastings talked mathematics.

'This – this is wrong,' he said, swiping at the whiteboard with a cloth. 'The relationship is asymmetrical – you see, here is the correct expansion, and this value falls out on the right side.'

Brohier frowned unhappily. 'Then the covalent function is indeterminate.'

'Of course. This entire recapitulation is unnecessary. Where did you get this?'

'That section provides the morphological inertia that restores the initial resonance matrix.'

Bennington-Hastings made a scoffing sound. 'Sheldrake. I'll erase it.'

'Wait – wait. If I lose that function, then there's nothing to restore the time-zero *eigenstate*. The material won't return to its initial condition.'

'There is nothing in what you've shown me to indicate that it should.'

'But would the new *eigenstate* be stable?'

'If the solution set for the resonance matrix is complete and meaningful – and if stability is a feature of the solution set.'

Pressing his right hand to his cheek, Brohier turned away and walked to his desk. He picked up his cup of Indian coffee and sipped at it as he considered both the threat and the opportunity in Bennington-Hastings's contention.

'I had been expecting – counting on – a morphological safety net,' Brohier said at last. 'To create a local change that lasts only as long as the input continues, and then to have the material revert to type under the influence of its universal resonance parameters. Peer pressure to conform, if you will.'

Bennington-Hastings glanced back at the whiteboard. 'As Descartes said of god, I have no need of that hypothesis.'

'We can change the information envelope permanently.'

'I see nothing here that forbids it.'

'Then we also could destroy the information envelope.'

'I see nothing here that forbids that, either.'

Brohier set his cup down with an unsteady hand and walked back to the whiteboard. Reclaiming the marker from Bennington-Hastings, he gestured at the lower right quarter of the board.

'Correct me if I'm mistaken, but this is consistent with the parameters of a matter-antimatter reaction,' he said. Erasing the morphological extension with his sleeve, he scribbled several mathematical symbols in the vacant space. 'You see? The values for particle and antiparticle cancel, and their bound energy is released in mutual annihilation. Remove the resonance matrix –'

'And we will have direct experimental evidence of the conditions at the beginning of the Universe,' said Bennington-Hastings. 'Sadly, our funerals would have to be closed-casket.'

'Brohier's Last Theorem.'

'Very much so.'

Their light tone belied a sobering realization – that an elemental energy discharge from matter stripped of its matrix would dwarf not only the largest man-made explosion ever, but every cataclysm Earth had witnessed since the Yucatan impact.

'Perhaps I'll take another look at the Sheldrake hypothesis,' Bennington-Hastings volunteered, breaking the silence. 'We wouldn't want to have any unexpected outcomes when you take this off the whiteboard and into the laboratory.'

'I'm going to revisit every piece of it, from top to bottom,' said Brohier grimly. 'My tolerance for uncertainty is suddenly very thin.'

He did not share the rest of his thoughts, which were to haunt him for days to come. *We are already running this experiment. We have altered the information envelope of human culture, and changed the behavior of its constituent matter. Have there been any unexpected results? Have we prevented many small calamities – or laid the groundwork for the one great calamity that will shatter everything?*

In the wake of the successful test of the Twins and the departure of Jeffrey Horton, the Annex had reached a cusp. The first question Leigh Thayer and Gordon Greene had taken up after taking over was whether the lab still had a mission – and if so, whether it was one that required the Nevada facilities.

'The problem is that this place is too big and too small at the same time,' Greene had explained to Goldstein and Brohier in a videoconference. 'Too many people spending too much time together too far away from civilization – the pioneering spirit eventually wears thin, especially when there's no place to go to get away from each other. At this point, these people feel like they've built the bloody bridge for the Colonel. It's time to either pack up and go home or turn the camp into a settlement.'

Thayer had a different perspective, but had reached the same conclusion. 'The test and development situation is impossible – my labs and the test range should have been isolated from everything else from the beginning. With the uprated Mark I and the Mark II, we're always impinging on the whole campus, including the apartments. At this point, I don't know if it's going to cost more to move the test units or the residences and support facilities, but somehow we have to separate them. If we don't, I can't see that it's worth keeping the Annex open.'

It was Goldstein who had reduced both their presentations to the essentials. 'So we either put more money into the Annex, or write off what we've already spent there. We need to decide whether to make the Annex a permanent part of Terabyte.'

'Exactly,' Greene and Thayer had said in unison.

'Very well. Karl and I need to talk. We'll let you know as soon as there's a decision.'

Two days later, Brohier had delivered the answer – the surprising answer, since it made no economic sense whatsoever. Goldstein was acquiring an additional nine square miles of property adjoining the Annex site, and opening the corporate purse for a thoroughgoing transformation of the facility.

'There are two conditions,' Brohier had informed them. 'One, that both of you agree to stay on at least until your recommendations have been implemented. And two, that you make certain we have at least one operational test unit available throughout the transition.'

Then it had been Greene and Thayer's turn to consult in private.

'What do you think?' Greene had asked.

'We're talking about a commitment of at least a year, wouldn't you say?'

394

'I'd guess two, allowing time for all the dust to settle. Can you stand the thought of another two years out here?'

She had shrugged. 'I'm ambivalent. I like the air. I hate the heat. I love the night sky – all the stars. I miss the color green.'

'What about the work – and the company?'

'I can see some potential in both,' she had said, with the barest hint of a hopeful smile. 'What about you? You're the footloose one. Aren't you missing Columbus, all those student dives filled with *Girls of the Big 10* candidates?'

Greene had laughed. 'I like the scenery here – and the challenges. I'm planning to stay.'

'Then I suppose I will, too.' Then she had smiled sweetly and added, 'After all – you'd be in deep trouble trying to handle it all without me.'

Nearly seven months had passed since then, and the first phase of the metamorphosis was now complete. Security chief Donovan King now had responsibility for an unfenced sixteen-mile-long perimeter guarded by four thousand sensors, five four-wheel-drive trackers, and a whisper-quiet cherry-red helicopter that mounted a million-candlepower light pod, rocket flares, and dye bombs. Donovan was unabashedly enjoying his new toys, and there had been several unconfirmed sightings of off-duty staff officers wearing black t-shirts bearing the puckish logo AREA 5.1 SECURITY.

In the southwest corner of the enlarged Annex site, a new Village had sprung up on the rise above a dry arroyo. It boasted three paved streets, twenty new homes, a half-acre of irrigated grass as park and playground, a general store and late-night grille, a fitness and recreation hall with a first-class minitheater, and the Family Center – one wing of which was a health clinic, and the other a day-care facility.

What the Village did not have yet was any residents, though many Annex workers had already packed their apartments in anticipation of the move. But they were at the mercy of the building inspector for Eureka County – a part-time post currently held by the owner of the largest building-supply dealer in central Nevada. The inspector had already canceled two appointments and failed to appear for a third.

Greene suspected they were being punished for a breach of

etiquette – namely, failing to properly grease the inspector's palm. With Aron Goldstein's bargain-hunting corporate buyers signing the purchase orders, very little of what had gone into building the Annex or the Village had been purchased locally, and none of it from Tillman Construction.

The suspicion hardened into certainty when Greene received the early-morning call from the gatehouse. 'Dr Greene, we have a Robert Tillman here – he says he's here for final inspection on a number of permits, and you're expecting him.'

Greene cast a bleary eye in the direction of the clock. 'Have someone take him up to the Village, and stay with him until Mr Colquit or I get there. Give him some coffee, but don't let him inside any of the buildings without us. In fact, give him a *lot* of coffee – it might help improve his opinion of the plumbing.' Closing the comset on the guard's laughter, Greene rolled onto his right side and nudged a sleeping Leigh Thayer. 'Lee?'

She stirred and turned toward him. 'The answer is no,' she murmured. 'Ask again later.'

'Tillman's playing some more games with us. I have to go down to the Village right now. Give me a tickle when you get up – if we're still at it, maybe you'll want to come join us,' he said as he climbed out of bed. 'Besides, I don't think you've been down since before the Family Center came in and the landscapers rolled out the sod for the playground.'

Yawning, she sat up, letting the sheet fall away with careless unconcern. The Tasmanian Devil grinned back at him from her sleepshirt. 'It's not like I haven't had any work of my own to do,' she said.

'I know,' Greene said, jumping into his pants. 'I just thought if we all could sign off at the same time, we might be able to give the green light to the people who've been waiting to move.'

'You actually think Tillman will let us occupy? I'm expecting him to fine-print us to death. But I'll come down anyway in a little while to lend moral support. – Comb your hair, hon, you look like you've been partying all night with some tart.'

By the time Thayer joined them two hours later, her prophecy had already been fulfilled. Tillman had torn open a finished wall and ripped up the subfloor of a carpeted room before red-tagging the California-built manufactured homes so heavily that the tags looked like part of the decor. But he had not dawdled in doing so; he was already on his way back to the gate when Lee found a glum Gordon Greene sitting on the porch steps of one of the two larger L-shaped prefabs.

'Bad?'

Greene waggled the sheaf of yellow deficiency notices at her. 'He rejected the manufacturer's certification papers because they weren't originals – hand-signed by the inspector, embossed seal, one copy for each unit.'

'That arrogant son of a . . .'

'The smaller the crown, the more petty the king. But this won't hold us up more than a couple of days. I've already contacted the manufacturer. They'll have new certificates couriered to us as soon as they can put them together.'

'I didn't know you were capable of being this philosophical,' she said with a wry smile.

'Some people just aren't worth the stomach acid,' Greene said. He jerked a thumb over his shoulder at the door behind him. 'Got a few minutes? I'd still like to show you this one.'

Her gaze narrowed. 'Why? Isn't this the administrative supply building?' Then she raised an eyebrow. 'Or is this your idea of asking me later?'

Greene laughed as he stood. 'No to both. Come on – I'll show you.'

It was obvious on first glance that the spaces inside were set up for a residence rather than for storage. But the structure was half again as large as the standard Village home. 'I don't understand. I was sure the site plan called for an administrative building here.'

'It did,' Greene agreed cheerfully. 'I think the director's residence qualifies as an administrative building, don't you?'

'The director's residence,' she echoed, as she peeked through a doorway. 'Hey, look at the size of that bathroom. You talked me into it – I'll take it. – So, where are you going to live?'

'Well – I'm afraid there's only one director's residence, and we happen to have two directors.'

'That was poor planning.'

'I agree. But it's too late now to do anything about it. So –'

he shrugged '– I'm afraid we don't have much choice but to share.'

She crossed her arms and leaned against the door frame, an amused expression on her face. 'Gordie, this is at once the sweetest and the dumbest way I've ever heard of asking someone to move in with you.'

Greene protested his innocence with raised hands. 'I'm just trying to carry out my responsibilities for efficient facilities management. Here we are, occupying two Cardinals, burning twice as many lights, using twice as many rolls of toilet tissue –'

Lee frowned. 'I suppose if we did move in together, we'd finally have enough pillows for the bed.'

'And we could return half of the silverware we've lifted from the cafeteria – more savings for Terabyte. What do you say, Lee?'

Her smile returned, at once tender and mocking. 'How can I resist a company man?'

Greene smiled back. But before either could say more, both their comsets began to chirp the priority page signal.

'I was thinking about coming over there and kissing you,' he said, 'but I suppose a company man would answer.'

Thayer was already reaching for her pocket. 'It's Karl,' she said, looking down at the display.

They hit their callback buttons together, and in moments they were connected.

'Gordie? Lee? This is Dr Brohier.' The senior scientist's voice was eager and vibrant. 'Whatever you're doing, drop it. Whatever you were planning on doing, forget it. I need you to build something for me.'

26:

'We cannot accept the doctrine that war must be
forever a part of man's destiny.'

— *Franklin Delano Roosevelt*

Aron Goldstein was one of the last of his breed, and he knew
it. He had watched the globe-trotting on-the-go CEO gradually
give way to the teleconferencing stay-at-home CEO, seen the
articles in *Fortune* and *Forbes* and *Business Week* lauding multimedia
interconnectivity as the essential management tool, noted the
ranks of the corporate jets thinning as stockholders and corporate
boards increasingly questioned the necessity of shipping proto-
plasm from here to there at company expense. When McNamara's
The Frugal Executive hit the bestseller list, airline stocks fell fourteen
percent in three days, and business travel fell twenty percent by
the end of the year.

But Goldstein remained a road warrior, spending an average
of thirty-five weeks a year away from his Maryland estate. That
included week-long visits to each of his companies, attending
international trade shows in North America, Europe, and the
Pacific Rim, and an annual two-week retreat aboard the rigid-sail
catamaran *First Love* he kept docked at St Thomas, in the Virgin
Islands.

He did it because he could – as sole owner of Aurum Industries,
the holding company which served as overseer of all his properties,
he did not have to answer to anyone but himself. He also did it
because he believed it was necessary – he would not trust even the
smallest of his enterprises to a manager whose measure he had not
taken in person. Nor would Goldstein assess an operation by the
numbers alone, or allow himself to be given a 'Stalin village' tour of
operations. Consequently, his unannounced visits had, over time,

become what Goldstein described as 'agreeably motivational' – not least because they were frequently followed by sudden promotions and summary dismissals.

But that was the quintessential Aron Goldstein – demanding and decisive. He had made his fortune and his reputation on two simple principles, and one personal gift. The first principle was 'Move quickly, whether pursuing an opportunity or being pursued by calamity.' The second principle was 'No one ever lost a customer by giving him too much value.'

Goldstein's gift was an uncanny ability to connect seemingly unrelated events and in doing so to pick up on the earliest signs of coming trouble – a knack for hearing the signal among the static, the off notes in the orchestra. It was said in jest that there was no need for smoke detectors when he was around, that the first warning sign would be Goldstein standing over the point of ignition with an extinguisher, waiting for the fire to break out.

The myth exaggerated the gift. Still, Goldstein had come to rely on that feeling of prescient certainty. But it took no special talent on Goldstein's part to recognize that when a Secret Service advance team showed up at his estate to arrange for an unexpected and off-the-record visit from the President, the disarmament initiative was in trouble.

Breland's visit was hidden as an unannounced stop on a routine weekend flight to Camp David. The giant props of the Marine Corps Osprey set it down gently on the rain-softened driving range a few minutes before Friday noon. The President alone emerged from the rear hatch of the tilt-rotor to join Goldstein and the Secret Service ground detail. Breland looked at once tired and tense, and snapped at the agents when two of them tried to follow him inside the house.

'This is a private meeting,' he said, stopping short and blocking the doorway.

'Mr President, we have to be close at hand if we're going to be able to respond quickly enough to protect you,' one of the agents protested.

'If the International Army of God is waiting in the wine cellar, we'll have learned something about my ability to judge character. In the meantime, you stay out,' Breland said, and closed the door in the agent's face. As he turned back to a wide-eyed Goldstein, he muttered, 'damn spiders. Ever since Starr got them to spy on Clinton –'

'Their discretion can't be taken for granted – I know. Shall we?' Goldstein asked, gesturing toward one of the exits from the expansive foyer.

'I wonder if there's a room with no outside windows where we might talk?'

Nodding, Goldstein said, 'If the irony isn't too strong for you, there's a chamber in the lower level which the original owner had built as a firing range. My elder daughter used it for archery, and I keep my trains there now. The accommodations are somewhat spartan –'

'It sounds ideal. Lead on.'

Goldstein's trains were a complete world in miniature – a great U-shaped landscape wrapped around a small raised observation platform with three swiveling seats. The moment he and Breland entered, a computerized controller brought the diorama to life. Lights came on in buildings, more than a dozen freight and passenger trains started moving along hundreds of meters of track, trolleys shuttled through the streets, and real water flowed through river channels. A matte painting which climbed half-way up the wall extended the landscape to a hilly distant horizon.

'Why, this looks like north central Philly – say, 1950 or so?' Breland said with surprised pleasure. He stepped closer and peered over the layout. 'Sure, there's 30th Street Station, and the Zoo. Which makes this the Schulkill River. Am I right?'

'Right city, wrong era. I went with 1935, pre-war, so I could bring the occasional steam engine into the city.' He pointed at the far left end of the diorama. 'I grew up eight blocks from Reading Station and the Chinese Wall. Every time I hear a train whistle, it takes me right back to my bedroom.'

Suddenly looking wistful, Breland settled into one of the chairs. 'I envy you, having the time for this – for something wonderful and frivolous and personal.'

Goldstein laughed. 'Don't be misled. You're looking at more money than time – and at that, the time is scattered across three decades, an evening a month, a weekend a year.'

'Ah. Still – I think I used to have hobbies. Surely one, at least.' Breland smiled wanly. 'But, then, it won't be too much longer before I'll have plenty of time to try to figure out what it was.'

'Now, Mr President –'

'Please – Mark,' Breland implored. 'I find I'm increasingly hungry for the sound of my own name.'

'Mark,' Goldstein echoed. 'As I was about to say, it's much too early to surrender.'

'I have a forty percent approval rating, Aron.'

'A passionate and unshakeable forty percent – the kind that can decide an election when half the population stays home.'

Breland laughed bitterly. 'I don't think anyone's going to sit out the next election. Whatever the modern record for voter turnout is, I'm sure we're going to see it broken.'

'And if that happens, all bets are off – the pollsters have no idea how to predict the behavior of a group that's never voted before.'

Holding up his hand and shaking his head, Breland said, 'Enough – enough, please. The only thing sadder than a young cynic is an old idealist.'

'With respect, sir, I would have said it the other way around. – But our time is limited, and I doubt you came here to trade aphorisms with me.'

'No,' Breland said. Shoulders slumping, he sat back in his chair. 'No, I came here hoping for your help.'

'Whatever I can do.'

'I don't know that there is anything you can do. But I'm desperate, Aron. Everything is spinning out of control. I have no authority over the Pentagon, no credibility in Congress – they've both decided that I'm the lamest of lame ducks, and can safely be ignored. The Joint Chiefs are preparing to rearm with tactical nukes and azide explosives. The House is looking for a way to ban privately owned LifeShields as public hazards. The NRA is suing to get rid of state-installed LifeShields as violations of the *Fourth* Amendment – unreasonable search and seizure. And I have no leverage with any of them.'

'That's not all – there's yet another front in this war,' Goldstein said. 'There're more than sixty liability lawsuits pending against

Aurum Industries, Terabyte Laboratories, Jeffrey Horton, and anyone else who had a hand in building the Triggers which are out
there now.'

'Sixty!'

'It's only the beginning, I'm afraid. I believe there's a coordinated
effort to get rid of the Trigger by making it prohibitively expensive
to build them or install them. And it's working as blackmail even
before the first case has reached a courtroom – we already know
of more than a hundred private installations that have been voluntarily shut down or removed.'

'Because the owners are more worried about being sued than
about someone being killed.'

'That's what it comes down to.'

Breland blew a sigh across a clenched fist. 'You know, Aron,
I've never had any faith in Freudian analysis, but in this instance,
I'm sorely tempted – the male fetish for guns, and the completely unreasoning way some men react to the prospect of giving
them up –'

'I know where this is going. As if they were being castrated,
rendered impotent.'

'It sounds absurd, and yet –' Breland shook his head.

'I suppose it's too late to add National Mental Health Insurance
to Medicare.'

That drew a brittle laugh from Breland. 'The other explanation
I've been offered is even more depressing – that we're fighting a
primal biological selfishness, an innate drive to acquire power and
defend the family. A British anthropologist sent me a long essay
with his analysis: The resistance is coming from men who see me
as a threat rather than as a higher-status male of their tribe. They're
refusing to place themselves under my protection, and clinging to
what they believe they need to protect themselves.'

'That sounds like the makings of a revolution.'

'Doesn't it, though? Maybe the only thing that's saved us from
that is how weak I look – how weak I *am*. They see me as
mortally wounded. They think they've already won. And right
now, I'd have a hard time arguing the point. Which is why I'm
here – looking for more leverage. Looking for a way to prove
them wrong.'

'I'm not sure I understand –'

'With your cooperation, I turned over the complete theoretical and technical record on the Trigger to five government research centers – four military, one under the Justice Department. I know now that I can't look to any of them for help. Their mindset is controlled by the people who feel threatened by the Trigger, and they're picking it apart to learn how to thwart it, not how to improve it. Nothing I can do will make any difference – it's like hiring wolves to shear sheep.'

'I understand now. You want to know what we can do for you.'

'I'd phrase it with a bit more desperation – I've come to beg you to *find* some way to help. I need a better Trigger, Aron. A better and a safer Trigger. I need one that works on all the exotic flavors of explosives we're rushing to bring into play. I need one that handles explosives the way the current version handles black powder. I need one that makes us feel safe enough that the generals can live without battlefield nukes and the rest of us can live without an arsenal in the closet. I need more leverage. I need an answer – if I can't find one, civil disarmament is going to end up side-by-side in the history books with Prohibition as a noble idea we couldn't live up to.'

A deep frown furrowed Goldstein's face with worry lines. 'Have you talked to Senator Wilman about this?'

'Grover came to me, earlier this week. He has his own concerns, and no answers. It was a very gloomy conversation.'

'But the foreign labs –'

'– Have so far been unable to do more than refine the original design. Grover spoke of a theoretical hurdle, a missing piece.'

'I assure you, Mr President, we didn't hold anything back.'

'I know that. But the original Trigger was your creation – no one knows more about it than your people.'

'Perhaps so. But Dr Horton's been on sabbatical –'

'Then it's time to get him back to work,' Breland said sharply.

Goldstein frowned. 'The fact of the matter is, Dr Horton hasn't been keeping very closely in touch.'

'You don't know where he is?'

'That's my understanding.'

404

Breland shook his head unhappily. 'Maybe it's unfair of me to lay this at your doorstep, Aron, but there it is – what you've done so far isn't enough. You have to take it further. You have to give me more, and sooner rather than later. If you can't, *we will fail* – and I know you don't want that.'

'Of course not. Of course not.'

Breland stood and edged toward the door, signaling his intention to leave. 'In fact, I remember very clearly something you said that day in the Oval Office – that even if our species is condemned to create murderers and warlords, the least the rest of us can do is make it as hard for them as we possibly can. Well, we aren't there yet. Help me. Push your people. Shame them, bribe them, scare them, inspire them – whatever it takes to extract the very best they can give us. Because it's getting very late, Aron – and we won't get a second chance in our lifetimes.'

'No,' Goldstein said slowly. 'You're quite right. This is a singular moment. We either make this work, or in failing confirm the pessimism that excuses us from asking more of ourselves. Either a civil society, or a cynical one.' He joined Breland in standing and offered his hand. 'Mr President, I honestly don't know how much we can do that we aren't already doing – but I'll find out, and I'll see that it gets done.'

Goldstein saw the President out and waited until the tilt-rotor lifted off before reaching for his comset. 'Captain Hill? Get the plane ready – we're going to Princeton.'

There were no other aircraft at the Princeton airport's modest commercial terminal, and consequently no limos waiting at the taxi stand. Rather than wait for a car to be called, Goldstein went straight to the only rental agency and pounded on the counter until a puzzled clerk, apparently roused from a mid-shift nap, emerged from the back room. Goldstein accepted a bland cream-colored family sedan without complaint, keeping to himself the facts that his license had a daytime-only endorsement and he hadn't been in the driver's seat for more than five years.

The only parking available in the visitor lot in front of the Institute's Fuld Hall was a handicapper space. Rather than risk the automatic impoundment, Goldstein left the car running at the curb.

'Excuse me,' he said to the woman in the reception office. 'Can you tell me where I can find Dr Brohier?'

'I'm sorry – Dr Brohier isn't available to see visitors. But you can leave a message for him right there.'

Goldstein glanced over his shoulder at the comstand. 'What does that mean? Why isn't he available? Does he have his "Do Not Disturb" sign out? Is he sleeping? Is he off campus? – or is it something else?'

'I'm sorry – I don't have any other information. I suggest you leave a message for Dr Brohier, and make arrangements –'

'Miss, if I wanted to leave a message for him, I could have done so. Dr Brohier works with me.'

'In that case, you probably have better ways of contacting him,' she said brightly. 'I'm sorry I couldn't help. You understand that the Institute is deeply committed to creating an optimum environment for –'

'Yes, yes, yes,' Goldstein said impatiently. 'Now you understand –'

'Excuse me, sir,' a new voice interrupted. 'Is that your Elite parked outside in the traffic lane?'

Goldstein turned to find himself looking up into the face of a tall man in a low-key tan uniform. 'Yes.'

'I'm afraid you're going to have to move it, sir. It's blocking traffic.'

Pursing his lips, Goldstein bit back his first thoughts. 'Very well,' he said with deceptive calmness. 'I'll move it.'

When he reached the car, he climbed in, slammed the door shut, and sat rock-still for a moment, burning a hole in the instrument panel with his gaze. He had intended his visit to be low-key and discreet, to slip in and out of town as invisibly as possible, trusting nothing to the ether, where it could be intercepted, recorded, and decrypted by those who might be taking a particular interest in the creators of the Trigger.

But Karl was locked away behind a wall – not only of etiquette and protocol, but of Terabyte's own precautions. Brohier's physical address appeared nowhere in Terabyte records. There was no need for it. Money found its way into accounts, information found its way to displays and printers, and there were package drops aplenty available for the delivery of merchandise.

There were only two choices – try to knock a hole in the wall, or wait until Brohier came out from behind it on his own. Which, insofar as Goldstein was concerned, was really only one choice.

With a screaming whine of motors and a squeal of rubber worthy of a seventeen-year-old, he sent the car lurching forward, then swerving sharply to the right. The front wheels jumped the curb and then dug in, hauling the vehicle up onto the grass. There Goldstein waited.

He did not have to wait long. In moments, the tall male security officer came rushing out of the building's main entrance, followed by a much smaller female officer. Both ran straight toward Goldstein, neither shouting orders nor drawing weapons as they approached. When they were close enough to stand glowering over him outside the driver's door, Goldstein lowered the window part of the way.

'Shameful – shameful,' he said, not giving them an opening to speak. 'Is this your idea of security, Officer Weiss? What if I'd been a terrorist car bomber? I could have driven right up the steps and taken out the entire building.'

'Sir, you need to move this car *now*,' insisted the female officer. 'If you don't, you're looking at being arrested for trespassing and destruction of property –'

'Bluster won't cover up the deficiencies. Good heavens, one medium-sized car bomb would drop the mean planetary IQ twenty points in an eyeblink. I know you don't have a LifeShield installed here, because your directors foolishly declined our offer. But hasn't anyone around here ever heard of controlled access, or barrier design? This road should be closed at both ends, and you need to have someone looking out for strangers who has more than a frown and bit of brass to call on if they're unfriendly.'

Officer Weiss tried the car door, but found it locked. 'You have more than a little brass yourself, sir. How about telling us who you are, and what you want here?'

'My name is Aron Goldstein –' He saw the skepticism in their expressions and sighed. 'Yes, *that* Goldstein – don't be misled by the car. It's a rental. I just flew in, and I have an urgent need to talk to Dr Brohier. Now, I understand that you try to protect your fellows or associates or what have you from being disturbed, but this is extremely important – important enough that if I don't get a little cooperation, I'm going to start looking for ways to vent my frustrations. I do that by spending money to make trouble for the people who make trouble for me. How much trouble do you think one day's profits will buy?'

The officers were exchanging questioning glances. 'Do you have any certified identification?' the woman asked.

Casually and wordlessly, Goldstein handed her his SmartID card. He watched her face as she swept it through her scanner and studied its display.

'It's Dr Brohier you want, eh?' the man asked.

'Willis – don't –'

'How many times do I need to say it?'

'I think you're too late.'

'What do you mean?'

'Dr Brohier gave notice this morning. I gather he and Dr Sam were headed out somewhere together.'

'Where? Who is Dr Sam?'

'Hold on a moment.' The officer nodded, triggering the chin switch for his radio. 'Steven, this is Willis – has Dr Sam signed out yet?' He listened a moment, then added, 'Twenty minutes ago? Thanks.' Another bob of the head, and Willis bent down to peer through the window. 'Maybe you aren't too late, after all. Try members' housing, off Olden Lane,' he said, pointing toward the east. 'Dr Brohier was in Fifty-one.'

Goldstein nodded as he put the car in reverse. 'My apologies about the lawn, officers – I lost my grip on the joystick for a moment. Send Aurum Industries a bill for the landscaping.'

Only knowing that he was looking for two men allowed Goldstein to spot them. Otherwise, he would have obeyed the stop sign at Olden Lane. Otherwise, he would have surrendered right of way and allowed the taxi to pass through the intersection instead of pulling out in front of it.

Brakes squealed as both vehicles swerved. The taxi ended up with its right front wheel against the curb and its left front fender kissing the passenger door of the Elite. Both drivers stepped out into the twilight, one cursing angrily, the other calmly retrieving a $100 bill from an inner pocket.

'Sorry about that,' Goldstein said, flashing and then handing over the money as he neared and then walked past the suddenly speechless taxi driver. He poked his head through the open door and looked into the passenger seat. Brohier was pale, and the second passenger was visibly trembling.

'You're very old for a hit man,' the stranger said with nervous bravado.

'I'm very unarmed for one, too,' Goldstein said. 'Karl, we need to talk.'

'Aron, what the hell are you doing here? And are you completely addled? You could have killed us!'

'Nonsense, taxi drivers have splendid reflexes. Just get out and get in my car, will you?'

The taxi driver shouldered in at that point. 'Look, if this is some kind of boyfriend-boyfriend thing, I don't want to be in the middle of it.'

'It isn't, and you aren't. Unload their bags – I'll take them where they're going.'

'Hey, I have a meter running here. I don't let anyone steal my fares, not even for –'

Goldstein silently pushed another bill at him.

'Fair enough,' the driver said.

'You don't even *know* where we're going,' Brohier protested. 'And we're already late – we're going to miss our plane.'

'I don't know where you *were* going. But I do know you're not going to miss your plane.' He peered at Dr Sam. 'You, I'm not sure about. Karl, my car – please.'

Brohier frowned, then threw his door open. 'I've never seen you like this, Aron – so I suppose I'd better find out what's gotten into you.'

'That's my boy.'

'Not likely. Give me the keys, Aron.'

First, Brohier drove the car forward to the curb, clearing the intersection. The taxi driver followed suit, depositing Dr Sam and the suitcases on the sidewalk, then driving off.

'Now – what's going on?' Brohier demanded of Goldstein.

The industrialist joined him in the front seat.

'Things are very grave, Karl – very grave. The playwright's begging for our help. The play needs a second act, and there isn't much time. We've invested so much in this production, and I don't want to see it close prematurely –'

Blinking in confusion, Brohier interrupted, '*What* play? What the devil are you talking about?'

Frowning, Goldstein leaned close and whispered. 'I'm talking about the President. I'm talking about what we're doing for him.'

'Then why are you talking in code? There's no one here but the two of us.'

'And your friend out there. Who is he? How well do you know him?'

'I was about to take him to the Annex – does that answer your question?'

'To the Annex –' Aron pursed his lips. 'Well, the fact of the matter is, that's exactly where I want you to go. I'm here to drag you away and get you back to work.'

'I never stopped working.'

'On the second act.'

'Well – the fact is, I think Sam and I may already have a working draft of it,' Brohier said.

'What?'

'We were on our way to a dress rehearsal. Would you care to come with us to the theater?'

Goldstein nodded, hope brightening his eyes. 'We can take my plane.'

'Good – because ours left ten minutes ago.' Brohier waved the young scientist into the back seat of the car. 'Aron, meet Dr Samuel Bennington-Hastings. Dr Sam, this is Mr Goldstein – he pays the bills. And he's going with us. Or should I say, we're going with him.'

Wedged in between two suitcases, Dr Sam cast a wary look in Goldstein's direction. 'Promise me he's not going to be the one driving.'

Chuckling deeply, Brohier clasped the joystick and eased the car

410

away from the curb. 'No problem,' he said. 'Aron and I have an arrangement – I do the driving, and he does the flying. So just sit back, and don't worry a bit.'

Dr Sam sighed expressively. 'I think I am about to make a very big mistake.'

'That's what youth is for,' Goldstein said lightly, smiling conspiratorially at Brohier. 'When you get to be our age, you don't get that kind of latitude.'

'I am worrying about altitude, not latitude. I think I will close my eyes now – will you please tell me when it's over?'

The other men laughed. 'Sure, Dr Sam,' Brohier said. 'As soon as someone tells us.'

Dr Gordon Greene bent forward and peered through the electronic binoculars at the test stand a thousand meters away. Taking advantage of a natural bowl that had been further sculpted by bulldozers and explosives, the new test range was set up for 360-degree testing. That arrangement pushed the observation and control station much farther away than it had been at the Annex's original test stand, to the top of a sun- and wind-exposed ridge a kilometer to the southwest.

'A lot of firepower out there,' Greene observed, focusing on some of the instrumented sample pedestals. The pedestals, each nestled against its own curved reinforced-concrete blast wall, not only surrounded the test stand but climbed the face of the bowl to an elevation of more than thirty degrees. Four sloping tunnels on the north side extended the test envelope to minus twenty degrees.

Greene had been speaking to no one in particular, but Val Bowden was standing close enough to hear. 'Yeah, Pete McGhan did a great job pulling things together for the test.'

'It helps to have an in with the Army quartermaster,' Greene said. 'Ninety millimeter, thirty millimeter, rifle grenades, C-4 – if even one of those goes off, we're going to be picking up the pieces of the test stand for a month.'

'Don't say that around Lee – not after the twenty-hour days she's put in getting this place ready.'

Greene grunted his agreement, and Bowden drifted away. He

411

found himself standing beside Dr Brohier, listening to two technicians calling off the instrumentation checks.

'A lot of firepower out there,' Bowden said, just to have something to say.

'Not for long,' said Brohier cheerfully.

At the other end of the platform, Samuel Bennington-Hastings had attached himself to Leigh Thayer. 'I'm deeply confused by the fact that we're preparing to test this device and we still have no proper way to measure its output.'

'That's probably because it doesn't have an output in the conventional sense – it has an effect,' she said. 'And that ordnance out there will measure the effect just fine.'

'Very well. As long as you know that this isn't science – this is merely fooling around with god's Legos.'

'Oh, Sam – you're so cute when you're jealous,' Thayer cooed flirtatiously at him. 'Everyone knows engineers have all the fun. Theoretical science is just a little squirt of information – it doesn't amount to anything unless an engineer is around to take it in, combine it with some practical science, and lovingly nurture it until it's a full-term newborn baby technology.'

By the time she was done, Bennington-Hastings was blushing. 'Well, I just hope you're practicing safe Annex.'

'You're a strange little man, Dr Sam.'

Bennington-Hastings beamed. 'Thank you very much.'

Aron Goldstein and the newest arrival, Grover Wilman, had found themselves a place at the back of the platform, safely out of the way of the pre-test bustle.

'I'm nervous,' Goldstein confessed. 'I wonder if they might be rushing things because we're here.'

'Are you afraid we might jinx them, Aron, just by virtue of standing here and wanting it so much? The preliminary tests were very promising.'

'My mother believed that god is very concerned with our humility, and metes out disappointments when we start to expect more than our share of good fortune,' said Goldstein. 'As a rule, I'd prefer having low expectations exceeded than high expectations disappointed – but on those occasions when I have difficulty keeping my expectations in check, I remember my mother's warning.'

412

Wilman grunted. 'Aron, if you think a good result down there would amount to more than our share of good fortune, you need to let me take you on a little refresher tour of recent history. You put two world wars, twenty regional wars, a hundred civil wars, and all the racial, religious, and political genocides – in and out of war – on one side of the ledger –'

'But how much of that bad fortune did we create for ourselves?'

'Oh, the men with the guns created all of it. They've had things all their way for a long time now. But we're not here for them – we're here for the rest of the world, the ones who've done all the bleeding and suffering and dying.' He rested a hand on Goldstein's shoulder and squeezed reassuringly. 'No, I promise you, this won't come close to balancing the accounts. We're not asking for too much – this is a crumb, a token payment on account, a single kiss after ten thousand beatings. Don't be afraid to wish for it with all your heart.'

Goldstein nodded toward where Brohier and Thayer were standing. 'They've started the countdown,' he said, reaching for his binoculars. 'We'll know soon.'

It was a day when what did not happen made history.

At exactly 2.10 p.m., when the sun angles were ideal for the video recorders, the J1 prototype mounted atop the test stand's Mark I Trigger was activated at full power for one-twentieth of a second. All of the tension was in the lead-up – the moment itself passed too quickly for so much as a breath held in anxious anticipation. But in that brief interval, the array of munitions and poppers on the sample pedestals was subjected to what Brohier cheekily called the bolometric intermodulating gauge-integrating field – the BIG-IF.

Of all the observers at the control station, only Brohier was equipped to visualize what was happening to the structure of those materials during that fleeting exposure. Bennington-Hastings thought in mathematics, not metaphor – he saw the balance and fit of the equations the way a deaf composer heard music without instruments, as a pure essence requiring no translation into something concrete. The others were prisoners of whatever schoolroom model of the atom had settled most firmly into their library of ideas, because there was no place in a world of either orbiting electrons or quantum uncertainty for the instantaneous transformation of elemental matter.

But in Brohier's vision, elemental matter had disappeared, exposed as a comfortable fiction agreeable to the evidence of the senses. Matter was a mere derivation, a subordinate phenomenon. The fundamental essences were energy and information. Information bound energy into form, as will bound volition into purpose. Alter the information, and the form is altered, while the substance remains unchanged.

It was, Brohier thought, as though information was the Universe's will, imposing order on the Universe's substance – order which had followed in the wake of the spontaneous and explosive transformation wrongly taken as the moment of creation. Energy was older than information, but formless and timeless without it – older than matter, but helpless and useless without it. In this new and provocative view, the Big Bang was not the birth of the Universe, but the birth of its consciousness.

And with characteristic human hubris, he and his team were trying to tap into the mechanism by which the Universe had created itself and by which it sustained itself. They were trying to whisper a suggestion in the ear of the universal mind, to replace one thought with another, one pattern with another. They were hoping to find that the properties of matter were as arbitrary in the present as in the first seconds of the cosmic inflation, to demonstrate that quantum uncertainty was merely a clue to cosmic plasticity.

Brohier already knew that they could scramble the information envelope of bound energy – that was, he now understood, what the Trigger did. The question to be answered was whether they could coherently *alter* that information envelope. But even asking the question presumed upon the resilience of the fundamental order, presumed that a local change would remain local, and that the energy would remain tightly bound as Dr Sam's equations promised.

If it did not, the test range, the Annex, the central counties of Nevada, and perhaps much more would disappear in the blue-white

414

heat of chaos's ultimate fury. *This day*, Brohier thought, *we will become like gods, or we will meet them.*

That was the drama of the moment for Brohier – not the presence of military munitions on the test range, or the equally explosive backdrop of power politics. And that prospect was what made the stillness and silence after the first phase of the test protocol so sweet to him. They would not know for a little while what had happened in that one-twentieth of a second, but what had not happened brought Brohier as much relief as any non-event possibly could.

It took nearly thirty minutes for Pete McGhan's ground crew, dressed in full-body bomb-disposal armor, to bring their new remotely-driven APC-117 forward into the test range and load into its rear compartment one-third of the exposed samples from each pedestal. They were being removed from the test range before the second phase of the test, some to be held for analysis and some to be delivered to the new firing range for use in the final phase of the day's protocol. There was little talk on the observation platform during that wait, as an almost superstitious caution prevailed.

When McGhan's crew had cleared the test zone, a new count-down started – this one leading to a simultaneous five-second activation of the test article and the Mark I together.

All of the test munitions should have been vulnerable to the Trigger, and more than one observer steeled himself against being startled by an imminent barrage of explosions. But once again, the moment came and went uneventfully. There were no explosions, no fires, not even the tendrils of white smoke which attended the decomposition of certain compounds.

It was harder to keep the excitement contained during the second break. The full-voiced talk was still all business. But Brohier heard whispers and murmuring on all sides as McGhan's team moved forward to remove another third of the test samples. Then Gordon Greene sidled up to Brohier and nudged him with an elbow.

'This is getting interesting,' Greene said under his breath. 'I especially like not being able to tell whether the last man off the range tripped over the extension cord and unplugged everything.' He smiled impishly and wandered off again, leaving Brohier with his thoughts.

Each of the day's three tests at the range had a different purpose. The first was about system safety, and from it they had learned that the J1 test article did not destabilize live explosives and propellants the way a Trigger did. The second was about system efficacy, and from it they had learned that even a Trigger could not destabilize the samples with the J1 exerting its calming influence.

The remaining question on the program was whether there was any memory effect. Looking at the mathematics, Dr Sam insisted that there would be; looking at the residue analysis from hundreds of Trigger tests, Dr Brohier had doubts. To settle the question, they had planned a series of exposures with the Mark I Trigger alone, from one-hundredth of a second at ten percent power to three full seconds at one hundred percent power. There were ninety separate exposures in the profile, but under computer control it would take barely five minutes to complete them.

'Sequencer is ready,' Leigh Thayer announced. 'Range is clear. Dr Brohier?'

'Don't wait on my account.'

'Then here goes nothing – or so we hope, eh?'

The moment she activated the sequencer, the chatter on the ridgetop ceased. Even the wind seemed to hold its breath as the seconds accreted into a first minute, then a second, then a third. Every available pair of binoculars was trained on the test stand; those without huddled around the data station and peered at the monitors.

Bennington-Hastings was among them, bouncing and rocking on his heels like a restless and impatient child. When he noticed Brohier looking his way, the young mathematician grinned broadly and offered a two-handed thumbs-up salute. Brohier answered with a cautionary look and both hands raised with fingers crossed.

'We're at full power,' Leigh Thayer announced, a tremor of excitement sneaking into her voice. Tentative smiles flickered on and off all around her.

Brohier found the last minute excruciating – a taut wire seemed to be wrapped around his chest, cutting deeply into him with each breath. Even if the entire test stand went up in the next second, they already had enough to call it a very good day. But he suddenly wanted it all, wanted Dr Sam to be right and the exposed munitions to be stable, just for the pure and beautiful symmetry of the equations, for the extraordinary perfection of the moment. Toward the end, he could not breathe at all. His lungs burned, his head pounded, even as his hopes soared, unchecked by any fear of the consequences of hubris.

Then, at last, it was over. 'That's all,' Lee said quietly. 'We're done.'

Cheers went up all around, anticipation transformed into celebration, irrepressible, giddy, proud. In the middle of the tumult, Brohier leaned heavily on a railing and somehow managed to force air from his lungs and draw a new breath. He heard the voices as though from far away.

'Got to call my broker – tell him to sell that Remington stock –'

'You're way too late – keep it and hope the certificates become collectibles.'

'Did we do it? Did we do it? I think we did it –'

'Yes, and I'll be collecting on those bets very soon indeed.'

'Hey, Gordie – are you sure you put the batteries in right-side-up?'

'Let's go to the firing range and find out.'

'That's right, people – we're not done yet. Control crew, close out your stations and get started on your test reports. Everyone else, the bus is waiting at the bottom of the hill.'

Brohier borrowed Val Bowden's arm for the trip down the long metal-mesh staircase and into the van. That prompted Leigh Thayer to turn sideways in her seat and peer quizzically back at him.

'Are you all right, Karl?' she asked. 'Do you want to go back to the complex?'

'It's the heat – it wears me out. And the sun has given me a headache. But I'm all right – the air conditioning is helping. Let's finish.'

She looked unconvinced, but turned back to the driver and waved him on. 'Let's roll.'

McGhan's crew had everything set up by the time the van arrived at the firing range. There was a weapon for each caliber of ammunition and each composition of propellant, and a man in body armor for each weapon. The explosive samples were in pits a hundred fifty meters downrange, equipped with fresh initiators and wired to the electrical detonator.

'Now, I'd strongly recommend that you ladies and gentlemen watch from inside Big Ugly there,' McGhan said, gesturing toward the armored personnel carrier. 'We have two periscope monitors set up inside, so you won't miss anything – but everything should miss you.'

Brohier clucked dismissively. 'I like the view from here,' he said. 'You can begin whenever you're ready, Mr McGhan.'

After that, there was no getting any of the others near the APC. They lingered near Brohier and the van while McGhan walked to the end of the firing line, consulted his safety supervisor by radio, then raised the red flag.

Because of the prospect of misfires, McGhan had equipped the firing line with an array of revolvers, lever-action carbines, and pump-action shotguns. Over the next few minutes, that proved to be an astute choice. One man after another clicked or racked his way through a full load of ammunition, then set his weapon down unfired, sometimes amidst a scattering of ejected duds.

It was no different with the high explosives. Three rocket grenades plowed into a hillside, each raising no more than a puff of reddish dust. Electricity surged impotently through the circuits in test pit after test pit. Untreated blasting caps shattered explosive samples, but could not shock them into detonating. Steel hammers fell feebly on the tips of warheads, and gas-fired rams quietly squeezed plastic explosives into heat-fused inert bricks.

With every failure, part of the weight on Brohier's shoulders lifted, until at the end he was feeling peculiarly light and tranquil, like a balloon resting against the ceiling. When McGhan dropped the red flag and unconstrained raucous cheers went up all across the firing range, Brohier did not join in. The most he could muster was a broad, happy smile – it felt as though yielding to any more ebullience would make him float away.

No one, including Brohier himself, was aware that his condition was in fact precarious. Gordon Greene suddenly appeared in front of him, grabbing his hand and pumping it. Grover Wilman was there, too, saying something Brohier could not quite hear. Then

Dr Sam sprang on Brohier from nowhere, assaulting him with a hug that nearly knocked him to the ground. Leigh Thayer came to his rescue, dragging Dr Sam away by the scruff of the neck – only to return a moment later to subject Brohier to a fierce chest-squeezing hug of her own. The circle of bodies closed tighter and tighter around him, until the touch of panic in his eyes attracted Aron Goldstein's notice.

'Away – away, away,' Goldstein chided, taking Brohier's arm and guiding him to the van.

They sat down together in the open sliding door of the vehicle, and Brohier clung to the weight and solidity of the metal.

'Are you all right, Karl?'

'It was all – just a bit overwhelming,' Brohier said, his chest rising and falling quickly with his sharp, noisy breaths. He tried a smile. 'Who knew – one could get this excited – over nothing.'

'Nothing? Hardly that, old friend.'

A shadow fell across them, and Brohier looked up to see Wilman standing a long stride away. 'They've called for the helicopter and the EMT. Karl, can I get you anything?'

'I'm all right,' Brohier insisted. 'A touch of heat stroke, at worst.' But he waved away an offer of water. 'One of us should call the President – tell him that we have an operational Jammer.'

'I thought I might fly back tonight and deliver the news in person,' said Aron. 'Security, and all that.'

'Probably the best way to go,' Wilman said.

'Security,' Brohier repeated. 'Yes – I'm glad you reminded me.' He looked up, squinting into the late afternoon sun. 'Grover – this goes out just as the last one did. Where is Gordon? Work with Gordon – he knows what to do. Do you understand? I don't care about the patents. I don't want to make a penny on this. Anyone who wants the Jammer can have it. Give it away. Give them a chance. Give them a chance to do better.'

'You know we will, Karl,' Goldstein said, finding Brohier's hand and squeezing it. 'You know we will.'

It took five weeks for the Annex to engineer an add-on Jammer module for the Mark I, and eight more weeks for LifeShield Arsenal to convert Plants 4, 5 and 9 to Jammer production.

Then the real work began – and there was more than enough to go around.

'Here we go,' said Tamara Dugan, tugging at the stiff collar of her new pale blue uniform as she studied the directory. 'Property manager, D. Wright, Three-A.'

Her partner shifted the tool case to his other hand. 'You do the talking if it's a guy – I'll take it if it's a gal.'

'Why not?' she said, hefting the equipment case. 'It's going to take any edge we can find to get these cold sites back online.'

D. Wright was a dour-faced, round-shouldered man twice Dugan's age and half her partner's size. 'Mr Wright – good morning!' she said, turning on her smile. 'My name is Tamara, and this is Tony –'

'There's no solicitors allowed in the complex –'

'I wish my apartment had that policy,' Dugan said smoothly. 'We're from LifeShield Technical Services, and we're here to upgrade your installation. I believe you were notified we were coming this morning?'

'Now, I told that girl, we don't use the Trigger anymore –'

'Is that so? Why is that?'

Wright snorted. 'As if you have to ask. Too damn dangerous. Why, we had a sixteen-foot moving van go up in flames, burn up everything the young man owned, just because he didn't know about our installation. Our insurance company had to settle on it, and then turned around and raised our rates twenty percent. I had it turned off that afternoon.'

'I wish you'd gotten in touch with us when that happened,' Dugan said sweetly. 'We could have put you in touch with a co-operating insurer – in fact, we still can help you with that. But this upgrade eliminates any chance of another incident like that –'

'I don't want it upgraded. I tried to tell that girl who called –'

'Mr Wright, if you'll read the agreement under which Bellwood Trace received its installation, you'll find that we retained the right of access and the responsibility for system maintenance. The notification was a courtesy.'

'Then I don't want you turning it back on. In fact, you ought to just take it out instead of tuning it up – that'll give me back a storage room, and we can use the space.'

420

'Mr Wright, have you had a chance to watch the DVD you were sent? It explains the new Jammer system we'll be installing today –'

'Don't you think I have work to do, miss? Do you think all I do is sit in front of a screen all day like some glass-eyed nethead?'

'I'm sure you work very hard, Mr Wright – we noticed right away how well-kept the property is. That's why we're sure once you understand that your liability situation has changed completely, you'll be glad we're here.'

He squinted suspiciously at her. 'What do you mean, changed?'

'Well, simply this – now that the LifeShield disables firearms without setting them off, the first time there's a shooting here and the victim's family finds out you pulled the plug, they're going to end up owning this place – and you.'

'Me?'

Her partner stepped forward. 'Absolutely. For us to remove the unit, you're going to have to personally sign a waiver acknowledging that the system was operational and that you chose not to activate it. It's all in the original agreement.'

'I – I'm going to have to talk to the management office,' said Wright nervously.

'By all means, do that,' she said. 'In the meantime, though, we'll get to work.'

'Now, hold on – management's in Bakersfield, so nobody will be in the office for a couple more hours,' Wright protested quickly.

She deftly retrieved a self-dialing identicard from a shoulder pocket and handed it to him. 'Here's a number you can call while you're waiting, then, to get answers to any questions you have. Our information office is open around the clock.'

'Look, miss –'

'Mr Wright, even if you decide to live dangerously and sign that waiver, we're going to have to upgrade that unit before we install it for someone else. So we're going to go ahead and do that now, so you have every chance to do the right thing for the people who live here.'

'All right, all right,' he said, frowning and scratching his forehead. 'I'll get you the key.'

'No need – we have ours. We'll come back and check in with you when we're finished. It's in the basement of building F, correct?'

'That's right. Turn left onto Foxtree Lane and follow it back.'

They bit their tongues until they were back in the privacy of the red, white and blue LifeService van. 'Oh, man,' Tony said with a sigh, 'I hope they're not all like that – a half-hour of yammering to get in to do a ten-minute job. They've got us scheduled for twelve of these today.'

'You know, he looked to me like the kind who'd have a forty-five in the nightstand that he never practices with,' said Dugan.

'If he does, it's a paperweight now,' Tony said, casting a glance over his shoulder. The status display on the van's Jammer showed nothing but green. 'If he doesn't go for reactivation, do we tell him?'

'We'll just tell him we had to turn it on for a few seconds to test it.'

They found that a key was unnecessary. The lock had been beheaded with a bolt-cutter. Inside, they saw that the same cutter had been used to remove a half-meter of the Trigger's jacketed power conduit. There were also four bright-metal concavities in the system enclosure – bullet holes.

'Okay, so I overestimated him – twenty-two caliber,' Dugan said, examining the holes. 'You know, this could turn out to be the first of a run of very long days.'

'Let's get it open,' Tony said with a sigh. 'I'll start making a list of parts.'

27:

'The greatest honor history can bestow is the title of
peacemaker. This honor now beckons America . . . This
is our summons to greatness.'

– *Richard M. Nixon*

The office of the Chairman of the Joint Chiefs was surrounded
by layers of protocol and decorated with icons of tradition. As
the office of the man sitting at the top of the military pyramid,
it was an intimidating environment for most visitors. But it was in
defiance of that protocol, tradition, and power that Roland Stepak
had invited himself there to confront the occupant of that office –
General Donald Madison.

'I was reviewing the latest readiness reports last night, General
Madison – and I have to tell you that what I saw didn't contribute
to a good night's sleep,' the secretary of defense said, taking his pick
of the armchairs. He looked expectantly at Madison, and waited
for the general to join him.

'I thought the numbers were very good,' Madison said. 'Eighty-
eight percent of our aircraft are combat-ready –'

'This is my meeting, General – don't try to take over the agenda.
And don't try making any more smoke. There was enough of that
in the readiness report.'

'Mr Secretary, I don't understand why –'

'Oh, you don't? You don't think counting the entire Special
Forces order of battle as ready for a Trigger-neutralized combat
environment is deceptive?'

'No, sir, I think that's absolutely legitimate. Every one of those
men gets extensive and intensive training with alternative weapons, particularly the knife and hand-to-hand.'

'And every one of them is still being issued a gun as their

primary weapon. Every sniper is still carrying a gun. Every unit is still giving first priority to proficiency on the firing range. And none of those units, not even the Rangers, are prepared to deploy in force to defeat an enemy that's in the field in force.'

'Mr Secretary, if the situation arose, there's no reason we couldn't use them that way –'

'Come on, Donald, you're not talking to some wide-eyed Iowa lawyer who just got into town,' Stepak said gruffly. 'You and I both know that the natural operational unit for Special Forces is something closer to the platoon than the battalion. You and I also know that using them as primary combat troops means losing them for SpecOps.'

'Why should that matter?' Madison said with undisguised bitterness. 'The President has had half of them standing post, babysitting, for the better part of two years now – so it's obvious that their primary mission isn't viewed as having any value.'

Stepak was shaking his head. 'General Madison, that's unworthy of you and of this office. But maybe it helps explain the rest of the readiness report. The Army has exactly one company training with bows, one company training with quarterstaves, one company training with electrical weapons, one company training with compressed-air dartguns – as if we were only ever going to need them in SpecOps numbers.'

'Those are developmental projects. We're still evaluating the weapons and the training models.'

'Of course you are,' said Stepak. 'But speaking of models – the Navy has given every carrier task force Trigger-equipped ASW pickets and RPVs, but hasn't taken the first step toward creating an alternative force projection model – something that could survive a Trigger attack, which none of our task forces could today.'

'It's impossible. We can put five, six, seven hundred ships in the water, but unless we can arm them, they might as well be yachts at a regatta. We can't go back to catapults and burning pitch, or rams and boarding parties.'

'Why not? In the country of the blind, the one-eyed man is king. In the new order of things, the primary role of the Navy may turn out to be delivering troops and materiel, and the primary threat may turn out to be small, high-powered, remotely-piloted vessels designed to punch holes in the hull, or tangle the props in a trailing cable.'

'What "new order of things"?' Madison asked, his tone contemptuous. 'The gun, the missile, the bomb, the torpedo, the artillery shell – those are still the "order of things", and they will be until long after both of us are gone.'

'Seen any horse-mounted cavalry lately, General? Times change. Your problem is that you refuse to see the change that's already here.'

He reached down beside his chair and lifted his oversized black briefcase onto his lap. Pressing his thumbs against the smart catches, he raised the lid, then turned the briefcase a half-turn so Madison could look inside it. The chairman stared uncomprehendingly.

'This is Terabyte's prototype for a briefcase Jammer,' Stepak said softly. 'A *working* prototype. I turned it on outside the main security checkpoint, and disarmed every weapon in this end of the building.'

'You did *what*?'

'I turned it on again just a moment ago. There isn't a working weapon within a hundred meters of this office, up, down, or sideways. If I plugged this into line current, I could make it three hundred meters and keep it that way indefinitely. You can check the pistol you keep in that safe in your desk, if you'd like. Or call in the guard. You're both disarmed.'

'What do you think gives you the right –'

'It's my goddamned *responsibility*, Donald – just like it was yours. But you bet on the wrong horse. You didn't like the direction things were headed and you took a chance that they wouldn't go any further. Now you know you were wrong.' Stepak closed the briefcase. 'It *has* gone further, and we're not ready.'

'I don't accept that assessment.'

'Where's your nearest alternative-weapons unit, General? What happens when the Pentagon security detachment reaches for their guns and finds them Jammed? You kept us in a conventional defense posture – which means you've left us vulnerable. You counted on your new explosives and new propellants to preserve the status quo, and you didn't prepare for the possibility of being wrong. That's inexcusable, General.'

Madison's face reddened and his right hand became a fist, but he said nothing.

Standing, Stepak dropped his voice to a level he was certain would not carry beyond the door. 'Now we have to make up for lost time, and transform our defense posture virtually overnight. The President and I need to have full confidence that the person in this office has both the ability and the vision to lead us through that process.'

He paused, giving Madison a chance to make the offer, but the chairman was stubborn to the last, and made Stepak say it.

'Donald, the President sent me to thank you for your service, and ask for your resignation.'

Madison blinked three times, then squeezed his eyes shut for a moment before rising from the chair. 'You may inform the President he'll have it by the end of the day.'

'I know he appreciates your cooperation, General.'

Stepak moved as if to leave, but Madison edged sideways and blocked his way. 'Roland – I did what I thought was right for the country.'

'If this wasn't moot now, I'd ask exactly how dragging your feet in complying with a directive from the C-in-C is more like loyalty than insubordination.'

'I did what my experience told me needed to be done,' Madison said angrily. 'I only wanted to ensure our security.'

'I know that, Donald. The problem is that none of our experience applies. Everything we know is wrong.' Stepak started toward the door once more.

Madison reached out and grabbed the secretary of defense's arm. 'Roland – you should understand. You've worn the uniform. I couldn't be the one to tear it all apart. I don't believe in it. We teach soldiers to love their guns for a reason – a good reason.'

'I do understand, Donald. I understand all of that.'

Emboldened, Madison added, 'I always figured, if you beat all the swords into plowshares today, you're going to find 'em fighting with plowshares tomorrow. You might as well keep the swords, especially if you're already good with them.'

426

'If swords were the worst of our problems, we wouldn't be having this conversation.' He shook his head. 'It's going to be a new world, and I don't know if fossils like you and me will ever be comfortable in it. But we can't stop it from coming. And if we can't bring ourselves to help, the only honorable thing left is to get out of the way.'

Madison sighed, and in doing so seemed to shrink. 'Yes. Yes, I suppose that's what it will take. Perhaps younger, more flexible minds may find opportunities where I can only see danger.'

'I'm sure they'll pleasantly surprise us,' Stepak said. 'They are our children, after all.'

Showing a wan smile, Madison retreated out of Stepak's way. 'If I might be allowed to make a suggestion regarding my replacement –'

'I'll be happy to convey your thoughts to the President.'

'Thank you,' Madison said. 'Would you tell him, please, that he would do well to consider the Vice Chairman – General Heincer.'

'And your reason for saying this? –'

'I know Bill's held his tongue in front of the President, out of deference. But in the chiefs' private sessions, he's been far and away the most vigorous defender of the President's viewpoint – so much so that I'm afraid the rest of us started calling him The Lone Ranger. Moving him up would send an unambiguous message. I expect it could change the outlook of the chiefs overnight, without changing any more of the faces.'

At Stepak's questioning look, he added, 'I'm not protecting anyone. The last thing we need now is to create the impression of a revolt of the generals, and to have the aftershocks of that propagating down through the ranks. That wouldn't be conducive to good order and discipline during what we both know will be a difficult transition.'

Stepak nodded appreciatively. 'I'll be sure the President receives the benefit of your perspective.'

Evan Stolta poked his head into Grover Wilman's office and rapped his knuckles on the jamb to get Wilman's attention. 'There's been a little movement in the numbers,' he said, his tone upbeat. 'You should take a look.'

Before Wilman could say anything, the senior strategic consultant was gone again.

Wilman sighed. That was the pace of life now at the Mind Over Madness site in Georgetown – nonstop motion. In less than three months, MOM had doubled in size, tripled in staff, and hived off StreetSmart and The Peace Library into their own facilities. The growth had come at the price of the atmosphere of earnest dedication which had formerly prevailed. It was now more campaign headquarters than foundation, more nerve center than think tank.

Something else had disappeared along with the opportunity for quiet reflection. That was Wilman's ability to maintain a hands-on, face-to-face familiarity with all aspects of domestic operations. There was too much going on in too many places, too many shoulders to peek over, too many obligations tying him to his desk comset, which had become the only window through which he viewed his work and his world.

'Polling, current, trends, on screen,' he said, and sat back in his chair to study the charts. The foundation was buying continuous polling from two different services on six key attitudinals, looking for weakness on either side of the great divide in public opinion.

On one side were those who saw guns as the greater danger, who would gladly live in a residence protected by a LifeShield, and who were reassured by the idea that the police had this technology and that public places were protected by it. After a steady slide from highs of sixty percent or better, those numbers had been stalled in the low forties for months. The demographics of this core group were slanted toward women, college graduates, parents, older adults, and suburban dwellers. The key value that unified them was the importance they placed on community.

On the other side were those who feared the mysterious and unfamiliar forces of the Trigger more than the familiar presence of firearms, who would rather keep and carry a gun than depend on anyone else's protection, or who were more worried about a police state than about crime statistics. The hardcore constituency for unrestricted gun ownership amounted to no more than twenty percent of the adult population – overwhelmingly white men,

428

many of whom had a silent agenda of racism, class warfare, or political dissent.

But this uncompromising nucleus had successfully exploited fear to build a majority allied against both government and private use of the Trigger. Their coalition drew heavily on rural families, single urban men, conservative Christians, the working poor, the disaffected, and young liberals deceived into thinking that they were defending individual liberty. But the true unifying value, the polls revealed, was the community of one – one man, one family, one color, one creed.

Winning back members of this swing group meant addressing their fears and awakening their consciences. Neither was an easy task. All too often, fear was deaf to reason, and conscience insensible to an outsider's plight.

But Stolta was right – the new dailies showed a little movement in the numbers.

Looking at the groups involved, Wilman thought he knew the reason. The Mind Over Madness action committee had been diligently digging up LifeShield success stories from around the globe, and aggressively promoting them to the media. In the last few weeks, the committee had scored several high-profile placements, largely due to events beyond America's borders.

In the Yucatan, the ancient Mayan cities of Uxmal, Labná, and Chichén Itza opened to both tourists and scientists for the first time in nearly a decade. The Trigger had brought an end to the civil war which had enveloped the archaeological treasures, but it had taken the Jammer to clear the sites without further damage to the temples.

Jerusalem, which had fourteen marked and six unmarked Jammer vans patrolling its streets on a daily basis, celebrated the first year in its entire history without a single bombing or shooting death. The highly-rated video columnist Regina Wickman did the best job with that story, demonstrating with dramatic then-and-now footage that the soldier with the submachine gun had disappeared from public view.

'I've been living out of a backpack for most of the last sixteen years,' said Wickman, standing in front of the Wailing Wall. 'I've walked the streets of two hundred cities in more than forty countries. But as an American traveler abroad, I've never grown accustomed to the sight of assault weapons slung over the shoulders of policemen, or carried casually in marketplaces.

'To some, those very visible weapons represent security – but they've always made me feel anything but secure. No matter how much I might find to like or admire about a Kinshasa or a Seoul or a Buenos Aires, I cannot say that I'm ever comfortable in such places. Guns are a blemish on the face of society – any society – and I've never seen a cityscape that wouldn't be improved by their disappearance.

'And that is exactly what has happened here in Jerusalem. In a city which has been fought over for millennia, there is now a strange and unaccustomed peace. It is not that the old antipathies have been resolved, or that the old adversaries have grown weary of the fight. But in a city diligently cleansed of firearms on a daily basis, we can see the promise of the new technology – killing has become so much harder here that it just might be easier to learn to live together.'

But even talented journalists found it hard to make news out of events that never happened. It was easier to note the failures than credit the successes. And under the seemingly immutable rules that governed human emotional identification, a thousand lives saved in Ethiopia counted for less than one life lost in Erie – so long as the face of the victim was the same color as the face of the person adding up the damages.

Glad as Wilman was for the good news from elsewhere, he prayed for a success story closer to home – preferably a very public one, with good camera coverage and a photogenic rainbow of grateful near-victims. Something at a marquee sporting event, perhaps, or a threat to Mardi Gras or the Oscars.

But while he was waiting to hear from god, there was more than enough to keep Wilman busy.

'Senator Wilman?'

The floor manager for Mind Over Madness's walk-in services had a curious note in his voice and a quizzical expression on his face. Neither seemed to match the priority cut-in channel through which the page had come.

430

'What is it, Donald?'

'Sir – could you please come down to the counseling bullpen? Right away, if at all possible –'

'I might. Could I have a reason?'

Frowning, the floor manager glanced sideways. 'Senator – it's the damnedest thing. Do you remember that conversation we had after last Monday's teleconference?'

'I think I do. We were talking about how to handle priority clients –'

In fact, the discussion had been on handling possible security problems, including a building incursion. Wilman brought up the coverage map for the building video intranet and began scanning through the stations nearest the one the floor manager was using.

'That's the one. There's someone down here asking to see you.'

By then, Wilman had found the view he wanted – one that clearly showed the young man with the short black hair and what looked like an Imperial stormtrooper's utility belt under his black-and-red flannel shirt. 'Someone with a serious problem, I take it?'

'Well, Senator, he clearly thinks it's serious. And he's asking for you specifically.'

'You can tell him I'll be down shortly. I have a couple of calls to make.'

It was not hard to get his calls taken by the right people. Wilman watched from his second-floor office window as the NV25 and ActionCam17 sedans screeched to a stop at the curb below. Soon after, a SkyEye remotely piloted hovercam – a civilian spinoff from a Hughes battlefield monitor – arrived on the scene and began peering in windows with its low-light camera and audio telescope.

But Wilman lingered, waiting until CNN2 went live with the internal security feed he had offered them. He paused before the wall-mounted flatscreen just long enough to hear the anchor solemnly intone the introductory voiceover: 'This is breaking news from CNN – Pacifists Under Siege in the nation's capital. The quiet, collegial community of Georgetown is holding its breath this morning as a bomb-wielding terrorist holds more than seventy people hostage at the headquarters of –'

Satisfied, Wilman headed for the stairs.

Up until the moment he announced himself to the tall man behind the reception desk, everything had gone as David Thomas Mallock had planned.

His ancient Tracker, bought at auction from a Dallas wholesale lot, had held together for the thirteen-hundred-mile drive from Palestine, Texas to Georgetown with only two minor breakdowns. He had kept his speed down and maintained a low profile on the road – though there had been one scare near Knoxville, Tennessee, when a state trooper settled behind him and tailed him for nearly two miles before taking an exit. Mallock had kept to the freeway motels and truck stops and off the money net, stingily doling out the cash he had collected from friends and family for his pickup, his stereo, and his computer.

The meeting in Rock Creek Park had gone off on schedule and without a hitch. With thundering Beltway traffic masking the few words needed for the transaction, Mallock traded the last of his cash for the 500 grams of plastic explosive.

'This is virgin?' he had asked.

'Absolutely – home-grown, off the books. I know the chef personally.'

Despite that reassurance, Mallock had been cautious. The FBI's involvement in the far-reaching Trigger fraud was not limited to inserting microscopic radio detonators into commercial explosives and surreptitiously irradiating gunpowder supplies. According to the Truth Hunters mailing list, the agency also had dozens of operatives in the underground, posing as the operators of small-scale 'patriot labs' but serving up the same doped formulas.

So Mallock had abandoned his Tracker in the park, and set off on foot for his target, following a carefully mapped serpentine path which took him along wooded trails and down quiet streets without ever passing near an embassy, tourist landmark, public building, or posted intersection. If he had been betrayed, and the explosives he was wearing were tainted, he had been determined not to discover it until he was standing outside the enemy's citadel.

432

But he had not been betrayed, either by those he depended on or by a misstep of his own. He had reached and entered the citadel, had looked on the clueless faces of the insects within and called down their king to an accounting. It should have been a moment of high drama – but it was playing out as anticlimax.

Mallock had waited in the short line at the contact island, enjoying the anticipation. 'I want to see the supervisor,' he had demanded when his turn came. When the floor manager had appeared and introduced himself, Mallock had steered him to one of the counseling cubicles along the west wall. There he had shown the manager the bomb and the controller taped to his right hand.

'I know the truth about the Trigger. I want to see Wilman. You get him here without making a fuss, or everyone in the room is going to be dead. You get him here, and I'll let these people leave.'

'I'm not sure where the Senator is at the moment,' the floor manager had said. 'Let me see if can reach him.'

'You'd better do more than try. I'm wearing enough live explosives to blow out these walls and bring this building down on top of us.'

'Can I tell the Senator that?'

'No. You just get him here. I'll tell him how things are going to be.'

He had listened in on the manager's conversation with Wilman and been satisfied with its direction. Then, at Mallock's insistence, the two returned to the reception island to wait. From there, Mallock had a clear view of both entrances to the room – the front doors and the stairwell on the left side of the back wall. He also had a substantial oak-and-steel counter and six employees available as shields should someone unwelcome or unexpected make an appearance.

There were still clients in the waiting area and at the counter, and Mallock had told the floor manager to see that his staff carried on with business as usual. But as one minute stretched into the next, and Wilman still had not appeared, Mallock began to rethink his tactics.

He had decided to announce himself only to a supervisor because he did not want to have to ride herd on a roomful of frightened people – they were just as effectively hostages while ignorant of the threat, and much less likely to do something stupid. He had decided to insist that Wilman should come to him rather than demand to be taken to Wilman because of the risk of ambush – he did not know the building, and did not want to invite any surprises before his mission was complete.

But the longer he waited, the more he realized that he had not given enough thought to the possibility that Wilman was a coward and might need to be shamed into acting honorably. The longer he witnessed the staff at work, the less harmless they seemed – more like termites than sheep, destructive in their own right, irredeemable by their nature. And the more people he watched pass through the main entrance, the more he worried that the latest arrivals were plainclothes police and special ops assassins.

'What's taking so long?' he demanded of the floor manager. 'Where is he?'

'I don't know,' said the floor manager. 'But I can page the Senator again –'

'No. What you're going to do is close the building. Get all those clients or customers or whatever you call them out of here, and lock the doors behind 'em.'

'What should I tell them?'

'I don't care what you tell them, so long as you get them out, and do it now. Gas leak, network crash, fire alarm – you people are good at lying. Improvise.'

But when it was done, Mallock felt no more secure. There were more than two dozen pair of eyes regarding him, some expectantly, some curiously, one with open amusement, but none fearfully.

'You don't know, do you?' he demanded. 'You poor fools – you don't know that it's a fraud.'

'*What* is?' asked the floor manager.

'The Trigger. It's a hoax. It doesn't exist – everything you've seen on the news has been staged by the FBI.'

'Oh, please,' a woman said, her voice dripping with disdain.

'It's true,' Mallock said hotly. 'Ever since they took over the ATF, they've been looking for a way to grab our guns. They couldn't find a way to do it legally, so they're trying to scare us into giving them up.'

Someone behind Mallock cleared his throat. 'Young man, have you been keeping up with your medicine?'

Mallock spun around, searching for the offender. 'The FBI's Section Zero started doping explosives almost two years ago. They've been recruiting Hollywood FX techs for twice that long. Everything that's happened was scripted months in advance by the United Nations.'

'And you know this how?' It was the same voice, and it belonged to a round-faced man with a gleaming pate and a short white beard.

'Do you people think you're so smart that no one could ever figure out what you're up to?' That was met with more laughter, and a cold fury crept up from Mallock's heart to take command of his features. 'You'll find out, in a little while. You'll find out the truth, and then you and me together are going to teach the rest of the world the truth.'

'That's what we try to do here every day,' said one of the woman at the reception desk. 'Maybe you should sit down with one of our counselors and talk out these paranoid conspiracy fantasies.'

It was his turn to laugh – a brittle, cynical laugh. 'Sit down with one of your hypnotists, you mean? Let one of your neurolinguistic programmers work me over? I don't think so,' he said, shaking his head vigorously. 'It's not really your fault if you've been lied to. I feel sorry for you, honestly. But you'll realize when you hear it from your own leader.' He turned on Donald and demanded, 'Why isn't he here? I want an explanation. I want Wilman, *now*.'

'I don't know why he isn't here. But he said he was coming. I'm sure he'll be here soon,' the floor manager said, his tone placating. 'And, everyone, please – Senator Wilman asked that we cooperate with our visitor. Let's do that without being argumentative or provocative.'

'Fine,' said a tall, slender black woman. 'I'm going to go co-operate from my cubicle. I have a lot of work to do.'

She started to walk away, and Mallock sprang after her. 'Nobody's going anywhere,' he said, grabbing her by the arm. 'Wilman's playing games. I want you all sitting up on the edge of the counter, facing out. You're going to be my shield. Come on – move!'

A few of the others started to comply, but the woman stood her ground and jerked her arm free. 'Honey, it's going to take more juice than you've got to get me to let you look up my skirt.'

'Nettie –' the floor manager said reproachfully.

'Boss, please – can't I just deck him? He laid hands on me –'

'Don't you get it?' Mallock screamed in her face. 'I'm wearing a bomb. I can kill us all, any time I want to – and if I don't start getting some fucking cooperation from you traitors, I'll goddamned well do it. And there aren't any magic rays that can stop me –'

Just then, he heard a pair of loud metallic clicks, and whirled toward them. He saw a well-dressed older man holding one of the front doors open as a SkyEye flew through the opening, followed by a man and a woman wearing Witness bands on their heads and transmitter packs on their upper arms.

'What are you doing?' Mallock screamed. 'That door's supposed to be locked!'

The well-dressed man turned his way, and Mallock recognized him as Grover Wilman. 'I'm letting the media in. You wanted an audience, didn't you? You wanted to make a statement, right? Well, CNN2 is listening now, and so is Reuters, and StarNews, and Associated Media. Speak your piece.'

The rest of the people in the room were suddenly invisible as furniture to Mallock. He crossed the floor toward Wilman, shedding his flannel shirt and raising his right hand to show the controller taped to the palm. 'You're the one who's going to make a statement. You're going to end this hoax. You're going to admit your part in the conspiracy. You're going to tell the world the truth about the Trigger. Or I'm going to set off this bomb I'm wearing, and the world can read the truth in our mangled bodies. Your choice, Senator. You decide if protecting the lie another five minutes is worth these twenty lives.'

Wilman folded his arms over his chest and shook his head slowly. 'Mr Mallock, someone has been feeding you a lie. The truth is that the Trigger works. The Jammer works even better. That isn't a bomb you're wearing – if it ever was one, it isn't one now.'

436

'You're a damned liar,' Mallock said, advancing another step. 'Tell them! This is a conspiracy to disarm the American people. President Breland has already made a deal to surrender sovereignty to the United Nations. But you have to take away our weapons before the blue helmets arrive – before the last day of Breland's term. So you cooked up this hoax to trick us into surrendering them. *That's* the truth, Senator Wilman.'

'Who sold you that bill of goods, Mr Mallock?'

'There was documentation for everything I'm saying on the Patriot Crier Web site. Of course, it wasn't there long – the site was attacked by mites and maggots, and then crashed by a gridlocker. But I imagine you know all about that, since it was your spooks who took it down.'

'You might want to work on developing higher standards of evidence, Mr Mallock. I'm afraid someone's been taking advantage of your gullibility.'

'You can insult me all you want – it won't change the truth. And if I have to kill all of us to get the truth to the people, then it's my obligation as a patriot to do exactly that.'

'Don't delude yourself, Mr Mallock – you're no patriot. You're just another man who's having a hard time dealing with the fact that he's not in charge,' Wilman said, and then looked past Mallock. 'Please return to your duties, everyone. This man poses no threat to us.'

'Stop!' Mallock screamed, raising his right hand high above his head. 'By god, I'll do it – I will!'

'Do what you think you must, then,' said Wilman. Then he turned away as if to leave.

Receive me with mercy, Lord, Mallock prayed silently. Then he squeezed his eyes shut and twisted the actuator.

It took Mallock a full second to realize that his life had continued a full second longer than it should have. Opening his eyes, he stared disbelievingly at the actuator, then reset it to try again.

'Do you need some help, Mr Mallock?'

Mallock sank slowly to his knees, wearing a mask of incredulity and despair. 'He cheated me. Blade cheated me – gave me –' He grabbed at the belt, fumbling with the catch, tearing open one of the pouches. 'What, what is this stuff? Play-Doh? School paste? It was supposed to be ammonium picrate and C-1 –'

'It is,' said Wilman, stepping closer. 'But it's been adjusted by our Jammer.'

Shaking his head violently, Mallock said, 'No – no, that can't be –'

'Why not? Because it would make it inconveniently difficult to upset the apple cart?'

'No, I must have done something wrong – a bad lead, the wrong connection –'

'The wrong connection is the one you made between weapons and security. Do you really think that those of us who are fighting to drive out firearms love freedom any less than you do, care for our families' safety any less than you do?'

'Your freedom – but what about ours? Your families – but what about ours? You throw us to the wolves to keep your-selves safe –'

'We're trying to muzzle the wolves, Mr Mallock, not feed them,' Wilman said. He offered Mallock his hand to help him up; after a long moment's hesitation, Mallock accepted it. 'If you really want to understand, I have a better answer for you than that.'

Mallock's face wore a scowl, but he quietly said, 'I'm listen-ing.'

'The only thing that keeps society from being a twenty-four-hour-a-day bloodbath is the fact that most men, most of the time, aren't willing to risk everything on a fight which might leave them crippled or dead. And most of the time, even when we do fight, we fight just long enough to settle the matter – somebody yields before it gets past the bruises and black eyes stage.

'We spent millions of years working out sane and survivable rules of conflict resolution – and then five thousand years breaking them by inventing ever-deadlier weapons that can kill more and more efficiently from farther and farther away.

'We're at the point now where all most of us can remember of the rules is, "It's good to be king" – a tragic abridgement. Too many fathers have forgotten the lessons they have to teach their sons, or abandoned their responsibility to impart them – honor to elders, service to the community, duty to the family. And too many men

438

around the world have seized on the mistaken notion that because they can bring down a prince, they deserve to be one.

'You came here with a bomb, intent on destroying me and claiming the power of my celebrity. If I were playing by your rules, I would now be obliged to have *you* killed, for trying and failing. But I'd like you to have the chance to realize there's another way, a higher ethic to aspire to. So you can go as you came – those D.C. police waiting outside would need my help to charge you with anything, and they won't get it.'

Mallock stole a look through the front doors to the street before answering. 'Do you think this ends it?'

'No. But I think that you can end it – you, and those who believe as you did when you walked in here.'

'Do you think that putting on a show of mercy makes us buddies? Do you think we're going to just accept the way things are?'

'You think of yourself as a religious man, Mr Mallock – do you know the prayer that begins, "God grant me the courage –"'

'I know it,' Mallock said sharply.

'Then you understand that I pray for wisdom, every night,' said Wilman. 'I pray you will, too.'

Evan Stolta was waiting for Wilman in his office when he returned to it.

'Well – how did it play?'

'Awfully well, I thought – even if you got a little preachy at the end,' said Stolta.

Wilman smiled faintly. 'Comes from having had too much time to think about what I'd say. I was beginning to think that no one would ever take the bait, and we'd have to go all the way and hire our own terrorist.'

'You realize that if it ever comes out that we planted that material on the Patriot Crier site –'

'It won't.'

'The media are going to swarm all over this story. I thought you were getting awfully close to taunting him with the truth – "Someone has been feeding you lies", that sort of thing.'

'I might have been enjoying myself just a little too much,'

Wilman admitted. 'But it'll be all right. They won't find our fingerprints at the scene of the crime.'

Stolta shook his head unhappily. 'If he'd managed to get his hands on an exotic, or a dust bomb –'

'Why are you agonizing about this now? It's over. It came out well.'

'I suppose it's because I still don't understand why you were willing to take such risks.'

'That's because we're different kinds of people. Can you see yourself betting a hundred thousand dollars against a million?'

'I don't think so. A hundred thousand dollars would be a very big piece of everything I have.'

'You see? You didn't even ask the odds.'

'The odds are irrelevant. My father taught me two rules about gambling – one, only bet on a sure thing. Two, there's no such thing as a sure thing.' Stolta flashed a rueful smile. 'All right, so I'm a careful man by nature. But I don't think you've really answered my question.'

'Did you ask a question?'

'I thought I did – why you were willing to risk a down side that would have destroyed twenty years of your work.'

'Ah. That question,' Wilman said, easing into a chair. 'Well, it's true that I was never much of a gambler. I can't stand to sit there passively waiting for the cards to come to me.'

'So why would you just up and decide to play a long shot?'

Wilman shook his head. 'This undertaking is more like combat than gambling, Evan – tactical, not statistical. And more often than not, the worst thing you can do in combat is let yourself think about the odds – especially if they're against you. If you do that, you never go over the top – you never charge the hill – and you never change the odds in your favor. What you do from one minute to the next can change everything.'

'That still doesn't explain why you decided to charge up *this* hill, at *this* particular time.'

'You're not going to let this go, are you?' Wilman studied the other man's face for a moment, then added, 'No, I see you're not.' He sighed. 'The truth of the matter is that I'm tired of waiting. I don't know how much time I have left, and I want to see the end of this. So I'm willing to take some chances.' He paused, as though weighing whether he wanted to say more. 'It's not the stuff of heroic legend, but a lot of battles are decided by someone who couldn't stand the waiting any longer.'

'I'll bow to your experience,' said Stolta, who had never worn a uniform. 'But, Grover – you don't think that you converted that mark, do you?'

Wilman smiled and shook his head. 'I'll be happy if I just discouraged him. It's the audience I care about. Speaking of which – let's find out how big it was.'

28:

'But man is not made for defeat . . . A man can be
destroyed but not defeated.'

— *Ernest Hemingway*

The walnut block with the bronze emblem of the Missouri State
Police on top had rested on John Trent's desk for more than
six years. Though awarded to him for 'Public Service' – the
KidSafe Firearms Education Program, introduced in the wake
of the Truman Middle School shootings – it was less a treasured memory than a useful desk accessory. Not as a paperweight, which the designer might actually have had in mind,
but as a front-line weapon in the NAR office's ongoing war with
red ants.

When the fist-sized award struck the wallscreen just to the
left of and slightly below center, it was moving at a velocity
commensurate with the arm strength of a former high school
quarterback who could still throw a football forty yards on a line.
The wallscreen shattered like a giant mirror, and the thump and
crash were heard four offices away.

The aftermath, though, was less satisfying. What remained on
the wall simply went opaque, without a single satisfying crackle
or tendril of smoke.

Trent's executive secretary and chief administrative assistant
reached his office door together. 'Are you all right?' Jolene
demanded. Kenneth was drawn to the debris on the floor.

'Did you see?' Trent shouted angrily. 'Were any of you out there
watching?'

'I saw it,' said Kenneth, retrieving the award and carefully
brushing off the splinters of plastic and glass. 'He made it look
like only crazy people want to be able to protect themselves.'

442

'You get out there and find out for me who Mallock is and what the hell he was doing there.'

'You think it was a set-up?'

'Hell, yes,' Trent said, weighting the words with all the contempt they could carry. 'Wilman's got four major newsfeeds there so quick they hardly miss a thing. Four newsfeeds that're covering and cross-promoting a live event for one reason only, they're hoping to show us a terrorist bombing, a mass murder, in real time. What's Wilman doing?' Trent threw his hands in the air. 'He takes the time to give us a university lecture on violence and fucking human evolution, knowing they'll broadcast every word because we're all tuning in hoping to see some carnage.

'He's not going to do that unless he *knows* there isn't going to *be* any carnage. You bet I think it was a stunt. And he's going to get away with it. It's a great story, courageous crusader, fanatic assassin, chilling brush with death. The son of a bitch.'

'I'll see what we have on Mallock,' Kenneth said, placing the block on the corner of Trent's desk. 'And order you a new Trinitron.'

That left Jolene standing uncertainly in the doorway. 'Is there anything I can do, Mr Trent?'

'I don't even know what *I* can do,' Trent snapped at her. 'Sons of bitches – he was laughing at us, Jolene, you could see it in his eyes. They're killing people, taking away our guns and sending us out to face the wolves – they're murdering the Constitution – and he's *lecturing* us on morality?'

He snatched up the walnut block and hurled it at the wallscreen a second time. This time he was rewarded by some arcing and an acrid puff of smoke, but it was not enough to satisfy him.

'Leave me alone, Jolene,' he said darkly.

The secretary hesitated, then obeyed, closing the door behind her. When she was gone, Trent leaned heavily on his desk, chest rising and falling, blood pounding in helpless rage. 'So help me god,' he whispered, 'he doesn't deserve to be sleeping well at night. Let me be the one to take that from him. Give me courage, and patience, and wisdom, and somewhere, somehow, just one clean shot –'

Then, with shaking hands, Trent sat down and started to write out his resignation from the post of President of the NAR.

Over the next few weeks, John Trent told the friends who called the same thing he told the leeches of the media – that he had been President for twice as long as his predecessor and was ready to look at the issues from a new perspective, that he wanted to take some time off to travel and attend to personal matters, that he remained committed to an uncompromising defense of the Constitution and the essential liberties of citizens, and that he was exploring the possibility of becoming more directly involved in politics in ways the NAR was forbidden to pursue.

It was all true, but he made certain that his friends understood it differently than the political media, which devoted a couple of news cycles to dissecting the history of and prospects for single-issue third parties, and then turned its attention elsewhere.

By that time, Trent had begun to quietly make contact with the people he had chosen to make part of his endeavor. He limited himself to individuals – no committees, armies, associations, or militias. Their record in recent months was uninspiring, displaying a sorry lack of professionalism.

Bob Bowman was dead, having hung himself in a Virginia state prison while awaiting trial for running a Jammer van off the highway near Raleigh. Zachary Taylor Grant's plot against Supreme Court Justice Hannah Loeb was betrayed by a Hedgehog who pocketed half a million in FoxMedia payoffs for a video exclusive. Mel Yost was publishing *Washington War Crimes* from Barbados.

Among others making the headlines, the Boston Riders stronghold near Lake Champlain had been disarmed by an FBI Special Tactics unit. Three straight failures had left enough forensic evidence to link the Riders to the 'red letter' abortion clinic bombings across New England. Kelly Martin and the Freedom Sword were still at large in the upper Midwest, claiming credit for more than twenty bombings. But their choice of targets – mostly restaurants and retail stores in smaller towns that had seen few if any Jammer installations – was a public relations disaster.

There were a total of sixteen would-be assassins in Federal prison in connection with five different attempts to get to the

President. There had also been three known attempts against Comrade Wilman, eight against the Jew industrialist, five against various members of the Cabinet. Most had received little attention from the general media, which had apparently concluded that men being willing to sacrifice their lives and liberty for principle was a non-story. The dead and the imprisoned were heroes to the liberty media, but without fad diets, sex and celebrities to pad the ratings, it hardly amounted to more than static.

Patiently and deliberately, Trent studied each operation and all of the elements which had figured in the outcome. Not all those studies were instructive – incompetence rarely is. But two patterns did emerge, one of excessive complexity, the other of insufficient boldness. Most of what people wanted to call bad luck, he concluded, was not really luck at all.

Trent took what he learned to Atlantic City – to the New Flanders Casino Hotel, a site recommended by Angelo DiBartolo – for the only meeting there would ever be of the entire conspiracy. It was to be an odd meeting, though. All four of the conspirators traveled some distance to be in the same city, the same building, but Trent had decreed that they would never be in the same room or at the same table together.

Trent's first recruit had been Terry Stewart, a thirty-eight-year-old former CIA contractor who'd lost a lucrative billet as a paramilitary unit 'advisor' when Grover Wilman had exposed President Engler's covert war in Colombia. Stewart (or 'Gooch', as he preferred) had the training of a Special Forces commando, the connections of a mercenary, and a profile so low that just contacting him had required three intermediaries.

The second-riskiest job was the one Trent called The Winkler, the advance man who would work with all the bureaucracies to make arrangements for the confrontation. The Winkler would need to know exactly what was planned – it was not a job Trent could hire out blind. But his open involvement meant The Winkler would also need to be able to deny having known Trent's intentions, to convincingly claim he was merely hired by a client to do a job.

That combination of craven commercial motive, well-scrubbed ruthlessness and fluent lying called for a Hollywood lawyer. Trent found one in Roy Carney, whose small but well-respected firm had represented a number of conservative clients, and whose middle son was a member of the California Border Guards, an anti-immigration 'posse' whose volunteer efforts had put dozens of Hispanics in the hospital (and at least three in the grave).

The last piece of the puzzle was Atlanta security consultant Ben Brannigan, the mystery man behind the net postings of 'The Equalizer'. Just days after the Trigger was announced, 'The Equalizer' had penned a speculative, seat-of-the-pants analysis of how it could be defeated. His postings since then had contained ever more elaborate and authoritative critiques of both the technology and the security strategies which depended on it. Calling himself 'a free library', Brannigan had devoted himself to becoming the uncontested civilian expert on Horton devices. There was no proof that he had ever done more than offer anonymous public advice, but Trent understood how to tempt a man who had pride.

They conducted their business entirely over the hotel's fiber-optic teleconferencing network, which DiBartolo had assured Trent was secure from snooping – even by the hotel's employees. Internally routed, a room-to-room call never went to either wire or air, and the PGP scrambler boxes in each suite thwarted local eavesdroppers.

'My family likes the Flanders,' DiBartolo had said, smiling genially. 'We've been holding reunions there twice a year for three years, and never had any trouble. They know how to be discreet. They know it's important to the health of their business.'

Taking that as gospel, Trent assumed that it was DiBartolo, then, who was responsible for the two microtransmitter bugs Trent's squealer found in his suite. Trent had gone to DiBartolo for suggestions for a safe meeting place, but had neither told the mobster the purpose of the meeting nor invited him to take part in it. In that light, DiBartolo's curiosity was understandable. But Trent flushed the bugs down the toilet all the same. From that point on, he swept the suite after each time he slept, or left it, or a housekeeper entered, though he never found any other placements.

If DiBartolo was listening, he learned everything he needed to know in the first ten minutes, save for the names of the other players, which were never used.

446

'I intend to kill Senator Grover Wilman on live television,' Trent said calmly. He did not bother to offer any justifications for his decision; either he had properly judged the disposition and mettle of the three, or he had not. 'Your part in this is to help place me, Wilman, a weapon, and at least one working newscam in the same room at the same time.'

'Wilman doesn't go anywhere without a Jammer van. He lives in Horton space,' said the Equalizer. 'Are we going to try to coax him out of it, or beat his strength?'

'I can make him take whichever card we want him to be holding,' said Trent. 'That's what we have to decide together. But my first choice would be as much like a replay of Mallock as possible – face to face, in space Wilman thinks he controls.'

'Psych ops,' said Gooch. 'I approve.'

'I have a question about your scenario,' said the Winkler. 'Why did you include yourself in it? Or the cameras, for that matter. Just putting the bomb and Wilman together would accomplish the same goal – and that might be hard enough to pull off.'

'Not hard at all,' said Gooch. 'Just takes a big enough bomb.'

'And a sacrifice,' said the Winkler. 'But why go there? There are other ways to get him. He receives constituents. He travels between home and office. He goes to church.'

'No, he doesn't,' said Trent. 'He's a humanist – an atheist.'

'Then we don't have to worry about god saving him, do we?' Gooch said with no hint of a smile. 'Look, a military sniper rifle has a useful range approaching a thousand meters. At anything under six hundred, even I can make that shot. He can't possibly be blanketed so deep under Jammer fields that he never pokes his head out, or wanders near the edge.'

'He almost never leaves the District of Columbia now, and D.C. *is* blanketed,' said the Equalizer. 'How are you going to get him out in the open for a head shot from five hundred yards?'

'No.' Trent was shaking his head. 'Listen to me, all of you. It isn't enough to kill him. There are a hundred ways we could do that and gain nothing. His death has to say that his cause is futile – if Grover Wilman isn't safe, how can any ordinary person hope to be? Better off with my own gun than counting on magic rays. And it has to be in public, with the cameras on. He loves the

447

cameras. Before he dies, I'm going to show everyone that under the bluster, he's a liar and a coward. An impotent coward.'

The Winkler pursed his lips. 'Are you at all afraid of making him a martyr?'

'No. No, not for a moment,' Trent said emphatically. 'The real martyrs are the people who're dying because Grover Wilman disarmed them. It's for them that this needs to be done. Someone needs to rescue all those people at risk. Someone needs to set the balance right again. We can do that, gentlemen. I believe we can do that.'

'You know we can,' said Gooch.

'All right, then,' said the Equalizer. 'We're going to need to get him out of Washington. The question is, where to? Then we'll figure out how.'

'Let it be somewhere he thinks he controls us,' Gooch said. 'We'll teach him he's wrong.'

It was the closest Evan Stolta had ever come to screaming at Grover Wilman.

'Why are you even considering this? He's a loser, Senator, and all you can do is give him credibility. He lost his big case, his big push in Congress lost steam, and now he lost his job – you know they pushed him out. Why rescue him? Why elevate him to your level?'

Wilman smiled tolerantly, infuriatingly. 'Why let what he says go unanswered? Why be afraid of a little debate, if we believe in what we stand for?'

'So why does it have to be you? Let Martinson or Rocannon or Schultz do it,' Stolta insisted. 'You've got enough on your table. Gil Massey is threatening to bring S.B. 50 back to the floor, and you could be doing filibuster duty again before you know it. In fact, what if John Trent is still working with Massey? What if this big public challenge is just a game they're running on you?'

'To get me out of town, and slip the bill through Congress while I'm not looking?' Wilman laughed. 'You're a bit of a nervous Nellie, Ev. The Senate doesn't move half fast enough to pull that trick. I won't be traveling by carriage and plank road.'

Wearing a grim frown, Stolta sat down on the arm of one of

the visitor's chairs. 'It's the traveling that worries me. Senator –' Stolta shook his head vigorously, searched for words. 'Things can happen. Why does this have to be done in person? You could have a huge audience in VR.'

'We can debate in person and still have a huge audience in VR,' Wilman said. 'What kind of things?'

'Grover –'

'I just want to see if you can say it.'

'All right,' Stolta said angrily. 'Because there are people who want to hurt you, goddammit. I don't think you should be giving them extra opportunities.'

'Do you think that's news to me, Ev?' Wilman said, his tone mild, almost diffident. 'I've been reading the hate mail every morning since before you came aboard. I know most of them don't mean it, and I know that some of them really do. I'm the lightning rod for every rabid-dog king-of-his-castle who thinks his world will collapse if he has to give up the right to shoot his wife, his kid, his neighbor, his boss, or the drunken tourist knocking on the wrong door.'

'I think you're stealing my lines, Grover. Isn't that my argument?'

'How do I win under those rules? Do I change what I believe, to try to make them love me? Do I go into hiding, so they can't touch me?' Wilman waved a hand dismissively. 'I know you know the answer. I have to be who I am, Ev. Living afraid is not my way. If it was, I'd be the one holed up in Nowhere, Idaho, sitting on a National Guard armory and eighteen months of stale crackers.'

A reluctant laugh softened Stolta's features.

'Besides, you're wrong about John Trent,' Wilman added. 'He wasn't fired. He really did resign.'

'Why would he do that?'

'So he could take the gloves off and call me out,' said Wilman. 'This should be fun. Work something out with that Roy Carney.' He laughed. 'Fifteen rounds of bare-knuckles should be just about right.'

There were eight hovering SkyEyes, nearly three hundred people, and three hundred empty seats in Tufts University's Cohen Auditorium for the debate between Grover Wilman and John Trent.

Ticket distribution had been handled by The Fletcher School of International Affairs, under rules intended to produce a diverse audience for what the dean had called 'an important affirmation of the democratic traditions of free speech and the marketplace of ideas'. He apologized to the participants backstage before introducing them.

'I'm terribly embarrassed – there was strong demand for tickets – our students are *not* apathetic, they're very socially and politically aware –'

'Maybe the rumors about a riot had something to do with it,' Wilman said, looking levelly at John Trent.

'Riot? My god! What rumors are you talking about?' the dean demanded.

'My staff tells me that in the last few hours, there's been anonymized netmail coming into your system, addressed particularly to ticket holders,' Wilman said. 'One version said that you weren't going to show up, Mr Trent. Another said it would be smart to stay away, that there was going to be a riot in the auditorium –'

'A riot at Tufts – absurd,' the dean expostulated. 'This is not some state university party school. This is *Tufts*.'

'The mail I was shown also included a bomb threat, naming me as the target.'

'That's shocking,' said Trent, though his face showed no shock at all. 'Has the university received any threats directly?'

'Oh, no, no,' said the dean. 'I spoke with the chief of campus security just a few minutes ago. Everything's quiet outside. We've been discouraging everyone who doesn't have a ticket from coming into the area. But if what you heard is true, Senator, perhaps it explains why some of our attendees decided to stay home and plug in instead.' He shook his head sorrowfully. 'It's very, very unfortunate, but I'm afraid it's too late to do anything about it. At least you can count on those who are here being highly committed – attentive listeners.'

'That's fine,' said Trent. 'I welcome an informed audience. My hope is that they'll be even better informed when we're done.'

The conspiracy's shortlist of prospective sites for the debate had included Princeton, the University of Pittsburgh, Columbia, Harvard, and even Carleton University in Ottawa – all home to notorious graduate schools of international affairs which would jump at the chance to bring Grover Wilman on campus. Brannigan had pronounced the logistics at Harvard and Columbia impossible, and Carney argued that Princeton had too positive a public image. Trent had ruled out Carleton on the grounds that crossing the border muddled the message, even though Brannigan had promised that an operation at the Canadian school would be a cake-walk.

The final decision between Pittsburgh and Tufts came down to two facts – that The Fletcher School had accepted nearly half a million dollars in research grants from Mind Over Madness, making itself a partner in Wilman's treasons, and that the campus, despite being cheek by jowl with greater Boston, had no permanent Jammer installations of its own. MOM's mobile unit was lined up with the SkyEye control vans in the nearly filled parking lot adjacent to Cohen Auditorium, perfectly accessible, the rear doors and half of the right side exposed. There were campus cops on foot on that side of the building, but they were paying no special attention to the Jammer, and the Jammer's two-body support crew was sitting in the front seats of the van, bored.

Brannigan's own van, bearing the logo of a German publisher's New York-based imprints, was just three spaces away from the Jammer van. More than close enough to get the job done without interference. Pretending to watch the opening statements on the full-screen comset on his lap, he mentally rehearsed his movements, waiting for the signal from Terry Stewart, analyzing his own chances of walking away when it was done. Better than Stewart's, whose were better than Trent's. There were advantages in being the one to strike the first blow.

It was clear early on that the audience in Cohen Auditorium was tilted in his favor, but, even so, Grover Wilman could not help but be pleased by the response to him. After a warm welcome, he had been interrupted by strong applause four times in five minutes. There had even been some cheering mixed in at the end, though the moderator quickly chided those who took part, reminding them of the ground rules. Even so, it was good theater, and presented Trent with a hard act to follow.

Surprisingly, he seemed almost oblivious to the audience, addressing himself entirely to Wilman.

'It was very clever of you, Senator, to try to frame the question as mind versus madness,' said Trent, without so much as a sideways glance out into the auditorium. 'If we let you get away with it, then anyone who opposes you has the extra burden of proving that they are not insane.

'You and your allies have worked very hard, in fact, to create a presumption that anyone who advocates private ownership of guns and the measured use of force is irrational.

'I'm here to refute that presumption. I'm here to defend the deep conviction of tens of millions of reasonable Americans that it's disarmament that's tragically, fatally irrational. I'm here to say without any shame or hesitation that picking up a weapon and killing someone can be an absolutely logical act, the product of the highest level of moral reasoning – and you are going to help me make my case.'

'I don't think so,' Wilman said, turning a smile toward the audience. A wave of titters swept the first several rows, and the moderator chided Wilman for the interruption. 'My apologies, Mr Trent,' said the Senator. 'Do continue.'

The expected angry flush did not appear on Trent's neck. 'Senator Wilman, in all the many times you've spoken on this subject, in all the propaganda you and your organization have showered on us, there's one question I've never seen you address. When you're all done disarming the men with guns, what do you propose to do about all the men with knives? You slide around the question, telling us that of course the police will still be armed, that of course we won't allow an enemy to gain an advantage, that we can still travel in groups and form neighborhood watches and study martial arts.

'But that means that your brand of disarmament is a fraud. You don't want to get rid of guns, Senator – just *our* guns –'

Though that sounded like a cue line, it was Stewart, not Trent, that Brannigan had been waiting for. He answered the chirping comset eagerly, impatient with waiting.

452

'I'm in position,' Stewart said.

'I'm moving,' Brannigan said. He purged the fullscreen comset's memory and left it on the passenger seat; like the van itself, it was borrowed property, and he had no further need of it.

He took only the long, black six-cell flashlight on which he had lavished so much time and attention. Stewart had mocked it as his 'sawed-off, two-stage stealth shotgun', but nevertheless appreciated the cleverness of the mechanisms they had worked together to fit inside it.

There was no one within thirty meters as Brannigan emerged from his van. He walked along the backs of the parked vehicles swinging the flashlight easily, moving in the general direction of the rest room being used by the media. As he crossed behind the Jammer vehicle, he suddenly changed direction and moved toward it. Two long strides was all it took to put him in arm's reach.

Holding the shaft of the flashlight with both hands, he pressed the wide ring of the lens flat against the left door and slid the switch forward. The tool jumped in his hands, and there was a sound not unlike a car door slamming. The sound was made by the hardened steel spike, punching a hole through the sheet metal on the strength of a compressed air charge.

The hissing that followed might have been mistaken for a tire going flat. That sound was made by the conductive aerosol blasting through the ruptured tip of the spike. In barely two seconds, it stopped. Everything stopped, waiting.

The right front door of the Jammer van was flung open with enough force to strike the adjoining vehicle with a crunch and slam shut again.

Brannigan dropped the flashlight and backed away. His glance went to the blind-spot mirror, and met the eyes of the driver.

A moment later, there was a muffled *whump* as the aerosol created dozens of arc paths for the high-voltage current flowing through the Jammer and its generator. Brannigan saw it in the mirror behind the driver: lightning, dancing furiously in its metal bottle. The throb of the generator became a whine, then silence. The men in the van were silent as well.

Brannigan turned and walked briskly away. A campus police-man wondering at something he thought he had heard passed within five meters, but did not confront him. As soon as he could, Brannigan made a beeline for darkness.

'Gooch, come on in,' he said into his personal comset.

That was his last obligation to the team. From there on, he could look out for himself. He had done his part. There was a breach in the shield around Grover Wilman, a breach that reached up into the night sky. And as Brannigan fled, a black ghost came spiraling down through that breach on black wings as silent as a whisper, carrying with it a round black bundle of death addressed to Cohen Auditorium.

The moderator's tone had turned sharp with repetition. 'Your time has expired, Mr Trent.'

John Trent reached down and stilled the comset vibrating against his thigh.

'I'm not finished,' he said. 'Senator Wilman, you're a liar.' His mic went dead then, but he did not need one in that room. 'You promise them that if we all gather together in a herd, no one will be in danger from the wolves. But the people who find themselves living on the margins are in danger. Some of them will die appeasing the predators. It won't be me, and it won't be you, because we know how to stay in the middle of the pack – we have alternatives.'

'We all have alternatives,' Wilman said. 'We can choose to be civilized.'

'More lies,' Trent said, stepping out from behind his podium. 'You don't want the animals on the edge of the herd to know what's going to happen to them. You don't want them armed and able to defend themselves, because they *might* just think to ask why it is that they're the ones at risk.

'Your entire posture is a fraud. It's based on the premise that *you'll* still be safe when we give up our guns.'

'I didn't know you were going to speak for both of us tonight,' Wilman said to laughter.

'I'm throwing your own words back at you – interdependence. Group hugs. Neighborhood watches. Multiculturalism in the schools. Global economic planning. International peacekeeping forces. Community, community, community. It's all about keeping with the herd. Conform and take your chances –'

'Families that work are made up of people who pull together. No household worth living in ever saw the parents armed against each other, the children taking orders at gunpoint.'

At that point the moderator threw up his hands and left the stage, eventually taking a seat in the sixth row.

'And we're just one big family here, aren't we, Senator? Grandpa's not a psycho – Sister's not a thief – Dad's not a rapist – Junior's not a murderer. We can all sleep easily in our beds. That's the *reasonable* thing to do. That's what logic dictates. We can all be happy here in the herd. It's madness to believe that there are wolves.'

'It's madness to try to face them alone,' said Wilman. 'Which is where your worship of self-interest always leads. Why do you think we invented families, and tribes, and nations? What's the value of group identification, if rugged individualism is really the winning hand?'

'You've lost sight of the real question,' said Trent. 'The real question is whether a reasonable man can find enough reasons to arm himself. The real question is whether a reasonable man can find enough reason to kill. Your entire argument in defense of disarmament rests on the answers. If the rational mind answers yes, then there's no madness in bearing arms – the madness is laying them down.'

The dean reappeared on stage while Trent was speaking, and drew Wilman away from his microphone for a hushed conversation. In the meantime, Trent turned his attention to the audience for the first time.

'And here we have a room full of reasonable people – smart, well-educated, well-to-do young men and women who are used to settling their disagreements with other smart, well-educated people though a war of words. You came to this arena to see your champion gird on his logic and ideas, his science and humanism and philosophy, and do battle. But not one of you gave any serious thought to the possibility his opponent was not going to play by your rules.

'No, because if you had, you would have listened to the warnings I sent you this afternoon.'

The dean had started across the stage, but Trent's offhanded confession stopped him short. 'You, too, Dean Franklin? And with all your worldly experience – oh, but I forget, you're a graduate of this university, too. Another smart, well-educated man living in a well-mannered world. Why don't you tell them all what you just told Senator Wilman?' Trent suggested. He found he was enjoying the moment immensely.

'Mr Trent, I think we need to wrap this up.'

'As you wish,' said Trent. 'I'll tell them. Ladies and gentlemen, Dean Franklin would like you to know that Senator Wilman's Jammer has experienced an unfortunate malfunction, and is not presently able to protect you.' He peered out at them, disappointed by the lack of reaction. 'Perhaps the Dean can tell us what the reasonable response to that news would be. Or the Senator? No?'

He turned back to his podium, grasped the sloping top with both hands, and twisted it. It came free, and he dropped it to the floor with a clatter. Reaching inside, he grasped the pistol concealed within and raised it over his head for all to see.

'How about now?' he said in the hush of their caught breath. 'How about now?' He pointed the weapon out at the audience, sweeping it slowly from one side to the other. There were no cries or screams, just a rustling and an angry murmur. 'I recall our President doing this in Congress, and thinking it was educational. So let's call this a lesson, too. You – you, on the aisle, sit down. You are not dismissed.'

Turning, he brought the pistol to bear on Grover Wilman's chest. 'You're a very thoughtful man, Senator Wilman. Everyone tells me so. I'd like you to analyze this situation and tell me – wouldn't you rather be the one holding this gun?'

'It's been here since before the Jammer went down,' said Wilman. 'Are you sure it still works?'

With the SkyEyes closing in and jostling each other for the best angle, Trent raised his hand slightly and fired a shot over Wilman's head. It buried itself in the mock wood paneling of the acoustic shell. The sound was convincing enough to embolden a dozen or so members of the audience to bolt for the doors. On stage, the Senator started but did not flinch, while Dean Franklin dropped to a crouch and stayed there.

'Azides,' Trent said by way of explanation. 'Dean, why don't you go take a seat with the other students?'

'What's this about, John?' asked Wilman.

'Don't try to "handle" me, *Grover*. Just answer my question,' Trent said. 'I want the truth – wouldn't you rather be the one holding the gun?'

'No.'

'Liar.' He looked out at the audience again. 'You know, they really don't understand the herd concept you've been shoving down their throats. If they were to all storm the stage, they could surely disarm me. If they were to all head for the exits, most of them would make it. Isn't it strange? They don't want to be one of the ones who'd die. Now, would you consider that a reasonable state of mind?'

'What is it that you're after, Mr Trent? Me? Then let them leave.'

'Sorry. I need their assistance to make a point. Yours, too,' said Trent. 'Here they are, just as you wanted them to be, unarmed and helpless in the face of aggression. Don't you think some of them wish *they* had a gun right now? Don't you think they're finally learning something about the real world? Tell the truth this time, Senator – how do you like being the one who's powerless?'

'I was just thinking,' Wilman said, still annoyingly calm, 'that I didn't choose which podium I was going to use until five minutes before we came out.'

Trent laughed. 'Good – very good! Then maybe you should look in your podium.'

With obvious reluctance, Wilman twisted the top of his podium. When it moved, he lifted it deliberately and gently set it aside. The SkyEyes swept stage left to peer over his shoulder as he frowned down at the contents of the compartment.

'For those of you not watching at home, Senator Wilman has now discovered he has a gun just like mine,' Trent said. 'Senator, what are your "rational" options now? Are you considering any new ones? What do you think your friends in the seats expect from you? How about a little Jimmy Stewart, *Liberty Valance*-style. How about a little John Wayne?'

'I always suspected that you learned everything you know about

457

guns from Westerns, John. Are we doing Shane now? "Pick up the gun, boy –"'

'Well, why don't you? Pick up the gun, and maybe you can rewrite this scene.'

Infuriatingly, Wilman lowered his hands to his sides and took a step away from the podium. 'Is that what this is all about? You need public justification, or you can't kill me?'

'You can't talk me down, Senator, so don't bother trying. I'm a reasonable man who's made a rational decision. Now I want to see how your moral logic works.'

'No,' said Wilman. 'I'm not playing.'

'If saving yourself isn't reason enough to pick up the gun, I can offer you more motivation.' Trent pulled his comset from its leg pocket and unfolded the antenna. 'I think the first use of a cordless comset as a remote detonator was the Mall of America incident, wasn't it? Of course, the poor fellow forgot to screen out those courtesy calls from his wife's credit card company, so things didn't work out quite as he'd planned.'

'You *are* insane, John Trent,' Wilman said with a gratifying hint of a snarl. 'Where's the bomb?'

The word alone was enough to elicit gasps and cries from a suddenly agitated audience. Trent allowed the warm glow of accomplishment to suffuse his being before answering. 'It could be anywhere, couldn't it? Outside a bar. Under a bridge. In a lecture hall where kids on dates are watching a film that's older than they are.

'But where would be the justice in that? What have they done to deserve it? Did they conspire to make America weak and its citizens dependent? Did they offer a false promise to a gullible nation? Did they deliberately set out to destroy a fundamental Constitutional freedom in order to secure their own power?

'No. You did that. You, and all your friends from The Fletcher School, and The Elliott School, and The Woodrow Wilson School, and The Kennedy School,' Trent said, indicating the audience with a sweep of his free hand.

'You didn't take that field down for these guns,' Wilman said slowly. 'You didn't need to.'

'That's right, Senator. Analyze the situation rationally.'

458

'It's here,' he said tightlipped. 'Goddamn you, it's here, where the cameras are.' Wilman started waving his arm in the direction of the audience. 'Get out,' he shouted. 'Go, get out now.'

A few started to move, but most were frozen to their seats.

'I don't think they should do that, Senator,' Trent said, taking a step toward the edge of the stage. 'I might get flustered and push the wrong button. Why not pick up the gun instead? Look at how many lives you could save by rearming.'

'You could save just as many by disarming,' Wilman shot back.

'True enough – but it would mean surrendering to something I believe is evil. And that is not my rational choice. Would a countdown help you focus, Senator? I don't intend to wait for the cavalry to arrive. Ten – nine – eight –'

Answering Trent's words with a look of rough, unvarnished hate, Grover Wilman at long last lunged toward the podium and snatched the pistol out of the clip that held it there. As he did, Trent lowered his own pistol to his side, squeezing and holding the trigger. There was no report. There were no more cartridges – the clip had been replaced by a transmitter pack, and the second trigger pull sent the arming command. When he released it, the detonation command would follow.

From barely five meters away, Wilman pointed the pistol at Trent's head. 'There,' he said. 'You have the picture you wanted. It's going out all over the world right now. You've won. So put those down, just set them down on the stage. Tell these people they can leave.'

'I can't do that, Senator. If I do, we'll never know if this was all just another pose.' He started to raise the comset to where he could read its display.

Wilman grimaced, moved his gun hand down and to the right, thumbed off the safety, and fired.

The bullet slammed into Trent's left shoulder, tore through sinew and vessel, shattered bone. The shock, not the impact, stole strength from his legs and staggered him backwards. He stumbled into the podium, dropping the comset from a numb hand. He was vaguely aware of the tumult in the auditorium, as a frightened exodus finally began.

'Thank you,' Trent gasped, still clutching his own pistol tightly.

'Now I know – you understand the calculus. Here's your Trigger, Senator.' Shakily, he raised his pistol overhead, pointed it up into the maze of catwalks and cables above them, and allowed his index finger to relax.

There was already a woman screaming, angry shouts, pleading. No one else could have heard the click as a lever moved, a ratchet fell, a contact closed. But it was thunderous in Trent's ears. He never heard the explosion itself, eight kilograms of shape charge blasting downwards toward the stage through the top of the fly. He heard only the cries, the choir of raised voices, that he thought were for him, on this, his day of triumph.

29:

'I like to believe that people, in the long run, are going
to do more to promote peace than our governments.
Indeed, I think that people want peace so much that
one of these days governments had better get out of
the way and let them have it.'

— *Dwight D. Eisenhower*

Over the years, the trees on the north side of the White House
had been allowed to grow to the point that there were only three
windows from which one could see Lafayette Park. But even before
the arrival of the Trigger, the landscaping had less to do with the
security of Presidents than it did with their insecurities.

Lafayette Park was, and had long been, the favorite gathering
place for America's political protesters and social reformers to
voice their complaints. They were there every day, in all kinds
of weather, raising hand-written signs on balloons, programming
electronic placards, and declaiming amplified diatribes. It was, in
the words of one pundit, 'Washington's permanent carnival side-
show — a motley collection of political and philosophical oddities
given dignity only by their earnest innocence.' President Engler,
whose policies had given almost everyone something to complain
about, had dubbed Lafayette Park the 'Thorn Garden'.

But in the wake of the Trigger announcement, there was a new
and larger presence in the park — a decidedly more mainstream,
middle-class population that looked more like families than fanatics. That presence had grown until it filled the park by day and
overflowed it on evenings and weekends. But it was a well-ordered
assemblage, so much so that even the Park Service was unable to
help the Secret Service by finding a pretext for closing the park
or thinning the crowd.

461

Calling themselves the Liberty Militia, the squatters provided their own toilets, picked up their own trash, stood patiently in line every day at Gate 5 to file their individual requests to see the President, and even sang respectably in tune during their nightly rallies. Raised on several thousand voices, those martial hymns and patriotic anthems could be heard anywhere on the North Lawn, for blocks in all directions, and inside the White House itself through any open window.

The only jarring note was that nearly every man, woman, and child in the park carried a firearm – a chaotic assortment of rifles and shotguns, pistols and revolvers, of all vintages and calibers. As a practical matter, none of the weapons posed a threat to anyone, because the park was well within the range of the White House's Jammers. But as a matter of the laws still on the books, every one of the Liberty Militia's weapons was a violation not only of Federal statutes (for possession on National Park Service property), but also District of Columbia ordinances (for transporting them there through the streets of Washington).

The militia's occupation of Lafayette Park could easily have become a public relations disaster on a scale unseen in the capital since the 1960s – the jails filled, open-air stockades being built, and still more protesters arriving to take the places of those arrested. But law enforcement officials had seen the civil disobedience trap being laid for them, and agreed among themselves to leave the 'broomstick brigade' unmolested. Even so, to have that citizen army camped on the White House's doorstep was still a powerful symbol. And to Mark Breland, it was also a troubling one.

At least once a week, the President found himself caught at one of those three windows, watching and listening as the militia prayed, sang, and marched in review down the closed block of Pennsylvania Avenue. He did not understand why they were there, not even after hearing the reports from the agents the Secret Service sent into the park. He knew only that he had failed to reach them with his message, failed to convince them that it was time to find another way.

Breland's brooding preoccupation with the Liberty Militia troubled his staff, but no one knew how to constructively address it. It fell to Breland's new chief of staff, Charles Paugh, to finally broach the subject. He did so after discovering Breland in the Lincoln Bedroom at dusk one evening, standing at an open window and staring out as the strains of *The Battle Hymn of the Republic* rode in with the breeze.

'Mr President, please. This does no one any good. And when they catch sight of you watching, it only encourages them.'

'What is it they want, Charlie?'

'Bullets, I believe,' Paugh said, with his characteristic bluntness. 'Why do you subject yourself to this? You'll never convert them. The gun lobby is immovable. Didn't Trent just teach us that? They don't recognize any middle ground.'

'I just can't believe that they'd feel safer down there if we turned off the Jammers, and tomorrow all those guns were full of live ammunition. I can't believe they'd *be* safer.'

'That's moot, sir. It's what they believe that matters.'

'I know, I know.' Frowning, he finally turned away from the glass. 'Unloaded or not, Charlie, I feel like all those guns are aimed at me.'

'They are. At you, and at the next person to sit in your chair.'

'But those aren't criminals out there. Those aren't extremists. I don't understand what I did that was terrible enough to make god-fearing, tax-paying families lay siege to the White House.'

'You asked them to trust people instead of shoot them. Come, Mr President – the New World Order Cabal is waiting for us downstairs.'

'I want to talk to them.'

'What?'

'I want to talk to the Liberty Militia.'

'Oh – oh, no. You really don't want to do that.'

'Charlie, you're my chief of staff, not the thought police. Get in touch with John Burke and tell him I'm going out to the park.' Burke was the senior agent in charge of the President's Secret Service detail.

'To the park? Jesus, Mark, do you have a death wish? If you're going to insist on giving them a free shot at you, at least do it here, where we can keep things more or less under control.'

'That won't do.'

'Sure it will. They file a thousand requests a day to see you –

so, okay, tomorrow we shock the hell out of them and pick three lucky lottery winners. We bring them into a conference room, let them curse you and yours for half an hour, and maybe you can let go of this thing you have about reason being the common language of society. And then we can get on with business.'

'Charlie –'

'*Bzzzzt*. Reality check. These are the people who send out cute pictures of their kids in camouflage and semi-automatic with their Christmas cards. They're not going to listen to you.'

'Then I'll listen to them,' Breland said. 'Find Burke. I want to do this now.'

'Mr President – this is not something to rush into. They'll be there tomorrow, and the next day, and the next –'

'Charlie –' Breland's voice had a warning tone.

Paugh raised his hands in resignation. 'Fine. I'll let Burke argue with you.'

'You do that. Oh, and, Charlie – let's leave the bullpen out of this,' Breland said, referring to the complex of tiny West Wing cubicles occupied by the press. 'I don't intend for this to become a media event.'

Paugh grimaced at the thought. 'Believe me, I'll do everything I can to keep it from becoming one.'

There was no chance that John Burke would ever say he was satisfied with the security arrangements for the President's startling proposal. But with Breland so stubbornly determined that he was prepared to enter Lafayette Park without any escort at all if necessary, Burke made the best accommodation he could under the circumstances.

He alerted the rooftop bow snipers, and doubled the patrol on the north fences. He sent a dozen crowd management specialists ahead into the park to scatter among and monitor the temper of the squatters. Finally, he assembled the six best hand-to-hand fighters on the night roster as an escort unit. Carrying quarterstaves which were a head or more taller than they were, Breland's entourage had a decidedly medieval aspect as they moved out toward the park.

By then, the rally was over, and most of the crowd had dispersed into the streets. Only a few hundred overnighters remained, staking down pop-up tents, laying out bedrolls, and completing the nightly cleanup. But Breland and his escort were spotted immediately by a militia sentry standing watch at the park's periphery.

'South Post One, hail the company,' the young sentry cried. 'It's Breland – the coward-in-chief.' He repeated his astonished call into a headset mic.

Breland changed direction and headed directly for the sentry who had given the alarm. As he came near, he received a sneering challenge. 'What do you want here?'

'Is someone in charge, son?'

'Colonel Harris is the watch commander.'

It was a name and face he knew from Secret Service security briefings on the Liberty Militia. 'That'll do. Where can I find her?'

'You don't. I notified the HQ tent. If she wants to see you, she'll come here. If it were me, I wouldn't bother.'

'If it were up to you, son, they'd have made you watch commander.'

By then, a small crowd had begun to converge on the spot where the two stood. Breland's escort did not allow them to approach too closely, but there were more hostile and mocking jeers. Breland tuned them out and continued looking past the sentry, scanning for Colonel Harris. He finally spotted her approaching in the company of her own entourage of broad-shouldered young men. Sidestepping the sentry, he went to meet her.

'Colonel Harris.'

She nodded, but did not salute or offer her hand. 'Mr President. You surprise me.'

'That's a beginning.'

'It might also be the end – I'd like to be able to say that everyone here respects the office even when we don't respect the man. But the truth is, that distinction gets to be pretty fine when your grievances pass a certain threshold. What is it you want?'

'To understand why you've given up your lives to be here. And maybe, if you care, to try to help you understand why I've given up mine to be in there,' he said, jerking a thumb over his shoulder toward the fence and the White House looming beyond.

'How much do you really need to understand when someone attacks you?' said a man to Breland's right.

Breland turned that way and found him – a gaunt-faced man with thinning black hair combed straight back from his wide forehead. 'Attacks you?'

'Goddamned right. You take away my ability to protect my family, my wife's right to protect herself when she has to work late and walk to her car alone – you take away my boy's chance to protect himself from homosexual kidnappers and drug addict muggers – you make us defenseless in our own homes, and you'd better believe that's an attack. That's an attack on the family, that's an attack on the Constitution, and that damned well makes it an attack on me.'

That speech earned the speaker some hearty applause and a few vigorous claps on the back. 'That's tellin' him,' someone called out.

Breland cocked his head. 'Your name is –'

'Larry Dillard. You can tell your IRS attack dogs to look for me in Cross Plains, Wisconsin.'

'I don't believe in punishing people for speaking their minds, Mr Dillard. Could I ask you a few questions, though?'

Dillard shrugged, though he looked vaguely uncomfortable at the prospect. 'Sure.'

'Is your family all right now? Everyone well, I hope?'

'As far as I know. My middle child's here with me – my sons are back home with my wife.'

'Good. Good – I'm glad to hear it,' said Breland, with a sincerity the audience was reluctant to credit. 'Can you tell me some more about these crimes, and how what I've done figured in them?'

'Watch it, Larry – he's baiting a trap for you –'

Dillard shook off the warning. 'Crimes – no, you weren't listening, how do you expect to understand? I didn't say we'd been victims. But you're setting us up to be victims. My wife weighs a hundred and sixteen pounds. How is she supposed to fight off a rapist your size? How's my son supposed to make it home if the Muslim gang at school decides to pick on him next?'

'Your wife went everywhere armed?'

'And shot at the practical range once a month for proficiency.'

'And your son took a gun to school?'

Dillard stiffened, but defiance won out over discretion. 'You're damned right he did – until one of your Gestapo squads showed up and turned the campus into a Constitution-free zone.'

'Wasn't taking a gun to school already against the law?'

'So's assault, but that didn't stop the damned Muslims from putting one of Ken's friends in the hospital for three weeks.'

'So you were willing to teach your son to break the law.'

'When the law's wrong. When the law's unconstitutional. That's a citizen's duty.'

'I see,' Breland said, nodding noncommittally. 'Did you like your odds better when the rapist and the gang were just as likely to have guns as your wife and son?' he asked. 'Did you think that kind of arms race improved their chances of coming home?'

'What choice did we have?' a woman nearby interjected. 'Never leaving home? Expecting the police to protect us, when they've told us that's not their job? Forming gangs of our own? Or maybe you think we women should just lie down for the rapists. Maybe that's your idea of a civil society.'

'What reason have I given you to think that?' Breland asked. 'Why would you believe that I *only* care about murder, and not about other kinds of crime?'

'How can we believe anything else?' Dillard demanded. 'You obviously don't care about the crimes that our guns *prevent* – if you did, you wouldn't have taken those guns away from us.'

'Mr Dillard, I'll thank you to let me speak for myself,' Breland said. 'I know there are studies which claim that arming good people thwarts two million attempted crimes a year. When I talked to the FBI director about it, he told me he believes the number was closer to five or six hundred thousand –'

'Making it easier for you to ignore the victims,' someone taunted from beyond the first circle.

'Now, now, that's not fair,' another voice called. 'Maybe he likes the idea of more crime. Disarm the public, and we have to come begging to the government for help and protection. This city loves us dependent.'

Breland spun around, searching for the speaker. 'Why is it you'd rather make up my positions for me than hear what I have to say? If it's because you've already decided not to believe me, why are you even here?' He turned a half-turn back and caught the colonel's gaze. 'I was on my way to pointing out that if you count the crimes guns prevent, then you also have to count the ones they permit.'

'That's nonsense,' scoffed a short woman at Colonel Harris's elbow. 'Guns don't turn people into criminals. That's magical thinking. My brothers and I were raised with guns. My husband and I've raised our kids with guns. Not a single bloodthirsty felon in either litter. Explain that.'

'Good parenting. Good sense about alcohol and drugs. A light hand with the kids and a kind word for each other. Enough control over your own lives that you've been content with them. No little bit of good luck,' Breland said. 'But we don't have to be naïve about this, do we? It's no accident that people reach for a gun when they want more say in how things are going to go. No difference between law-breakers and law-abiders there.'

At that, Colonel Harris's expression frosted over, and hers was not the only one.

'Well, that explains a lot,' Dillard said, 'that you can't see any difference between the murderers and people like us. I think we all understand you a lot better now.'

The President scowled. 'That isn't what I said. Come on, there's no audience to play to – these people are all with you already,' Breland said, making a slow circle with hands extended to both sides. 'Can't we have a little honesty? Whether it's a bad guy sticking a gun in a good guy's face or the other way around, you all want the same thing at that moment – juice, leverage, weight – *control*.'

'I'm one of the good guys,' said a round-bellied man carrying an enormous shotgun. 'I just want to be left alone.'

'Which is wanting the world to be the way you want it to be – which is control. This isn't some secret truth that can't be spoken, is it?' Breland appealed. 'Guns are just like armies – there's only two reasons you point them at someone –'

'Coercion, and deterrence,' said Colonel Harris.

'Yes. You pick up a hammer to drive a nail. You pick up a gun to make somebody do what you want them to.'

468

'Now, wait a minute,' called a short young woman with long straight hair. 'You're making it sound completely grim and serious. What about target shooting? Skeet? Trap? What about the history, the lore, the reenactors? What about hunting? Guns are *fun*. Is there anyone here who didn't get a rush the first time they fired a gun?'

'Got a bigger one the first time I hit something I aimed at,' some wag said dryly. The laughter of self-recognition broke the tension that had been building.

'There's a little honesty, thank you,' Breland said. 'Look, maybe you can help me understand something. What have you really lost that would make you want to go back to the way things were before the Trigger appeared? Because everything the FBI can tell me says that crime *isn't* going up –'

'I haven't heard that,' Dillard said. 'What I hear is that we're seeing two, three, four or more lowlifes working together, breaking into houses, mugging people at ATMs, dragging women into cars –'

'You're right,' Breland admitted, to his counterpart's evident astonishment. 'Team crime – that's what the FBI has decided to call it. We *are* seeing more team crime, and I'm not sanguine about it. I don't know what the solution is –'

'How about the team of Mr Smith and Mr Wesson?'

To Breland's surprise, it was Colonel Harris, frowning across the circle toward Dillard, who took that rhetorical bullet for him.

'The truth is, the President's right,' she said. 'You can find yourself on the short end even when you're carrying. And being outnumbered with guns isn't any better place to be than being outnumbered without them – especially since carrying just gives them reason to shoot first.'

Dillard spat angrily. 'Goddamn – Colonel, don't give this fascist aid and comfort.'

'I'm not giving him anything. The truth is the truth. Speaking of which –' She looked to Breland. 'When the FBI didn't come out with its preliminary crime stats for last year at the usual time, a lot of us thought we knew the reason – they were bad, and you were trying to figure out how to clean them up.'

Pursing his lips, Breland shook his head slowly. 'No, if anything, the numbers are too good. Even with some criminals changing tactics, the final figures should show homicide down fourteen percent, rape down at least ten, aggravated assault down nearly twenty, armed robbery down almost a full third, most of it in the commercial sector –'

'Oh, this is pure propaganda,' Dillard said in disgust.

'No, this is good news,' Breland shot back. 'It means we can still hope that Americans are as civilized as the people of Europe or industrial Asia or Canada. It means we found a way to change the rules and make things harder for criminals, and some of them lost their nerve, or their angle. It means the Trigger and Jammer saved a hundred thousand or so of your countrymen from becoming victims.'

'Then why are you holding it back?' Harris demanded. 'Why hasn't this been all over the media?'

'Because I ordered the FBI not to release anything until all the numbers were unimpeachable. Because I knew some people would be skeptical, and I don't want to help anyone convince themselves that the numbers were cooked.'

'Well, I don't believe them, not for a minute,' a young man interjected angrily. 'This is the big lie, your reelection strategy – to piss on us and tell us it's raining –'

'That's enough, Private Terrell,' Harris said sharply.

'What?

'This is the President of the United States. You *will* show respect.'

'Respect? Oh, this is insane – I can't believe what I'm hearing. I'm supposed to respect a coward – a traitor? This man cut the heart out of the Second Amendment, and the watch captain's falling all over herself to make nice to him. It makes me want to puke.'

'Master of Arms, escort Private Terrell to the galley area –'

'No, it's all right,' said Breland, stepping closer. 'I want to talk to him. What's your name?'

'Steve Terrell.' Defiance blazed in the young man's eyes.

Breland nodded. 'You've got your facts wrong, Steve Terrell. This technology came out of the private sector, without a penny of tax money or a whisper to Washington that it was coming. It's the private sector that's been making it go. And the reason is something you don't want to admit to yourself – that most

470

people don't want to have to be gunslingers to get by. That's not how they want to live.'

'I'd bet even most gun owners don't want that,' someone said quietly.

Breland went on, 'Now those people have a weapon of their own, one that turns that Winchester you're carrying into a museum piece, or at best an expensive club. Everything changes. The Bill of Rights didn't promise you eternal technological superiority for smokeless powder and the rifled barrel.'

'It damn well did promise that I could keep my gun, so I could blow away any fascist traitor who tried to take it away from me.'

'Is that why you're here, Mr Terrell? Are you hoping for a second chance?'

'I'm here to defend the Constitution from all enemies, foreign and domestic. You were supposed to do that, too.'

'I did,' Breland said. 'If we were the fascists you think we are, we could have taken this technology, put together a fleet of stealth helicopters and black vans, and disarmed whole cities overnight –'

'If you were the patriots you should be, you would have grabbed up this technology and lost it at the bottom of Lake Superior.'

'So you expect us to disarm your neighbor, but not you?' Breland asked, cocking his head. 'That's an interesting double standard you're setting up there. Unfortunately for you, the Supreme Court didn't go for it.'

Terrell scowled. 'That decision was bought and sold by the power brokers – the elite has never wanted the common man armed.'

Breland's stare was an indictment. 'You are much too fond of your fantasy of persecution, Steve Terrell,' he said, and turned back to the colonel. 'I did not disarm you. You can still have your guns on your own land, if that's what you and your family choose. You can still take your guns into the wilds to hunt. You can still go to the firing ranges and shooting clubs. If you live and work and play in the empty spaces of the continent, you can still lead the self-reliant life of the frontiersman. None of that's been taken away.

'But when you come out of your private spaces and down from

the hills, when you come into the villages and towns and cities where most of us live, you're going to find more and more places where your guns are neither needed nor welcome. And you're going to have to make a decision.

'Are you going to turn away, and stay outside? Are you going to join us, and accept our rules? Or are you going to push your way in and try to make yourself and your guns the new rules? That's what I wonder when I look out from those windows back there – which choice you'll make.' He slowly surveyed the circle, trying to read the unreadable expressions in the darkness. 'When you've made it, I suppose you won't be here any longer.'

'You're not going to be in *there* much longer,' someone shouted gleefully from the dark.

'Probably not,' Breland agreed. 'And I know you won't miss me. But wherever we go from here, we're all going to keep living in the world we create with our choices. You can make that a world of individuals, with everyone looking out for his own. Or you can take a measured risk, throw in with the rest of us, and try for a community.'

'Collectivist pap.'

'No – it's something called teamwork,' Breland shot back. 'I know how much it can do. I'm sorry you don't. I don't think human beings were made for living alone in fear of each other. I think all of our best moments have come when we let go of that fear and come together – even though there *are* predators out there, and some of us will lose our gamble.'

'You volunteering?'

'If it comes to that,' Breland said. 'If all we think about is ourselves, what do we have? Think bigger. Kant called it the moral imperative: Act in such a way that what you do might serve as a universal law. Do you want to live in a world in which ten billion other humans follow your lead? That's the real test to apply. That's the choice we're really making.

'And that's all I came out here to say – though I didn't know it until just now. Be sure you know what choice you're making.' His eyes sought Colonel Harris's, and he smiled a tight smile. 'Thank you for hearing me out.' She nodded acknowledgement, and he turned away.

Inevitably, there were some in the crowd unwilling to give Breland the last word. He was followed to the edge of the park and beyond by a small coterie of detractors who shouted their challenges and imprecations from beyond the ring of Secret Service escorts.

One young man in fatigues wasn't content to hurl words. As the President neared the gate, he came charging up from behind with a fist-sized rock clutched in each hand.

'You think you're safe? You're not safe!' he shouted from ten meters away, then wound up and let fly.

But by then one agent had already shifted into a blocking position, and successfully deflected the missile with his staff. It clanged harmlessly against the steel fence. At the same time, a second agent charged the attacker with his staff lowered like a lance. The agent dropped the young man with a single blow to the abdomen, then retreated to close the circle around Breland.

That was all Breland saw – he was surrounded, pushed forward through the gate, and hustled across the grounds by his escorts. Charles Paugh met him on the walk, and his chiding tone was little different from those who had reproached the President on the other side of the fence.

'Predictable. Completely predictable. You disturb hornets in their nest, and they're going to attack. I hope you satisfied your curiosity, because John Burke is going to want to throw a bag over you and lock you in the basement for a month.'

'I still think it was worth doing,' said Breland. 'It just ended badly.' But he could not pretend that the attack had not unsettled him. 'I'm going upstairs. Tell John if he wants to spank me, he can do it in the morning.'

'I'll tell him. – Hey, and stay away from the windows for the rest of the night, will you?'

But John Burke did not take the hint. A half-hour later, he was on the phone with the President, asking for ten minutes. 'I want to show you something that I think might let you sleep a little easier.'

'You have the guy?'

'The assailant is in custody, yes.'

'That's good enough for me.'

'I can do better, Mr President. You won't regret it.'

Breland relented, and shortly thereafter Burke emerged from the elevator with a memory block in his left hand. 'Your study?' he asked.

'Whatever.'

Burke led the way and settled himself, control board on his lap, in the chair nearest to the media center's wallscreen. Breland stood near his favorite working chair, a well-worried leather recliner.

'This is the attack, from camera sixteen,' Burke said as a ghostly low-light image appeared on the display. 'Watch the upper left corner for the assailant – there, and now he stops to shout at you – that's Agent Frank Baines who steps in and fouls off the fastball –'

'Good stick,' Breland said approvingly.

'I'll tell him you said so – he'll like that, he's a Dodgers fan. Now here's the part you didn't see. That was Agent Toni Waters who laid the assailant out. The reason she did not pursue and restrain is me – my orders to the detail were that getting you inside took precedence over everything else. So the assailant had an opportunity to get his legs back under him and run – getting a little help there from a couple of buddies. I'm sure we would have found him – the dye mark from the stick goes right through clothing and deep into the skin –'

'Wait a minute – "would have"? Didn't you say you had him in custody?'

'I did. This is the view from camera eighteen, about ten minutes later. Those are our people, at the bottom, organizing to sweep the park – there, top center, that's what I wanted you to see.'

Breland squinted. A clot of six people was emerging from the park, and it was apparent that one of them was being dragged along against his will. 'Is that our guy?'

'That's him – David Joseph Markham.'

'Your people in the park grabbed him, then.'

'They didn't get a chance to,' said Burke. 'The militia grabbed him for us – citizen's arrest. That's the night commander and the sergeant-at-arms, there, bringing him out and turning him over to the agent in charge.'

'I'll be damned –'

474

'When I first saw this, I thought maybe they could see we were getting ready to roust the lot of them, and that they weren't going to be able to hide him, so they might as well surrender him. But then I heard from our agents in the park – the guy wasn't stopping, he was heading straight for Liberty Avenue, yelling for his buddies to run interference. I guess he had fewer friends there than he thought. They took him down north of the fountain.'

'I would never have expected this,' Breland said, shaking his head. 'I wouldn't have expected any help from them.'

Burke turned off the replay, which had frozen at the last frame. 'Well, maybe that's why Colonel Harris said what she said. I didn't quite know what it meant.'

'What are you talking about?'

'When she surrendered Markham, she gave the agent a message for you.' He pulled a white card from a hip pocket and squinted at the scrawled handwriting. 'She said, "I'm taking a chance on you, and Kant, and community – and hoping there's more here than fine words." I guess this is her signature here.' He dropped the card by the console and looked up. 'Who's Kant?'

But by then, the President was no longer listening. He had turned away and was looking out the window toward the park, even though the dense leafy boughs of a sugar maple blocked his view.

'Me, too, Colonel,' Breland said softly. 'Me, too.'

Breland sat up alone for nearly an hour, thinking about Grover Wilman, and letting himself shake just a bit over his close call with the Liberty Militia. Now that his frustration had been displaced by a weary resignation, going into the park seemed like a damned reckless thing to have done.

Not until he finally rose to leave the room did he touch the card Burke had brought him. He picked it up meaning to pocket it, giving it only a casual glance.

But that glance fell on an embossed silver Q with an arrow pointing to the right. Beside it was the name *Carol Westin Harris*, and below that a Net address. On the back, what Burke had called her signature was an echo of the printed sign, squeezed into the lower right-hand corner.

'What the hell – Burke!' he shouted, starting toward the door.

By the time he reached it he was running. 'Charlie!'

No one answered. Breland ran back into the media center and vaulted into the lounge chair in front of the wallscreen. 'Vox. Log on. Security, Post 1.' A low-resolution image of a young Marine seated at a desk flashed on the upper right quarter of the screen. 'Who is that, Corporal Mackie?' he demanded of the guard. 'Who's in the house, Corporal?'

'Mr President, sir. You can see the gate log on channel thirty from any command node. Sending a snapshot now.'

The list of people in the White House filled the entire right-hand side of the screen. 'No, dammit, just staff – executive branch. Where's Charlie Paugh?'

'Gone, sir.'

'Burke?'

'Captain Milton has the watch tonight, sir.'

'Mrs Tallman? Oh, hell, I sent her home, she was having company for dinner. Is there anyone over in clerical? In the library? What time is it, anyway?'

'I show an imaging technician in the clerical suite, no one in the library. It's oh-two-ten hours, sir.'

Breland waved a hand impatiently. 'Vox. Close and clear.' He pondered for a moment. 'Vox. Net search. Quote – Futurians – close quote.'

Twenty minutes of brute-force Net-sifting turned up a comedy ensemble, a keyboard trio, two groups of science fiction fans (The New Futurians and The New Original Futurians) and one of dead writers (but not including Sturgeon, the one Wendell Schrock had mentioned), two novels, a 2-D film, a VR adventure game, and a superhero comic book series – none of which seemed to be associated with the Q-and-arrow symbol.

That he found on several of the sites devoted to Sturgeon, along with some appealing quotes on the subjects of love, reason, and world peace. But there were no ties to Schrock or Harris, no mention of an Alliance for a Humanist Future – which had no presence on the Net at all, which Breland found baffling. And even the high-powered Net agents supplied for his account by the National Information Office couldn't connect Wendell Schrock and Carol Westin Harris.

476

The hell with etiquette, Breland thought, and placed a call to Schrock. It took another toy from the NIO's toolkit to punch through the analyst's messaging system and force his phone to ring.

'What's going on? Who is this?' Schrock demanded sleepily.

'I need to talk you, Wendell,' said Breland. 'Vox. Send video.'

'Mr President.' Surprise was audible in Schrock's voice.

Breland reached out and held Harris's card in front of the close-up lens. 'I had an unexpected favor done for me tonight,' he began.

'Yes, I *heard*,' Schrock said.

'What – you say you heard? How?'

'There were at least three minicams in the park, Mr President. It's a top story on the overnight news.'

'Son of a bitch –'

At that moment, incoming video put Schrock's tousled-hair countenance on the wallscreen. 'It's actually playing fairly well, sir. Also, I heard about it from Carol, in meetspace.'

'She *is* one of you, then. Is this what we talked about before? Is this the help you said might be there?'

'No, sir. You were just damned lucky.'

Breland glanced away, gave his head a little shake, and then looked up again. 'Wendell, I really would be grateful for an explanation. Who are you? You know, there's no flipping way to enter that symbol of yours in a Net search.'

Schrock laughed lightly. 'You just have to know how. All right, an explanation. There's no creed or charter I can quote from, so you'll have to settle for the Gospel according to Wendell. I'll tell you how it was, and then I'll tell you what's changed in the last two days.

'The Futurians were born on the Net, and couldn't exist without it. The Net is where the founders met and where today's members keep in touch and do most of their work. It happened that way because the Net is drowning in ignorance, misinformation, hostility, quackery, propaganda, credulous pseudoscience, rationalization, and just plain sloppy thinking. Futurians are people who find that all dismaying, because we think we can reach a little higher, ask a little more of ourselves and each other.'

'You said something about that after you briefed me.'

Scrock nodded. 'We think there's a spark of reason in every human being – and in its light you can catch a glimpse of the commonality of humankind and the road to our future.'

'I may have to steal that.'

'Please do. So to belong, you don't have to say you believe A, or not-A – just that you know there's a rational way to choose between them. Being a Futurian means making a commitment to ask the next question, to keep an open mind, to test ideas – especially the comfortable and appealing ones that so often slip past the logical defenses. We profess an irrational faith in the power of reason. Passion may take us farther, but reason takes us higher. So we try to be the friends of reason wherever and however we can.'

'How many of you are there?'

'Not many. A few million who know they're members. Optimistically, a few billion who don't – like you.'

'International –'

'Of course. That's the unrealized promise of the Net – a stateless community of educated people working toward enlightened goals, including the pursuit of truth. A civilized New World Order in which you don't kill people for believing differently than you – you *educate* them if you can, learn from them what you can, and promote mutual tolerance.'

'I hear no small amount of idealism there.'

'Idealism is the horse,' Schrock admitted. 'But reason is the rider. Well, that brings me to tonight.'

'You said something had changed –'

Schrock nodded. 'Some of us – a lot of us, I think – have been working the disarmament issue for some time. But the events of the last two days have galvanized the membership in a way I've never seen. We've been meeting continuously in the well since Senator Wilman was murdered, and I've seen as many as thirty thousand avatars logged in at once. And out of that came something I never expected – we formed a committee. We're going to organize a coordinated effort in support of you and Mind Over Madness – there are already thousands of volunteers.'

'To do what?'

478

'To resist those who want you to fail, who want disarmament to fail, who think loss of privilege is too high a price for peace. They've been out there for months, pushing hard. We know they're organized – everyone speaking with one voice, making the same monkey-brain appeals. They don't debate, they propagandize. And they're very good at making themselves heard.'

'We're going to bet on reason winning out over propaganda. There are countless places in the real and wired worlds where people gather to talk – chat rooms, public meetings, reader forums, talk Web, bars, park benches. We'll be there. We'll make sure that there is a patient, thoughtful voice speaking up for sanity. And we will make *ourselves* heard.'

'I envy you your optimism, Wendell. I confess I've been struggling to find mine.'

'Don't give up, sir,' Schrock said earnestly. 'I could not have been more proud of my President than I was watching you wade into that crowd just forty-eight hours after your friend was murdered. You changed one mind tonight. We'll change ten more tomorrow, and a hundred the next day. Just keep speaking to that spark of reason, and little by little we'll breathe life into it.'

The briefcase Jammer made its debut at the Consumer Electronics Show in Las Vegas. Toshiba showed a slick three-piece system with a powered docking cradle for the home, another for the car trunk, and an eight-kilo briefcase capable of an hour of continuous operation at short range or three long-range bursts. It was aimed at executive anxieties and came with a five-figure price tag which did little to dampen interest. Safeco introduced the Safe Passage, a civilian version of the Suppressor backpack which police forces in twenty-eight countries had adopted, and the Sentry, an add-on to its modular home-defense system.

But the runaway hit of the show was the Celestial Silver Shield, a bare-bones Jammer packaged for the home. Built from less-refined components than the other offerings, the Silver Shield was the size of a small end-table and the weight of a small refrigerator, with the voracious electrical appetite of a resistance heater when set in 'continuous' mode. But it was offered for the price of a good television, and the packaging and positioning – straddling the line between an appliance and furniture – was inspired. Show preorders soared to record levels, and within six weeks Celestial had sold the entire first year's projected production, sending Goldstein to the Asian Rim on a quest for more capacity.

The sudden emergence of Horton devices as a commodity brought a swift response from Congress, which tried to strangle the infant market with regulation. Senator Hap Neely's 'Self-Defense Parity and Fairness Act' was a bald attempt to hamstring privately-owned Jammers by limiting them to a range of thirty meters or the nearest property line, whichever was less. It passed with a veto-proof margin, but lawyers for LifeShield Arsenal buried it in paper before it went into effect.

'If the authors of this legislation want to come forth to publicly demonstrate that the firearms and ammunition commonly in use have a range of only thirty meters and respect property lines,' the lead attorney said from the courthouse steps, 'the plaintiffs will gladly withdraw their petition. Otherwise, we count on the court to expose this law for the sham it is.'

The district court came through, but Congress went right back to work. This time, it was a triple-barreled attack using the Federal bureaucracies.

A House committee ordered the Federal Trade Commission to investigate 'health and safety issues' regarding prolonged exposure of young children and pregnant women to Jammer fields. A Senate panel directed the Federal Aviation Administration and Federal Communications Commission to jointly investigate the possibility that a VentureStar crash in Dallas was caused by interference from the Jammer installations at the spaceport. And the Food and Drug Administration was asked to look into reports that Horton devices were killing people by damaging the microprocessors in medical implants.

Each and every charge was specious, even fraudulent. But together they offered not only the prospect of months of bad publicity, but of the whole spectrum of regulatory actions from recalls to outright bans.

It was all part of the ongoing war of perceptions being waged on every front where public opinion was shaped. But as the year wore on, that struggle more and more strongly resembled a desperate endgame with an outcome that was foreordained. There was not going to be a grass-roots revolution against the government. The middle class was not signing up for a civil war.

Instead, there were signs of an evolution in public attitudes toward not only guns but violence – an awakening of outrage and revulsion, a retreat from the casual cynicism which had allowed the country to accept the slaughter with a shrug of inevitability.

'Now that we finally know we're sick, how will we know if we're getting better?' asked the hero of the sell-out stage hit *Asylum*.

Little by little, an answer emerged.

30:

'Making peace is harder than making war.'

– Adlai Stevenson

For the first time in history, the number of Federally licensed firearms dealers fell below the number of National Health Service crisis counselors. By then, storefront gun dealers were already an endangered species. In the span of only a year, one out of every three had closed up shop, and only stubbornness was keeping many others open in the face of unrelenting red ink. The gun-show circuit simply imploded, with sellers outnumbering buyers and prices in free fall.

The firearm and ammunition manufacturers were scarcely better off – a wave of mergers, acquisitions, and bankruptcies had thinned their ranks, and still no one could say how many bullfrogs the shrinking pond would support. Remington-Colt went through four rounds of layoffs. Winchester's parent company spun it off to a German tool-and-die concern more interested in its factories than its products.

Seeing the criminal use of firearms plummeting, the State of Massachusetts repealed all of its 'time, place, and manner' regulations on firearms – and added a law which made disabling or deactivating a Horton device a felony. Within a month, thirty-five other states followed a similar course.

Ordinary citizens were seeing less crime as well. Millennium Media, the largest English-language program syndicator and push-cast server, dropped the *Crime Witness* channel from their Home Essentials lineup due to 'ratings erosion'. *Crime Witness* had featured around-the-clock live video of crimes in progress and police pursuits from six continents. It was replaced by Wonderful Planet, a new virtual-tourism feed from National Geographic.

The bad news continued for *Crime Witness*, which was forced to cut its rights payments by a third and go to a 'deja vu' schedule with twelve hours of repeats a day. Those steps were not enough to save it. Two months later, after a key advertiser bailed out, *CW* tried to carry on as a subscription service. In another six weeks, it was in bankruptcy.

That key advertiser had been rental property and relocation giant Halstead Homes, which had been pitching the security features of its premium rental communities with the slogan 'Sleep easy – come home to a Halstead Home'. With occupancy rates falling, Halstead's president announced that the company was repositioning itself as the 'middle-class luxury and convenience alternative'.

'You can't sell people what they already have,' she told the *Wall Street Journal*. 'We need to offer more than personal safety to entice the step-up relocator to move.'

Whether all those developments were truly as connected as they seemed was open to debate. But the debate did little to stop the connections from being drawn, or hope from starting to bloom.

To be sure, there were still places which were not safe, and people who could not be trusted. But there were signs of a determined search for ways to address that reality without recourse to the gun.

In the often-quoted words of New York City's 'blue ninja', Detective Sergeant Jan Flynn, 'Being armed isn't the same as being safe – and being unarmed isn't the same as being helpless.' The petite, blue-eyed Flynn made herself into a symbol of the new attitude, tirelessly demonstrating both propositions in auditoriums and studios throughout the northeast. Hundreds of community-ed programs adopted the *NYPD Guide to Self-Defense* as the Bible for their new adult classes.

The Commonwealth of Pennsylvania went a step further, making not only self-defense but anger management training part of their new common-schooling curriculum for children aged five to fifteen. Incorporating scream-offs and foam-bat duels, the training copied successful pilot programs in Youngstown, Ohio, and

Baltimore, Maryland, where juvenile assault rates were down more than ten percent.

In Los Angeles, the charismatic leader of the Islamic Confraternity declared that Allah had blessed husbands and fathers with 'the antidote to emptiness, the essence of togetherness, and the key to righteousness.' Warning that the 'idle hands' of a man who was not married by age twenty were a danger to himself and his community, Benjamin Muhammad announced that the Confraternity would begin arranging marriages for single men as young as fifteen and single women as young as fourteen.

'It is only when we know our place that we can find our way,' he proclaimed at the mass wedding of the first twenty-one couples joined by the matchmakers. 'Love civilizes us, and marriage fulfills us, and faith uplifts us.'

In Atlanta, an alliance of Southern Baptist churches recruited a team of ministerial mediators with the idea of doling out a different flavor of street justice. Armed only with a folding stool and the moral authority of the collar, the mediators set about to resolve conflicts where they arose, conducting their cleric's court on street corners and playgrounds and front porches. The compromises they arbitrated were sealed with a handshake and a hand on a Bible, and enforced by the expectations of the witnesses to that oath.

In community there was conscience, and in conscience, community.

But however many such collective affirmations could be found, in the end change depended on individual acts of courage and commitment. Most such acts were private, invisible, and uncelebrated. But some found a place in the public spotlight, and their influence went far beyond mere example.

Fifty-eight-year-old widow and grandmother Marge Winkins, a branch bank manager from Rochester, New York, awakened to the sound of breaking glass in the rental half of her duplex, occupied by a sixty-six-year-old retired schoolteacher with osteoarthritis. Concerned for her tenant, Marge picked up a can of wasp spray and an Indian juggling club and went to investigate.

484

She surprised two teenage intruders armed with knives. One burglar went to the hospital with severely bruised testicles; the other, blinded by poison and bleeding above the ear from Marge's blows which gave him his concussion.

'I'll say you surprised them. But why didn't you call 911 first?' every interviewer asked as Marge made her tour of the talk shows.

'Why, because I was there,' Marge would reply. 'You would have done the same for your friend, wouldn't you?'

Pop music idol Kip Knight, lead guitarist for the power-improv quintet Mach 5, shattered his own devilish playboy image with a video confession on the front page of the Mach 5 Web site. 'I'm a drunk. And when I'm drunk, the nasty shit I carry around inside me leaks out. I've hit and hurt every woman I've ever cared about. And a lot of the women I didn't care about – all those eager women who got the nod from the manager to come backstage and come back to the hotel – got the same treatment.

'I'm not gonna talk about why, about where all the anger is coming from. But I want to apologize to those women – to Dove, and Paula, and Noria, to Sam and Mackie and all the rest – for not finding another way to handle it, for taking advantage of you that way, because I was Kip Knight and you knew there was a long line of women waiting to be where you were. I shouldn't have done it. I wish to Holy Pete I hadn't.

'And I want to say something to the guys. This'll be short, because it's not at all complicated. But listen hard, because it's important: of all the stupid things we do, the worst of all stupidities is to raise your hand to someone who loves you. Whatever your problems, whatever your demons, whatever flavor of poison you've been sucking up, don't do what I've done – don't throw away those gifts. Find another way. That's what I've got to do now – find another way.'

The response to that appeal was so extraordinary that Knight joined forces with three other celebrities to found Another Way, a 'no-support group' for abusive men.

No one, however, surprised more people, stirred a stronger or farther-reaching response, or more aptly symbolized the evolution than media commentator Herbert Rogers, whose top-rated broadcast *Funhouse* was almost as influential in the entertainment industry as it was with the consumers who checked in twice a week to hear his opinions.

'Those of you who can remember the twentieth century know I've been reviewing popular entertainment since the days when "movie theater" meant a projector and a flatscreen and "home video" meant VHS tape and a nineteen-inch television in 4:3 aspect ratio,' a somber Rogers said at the opening of his *People's Choice Awards* special.

'In that time, I've willingly allowed the images of the murders of tens of thousands of human beings to enter my eyes and thoughts. By my calculations, I've seen more crime scenes than any detective, more combat than any career soldier, and more corpses than any pathologist.

'I'm embarrassed to remember how many times I sat here and recommended that you pay someone money to push those same brutal images into *your thoughts*. But I'm far more troubled by the realization that, over the years, I became so numb to violence that more often than not I sat in the screening room watching blood fly and bodies fall and was bored.

'Along the way, I shrugged off complaints that the film industry had turned killing into a spectator sport. It's a violent world, I told myself, and these films are only mirroring reality.

'I dismissed charges that those action-adventure blockbusters cater to paranoid power fantasies, that they're a pornography of violence. These films are cartoons, I told myself, that no one could take seriously.

'I shook my head at the idea that the mutilation and execution of men for entertainment was the product of a vicious sexism. I told myself that the real sexism was selling tickets to see young actresses' bare breasts.

'I was wrong. I was wrong right down the line.

'Our entertainments depend on our willing suspension of disbelief. We trick ourselves into thinking that what we're seeing and hearing is real. Well, it's worked too well. It's worked so well that we can never quite get those images out of our heads. When I wonder if I remembered to lock the back door, it's not the reality of my life that makes me bounce out of bed to double-check –

it's the demons from a thousand horror flicks and crazed-killer mysteries, still alive in the back of my mind.

'We all want to hear stories that confirm our view of the world – but we've turned things upside down, and now expect reality to be like our fiction. Fact: even before the Trigger showed up, most police officers went their whole career without firing their weapon at a suspect, much less shooting or killing one. Where can you look in the Blockbuster catalog to discover that reality?

'Many of us firmly believe we live in a dangerous place at a dangerous time. But the truth is that only a few of us actually do. How many real people did you see beaten or stabbed or burned or blown up or shot this year? How many imaginary people? Now think about the body counts you'd run up in a lifetime of "entertaining" yourself.

'Why have we allowed the lie to drown out the truth? Why are we assaulting our senses and poisoning our sensibilities this way? I can't find a good answer – and that tells me that it's time to stop. It's nothing more than an addiction to adrenalin.

'Well, enough, then. I'm going into detox. I'm giving up the juice. I've seen enough of war and murder and deaths that only matter because they connect page two of the script with page four, enough of gangs and gangsters, ruthless terrorists and crazed serial killers.

'I want to hear from writers and directors who know something about the rest of our lives, about all the kinds of moments that fill our days and make being human so glorious and perplexing and tragic and paradoxical. That's this man's choice. From here forward, I want to be connected to life, not disconnected from death.

'Meet me here next time if that's what you want, too.'

Not every viewer did – *Funhouse*'s ratings dipped sharply at first, and Rogers's mail was full of complaints about 'censorship' and 'paternalism' and even 'creeping cultural fascism'. But after the first wave of defectors had departed, *Funhouse*'s ratings began a steady climb to levels that equaled and then exceeded the old numbers, and the mail started to praise Rogers's 'uncommon sense' and applauded the 'outbreak of sanity'.

Still, a thousand philosophical miles away from Jan Flynn and

Herbert Rogers, there were those who viewed any accommodation with the new order as treason, and who were inalterably opposed to allowing it to become the status quo. These dissenters had been unaccountably silent, but they were about to be heard from.

'You're paying with *cash*?'

Jeffrey Horton nodded wordlessly and fanned six twenty-dollar bills out on the check lane. The young grocery clerk's surprise was nothing new to Horton. Even in the small nowhere towns to which he had been restricting his visits, buying more than a few dollars of goods with cash marked one as, at best, an eccentric. Ever since thumbprint-secured debit cards had become the principal medium of exchange, the shrunken remnant of the cash economy belonged to small-time tax evaders, anti-establishment iconoclasts, debtors on the run, and other assorted cranks and petty criminals.

Horton did not mind being thought of in that company. Indeed, his beard, now full enough to dramatically change the shape of his face, and unfashionably long hair invited the association. An unsavory image brought a certain kind of privacy – while people might stare and regard him warily, they were less inclined to approach and engage him in conversation.

Besides, there was really no choice – green-palming was the only way to escape his notoriety. All but invisible in the digital transaction registers which could document most lives in startling detail, he moved through the Northern Tier states as a ghost, leaving as few traces of his passing as possible. He no longer used commercial transport of any sort, or public accommodations – his *Nomad* pop-up van conversion fulfilled both needs, and much more discreetly. He could go weeks without needing to use his identity, and months without hearing his own name.

True, the periodic cash withdrawals did momentarily betray Horton's location to anyone with access to his bank records. But those withdrawals were always the last thing he did before hitting the road, supplies replenished, for a new and isolated locale which might be 500 klicks or more in any direction. He would then stay in that spot until his privacy was invaded or his supply of cash exhausted, at which point he would return to town and begin the process anew.

He had been robbed once, by someone who had taken note of the thickness of his billfold and followed him back into the woods. He had had three close calls with bears, the last of which had found him wishing for a gun as a seven-hundred-pound black bear threw himself against the camper and tore pieces of trim and the spare tire off the rear door. He had been rousted by rangers and game wardens more times than he could count, though less often since he had acquired the 200mm widefield autocorrelating telescope.

But none of those dangers was nearly as threatening as the prospect of reentering his old life. Even on the worst days, that option had no appeal, and he gave it little thought. The camper had become a cozy home base, especially now that he was working again.

For the telescope had given him more than a plausible excuse for being where he was. It had allowed him to reenter the world of science in a comfortable way, challenging his mind and keeping his hands busy. He was still learning both the sky and the instrument, but had already begun taking advantage of the clear, still North Woods nights to go comet-hunting and count meteors.

Beyond that, he had his books – a lifetime archive of fiction and nonfiction for which there'd never been time – and a Martin steel-string acoustic guitar which he'd always been too busy to master. When he got lonely for the sound of human voices, he could pull in a zonecast from the Netcom 9 platform or Canada's CBC-West satellite, or use his anonymizer and find a chat online. When he grew hungry for human touch, a truck-stop brothel was never very far away.

If he could not quite call himself happy, he could at least take comfort in having found enough purpose to keep getting out of bed at the start of his day, and enough peace to get to sleep again at day's end.

Then came the call that turned everything upside down.

His comset was still configured to defer all calls to v-mail, and to automatically purge all mail with no priority flag. There were very few people who had Horton's current priority key – Lee, his family, Karl Brohier, the Terabyte business office, his lawyer, his accountant, his personal DataSearch librarian – and he still had the priority alarm disabled. Once every few days, usually in the middle of the night, he would check the queue of waiting messages, replying to some, archiving others, disposing of the rest.

The message tagged as USGOV | TREASDEPT-MOST URGENT-TO:JHORTON had been waiting for two days before Horton saw it. Its envelope was double-encrypted, both Personal and Secret. Both bindings dissolved with no alarms, leaving a short but chilling v-mail.

'Dr Horton, this is Agent Keith Havens of the Special Protection Division of the Secret Service. Please contact me immediately when you receive this message. Dr Karl Brohier is gravely ill, and insists on seeing you. I'm to arrange your transportation to the secure facility where he's being cared for.'

Horton tried calling Brohier instead. There was a personalized message waiting for him.

'Jeffrey – it's just my luck that when you finally do decide to call me, I'm indisposed. Count it as payback for making yourself such a hermit these last few months. Pour yourself a glass of wine – I'll call you back before it's gone.'

It sounded like something that had been recorded a long time ago, and Horton did not trust Brohier's promise. He reopened the Havens message and clicked the SecureCall icon.

'Dr Horton.' Havens was wearing an olive-green t-shirt, and his crewcut hair was matted. It was obvious he had been sleeping. 'Thank goodness. Where are you?'

'Wisconsin.'

'What's the nearest town?'

'Eh – Grandview.'

Havens looked away and squinted, as though at another display to the side. 'Chequamegon area?'

'Yes.'

'Do you have a vehicle available?'

'Yes. A camper.'

'Very good.' Havens looked back toward Horton. 'There's a civil airport at Hayward, on County Road Twenty-Seven. We can have someone there in two hours. They'll identify themselves to you with the codeword "Candyland".'

'Like the game?'

'Like the game.'

490

'I'll be there.'

Havens nodded approvingly. 'Dr Horton, there's a great deal at stake – personal considerations aside, it's extremely important to the security of the nation that we get you and Dr Brohier together in the same room. I strongly recommend that you try not to call attention to yourself while you're out there alone. Stay off the air – stay in your vehicle until you're contacted. You'll have answers to all your questions in a couple of hours.'

It was a perfect set-up. Worry clouded Jeffrey Horton's thinking; it did not even occur to him to doubt the authenticity of the message. Though Brohier himself had never spoken of it, Horton knew from Lee's letters that the senior scientist was being treated for an enlarged heart, and that he had been 'swallowed up by Washington' after the successful Jammer tests.

So neither the news nor the source of it raised any warning flags, especially since all of the security keys on the message behaved exactly as expected. When a dark blue SUV turned into the air-field's grassy parking area a few minutes after sunrise, Horton regarded it hopefully. When two men with military haircuts and a wary, alert bearing emerged and approached, Horton felt an eager relief.

'Good morning, Dr Horton,' said the older of the two, bending at the waist to peer through the partially-lowered driver's window. 'We're your escort to Candyland. You can call me George.'

At that point, Horton experienced his first and only quiver of uncertainty. 'I was expecting a helicopter, or something.'

'It's en route – there was nothing suitable for this field at Grissom, so we had to go all the way to Scott for a C-12. You managed to pick a state where we don't have many resources.'

'Sorry about that.'

'It'll be fine. Are you ready to go?'

Horton patted the soft-sided sport bag on the seat beside him. 'This is all I need.'

'Good.' George jerked his thumb in the direction of his companion. 'This is Agent Loomis – he and another agent are going to drive your vehicle in, so you'll have it available to you when you're ready to leave Candyland. If you'd care to wait with me in the four-by-four, we can let them get started – they have a long drive ahead of them.'

'Of course,' Horton said. He climbed out, bag in hand, and surrendered the keys to Loomis. 'The papers are in the door pocket. Oh, and watch it – the parking brake sticks.'

'We'll be careful,' said Loomis, who nodded – more to the other agent than to Horton – and clambered into the seat.

Horton would end up replaying the next few seconds over and over in his mind. While he crossed the grass to the passenger side of the SUV, Loomis backed the camper out as if to leave. But at the last moment, he braked hard and stopped short behind the second vehicle, blocking the view from the main road.

'Hurry, Doctor – we have company,' said George, grabbing Horton and shoving him forward. Horton did not resist, thinking that the agents were protecting him. The door in front of Horton flew open, and other hands reached for him and hauled him inside. Lying on his back on the floor, Horton looked up into the face of the man who had called himself Keith Havens.

'Change of plans, Doctor,' the man said, and sprayed a bitter-tasting aerosol in Horton's face.

The next thing he knew was blackness and silence.

Jeffrey Horton's senses returned one at a time. At first, everything they told him only confused him. Even once the messages became persistent enough that he had to accept them as real, his staggered mind had trouble assembling them.

He seemed to have no limbs. There was a constant roar, punctuated by creaks and banging. He was being violently jostled within a confined space made of hard, irregular surfaces. Burnt oil and mildew jousted in his nostrils. His face was frozen into a mask that had no mouth. He was in darkness, but there was light just beyond. There were voices, but none of the words made sense.

Then there was a sound he recognized – car doors opening and slamming shut.

And something that was not quite silence, but passed for it after the bath of noise in which he had been submerged.

More door sounds, much closer.

492

Sudden light, blindingly intense, as the blanket covering him was jerked away.

A rush of clean, sweet air.

At last, recognition: he was lying on his side in the rear cargo area of the SUV, wrists and ankles taped.

'Dr Horton. Not too uncomfortable, I trust.'

It was a now-familiar voice. Squinting out through the open rear doors of the SUV, Horton recognized the face that went with it. The duct tape across Horton's mouth would have prevented any reply, even if he had not still been too stunned to speak.

'Get him out of there.'

Two men moved forward, grabbed Horton's elbows, and hauled him out and to his feet. Horton's legs almost buckled under him; only the hands firmly holding him kept him upright.

'It's time for a proper introduction,' said the man who had spoken – the man whose v-mail had precipitated everything. 'I'm Colonel Robert Wilkins, regional commander of the People's Army of Righteous Justice. And you, Dr Horton, are a prisoner of war.'

It was only then that Horton could identify a sound which had been pushing at his awareness since the vehicle's doors had been opened – the intermittent sound of gunfire, coming from beyond the trees.

31:

'War is not the normal state of the human family in its higher development, but merely a feature of barbarism lasting on through the transition of the race, from the savage to the scholar.'

– Elizabeth Cady Stanton

The tape came off Jeffrey Horton's ankles and knees, but remained on his wrists and across his mouth for the walk through the forest compound of the People's Army of Righteous Justice. Along the way, Colonel Wilkins said nothing, but allowed Horton to see enough to raise his already high level of apprehension to the level of near-panic.

There were camouflaged vehicles – SUVs, pickups, one Hummer, and two vans – concealed under netting at the edge of the woods. At least three of them had mounts for automatic weapons. Others had metal-plate armor around their engine compartments, and flak batting on the doors and tailgates.

The sounds of gunfire were coming from a marksmanship range with six shooting stations on one side of a sloping clearing and a banked-earth target barrier on the other side. Nearby, Horton caught a glimpse of a practical shooting course set up amongst the trees, with pop-up and drop-down targets in human silhouette.

Even away from the ranges, there was plenty of firepower in evidence. Every adult male was armed, most with both a rifle and a sidearm. The rifles tended toward Colt AR-15s and other military-style semi-automatics, though Horton spotted more than one true assault rifle. At the other extreme, several of the older militiamen had bolt-action deer rifles, and one short-legged, round-bodied gnome carried a Winchester lever-action carbine.

In all, Horton counted at least twenty-six armed men and

a dozen or more women. He heard children's voices, but the youngest person he saw was a boy of twelve or thirteen, and as he was armed, Horton counted him with the men.

Above ground, there were two long buildings that Horton took for bunkhouses, a cook tent surrounded by split-log benches, a bathhouse, and a rank of portable toilets in drab olive green. The bunkhouses were old, and reminded Horton of a seedy summer camp. *Summer camp for toy soldiers –*

Some distance from that cluster were two new steel sheds with guards posted outside. All the structures were hidden in the trees, invisible from above.

At ground level and below, the compound boasted slit trenches on its perimeter, foxholes in its interior, and half a dozen low earthen mounds with metal storm-shelter doors. It was to one of these that Horton was led.

Wilkins opened the single metal door, then turned back to Horton.

'It can get a little close in there, and I don't want you choking on your vomit,' he said. Then, with one quick motion, he reached up and tore the wide band of tape off Horton's mouth.

It took patches of beard and skin with it, leaving Horton gasping with sudden pain as the escorts pushed him through the open door and into the pit below. He rolled over twice, awkwardly, and ended up face-down in a dank, fetid mat of sodden wood chips and mud. When the door clanged shut above him, he was in darkness once more.

By the time they returned for him, it was nearly as dark outside the pit as in. The cool night air that swirled through the opened hatch brought his own humiliating stink to his nostrils – he had lost the fight and fouled himself hours ago.

'Get him out of there,' someone said from above, and hands reached down to grab him by the arms and drag him roughly up through the hatchway.

'He's seriously skunky, Colonel. I pity the next person who has to use Shelter Six.'

Horton swung his head around, searching for Wilkins. He found him when the Colonel spoke again.

'Clean him up and bring him to the men's cabin,' Wilkins said, meeting Horton's angry gaze with a cool detachment. 'And then burn his clothes.'

There were too many strong hands to struggle against. Horton was stripped, stood up against a tree, and doused with bucket after bucket of well-cold water. Then, naked, dripping wet, and shivering uncontrollably, he was quick-marched to one of the long houses and ushered inside.

By the light of three single bulbs hanging below the roof trusses, he glimpsed a long wall of triple bunks, a desk with a comset, an empty rifle rack, and a silent half-circle of men awaiting him. In the middle was Wilkins, his expression unreadable.

'Vincent, get Dr Horton a towel,' he said quietly.

The balding man at the right end of the circle brought Horton a rectangle of cloth no bigger than a kitchen towel. Still shivering, Horton dabbed at his sodden hair and wet shoulders, trying unsuccessfully to forget his nakedness. As though reading Horton's thoughts with his coolly appraising gaze, Wilkins raised a hand in signal to someone standing behind him.

'Some clothes for Dr Horton,' Wilkins said.

The clothing was a prison-style jumpsuit in bright hunter orange, but Horton was grateful for it nonetheless. He was also puzzled by the consideration. Forcing him to stand there naked and chilled to the bone would have been more in keeping with the treatment he'd received so far – and probably recommended by whatever psych-war handbook Wilkins had learned his trade from.

'Did you all know that Dr Horton and I have an acquaintance in common?' Wilkins asked, glancing sideways at his companions. 'Did you know that, Dr Horton?'

'It's a small world,' Horton said with a shrug, refusing to be tempted into asking.

'She goes by Pamela Bonaventure now – but that's her married name, right, Jeffrey? When she won her Olympic shooting medal, she was known as Pamela Horton.'

Hearing his sister's name from Wilkins's lips made Horton acutely uncomfortable. 'Where would you know her from?'

'Well, unlike you, Jeffrey, she's not in hiding. Our paths crossed at the NTSA Sport Pistol Nationals. She shot very well, considering she's only had the Weiss-Cushing for a few months.'

The discomfort exploded into a fearful rage. 'What – have you been spying on her?'

'No, hardly. We had a nice lunch together after the match, that's all.'

'You?'

'Why not me? And then we went out to the range and traded pistols for a couple of dozen rounds.' He laughed to himself. 'I'm afraid she very much had the advantage over me – the targets I practice with have bull's-eyes the size of a head.'

'If you're trying to tell me you can get to my family, too –'

'Get to your family – oh, no, Dr Horton, you misunderstand. I simply want you to know that we're aware of your background. We know that you and your family are shooters. We know about Pamela. We know that your father is a Life Member of the NAR.'

'And what does all that mean to you? What does that have to do with my being here?'

'It means that we're prepared to believe that you were an unwitting participant in Breland's great treason,' said the man sitting to Wilkins's left. He had a crooked nose, an American flag pin on the lapel of his dirty yellow shirt, and a restless right hand. 'It means that if you tell us you didn't know what they intended to do with your research, you'll find that we're disposed to believe you.'

'And then I can leave?'

'And then you can join us,' said Wilkins. 'You can help us put things right.'

'How can I do that?'

'Tell us the secrets of the Trigger and the Jammer. We'll take care of the rest.'

'The secrets of the Trigger,' Horton repeated slowly.

'Yes,' said the second man. 'How to shield an armory, and how to detect a Jammer field before you're inside it.'

'What types of explosives are immune –' offered a third man, and others joined in.

'The true maximum range.'

'Which of the new satellites contain the big zappers.'

'What the UN troops are going to be using in place of gun-powder –'

'There are no secrets,' Horton said, interrupting.

'Excuse me?' said Wilkins.

'There are no secrets. I released everything. Nothing was held back. It's all in the packet we published to the net.'

'What about the Jammer?'

'I didn't work on the Jammer,' Horton protested, then frowned. 'But it's no different – it's just a refinement of the Trigger. It works on the same nitrate chemistry. It must have the same attenuation curve. The electronics must be vulnerable to an electromagnetic pulse, just like the Trigger and your comset and most everything else that goes into civilization – you don't have any nukes, do you? I suppose not.'

'You're not telling us anything that we couldn't have found in *Popular Science*,' the man with the crooked nose said, scowling.

'Don't you understand? That's the point,' said Horton. 'There isn't anything to know that hasn't been in *Popular Science*. I gave it away so everyone could have it. I wasn't going to let it disappear, and I wasn't going to let it be controlled by the people who liked the status quo. If that means I'm back on your traitor list –'

He shrugged, affecting a casualness he did not feel. If his life depended on being useful to them, there was not much cause for hope.

'If you don't try to help resist a tyrannical government that's disarming and enslaving the people, then you *are* a traitor.' The speaker spat contemptuously.

'I disarmed *them* first. Isn't that enough?'

'Hell, no!' one of the men tersely. 'Our arms are what gave us a chance against them. They can replace their guns – they have all kinds of power. They can replace them with sheer numbers. They control the media, and the purse-strings, and a nation of sheeple sucking at the tit of statism. We have to have our guns, Doctor, to break their hold. We have to be able to count on our guns if we're ever going to be free again.'

'There's no way to shield an armory. We never learned how to remotely detect a Trigger field. So if that's what you expected from me, you made a mistake bringing me here.'

498

'If we made a mistake, we'll correct it,' said Wilkins. 'But are you absolutely certain you have nothing for us?'

It was a question with ominous overtones, and Horton cast frantically about for some bone to toss them. 'I can tell you that you can stop worrying about satellites. The range varies with the cube of the power, just like it says in the manual – so it's easy to make the little ones go and just this side of impossible to make something that'd work from orbit.'

'Not even powered by a nuclear power plant?'

'The kind we have down here, maybe. Not the kind we can put up there.'

'So it *would* be possible, with enough power.'

Horton turned his head in the direction of the voice. 'But there isn't enough power – that's the point.'

The man's expression turned to one of disgust and contempt as he looked to Wilkins. 'How can we believe anything he says? Either he's not far enough inside to know about Pink, or he's so far inside that he's gonna lie about it.'

Horton also looked to Wilkins. 'What is he talking about?'

'DARPA has had an operational deuterium microfusion plant for twenty years,' the colonel said slowly, stretching his legs out.

'Oh, that's nonsense. An Internet hoax.'

'Hardly. It was developed for the Shark and Falcon long-duration stealth spycraft. Project Pink Drum. But they're everywhere now – key government installations, radio stations, anything they're going to need when they start the blackouts. You can detect a Pink with an old-style AM radio – you pick up an interference band at twelve-forty when you get within a couple of miles.'

'*What* blackouts?'

'It's part of the Federal pacification strategy, in case of civil disobedience.'

As far as Horton was concerned, the conversation had abruptly veered off the road and into the deep underbrush of surrealism. 'Are you getting this from a newsfeed, or your kid's comic books?' he said, his contempt getting the better of his caution.

But Wilkins did not show any sign of having taken offense. 'Even someone of your intelligence and accomplishments can be compartmentalized and propagandized – our enemies are very practiced in mind control and deception. We will help lift the fog from your eyes, Dr Horton – and when you are seeing clearly, I have no doubt that you will apply yourself and your talents to our common cause.'

'So am I a prisoner of war, or a recruit?'

'Which do you want to be?' Wilkins said, standing to signal the end of the audience. 'We will give you the facts – the real truth. You will make the choice.'

As they ushered him out of the long house, Horton took notice of the time displayed on the comset's screen-blanker. With that piece of information, it would take only a few seconds' glimpse of open sky for him to gauge how far he had been moved, and in what direction – the rotation of the bowl of the sky would reveal all to those who knew how to read it.

But the group's anxieties about being spied on from above thwarted him. The heavy canopy of leaves under which the camp was hidden yielded him only a fleeting glimpse of a tiny patch of night sky on the way back to Shelter Six.

Horton begged a side trip to the latrine before they locked him back underground, but all he gained from it was a peek at his own face in a metal mirror. He looked haggard, haunted, and unaccountably old.

'Do you have Dr Brohier, too?' he asked as he was led back to his tiny prison. 'Is he in another one of these holes?'

'If I knew, I wouldn't be authorized to tell you,' one of his escorts said affably as he threw open the shelter door.

They left his hands unbound, which was as great a mercy as the fresh layer of wood chips.

He fell asleep to the sound of distant voices singing hymns to the glory of god.

Monica Frances could not believe what she was reading. The weekly surveillance report on Dr Jeffrey Horton had been tendered with standard priority, even though its contents were potentially explosive. After securing her desk comset, she stormed down the corridor of Section 7 in pursuit of the report's author. It was not enough to sit there and send her sprites after Benhold Tustin – she needed to breathe fire in his face.

She found him in the 'cave', the windowless home of the Technical Services Division and its ultrasecret data-gathering technologies. He was in a secure booth with a Techserv resource librarian, and the expression on Tustin's face when he saw her told the rest of the story: he knew how serious the problem was, and had been hoping to resolve it before it came to her attention.

'What happened?' she demanded. 'You were supposed to maintain contact with him. That was the President's direct and explicit order.'

'I don't know what happened. We're just not getting anything back from our pings.'

'What does the tracings book say?'

'No activity on any of his comm accounts. His credit card was used a few hours ago in Evanston.'

'Chicago! He hasn't been near a city bigger than Fergus Falls for as long as we've been tracking him.'

'I'm aware of that,' Tustin said grimly.

'Could he have discovered our trackers?'

'He's not supposed to be able to.'

'Is there anything else in the tracings book?'

'Just the GPS history for the transponders. The comset trace ends north of Eau Claire, a day and a half ago. The camper trace terminated about sixteen hours ago, near Iron River, in the Upper Peninsula. It's just possible that those are two points on the same route'

'So the van went to Michigan, and the debit card to Illinois?'

'I suppose he could have sold the van –'

'To finance an irresistible craving for Chicago stuffed pizza, I suppose? Why didn't you bring this to my attention sooner?'

'We really don't *know* that there's a problem –'

She looked past him to the librarian. 'Check that Evanston transaction – find out if it was thumbprint verified.'

A few moments later the librarian had the answer. 'It was a no-contact purchase – gasoline and a car wash at an automated station.'

'I'd say we have a problem, Mr Tustin. How long has it been now?'

Tustin glanced at his watch. 'Forty-four hours, give or take.'

501

She shook her head. 'We'd better go see the Director.'

Jacob Hilger, director of the Defense Intelligence Agency, studied the incident map and timeline Monica Frances had thrown together.

'This has been a strictly routine tracking job from day one, correct?'

'Absolutely,' said Tustin. 'There's never been any interest from the White House. We've never gotten a request to get any closer. I don't even know that anyone other than Mrs Frances has ever seen our reports.'

'What about that?' Hilger asked, looking to the project security supervisor.

'He's right. By the time we located and tagged Dr Horton, Dr Brohier already had the Jammer operational and had brought in Dr Bennington-Hastings. The other shoe never dropped. We kept up with Dr Horton anyway, just in case.'

'How?'

'Piggyback transponders on the global-position circuits in Dr Horton's camper and comset. Our agents did a black-box swap on the van and replaced the comset with a doctored dupe. At every tenth refresh, we received a location report. And we could ping the transponders at any time for a real-time fix.'

'So long as the parent systems have power,' Tustin added.

'Did you ever have a data blackout before?'

'Just one, on the camper, about seven hours long. But that same day he had an emergency road service call and a repair bill for a new alternator.'

Pursing his lips, Hilger shook his head. 'I can't see the same scenario here.'

'No, sir,' said Frances. 'I think someone's grabbed him.'

'I read it the same way. Do you have anyone in the field on this yet?'

'Three teams – one in Chicago, one en route to a trace in the U.P., and one heading for Dr Horton's last known fixed location in northern Wisconsin.' Frances glanced at the clock. 'They should be arriving on site just about now.'

'They won't find Horton,' Hilger quietly predicted.

'Probably not, sir. But maybe they can find something that'll lead us in the right direction.'

'Finding the camper would be a good start. Who's coordinating on the ground?'

'Captain Whalen, with the Crequamegon Forest team.'

'How about on the water?'

'Excuse me?'

Hilger traced the serpentine Lake Superior shoreline of northern Wisconsin with a fingertip. 'Look where he was. This is the gateway to the Atlantic – not a single security checkpoint between here and Europe, or Africa, or South America. Dr Horton could have been put on any boat bigger than a Boston Whaler that put out from any dock along here in the last two days. And he could have been moved to any other boat since.'

'Or to a float plane,' said Tustin.

'Bite your tongue. It'll be hard enough if he's still on the water. You'd better bring the Coast Guard in, have them get some people to the Soo Locks fast, try to keep the cork in the bottle. And in the meantime, get with the National Reconnaissance Office to see what they can tell us about traffic on the lake.' Hilger sighed. 'Summer on the Great Lakes. We may need to call in the whole Section.'

'Are you going to notify the White House?' Frances asked.

Grimacing, the director said, 'Let's see if we can't find out what's happened first. Let's wait for the first reports from the field.'

The first reports were in by midnight, and the story they told brought a reluctant and unhappy Jacob Hilger to the White House gates. He showed his ID to the scanner and his face to the security detail and was directed to the East Wing gym – a former staff office Breland had had outfitted with Nautilus gear, a treadmill, and a rowing machine.

Before Hilger reached the gym, he passed through two more Secret Service checkpoints and was joined by Chief of Staff Charles Paugh. 'Leaving Amanda to fend for herself with the new baby tonight, eh, Jacob?' Paugh said cheerfully. 'How is Gavin?'

'Growing like a weed,' Hilger said. 'Do you ever go home, Charlie?'

'Why would I? I have a closet under the stairs, a bedroll, and my very own flashlight – plus I know where the State dinner leftovers are kept. Here we are, right through here.'

They found the President sitting on the end of the back bench, mopping up perspiration with a small towel. His gray Philadelphia Phillies workout jersey was soaked almost to his waist.

'Has either of you gentlemen noticed that once you're north of forty, you end up just as tired and twice as sore doing half as much?' Breland asked, dabbing at the side of his neck. 'I don't know how Ryan and Spahn played as long as they did.'

'I don't know who Ryan and Spahn are,' said Paugh. 'Did either one of them have a decent jump shot?'

'Heathen,' said Breland. 'Jacob, what do you have for me?'

'Jeffrey Horton has disappeared. It looks like he's been abducted.'

Breland let the towel drop to the floor. 'The hell you say. What happened?'

'I'll tell you what I can, which is less than we'd like to know,' said Hilger. 'Two days ago, Dr Horton had a secured conversation with someone who was spoofing a DOD account. We don't know who he was talking to or what was said, but it appears that shortly afterward, he packed up and drove to Hayward Municipal Airport. Something happened there.'

'How do you know?'

'From that point on, the traces for Dr Horton's comset and his camper separate until they're about twenty-five kilometers apart, heading south on US Fifty-Three toward Eau Claire.'

'Two vehicles.'

'Presumably – and no telling if Horton himself was in either of them. The trace for the comset vanishes around Chippewa Falls. The trace for the camper continues east to Wausau, then back north again into Michigan.'

'Wausau? That takes us pretty close to Tigerton, doesn't it?' asked Paugh.

'Yes, we noticed that.'

'Tigerton?' asked Breland.

'Former home of the Posse Comitatus,' said Hilger. 'If they still existed, they'd definitely be on the list of usual suspects.'

'Are we sure that they don't?'

'Well – the JATF should be able to tell you better than I can,'

Hilger said, looking uncomfortable. 'What we do know is that the camper was abandoned on a dirt road on the edge of the Ottawa National Forest. It had been stripped, and someone had tried to burn what was left with an incendiary bomb – the smoke attracted a Forest Service ranger, which is how we got our hands on it so quickly.'

'A bomb? Not a match in the gas tank?'

'No – military-issue magnesium flare, probably with a timer or a fuse, so they're long gone when it goes up. We had to take a serial number off the rear axle to identify it as Horton's.'

'Jesus,' said Breland.

'I need to know how far you want us to go with this,' said Hilger. 'We really don't have the expertise or the authority to do criminal investigations – though we're ready to support one with all the domestic intelligence assets we have. But somebody else needs to take the point.'

Breland looked to Paugh. 'What options are there? FBI?'

'Going by the book, we should give it to the FBI,' the chief of staff agreed. 'But their rule book is the thickest, which means they can't always move the fastest. What's at stake – Horton's life, or some larger national security interest? What good is he to whoever grabbed him? What does he know?'

'Not very much,' Hilger said. 'By his own choice, he's been out of the loop for some time. Besides, most of the Trigger material has effectively been declassified already, thanks to those Terabyte people giving away the store. I'd judge the national security risk slight.'

'But would whoever grabbed him necessarily know that?' Breland asked.

'They might. They knew enough to get Horton's private address and flag codes, and to spoof a secure DOD commlink. That's the real national security issue here – that whoever grabbed him had help from someone inside the Pentagon's comm net. That's reason enough to go hard at this.'

'Dr Horton's life is reason enough,' Breland said sharply. 'He may not have been kidnapped for information. There's more than a few people who might want revenge.'

'If you want revenge, you kill him nasty and then leave the body where it'll be found,' Paugh said grimly.

'And what's to say that's not where this is going?' asked Breland. 'What are the other options, Charlie?'

'Army Intelligence could take it on the strength of the DOD penetration. For that matter, so could the CIA, if we're willing to pretend to know that the penetration was foreign, not domestic.'

'If it was your brother – or your son – and your first consideration was finding him and getting him back safely –'

Paugh and Hilger exchanged glances. 'I'd want to keep it all as quiet as possible, so as not to spook them,' said Hilger. 'Zero public profile, completely compartmentalized within the intelligence and law enforcement communities. I'd say Unit Thirteen – the Special Forces Unified Command domestic counterterrorism team. We plug them in with Defense Intelligence, CIA, National Recon Office, NSA, and give them their head. Odds are that they might have a list of likely suspects already in hand.'

'What will it take to get that started?'

'General Stepak can coordinate,' said Paugh. 'Everyone we want involved already reports to him, except the Company – and that can be worked out.'

'All right. If I have to sign something, get it drawn up.'

'That can be taken care of later,' said Paugh.

'I have a question –' Hilger began.

'Go.'

'Dr Brohier. Should he be notified? Should any of the Terabyte people be involved?'

'Where is Dr Brohier now?' asked Breland.

'He's been staying with Aron Goldstein in Maryland, working there in the mansion. As fragile as he is, he shouldn't be working at all – he should be in a hospital. But he won't stand for it.' Hilger chuckled ruefully. 'So Mr Goldstein has turned two rooms at the far end of his mansion into an emergency medicine field hospital, with a full ER staff – including a cardiologist – on duty around the clock. Last I heard, Dr Brohier still has no idea that they're there, or that he has a full suite of biomonitors in his bed.'

'I think he would want to know about Horton,' said Breland.

'What use could he make of the information?' Paugh asked. 'Is there some up side here that I'm not seeing? We can tell him when it's over, one way or the other – and spare him the suspense.'

506

Breland looked unhappy at that, but did not argue. 'I guess I'd better go wake up General Stepak.'

Dawn gave Jeffrey Horton his first look at his prison cell. He had already explored it with his hands, but only his eyes could make it real.

The soft glow of daylight leaking in revealed the three gun slits which also served as air vents, and the fist-sized chimney overhead which provided the draw. The steel cone which formed the ceiling also had empty spring clips which might have been meant for water bottles, lanterns, and other supplies. Three rungs of chain ladder dangled below the door.

Below the ceiling cone, the walls were packed black dirt threaded through with wiry, shovel-cut tree roots. Shelter Six was just deep enough for a standing adult to fire through the gun slits at shoulder level, and just wide enough for a family of four or five to huddle around the shooter's legs.

The presence of the shelters in the living area of the camp spoke volumes to Horton about the outlook of those who had built them. To Wilkins and his army, it was perfectly conceivable, an ordinary expectation, that if they were discovered they would be attacked with deadly force. Horton doubted they saw any other possibility. And if they were attacked, surrender was not an option – they were prepared to send their families to the shelters and resist to the death.

Those were the rules of engagement they had prepared for. They were already at war – at war against the world he had forsaken.

And, realizing that, Horton understood that his only choices were to join the revolution, or rejoin the world – and that he would pay a terrible price if he made the wrong choice.

They came for him early, and allowed him to use not only the latrine but the shower before bringing him to the meal circle for the last plateful of eggs and hash scraped from an enormous skillet. It was the first food he had had since the Reese's cups he eaten while waiting in the camper at the airport, two days ago – or was it three? He ate greedily, barely tasting what passed his lips, and washed it down with mug after mug of bottled water, until his shrunken stomach felt uncomfortably full.

He had nothing to say while he ate, and the women and children who were finishing up their meals as he arrived had nothing to say to him. Their quiet conversations were so self-consciously banal that they made him acutely aware of his status as outsider and pariah.

It was not until Colonel Wilkins appeared and settled on the bench to his right that Horton felt the chill begin to thaw. 'Feeling a little better with a little something in your stomach?'

'Almost civilized,' Horton said. He hesitated, then added, 'Thank you.'

'Oh, it's Jean here that you should thank,' Wilkins said, gesturing toward a wide-hipped woman sitting half-way around the circle, quietly sipping at a cup of coffee. 'The menu's short at Cafe Bivouac, but Jean has a way of turning plain into fancy, even when we won't let her have more than one pot and one skillet.'

She blushed at the praise, but her features frosted over when Horton tried to meet her eye and add his thanks. 'Your first thanks should be to the Creator, not to me.'

Wilkins laughed lightly. 'Skipped grace, did you, Jeffrey? You'll discover that's not done lightly at Jean's table.'

'I'm out of the habit, I'm afraid.'

'We can help you with that,' Wilkins said. 'All done there?'
'Yes.'

'Then let's walk.'

Wilkins dismissed the two men who had been standing guard over Horton, and led him eastward along a wooded ridge line at a leisurely pace. 'I understand you've been asking about Karl Brohier.'

'I want to know if you have him. I want to know if he's all right.'

'I can answer the first of those with more confidence than the second. No, we do not have Dr Brohier. His age, his socialist political views, and his unreconstructed atheism made him unattractive.'

'Then explain to me how you knew that your lie about him being sick wouldn't trip you up. If I'd gotten Karl instead of that message –'

'Your calls were diverted at the satellite. A simple matter of

508

incrementing the address with a virus. You never had any chance of talking to anyone but the voice files on a comset closer to the Rockies than the Smokies.'

'So Karl is okay?'

'I don't know,' said Wilkins. 'The fact is, he dropped out of sight about eight weeks ago. Maybe if you tell us where he is, we can try to find out how he is.'

'I don't know where he is.'

'I see,' said Wilkins. 'Are you a student of history, Dr Horton?'

'No more than I had to be to satisfy my undergrad social studies requirements.'

Wilkins nodded thoughtfully. 'That makes you a perfectly average American, I'm afraid – blissfully ignorant. The rigorous study of history was chased out of the schools by feminists and black racists, on the grounds that we had nothing to learn from the lives of dead white men. You were probably subjected to Contemporary World Studies or some other flavor of fuzzy feel-good multiculturalism.'

'SS-201, "Contemporary Problems in International Relations".'

'Where "contemporary" means "within the lifetime of the teenaged students". You see, they really don't want the public to understand. It isn't education they're offering – it's programming. You can be sold any sort of spoiled fruit if they can keep you from remembering what the real thing tastes like.'

'So what's the missing context for this?'

'That every genocide of the twentieth century was preceded by gun control. That every totalitarian regime of the twentieth century sought a monopoly on the power of arms. That history reveals there is a natural affinity of governments for tyranny, and demonstrates the only hope of successful resistance lies in the natural right of free people to keep and bear arms.

'That's the only reason the Constitution contains a Second Amendment. It's not so the hunters can keep their sport, or the wealthy can keep their possessions. It's not even so women can fight off rapists, or men can defend their families from predators – human and animal.

'No, we need our arms because we want the government to be afraid of us. And if they forget to be afraid of what three hundred

509

million weapons in the hands of seventy million patriots can do to police who won't protect and judges who won't punish and lawmakers who make rules for everyone but themselves and soldiers who obey unconstitutional orders, then we are morally bound to remind them.'

'"The tree of liberty –"'

'" – must be refreshed from time to time with the blood of patriots and tyrants."' Stopping, Wilkins rolled up his right sleeve to reveal a tattoo of a tree with red roots just below his shoulder. 'Dr Horton, those words should have been written into the Constitution – into the Second Amendment itself. The Founding Fathers missed a chance to make their meaning inescapably clear. But those who study history know that the Second Amendment was meant as the central government's self-destruct button. And I'm afraid you are responsible for cutting the wires.'

'That's not fair,' Horton said. 'The Trigger was discovered by accident – scientific serendipity. We weren't working on disarmament. We weren't working for the government. Discoveries come when they will. If it hadn't been us, it would have been someone else, and not long after.'

'I have no complaints with your conduct as a researcher, Doctor. It's your conduct as a citizen that I have to question. Just imagine what a powerful tool for democracy the Trigger would have been in the hands of the patriot militias. The next time the government dared to send out its armies of oppression, we would have been able to send them back disarmed, disabled, and disheartened – with no idea how it had been done.' Wilkins smiled wistfully at the thought. 'Oh, to see that day –'

Then he shook his head. 'But giving it to Washington – no, that was a horrendous mistake. And unless you act to undo your mistake, you'll also be responsible for the tyranny that's sure to follow. They have nothing to fear now.'

'I gave the Trigger to everyone,' Horton said. 'Karl did the same with the Jammer. That's the way it should be. No monopolies. No imbalance of power. No secret weapons.'

'I'm sure you thought that that would be the result. But you still haven't gauged the depth of their deceit. You were betrayed.'

'What are you talking about?'

510

'The *federales* haven't canceled or retired a single weapon system. Every grunt still spends as much time training with his M-16 as ever. The Lake City Army Ammunition Plant in Missouri is still going strong. Every major police force in the country still has a Gestapo unit with a rack of AR-15s.' He stopped walking and turned toward Horton. 'Now, why are they going to all that expense and trouble, if these tens of thousands of Triggers and Jammers in basements and closets and trunks and briefcases have rendered the gun obsolete?'

'Inertia. Familiarity. Professional caution. Future shock. Political clout of enormous military contractors –'

'You're overlooking the obvious explanation.'

'Which is –'

'The government got the public to bring the Trigger into their lives like it was some sort of cute puppy that would grow up to be their kid's friend and protect the house at night. The only problem is, the government had already trained it to lie down on command – so it's no threat to them.'

Horton squinted at the militia commander. 'Sorry, I'm not following.'

'They kept their guns because they know they're still going to be able to use them. They allowed us to have Horton devices because they know they can shut them down at any time – which they'll do as soon as we've finished disarming ourselves for them. They were never going to let us disarm them, Dr Horton. Never in a million years.'

'You think there's some sort of remote control circuit in the civilian Triggers? A secret kill switch?'

'It's the only reasonable explanation. But in all of them, not just the civilian model – weapons have a way of changing sides during a war.'

'I don't believe this.'

'Oh, it's there. And you can find it for us, Dr Horton – if you don't already know where it is.'

Wilkins resumed walking, giving no sign he noticed or even cared if Horton was following. The physicist took a quick survey around him to see if anyone else was watching; when he found no one in sight, he gave a passing thought to bolting into the woods.

But it was too early. He had no resources, no firm idea where he was, and therefore no real chance of escaping – especially wearing a bright orange jumpsuit. Instead, he made himself hurry after Wilkins.

'Look, Colonel, this just isn't possible. Those systems were made by Aurum Industries. I can't believe Aron Goldstein would have any part in such a wild scheme.'

'Why not? The propertied elite have always supported gun control. If you own factories and banks, you have the army and the police to protect you and yours – and every reason to want the poor and the wage-slave working poor disarmed. The wealthy are the government, Dr Horton.' He sniffed disdainfully. 'Besides – a Jew, selling merchandise at cost? What more do you need to hear?'

'He's a humanitarian, for Christ's sake – he believes that guns are tools of oppression, not liberation. And with no small reason.'

'The proof of what he really believes is etched in the control circuits of every Trigger and Jammer he sells.'

'I'm sure it is – and just as sure that you're wrong about what it is.' Horton felt the flush of anger creeping up his neck. 'Do you have one here?'

'A Trigger? Yes, of course. Knowest thine enemy, says the Good Book. Ah – here, come this way. This is what I wanted to show you.'

With an exasperated sigh, Horton followed Wilkins through a nearly solid wall of brush that blocked their way. At the other end of the invisible trail, the ground fell away before them, descending steeply to a rocky valley meadow cut in half by a shallow stream. Beyond were more hills, some heavy with trees, some as bare as the slope at their feet. Wilkins had wedged himself into a perch between the trunk of a hickory tree and a large rounded boulder bulging out of the ground.

'You could have just sent me the postcard,' Horton said. 'I don't know what I'm looking at.'

'I know you don't,' said Wilkins. He swept his hand from side to side, taking in the entire panorama. 'This is what it all looked like before human beings arrived. Not a sign anywhere of our hand on the land. Do you know how rare that's become?'

512

'Are you a conservationist, then? I wouldn't have guessed that as your motivation.'

'There's a great lesson in front of you, if you'll allow yourself to see it –'

'"Mind your step" is the first that occurs to me.'

'The essence of nature is freedom. There are no statutes and ordinances and treaties out there, no forms and lists and taxes. Man, in his natural state, is also free. That's what our natural rights are, Jeffrey – God's guarantee that we have a place in His creation, and the necessary tools to fulfill our part in His plan. That's what the Constitution was supposed to protect – the right of free Christian men and women to follow their faith and conscience. No laws but His holy law. No authority higher than His truth.

'We strayed from that purpose, and our people, our nation was cast into the darkness. But we have found our way back, and we will lead the way for others. We are living in the Light, Jeffrey – the Light of His love. You have to choose whether you want to live in the light, or return to the darkness.'

Was it a threat, or merely the fervent rhetoric of a True Believer? Horton could not tell, but it did not matter. He had already made his decision.

'You said you have a Trigger back at the camp?'

'A Trigger and a Jammer both. – Defanged, of course.'

'I'll look at them,' he said. 'I'll see if I can find your remote control. But I want it understood I fully expect to prove to you that you're wrong.'

Wilkins showed a tolerant smile. 'And if you should happen to find that I'm not – will you allow yourself to accept it?'

'I can promise you that my mind is at least as open as yours is, Colonel.'

'Is it?' Wilkins said. 'Let us see.'

Mark Breland had instructed General Stepak to bring him updates three times a day – at eight in the morning, two in the afternoon, and eight at night. But it was hard for him to stay away that long from the lower-level Situation Room from which Stepak was directing the search for Jeffrey Horton.

The rest of Breland's schedule was not compelling enough to fully distract him – a preliminary face-to-face meeting with Congressional leaders on the budget, a weekly teleconference with Party leaders on the fall campaign, a ceremony in the Rose Garden honoring the year's Presidential Scholars, a private luncheon with Aimee Rochet, a softball game on the South Lawn with the outgoing Presidential pages.

But only the luncheon could be canceled without complications, and Breland did so, with a kiss, an apology, and a promise. He took advantage of the hour thus freed to go to the Situation Room, which by then had been transformed from its usual somnolence into a busy crisis management command center. More than a dozen intelligence specialists were staffing com stations, with a variety of senior suits and uniforms peering over their shoulders, huddling together over display tables, and consulting with Stepak.

'Any progress, General?' Breland asked as he joined the secretary of defense, who was standing with the CIA domestic intelligence liaison by the map board.

Stepak whirled around in surprise. 'Mr President, good afternoon – I'm sorry, I didn't see you come in.'

'Well, it's my fault. I won't let them pipe me aboard.' Breland looked past Stepak to the thin-faced man with the intensely alert eyes. 'Mr Thorn, isn't it?'

'Yes, sir. I was just telling General Stepak about the assets now on task.'

'By all means, continue.'

Thorn nodded. 'We now have eight Global Hawk RPVs in the air over Wisconsin, Illinois, Minnesota, Indiana, Michigan, and south-central Canada. The Keyhole-15 satellite has also been repositioned to give us better coverage in the primary search area. We're concentrating our attention on known anti-government groups operating in the five-state region, using information provided by the Joint Anti-terrorism Task Force. But we're also allowing the operators some latitude, since a new group might be involved.'

'Any possible sightings yet?'

'Not in real time. But an analyst at NSA dug a couple of images

514

out of the archives – Horton's camper at the Hayward airport, and then traveling in convoy with an SUV on US 53 about ninety minutes later. We lose them both under some cumulostratus that had everything from Eau Claire west to Sioux Falls blacked out. But we got a good infrared profile on the SUV – if we see it again, we should be able to recognize it.'

'What about the search on Lake Superior?'

Stepak said, 'The Coast Guard's handling that, though they're short-handed enough we've put all of UDT-12 and SEAL Teams Four and Six on the water in four-man boats and borrowed three float-copters from the Canadians. Nothing so far, though. My gut feeling is that our perpetrators are home-grown, and they and Horton are still in the neighborhood. The problem is that with every passing hour, the neighborhood gets bigger.'

Breland looked across the room and allowed his gaze to settle on Monica Frances. 'How did this happen, Roland? The DIA was supposed to keep contact with Jeffrey. I gave Hilger that order personally.'

'It's hard to keep contact with someone who doesn't allow a lot of contact,' said Thorn, answering for the general. 'You end up having to rely on technical rather than human resources, and by the time you know you've had a breakdown, you've lost them.'

Still frowning, Breland sighed. 'Maybe it's time to come up with some sort of personal tracer you can put right in the body.'

'In inventory, Mr, President. But using 'em generally calls for the cooperation of the person being traced,' Thorn said without missing a beat. 'The ingestible version passes in a few hours. The injectable requires an incision and periodic induction recharges.'

'I guess I haven't been keeping up on spycraft.'

'There's a way to do anything you can imagine,' said Thorn affably. 'What you need is a reason.'

For two days, Jeffrey Horton enjoyed what he thought of as a probationary membership in the People's Army of Righteous Justice.

While he was still obliged to wear the walking-target orange jumpsuit, he was given a bunk in the men's long house, the right to take first meal with the men, and the freedom to go back and forth to the bathhouse and latrine unescorted. He earned those privileges by spending the greater part of both days inside a stuffy, windowless metal shed, analyzing the command and control logic of a late-model Trigger from Sears and an early-model Jammer from ADT.

The output stages of both units had been replaced with simple status lights by Wilkins's chief technician, Frank Schrier. Schrier also hovered at Horton's elbow the entire time he was in the shed. The combination of the tech's preemptive tinkering and his constant presence made Horton's faint hope of using the devices against his captors vanish.

That left the even fainter hope of emerging from the makeshift laboratory with the kind of incontrovertible proof that would change Wilkins's mind – or his own.

They had, at least, provided him with a table full of the best tools. The logic probe was a PM Technologies CodeBreaker, found in reverse engineering labs around the world. The diagnostic analyzer was Zoftwerkz Mastermind, favored by designers and code thieves working on both sides of the law. And the benchmark reference was familiar enough – it was Horton's own public domain release of the Trigger technical guide.

Even so, it was a job that either Gordie or Lee would have been better equipped to tackle. Both were more familiar with not only the original designs, but the process of reading another designer's firmware from the inside out – in this case, in search of anomalous code. Horton tried to use his inexperience to lower expectations, but Schrier warned him that Wilkins would not stand for footdragging.

'One of the reasons I'm here is to keep things moving forward,' Schrier said. 'The Colonel always has a timetable, and it's not a good idea to be the one who's holding him back.'

'Have you already gone through these systems? Do you know if what I'm supposed to be looking for is here?'

'If they'd been sloppy enough that it was something I could spot, we wouldn't need you, would we, now?'

Horton began to see signs of Wilkins's impatience by the end of the second day. After leaving them alone on the first day, he stopped by the shed three times in the course of the second to

516

check on their progress. When he showed up for the last of those, Wilkins's mouth was pinched, and he spoke only to Schrier. He was not at all happy to hear that they had only begun work on the second unit, the ADT Jammer, at midafternoon.

'How much longer?' Wilkins demanded.

'At this pace, Colonel, it could be three more days. The Trigger was open and basically clean. The Jammer has logic traps and looks like it's full of junk.'

Wilkins held Horton in a coldly appraising gaze. 'Services are in twenty minutes. I expect to see you both there. Then you can return to your work and see if you've been blessed with the guidance you need to bring it to a speedier conclusion.'

Horton had heard the communal singing every night since he had been brought to the camp, though the preaching and praying interspersed between hymns did not quite carry to the depths of Shelter Six. But on his first night of 'freedom', he had gotten an earful, even though he had exercised that freedom and stayed behind in the men's long house when services began. The preaching was one of two reasons he shortly thereafter left the long house and struck out into the woods.

The other, more important reason was to see if the camp's perimeter security was more porous during services. If he had not come across any of Wilkins's men, Horton might have just kept walking. As it was, he had come close to getting himself shot by a two-man foot patrol for whom he had no good explanation for his wandering.

'At night, Dr Horton, you want to make sure you stay inside the green perimeter,' the militiaman had said from behind his bug-like night-vision goggles. 'Another ten steps, and you would have been in our free-fire zone.'

'I lost track of where I was,' Horton had said weakly.

'That's a mistake I'd try not to repeat, Doctor. We'll escort you back.'

Wilkins had not said anything to Horton about his perambulation, but his hard look and pointed invitation said enough. The next evening, the physicist made sure that he was among the early arrivals when the women's long house began to fill in response to the call to worship.

Horton had not been inside a church since forsaking his parents' low-key Lutheranism at age fourteen. He was surprised at how many of the melodies were still familiar – some because they were borrowed from German Romantics and English folk tunes he now knew better from a different context, but others awakened unexpected echoes of childhood Sunday mornings.

The words, however, were another story. No congregation Horton had ever been part of before had sung 'Onward, Christian Soldiers' with a verse about the 'martyrs of Waco' or 'the heroes of Tigerton Dells', or 'The Ballad of Gordon Kahl' to the tune of 'This Is My Father's World'. But almost as startling was how martial some of the unaltered lyrics were, straight from the well-worn reprint of the 1933 *Hymnal* someone helpfully gave Horton when they saw that he was not singing:

Soldiers of Christ arise, and put your armor on.

Leave no unguarded place, no weakness of the soul.

Tread all the powers of darkness down, and win the well-fought day –

Once, Horton would have read those as metaphors. But surrounded by the people of the Army of Righteous Justice, seeing not only the fervent and unquestioning commitment on their faces but the weapons cradled in their arms, he knew that that distinction did not apply. He mouthed the words, unwilling to give them voice.

The service went on for nearly two hours, with more than a dozen men and women rising to offer witness and lead the group in prayer. Horton wondered how much of it was for his benefit, or because of his absence the night before. It was almost as if they were testing him, expecting the power of their own faith to bring about a public conversion, hoping to see him suddenly filled with the Holy Spirit and recanting his scientific sins. And while he could not say that he felt like the center of attention, he could not shake the feeling that everyone in the room was aware of him – especially when Colonel Wilkins rose and led the final responsive reading.

'The Lord My Strength,' he announced, looking directly at Horton.

The entire group answered with thunderous and unselfconscious vigor. 'The Lord is the strength of my life – of whom shall I be afraid?'

'When my enemies and my foes came upon me to eat up my flesh, they stumbled and fell.'

'The Lord is the strength of our family – of whom shall we be afraid?'

'Though war should rise against me, my heart shall not fear.'

'The Lord is the strength of our church – of whom shall we be afraid?'

'My head shall be lifted up above my enemies round about me.'

'The Lord is the strength of our tribe – of whom shall we be afraid?'

'The kings of the earth set themselves against the Lord, and against His anointed.'

'The Lord is the strength of our nation – of whom shall we be afraid?'

'We shall break them with a rod of iron, and dash them in pieces like a potter's vessel.'

'Blessed are they who serve the Lord with fear, and rejoice with trembling.'

'Blessed are they who put their trust in Him, from whom nothing is hid, and whose judgements are altogether true and righteous,' Wilkins proclaimed. 'Amen.'

The cry came back: 'Amen, and praise be to God.'

Horton shuddered involuntarily, his skin prickling with goose-flesh despite the heat in the long house. He was almost insensible to the words of fellowship being offered him as he stood and headed for the doorway. Outside, he sought out Schrier, seizing him by the arm and turning him away from the woman he was speaking to.

'I had a thought,' he said. 'The same code would have to be in both units. Can we just run a compare on the Jammer using the anomalies we found in the Trigger? That would save us from having to work through the Jammer's base code.'

'But the override command could be part of the base code.'

'It's not,' Horton said firmly. 'The base code is my lab's code. If this thing is there, it's something that was added later.'

'How sure of that are you?'

'As sure as I am of anything at this point,' said Horton. 'Come on, we have a couple of hours until lights-out.'

More than twenty years had passed since Roland Stepak had given up the cockpit for a desk, but he had retained one essential skill of the combat pilot – 'power napping' or 'sleeping fast', the knack of diving deep into sleep whenever and for however long the opportunity presented itself. His four-hour nap in one of the Japanese-style capsules attached to the Situation Room was enough to sweep the weight from his eyelids, and a hot shower helped wash the vaguely sick ache of fatigue from his limbs.

He had left a lieutenant colonel from Army Intelligence in charge while he napped, so he was surprised to find Morton Denby of the CIA riding the hot seat instead.

'Caught a small break, General – we've identified your mole in Defense Communications,' Denby said, rising to surrender the chair.

'Is that where Lieutenant Colonel Briggs went?'

Denby nodded as he slid sideways into the next seat. 'The mole is one of theirs – a civilian technician attached to the Signal Corps, working the graveyard in the GLOCOMNET traffic management center. David Luke Wickstrom, age thirty-four. It looks like he managed to access secure addresses and verifiers for several Terabyte principals, and upload a routing filter to the satellite network.'

'You should have wakened me,' Stepak said. 'Where is the mole now?'

'That's the thing – there was no point in waking you. Wickstrom's scampered. He may have been tipped off when GLOCOMNET security spotted the virus and started taking the satellites offline to flush it out. He took a sick day yesterday, and last night his apartment building was gutted by an arson fire that started in his apartment.'

'Let me guess – military-grade magnesium flares on a timer.'

'Looks like,' said Denby. 'Army Intelligence is on the scene, going through what little is left. FBI is going into his background, trying to get the egg off its face for clearing him for the post.' He clucked and shook his head. 'Pretty cold business, General – the fire killed three kids, burned out half a dozen families.'

'Any sightings or traces on Wickstrom since?'

'Nothing. Personally, I wouldn't bet on him going anywhere near wherever Horton is being held.'

'No,' said Stepak, leaning back in his chair with a deep frown creasing his face. 'But he'll be in touch with them – which means that they now know that we know. And I don't think that's good news for Jeffrey Horton.'

32:

'There never was a good war or a bad peace.'

– Benjamin Franklin

It was midmorning, and the light rain which had been falling since dawn had finally percolated down through the trees to land on the work shed's metal roof as fat, percussive drops. The sound was grating on Jeffrey Horton's nerves, already stretched taut by the cumulative stress of imprisonment.

'Nothing,' Horton said, pushing back from the table where the analyzer and the Jammer sat side by side. 'There's nothing there. Right? You didn't see anything, either, did you?'

'There were no matches –' Schrier began.

'I expect you to tell Wilkins that.'

'– But that doesn't mean there's nothing there. The code might be different for a Jammer. Or you might be wrong, and it could be hidden in the base code.'

'Or I could be lying.'

'Or you could be lying,' Schrier agreed. 'But I think you're too smart to lie about something when you might be caught at it. I think you're too smart to underestimate us.'

'I'm not the enemy,' Horton said, shaking his head. 'I just want to go back to my life. But if Wilkins makes me choose, he could turn me into one.'

Schrier pursed his lips and said nothing.

Horton sighed. 'What now?'

'Keep looking. Who knows how many add-ons there are in this system? From what we've seen so far, I have a feeling it's a junkpile.'

Easing his chair forward, Horton said tiredly, 'Eeny, meeny, miney, moe –'

They had only another hour to themselves before Colonel Robert Wilkins threw open the door to the work shed and filled the opening with his silhouette. 'Report,' he said curtly.

'Yes, sir, Colonel, sir,' Horton muttered under his breath.

'Nothing to report, Colonel,' Schrier said, standing. 'No matches between the two systems that aren't covered by standard control functions.'

'You have nothing to show for three days' work? You're letting this man stall you.'

'Oh, we can show you a lot,' Horton said, coming to his feet behind Schrier. 'We can show you a little picture of the project supervisor for ADT, complete with horns and a funny mustache. We can show you the scores of the last ten football games between Texas and Texas A&M, the phone numbers of three women of dubious virtue, and about five hundred words of *The Rime of the Ancient Mariner*.'

Horton stepped around the technician and stood face to face with Wilkins. 'Oh, no, we didn't miss anything – we found the places where people slipped in their kids' names, or their tribute to a sex star, or their favorite quote from *Calvin & Hobbes* or *In Sanity*. But what we didn't find is any goddamned secret back-door boogeyman-conspiracy remote-control kill-switch gateway, because there *isn't* any. It only exists in your paranoid fantasies. No, not paranoia – wishful thinking. I'll be damned if I know why, but you love this – you actually want this war.'

'War is a moral necessity, Dr Horton, when you're faced with an immoral enemy. There's no pleasure to be taken in it.'

Horton's eyes poured out his contempt. 'You think you're fit to judge what's moral? You think you're sitting high enough to judge me? Have you looked in a mirror lately?'

'Have *you*, Doctor? Your march-of-progress pose doesn't wash with me. You scientists gave us Zyclon-B, AIDS, abortion on demand, evolution, and now this. You never count the cost. And you, Jeffrey Horton, personally betrayed seventy million law-abiding American families. You condemned ten thousand good people to death at the hands of thugs and thieves. Don't strike a noble pose with me, Doctor. You're as guilty as if you murdered them yourself.'

The militia leader's impenetrable self-assurance roused a terrible fury in Horton, and he struck out at Wilkins with a torrent of angry words. 'You need to be a hero so badly that you're making up enemies as you go. But if that's what you want me to be, all right. I'm sorry that what I discovered cost some good people like my father their hobbies. And it does bother me that there's other people out there who got hurt because they didn't have a working gun to protect themselves. But I'm damned proud to have gotten in the way of a terrorist like you. You're a selfish little man with a head full of delusions, and anything I can do to put a crimp in your plans is a public service. Your revolution would be a disaster –'

Something Horton said must have found a weakness and pierced through Wilkins's armor to his tender pride. The colonel slammed both his palms against Horton's chest, driving him backwards into Schrier. 'You think you've accomplished anything? You think you've disarmed us?' He turned away into the drizzle. 'Bring him!' he snarled to the guards.

Horton was seized by both arms and dragged bodily along in Wilkins's wake, scrambling to get his feet under him and his emotions under control. *Don't beg*, he thought. *Don't give him that –*

Wilkins's long strides led them to the second metal shed, standing by itself a hundred and fifty meters from the main camp. 'Cuff him and control him,' he said as he bent to the lock.

In the next moment, Horton found himself dropped face-down in the grass, with a booted foot on the back of his neck to hold him there. His arms were twisted behind him and his wrists bound together by a thin plastic tie that cut deep into the skin. He heard the door squeak and then clang open.

'Bring him in,' Wilkins said.

Hauled upright once more, his shirt and the side of one face painted with mud and dead needles, Horton fought the impulse to resist. Unaccountably, a quatrain from Matthew Halverson came to mind:

Control is an illusion,
order our comforting lie.
From chaos, through chaos,
into chaos we fly –

As he was pushed through the doorway, the lights inside the shed came on. They revealed it to be an armory, with the four walls hung with assorted weaponry, all military grade, all heavier than the personal arms carried by the militia – SAWs, light machine guns, grenade launchers, a 40mm mortar, a pair of Stinger antiaircraft missiles. The base of each wall was lined with ammunition boxes stacked two and three high.

The middle of the floor was empty except for four square panels of wood slats, each with a rope pull. Wilkins stood on one of those as he turned to face Horton. 'You say you've stopped us, and yet every weapon in this armory is fully functional. I'm sorely tempted to prove it to you using your own flabby body as the target, but that would keep you from appreciating the fine irony about to be revealed to you.' Then he called an armory guard in, and gestured toward one of the wood panels. 'Bring up a canister from Bunker Two.'

'Yes, Colonel.' The guard pulled up the panel, revealing a man-sized tunnel opening into the ground below. He dropped through the opening as though it were a practiced thing, and returned not long after carrying a cylinder as long as his forearm and the diameter of a tennis ball.

'Now one of the aerosols from Three,' Wilkins said, taking the cylinder from the guard and moving toward Horton. 'You see, Doctor, we're very, very good with our guns, and we hardly ever hit anything we haven't aimed at. But if you do manage to take our precision tools away from us, don't ever think that leaves us unarmed.

'Maybe you've forgotten that gasoline makes a perfectly fine explosive, and it's conveniently available most everywhere.' The guard reappeared then, holding what looked like a small pressurized bottle. 'And when it comes time to start killing traitors faster than we can do it with K-Bars and garrottes, well, the Lord shall provide.'

He held the olive-drab cylinder up in front of Horton's face, allowing him to read the words and numbers stenciled on the side. Beside him, the guard did the same with his burden.

'What is this?' Horton asked.

'Chemical weapons and biological aerosols don't require

conventional explosives, Dr Horton,' Wilkins said with smug triumph. 'What do you think about that?'

Horton slowly raised his gaze from the stenciled lettering to Wilkins's chiseled face. 'I think it means my work's not finished – and the sooner I get back to it, the better,' he said quietly.

'Son of a – get this bastard out of my sight,' Wilkins said, the cold malevolence of his soul finally revealed in the bloodless hate in his eyes. 'Throw this animal back in his cage – now, before I rip his fucking throat open.'

'Yes, sir!'

Horton was unceremoniously dragged backward out of the shed. Wilkins's voice followed him, rising in pitch and volume with each succeeding word. 'You better think about this! Think long and hard, Mr Fucking Boy-Genius Presidential Hero. You're gonna decide which of these weapons gets used – the ones on the wall, or the ones in the hole! You, Jeffrey goddamned Horton, you're going to decide how many we have to kill and how ugly they die. Think about *that*, Doctor – you think about that!'

But all Horton could think as they threw him down into Shelter Six and clanged the hatch shut above him was, *I got to you – I finally got to you – and now I know exactly who you really are –*

Aron Goldstein watched as the Pennsylvania Railroad GG-1 electric eased into Broad Street Station pulling a string of six purple and white passenger cars – the 8.40 from Newark. Just below it, a long slow freight made up principally of Erie & Lackawanna boxcars trundled northward along the river.

On the broad panel display before him was the engineer's-eye view from the tiny camera in the scale model GG-1. Since it would be stationary for several minutes while the mail was unloaded, Goldstein touched a control bar and changed to the view from the freight's Number 1 engine, just before it passed under a stone trestle. The track ahead included a pair of tunnels and a glimpse of the Zoo – one of his favorite sections of the lay-out, and an agreeable meditation to distract him from other matters.

But before the freight reached the first tunnel, Goldstein was disturbed in his sanctuary by one of the nurse-practitioners who had adopted house staff attire so that they could monitor his house guest in person. 'Mr Goldstein, Dr Brohier is asking to see you.'

'Thank you,' Goldstein said, starting to shut down the running trains. 'Is he in his workroom?'

'No, he's still in bed.'

That report hastened Goldstein's hands. 'Has he said anything else?'

'Only that he's tired. He ate almost none of his breakfast.'

'Let's get Dr Hubbs up there, now,' Goldstein said. 'I've given that old curmudgeon his way long enough.'

'I'll go get the doctor.'

Goldstein found Brohier lying propped up against a mound of pillows, his digital desktop resting untouched beside him on the blankets. His gaze tended in the direction of the east window, but seemed slack and unfocused.

'And what's with you this morning, Karl?' Goldstein asked gently, approaching the foot of the bed. 'Too much wine with your veal marsala last night?'

'Ah – Aron. There you are. What did you ask me? Oh, the food. No, I do not blame your cooks.' The effort expended for just a half-smile and those few words left him momentarily breathless, and the deep breath he drew to catch up started him coughing. 'Nothing feels right, and I hardly have the energy to care. If I were younger, I might suspect something like the flu. Of course, in my dissolute state, the flu can surely kill me as well as anything.'

'I've asked Dr Hubbs to come over and take a look at you,' said Goldstein. 'I expect you to behave when he gets here.'

'Witch-doctor nostrums,' Brohier said disdainfully. 'There is no antidote for entropy, Aron.'

'Perhaps not. But there's no substitute for letting a good geriatric diagnostician have a look at you now and again.'

'I already know everything he can tell me, and none of it is important,' said Brohier. 'But I'll let him poke and prod me if that means we can talk about something else.'

'Of course, Karl.' Goldstein moved to the side of the bed and sat down. 'Been doing some work?' he asked, nodding toward the digital desk.

'I was trying to write a letter,' he said. 'Where did you go last night? I heard the helicopter.'

'Washington,' Goldstein said. 'Another boring meeting.'

'Meetings – yes, thank you, now I remember what I wanted to say. Aron –'

'Right here, Karl.'

'Don't turn Jeffrey into an administrator. Don't let him do that to himself. Find someone else to write the letters and run the meetings. He needs to be in the laboratory. He needs to hear his own voice above the noise.'

'All right, Karl.'

'That's what he's been having trouble with. That's why he went away, you know. I want to know that you'll keep the door open for him to come back.'

'Of course. Only –' Goldstein sighed. 'Karl, at that meeting last night – I'm not supposed to tell you, but I don't know how they can expect me not to. Although maybe that's why they didn't tell me until now.'

'Stop babbling, Aron, or I may not be here when you finish.'

Goldstein nodded apologetically. 'Karl, I have some news about Jeffrey. He's missing. He was kidnapped a week ago – they think possibly by some sort of domestic terrorist group. There's been no word of him or from him.'

The only visible reaction from Brohier was the way his gaze darted about the room. 'That's all right,' he finally said.

'A week's a long time for a kidnapping,' Goldstein said, shaking his head. 'They're doing everything, but – Karl, the FBI didn't hold out much hope.'

'Jeffrey will be all right.'

'Of course that's what we all want,' said Goldstein. 'I just thought we might talk about what we'd want to do with Terabyte if for some reason Jeffrey doesn't come back.'

'A waste of time and energy – something I find myself rather sensitive about at the moment. He'll be back, Aron,' Brohier said. 'He knows where he belongs.' Then he let himself sag into the pillows, almost as though he were attempting to hide under them. 'Your doctor friend is here.'

528

Goldstein looked behind him to see Dr Hubbs standing just inside the doorway.

'I have your word, Aron?' asked Brohier.

'Yes, Karl.'

'Then come on, Doctor, and don't tarry. You're the last promise I have left to keep.'

For more than a day, Jeffrey Horton was left alone in the dank, claustrophobic confines of Shelter Six. No one came to check on him, or take him to use the toilet. No one brought him food or drink. No one threw open the metal hatch to allow so much as a few seconds of light and fresh air to relieve the gloom.

He made the best use he could of the neglect: within an hour of being returned to the dirt-walled cell, he started trying to dig his way out.

The only tool available was one waffle-soled ankle-height hiking boot. His captors had taken his boots along with his clothes on the first day, but had returned the boots to him – sans laces – during his probation. Somehow, he had managed to keep the right boot on while being dragged to and from the armory shed. Where the left boot had ended up, he did not know, but the right had kept him company when he was enthusiastically and unceremoniously dumped through the hatch.

After seeing the tunnels in the armory, Horton wondered if all the camp's structures were connected underground, even the shelters – especially the shelters. But rather than search for a sealed-up tunnel that might not be there, he chose what he hoped would be the fastest and shortest way out – making a shimmy-hole under the edge of the steel cone roof. He started at the top of the wall directly beneath the hatch, where it would be hardest to see from outside, and spread the dirt evenly across the shelter floor with his bare feet as he worked.

Even near the surface, the soil was dense and claylike. The boot quickly proved better suited to scraping than digging, and not terribly well suited to that – the cleats clogged up after only a few passes, and it took longer to clear them with his fingertips than it did to fill them again. After a while, he stopped bothering, finding that the edge of the heel gave him the best leverage, and the two-handed grip that required gave him the best results for his effort.

The one advantage of the boot was that it was virtually silent, no matter how hard or how quickly he worked – even when he accidentally struck the metal roof itself. So it did not take him very long to find that the way was blocked – the roof did not merely rest on top of the ground, but atop a circular steel collar that extended down into the ground. There would be no quick and easy shimmy-hole.

Undeterred, he scoured his way down the wall until he found the bottom edge of the collar. There he started working his way sideways again, worrying out a hollow that slowly grew into something that could aspire to be called a tunnel. He worked until his face was streaming with sweat and his arms were screaming with fatigue, and then a little longer. He rested until his chest stopped heaving, and then started all over again.

They were singing hymns in the women's long house when Horton started to uncover roots. The farther he went, the thicker and denser they got, until he could no longer tear them away with his aching hands. Trying not to think about the wasted effort, he turned to another part of the wall and started over.

By the time morning light showed at the vents, the tunnel was half as long as Horton was tall, and, by his guess, a little more than half-way to the surface. It was not enough. He sat atop a mound of freshly dug earth, exhausted and discouraged, fully expecting his efforts to be discovered at any moment, and, in discovery, defeated.

But they did not come for him. And when he belatedly realized that the moment had not yet passed, he attacked the tunnel with renewed vigor. The boot was long past being useless – squeezed into the confined space, he clawed and dug at the packed dirt with his bare hands, nails bitten down to the quick to try to save those he had not already torn and bent back. The dirt caked his face and hair, choked his every breath. But he did not stop until his fingers reached the outside edge of the conical roof, and he knew that all that separated him from the surface was a few inches of overburden he could clear in minutes.

He stopped then because he had a decision to make – whether

to chance an escape in the daylight, or chance waiting until night returned.

If their neglect of him was the product of nothing more than Wilkins's rage, then it could end at any moment. But if it was the beginning of a calculated effort to break him, it was likely to go on for days.

Horton guessed the latter, and decided to wait.

He guessed wrong. They came for him just before the dinner hour.

Colonel Robert Wilkins cocked his head questioningly at Jeffrey Horton's appearance as his guards pushed him down on the log bench. 'What's this about?' Wilkins said, gesturing at Horton's filthy clothes.

'We found him trying to tunnel out of the shelter, sir.'

The militia leader clucked disapprovingly and shook his head. 'Really, Doctor, you should have known better –'

Watching Wilkins's eyes, it came upon Horton with a sudden sinking certainty that this was not news to him. 'You have some kind of monitor in the shelter.'

'That would be telling.'

'You just wanted me to start to think I was going to make it, so you could take it away –'

'Dr Horton, the only reason I have for locking you up is to keep you from getting hurt. Honestly, now, you're only a threat to yourself. And if you happened to wander away without telling anyone, you'd stand an unacceptably high chance of getting yourself shot. Have you ever been shot, Dr Horton? Have you ever seen anyone shot with a NATO round from a combat rifle?'

'No,' Horton said quietly.

'Well, I hope you'll take my counsel on this – it's definitely something you want to avoid.' He looked up and away toward the three other men standing nearby. 'Frank, are you ready?'

'Yes, Colonel.'

'Let's have it, then,' he said, patting the bench beside him.

Schrier came forward and laid a Celestial 3000 comset and its battery pack on the bench. There was a familiar scuff mark on the edge of the comset's plastic case – it was Horton's.

531

'Thank you,' said Wilkins, making no move to pick up the unit. 'Would you tell Dr Horton what it is you've done to his property?'

'I pulled the GPS locator module and then dropped a dummy module in its place. That way the system diagnostics won't know the difference, and there won't be any fault messages sent to your provider.'

'And this is the same treatment you give all our comsets, correct?'

'Yes, sir. Nothing special. Takes more time to set up the work-bench than it does to do the work. But remember, we don't have any helpers upstairs anymore – they can still triangulate on a comset call if we give them enough time.'

Wilkins nodded. 'That's all for now, Frank.' He turned his attention back to Horton. 'People don't think about the fact that every time they use their comset, they're notifying the government where they are – all because some dumb bitch with a cell phone got herself lost in a snowstorm and almost died, twenty-five years ago. Every time something bad happens, you can count on some liberal to come along with an idea about how, for just a *little* bit of our freedom, we can keep this terrible calamity from ever happening again. Personally, I have a philosophical objection to advertising my location to anyone who might be interested. You can understand that, I expect.'

'I can sure understand why *you* wouldn't want your location known.'

'I hope you're not holding a grudge over words spoken in anger, Dr Horton – especially since I had the fellows fetch you here as a courtesy.'

'A *courtesy*?'

'That's right. A little while ago, I got word that Dr Karl Brohier has died –'

'That's a good start,' one of the guards said snarkily.

'Now, Michael, don't be insensitive,' Wilkins said. 'Dr Horton and Dr Brohier were friends.'

'Why should I believe you?' Horton demanded. 'You've lied to me before to get me to do what you wanted.'

'I anticipated you might have a certain degree of skepticism.'

Wilkins picked up the comset and slid the battery into its recess. 'So I'm going to let you call the President, and hear it from him. And while you have him on the line, I'll have a few words with him myself.' Cradling the comset loosely in his right hand, he offered it to Horton.

Horton's hands stayed in his lap. 'The fact that you want me to do this is enough to make me want not to.'

Wilkins gestured with his other hand, and the rifles of the two men standing with Schrier came down off their shoulders. With no further warning, one fired a three-round burst that whistled just above Horton's head and thudded into the trunk of a tree a dozen meters behind him.

'Please,' said Wilkins.

His heart racing and his mouth suddenly dry, Horton took the comset.

'An authenticated call, please, so you can both be sure who you're talking to.'

'What makes you think the President takes my calls?'

'I think he will,' Wilkins said. 'I'll even bet that his address is in your personal directory.'

'Do you really think I'm worth enough to them that they'll give you what you want?'

'With Dr Brohier dead, I should imagine your market value has gone up considerably. And I don't intend to ask for very much. Besides, isn't that the liberal mantra? "If it saves one person's life –" They can save yours.'

Horton placed the comset back down on the bench and pushed it toward Wilkins. 'No, thank you. The price is too high. You can call the President yourself. I'm not going to help.'

Wilkins moved with catlike quickness – Horton never saw the blow coming. One moment they were both sitting on the bench, and the next Horton's head was snapped sideways by a slap so powerful that it knocked him to the ground. Dazed, he tried to struggle to his hands and knees, only to have Wilkins shove him back down with his foot.

'Do you think you're too valuable to hurt?' the colonel screamed, standing over Horton. 'Is that it? You think you're something precious now?' The kick to the abdomen that followed was hard enough to nearly lift Horton off the ground. Gasping for breath, he tried to roll away from the next assault. As he did, Wilkins grabbed his right hand and bent the thumb down toward the wrist until Horton could not hold back any longer, and screamed in pain.

'There, that's better, now you're starting to understand,' Wilkins said, maintaining the excruciating hold as he settled back on the log bench. 'Doctor, there are a lot of ways to hurt you that will leave you quite capable of coming back an hour later to be hurt some more. I've been giving you benefit of the doubt, assuming that as an intelligent man you'd be insulted by such crude tactics. But maybe I've overestimated you. Right now, you don't seem nearly as bright as your press clippings claim.'

Every word of Horton's answer was an effort. 'What do you want from me?'

'You're not paying attention, Doctor,' Wilkins said, squeezing harder. 'I want to know how to beat the Jammer. I want that goddamned disable code.'

Horton squeezed out his answer from between clenched teeth. 'There – is – no – *code*.'

'Your credibility is suspect, Doctor. I want to ask someone else – someone who might value your life a little more than you seem to.' Abruptly, Wilkins released Horton and walked away toward his men, leaving Horton writhing in the dirt. 'Gaylord, you keep up with these things. Has anyone tested to see how long an amputated thumb will green-light a comset's fingerprint authenticator?'

'It's longer than you'd think,' said the soldier. 'Ten, twelve hours if you take steps to keep it from drying out.'

By then, Horton had hauled himself up to a sitting position, cradling his injured thumb in his other hand. 'Let me get this straight – the way your mind works, you now expect me to be *more* cooperative?'

'I *expected* the same finely-tuned sense of self-preservation that makes you gun-grabbers afraid to live in a world of armed free citizens to kick in,' Wilkins said. 'But since you're having trouble getting there, let me simplify things for you. We're the bullies. You're the geek. Nothing's changed. You're still in high school, and we're still on top. If I want your goddamned lunch money,

I'm going to get it. The only question is how much pain you want before you give it up.'

Horton slowly pulled himself up off the ground and onto the bench. 'You want the President to know you have me, right? That's what you want now.'

'That's right. That way I know they'll listen to what I have to say.'

Nodding slowly, Horton said, 'I don't suppose I really have anything to lose.' He sighed heavily, then pointed at the comset, which had been knocked off the bench into a clump of grass beside it. 'May I pick that up?'

'By all means.'

Moving gingerly, Horton hobbled the couple of steps, then crouched down and clasped the comset firmly in his good hand. He started to rise, grimacing as he did. His thumb slipped easily into the hollow on the side of the unit where the personal authenticator grid was located.

'Personal directory,' he said. 'Open secure folder. Scroll to Breland.' As he did, he saw in their faces that they were enjoying their triumph, saw them relax that little bit he had been hoping for. He reached up as though to enter a number on the datapad.

But, instead, he grasped the comset firmly with both hands, and allowed his legs to turn to rubber beneath him. Adding his falling weight to every bit of strength remaining in his arms, he smashed the unit against the edge of the log bench. The blow was agony to his injured hand, but produced an agreeable scattering of plastic and metal bits. A second blow, struck from his knees, shattered the guts of the comset and spilled them into the dirt.

The nearest guard tackled him before he could complete his demolition. The impact drove him backwards onto the ground, and he quickly lost the fight for what was still clutched in his left hand. But it didn't matter – the largest piece remaining was the battery pack.

From his back, oblivious to the weight on top of him, Horton searched for Wilkins, and met his disbelieving stare with a lopsided smile. 'To hell with you,' he said. 'I never could respect a bully.'

They beat him until he nearly passed out, then bound him facing a tree trunk while they argued about what to do with him. He tried his best to follow the argument, but his guards made it difficult – any time he stopped moaning long enough to hear the voices clearly, one of them would hit him again.

They left him hanging there while they broke bread together, the smell of food drifting in the evening air almost as great a torment as his aches and bruises. They left him hanging there while they prayed and sang in fellowship, washing the blood from their hands with the bleach of ideology.

Then they came back to him, surrounding the tree as they cut the nylon cords that held him. With Wilkins leading the way, they took him a long five minutes into the woods, away from the camp. Horton was certain that they had decided to kill him, but the truth was far worse.

When they stopped, he was pushed down to his knees in a large patch of bare earth, and made to watch while four men with long-handled shovels dug a shallow trench directly in front of him. The rest of the gathering stood shoulder to shoulder in a circle around the spot, with even the children clasped in arms or peeking between legs eerily silent.

'That will do,' Wilkins said finally, unholstering his pistol as he stepped forward.

Horton found it almost impossible to breathe. Strong hands on his shoulders made it impossible to run.

'Bring the first one in,' Wilkins said.

The circle opened, and two militiamen dragged a slightly-built woman to the center, forcing her to her knees on the other side of the trench. Her arms were bound behind her, and she was gagged with duct tape as Horton had been that first day. Blood from a gash on her temple had stained the breast of her pale brown uniform. He did not know her, but he knew all the colors of fear and confusion in her pleading eyes.

'What is this?' Horton demanded. For his curiosity, he earned a rifle barrel jammed sharply into his ribs from behind.

Wilkins raised his left hand in rebuke. 'No need for that. I'm sure I have Dr Horton's full attention,' he said. 'Jeffrey, I'd like you to meet Sheriff's Deputy Shannon Drayton. She's twenty-eight years old, the single mother of two children.

'That's offense enough against God's plan for us. But she also works as a dispatcher, helping the local thieves in uniform confiscate the property and curtail the freedoms of sovereign citizens. That makes her a traitor, and we have every right under the rules of war to execute her on the spot.'

Drayton could not answer with more than a whimper, but her eyes were pure, wild terror, searching for understanding, pleading for mercy. Strangely, she did not struggle against her restraints – her limbs seemed to have no will left in them.

'This is insane –' Horton began.

'Listen carefully, Jeffrey, because the offer I'm about to make you is available for a limited time only. I'm going to give you a chance to save Shannon's life –'

'How can you expect anyone to follow you down this road? You're far more of a tyrant than Breland could ever be.'

'– and return her to her children. Since the lives of innocents mean so much to you, I am giving you the chance to intervene in those lives. Tell me what you've been holding back, *everything* you know, and I'll pardon this woman.' He raised his pistol and pointed it at the woman's midsection.

'Colonel – Robert – for mercy's sake –'

Wilkins held up his hand. 'No, you're right, that wouldn't be humane. Belly wounds hurt so much and take so long to kill. This is better.' Wilkins moved to the side and raised his arm until the barrel of the pistol was a hand's-breadth from the woman's ear. 'Talk to me, Jeffrey.'

'Don't do this –'

'You can stop me. Tell me how to block a Jammer. Tell me how to neutralize a Trigger. I hold the gun, but you hold her life in your hands.'

'For mercy's sake, there are *children* watching.'

'Good. Let them learn the price of treason.'

'This is pointless! I can't give you what you want! It doesn't exist – it's nothing but your fantasy!'

'Shannon is real. Where's your compassion for her, Jeffrey? Here you are with a golden opportunity to prevent a needless firearm death. But you're running out of time. When this offer expires, so does she.'

'You don't want to do this,' Horton said, desperate to believe his own words. 'You don't *need* to do this. There's no goddamned code! Ask me for something I can give you. Give me a real choice –'

'I think I know what your problem is, Jeffrey. I think that on some level, you just don't believe.'

'No, no, no, don't,' Horton pleaded. 'Please – Wilkins!'

There was no sign that Wilkins was even listening. In the span of a few seconds, with a chilling deliberateness, he bent the woman forward with a foot planted in the middle of her back, then reached down and fired one bullet into the base of her skull.

The report seemed thunderous, and yet the trees swallowed it up almost at once. Something warm and wet flew through the air and spattered Horton's face. He began to retch as the shattered, empty flesh that had been Shannon Drayton toppled sideways and slumped half-way into the trench.

Unbelievably, Horton heard cheers.

Tears were running freely down his face by the time Wilkins looked up from his handiwork. 'You bastard,' the physicist whispered. 'You're damaged goods, Wilkins. You sick, murderous bastard.'

But Wilkins's affect never changed, not the slightest bobble. 'In my world, that was an execution, for good and just cause. But you murdered her, Jeffrey – you made the choice. I only held the gun for you.' He looked away to the circle. 'Bring in number two.'

'No!' Horton shouted. For just one brief moment, he managed to fight free of the hands holding him, long enough to stand and advance a step. Then something hard struck him behind his knees, and he toppled face-forward into the dirt and gore, only inches from the edge of what was now a grave.

'Ah, so you do care,' Wilkins said, crouching beside him. 'And I can see that you now do believe. Maybe that will make the next decision easier.' He waved a hand, and Horton was hauled backward and again forced to kneel and face another hostage. 'This is Ray Macey, Jeffrey. He's an appraiser for the county tax assessor –'

'No!' Horton shouted once more. 'I will not play your game. You can't shift the responsibility to me – you're responsible for everything that happens here. This is your little cult, and these are your crimes. And you'd better kill me next, because if you don't, I'm going to be the happiest witness you ever saw when I testify at your trial – all of you, every one of you standing here who could have stopped this, except you were too much of a coward or too much of a robot to do anything –'

Wilkins said nothing. He simply walked behind Ray Macey and pressed the barrel of his pistol against the base of the visibly shaking hostage's skull. Then Wilkins looked across at Horton with a defiant gaze that said *Choose*.

Closing his eyes, Horton drew a deep breath and let it out slowly. When he opened his eyes again, he had calmed himself enough to speak the thoughts screaming inside his skull.

'You really don't understand how little power that gun gives you,' he said. 'You've fallen for your own myth. You're trying to use guns to control people, when all they're really good for is killing them.'

'That'll do until something better comes along!' a voice called from the circle.

'Something better *has* come along,' Horton retorted, then fixed his gaze on Wilkins. 'But even if it hadn't, you'd still be wrong. All you have in your hands is the power to inflict death, and that's nothing special. That's something so ordinary that every living thing and most of mindless Nature has it, too. And it isn't nearly enough to make me into someone else. It isn't enough to make me into you.

'I don't have what you want, Colonel Wilkins – no one does. But if I did, that gun couldn't make me give it to you. It's fear that controls us – it's controlling *you*, right now. But I'm not going to let myself be afraid of you, or what you decide to do. I know where my responsibility ends, and yours begins. And this poor woman is on your ledger, not mine. Come on, point that damned thing at me, instead, so I can say "Go to hell" one last time and be done with you. You know you'll enjoy killing me much more than you will killing him.'

'Nice speech. Very philosophical. Here's my rebuttal,' Wilkins said, and pulled the trigger –

– to silence.

Macey whimpered and snuffled.

Frowning, Wilkins racked the slide and cleared the misfire, then once more jammed the barrel against the appraiser's skull. In the held-breath silence, the entire circle heard the tight metallic clank of the hammer falling, but nothing else.

'What the hell –' Wilkins said.

Then Horton heard the whisper of the helicopter blades, and a few seconds later the roar of the downdraft. Then came the cracking of branches overhead as the weighted lines tore through the canopy, with a Special Forces commando riding each bucket to the ground.

'Maintain the formation!' Wilkins screamed. 'Shooters, face out – everyone else, move to the center and get down on the deck! Fire at will!'

The unit discipline of the Army of Righeous Justice lasted just a few seconds. That was all it took for its members to realize that they had been Jammed, and none of their firearms were going to work. Then the circle broke and scattered like insects from under a rock that's been kicked over.

Wilkins screamed at them to fight, and a few battle-eager militia-men responded by drawing knives or fixing their folding bayonets to charge the invaders. But Horton saw more of them reaching for their wives and children instead, and retreating in the general direction of the long houses. Some merely huddled on the ground where they were, arms raised in surrender.

Those who did go on the attack found themselves facing what seemed to be an ever increasing number of opponents, not only sliding down the bucket lines, but closing in through the trees from every point of the compass. The commandos were armed with quarterstaves and compressed-air dart guns, and wielded the former with such skill and efficiency that the latter were superfluous.

And as the short-lived battle began to wane, Wilkins and Horton found themselves momentarily alone in the middle of the chaos, one man's face painted with incredulity, and the other man's painted with delight. Their eyes met for a moment, and in that moment both men remembered things they had momentarily forgotten.

540

In the next moment, Horton lunged for Wilkins. His charge was turned aside with embarrassing ease, and Wilkins compounded the insult by paying him no further attention. As Horton lay gasping on the ground, Wilkins broke into a run, angling off into the trees.

'Stop him,' he croaked, pointing after Wilkins.

No one took notice. Horton pulled himself up to his hands and knees and tried again. 'Please – listen – you can't let that man get to the armory! There are chemical weapons. Stop him!'

His voice was stronger now, but there was no one to respond. The scattered fighting had moved past him. The only commando within twenty-five meters was fully occupied, herding at least a dozen prisoners.

Grabbing a long-handled shovel that was lying abandoned on the ground, Horton staggered to his feet and set off in pursuit of Wilkins. He was still wheezing, and he knew he had no chance to overtake the rangy, fleet-footed colonel. But he did not know what to do except try. He stumbled on roots and rocks in the gathering darkness, falling headlong before he had gone twenty strides. Gathering himself to his feet, he went on, barely noticing that the blade of the shovel had deeply gashed his forearm.

By the time the armory shed came into view, Horton had long since lost sight of Wilkins. But the physicist's persistence had finally attracted the attention that his pleas had failed to. Two commandos appeared from nowhere, and one took Horton's legs out from under him with his staff while the other struck the shovel from his hands. He fell hard, but made his first words count.

'Let's take it easy, now, your war's over –'

'Soldier, there are chemical and biological weapons in that shed,' Horton gasped. 'If the door's unlocked, it means the militia's in there after them.'

One of the commandos shined a hand flash in his face. 'This is the hostage – this is Dr Horton,' he said in surprise.

'Stay with him. I'm on it,' the other said, and sprinted away toward the shed.

'I'll try to get you some backup, Badger,' the first said, and reached for his throat mic. 'Warthog to Lord of the Forest – I have the package in hand, repeat, package in hand. We have a structure unsecured, northwest section, reported possible Charlie Bravo munitions.'

'We're coming, Warthog. Get the package out of there.'

'That's you, Doctor,' the commando said. 'Can you walk? Sorry about the takedown – we didn't know.'

'I can walk,' Horton said. 'But, look, that armory's more important than I am –'

'Badger is a Recon Marine, Doctor,' the commando said. 'He'll get it done.'

By the time Horton's escort located the assault commander, a bank of portable floodlights was turning dusk to midday. The commander took one look at Horton, insisted that he sit down, and called for a medic. The medic, in turn, took one look and called for a stretcher.

'I'm Captain Sandecki of Unit 13, attached to the 641st Tactical Brigade,' the commander said, squatting on his heels and offering his hand. 'You look like hell, Doctor. I'm damned sorry we weren't fast enough to spare you some of that. But it's over now, and I can tell you that your friends back East are going to be real pleased to hear that you're okay.'

'How did you find me?'

'Got a ping from the backup locator DIA put in your comset. Then a Global Hawk out of Minot located the camp and kept the area under IR and SSR surveillance until we could hoof it up here.'

Horton nodded, though he understood hardly a word of it. 'Captain – where's here? Where the hell am I?'

'The nearest town is Babbitt, Minnesota – about ninety klicks and a hundred years north of Duluth.'

He took a moment to absorb that. 'Can you arrange me transport to Columbia, South Carolina?'

'I sure can – so long as you don't object to an itinerary that includes stops at the nearest military hospital and a hotel suite in Washington. There's some folks at both very eager to see you.'

'I just want to go home,' Horton said.

Sandecki smiled understandingly. 'You have family in Columbia, then?'

'Not to speak of. Not at the moment,' Horton said, lying back and

542

allowing his eyes to close. 'Seems I managed to leave the pieces of my life scattered so far apart that I'm not sure where home is. But maybe I can put them back together, if I get a second chance.' He grunted, then added. 'Not sure I deserve one.'

'Well, hell, Doc, who really does? But it looks to me like that's what we're all trying to do, make the most of a second chance,' Sandecki said, and patted Horton's hand. 'You and your friends gave us that chance. If there's any justice – and today, I'm willing to say maybe there is – you've got one coming, too.'

III: Killer

Even though the narrow gravel path took the most direct route through the campus woodland, it was still nearly a kilometer's walk from the main complex of the Terabyte Corporation's Columbus facility to the contiguous Brohier Foundation Laboratory for Peace Technology.

The isolation gave the twenty-two researchers at PeaceTech the elbow room they needed for advanced work in H-wave mechanics and defense engineering. The gravel path gave Terabyte research director Jeffrey Horton a reason and a place to find a few minutes of solitude and exercise in the middle of the day. Except in the worst weather, he made it his habit to walk back and forth between the two nodes of the campus at least once a day.

He did so despite a slight limp and the ever-present aches in his legs and right hip, in part a legacy of a nightmare now almost two decades removed. He did so despite the campus's cutting-edge communications net, which could drop him into a high fidelity VR space with anyone on Terabyte payroll, from the office next door to the Nevada Annex or the Joint Materials Process Module orbiting 12,000 kilometers overhead.

He did so because he liked the woods, and because he did not want to surrender to time or to the pain, and because the walk had become a mind-clearing meditation. He invariably left his comset behind in his office, and his staff knew better than to disturb him on 'his' trail, even on those occasions when he loitered an hour or more in making the transit.

That morning, however, he was not loitering. The message from Jordan Kilmer, a member of the Biophysics workgroup, had been equal parts urgency and intrigue: 'Director, we've had an unexpected development in the TOCS project. Please come to the lab at the very earliest moment possible, so I can brief you –

and you can advise me. I'm sending the rest of the team home until we talk.'

TOCS was the Trace Organic Contaminant Separator, a direct descendant of Horton's modification of the Mark V Trigger for deactivating chemical weapons. The goal of the TOCS project was to produce an analyzer-projector which could swiftly break down poisons already ingested by a living organism. The unsolved challenge of TOCS was to refine the selectivity of the projector to the point where only the contaminant was destroyed – and not any structurally similar compounds necessary for life. The toll in research animals had been so high that Kilmer's nickname was 'Killer', and Biophysics was commonly referred to as the Morgue.

Horton found Kilmer tuning his test rig in Biophysics 3, an otherwise deserted lab whose high windows admitted light but allowed no view. The test rig filled a large utility cart. Five meters away, a cage containing a dozen guinea pigs rested atop a lab stool.

'Hey, Jordan. I thought you were working in Two,' Horton said.

'Director – Christ, I'm glad you're here. I got this out of Two and locked it up as soon as I realized what was happening,' Kilmer said, straightening up.

'Why, what's going on?'

'We upgraded the analyzer with the new long-molecule smart filters yesterday. I've had three people working on them for four months – organic chemistry married to high-level Boolean logic –'

'I remember. Teething pains?'

'Not exactly.' Kilmer moved around to the other side of the test rig, and waved Horton to follow. 'Watch the cage. Keep your eye on the big one on the right.'

'With the mostly black face?'

'That's the one my sample came from,' Kilmer said, and started the analyzer. The test rig's displays were busy with numbers and waterfall graphs for more than two minutes, then became quiet again. 'The system's locked in on the sample, and selected an H-wave profile. I'm going to give the go-ahead for treatment.'

'Okay.'

Kilmer pushed a safety interlock and turned a spring-loaded knob. The test rig hummed briefly, and as it did, the black-faced guinea pig collapsed.

'That was fast,' Horton said. 'Is it dead?'

'Extremely,' said Kilmer.

Horton was a touch surprised by the indifference of the other guinea pigs, which continued to nibble lettuce unconcernedly. But the result itself seemed quite in keeping with TOCS's previous problems.

'That was the only one of the group contaminated, I take it?' he asked.

'None of them were contaminated,' Kilmer said, shutting off the test rig.

Horton's eyebrows narrowed. 'Then what was your sample?'

'One strand of fur plucked from its back.'

Horton stared at Kilmer, then at the cage. 'What happened, Jordan? Explain this to me.'

'A single simple error in twenty-six billion bits of code – a NOT where there should have been an AND. The analyzer selects for the DNA pattern of the sample, instead of excluding it. It's almost like a mutation, really. But you see why I had to close up shop. One microscopic flake of someone's skin hitting the open sample tray, and –'

'Are you saying that you can selectively tune for any DNA pattern with this?'

'Yes.'

'How selectively?'

'I don't think it could distinguish between identical twins,' he said. 'But other than that – well, all of those animals are litter-mates.'

'Sweet mercy,' Horton said. He cautiously approached the cage, his eyes wide with awe and dismay. 'So, in theory, you could target any individual organism –'

'Not in theory,' said Kilmer, following. 'I just did it. I did it three more times this morning, and twice yesterday. Given enough markers from a DNA profile, it will zero right in on a single individual. All it takes is a drop of sweat or blood, a flake of skin, a hair –'

Standing on opposite sides of the cage, they stared long and hard at the dead guinea pig and its unknowing siblings. 'The perfect murder weapon,' Horton said hoarsely. 'An assassin's dream. It'll kill only the person it's tuned for, and no one else in the entire world –'

'You see why I had to lock it up?'

'But you can't lock it up, Jordan. Don't you understand?' There was anger in his voice, and fear. 'Nature doesn't keep secrets. She won't play along, no matter how you cozen her.'

Horton turned away suddenly, and in doing so his gaze settled on the brass plaque beside the lab door – the plaque which bore the face of PeaceTech's benefactor, and his old friend and mentor.

'What now, Karl?' he asked despairingly. 'Now what shall we do?'